BERIA

MANCHURIA

W9-ACB-180

Vladivostok

CHAHAR

JEHOL

Mukden

SUIYUAN

Peiping • Shanhaikwan

Tientsin

KOREA

JAPAN

HOPEI

Yenan

SHANSI

SHANTUNG

Tsingtao

Sian

HENSI

KIANGSU

HONAN

Nanking

ANHWEI

Shanghai

HUPEH

Hankow

CHEKIANG

HUNAN

KIANGSI

Juiking

FUKIEN

TAIWAN
(FORMOSA)

PACIFIC
OCEAN

WANGSI

KWANGTUNG

Canton

Hong Kong

HAINAN

THE
PHILIPPINES

THE LANE OF
ETERNAL STABILITY

The
LANE
of
ETERNAL STABILITY

a novel by
K. C. WU

CROWN PUBLISHERS, INC.

NEW YORK

To my wife,
who has given me
love in marriage,
happiness in life,
counsels of moderation and restraint
in moments of seeming success,
and
understanding, strength, and faith
in times of adversity.

© 1962 by K. C. Wu
Library of Congress Catalog Card Number: 62-11797
Printed in the United States of America
By American Book-Stratford Press, Inc., New York

This is a story of China and the Chinese people in the first half of the twentieth century. During this period a tremendous and incredible change occurred in the basic structure of China—from the old tradition-bound Confucian society into the present Communist-dominated state. This work attempts to trace and illustrate how the change was brought about, stage by stage.

This, however, is not a history; it is a novel. Though the plot faithfully follows the charted course of historical events, except for occasional mention of a few real names, all the characters are purely fictitious and bear no relation to any person or persons, living or dead.

For ages China had been living in grand, contented, but stagnant isolation. Then, in the early nineteenth century, the West arrived in force, and she staggered under the impact.

Unequal in modern technology, she was defeated by Great Britain in the so-called Opium War, 1840-42; and again by Great Britain and France in another war, 1856-58. She suffered territorial losses (i.e., Hong Kong), and was forced to cede special rights—rights which were soon extended to other Western nations, and later to Japan. Foreign nationals, though they traded and resided in China, were no longer subject to her laws. Foreign vessels, merchant ships and men-of-war, could navigate freely in her inland waters. And in important "treaty ports" such as Shanghai, Canton, Tientsin, and Hankow, sizable areas of land were leased as "Concessions," in which the foreign powers could station troops and set up local governments independent of Chinese control.

1861   Emperor Hsien Fung died; ruling power of the Manchu Dynasty passed into the hands of Empress Tse Hsi, known to the West as the Empress Dowager.

1893   Sun Yat-sen organized the Hsin Chung Hui (Regenerate-China Society) to plot the overthrow of the Manchu rule. He changed its name later to Kuomintang (the Nationalist Party).

1894–95   Chinese-Japanese War. China lost again and ceded Formosa to Japan.

1894   Ho the Central Hall, a Minister of State of the Manchu Court, retires to his native home on the Lane of Eternal Stability in the inland city of Yi.

1897   Fucho, son of Ho the Central Hall, goes to Japan to study.

6

1900   "Boxers' Rebellion." Eight foreign powers sent an expeditionary force and captured Peking.

1901   Peace made with the foreign powers.

The Manchu Court attempted some half-hearted reforms: The old literary examination system was abolished to make way for a more modern school system; a new army was organized under General Yuan Shih-kai, and soon became Gen. Yuan's personal tool.

1908   The Empress Dowager and the nominal Emperor Kuang Hsu died.

The Boy Emperor Hsuan Tung, better known to the West as Henry Pu-yi, ascended to the throne.

Fearful of the ambitious Yuan Shih-kai, the Manchu Court forced him into retirement.

1911   On October 10, after nine unsuccessful uprisings organized by Sun Yat-sen, the tenth broke out in Wuchang and was called by the Kuomintang the First Revolution.

The Manchu Court recalled Yuan from retirement to put down the revolution.

1912   Yuan Shih-kai reached an agreement with Sun Yat-sen. The Manchus abdicated, and Sun yielded the Presidency of the Republic to Yuan.

1898   Ho the Central Hall rescues Widow Lan.

1899   Old Ma takes Jasmine to be his sixth concubine.

Later that year the Reverend Dr. Logan J. Holt, the missionary, arrives at Yi.

1900   The Reverend Holt has a narrow escape from a band of Boxers led by Fong Tienpa.

1902   Widow Lan learns surgery from Reverend Holt.

Old Ma packs his two sons, Pingnan and Pingshi, off to Europe.

1905   Ho Fucho returns from Japan and is married to Delicate Blossom, to whom he had been betrothed since childhood but whom he has never met.

Fong Tienpa the Boxer changes his name to Tien Fong and joins the New Army.

1909   Johnny Hunt, the American trader, brings his unsavory wares to Yi.

Chi Teh-shan (the Mountain of Virtues) becomes undisputed leader of the Secret Society in the big port city in North China.

1911   Ho Fucho stages a revolt in his native province and makes himself Governor—thus precipitating an insoluble conflict of loyalties, between a loyal father and a loyal son.

1912   Ho Fucho recommends Tong Hsi, a Kuomintang comrade and husband of Amy, his former girl friend, to be appointed Mayor of the port city.

1913   Yuan cherished secret designs to make himself Emperor. The Kuomintang launched the so-called Second Revolution against him, but was quickly subdued.

1914   Japan presented twenty-one demands to China, which, if accepted, would have made her a satrapy of the Mikado.

China torn by turmoil.

1916   Yuan declared himself Emperor on January 1. Widespread revolt ensued. He abdicated on March 22, and died three months later.

Vice President Li Yuan-hung succeeded as President.

The Period of Warlords began in China, when every province, under a warlord, became virtually independent of the Central Government.

1917   Following the advice of President Woodrow Wilson, the Central Government made a nominal declaration of war on Germany.

1919   After World War I, the Treaty of Versailles gave to Japan the special rights Germany had acquired in China.

Chinese demonstrations against the Treaty were widespread.

1913   Return of Ma Pingnan to Yi. Natural and unnatural developments in a house of eleven concubines.

Jasmine, the sixth concubine, leaves Yi for the port city, unaware of the fate awaiting her.

1913   Treachery dogs the footsteps of Ho Fucho. Tien Fong replaces him as Governor of the Province.

Ta-kong, grandson to Ho the Central Hall and nephew to Fucho, enters into sworn brotherhood with Lan Yuwen (Widow Lan's son) and Li Chien.

1914   Ta-kong meets Yin Mei-yin, the brilliant girl agitator.

Ta-kong joins Chi Teh-shan's secret Society.

1915   Ma Pingnan leaves Yi under most unpleasant circumstances.

1917   Ho Fucho goes into self-imposed exile in Malaya.

1918   Ma Pingnan changes his name to Nan Ping and teaches in the university where Ta-kong is a student.

Lan Yuwen leaves for the United States to continue his education.

1919   Ho Ta-kong learns the trick of inciting a mob, almost at the cost of his life.

8

1920   In Moscow, the Second Congress of Communist International decided to create a Committee on Nationality and Colonial Problems under the personal direction of Lenin to "promote the closest contact with revolutionary forces in the politically and economically oppressed nations." Lenin sent Grigori Voitinsky to China.

Chen Tu-hsiu, a former Professor of Peking University and editor of the monthly "La Jeunesse," formed the Society for Study of Marxism in Shanghai.

1921   The Chinese Communist Party was formally organized in Shanghai.

1923   Soviet Russia offered aid to Sun Yat-sen and sent Adolf Joffe to negotiate with him. Agreement was reached on January 26. The Kuomintang permitted Communists to join its ranks as individual members; and Russia dispatched Borodin to act as Political Advisor, and General Galen as Military Advisor, to Sun's Government at Canton.

1924   The Kuomintang was reorganized, and held its First National Congress in January. Many Communists, concealing their true party affiliations, were elected to the Central Executive Committee. Among these was Mao Tse-tung.

With Soviet help, Sun established the Whampoa Military Academy and named Chiang Kai-shek its Superintendent.

1925   On March 12 Sun Yat-sen died. Anti-Communist feeling grew within the Kuomintang. On November 23, many of the older leaders met at the West Hill near Peking and advocated the expulsion of Communists.

1920   Ho Ta-kong organizes a branch Society for Study of Marxism in the big port city university.

1921   Ho Ta-kong and Ma Ping-nan are initiated into the Communist Party. Li Chien joins afterwards.

1924   Under orders of the Communist Party, Ho Ta-kong and Li Chien enroll in the Whampoa Military Academy as cadets.

1925   Both the Rightists and the Leftists seek support from Ho Fu-cho, who is still in Malaya.

1926   The Second National Congress of the Kuomintang, convened at Canton, was dominated by Communists. It dropped members of the West Hill Conference Group from the Central Executive Committee and adopted disciplinary measures against them. Chiang Kai-shek was made Commander-in-Chief of the Kuomintang Army, Mao Tse-tung head of the Kuomintang Publicity Department.

July 9. Chiang Kai-shek launched the Northern Expedition to overthrow the Warlords and unify the country.

September 8—the capture of Hankow by the Kuomintang Army.

1927   In January the British Concession in Hankow was seized by a mob. In April Nanking was taken by Chiang. Chiang then set up a new Government, broke with Russia, and purged the Communists from the Party.

Mao Tse-tung organized a Communist revolt in Hunan Province, failed, and entrenched himself in the mountain fastnesses of Chingkangshan.

1928   In July, Peking was captured by the Kuomintang forces, and China was nominally unified under the Kuomintang.

1929/30   Not heeding the Communist danger, the Kuomintang generals fell out among themselves. After having defeated the Kwangsi generals in 1929 and Generals Yen Hsi-shan and Feng Yu-hsiang in

1926   Ho Fucho returns to Canton and at once becomes a victim of political trickery.

Ho Ta-kong, now serving as a Political Commissar in the Kuomintang Army, is again confronted with the problem of family loyalty versus Party loyalty.

Ho Fucho plans an independent revolution of his own.

Ho Fucho meets Johnny Hunt for the second time.

1927   Ho Fucho's unexpected reception in the north.

Ho Ta-kong and Li Chien follow Mao Tse-tung.

1928   Like many other warlords, Tien Fong acknowledges allegiance to the Kuomintang Government in Nanking and is permitted to remain as governor of his province.

Lan Yuwen returns to Yi from the United States.

1929   Lan Yuwen's romantic adventures in the port city force him to flee to Shanghai.

Yuwen encounters a childhood friend.

10

1930, Chiang Kai-shek became the undisputed master of the Kuomintang Government in Nanking.

Communist strength kept growing. With their base established at Juiking, Kiangsi, Communist hordes overran several provinces. Finally, late in 1930, Chiang turned on them in force.

1930   Ho Ta-kong is appointed head of the Communist Eastern Bureau in Shanghai. Li Chien is his assistant. All three sworn brothers are now in Shanghai, but between them stands an insurmountable barrier.

Yin Mei-yin and Ma Pingnan give a demonstration of Communist attitudes toward sex, marriage, and mutual spying.

1931   On September 18 Japan seized Mukden and started occupying all of Manchuria.

1931-34   In 1933 Japan extended her control to Jehol outside Manchuria. In 1934 she established "Manchoukuo" and placed the puppet Henry Pu-yi on its throne.

Chiang temporized with the Japanese, but reinforced his campaigns against the Communists.

October, 1934—December, 1935
The "Long Trek" of the Communists. They were forced to abandon their lair in Kiangsi, trudge some 7,000 miles, and finally take refuge in Yenan, Shensi Province.

Chiang pressed on in pursuit. To persuade Chiang to cease his attacks, the Communists stepped up propaganda calling for the end of civil war and the formation of an "Anti-Japanese National United Front."

1936   The Japanese extended their aggressions into North China. The Communist propaganda worked on some of Chiang's troops; in December a mutiny took place in Sian and Chiang was made prisoner.

1931   All the oaths of sworn brotherhood come to naught.

1931-34   The trials and tribulations of Ho Ta-kong as a Communist.

October, 1934—December, 1935
Ho Ta-kong distinguishes himself in the "Long Trek" and is reinstated in the Communist Party.

1936   Ho Ta-kong participates in the Sian Incident.

11

1936 (cont'd)   On direct orders from Moscow, Chiang was released after he had agreed to form the United Front. The Communists, for their part, promised to abandon their ideology, incorporate their troops into Chiang's Nationalist Army, and obey Chiang's orders.

1937   On July 7, the Japanese opened fire on Chinese troops at the so-called Marco Polo Bridge near Peking. War between China and Japan began.

The Kuomintang Government convoked a "Political Advisory Council."

1938   China lost all her coastal provinces and moved her capital to Chungking.

1939   On May 3 and 5 the Japanese bombed Chungking by air. Casualties ran into tens of thousands.

The Communists expanded their guerrilla activities behind the Japanese. Within these territories they tolerated the existence of no other guerrillas, and attacked both regular Nationalist troops and independent local units alike.

December 7, 1941   Pearl Harbor.

1937   Yi falls to the Japanese. Governor Tien Fong flees into the mountains.

The Reverend Holt tries desperately to save the women refugees in the Mission Compound.

Widow Lan embarks on unsought adventures.

Lan Yuwen, Chi Teh-shan, and Chang Fa-foo (a nominal Kuomintang but a concealed Communist) are among those named Councilors.

1937/38   Widow Lan thwarts Japanese attempts to dislodge her from her mountain base.

1939   Chang Fa-foo finds a means to blackmail Amy, the wife of Tong Hsi, now a powerful minister of the Kuomintang Government.

1939/40   Advanced Communist troops, led by Ma Pingnan, are frustrated by Widow Lan's base.

The Communist High Command gives an assignment to Ho Ta-kong.

December, 1941   The Reverend Holt is sent to a Japanese concentration camp.

1942   The Reverend Holt is transferred to a concentration camp in Shanghai, where he chances upon an old acquaintance.

1945   On August 6 an atomic bomb was dropped on Hiroshima. On August 8 Russia declared war on Japan and swept across Manchuria. On August 14 Japan surrendered unconditionally. On the same day Soviet Russia signed a Treaty of Friendship with China, pledging full support to the Nationalist Government.

Shortly after, however, Chinese Communist forces poured into Manchuria under Russian protection. They were given the stockpiles of arms the Russians had captured from the Japanese.

General George C. Marshall arrived in China, his mission to arrange a peaceful settlement between the Kuomintang Government and the Communists.

1947   On January 7 General Marshall left China. Hostilities were resumed openly between the Nationalist Government and the Communists.

1948   Under the pressures of acute inflation, the Government issued a new currency in August. By October the new currency had failed miserably. In the same month Manchuria was lost to the Communists.

1949   Peking and Tientsin fell in January. The Communists crossed the Yangtze River in April. Before the year was over, they had occupied the entire mainland. Chiang fled to Formosa.

1950   The Communists started mass liquidation in China, and the "Hate America" campaign.

1945   Lan Yuwen returns to Yi with the Reverend Holt and discovers a tragic truth.

1946–48   Lan Yuwen wages a private fight against Communist infiltration in Shanghai.

Chang Fa-foo plots against Yuwen's life.

1949   Lan Yuwen's last days in Shanghai.

The Reverend Holt remains in Yi against all warnings.

1950   The Reverend Holt is arrested. A confession is wrung from him at long last, only to lead to unexpected developments.

Prologue

THE TOWN OF YI lies inland. It was a place of great antiquity when the Reverend Dr. Logan J. Holt—formerly of Newton, Iowa—first went there more than sixty years ago to work as a medical missionary. The town had charm in those days just before the turn of the century; unlike the large port cities, it had not been influenced, architecturally or otherwise, by what is called Western civilization. Its roots were in the old culture and the time-honored conventions. Filial Piety was only one of the ancient virtues; a man could honorably grow old and be all the more venerated and loved and heard in council. There was pleasure in conversation and bowls of tea. Life was as leisurely and graceful as sedan-chair travel; and under the Empress Dowager, as they had for centuries before, scholars ranked as the highest class in society.

It is sadly changed now, by revolution and the inexorable advance of what passes for Progress. The Reverend Dr. Holt—if he could return—might hardly recognize what he once knew as dear and familiar. Coming up by bus through the communized farms, he would be told, proudly, that much more rice is being raised, that there are no longer any coolies, and no flies. . . .

There are no flies because China has so many millions of people that if each one swats a few flies every day, flies cannot survive. There are no coolies because the common denominator of Communism has reduced every man to coolie status, and calls him "Comrade" instead. Perhaps more rice is being raised, but no one seems to know where all the foodstuffs go, and everyone is fed less and less. The people all eat the same scanty food, wear the same drab clothes, perform the same collective labor, speak the same Party line; and are robbed of an ancient heritage that once was the pride of their race, that used to pay special homage to Wisdom, Virtue, and other such rare attainments of Man.

Nobody, now, in Yi, dares to dream.

There is a mill of some kind by the compound where the Reverend Dr. Holt had his mission, on that short but rather wide thoroughfare called Yun Ting Hong—the Lane of Eternal Stability. The Mission itself is a school that trains young Party cadres.

It has been a long time since two strangers, meeting in Yi, had the grace to ask, "How high, sir, is your Honorable Age?" so that the younger might properly defer to the elder. It is long since anyone mentioned Fidelity, or Filial Piety, and paid attention to the teachings of Confucius.

A few wrinkled and toothless Honorable Elders are left to drag out their days in the town of Yi. They are of no use to the Party.

"Eh?" they say, dim eyes suddenly becoming bright. "You ask about Ho-Lo-Teh? He was an American, and we are taught to hate the Americans now, you know. But he was a brave man. He was the first foreigner we ever saw, and his hair was most uncommon. When he was a young man, his hair was the color of a leaping flame. . . ."

BOOK I

One

THE YOUNG AND redheaded Dr. Holt had been in Yi nearly five
months that day when he looked out from his room to the courtyard, and to the Lane of Eternal Stability, and asked himself why
he had failed. He was a dedicated man. Orphaned early in childhood, he had shaped his course with almost fanatical determination:
first, medical school, and then missionary work in China. He had
resolved, long before, never to marry. Back in Baltimore, while
studying at Johns Hopkins for his degree as Doctor of Medicine, he
had met a girl and was tremendously attracted to her. But he put
romance sternly aside; the life he planned might be suited to himself but not to a woman; and he had no right to ask her to share it.

So he had come to China alone, first to undergo a long and intensive novitiate in the big port city, where he creditably mastered
the Chinese dialect he would need at Yi, and then to move to the
inland town to establish his little stronghold of Christianity in a
sea of heathen.

He loved the place. The Mission compound had been bought, not
built; it was not like the houses in the port city, which had surrendered to Western influence. It was a typical house of inland
China, constructed entirely according to the traditional architecture
the Chinese had used for centuries. Actually, it was not a single

17

building, but a large compound circumscribed by an outer wall. The pedestrian walking along the street saw no individual houses, merely ranges of walls, bare, grayish to monotony, with the tiled roofs of one-story houses beyond. The drabness of the scene was relieved only by intermittent gates painted bright vermilion. But beyond the walls was the beauty of gardens.

The compound proper was divided into courts, which were con-nected by a labyrinth of verandas; the rich had dozens of such courts, separate but still joined, surrounded by gardens, ponds, and pavil-ions; not infrequently a single large Chinese family with four or five generations, hundreds of individuals, would live together in the same compound.

The Mission compound was not that large. It had three courts, in addition to the newly constructed church. It could hardly compare with the extensive mansion just across the street, or with the house next door to the Mission—reputedly owned by the richest man in Yi. At the same time, it was a far cry from the one thing that marred the respectability and serene beauty of the Lane of Eternal Stability —a lone dilapidated shack which shouted poverty.

The sun climbed a spring sky; another day of frustrating idleness. A man who could leave a girl behind in Baltimore was not inclined to be impetuous or impatient; yet after five months the people of Yi should have been coming to the church and to the medical clinic. They came to neither. Holt had been instructed concerning the prejudices he might expect against his Christian doctrine; he had also been taught the best methods of overcoming prejudice and been warned to be patient and to persevere.

But he had had five months of apathy and indifference; he and his Christian God had been totally ignored. He had paid his respects to the Prefect of the Prefecture, and from him had obtained a full list of all the important people in Yi. He had called upon these, one by one. Nobody was at home. Moreover, the people of Yi appeared to have forgotten the proverbial politeness of the Chinese—not one returned Holt's call. He had then tried dealing with the tradesmen in the marketplaces. Here he found courtesy, as long as he dealt in purely business matters, and shrewd but not dishonest bargaining. But the tradespeople said they had no time to visit the Mission compound.

For a little while, the Reverend Dr. Holt and the Chinese assistant who had come up with him from the port city—Ah Wong—resorted to Salvation Army tactics: Ah Wong beat a drum and blew a trumpet, and when a crowd had gathered, the missionary passed out pamphlets and preached. . . . And then the crowd would drift away, smiling mysteriously.

Five months without a convert, without a visitor to the compound, without even a patient in the well-equipped medical clinic—this was a long time.

Holt looked out on the Lane of Eternal Stability, and as he did so, tried to imagine a street named that in Newton, Iowa. He wondered if there ever could be eternal stability on earth? Surely not, he thought, until the Kingdom of God came.

The Lane of Eternal Stability was the most respected part of Yi. The mansion across the street was owned by a man known as Ho the Central Hall, who had refused to receive Holt. It had become clear to the missionary that Ho the Central Hall was the principal impediment to any progress, and his chief obstacle. Ho had consistently ignored him, and the whole town had followed Ho's example.

On the same side of the street with the Mission compound was the house of Ma. Holt had already learned from Gatekeeper and Cook— these worthies were known by their occupational titles, and not by their names—that Ma was the richest and meanest man in Yi. His whole purpose in life was to acquire money, and more money—he should have been born in the United States, Holt thought, not in China.

Even though he was rich, Ma was looked down upon by the people of Yi. In addition to his obsession for money, he was known to have a weakness for women. He was stingy toward himself, never wore the silk he could well afford, but where women were concerned he was not niggardly. He did not spend money on singsong girls but bought his women outright, acquiring a new concubine almost every year, and adding court after court to his compound to accommodate them and the continuing crops of children.

From all that Holt had been told, Ma was indeed a strange man. He took great pleasure in lavishing gifts upon his concubines— dresses, furniture, and jewelry—and just as strangely drew the line at providing food. When the women and children complained at the coarse and frugal fare, Ma would say, "Why do you grumble? Have I not kept you from hunger? There is food in sufficient quantity, isn't there? You must remember that food is not like things with durable value. Food has no durable value. There is no difference between good and bad food—when you have consumed either, it will come out of your bowels just the same."

19

Holt had also learned that though Ma was despised by most of the people in Yi, he had too much money to let his unpopularity worry him. If people wanted to do business in Yi, sooner or later they had to come to him. But according to the gatekeeper and the cook, there was one man in Yi of whom Ma was genuinely afraid.

This was Ho the Central Hall, who lived just across the street. If it had not been for Ho, the missionary was told, no telling what Ma might have done. "He could have sold us all off as slaves," Gatekeeper would say, and Cook would nod agreement.

"But why should a man like Ma fear Ho the Central Hall?" Holt asked. "Why does everybody in Yi seem to fear Ho the Central Hall? Is he richer than Ma?"

"Oh, no!" Gatekeeper would answer. "Ho the Central Hall is by no means as rich as Ma—not even half so rich. True, he has held high positions, but he is in retirement now. Undoubtedly he has great influence, but he has never used it. Why, when Ho the Central Hall is walking, he takes care not to tread on an ant. Fear him? Oh, no—we people of Yi certainly do not fear him! But we respect him. He is a good man, a righteous man—Confucius would have called him a gentleman. Of course Ma has reasons to fear Ho the Central Hall. As we say, 'The sly can never hold a straight face to the proper.' Ma is sly. Ho the Central Hall is proper. . . ."

Thus the Reverend Dr. Holt learned, in his persevering and dedicated way. In time, he inquired about the shack that was so out of place in the Lane of Eternal Stability.

"Eh?" said Gatekeeper. He was tall, slender, and rather hairy for a Chinese. He had no letters but took pride in his hearsay knowledge of the classics, and being in his thirties, a little older than Holt, he was inclined to be somewhat patronizing toward his foreign master. "Eh?" he said. "You mean Widow Lan's shack? She is a protégé of Ho the Central Hall, and has no one except her child—a boy, fortunately. When he grows up, her troubles will be over. Now she lives a hard life selling embroideries and dumplings, but at least Ho the Central Hall gives her a roof over her head. He is like that—he goes out of his way to find a destitute widow from Heaven knows where, and helps her."

Cook was short and chubby. He was conscious of his inferiority to Gatekeeper by ten years in age, but was unwilling to concede this too openly before their employer.

"Master," he said, "you must taste her dumplings. She makes them better than anyone else. They are almost as good as her own good looks!"

"Hold your tongue!" said Gatekeeper. "Has Widow Lan, by her conduct, given you cause to gossip about her looks? Looks are given by Heaven, and she cannot help it if she is particularly favored. Has she not always behaved as properly as any widow should? Ho the Central Hall thinks highly of her!"

Cook mumbled contritely, "I spoke hastily, but meant no ill to Widow Lan. Is there not an ancient adage about women like her? Does it not say, 'From time immemorial Fate has always dealt harshly with those who are endowed with excessive beauty'?"

Placated, because the quotation had been directed to him, Gatekeeper nodded. Then Cook turned to Holt. "Please sample Widow Lan's dumplings. All Ma's concubines and his children are her regular customers, but a great storm would break loose if Ma knew. That stingy miser!"

So it came about that, accompanied by Ah Wong, Holt went to the Widow Lan's shack. It was furnished with the barest necessities. The floor was hard earth, and a rough wooden table stood near the entrance, with benches for customers to sit. A charcoal stove and a cupboard completed the furnishings. The walls were bare except for a piece of paper which said, "Ten dumplings, one copper." But everything was meticulously clean.

When Holt and Ah Wong entered, Widow Lan was doing embroidery work on a stool, with the boy toddling about the room. She was neatly dressed in a gray jacket and black skirt. Although she stood up when the men entered, she neither looked at them nor spoke any words of welcome.

Ah Wong ordered twenty dumplings. And as Widow Lan moved to prepare them, the Reverend Dr. Holt watched her. Never had he seen anything to compare with her feet, which, according to custom, had been bound in early childhood. They were no more than an inch in breadth and three inches in length. On her way to the cupboard she tripped, and his sense of chivalry made him forget where he was. He stepped forward to assist her, but Ah Wong restrained him with a strong hand and shook his head gravely to remind Holt that it was unthinkable for a Chinese woman to have physical contact with any man other than her husband or her closest blood relations. Holt stopped short. Even so, Widow Lan stiffened and looked at him with an expression of half sorrow, half disdain. He was ashamed.

Holt studied the boy, a well-formed and intelligent-looking child, who was now playing with the toy figure of a mandarin. In his red coat and red breeches, he was extremely well dressed in comparison to his mother's garb. Around his neck he wore a gold chain with a pendant that said, "Long life, great wealth, and high position."

Holt saw the round plaster on the child's forehead at the same time that the youngster noticed Holt's red hair, and fled shrieking to his mother's skirts, asking if this was a man or a demon.

"Hush, hush, my heart!" she said, taking care not to look at Holt. "Be not afraid. The man is not a demon. He is only a foreigner. . . ."

She served the dumplings with vinegar, sliced ginger, and soya sauce. They were delicious. Finally Holt went contrary to Ah Wong's counsel, and asked her about the boy's forehead.

She hesitated a long time, and then said, "It is a boil."

"I am a doctor," Holt told her kindly. "I do not say that your doctor is not good. I wish him success, and your son speedy recovery. But if the boil does not heal, then please come to the Mission compound across the street. I will do my best to cure your child, free of charge."

There was no answer. The two men withdrew and returned to the Mission compound. There, Ah Wong said, "What a character we have just witnessed! It is indeed as the poets sing, 'Beautiful as peach and plum blossoms, but cold as frost and ice!' "

2

THE WIDOW LAN did not come to the Mission compound to have her child treated, nor did Holt go to her shack again. He had his own frustrations and worries during the next several days.

Then one night when he could not sleep, the missionary left his bed to walk alone in the compound, hoping to grow tired. As he approached the school court, which had a side door opening onto the street, he heard a strange, anguished moan. He listened intently for a minute, and the eerie sound came again. This time it was nearer, and he knew that it came from the Lane of Eternal Stability. He went stealthily to the side door, unbolted it silently, and peered out into the night.

What he saw made his blood run cold. Some ten paces to his left, on the ground, was what appeared to be a dark, furry creature. Projecting from it were two pinpoints of light, as if the creature's eyes, like those of some insects, were on sticks. The dots of light moved; the apparition was bobbing up and down. Then it rose erect and hobbled toward him, coming out of the wall shadow and into the faint moonlight.

Holt breathed again. It was only a woman wearing a black shawl around her head and carrying a burning incense stick in each hand. It was Widow Lan!

She seemed to be in a trance. Apparently not seeing him in the doorway, she walked painfully on her incredibly small, bound feet, counting aloud with each step. When she came to the number nine, she sank down onto her knees, uttered the weird moan, and began the prelude to a prayer, speaking so fast and in so low a tone that Holt could not understand her words. Presently she took both incense sticks in one hand and prostrated herself on the earth. Nine times she kowtowed. Then she stood up and limped forward for nine steps, passing the school court door. Once more she sank to her knees, again she prayed and kowtowed nine times.

Holt stood watching, in fascination and pity, for at least fifteen minutes. By that time Widow Lan was at the far end of the street; there she turned and was lost to his sight, and he knew it would not be proper to follow her. But if he had been unable to sleep before, sleep now was out of the question, and he went to awaken Ah Wong and relate what he had seen.

Ah Wong's eyes were heavy. Blinking and managing an owlish solemnity, he reflected on the matter for a moment. "Did you say she was going away from her shack?"

Holt nodded.

"Then even as she goes, so must she return," Ah Wong said in his pontifical manner. "Therefore, we can observe her again."

It was nearly three hours before Widow Lan reappeared. She was staggering with pain and weariness now as she went through the nine-step ritual, and the incense sticks, originally more than a foot long, were about to burn her fingers. When she prayed just outside the gate of the Mission compound, Ah Wong's ears were able to pick up a soul-rending cry:

"O Goddess of Mercy, Thou Thousand-Eyed and Thousand-Handed, have mercy upon me and my son!"

The Reverend Dr. Holt was moved by a great compassion to learn more. It was not easy. With great tact Ah Wong told the cook, who was instructed to tell his wife about it. The cook's wife had a maternal aunt who was an amah to the fourth concubine in the House of Ma. By visiting her aunt on some plausible excuse, the cook's wife managed to arrange a meeting with Mistress Chow, amah to Ma's sixth concubine, and known to be a trusted friend of Widow Lan.

Mistress Chow told the story with relish. It all had to do with the boil Holt had seen on Boy Lan's forehead. . . .

Ah Wong had to explain some of the things the cook related. The Chinese believed implicitly in the "Science of Physiognomy." From a study of facial features and the shape of the body, personal character readings were made and fortunes foretold. The forehead was considered one of the most important parts of the anatomy, and was known as the "Seat of the Seal." Seals were always employed as insignia for high offices, and no one without a good and proper forehead could aspire to lofty position. Even ordinary persons carried seals as means of identification; to be without a personal seal would be to be without a personality. Unless one had a clear and unmarred forehead, one could not hope for a bright future, and so Widow Lan was grievously troubled by the boil that persisted on the Seat of the Seal of the child upon whom her whole life was centered.

The boil had been there during all the five months of the Reverend Dr. Holt's frustrating stay in Yi. Widow Lan had finally called upon her protector, Ho the Central Hall, who sent over his personal physician. This learned doctor was not optimistic. Too many kinds of plaster had been used, he said, and perhaps by now the boil had become resistant to all medicine. Furthermore, even if it healed, he feared it might leave an ugly scar. Widow Lan's heart sank.

And then Mistress Chow made her frightening discovery. Ever since she had entered the service of Ma's sixth concubine, she had been a regular purchaser of Widow Lan's excellent dumplings to help piece out the niggardly meals served at the House of Ma, and she had developed a warm affection for the Lans. A widow herself, middle-aged and childless, she liked to fancy that the comely young woman was her own daughter, and the boy her grandson. During the time of Widow Lan's great anxiety, Mistress Chow had visited her frequently, trying to comfort her.

One day when she was helping to change the plaster on the boy's head, she gave the boil a sharp look, and then gasped: "O Goddess of Mercy! What is this we find here?"

"What, Mother Chow?" the boy's mother cried. "What do you find?"

"Look, my child! There are three openings on this thing, oozing pus. The two on the top are at the same level, like eyes. The one below is bigger—it is like a mouth. O Goddess of Mercy, this is no common boil. It is the dreaded Human-Face Carbuncle!"

Widow Lan wept, though still not fully comprehending, and Mistress Chow went on to explain that the root of the trouble had to be sought in the past incarnations of the widow and her son. "In your past incarnations, you must once have committed a terrible wrong against someone. The spirit of that person has now come back to wreak vengeance, in the shape of the Human-Face Carbuncle."

"But what? What could I have done—what could my child have done—to deserve this?"

"Of course you do not know," said Mistress Chow by way of consolation. "You can never know. But you can cast out the evil spirit by doing penance."

Widow Lan dried her tears with this new hope. "Tell me how!" she begged desperately. "I will do anything!"

"I am afraid that it calls for a penance much more severe than usual," Mistress Chow said. "It would not help to do as I do. I worship Goddess of Mercy, you know. I wear these fifty-three beads around my neck and count them at least three times a day. I abstain from meat on the first and the fifteenth day of every month, and offer incense in every temple I pass. But that would not be enough."

"I will do anything—anything!" Widow Lan repeated.

"I saw a monk do penance once," Mistress Chow recalled. "Yes, yes—it would work, but it is very severe! Listen carefully. Outside the East Gate of the city wall, there is a temple of the Goddess of Mercy. Go there and do this penance. First, you must not eat meat for three days, and you must wash your body thoroughly every morning and every night. At the twelfth hour of the fourth night, you must set out alone for the temple, holding two incense sticks burning before you. You must walk straight ahead, counting every step you take, and at the end of every ninth step you must fall on your knees, cry pitifully to the Goddess, pray to her, and then kowtow nine times before you rise again.

"At the temple, you must walk around the image of the Goddess three times, and each time you are directly before her, pray and kowtow nine times. Come back in the same manner, but remember this: you must return here before the cock crows. The Goddess heeds most the prayers spoken in the stillest hours of the earth."

Then Mistress Chow looked at Widow Lan's tiny bound feet and sighed. "At times," she confessed, "I have had sinful and earthly thoughts, may the Goddess of Mercy forgive me! I have wished that I had your bound feet—they are so tiny, so beautiful. But now, for *your* sake, I wish that you could exchange my bigger, ugly feet for yours, because it is three li each way, to the temple and back. Such a long distance! My child, do you really think you can undertake the penance?"

3

THE VIGOROUS AND strong Reverend Dr. Holt felt a sense of shame when he heard the story of Widow Lan's cruel penance. He gave some thought to the ancient Christian martyrs, and told himself that Widow Lan's faith was the kind that moved mountains—and he wished that he might convert her to Christianity. But Holt was both human and humane. The paramount thing now, he knew, was to do something for that small and appealing boy.

Four days had passed since the penance. Mistress Chow was visiting Widow Lan, and feeling both embarrassed and uneasy, for there had been no perceptible improvement in the child's condition.

The Reverend Dr. Holt, with Ah Wong following, entered the shop. Mistress Chow took the boy by the hand and went into the bedroom to give more space to the customers. Widow Lan, head bowed and eyes on the ground, waited for their command.

"We do not come for dumplings, ma'am," Holt said meekly, clasping his hands one inside the other in Chinese fashion. "We are here to offer our services. I am sure I can cure your son of his boil."

Widow Lan did not move. This was the foreigner with whom nobody in all Yi would associate, because all Yi was following the personal example of her protector, Ho the Central Hall. Since the foreigner also was a young male, she, a widow, could not properly have any dealings with him at all. But how wonderfully sweet were his words—he was sure he could cure her child of the Human-Face Carbuncle.

She wavered. Of course the thing was impossible. What would Ho the Central Hall say—even though his own doctor, and others, had failed? And what if the foreigner's skill or his magic could not match his boast?

26

She stood undecided, torn in heart, her feet still paining her terribly. And suddenly Mistress Chow, who had heard everything, opened the bedroom door. The boy shrank back at the sight of Holt. "O Grandmother Chow, close the door quickly!" he shrilled. "The red-haired demon is there!"

"Come in here and attend your child," Mistress Chow bade Widow Lan. Then, with the door still open, she said, "Sirs, please have the goodness to wait but a moment while I talk with the boy's mother."

After she had closed the door, she turned to Widow Lan with an air of great and dramatic excitement. "Congratulations, my child—a thousand congratulations!" she whispered exultantly. "Your prayers are answered! The Goddess has heard. She has sent the foreigner to cure the Human-Face Carbuncle!"

"But Mother Chow—the foreigner does not worship our gods. If he does not believe in the Goddess of Mercy, then how could she send him?"

"Do not be so presumptuous, my child—none of us can judge the actions of gods. Who are we to say what the Goddess of Mercy can and cannot do? For us humans, it may be quite impossible to order people around who are not our servants, but for gods and goddesses it may be a very simple thing. Ho the Central Hall—or even Ma—could borrow a servant from somebody, to run an errand. So it stands to reason that the Goddess of Mercy can also borrow the foreigner from his god, to do her bidding. No—you did your penance four days ago, and now comes the foreigner to offer help. This cannot be a coincidence—it is divine providence!"

Mistress Chow, driven to save face for her goddess, argued long and earnestly. After what seemed an age, she emerged from the bedroom to state conditions and terms: Widow Lan would accept the foreign doctor's offer only if he would guarantee to cure the boil within three days, and only if there would be absolutely no remaining scar.

Holt saw the solemn disapproval printed on Ah Wong's face, and certainly he himself was aware that his chances of meeting such terms were slender indeed. He never understood, in later reflection, just why he took such a desperate gamble. But with less than a minute's hesitation he gave his promise.

At once he ran into fresh difficulties. Widow Lan stubbornly refused to take her child to the Mission compound. As a widow, she could not enter a house inhabited only by men. Would she come with Mistress Chow as escort? Mistress Chow was quite well-disposed toward Holt by now, since she considered him a servant borrowed by the Goddess of Mercy. But she too was a widow and governed by the same rules of propriety.

Holt suggested that he could take the boy alone to his clinic, but this offer was also promptly rejected; it was unthinkable for Widow Lan ever to permit her child to leave her sight. So the missionary reluctantly proceeded with his treatment in the shack. He had craftily brought along some chocolates, and after the first one the child smiled and was no longer frightened by Holt's red hair. After the second chocolate, he told the American his name. It was Lan Yuwen. Three chocolates, and he was sitting on Holt's lap, touching the strange red hair and finding that, after all, it felt not much different from his own.

Notwithstanding, the third day came, with no evidence of a cure. To the Reverend Dr. Holt, this was the day in which he very nearly regretted ever having come to China. To Widow Lan, it had become increasingly clear that the foreigner could not effect a cure, and now Ho the Central Hall must have heard about the affair. If there had been an accomplished cure, it would have been much easier to face her protector. Without it, what could she say to Ho the Central Hall, or even to any of the people of Yi?

Mistress Chow was still clinging to her belief that the foreigner was an agent of the Goddess of Mercy, but her face-saving trust was worn thin. She could offer no solace.

When the Reverend Dr. Holt arrived at the shack, with Ah Wong, Widow Lan made it clear to him that this was his last day, his last chance. It was an ultimatum.

And then Holt spoke with an inspiration born of desperation. "I understand, and I shall fulfill my part of the agreement. But you must fulfill yours. I promised to cure the boil in three days, and not leave a scar behind. That I shall try to do. In our original agreement, no restrictions were placed upon the manner or place of my medications. I now insist that I be allowed to take Yuwen to my clinic, and treat him there!"

Widow Lan was again indecisive, but Mistress Chow snatched at this last straw of hope. As for little Yuwen, he knew that a visit to the Mission compound would mean chocolates. Holt carried the boy over in his arms, with Widow Lan and Mistress Chow following, to wait at the compound gate. Ah Wong was filled with solemn misgivings.

Inside the clinic, the redheaded American became less the man of God and more the man of medicine—though who can say it was not quite the reverse? After examining the child's forehead with minute care, he took a piece of paper and cut it into the exact size of the boil. Then he rolled up the left leg of his own trousers. He washed an area thoroughly with alcohol, applied the paper to the flesh, and traced its outline there, a little larger than the area of the boil. He was ready.

Coaxing Yuwen with brave and flattering words, sweetened with chocolates, Holt applied local anesthesia to the sore forehead. Carefully, he opened the boil, cleansed the pus, and scooped out the rotten flesh.

Then, while Ah Wong busied himself in comforting the child and keeping him still, the Reverend Dr. Holt did something which the learned faculty of Johns Hopkins University had never taught him. He seated himself behind Ah Wong, placed his left leg on his right knee, and with a quick and deft stroke sliced off the piece of flesh he had outlined. Paying no attention to the grievous wound he had inflicted upon himself, he stepped in front of Ah Wong and pressed the piece of his own living flesh into the boy's forehead, exactly fitting the spot where the boil had been.

Quickly he dressed and sutured the wound. Only when he was applying the bandage did little Yuwen look down and see the ugly wound in Holt's leg. At the sight of the blood streaming downward, the boy burst into a loud and terrified howl.

Everybody heard the cry. Forgetting all rules of propriety, from outside the main gate Widow Lan charged forward, dragging Mistress Chow with her. They dashed through the second gate, heading toward the clinic. The gatekeeper did not know whether to stop them or not, and finally decided he should follow them. Cook heard the cry in his quarters, and likewise gave chase.

Mother love swept Widow Lan on, and in spite of her bound feet she and Mistress Chow were the first to reach the clinic. The mother had eyes only for her son, who, at first glance, looked none the worse for his experience. But when he saw his mother, he let out another frightened howl.

Widow Lan gathered him in her arms, and angrily faced the missionary. "What have you done to my child?"

Holt did not know what to say. But Ah Wong, for once, threw

solemnity to the winds. "What has he done?" he asked excitedly. "You ask what he has done? You should ask what it is that he has not done for you and your boy, ignorant woman! Look, ungrateful one! He has cut out a piece of his own skin and flesh to cure your son of the boil! Does this mean nothing to you? Your troubles will soon be over, but he who mended them will have a terrible wound to heal! Never have I seen such an ingrate!"

The gatekeeper and the cook came up, panting, in time to hear Ah Wong's diatribe. They looked at the Reverend Dr. Holt's angry wound, from which blood was still streaming, and then Holt himself seemed to become conscious of it, and somewhat wearily began to give it professional care. The women, too, looked for a moment, but either because of the sight of blood or because suddenly it came to them that it was indecent to look at a man's naked leg, they quickly turned their backs. Mistress Chow took Widow Lan's arm, and they carried the boy away without a word.

Holt approached the postoperative care with some misgivings. Widow Lan, however, permitted him to change Yuwen's dressing without protest, and it was apparent from the first that the skin graft was going to be successful. The visits continued for several days, and during them she hung her head, kept her eyes on the ground, and spoke no word either of accusation or gratitude. Even when Holt removed the bandage and pronounced the boil completely healed, and said there would be no scar, she remained silent. He had not expected to hear any expression of thanks, but he had anticipated something in the way of a friendly farewell.

The Widow Lan said nothing at all.

Holt was bewildered. Going back to Ah Wong, he asked, "What is the matter, here? Did I do right, or wrong?"

Ah Wong cocked his head to one side, and became solemn. "You know my origins. Though I am Chinese, I was a foundling brought up by you missionaries, and now I am not sure I think altogether like other Chinese. So whether *I* think you have done right or wrong is not pertinent in this case."

"But look!" Holt exclaimed. "I can't understand this. If I helped the boy—"

"I have consulted with Gatekeeper and Cook, separately," Ah Wong went on. "They are Chinese in their thinking. If what they say is an indication, it does not augur well."

"What do they say?"

"Gatekeeper says that although he has heard you quote from

30

Confucius, this incident, more than anything else, proves that you are still a foreigner—a barbarian. There is this passage in the classics concerning Filial Piety: 'The body, the limbs, the hair, the skin—all these we receive from our parents. Not to dare hurt and harm them, that is the beginning of the sense of Filial Piety.' There is no question but that you have violated that!"

"And what does Cook say?"

"He says it is witchcraft you practice, and he is sorely afraid for young Yuwen's sake. He thinks you have stolen the boy's soul by engrafting your piece of flesh on his head. He says that if there is anything Ho the Central Hall detests, it is sorcery. Now that you have performed sorcery at his very door, Cook believes that the great man will have to take some drastic action against you—he can no longer ignore you here in Yi."

The very next day, Ho the Central Hall sent a messenger to ask the missionary to call upon him.

Two

THE ALARM CLOCK woke Holt before daylight, and he sprang immediately from the hard brick bed the Chinese called a *kong*. The kongs in the Mission compound were anything but luxurious, no matter how much bedding one used, but each one had a built-in charcoal stove underneath. During the previous winter, Holt had found the weather in that part of China to be somewhat more severe than any he remembered from his boyhood days in central Iowa, and he had been grateful for the kong's warmth. Even so, he was not yet used to the idea of sleeping on a stove.

Remembering how crucially important this day and the call on Ho the Central Hall might be to him, the missionary at once knelt on the cold tiled floor and prayed earnestly. Then, lighting a candle, he began dressing carefully.

It was no familiar task. His faithful assistant, the solemn Ah Wong, had insisted that to call on a man of the eminence of Ho the Central Hall, the young Reverend Dr. Holt must be arrayed like a respectable and conservative Chinese gentleman. In fact, he must wear the garb of a scholar, Ah Wong said. In the China of that time, scholars ranked higher than any other class—and, indeed, was not Ho-Lo-Teh a scholar in his own right?

Holt first donned some inner garments that looked like pajamas, except that the coat had an erect, stiff collar. Then he pulled on a pair of cloth stockings, tucked them up beneath the loose trousers, and bound trousers and stockings together above the instep with a specially woven satin band. He thrust his feet into slipper-like shoes with black coverings and white soles, both made of durable nankeen, and then put on a long, flowing gown of bluish silk that hung down to his feet. Around his waist went a belt of fine brocade two inches wide. It was not gaily colored like those fancied by Chinese dandies, for again Ah Wong had counseled the somber hue worn by scholars. Over the gown went a black satin jacket, fastened in front with a row of frogs made of knotted silken braids. Into the fabric were woven circular designs symbolizing good luck and long life.

Holt studied his reflection in the mirror from various angles. The costume left nothing to be desired. It was conservative, it was in good taste. But for a moment the missionary wished the Almighty would work a minor miracle and make his complexion a shade more yellow, his nose not quite so pointed, his eyes brown instead of blue, and—above all—change his hair from flaming red to black. The wish was fleeting; Holt discarded it as a vanity, unworthy and sinful, and told himself that what the Lord had ordained none could alter. And then, being possessed of a sense of humor, he was unable to keep his handsome mouth from smiling mischievously.

The Chinese all had queues in that year of 1900. Queues were, in a sense, cultivated by men—they were not made by God. And if the Chinese wore queues, so could the Reverend Dr. Holt!

It was the custom of Chinese gentlemen to wear a close-fitting type of skullcap known as a "melon skin." This was fabricated out of black silk, with a braided button on the top. It was not even removed inside the house in the daytime. Ah Wong and Holt had bought a "melon skin" months before in the big port city, when both were undergoing their training at Mission headquarters. Holt had had a false queue sewed into this cap. When he wore it for the first time, his fellow novitiates laughed outright and the head of the Mission frowned deeply. He had not worn it since, but now it would add the crowning touch to his dress.

He took the "melon skin" from a drawer, put it tightly on his head, and carefully tucked up a few betraying strands of red hair. The long glossy black queue dangled down his back in a most satis-

factory manner, and Holt chuckled at his reflection in the mirror.

It was still not full daylight. Looking out from his room to the courtyard, he could see the shadowy columns supporting the roofs of the verandas on the other side. The forsythia was in bloom in the yard, and lording it over these shrubs was a Chinese elm. It was curious, Holt thought, that these elms bore a growth something like pine cones, but looking for all the world like strings of nickel-sized coins. Ah Wong had explained that these were called "elm-coins."

He had time to wait, time to reflect that northern China was lovely in the spring, that the Mission compound was a charming place. Before he had met with such frustration in Yi, Holt had had ambitious plans for the use of the courts. He had taken the hindmost —it also was the smallest—for his own living quarters. Ah Wong, whose real name was the Reverend Wong Ming, shared these with him. Holt had marked out the court nearest the church on the far side as the site for a school—as yet it had no students—and the third one, immediately in front of his living quarters, had been outfitted for his medical clinic.

The door across the courtyard swung open. Ah Wong emerged from the suite opposite, lanky and serious of countenance. Holt stepped quickly out of his room and said, "Good morning! Well . . . what do you think?"

Walking over gravely, Ah Wong cocked his head and inspected Holt with a melancholy mien that was almost ludicrous.

"Will you please turn yourself around once or twice?"

Holt turned three times. There was no comment.

"Will you walk down the steps of the veranda into the center of the yard?"

Holt walked, Ah Wong following behind. "That's it! That's it!" he said after a moment. "It is not the way you dress. It is the way you walk. You walk too fast—you don't walk proper."

"Then I'll slow down my steps. But what do you mean by not walking 'proper'?"

"You walk like a coolie, not like one of the gentry. You walk like a sedan-chair carrier, not like a man accustomed to being borne in a sedan. I will show you."

Ah Wong took a few steps. "See? Do not point your toes straight forward. You must point them thirty or forty degrees outward, like this. Remember the Chinese character for 'eight'—it is somewhat like your letter 'V,' and your toes must be pointed that way. This is the so-called 'Eight-Character Gait' that all the scholars assume these

33

days. Please put your heel down first, and allow the toes to fall gradually. See? It gives you a willowy, contemplative, and unhurried air. . . ."

Holt sauntered leisurely up and down the walk, with Ah Wong coaching him.

"Now you are really improving!" said Ah Wong. "Remember to walk with the Eight-Character Gait, and nobody will doubt that your ancestors have been borne in sedan chairs for generations. Permit me, now, to go to the gate and watch for the sedan chair we have hired. They promised to be here at sunrise. Perhaps they would not do this for us, but they certainly will, knowing that you are going to call on Ho the Central Hall."

"But Ah Wong," Holt said, "why must we have a sedan chair just to cross the street?"

"Ah," replied Ah Wong gravely, "that is precisely why a sedan chair must be used. Confucius says, 'When a gentleman wishes to study the character of a person, he must look for revelations in trifles.' Then says the great master again, 'When a gentleman walks, he never takes a short cut.' The meaning is that one must not do a thing simply because it is convenient and expedient. One must always do things in the proper way. Now, to walk, in this instance, is undoubtedly convenient and expedient. But to take a sedan chair is proper. We know Ho the Central Hall has been studying us with great care these last few days. Would he not read in the lack of a sedan chair a disrespect for himself? For who has heard of anyone calling formally upon His Excellency the Central Hall without being borne in a sedan chair?"

That closed the argument to Ah Wong's satisfaction. He left his companion practicing the Eight-Character Gait, and went to await the chair and its four carriers.

2

THE MORNING WAS brightening; sunrise would come at any moment. To the Reverend Dr. Holt, sunrise seemed an odd time to pay a formal call, but this, too, was apparently "proper." He heard sounds outside the second gate, and presently Ah Wong returned to say that the sedan chair had arrived.

Holt made his way to the second gate in his newly learned, leisurely and willowy manner. The waiting sedan chair had not four men but five. "This is the proper form," Ah Wong whispered reas-

suringly. "When you hire a four-carrier chair, you really hire five men. One is a forerunner, who carries visiting cards for the master. See, that one—I have already given him your card."

Holt glanced at the forerunner, and could not suppress a smile. The card Ah Wong had given him was fully eight inches long and four wide, with one side painted crimson. On that side three large characters were printed in black—"Ho-Lo-Teh." Ah Wong had already explained to him that he was indeed fortunate to have Holt as a surname. Rendered into monosyllabic Chinese, Ho-Lo-Teh was a fine name, not at all foreign to the Chinese ear. "Ho" is a regular Chinese surname, the same as Ho the Central Hall's. "Lo" means delight, and "Teh" means virtue. Taken as a whole, the name meant Ho-Who-Delights-in-Virtue, and the Reverend Dr. Holt was already quite proud of it.

The forerunner helped him take his seat in the sedan chair, and fastened a half-curtain across the front. Then the four carriers took their posts, each at an end of the parallel bars. When the forerunner gave the word, the chair was hoisted to the men's shoulders.

It took only a minute to cross the Lane of Eternal Stability and reach the main gate of Ho's mansion. The forerunner advanced to give Ho's gatekeeper the visiting card, the main gate swung open, and with an easy gait the sedan chair was carried into the yard. At the second gate it was lowered gently to the ground. The forerunner helped Holt out, while Ho's gatekeeper stood respectfully at the side.

"His Excellency the Central Hall is waiting for you, sir, at the Eastern Court. I shall have the honor to take you there."

The gatekeeper led the way, walking a little sidewise, in advance of but not directly before the visitor. The Reverend Dr. Holt followed, looking straight ahead because to show curiosity was not good manners. Even so, he got an impression of the spaciousness of the court and of the height of the surrounding buildings, as well as of the over-all quiet dignity pervading the air. They reached a moon gate with another court beyond, and Holt heard the singsong voices of children coming from within one of its suites. They were reciting Chinese classics.

"We must wait here, sir," said the gatekeeper. "This is an inner court." Then, seeing Holt understood that only maidservants and boy attendants were permitted in the living quarters of the master, he added: "His Excellency the Central Hall spends much of his time teaching his grandchildren and grandnephews the classics, sir."

No one appeared until the gatekeeper uttered a loud cough. Then out came a boy of about fourteen, wearing two short queues, each tied at the end with red silk tassels. The gatekeeper handed him the visitor's card, and spoke briefly to him. Nodding in reply, the boy went into the suite from which the singsong voices came. As soon as he entered, the voices ceased. Then he returned to usher the visitor into the inner court.

As Holt moved forward, remembering his slow and willowy gait, an old man stepped out of the suite onto the veranda. He was of medium height, and nearly seventy; his queue was all white, and he had a small white beard, but his face, singularly free from wrinkles, was a healthy reddish color. He wore a blue silk gown topped by a yellow brocade jacket. The latter denoted the high official rank he held in the Empire—it could be worn, Holt knew, only by the special grace of Her Imperial Majesty, the reigning Empress Dowager.

When Holt was at the foot of the veranda steps, the boy announced the obvious. "Master, your honorable guest is come."

The missionary stretched forth both hands so that the fingers touched, then bowed low, the tips of his fingers nearly reaching the ground. Straightening, he lifted his hands to the level of his nose before lowering them. This was the simplest form of respectful salutation. In reply, the old man did the same, except that his bow was not as low as his visitor's. Holt thought he saw the trace of a wry smile on his face—whether in welcome or in mockery, he could only guess. Ho the Central Hall was gesturing for him to enter the suite, and Holt mounted the steps and crossed the veranda in his best Eight-Character Gait.

This was the central room of the suite, simply and symmetrically furnished. In the middle of the wall that faced the entrance was a wooden alcove embellished with delicate carving. Inside the alcove stood a gilded tablet bearing five Chinese characters in red, reading downward: Heaven, Earth, Sovereign, Parent, Teacher. Beneath the alcove was a long narrow table on which were a three-legged censer, with a candlestick at each side, and two porcelain plates piled high with fruit. These were offerings to the tablet that reminded the household of the five factors to which they owed daily reverence.

Along each of the walls flanking the alcove were aligned four stiff-backed chairs, interposed with tea-stands. Four scrolls hung on these walls—two of painting and two of calligraphy. The room was austerely furnished, but the table and chairs were made of teak, and the carpet on the floor was the best that could be found in Peking.

Ho the Central Hall motioned the Reverend Dr. Holt to take the chair on the left side, nearest the alcove. Knowing that this was the most honored seat in the room, Holt declined with a polite gesture and took the chair on the left that was nearest the entrance. Again the wry smile came and went on the old man's face. He seated himself on the other side, opposite his guest. The boy with two queues brought cups of tea on a lacquered tray, and when he had bowed out of the room, Ho the Central Hall opened the conversation—in a manner Holt had never anticipated.

"Pray, sir," he said, "forgive an old man his curiosity. Tell me, why did you not take the seat I asked you to take?"

"With your age and with your position, Your Excellency," Holt said, "I would not dare presume to sit on the most honored seat in your presence."

"And how is it that you walk in the way I noticed? Is this your natural way? Or have you learned it here for a purpose?"

"I have learned it here, Your Excellency. Back in my own country we have a saying, 'When in Rome, do as the Romans do.' Since I am in China, I believe it is proper for me to walk in the way Chinese scholars do."

Ho the Central Hall smiled his wry smile. "But I do not walk that way. It is too affected."

Holt lifted his eyebrows, nonplused at this remark. Before he could think of anything to say, Ho the Central Hall had another question.

"I am told you have come to my house from across the street in a four-man chair. Why have you done so for such a short distance?"

"I was informed," Holt said after a slight hesitation, "that it was the only proper way to call on Your Excellency."

"And the Chinese dress. And the Chinese name—my surname, too! I suppose all these are because you think they are proper?"

"Yes, Your Excellency."

The old man now permitted himself an unmistakably mischievous smile. "But that queue of yours! That cannot really be your hair. Do you think it proper to assume false appearances, sir?"

"If you deign, Your Excellency, to consider the queue in the same light as the dress—as a sort of personal apparel—then it is just as proper for me to wear the queue as the dress, both being Chinese."

Looking Holt full in the face, Ho the Central Hall now raised his voice. "Proper! Proper! You seem, sir, to know all that is proper. Then let me ask you this. A few days ago, I understand, you deliberately cut a slice of skin and flesh from your own person. Do you consider *that* proper? Do you think it right to inflict such grievous injuries upon the body you received from your own parents?"

"I did it for a good purpose, Your Excellency—to cure a little boy of his illness. The injury done to myself is small. The good done to the child, I hope, is much greater."

"Would you do this a second time, should a similar situation arise?"

"I hope there will not be another such occasion. But if need be, I would not hesitate to do it again, Your Excellency."

Ho the Central Hall studied Holt thoughtfully. Then he began softly, as if speaking to himself: "And to think that you are a foreigner! We have a saying, 'A doctor must have a heart to be willing to cut off his own limb for his patient.' I have lived almost seventy years, and only now have found a doctor who lives up to that proverb. And a foreigner, at that. And our Great Master, Confucius, said, 'What is a gentleman? He is a man who has an overpowering love for his kind.' Sir, you have that overpowering love, and yours is such a heart. Why, then, should you bother about minor proprieties? With a heart like your, you will never go wrong—you will always be right and proper. Our Great Master would unquestionably have called you a gentleman."

This left Holt speechless. He shifted awkwardly in his chair, embarrassed by the sudden turn, but Ho the Central Hall was not through. "Forgive me, sir," he went on. "I have misjudged you in the past. I thought you no different from the other foreigners I have had the misfortune to meet, but I was mistaken. I shall consider it an honor if you will allow me to be your friend."

The Reverend Dr. Holt now had to guard against his emotions. He was at the point of pledging undying friendship to the old man, but he remembered the Chinese custom of dividing all society not into classes or castes but into generations. Outwardly, the Chinese acknowledged four classes—scholars, farmers, artisans, and tradesmen, in that order. But these were not sharply delineated, and it was perfectly possible and easy for a man to change his class just by changing his occupation. Not so with his generation. If a man met a friend of his father's, he addressed him as "generation-uncle," and was in turn called "generation-nephew." There was an entire scale of such titles to govern one's speech and conduct, since in a normal course of life a man would have known five different generations.

Holt was not yet thirty. Ho the Central Hall was more than old enough to be his father.

"What a great honor that would be!" Holt finally said. "But it cannot be, Your Excellency. Your age is too high. I dare not reach to it."

"Oh, a pest on those minor proprieties!" Ho dismissed them with a wave of his hand. "However, I am glad you know about them. You may not have heard of another convention practiced by learned scholars in the past. It is known as 'Age-Forgotten Friendship,' and it means that in cases of mutual high esteem between an old man and a young one, the disparity in their ages is completely forgotten. It applies precisely to our own situation. Of course, as the convention goes, only the older man can make the proposal I am making now. But, mind you"—and here Ho's eyes twinkled merrily—"once such a proposal is made, it would be most improper for the younger man to refuse!"

The Reverend Dr. Holt had been trained well back at Mission headquarters in the port city. Bowing his head, he made the perfect answer, the common Chinese saying: "To show my deference to you, I can do no better than obey your command."

Ho the Central Hall broke into loud, joyous laughter. Then he smiled that smile of mischief again as he said, "Now that we are friends, may I say something you may not regard as proper?"

"Between friends," Holt said, quoting another popular proverb, "there should be nothing left unsaid."

"It must be extremely uncomfortable to wear that false queue. Why don't you take it off?"

It was Holt's turn to laugh. He removed his special "melon skin" with its dangling queue, and placed it on a tea-stand. His crop of red hair blazed in all its unusual glory—and immediately there was a sound of giggling behind a closed door.

"My pupils must be playing truant," the old man remarked. "They have been peeping at us. And I know who the giggling one is—my youngest grandson, Ta-kong. I am afraid I have spoiled that little imp—he has not even learned his manners." Then, turning his head, he called, "You children! Since you have already forgotten your books, you may as well come out and pay courtesy to your new grand-generation-uncle."

For a moment no noise was heard from inside the adjoining room. Then the side door opened, and about a dozen small boys came forth quietly in an orderly single file, led by a lad in his teens. The toddler who brought up the rear could hardly have been more than four. There was no doubt that this was Ta-kong. The others managed to look dignified and solemn—even a little remorseful at their discovered guilt—but Ta-kong's dark little rolling eyes were bright with undisguised mischief.

The procession ended, and the boys filled a whole corner of the room as they faced the Reverend Dr. Holt respectfully.

"Pay your courtesy to your grand-generation-uncle," ordered Ho the Central Hall.

Before Holt could rise to acknowledge the courtesy, the boys fell to their knees, kowtowed, and chorused shrilly:

"Salutations to you, grand-generation-uncle!"

Three

THE NAME GIVEN to Ho the Central Hall by his father was Ho Tao. This was indeed a fitting name, for of the more than eight thousand common characters in the Chinese language, Tao is perhaps among the most sublime and mythical. In ordinary usage, it means Reason. For scholars, it signifies The Way, meaning the way of righteousness, the one and only possible way of living—very much like what present-day Americans mean when they speak proudly of "the American way of life." And in the vast lore of the nebulous Chinese mythology, Tao means also Truth—the mysterious Truth that is so difficult to attain.

Ho Tao was called Ho the Central Hall because he had been a great minister of state in the Empire. In the old days, the buildings of the Imperial ministries were always symmetrical, usually with three main halls, one in the center and two on the sides. These were the private offices of the Minister and the two Vice-Ministers. So in time their subordinates, and then the common people, learned to address these dignitaries not by their names, for that would be too disrespectful; nor by their titles, for they might be too long and cumbersome; but simply to call them the Central Hall, the Left Hall, and the Right Hall respectfully, with the Left taking precedence over the Right and with the Central over both. Though Ho was living in retirement now, he was still known by that designation—once a Central Hall, always a Central Hall.

By the time the Reverend Dr. Holt came to Yi, Ho the Central

Hall had already become a legend to his people. They even took pride in relating what happened when, still a small boy, he learned his first four characters. And that story, indeed, was revealing of his personality:

The Hos had been living on the Lane of Eternal Stability for generations. They were typical of the Chinese landed gentry. On the one hand, they owned farmlands in the countryside and made a living by letting them out to tenant farmers. On the other, they worked hard at studying the classics, in the hope that they could pass the Government-conducted literary examinations, which in those days provided the only entrance into officialdom and the only sure road to position and wealth. Over the last two hundred years, the fortunes of the Hos had fluctuated greatly. Sometimes a Ho had risen to eminence, though none before him had ever attained such a high position as Ho Tao did. Then, for a generation or two, the Hos would remain obscure scholars who barely squeezed through the preliminary examinations. At times, the Hos were so prosperous that their possessions extended to hundreds and even thousands of acres; again, their circumstances were so reduced that they had to mortgage or sell most of their properties. But somehow, through good and through ill, they had clung to the house on the Lane of Eternal Stability.

Ho Tao was not especially favored from birth. To begin with, he had three brothers, two older and one younger. All three had been born to his father's wife; only he himself to a concubine. Though this did not deprive him of substantial rights as a son, it did carry some stigma. For instance, he had to call his real mother, "Aunt," the title "Mother" being reserved for his father's wife. A sensitive child like Ho Tao, understandably, was unhappy with this unique position in the household.

At the time Ho Tao came into the world, the fortunes of the Hos were sharply on the decline. Ho Tao's father was a spendthrift, and when he died shortly after Ho Tao's birth, he left the family estate in a sorry plight. He was survived by a wife, several concubines, and four sons, the oldest scarcely knee-high. He left no brothers to look after the family. Thus, the entire burden of managing the wretched estate and carrying on the name of the House of Ho devolved on the slender shoulders of the wife—a woman who had never been instructed in conducting any business other than domestic; and, moreover, a widow whose freedom of action was severely restricted by convention.

41

It was a tribute to Ho Tao's "mother" that she fully rose to the occasion. From the very start, she took drastic measures. No sooner seven times seven days—the proper period for mourning—were past than she told the concubines they were free to return to their own people. They were free to remarry, and free to be resold. However, to Ho Tao's "aunt"—since the woman had given birth to a son of Ho—she gave a choice. She could either do as the other concubines or choose to remain for her child's sake. But should she decide upon the latter course, she must renounce her style of living as a concubine and do the menial work of a servant. It was a tribute to the woman who bore Ho Tao that without the least hesitation she elected to stay.

Presently, the family fortunes fell so low that portions of land within the compound on the Lane of Eternal Stability, originally reserved for flower gardens, had to be put to more practical uses. Pigs were raised and vegetables grown to increase the food supply, and Ho Tao's "aunt," a farmer's daughter, was entrusted with the chore. Those who had known her as a concubine hardly recognized her now. Her face was tanned, her hands chapped. In spite of her bound feet, she shuffled back and forth on the vegetable plots carrying pailfuls of manure for fertilizer. She worked as hard as any peasant woman, and never complained.

Meanwhile, Widow Ho bravely undertook to continue the traditions of the House of Ho. As soon as the boys were of the age to study, she sought out the best possible tutor within her limited means. And she showed no partiality toward her own children. When Ho Tao reached six, he joined his two older brothers.

All the townspeople of Yi knew the story of the first day Ho Tao went to school. Before sunrise, he was taken by his two older brothers to the family temple and bidden to kowtow to the ancestral tablets, reporting the memorable step he was about to take in his young life. Then he was led to the tutor, an old man of some sixty years, even more impecunious than the Hos but widely known for his scholarship as well as his personal virtues. Ho Tao had long since been taught the proverb: "If a man is a teacher to you but for one day, he is a sort of father to you throughout your life." The little boy knew what was expected of him. He fell down on all fours and kowtowed to the tutor nine times. This ceremony over, he seated himself meekly beside his brothers.

The tutor cleared his throat. "Ho Tao," he said, "this is the first day that you come to learn from me. Though you are only six years old, it is not too early to let you know of the things that are important in life. Before we start on your regular lessons, I want to teach you four characters. I shall write them out. I shall explain their meanings. If you don't understand, ask me questions. If you do understand, then remember the significance of the words as long as you live. And you must do more than remember them; you must also forever live up to their standards."

At that time blackboards had not yet come into use in China, and the tutor took out a brush, dipped it in black ink, and wrote four large characters on a sheet of paper. He held up the paper and asked the two older boys to read the characters aloud one by one. To the envy of Ho Tao, his brothers pronounced them correctly.

Then turning to the younger boy, the old man said, "Now I shall explain these characters to you. I shall give their meanings in the simplest form.

"The first word is CHUNG—Loyalty. You must be always faithful to your sovereign, the Emperor. You must never fail to carry out His Majesty's orders.

"The second word is HSIAO—Filial Piety. You must love, honor, revere, and serve your father and mother. It is they who gave you birth. It is they who take care of you when you are young. It is therefore fitting that you requite them with filial deeds as soon as you are able to.

"The third word is CHIEH—Fidelity. This mainly concerns womenfolk. I am most honored to be a tutor in your house, Ho Tao, for what your 'mother' and your 'aunt' have been doing is an excellent example of Fidelity.

"The fourth word is YI—Integrity. You must be always honest with yourself and true to others. You must not lie. You must not cheat. You must never speak one way and act differently. You must do what you believe is right.

"These four words form the essence of our culture, the core of the teachings of our ancient sages. If you can remember them, live up to them, and help to uphold them in every way, then you will grow up a better man and our society will become a better society. Do you understand me, Ho Tao?"

Ho Tao thought as much as a boy of his age could. Then he shook his head.

"Which of the words don't you understand?" asked the tutor.

The boy pointed his little finger at the second character.

"Filial Piety?" The old man was a little surprised. "Why, that is the easiest of the four to understand. As I said before, it means to honor, love, and serve your father and mother. It means to anticipate their wishes and to try to fulfill them. It means to care for your parents as soon as you are grown up and able to do so. Let me give you some examples, very simple ones. Suppose you have good food. You should not eat it yourself. You should offer it first to your parents. Or suppose there is some work to do in the house. Before they think of doing it, you should have it done for them. These are small matters. But they represent roughly the idea of Filial Piety.

"And mark you, my boy, don't overlook the importance of Filial Piety. It is the greatest thing in our life. It is the one thing which separates men from the lower animals. In many respects, the lower animals are not different from us humans. When they are hungry, they want to eat, like us. When they are thirsty, like us again, they want to drink. But they do not have a sense of Filial Piety, and we do. The lower animals know only of their mothers, and not of their fathers. And even with their mothers, they cling to them only so long as they are young and need their milk. As soon as they grow up, they leave their mothers and recognize them no more. But not so with us humans. And if we do not have a proper sense of Filial Piety, and we neglect our fathers and mothers, then we will be degrading ourselves to the level of lower animals. You don't want to do that, Ho Tao, do you?"

The little boy shook his head violently. But at the same time he said, "I don't know my father, master."

"True, your father is dead," answered the tutor. "It is a pity he should have died when you were too young to know him. But his name is known to you. If you become a good man—one who lives up to the standards of Loyalty, Filial Piety, Fidelity, and Integrity—you bring honor to his name. If you become a bad man—one who does not live up to those standards—you bring shame to his name. The way to render Filial Piety to your deceased father is to try always to bring honor and not shame to his name."

"But I have also a 'mother' and an 'aunt,'" the boy stumbled. "To which of these should I render my Filial Piety, master?"

The question caught the tutor somewhat unprepared, but he answered solemnly: "To both, Ho Tao. Your condition is not uncommon. There are many like you who have both a mother and an aunt. Your 'mother' is the one who has taken care of you. Your 'aunt' is the one who has given you birth. You owe much to both, and to both you ought to render Filial Piety."

44

The next day Ho Tao would not go to school. Unbeknown to his "aunt," the little boy had gone to the back yards of the compound and fertilized the vegetables and fed the pigs. When he was discovered, he could not be dragged away. He insisted that he was following the teachings of the tutor and that he wanted—oh, so much—to show his Filial Piety toward his "aunt." It took quite a few tears from his "aunt," a severe scolding from his "mother," and the strength of his two older brothers to persuade him to return to the schoolroom.

The tutor did not reprimand Ho Tao for his truancy. He simply told him that the proper way to render Filial Piety to his 'aunt' just now was to apply himself diligently to his studies rather than to save her labor in her chores. As the old man remarked then, he was singularly impressed with the boy's strong "virtuous roots." And in later years the townspeople of Yi were similarly impressed.

Ho Tao never forgot those four characters. Whatever his ups and downs in life—and his career was on the whole exceedingly fortunate—he always strove hard to live up to their ideals.

Ho Tao was the only one among the brothers who passed the three literary examinations to qualify for official appointment. But at first he was not at all successful as an official. He was a very conscientious public servant, but altogether too honest and upright. He did not know how to flatter his superiors and curry favor with them, nor did he remain silent and evasive even when it was clearly not to his interest to be straight and outspoken. Indeed, he would have been consigned to oblivion had he not received unexpected outside help. And strange as it might seem, he owed his rise entirely to a woman—none other than the reigning Empress Dowager.

Unscrupulous and capricious, the Empress was everything that Ho Tao was not, yet somehow she discerned in him the solid qualities she herself lacked but valued highly. From the moment she chanced upon that discovery, Ho Tao's fortune was as good as made. Quickly he was lifted from obscurity to prominence. And after serving in a variety of important posts, he was finally named a Minister of State—the highest honor a subject of the Empire could ever hope to attain.

Ho Tao served Her Majesty truly well. Not once in his long, distinguished service did he permit the thought of losing her favors to interfere with his own sense of Loyalty. In time, he became known as the only person in the Imperial Court who was not afraid of speaking his mind and incurring her displeasure. And luckily for Ho Tao again, where Her Majesty would not tolerate others, she tolerated him. She might not follow his advice, but at least she let him have his say, and that in itself was considered an extraordinary favor on the part of Her Majesty.

There was no question but that Ho Tao lived up to the standards of Filial Piety. He did well by both his "mother" and his "aunt." When he got his first appointment away from home, he took his "aunt" to live with him, with his "mother's" permission, and for many years thereafter he cared for her with all respect and affection. It grieved him deeply that, her life abruptly cut short by a dreadful tragedy, she did not live to see him become a Minister of State; but so it was ordained by Heaven. As for his "mother," he regularly sent her a sizable portion of his salaries. These sums were considerably increased later by the large monetary rewards Her Majesty graciously granted him. Thus, his "mother" was enabled not only to pay off all the old mortgages but also to acquire many new properties. By the end of the old woman's life, she had the satisfaction of knowing that under her management the House of Ho had surpassed all its former glories and was reputed to be among the richest families in Yi.

Ho Tao's married life was also exceedingly happy, and in it he showed a unique understanding of the virtue of Fidelity. It was the custom in China that all marriages of young people were arranged very early by parents through go-betweens. Ho Tao's marriage was no exception. His wife—her name was Orchid—was descended from an impoverished scholar's family. Until they were joined in nuptial ceremonies they had never seen each other, but theirs was indeed a union contracted in Heaven. Though concubinage was common practice, especially among men of position and wealth, because of the great love he bore for Orchid and because of the sad memories of his "aunt," Ho Tao never once considered taking a concubine.

Finally Ho Tao's "mother" passed away. That worthy woman had lived to a ripe old age and had seen her two older sons die before her. Though none of her own three offspring had been much of a success, she had enjoyed all the fruits of Ho Tao's honor and wealth. According to Court etiquette, the death of a parent required the surviving oldest son to retire from officialdom for three years as a symbol of Filial Piety. Ho Tao, knowing how stormy the waters of politics could be, and realizing that his fortunes depended on the caprice of a woman, gave heed to the wisdom of an ancient saying:

46

"When the current flows swift, it is not the man who swims along with it who is brave, but the man who retreats away from it." He petitioned to make his retirement permanent. The Empress Dowager was reluctant to let him go and wanted to waive his retirement by an Imperial Decree of special dispensation. But Ho Tao insisted, and Her Majesty acceded.

It was not simply the material benefits Ho Tao gave to the people of Yi that earned him their recognition and respect—the many public works, such as bridges and roads, which he built at his own expense, and the many charities, known and unknown, which he endowed with his private funds. These material services, though worthy, were nothing to compare with his spiritual leadership. True, Ho Tao did nothing more than strictly follow the old teachings and conventions. But whereas to others the teachings might be mere dogmas, and the conventions rituals that were quoted or practiced perfunctorily through force of habit, to Ho Tao they were real, living, and meaningful. In observing them, he was not only conscientiously striving to raise himself to their standards, he was also trying by his personal example to persuade others to do the same.

Indeed, nothing gladdened him more than to see this improvement in others. For instance, when he heard of a notable act of Filial Piety, even though the man might be only a poor peasant living in a remote village, he, a Central Hall of the Empire, made a special journey to call on him and offer his friendship. Or when he noticed a widow practicing Fidelity, he had Orchid visit her with gifts and help her in every way. Or when he heard of a righteous deed, he would sing praises for days of both the man and the deed.

He was quite a busybody, but one people understood and appreciated. He never spoke of the bad things men did; he spoke only of the good things they either did or could do. He never condemned, he always praised. And as he continued tirelessly in his efforts, the people of Yi began not only to value what he praised but also to abstain from what he would not praise. Without his issuing any instructions, they did what he approved and shunned what he disapproved. They did not think they were giving him obedience. They regarded him as their own conscience.

The people of Yi felt they knew all about Ho the Central Hall. Actually they did not. This was because, though he was ever eager to speak of the good deeds done by others, he was invariably silent about his own. Besides, his good deeds were so manifold that the people came to take them for granted and were not curious. That is why the story of his saving Widow Lan came to be known to only a few.

It had happened about two years before the Reverend Dr. Holt arrived in Yi. Ho the Central Hall was taking a trip to the mountains lying to the southwest of the prefecture to see what he could do to improve communications for the villagers there. He was exploring a lonely trail, and for a short while had lost the company of his attendants, when in a dense wood on a deserted hill he found Widow Lan.

She had not expected anyone to find her in that solitary spot. With her baby in her arms, she was huddled under a tree over which a rope had been swung. The only thing that had deterred her momentarily from hanging herself was the agony of parting with the child. She was crying her heart out, and when Ho the Central Hall made his presence known, she was taken completely by surprise.

Little by little he succeeded in prying the story out of her. She had been living with her husband in a village near the mountains. They owned a few acres of land and had managed to be quite happy and comfortable. Then, a few months before, a stranger had ridden into the village and, seeing her, had approached and said that he was thirsty. Though her husband was out working in the field, she brought the stranger tea. She never spoke so much as a word to him, but he kept on telling her about himself. He bragged about his riches, and said that he lived in the City of Yi and his name was Ma Teh-lin.

Shortly after the incident, her husband fell into bad company and began to frequent the local gambling house. The first few times he brought home some winnings; then his luck changed, and finally he had to deed his entire property—the few acres of land and the little dwelling in the village—to pay his gambling debts. She had learned about this only ten days ago—after her husband had hanged himself at this same spot in the wood.

She did not want to die. She wanted to take care of her child, and was willing to work her fingers to the bone for its sake. But at this juncture Ma had turned up, not only holding the deeds to the properties but claiming that her husband owed him much more besides. According to law husband and wife were held equally re-

48

sponsible for debts, and Ma told her that she must either pay up within ten days or become his concubine.

She now had only one day left. Pay she could not; she was penniless and had neither relatives nor friends to help her. To become Ma's concubine—that was out of the question. She had not read the Books, but she knew what Fidelity meant. Hence, she had come to this spot, prepared to follow her husband.

When she finished her story, Ho Tao was filled with as much indignation at his neighbor Ma as compassion for her. Legally, Ho was aware, nothing could be done against Ma, but socially was another matter. It would be easy for Ho Tao to proclaim Ma's knavery and have the wicked man ostracized by the society of Yi. But such conduct would not be in line with his own ideal. Said Confucius, "A gentleman must always blazon the good and conceal the evil in others." And this precept was the one he had always followed.

So, confidentially, through an agent, he paid Widow Lan's debts to Ma and brought the young woman herself back to Yi. Bidding her not to tell her story to anyone, he built her the shack directly in front of Ma's house—with a twofold purpose. On the one hand, it would enable Widow Lan to avail herself of his protection whenever necessary. On the other, it would serve as a constant silent reminder to Ma that he had better mend his ways.

Four

To THE PEOPLE of Yi, it was unthinkable that anything could ever trouble the wise and tranquil mind of Ho the Central Hall. Since he kept his worries to himself, nobody ever knew that he was greatly concerned about his youngest son, Fucho.

Orchid had borne Ho three sons and a daughter. At the time of his retirement, the two older sons were doing well. Both had passed the examinations; one was a minor official in the Imperial Court, and the other was serving as prefect in a distant province. The daughter had been married to the son of a Viceroy. When Ho Tao and Orchid came back to the Lane of Eternal Stability to live, only Fucho was with them.

This was some two years before the Reverend Dr. Holt came to Yi, and Fucho was fifteen. He was brilliant and industrious at that time, and had made great strides in his studies of the classics. His father was happy in the thought that in two more years Fucho would be able to pass the preliminary examinations. But in just half that time his dream was rudely broken. China and Japan fought a short war over Korea, and the Celestial Empire was humbled by her upstart island neighbor. Ho the Central Hall was grieved sorely by this defeat, and even more so by the fact that from then on Fucho lost all interest in his studies.

Ho waited for a moment when they were alone and then asked Fucho if he was having some trouble with his health. "You have not been making much progress in your studies of late," he said carefully.

"There is nothing wrong with my health, Father," Fucho said, looking down his nose.

"Then is there something troubling your mind?"

The boy hesitated. "Father, you named me Fucho. It is not an ordinary name. It means 'vengeance.' Why was I named that?"

"But you know the story, my son. You have heard it from your mother, and from your brothers."

"I have not heard it from you, Father," Fucho said stoutly.

"Very well," and Ho sighed. "You were born just after your 'grandaunt's' death, when I was Prefect of Fuchow, capital of Fukien Province. The Men from the West were making trouble. One of their warships came into the harbor of Fuchow under false pretenses of friendship, and suddenly opened fire on the city. Your 'grandaunt' was killed by a cannon shot."

"You named me Fucho so I would not forget—you wanted me to revenge my 'grandaunt's' death when I grew up?"

Ho the Central Hall nodded. "Yes, but now—"

His impatient young son forgot his manners, and interrupted. "Why have the Men from the West made war on us so frequently, Father? Why has the Empire signed the Unequal Treaties and given them land in the port cities—why do they have so many privileges when they are still not subject to our laws?"

"It began more than fifty years ago," Ho said sorrowfully. "That was when they came from the West Ocean in great numbers, bringing opium from India—our people had not had the evil drug before. A Viceroy seized one of their ships and burned its cargo, and that

50

started the first war. China was badly beaten. Finding us weak, they have used force again and again."

Fucho bristled with the anger of youth. "My tutors have told me that ours is the oldest and greatest culture, and that our Empire is the biggest and most populous. How can they defeat us?"

"They have better firearms, my son. Even the Japanese—even the islanders we used to call Dwarf Barbarians—have defeated us. In the past they came to learn from us, eagerly, and we looked down on them as an ignorant people. More the shame on us, now. They also learned from the Westerners—they learned how to make better firearms."

Fucho came suddenly to the point. "Then, Father, let me go across the West Ocean and learn the same things the Japanese have learned!"

"No—never will I allow that!" Ho said positively. "Even when I was Minister of State, I did not want any of our young men to learn Western ways, and I hold that opinion now. You are perhaps too young to understand, Fucho, but I tell you this: Even though the Westerners are more capable of fighting wars, our culture is still far superior in that it teaches basic human virtues. It aims at contentment for the individual, and stability for society. This is not true of the Western culture. It does not even teach Filial Piety. No—I shall never let you go to the Western countries where you would lose our ethical values."

"Then let me go to Japan, Father. Their culture is based upon ours, and cannot be too much changed. I would not lose our ethical values there, but I could learn about firearms, and defense. Father, you gave me my name. I owe this to you—I owe it to my 'grand-aunt'!"

For a moment, Ho the Central Hall was speechless. Then he said remorsefully, "I intended to explain more fully when we began this conversation, but you interrupted me. Yes, I named you Fucho—nearly sixteen years ago in a moment of anger. I have regretted that. It is not right for an individual to wreak private vengeance, taking the law into his own hands. It is even worse for nations to do so. Under the teachings of Confucius, we have always been a peace-loving people. I don't want to talk about wars or vengeance any more, Fucho. I wish we could build another Great Wall and keep the Westerners out, just as the First Emperor kept out the Northern Barbarians so long ago."

51

Fucho smiled, and shook his head. "But we can no longer build a Great Wall high enough or thick enough, Father. Please let me go to Japan and learn the arts of defense!"

Ho the Central Hall turned to another argument. He had years before affianced Fucho to a girl of the Tan family. Her name was Delicate Blossom, and her father was still in active service as a Minister of State. It was the dearest wish of Ho and Orchid to see the young couple married before they died.

"But you should wait a few years, Fucho," he said. "You are nearly sixteen, and Delicate Blossom is twelve. In four more years you can be married. Then if you are still determined to go to Japan, you can take her with you."

Fucho was stubborn. "It is difficult to study with a woman at one's side. You yourself have told me of the famous general of the Han dynasty who drove the Tartars out of Mongolia. You told me that he said, 'While the Tartars remain undestroyed, what is the use of my getting married?' I want to be like that heroic man!"

In the long run, Ho Tao consented. Orchid shed many tears. But before Fucho was seventeen, he left for Japan.

2

FOR A LONG time after Fucho left, Ho the Central Hall suffered that loneliness which must be endured by the great. All the people of Yi honored him, but his position was such that he could not exchange intimacies with any of them. His two older sons knew of his loneliness, and followed a custom of the times by sending several of their children to be reared by Ho Tao and Orchid—to comfort them, the sons said, in their Honorable Age. Ho was grateful. He loved all his grandchildren, and especially adored that bright-eyed little imp named Ta-kong, who reminded him very much of Fucho. But although he could play with Ta-kong, he could not yet discuss the classics, or carry on other satisfying conversations, with him.

Ho the Central Hall was most of all lonely for the friendship of someone near his equal as a scholar. Thus, after he met the Reverend Dr. Holt—and after the "Great Wall" between them was broken—the two men profited mutually. Once Ho the Central Hall had received the American, all the notables of the town called at the Mission compound. Now that Ho's older grandchildren and grandnephews were permitted to study English at Holt's school, it was possible to set up a sizable class. And when word got around of the surgery that had cured Widow Lan's son, people even began coming to the missionary's medical clinic.

Ho the Central Hall found pleasure he had not known for a long time, in theological and philosophical discussions with the red-headed young man. But for Holt there was one disappointment. Six months—seven months—in Yi, and he had not converted a single soul to Christianity.

"It is necessary to have patience," the lanky, solemn-faced Ah Wong told Holt. The two had already given up their Salvation Army street tactics for more dignified methods. "Of course, if you could convert Ho the Central Hall . . ."

At last, the Reverend Dr. Holt succeeded in persuading Ho to read the Bible from cover to cover.

"What did you think of it?" he asked the older man when he had finished.

"It is very interesting," admitted the Confucian scholar, drawing his blue silk gown closer around him. "The Old Testament is very much like the Book of History in our classics. The New Testament is like the Analects of Confucius, except that Confucius attributes his teachings to a study of basic human relationships, and not to a divine origin."

He smiled benignly at his new friend, who seemed somewhat taken aback.

"But the Bible *is* divinely inspired!" Holt said.

"I found it instructive and interesting," Ho the Central Hall went on blandly. "It helped me to understand you and your people; it gave me comfort to know that there is some spiritualism in you, not merely materialism."

"Ah!" said Holt. "If you are spiritualistic, why can't you believe in the divine origin of the Word—in the divinity of Christ? Why not believe in the one and only true God?"

"But there are limits, my friend. I cannot believe in what I do not know."

"But you do know! You are too intelligent not to realize that the world would make no sense if there were not a Supreme Being!"

"Oh, I believe in the existence of a Supreme Being. So did our Great Master. In his Book of Odes, Confucius sang, 'How bright and fearful is the God who sees all within the four directions!' "

"Then why can't you crystallize your belief in Him?"

"Ah, but Confucius also said, 'I do not know enough of this world;

how can I tell of the next?' And it is recorded in the Analects: 'The Master never speaks of strange forces and false gods.' I think this —if I do everything right by men, I shall not be denied by the true God even if I do not recognize Him. But if I fix my eyes only on God, and do not do right by men, then even the God I believe will spurn me."

Holt found that philosophy nearly unanswerable. "You are very fit to be a Christian, you know," he said. "In the Faith, your belief in doing right by men would be greatly strengthened."

"No, I do not think it would," Ho Tao said firmly. "You Westerners say you are Christians. But have you conducted yourselves in accordance with the teachings of this book? Have you turned the left cheek when the right cheek is slapped? No, you have slapped us, instead, on both our cheeks. You have sold opium to our people, and warred on us without provocation. Even your own God does not know what your countries will do to us next." He smiled again at the missionary, and continued gently, "No, unless these things are changed, you can never persuade me to become a Christian. . . ."

The year 1900 brought terrible drought to that part of China. Ho the Central Hall read the signs in the burning sky and the windless nights loud with cicada shrilling. He began making inspection tours of the countryside, and frequently took Holt with him. The fields were parched and the crops stunted. Fear of famine returned to memory, and there was little laughter in the villages. By August, the situation had become desperate.

The House of Ho had always collected rent from many tenant farmers, but Ho the Central Hall waived the rent payments for that year, and on his recommendation the Prefect asked that all landowners do the same. It was noted that among those who did not heed the Prefect's plea was Ma Teh-lin—the keeper of many concubines and the richest man in Yi.

People thronged to the temples, Buddhist and Taoist alike, to burn incense and pray for rain. The Prefect erected a huge bare scaffold in front of his yamen, and sat there, bareheaded in the scorching sun, to pray continuously for three days. Despite his age, Ho the Central Hall joined the Prefect in doing this penance.

Holt went to see them, and was not a little moved by their faith, even though it was not the same as his own. He asked what he could do.

54

Ho's voice was hoarse with dust and thirst. "Go back, my friend!" he begged. "Go pray to your Christian God to give us rain!"

The Reverend Dr. Holt prayed long on his knees, and the young-old Ah Wong, saying nothing, knelt beside him.

But no rain fell.

In September, it was estimated that the harvest would be only a third of its normal yield. Holt was invited to a select gathering at the central court of Ho Tao's residence; he had not seen Ho the Central Hall for several days, and did not know the purpose of the meeting. When he arrived, he found the Prefect there and all the leading citizens of Yi. As the missionary entered, there was a stir of surprise.

Ho the Central Hall introduced the Prefect in a short speech, saying that many people would go hungry through the long winter unless something were done. His Excellency the Prefect, Ho said, had done all he could; the Imperial Court had mercifully waived all taxes. Even this was not enough. He called upon the Prefect, who presented statistics and outlined a well-organized plan for the equitable distribution of food to the needy—provided such foodstuffs could be raised by popular subscription.

Now, Ho the Central Hall spoke again.

"Confucius," he said, "exhorted us to live by the principle of Benevolence. Mencius has said, 'The sense of pity is common to all men.' Heaven has blessed these here with fortunes, and it is time for us to share with those less fortunate. I ask you, honorable sirs, to give. Give to the limit of your capacity! Give until your conscience tells you that you have earned the dignity of man! Give no less!"

The Reverend Dr. Holt listened with a new and growing awareness of the old man's stature, of his humanity and the philosophies by which he lived; the tenets of Ho the Central Hall would put many a Christian to shame. Holt felt a lump rising in his throat, and when Ho ended his poetic plea with a call for donations, the redheaded missionary stood like a torch over his Chinese neighbors.

"Honorable sirs," he said, "I did not know, before my coming here, the purpose of this meeting. So there has been no time to ask my Mission how much it can give, although I have written to headquarters about the need. On my own part, I want to give my humble share. It is nothing—it is an inadequacy. I wish to contribute fifty piculs of wheat."

Ho the Central Hall beamed at Holt, and turned to write on a large sheet of paper, "Ho-Lo-Teh, fifty piculs." He faced the assemblage again. "You have heard!" he said. "I know the Reverend Dr. Ho-Lo-Teh's circumstances—he has nothing but his salaries, and this represents half his earnings for a whole year. That he was the first to speak is also significant. Did not Confucius tell us, 'In pursuing a righteous cause, one must not lag behind others'? Who will be next?"

The crowd fidgeted, but remained silent. Ho smiled. "Perhaps, honorable sirs, you are being polite to me. Because of my age and my unworthy achievements, you wish to accord me the privilege of being the first to follow the Reverend Dr. Ho-Lo-Teh. All of you are familiar with my circumstances. Then name the amount I should give!"

Again there was silence. Ho the Central Hall turned to an old gentleman with rheumy eyes and a long white beard. "You are a good and dear friend of my family. What should I give?"

"In my opinion," the old man quavered, "a thousand piculs. More than that would deprive your family."

Ho smiled again. "You are too good a friend," he said. "You think too much of my family and not enough of the hungry people. I am sorry to cast aside your advice. I donate three thousand piculs."

The central court murmured with astonishment as he wrote this down. Then he lifted his head, and said, "Who will volunteer next, honorable sirs?"

Holt studied the crowd. Everybody was visibly engaged in mental calculations, readjusting figures in an effort to meet Ho's surprisingly excessive donation.

After a moment, the Prefect raised his voice. "Perhaps we should go about this another way. Who is the richest man among us? Let him make his donation now."

The entire assemblage looked at Ma. Holt saw him, ill at ease under the mass scrutiny, a sallow man of about fifty with shrewd, piggish eyes. He was trying to pretend that he did not see the stares.

"How do you answer, Mr. Ma?" Ho the Central Hall asked quietly.

"But—but *I* am not the richest man in Yi!" Ma protested. "It is true that I have properties, but they are not profitable. I am by no means a rich man!"

"Come!" Ho said gently. "We will not argue about your wealth. If you are not the richest man in Yi, then here is your opportunity to be the most generous one. Pray, what will you give?"

"I—I will contribute five hundred piculs, Your Excellency the Central Hall."

Seeing the contemptuous glances of the gathering, the Reverend Dr. Holt almost felt sorry for Ma Teh-lin. The character of the man was being pitilessly laid bare before all of Yi.

The Prefect rose to save Ho the Central Hall from having to challenge his miserly neighbor. "Do you mean, Mr. Ma," he asked, "that your net earnings for half a year are only ten times those of our foreign friend, Mr. Ho-Lo-Teh?"

Ma's sallow face paled. "For your Excellency's sake, I will increase my contribution to a thousand piculs."

"No, no!" the Prefect said. "Do nothing for *my* sake. Our records show that you own much more land than the House of Ho. Yet His Excellency the Central Hall has donated three thousand piculs."

"But my lands are heavily mortgaged!" Ma whined. "A thousand piculs is, in truth, the utmost I can give!"

Holt heard a murmur swelling through the crowd. It was evident that nobody believed Ma. Then someone shouted a demand that he produce records of the mortgages.

"You want to bankrupt me!" Ma shouted desperately. "I hope you will be satisfied when I am a pauper. Very well—*two* thousand piculs!"

The redheaded missionary was suddenly enjoying himself hugely, thinking that people were the same the world over, remembering that he had seen this sort of gambit back in the Middle West.

Ho picked up his pen, and then put it down again. He leaned forward and said in a very gentle voice, "Could you go a little higher, Mr. Ma? Couldn't you make your sum equal to mine?"

"No, no!" Ma squealed, shaking his head vigorously.

"A mere thousand piculs!" Ho said. "That would not cause much privation to your family, but it would make a tremendous difference to people who are starving. Think of the men who will commit suicide! Think of the women who may be sold as concubines and prostitutes—of the children who cry with belly hunger! Shall I put you down for *three* thousand piculs, Mr. Ma?"

Ma was sweating terribly. Watching him, the Reverend Dr. Holt saw that Ho the Central Hall had struck home with that reference to concubines. Ma lived in mortal fear that his conduct toward Widow Lan would be exposed.

Ma wavered, then dropped his head low and said in a choked voice, "It shall be as you wish, Your Excellency. Three thousand piculs."

Ho wrote that down with a smile. Holt saw the look on Ma's face;

57

black hate contorted the miser's features into something inhuman.

After that, the subscriptions proceeded swiftly and well. The Prefect closed the meeting with more than the minimum pledges he had asked, and Ho the Central Hall signaled the Reverend Dr. Holt to stay. When the two were finally alone, the older man said, "You more than came up to my expectations, my friend. Do you know why I asked you here?"

"No," Holt said. "But I am more than happy to do my share."

"Let us have some tea," Ho suggested, and led the way to another room. "Has your Mission warned you about the organization called the Boxers?"

"I have heard of them," Holt admitted, "but only casually. As for a warning—should there have been one from my Mission?"

The tea came. The boy who brought it bowed deeply and departed.

"Let me tell you some things, my friend," Ho said. The old man's face was lined with troubles. "We are a peace-loving people, but your people—the Westerners—have invaded our land, have humbled us repeatedly. So village bands have been started, much like your militia, which, among other things, practice one of our traditional sports, boxing—partly for good health, partly in self-defense. These bands—the I Ho Ch'üan—have been called the Righteous Harmony Fists, or simply the Boxers. They have formed secret societies; they even believe their skill in this sport, plus our overwhelming numbers, can defeat you."

Holt put down his teacup and stared at Ho the Central Hall. "Do you mean fists against firearms?" he asked incredulously.

"Hear me," said Ho. "We have some people in the Imperial Court who are selfish and ambitious, and they have been encouraging the organization of bands of Boxers throughout the whole country. It might have been a harmless patriotic movement—perhaps even a good one, with proper direction. But no, it has already, without having been tried, become an antiforeign effort. I have had reports of riots in many places—most of them to insult foreigners in public, to molest your churches and trading posts. And this terrible drought does not help the cause of peace. It makes men desperate. I fear that the Boxer movement will spread like wildfire, and under unscrupulous leadership."

"I am grateful for your telling me all this," Holt said slowly. "But it is not my business to interfere in the political affairs of China. I am here only to try to save souls for Christ. So what should I do?"

"Nothing," said Ho. "I hope I have done it by inviting you to this meeting today, and that you have done it with your generosity— I think, now, the people of Yi are behind you. I do not think any harm would come to you so long as I am here, and I have already advised the Prefect to forbid the formation of any bands of Boxers in the Prefecture. But, my friend, I am going to Peking to ask an audience with Their Majesties, so that I can give them my opinions on this very serious situation. While I am gone, I would be worried about you if it were not for today . . ."

"Thank you, Ho the Central Hall!" Holt said warmly. "I don't know how I can ever express my gratitude."

"Between friends," Ho answered, "there is no call for gratitude. Indeed, I should be thankful to you, not for myself but for the hungry people. You are a stranger to our land, and your fifty piculs should mean much more than my three thousand."

The teacups were empty. The Reverend Dr. Holt rose to leave, thinking that every day he learned more about the old man in the blue silk gown, and always to Ho's credit.

Now Ho the Central Hall added with obvious pride, "And when I return from Peking, I shall bring with me the one of whom I have spoken so often—Fucho, my youngest son!"

"It will be a great pleasure to meet Fucho," Holt said, bowing. "Has he finished his studies in Japan?"

"No, he has finished only a preparatory school, and will go back to enroll in the Japanese Military Academy. But we hope that his wedding will take place during his short leave—and you, my friend, will be invited as an honored guest!"

Five

SHORTLY AFTER HO TAO's departure for Peking, the Reverend Dr. Holt received an urgent communication from Mission headquarters confirming all his friend had told him, and painting a far worse picture. After foreign nationals, the Christians were ranked as a secondary menace by the Boxers, it seemed, and several missionary outposts had already been burned by unruly mobs, and a few missionaries killed. Yi was considered no longer safe, and Holt was advised to evacuate at once to the big port city, where the foreign powers maintained armed forces in the Concessions.

But Holt declined to follow the instructions; he felt perfectly secure in Yi. Following Ho Tao's advice, the Prefect had publicly banned the formation of Boxers' bands in the Prefecture. And people were trooping as usual into his clinic for the treatment of their ailments—in fact, the number of his patients had lately increased, for the famine was exacting its toll, and with the general lack of nutrition sickness became widespread.

Yet, as days went by, Holt began to lose his self-assurance. He felt his first uneasiness when, upon hearing that illness was even more rampant in the countryside, he offered his services to the Prefect to take a tour outside the city. His Excellency politely refused the offer, saying that it would be unsafe for Holt to go. Then, without warning, two pupils in his English class stopped coming. They were Ma's two older sons—Ma Pingnan, a blustering bully, and Ma Pingshi, a sullen stripling. They had been among the first to enroll in the class, and although Holt had no particular liking for them, their abrupt, unexplained abstention troubled him. As if their truancy were a signal, the stream of his patients suddenly dwindled to a trickle. Now when he went about the city he felt an indescribable tension. He was still greeted everywhere, but only in recognition, not with cordiality. The people were no longer sure of themselves. The antiforeign sentiments of the country had infected them. Deprived of the enlightened guidance of Ho the Central Hall, they did not know what to do with this foreigner, who was acknowledgedly a good foreigner but a foreigner nonetheless.

Holt discussed his anxieties with Ah Wong. But that faithful and solemn assistant could offer no better counsel than caution and patience—platitudes Holt already knew. Ah Wong, in turn, sounded the gatekeeper and the cook. Gatekeeper showed a stout heart. He said, "Whom Ho the Central Hall favors, nobody can harm in this city. Have no fear! We shall all protect our foreign master."

But Cook's remarks were not so reassuring. "Hasn't our master got his witchcraft?" he asked, and then continued, "I hear the Boxers say they are immune from bullets of foreign guns. You can fire at them point-blank and you cannot kill them. If that is not good magic, I don't know one! If I were His Excellency the Prefect, I wouldn't ban the Boxers. I would let them come in and match their magic against our master's. If they win, then it proves that we Chinese are after all better than the foreigners. If they lose, then our

60

master is superior. I wager that our master will come out of the contest the better of the two!"

Though Holt laughed at the reported conversation, he was nevertheless disturbed. The Boxers' movement was manifestly sweeping across the country, gathering momentum. Could Ho the Central Hall persuade the rulers of the Empire to check it in time? And how long could the Prefect of Yi keep the Boxers out? Holt was aware that tremendous forces had been let loose by the movement—rightly or wrongly, it was the first awakening of national consciousness in a proud people. It was like a stupendous volume of waters long dammed up. While it was secured within confines it looked harmless, but with the bounds broken it would rush down to drown everything.

He could not sleep easily any more, but spent much of his nighttime reading the Scripture. One night, long after Ah Wong had gone to bed, he was still reading when he heard someone tapping at his windowpane, and saw two dark shadows on the veranda.

"Don't move, honorable sir!" a voice said. "It is I, Widow Lan. And Mistress Chow is with me. If we were found here, it would be the death of us—but we had to come. You are in mortal danger! You must flee! Tonight! Tomorrow will be too late."

The Reverend Dr. Holt had not tried to see Widow Lan after curing her son of the boil. But from time to time she had presented him with dumplings as gifts, through Ah Wong, when she chanced upon the latter on the street. Knowing well the rules of propriety that governed the conduct between a young man and a young woman, especially a widow, Holt did not seek her out to thank her. And thinking of those rules now, he realized what desperate courage the women must have summoned to come at this hour.

"Why must I flee?" he asked.

In hushed whispers Widow Lan told her tale. She had just learned it from Mistress Chow, and Mistress Chow from her mistress, the sixth concubine of Ma. This sixth concubine was a good woman. She had heard how the redheaded foreigner had cured Yuwen's boil, and had been well-disposed toward him ever since. Though she was Ma's favorite, she had no sympathy with many of her husband's doings. Tonight, about an hour ago, Ma had come to her chambers after a riotous banquet, very drunk, and had blabbed a terrible plot:

His public professions to the contrary, Ma nursed a secret hatred for Ho the Central Hall. He had long desired to harm the great man, and after his return from the meeting in which funds were raised for the drought, he smouldered in fury for days. Besides the agony of parting with three thousand piculs of wheat, he felt himself publicly humiliated. He hated Holt too, because Ho the Central Hall had bestowed so much honor upon the missionary at the meeting. Now he had discovered the Achilles heel of Ho the Central Hall. The sentiments of the country had turned antiforeign, and yet Ho the Central Hall had befriended a foreigner. If Ma could not harm the great man, he could harm Holt. . . .

Ma would not have dared make a move had Ho not been in Peking and the Prefect away on an inspection tour. For some time now, Ma had sought the friendship of one Fong Tienpa, chief of the Boxers in a large area surrounding Yi. Fong bore a grudge against Yi because the Prefect had so far thwarted all his attempts to organize the Boxers here, and he was eager to conspire with Ma. In the last few days, hundreds of Boxers had been brought into the city in disguise, and this evening Fong Tienpa himself had come to Ma's house; it was in his honor that Ma had given the banquet. And it was at the banquet that the conspirators decided to surround the mission compound early in the morning, kill the foreign missionary, and raze all the buildings.

Widow Lan finished with a plea, "We cannot stay here any longer. We cannot risk being discovered. For your God's sake, flee! Flee at once, while there is yet time!"

And Holt heard an added whisper from Mistress Chow, "May the Goddess of Mercy grant you fleet foot and safe flight!"

Then, before he could thank them, the two women vanished as silently and as furtively as they had come.

2

FOR A MOMENT Holt felt utterly confounded. Then gradually he collected himself. Flee where? To the big port city? That was three days' journey by horse. The country outside Yi was swarming with Boxers. It was no use trying to disguise himself; with his physical features, he would be recognized anywhere along the way and put to death at once. Flee? Yes, there was a place, right across the street— the House of Ho. But the Central Hall was not there, and his younger brother had always impressed Holt as a weakling. Would the brother grant him refuge? And what about the building and other properties of the mission compound? Would not he, leaving them to their fate, be like a rat deserting a sinking ship? Further-more—a more frightening thought—these wicked and ruthless people harbored no love or respect for Ho the Central Hall. What if, for the sheltering of a foreigner, they shifted their anger and destroyed the House of Ho?

Holt fell on his knees and prayed hard, holding the Holy Book in his hands. Peace came to him, and a plan developed in his mind. Come what must, he was no longer fearful of his fate.

He got up, stepped calmly out of his suite, and awakened Ah Wong. Then he went to the gatekeeper's quarters and roused his two domestics from sleep. He summoned them all to a meeting and told them to what dangers the Mission compound was exposed, but gave no inkling as to how he had come by the information. Then he advised them that as there was little time left, they should all make their escape while they still could. As for himself, it was his church, his mission. He would remain at his post.

Ah Wong spoke first, slowly and solemnly as usual, his head cocked to one side: "Certainly, sir, you don't mean that I should flee too?"

"Yes, I do, Ah Wong," said Holt. "You are a Chinese. You can easily hide yourself somewhere."

"But that I cannot," said Ah Wong intensely. "No matter where I go, I cannot hide myself from God. I was a foundling, I never knew who my parents were. The church brought me up. The church is father and mother to me. I was asked by the church to assist you in this mission. If I cannot assist you in life, then I shall do so in death."

Holt cast a long glance upon his companion and hung his head. Then he heard the gatekeeper speak.

"I am not affiliated with the church, but I know our ancient teach-ings of Loyalty. What would Ho the Central Hall think of me, were I to desert you now? You have been a good master, sir, and I shall be a good servant. Besides, I don't see much danger for myself and the cook. We are not Christians, and we are Chinese. At most, the Boxers will only give us a beating. They will not kill us. I shall stay with you to the end, sir."

The cook took a side step as though he were about to accept the master's advice. Then he drew himself to an abrupt halt as the gate-keeper spat loudly and then said with utter contempt: "Think what a blind fool I have been! There are indeed people who talk like scholars about virtues, but who never put them into practice. They would slink away at the first sign of possible disadvantage to themselves."

The cook turned about and said excitedly, "Me? Me? I know the virtues as well as any scholar. I conduct myself as properly as any scholar. He is a blind fool indeed who thinks I am slinking away. No, not I. If I moved at all, it is because I couldn't help speculating on how bad a beating I may get at the hands of that Fong Tienpa. It is said that he has killed many a person without batting an eye. But I have come to this conclusion—the worse a beating I get from him, the more virtuous a scholar I become!"

And he spat back as forcefully as the gatekeeper had.

"But you are perfectly free to go," said Holt. "In fact, I want you to."

"Never, sir!" insisted the cook. "Before Fong Tienpa comes and slays me, you will have to kill me first, sir! Besides, I want to see you match your magic against his. I am sure you will come out the better of the two, sir!"

Holt did not think it fit just then to chide the cook on that point. Moreover, to carry out the more effectively the plan he had in mind, he would need the assistance of all three of them. So he agreed to let them stay, and unfolded his scheme. It was not a good scheme— it might not avert the dread eventuality, but only delay it. However, after he finished his instructions, they all set about their various assignments quietly.

In the gray light of the dawn the Boxers converged on the Mission compound in four groups. Each consisted of fifty men, and each was led by a chosen disciple of Fong Tienpa's. The men all carried spears, with red tassels hanging loosely behind the sharp-pointed tips; they wore a sort of uniform, a red kerchief wrapped about the head, a suit of black pajamas closely fitted to the body, with long white frogs knotted in the front of the jacket. As they marched, the flag of the Manchus—the Yellow Dragon—waved at the head of each group. This signified that they acknowledged allegiance to the ruling dynasty; they pretended that they were acting, if not with Their Majesties' approval, at least in their name. Then followed a huge white banner with one gigantic Chinese character embroidered in black in its center—Fong. But the chief, Fong Tienpa, from whose surname the inscription was derived, was not with his troops. He was still sleeping soundly at Ma's house, for he considered this expedition too trifling for his personal attention. He had issued his orders, and his four disciples knew what to do.

It had been the Boxers' original plan to assault the Mission by surprise, to storm into the compound, to kill the Reverend Dr. Holt on the spot, to loot the place, and to put the buildings to flames. They were prepared to batter open the gates. However, to their astonishment, both the main gate and the two side doors were wide open. And on the walls were pasted large scrolls with bold Chinese characters which read: "Welcome to Honorable Fong Tienpa! Welcome to all Boxers! Please enter. We have food for you."

The Boxers hesitated. How could the foreign devil have known they were coming? What dire trap could he be laying for them? Hastily the four disciples put their heads together, and then two of them repaired at once to Ma's house to inform their chief of the matter. When Fong was roused from his slumber, he excitedly consulted Ma. But Ma could not advise him.

"So the foreign devil knows my name and sends me a personal invitation!" Fong Tienpa exclaimed. "Well, since he requests my personal attention, it would be impolite to disappoint him and so I shall go there. I shall have my little amusement with him." And he roared with laughter.

Thus swaggered Fong Tienpa toward the Mission compound. He was then about thirty, a giant of a man with the reputation of being one of the mightiest Boxers and also one of the cruelest. It was said of him that once, when infuriated, he had thrown a man bodily into the air, caught him by the legs on the fall, and torn him savagely into two parts. It was also said that not a hundred men could match his strength and dexterity in boxing. He himself claimed that his whole person had been so toughened by exercise that he could withstand bullets fired at close range. Since nobody had ever summoned enough courage to put him to the test, his contentions had never been disproved. He also wielded a unique weapon of his own design, a huge piece of fine steel beaten into the image of a man, but with only one leg. It was three feet long and weighed some eighty pounds. When he held it by the leg and brandished it in a fight or in exercise, it whistled in the air. Armed with this weapon now, he sallied forth to meet his intended victim.

The Boxers lined up in front of the main gate yielded a passage at his approach. He planted himself in the center of the wide-open gate, his four disciples close behind, and looked about. Inside the compound there was absolute quiet. He made a move to enter, then hesitated and shouted in a stentorian voice, "Anybody there?"

From the gatekeeper's quarters emerged the gatekeeper. "Ah, I take it," said he politely without any semblance of alarm, "that you are Honorable Fong Tienpa. If you are truly he, then my master is waiting for you."

"Of course I am Honorable Fong Tienpa, you blind fool. Look at me closely. Can there be anyone like me? Has anybody a weapon like mine? But to Hell with your master! Why doesn't he come out and welcome me himself?"

From behind the second gate appeared the Reverend Dr. Holt. He took a few steps forward and bowed low.

"A thousand pardons, Honorable Fong Tienpa," he said. "It is truly a great honor for me that you have condescended to come to my humble compound. I am afraid that my means are too limited to provide you with proper entertainment, but I have a meager feast prepared for you and a few of your chosen followers. I myself and my assistant will wait upon you. For the rest of your Boxers, I have arranged to have stewed rice and preserved vegetables served in the school court. My gatekeeper and my cook will attend on them. Forgive me my poor offerings. Had I known of your visit earlier, I would have done better."

"What ugly plot are you hatching against me and my men?" Fong shouted suspiciously. "Are you trying to poison us?"

Holt shook his head and imitated the Boxer's jargon. "Even if I had eaten a tiger's heart or a leopard's liver, would I dare try to poison you? We have only four men in the compound. And we will taste all the food before you eat. Can it be possible that the great and mighty Honorable Fong Tienpa is a little afraid?"

"I, afraid!" Fong Tienpa laughed aloud. "Even if your compound be a lair for dragons or a den for tigers, I will come in." Wheeling about, he waved to his followers. "You all have heard what this foreign devil says. Go to the school court, wherever that may be, and enjoy yourselves. Before an execution takes place, the condemned is usually given a feast by the executioner, but now it is the executioners who are feasted by the condemned!"

3

WHILE THE GATEKEEPER ushered the other Boxers to the school court, Holt led his principal guests to the waiting room of the clinic, where a banquet had been spread on the table by Ah Wong. The missionary seated them one by one, observing every minor detail of courtesy which etiquette required, Fong Tienpa first at the top of the table facing the entrance of the room, the others at the two sides. Holt himself sat opposite Fong Tienpa, and Ah Wong served as waiter.

Fong Tienpa glared at his host. "Now, foreign devil, don't think that because you are treating us with such niceties, we are going to let you off. We are going to kill you!"

"Oh, that is understood," answered Holt airily, "but you have plenty of time. First, let me have my last meal with you. And in order to quiet your apprehensions, may I take the liberty of tasting every dish first?"

"You do that, foreign devil." Fong Tienpa leered cunningly, then pointed at Ah Wong. "And let that assistant of yours—that second-class foreign devil who has our blood but a barbarian heart—let him also sit down and taste the dishes before we eat. Who knows what diabolic plot you may have hatched in your devilish mind? For all we know, you may think that since this is your last meal, you will poison us together with yourself."

Holt laughed outright, much to the discomfiture of his guests. But he beckoned Ah Wong to sit down by his side and the two of them proceeded to attack the dishes. Seeing them do so, Fong Tienpa and his disciples ate voraciously.

When he had finished, Fong Tienpa wiped his oily mouth with his sleeves and growled, "Thanks, you condemned foreign devil! Now, have you anything to say before we dispatch you back to the West—to the eighteenth grade of Hell from which you will never return?"

Holt smiled. The Boxers who had been entertained in the school court had also finished their repast, and they were now returning in droves, filling the courtyard and watching the scene expectantly.

"You, Honorable Fong Tienpa, and you, Boxers!" the missionary called loudly. "You are all just men. I ask you—has a man a right to know for what he is to be killed? If you think he has, then tell me what crimes I have committed."

"The crime of being a foreign devil!" roared Fong Tienpa, thrusting his one-legged weapon aloft threateningly. "Is that not crime enough?"

"That is not a crime, Honorable Fong Tienpa. Though I am a foreigner, I am not a devil. I have come to this country to do good and not harm. I believe in a God who knows only love, and I preach and practice His Faith of Love. Ask the people of Yi. Since I came here, have I done them any evil? When they are sick, I try to heal them. When they are in distress, I—"

"Enough!" thundered Fong Tienpa, jumping up from his seat. "You missionary foreign devil—you are the worst of foreign devils. Nothing but a spy for your breed. You come and do your little goodnesses so that your breed can do us greater harm!"

He turned to the Boxers: "Tie up the foreign devil and take him outside the main gate. I shall have him executed publicly on the street."

Ah Wong spoke up firmly, "If you want to kill him, kill me too."

"It will be as you wish," Fong Tienpa sneered, "you shameless second-class foreign devil. Boxers, do the same to him!"

Quickly the hands of the Reverend Dr. Holt and Ah Wong were tied behind their backs, and they were half pushed, half pulled, through the gate. Holt caught a glimpse of the sad-faced but determined gatekeeper, about to jump forward and attempt his rescue, and he shook his head violently. In the general confusion, neither his movement nor that of his faithful servant was noticed. The cook was not in sight, and Holt was glad that at least that one had kept his senses.

Fong Tienpa ordered the prisoners taken to the center of the street. He apparently expected to attract a crowd of spectators to watch the execution, but in this he was to be disappointed. The Lane of Eternal Stability was located in an exclusive residential area, and even in ordinary times there were not many passers-by. This morning the street was deserted. The few people who had happened along were frightened away by the sight of the Boxers. At the first sign of commotion, Ho Tao's younger brother had ordered all the gates of the House of Ho closed tight. Ma had cunningly followed suit with respect to his own house after Fong Tienpa left. He did not wish it to be known, any more widely than necessary, that he had anything to do with the plot of the Boxers. The only person on the whole street who felt genuine concern about Holt's well-being was Widow Lan. She had locked herself inside her shack, to hold Yuwen in her arms, to lament bitterly that her benefactor had not heeded her warning, and to pray earnestly.

Fong Tienpa waited until all his men had trooped out of the Mission compound and lined up on the two sides of the gate. Then he approached Holt. "Foreign devil, I shall do you the honor of killing you myself. What is the last thing you want to say before you are executed?"

"I do have one last request. Let me kneel down in peace and pray to my own God."

"Foreign devil though you are," said Fong Tienpa, "you have given me a feast. I shall grant you this request. Stand back, Boxers. Leave the prisoners alone for a minute."

The guards withdrew a few paces until only Fong Tienpa hovered near the prisoners.

Holt turned to Ah Wong, smiling wanly, and said, "Let us pray."

Their hands tied behind them, they fell to their knees and bowed their heads. The missionary knew that everything was lost. He had played for time—that was the purpose of his scheme—and time was now at an end.

"Our Heavenly Father," he began, "if it be Thy will—" and then there seemed to be a growing thunder of drums above the pounding of the blood in his temples. He said his "Amen" hastily, and opened his eyes to see a cavalcade of a dozen or more horsemen sweeping into the far end of the street, throwing up a great cloud of yellow dust.

Fong Tienpa swore, and shouted a sharp command. The Boxers scrambled hurriedly behind their leaders in a sort of military formation, as if ready for battle. Those guarding the prisoners also joined the ranks. Only Fong Tienpa remained at his post, waiting expectantly.

When they saw the Boxers, the riders reined their horses to an abrupt halt, then started to advance again, slowly and cautiously. At their head, Holt could see distinctly, rode Ho the Central Hall. A dashing young man, who would be Fucho, his youngest son, was at his side. All the riders were armed with pistols.

Fong Tienpa brandished his weapon menacingly and took a step toward the kneeling missionary. He roared to the horsemen, who were pressing forward, "Advance no further, or I will strike!"

It was then that Fucho fired. The boy had not studied in Japan in vain; he had learned marksmanship. Fong Tienpa staggered backward, dropping his one-legged man of steel into the dust.

A moment of stunned silence ensued. Then a short, chubby man dashed from inside the main gate of the Mission compound. It was the cook. He planted himself in the center of the gate where all the Boxers could see, and waving his hands wildly, he shouted at the top of his voice: "Look! Look at Fong Tienpa! He is hit! He is bleeding! He is not safe from bullets! His magic is no good!"

The Boxers craned their necks to look at their leader, who was nursing his bleeding arm. All were struck with fear.

Ho the Central Hall spoke with a voice accustomed to authority. "I am Ho the Central Hall. Get out of here, all of you, or we'll fire!"

The Boxers turned into a frightened rabble as they took to their heels. Even Fong Tienpa vanished, leaving his unique weapon behind.

Ho the Central Hall's eyes pursued the fleeing figures until they disappeared at the turn of the street. "What riffraff they are!" he said with disgust.

"That they are, Father," replied Fucho at his side. "Even so, I believe they can be put to good use."

The old man did not hear this rather curious remark. His whole attention was concentrated on the missionary, who was getting up from his kneeling position and straightening himself.

"Thank Heaven and thank Earth," Ho the Central Hall cried out joyously, "you are safe and sound, my friend!"

Six

IT WAS NOT until some time later that Holt learned the narrowness of his escape. Ho the Central Hall had failed in his mission to Peking; many influential men sympathized with the Boxers, and their counsel, not his, prevailed with the Empress Dowager. She took no action against the movement, and Ho had hurried back to Yi, worrying about the safety of his American friend.

Now the Boxer Rebellion moved swiftly into history. Though the Empress Dowager was cunning enough in domestic intrigues, she lacked statecraft and could not cope with the situation. The Boxers went from success to excesses, and ran wild; the foreign powers landed an expeditionary force, and the Imperial Capital—Seat of the Son of Heaven—fell into alien hands. Their Imperial Majesties fled inland—no one knew where—and finally the ultimate humiliation was reported: The chief of the foreign invaders was openly sleeping with a notorious courtesan of Peking named Peerless Golden Flower, on the Imperial dragon bed.

Still, China was so vast and communications so scant that things went on as usual everywhere except in the small area under foreign occupation. Ho the Central Hall worked night and day to correspond with the viceroys of far-flung provinces, striving to raise an army to drive the foreigners into the sea. Before anything could be accomplished, Their Majesties suddenly turned up at Sian, an inland provincial capital, and the Empress Dowager hastily concluded an ignoble peace by bowing to every demand the foreigners dictated. And so the first faint stirrings of a would-be revolution were over.

Ho the Central Hall felt that both he and the Empire had lost face, and he shut himself in his quarters and would not even go to see the Reverend Dr. Holt. Meanwhile, the missionary was surprised to find that the status of foreigners had undergone an abrupt change for the better, and that he had many more friends than before. The first Chinese to pay him a visit, strangely enough, was Ma Teh-lin.

Ma came, giving the lie to his miserly reputation by bringing many gifts. He professed eternal esteem for Holt. He begged forgiveness for not coming to the aid of his honorable neighbor during Fong Tienpa's dastardly attack; he had neither pistols, he said, nor Ho Tao's mighty prestige. Now he hinted that since it was the Empire's policy to give foreigners complete freedom, he and Holt might profitably go into secret partnership for trading purposes. Holt needed only to furnish his name; Ma would provide the capital.

The missionary met this sly overture with such frigid politeness that Ma quickly laughed and said he was only joking. Next day, his two sons returned to Holt's English class just as suddenly as they had left. Ma Pingnam, the elder boy, began addressing his teacher as "generation-uncle," thus raising himself one generation higher than the Ho boys, much to their chagrin.

Since foreigners were again in good repute, the sick and ailing began to pour into the American's clinic in ever-increasing volume.

Although the Central Hall did not call, his youngest son, Fucho, was a frequent visitor. This young man's attitude was strange, indeed. Now that all the townspeople of Yi treated Holt with warm friendship, Fucho became unpleasant to the point of rudeness. There came a day when an Imperial Decree guaranteeing protection for all foreigners was publicly proclaimed, and that evening the Reverend Dr. Holt found Fucho striding angrily into his suite without being announced.

"Now you have no need of us any more!" Fucho exclaimed, scowling. "You have the freedom of the whole Empire—you can do anything you wish. You can violate all the laws of the land without fear of retaliation!"

Holt deliberately did not answer for a moment. He gestured for Fucho to sit down, but the young man ignored the invitation.

"Don't think you have really defeated us!" Fucho went on passionately. "It was only a mob of unorganized Boxers you defeated. If the old Empress Dowager had not weakened—if my father's plans had materialized—"

"Must we fight each other?" Holt asked gently. "Can't our two nations be friends, even as you and I?"

"Ah, we believed that in the past, but we learned better. We learned from you foreigners. If you Christians have taught us one lesson, it is that might makes right!"

"We do not teach that," Holt protested. "Nor do you believe it, Fucho. You and your father risked your lives to save mine. Was that because you wanted to fight the Boxers, or because you thought it your duty to protect me?"

"That proves my point exactly," Fucho said bitterly. "We were stronger than the Boxers because we had pistols. If we had not been armed, Fong Tienpa and his men would have torn you to pieces, and us, too. Might makes right. If we had a modern army as well-equipped as yours, we would not have this proclamation today—this public avowal of our humiliation—this national disgrace!"

Holt shook his head, marveling at the fires burning in Fucho, seeking to understand the youth. There was a force here to be harnessed, a power to be used, a talent for leadership to be directed. Still speaking gently, he said, "But Fucho, the proclamation only guarantees protection to aliens in your country. You Chinese have always been famed for politeness. Isn't this just an official expression of politeness?"

Fucho looked up truculently, his eyebrows drawn together. "It could have been, if we had done it of our own accord. But no—it was rammed down our throats!"

And turning away haughtily, he left as discourteously as he had come. Holt thought about the visit for a long time.

2

THE MISSIONARY WAS not the only one troubled by Fucho's morose behavior. Ho the Central Hall was most disturbed, although his son had not dared confide to him his turbulent political thinking. The dispute between them took another course, centering on a matter dear to the father's heart, the marriage of Fucho to Delicate Blossom, to whom he had long been betrothed.

Fucho rebelled. Delicate Blossom, he said, was not of age to marry. He had not finished his studies; there would be time for the wedding after his graduation from the Japanese Military Academy.

Ho countered that Fucho's mother, Orchid, had married when no older than Delicate Blossom. He reminded his son that it would be four years before his graduation. "Who knows," the old man was driven to say, "whether your mother or I will live that long? You may return to find us both gone."

Fucho found it difficult to answer such pleading. He was relieved when Minister Tan, Delicate Blossom's father, wrote that the Tan family was not yet ready for the wedding, since Minister Tan himself had just returned with Their Majesties to Peking, and there was much to do to rehabilitate the Imperial Capital.

The marriage, therefore, was postponed, and Ho said nothing more of it. Yet Fucho remained restless and moody by turns, and always withdrawn. Orchid, whose woman's intuition made her suspect he had had some affair of the heart in Japan, urged Ho Tao to have a frank talk with their son, but he waited until the day before Fucho was scheduled to leave for Japan to resume his studies. Then he asked the boy, tactfully yet forthrightly, if there was some trouble concerning a young woman.

To his surprise, an involuntary smile flickered in Fucho's eyes. "Not a young woman, Father," he said unthinkingly. "An old one."

No sooner had Fucho spoken than he bit his tongue. This was a matter he did not dare speak of to his father, but mindful of his filial duties, he awkwardly attempted a plausible explanation.

"I am making a poor joke, Father. I have, in fact, been wondering about some questions of life which I cannot answer. In Japan, when I am studying again, I will forget them. Please do not be concerned."

"Ask me those questions then, my son."

Hating himself for lacking the inventiveness to disguise his thoughts, Fucho protested, "But the questions may sound absurd and ugly to you, Father."

"Our Great Master Confucius said, 'No father will ever think his son ugly.' You may confide in me, Fucho."

Suddenly, in desperation, Fucho blurted out, "Then please tell me this, Father. The queue we wear—isn't that a Manchu custom, and

73

not a Chinese one? Isn't it true that we Chinese never wore queues until the Manchus forced us to do so?"

"Well . . . yes," answered the old man, taken aback at this simple question.

"Then, to the Chinese, is not the queue a symbol of humiliation?"

"No, no," said Ho, frowning. "It would be much more appropriate to regard it as a token pledge of our allegiance to the Dynasty."

"But before the Manchus conquered our Empire, they were barbarians, from the northeast—just like the foreigners who now come to threaten us from the west. Is that not true, Father?" Fucho persisted.

"Historically, that is true," Ho Tao admitted. "But the Manchus did not really conquer us, directly. At the end of the Ming Dynasty, the country became infested with bandits. The bandits overthrew the Mings. The Manchus rid us of the bandits and established the Ching Dynasty." Ho Tao was beginning to feel apprehensive about what his son was implying.

Fucho went on recklessly, "In Japan, I found books that have been suppressed here. The Manchus committed many unspeakable atrocities against us Chinese—in Yangchow, in Kiating, which they razed. Did you know that, Father?"

"Yes." Ho Tao sighed. "There is some truth, and some exaggeration, in what you have read. But in three hundred years we have assimilated the Manchus."

The boy rose, tense, burdened by the terrible seriousness of the young. "Father, Their Imperial Majesties are still Manchus!" he declared. "The Imperial Throne has been occupied by none but Manchus. Why should we Chinese owe them allegiance?"

Ho the Central Hall stood up too. "Be mindful of your speech, Fucho. Our ancestors gave our allegiance to the Ching Dynasty three hundred years ago. Their Imperial Majesties are our sovereigns."

"But what if they are unfit to rule?" demanded the impassioned Fucho, unable to restrain himself. "I told you, Father, that it's an old woman who has been bothering me. It is the Empress Dowager! She has deprived the Emperor of all rights. She has squandered on a Summer Palace the money meant for a navy. She has lost us the Japanese War. And now she has bungled the whole affair of the Boxers' Rebellion. . . . Father, no one knows her incompetence and her corruption better than you do. For our present humiliation, I cannot blame the foreigners as much as I blame her. That old woman, with her rotten Manchu Court!"

74

Ho the Central Hall stared, disbelieving his ears. "Stop it," he ordered angrily. "You are talking treason. Remember the ancient saying, 'A sovereign can do no wrong; it is only his ministers who fail him.' And remember this too: Not only is Her Imperial Majesty our lawful sovereign, but it is to her, personally, that the House of Ho owes everlasting gratitude. I would sooner kill myself than have a son who whispers one word against her!"

Fucho saw that he had gone too far. "Forgive me, Father," he muttered, bowing his head low. "I know these thoughts of mine are wild, but they have upset me greatly. There seem to be two Loyalties struggling to possess me—the one to Her Majesty, to whom we owe so much, and the other to our people, to whom we belong. Father, forgive me for ever thinking such thoughts. Forgive me for causing you uneasiness."

Ho the Central Hall gave a sigh of relief, and his heart went out to his son.

"I can understand your feelings a little, Fucho. But never again, please, give free rein to such wild thoughts. Do not make a distinction between Their Majesties and the Empire and the people; they *are* the Empire and the people. Besides, you must not think of yourself only. You must think of the House of Ho. Our house has always prided itself on observing the ancient virtue of Loyalty—let it not be said that a Ho has ever violated it. As I have a right to ask you to be a filial son, so I beg of you to be a loyal subject."

"I understand. And I'll ever try to be a filial son to you, Father," Fucho said meekly.

The next day he left for Japan, and he was to stay there four years.

Four years meant little to the Reverend Dr. Holt, who was devotedly pursuing his task of healing the sick and spreading the Gospel. It meant a great deal to the Chinese Empire, and the town of Yi. . . .

A new army had been planned under the leadership of Yuan Shih-kai, Viceroy of the province where Peking is located; Ho the Central Hall, judging Yuan to be overly ambitious and unscrupulous, had little liking for him.

There was also talk of a constitutional system of government. And as a forerunner of things to come, the custom of literary examinations was abolished, and schools were established as a substitute. Ho the Central Hall protested by written petitions to Her Majesty, but his protests went unanswered. He believed in private tutors who, besides instilling knowledge, could by personal example inculcate in the pupils the standards of virtue. Admittedly, this kind of instruction was not available to the people as a whole, yet even under the new system the town of Yi, with thirty thousand people, obtained only one poorly conducted grammar school.

Ho the Central Hall began to feel that the once-solid earth upon which he stood was slipping from under his feet. Not only did the Empress Dowager no longer heed his counsel, but the people of Yi also no longer seemed to listen to his opinions with the former respect. Over and above these, he worried about his youngest son, Fucho.

And there was his grandson, that young imp Ta-kong, at his side daily, reminding him of Fucho. The boy would come up with strange requests, such as that he be allowed to stop private tutoring and go to the public school, where Lan Yuwen, Widow Lan's son, had already enrolled.

One other thing. Though the Imperial Court enforced censorship as best it could, there were disquieting rumors of a man named Sun Wen, otherwise known as Sun Yat-sen, who was openly advocating revolution and had been forced to flee to Japan as a consequence. The rumor said many hotheaded Chinese students in Japan were rallying to him. Ho Tao worried that Fucho might be among those so misguided.

Ho's health declined too. He visited his friend the Reverend Dr. Holt only seldom, and went nowhere else, but withdrew into himself, read the ancient classics, and lost touch with the outside world. It was only natural that the people of Yi also lost interest in him.

As Ho the Central Hall shrank, Ma Teh-lin blossomed.

Ma came, one day, to the Reverend Dr. Holt for advice about sending his two sons abroad to study. But apparently the boys' minds were already made up. The oldest son, Ma Pingnan, having heard reports of gay life in Paris, was bent on going to France; and the second son, Ma Pingshi, sullenly proclaiming his ambition to become a Blood and Iron Chancellor of China, another Bismarck, was equally determined to go to Germany.

Ma did then a singular thing that belied his reputation as a miser. He gave a big banquet—long remembered in Yi—as a send-off for the two boys, and it was well attended even by those who had formerly held Ma in open contempt. The social life of Yi was indeed changing.

The Reverend Dr. Holt could look back on this time, later, in his mellow years, and realize what had been happening. But at the moment, he was doing well and was so completely absorbed in his daily routine that he had no time to wonder. Besides, he was occupied with an urgent problem. Though there were as many sick women as sick men in Yi, only male patients came to his medical clinic because there was no woman in attendance.

"Ah Wong," Holt told his assistant, "you must get married."

Ah Wong received this command with his usual calm, but it set forces in motion. In due time he repaired to the port city, where a girls' orphanage was run by the Mission, and returned with a bride. Her name was Anna, which in Chinese means "The Maiden of Peace."

Anna was a good wife to Ah Wong, and at once started calling on women and inviting them to tea parties. Thus it was that Orchid, the wife of Ho the Central Hall, came to honor the Mission compound with her presence for the first time. But Anna's inexperience inevitably caused some embarrassing moments. She did not know about proper social mixing. Although she had some idea of separating the rich and poor, she was negligent in the most important matter—separating the wives from the concubines. Once she mastered that, however, her tea parties became very popular.

On the occasions Anna could always depend on Widow Lan for able and willing assistance. Taciturn and aloof as Widow Lan remained even with her own sex, her delicious dumplings were widely known, and many of Anna's guests accepted the invitations just to enjoy the refreshments.

Now that there was a woman in the compound, Widow Lan came often. She had her son, Yuwen, teach her to read the characters in the Chinese Scripture, thus beginning Bible study in earnest, and soon she became the Reverend Dr. Holt's first convert to the Christian faith in Yi. When she was baptized, so was Yuwen. His forehead now bright and clear, without a trace of scar from the boil, the boy was fast growing into a comely youth as strikingly handsome as his mother. He made the best grades in the Government Grammar School, and took English lessons from Holt besides.

But still no woman would come to the clinic for treatment because the doctor was a man. Thus, it occurred to Holt that he should try to teach Anna the rudiments of medicine so that she could handle minor cases and draw female patients into the clinic. Anna did not, however, prove to be an apt student. But one day while watching Anna take a lesson, Widow Lan showed great interest and expressed a wish to be allowed to study the same course. She was a born doctor, and in a short time not only outdistanced Anna but exceeded Holt's utmost expectations. She revealed a superb talent for surgical work, the hands that were so adroit in using needle and thread being equally gifted in wielding a lancet or a scalpel.

Though she could not at first bring herself to treat male patients, Widow Lan treated women with amazing success. In time, Holt asked her to give up her dumpling and embroidery business and serve instead in the Mission clinic as a doctor for women, with a stipend. Widow Lan agreed. A separate office was set up for her, and soon women patients began to troop into the Mission compound.

Seven

FUCHO HAD RETURNED from Japan, and a day had been set for his wedding with Delicate Blossom.

Before his return, a large new court had been added to Ho's mansion, ready for him and his bride-to-be. Ho Tao and Orchid, who had always had a special affection for their youngest son, had taken great pains to furnish this with taste and splendor. And as was the custom, Minister Tan—Delicate Blossom's father—had sent the bride's trousseau in advance of the wedding. It was worth a fortune, becoming the station of such a house as Tan's.

In the general bustle of preparation, however, the prospective bridegroom was all but forgotten. To be sure, he was the sun of the universe, about which everything revolved, but like the sun, he was expected only to shine, not to take a direct hand in the common chores of the day.

Ho Tao had not as yet found time for any serious talk with his son. And Fucho was glad that his father was so preoccupied—too busy to question him about his past activities in Japan or about his future plans. But he had schooled himself for the ordeal. He remembered well his last serious conversation with his father, and was deter-

78

mined to avoid a recurrence of that experience. In the same breath, he cursed the times and the circumstances that were going to force him to practice deception upon his own parents.

Fucho was too truthful a man to like the part he was playing. The more his father lavished affection upon him, the bitterer he felt in his heart. Even though he had made up his mind not to be a loyal subject to Their Imperial Majesties, he wanted to be a filial son. For his father, he would willingly lay down his life. Yet in the one thing on which his father set high value, he could not accommodate him.

As the days drew past, the necessity to pretend constantly to be what he was not, grew increasingly irksome. The man in whose company he needed to dissemble the least was the Reverend Dr. Holt, and Fucho sought him out often as a sort of refuge. Idly, he would watch the foreigner treat his patients in the clinic; he would join him in his English class, though his own knowledge of the language was far beyond that of the pupils. And in the evenings, whenever he could, he would steal over to Holt's suite and visit with him.

It was two days before the wedding, and the day had been an especially trying one for Fucho. Minister Tan and his wife had arrived with the bride, accompanied by a large retinue. For the convenience of both families, the Tans had borrowed an extensive section of a very large house in Yi, and shortly after they were settled, Ho Tao and Orchid paid them a visit, taking along the prospective bridegroom, who of course was not permitted a glimpse of Delicate Blossom. Fucho had a difficult time behaving becomingly toward the father-in-law, mother-in-law, and the many brothers- and sisters-in-law. It taxed his self-discipline to the utmost to put on the appearance of an exhilaration he did not feel.

Orchid was the only one who had seen the bride, and as soon as she was alone with her husband and her son she could hardly cease praising the charms of her future daughter-in-law. If Fucho's mother had sought to please him in this manner, she was greatly mistaken. The more he heard, the unhappier he felt. Why should Heaven cruelly destine two people to be so miserable as they were bound to become?

In despair, Fucho fled to Holt's suite that evening, his dejection written large on his face. Accustomed to his ways now, Holt let him sink listlessly onto a chair, and did not speak until Fucho had somewhat collected himself.

"You must be excited about the forthcoming happy event," ventured Holt finally.

"Excited?" Fucho gave a start. "Why should I be? It's all arranged. And happy? What happiness can come from an arranged marriage?"

"I take it, then, that you are opposed to the marriage system of your people."

Fucho hesitated over a possible answer, but his extreme nationalistic sentiments would not allow the missionary's remark to go unchallenged.

"Why should I be? It's a perfectly good system."

Holt was taken aback by this transparent self-contradiction. "You mean it is all right for two people to marry without even knowing each other? You mean it is good to have marriage without love?"

"Love!" Fucho was scornful. "What is love? It is a feeling that is cultivated. It is an animal magnetism brought about through personal contact. Without personal contact, no love can be generated. You think your system is better because you have personal contact first, then love, then marriage? Why should our system fail to work equally well simply because we have changed the order? We have marriage first, then personal contact, then love. Indeed, I think our system actually works better. People are like water, love is its boiling point. You have love before marriage. So when your couples are married it is like water already boiled. But it is not human nature to maintain a climax long. Thus, in your system, love soon cools down after marriage, and what God has joined together men often rend asunder. Our system is different. Our couples meet like cold water. Marriage serves as the first application of heat. When people get married, they cannot but begin to bubble and boil. And this kind of marriage will last longer, not only because love comes afterward but because they know that only through marriage has their love been brought into being—therefore they treasure their marital status more highly."

"Then," retorted Holt, amused, "if you are not satisfied with your marriage, you just go ahead and take concubines. At least, we don't do that in the West."

"What's wrong with our system of concubinage? When your people are dissatisfied with marriage, they separate and divorce each other. Your men don't do justice to the women who have given them all a woman can give. And infinite harm is done to your children because they cannot be brought up under proper parenthood. If your men don't divorce they take mistresses, and that's as bad as taking concubines—even worse, because it's done on the sly. Your system neither

80

gives consideration to the position of the wives, nor provides sufficient security for the mistresses and the children born to them.

"Concubinage is different. The concubines live in the same house as the wife, with her acquiescence and sometimes her approval. They have security and a certain recognized position in society. Their children are cared for exactly like the wife's, and are always brought up under the watchful eyes of the parents. As for the wife, her pre-eminent status in the household is accepted by all, and her well-being is in no wise threatened as it is in your system of mistresses. Your system works to the disadvantage of all parties concerned, whereas ours actually works to the disadvantage of none. Furthermore, remember there are more women than men in this world. In your countries many women never get a chance to live a real woman's life, but here we seldom neglect to provide them with such chances."

"Well, then," said Holt reasonably, "if you like your marriage system so well, why do you feel so glum about your own arranged marriage?"

Fucho remained steeped in thought for a moment. "It's the cursed condition I find myself in—knowing both systems, yours and ours," he said. "I could have lived happily in either, to the exclusion of the other. But I cannot do so with the knowledge of both."

Holt did not know what comment to make.

After a pause, Fucho asked, "Why are you not married? Have you never been in love?"

Because the question was so sincerely put, because Fucho was such a good friend of his, and because he was young and lonesome, Holt told him the story that he had never told anybody—the story of the girl in Baltimore.

"So"—Fucho nodded his head in approbation—"it is self-sacrifice on your part that you have not married. If you can renounce marriage for the sake of one cause, know then that others may accept marriage for the sake of another."

What he did not tell Holt was that just as the missionary had had a romance back in the United States, so had he had one in Japan, with a girl named Amy.

2

THE BRIDEGROOM HAD gone to the house temporarily borrowed by the Tans on a ceremonial journey called "Personal Welcome." All the relatives and friends were gathered in the great hall of Ho's mansion awaiting the return of Fucho with his bride so that the rituals and the feast could begin. The Tans were not expected—it was the custom that no member of the bride's family, except for the few specially designated matrons of honor, should be present in the bridegroom's house during the three-day celebration. But nearly all the other relations were there.

Weddings were the most festive occasions of a Chinese society otherwise noted for its severe regulation. For three days all the proprieties would be forgotten, and also the distinction among the generations. Everyone might get as drunk as he wished, and the young could freely and safely make fun of their elders. Of course, the children would be the gayest and noisiest, but the grown-ups would unblushingly exchange the bawdiest tales.

Ta-kong had a small "melon-skin" perched carelessly on his head, a tiny queue enmeshed with red tassels dangling wildly behind; he wore a red jacket, and red trousers and red slippers to match, red being the color of felicity. Darting about with a merry twinkle in his eye, a string of firecrackers in his hand, he looked like a little red devil. He exploded a firecracker behind an elderly guest's back, startling him fearfully, and then fled behind his mother's red skirt, thrusting his tongue out, laughing at the furious old man.

The heralds now announced that the bridegroom was returning with his bride, and the guests stood up and took their posts; they did not go outside but waited in the great hall. Before long, exploding firecrackers signaled that the bridal procession had arrived at the main gate. In the street, a huge crowd had gathered to watch the wedding of a Central Hall's daughter to a Central Hall's son.

The bridegroom arrived first with a cavalcade. When he had taken up his station at the center of the main gate, an attendant handed him a bow and three arrows, all painted crimson. The bridal procession now came, moving slowly. There were hundreds of retainers, some playing music, others carrying bunting, the rest bearing additional trousseau. Finally four sedan chairs appeared, each enclosed with silk curtains gorgeously embroidered in red and gold, but the last one exceeded all the others in splendor. The first three carried the three matrons of honor, the last the bride. The matrons got out in succession, and a dozen or so servitors rushed forward to spread out roll upon roll of red carpet, covering the ground from the center of the street, past the main gate and into the house.

The bridal chair was lowered to the street at the end of the red carpet. The bride could not be seen, for the curtains were drawn tight. The crowd looked to the bridegroom, who took up the bow and discharged the three arrows one by one, pretending to take aim at the bridal chair. This was an ancient superstition meant to fend off evil spirits that might become too jealous of human felicity. Everyone in the crowd knew that the arrows were made of soft wood and not pointed; why, then, were the bridegroom's hands shaking so visibly as he let fly the missiles? His face had actually turned pale; this was unbecoming for a man reputed to be a dead shot with a pistol. Was he already so enamored of his bride that he feared even the innocuous arrows might harm her?

But now Fucho advanced toward the sedan chair, and with the help of the head matron of honor, removed the front curtain. Assisted by the other two matrons, the bride stepped out. Everyone cast his eye on her, though all knew that not much of her person could be seen. She was only a vision of exquisite embroidery, all in red, her head completely covered by a long crimson silk veil, which drooped far below her shoulders. She evidently found walking difficult, being hampered by her bound feet and the stiff ceremonial dress. The thick veil entirely obstructed her view, but two matrons of honor were at her side, holding her by the arms and guiding her gently. They helped her move forward on the red carpet as gracefully as she could. Behind them came the head matron, and then the groom.

To the accompaniment of exploding firecrackers they reached the main hall, where an open space, covered with a thick red carpet that bore special inlaid designs of good fortune and long life, had been reserved in the center of the room. It faced the alcove containing a gilded tablet with the familiar legend—Heaven, Earth, Sovereign, Parent, Teacher. Ho the Central Hall and Orchid were standing at the left of the alcove, and Ho's younger brother and his wife, Fucho's only remaining uncle and aunt, at its right. On the flanks, in row upon row, Fucho's kith and kin were lined up in the order of their seniority, first in generation and then in age. Behind them thronged the other guests. Because the Reverend Dr. Holt was a special friend and because he had come to Yi from such a great distance, he was allotted a position of honor behind Ho the Central Hall and Orchid; His Excellency the Prefect and his wife were placed behind Fucho's uncle and aunt.

The bridal procession gained the open space. Though firecrackers continued to crackle loudly outside, the Master of Ceremonies made his voice heard to proclaim the commencement of the rituals. An usher at once stepped forward and led Fucho to a position alongside his bride. The Master of Ceremonies unleashed a torrent of well-chosen phrases in rhyme, invoking Heaven and Earth to bestow all the blessings—longevity, wealth, honor, and happiness—upon the man and woman who were to be united in marriage. Then he gave a command. Fucho knelt down on the carpet, and assisted by the matrons of honor, Delicate Blossom knelt beside him. Thrice the Master of Ceremonies called out his orders, and thrice the groom and the bride kowtowed to Heaven and Earth. Then they were bidden to rise.

The Master of Ceremonies gave another rhymed recitation, this time extolling the virtues of the illustrious House of Ho, calling upon its various ancestors, one and all, to bless this descendant of their loins and his lawful wife, married with the consent of their parents. Then the kowtowing was repeated, and thrice also the groom and his bride kowtowed to their ancestors.

No sooner had they arisen than the attendants placed two chairs richly decorated with red satin embroidery in front of the alcove, facing the couple. The Master of Ceremonies recited another canto in rhyme, and with smiling dignity Ho the Central Hall and Orchid seated themselves upon the chairs. At the command of the Master of Ceremonies Fucho and Delicate Blossom kowtowed three times to their father and mother.

The parents then vacated their seats and returned to the left side of the alcove, and the Master of Ceremonies spoke again. Though Fucho's uncle and aunt feigned to be unworthy of the homage and muttered a wish to remain standing where they were, they were not permitted to do so. After a short exchange of remarks with Ho the Central Hall and Orchid, they drew forward to the chairs, but that was as much as they would do. In spite of all urging, they would not sit down but stood smiling, each by the side of a chair. When Fucho and Delicate Blossom kowtowed to them three times, they inclined their heads in return, saying repeatedly, "Thanks. Many thanks. May you two have great blessings, a long life, and many children!"

By this time Fucho was beginning to be worn out by the genuflections. He stole a glance at his bride, thinking how much more tired she must be, feeling a great pity for her. It might all have been worth while if this were to be a true marriage, but even that was to be denied her. For her sake he wished the rituals could be over more quickly.

But the rituals were far from finished; there were still many kowtows to do. The Master of Ceremonies no longer recited long

84

verses, though he still called out the names one by one, or couple by couple, where there was a couple. However, he did not begin with Fucho's oldest brother and his sister-in-law; he started with the first son of Fucho's first uncle, now deceased, and his wife, he being the oldest member of his generation. Fucho was glad for Delicate Blossom's sake that they were required to kowtow only once to each of these elders, who kowtowed in return without stepping forward. But looking at the long rows of his elderly relations, he could barely repress a shiver. How long would this last? Could Delicate Blossom stand it? Might she not faint or collapse? He kept stealing uneasy glances at her and finding comfort in noting that she was doing tolerably well.

Finally, they had kowtowed to Fucho's sister and her husband— the last of their elders. From there on his relatives were either younger than he or of a generation lower than his, and they need not pay them respects. But now the Master of Ceremonies began to call out the names of the guests, commencing with the old man Ta-kong had startled with the firecracker, who insisted that he was unworthy of such attention. Then His Excellency the Prefect and his wife did the same. At last the Master of Ceremonies pronounced a eulogy of all the guests who honored the house by their gracious presence. At his bidding, Fucho and Delicate Blossom kowtowed thrice to their left and thrice to their right, and the guests bowed their heads low in response. And then, to Fucho's infinite relief— more on account of his bride than himself—the formal part of the ceremony was concluded.

3

THE GUESTS WAITED until the bridal procession departed from the main hall before they dispersed to the other rooms to enjoy the feast. Day was now drawing to a close, but the endless verandas were brilliantly illuminated by hundreds of red hanging lanterns. The fortuneteller whom the two families had consulted prior to the wedding had certainly chosen a most propitious date, for a full moon was shining and there was not a wisp of cloud in the sky. As the bridal procession moved slowly through the verandas, Fucho felt the romance of the scene and wished that the veiled figure walking ahead might have been Amy rather than Delicate Blossom. But he and Delicate Blossom were now man and wife.

The younger children followed, running back and forth, shouting and laughing, setting off firecrackers and making as much noise as they could. Ta-kong even tried to peep inside the bride's veil, but the matrons of honor pushed him away.

Once inside the bridal suite and the bedchamber, the matrons seated the couple side by side on the four-poster. It was time now for Fucho to take off his bride's veil with his own hands—the matrons were pressing him, no evasion was possible. Reaching out somewhat uneasily, he gently lifted the veil aside and was instantly dazed. His mother had not told even half the truth about Delicate Blossom. She was the most exquisite woman he had ever seen!

The bride continued to look modestly at the floor, and Fucho saw that her raven-dark hair was unusually silky and shining. Her complexion was fair, tinged with a becoming red that was more due to her recent exertions than to artifice. It was so finely-textured, so flawless, that it had the translucence of priceless ivory. Though Fucho could see only her profile, he felt that no artist could have created more perfect features. Her forehead was neither too high nor too low, her eyebrow like the soft curved wing of a moth, her long eyelashes like glimmering threads of cloud over a twinkling star. Her cheek was not wide and prominent as is common with her race, but like a piece of gently rounded jade. Her nose was straight, yet so tenderly padded and so lovingly tipped that Fucho longed to touch it. But Delicate Blossom's tiny, cherry-red mouth distracted his attention, and below it, her divinely chiseled chin.

Fucho was so absorbed that the children burst into roars of laughter, and even the matrons of honor were shaken by giggles. Involuntarily Delicate Blossom smiled, her eyes shining; Fucho recovered and drew back with a start. Suddenly he felt all the more hurt because he knew that eventually it was he who would do the hurting. Why should Heaven be so cruel? Why had Delicate Blossom been made so excruciatingly beautiful?

The matrons of honor handed the groom and bride each a cup of wine. Fucho was aware of the custom. They were to drink with their hands intertwined, he from her cup and she from his. But his hand was like a dead weight; he could hardly lift his cup. The children attributed this to bashfulness and laughed again. Ta-kong jumped forward and held his uncle's hand aloft, twisting it around Delicate Blossom's. As their arms touched, Fucho's whole body went taut.

"Drink!" the children urged. "Drink!"

Fucho knew the superstition—the one who drank first was fated to be afraid of the other for life. Without hesitation he finished Delicate Blossom's cup in one gulp.

Ta-kong rolled on the floor with delight, shrieking, "My uncle is willing to be henpecked! Look at my henpecked uncle!"

Now that the little ceremony was over, the head matron reminded Fucho of his other duties. While the bride changed into a less formal dress, took refreshments, and rested, the groom must go outside to help his parents entertain the guests.

Like an automaton, deprived of his senses, Fucho left. He spent three hours going from room to room, from table to table. If Orchid had not seen to it that his cup was filled with tea instead of wine, he would have been dead drunk rather than merely exhausted. All the time he kept a smile on his face he was asking himself, "Shall I tell her? What will it do to her?"

There was no answer.

The guests started to take leave, and finally his younger cousins escorted him back to the bridal court. Orchid sent word that the hour was late; the children could have their fun in the next two days, but now they must retire and leave the couple alone. They obeyed, half under protest, and the matrons of honor also discreetly took their departure. For the first time Fucho and Delicate Blossom faced each other alone, total strangers up to now, but as much man and wife as the holy rites of their ancestors could make them.

At first Fucho tried to pretend he was drunk, and did not even look at Delicate Blossom. But she sat demurely at the other end of the bed, in a less formal dress that showed her figure well. Fucho knew he had to make the first move, and he was determined to save her as much pain and embarrassment as possible.

"You must be very tired," he said. "Would you like to retire?"

To his surprise Delicate Blossom did not answer, but with a twinkle in her eye directed his attention under the bed. Fucho bent down and held up the curtains that screened the lower part of the four-poster. There was Ta-kong staring in his face. Dragging the boy out, he ordered, "Be gone, you little imp!"

Ta-kong ran out of the room in great hilarity, shouting, "You are not so smart as my new aunt, henpecked uncle! If it hadn't been for her, you wouldn't have found me!"

4

Fucho bolted the door of the bedchamber, chuckling. He straightened his face, however, as soon as he saw Delicate Blossom.

"The children must have their fun," he said stumblingly. "Would you like to retire now?"

Delicate Blossom rose slowly. She turned her back on Fucho and went to one of the candles and gently blew it out. Fucho extinguished all the other lights, but moonlight from the windows gave the chamber a silver sheen crisscrossed with shadows, very much like fairyland. For a moment the whole person of Delicate Blossom was bathed in it, and Fucho thought he had seen nothing so beautiful. Suddenly he felt an irrepressible urge to rush forward and take Delicate Blossom in his arms. Wasn't she his lawful wife, before Heaven and Earth, and before all men? He dug his fingernails so deeply into his palms that he felt pain, until he was sure of himself once again.

He undressed quickly. The underclothes the Chinese wore were like pajamas, and he needed to take off only his outer jacket and long gown. He saw that Delicate Blossom had done the same, but she was still standing a little uncertainly before the bed.

One side of the four-poster was against a wall, and with curtains all around, the only way in and out was from the front. Fucho did not wish to be on the inner side of the bed, deprived of freedom of action.

"Would you go in first, please?" he asked.

Without a word Delicate Blossom got in and covered her body with the silk quilt. She lay on her back, motionless, her eyes half-closed. Fucho moved in under the same quilt, but squeezed himself on the outer edge of the bed as far from her as possible.

He thought three times. Another three times. And still another three times. Then he spoke.

"I have something to tell you."

There was no answer. After a while he went on, "It is very difficult for me to tell you."

Delicate Blossom replied, rather hesitantly, "There should be nothing difficult for a husband to tell his wife."

This was the first time Fucho had heard her voice, and he thought it was like soft music. His heart beat wildly.

"But it's going to be unpleasant, very unpleasant. Very painful. Especially for you."

88

Quite a few seconds elapsed before Delicate Blossom answered, "Nothing that a husband tells his wife can be unpleasant or painful to her."

"But that's it," Fucho told her bitterly. "We cannot be husband and wife. We cannot be married."

Delicate Blossom did not stir. Fucho dared not look at her. Finally, in a voice that was even more gentle, she asked, "Aren't we already married? Already husband and wife?"

"Yes," said Fucho. "In name, but not in fact. I don't mean all these ceremonies we have gone through. I mean what makes man and woman truly husband and wife."

Why did she not answer? Why did she show no sign of emotion? Could she be thinking that he was impotent? Fucho's whole manhood revolted at the thought.

"Not that I cannot be a husband," he added quickly. "In that respect, I am like any other man. But I am bound by my own word. I have given my promise to another."

There was an abrupt movement, and then Delicate Blossom lay completely still. Fucho knew he had hurt her terribly, she, the most heavenly woman of all!

"I would like our marriage to be a genuine marriage," he went on, in a hasty effort to console her. "But it cannot be. There is another girl—and I have given her my word."

Delicate Blossom's voice was so low as to be almost inaudible. "Tell me about . . . about this girl."

"There is not much to tell. Her name is San Ai-mei. But she calls herself Amy San, after the Western fashion. She is in Japan. I met her there."

"Is she good-looking? Better-looking than I am?"

"She is not bad-looking, in her way—but she is nothing to compare with you. I know no one who can compare with you—believe me when I say this; I do not say it to please you. I say it with all the sincerity of my heart. Amy is pretty, charming, vivacious. But you—you are beautiful."

Delicate Blossom asked him to tell her more about Amy. "How did you first meet?"

Fucho told as much as he could. He had met Amy in connection with his revolutionary activities in Japan, but he could say nothing about them. Amy was involved in the cause of Sun Yat-sen, and it was natural that young people, so thrown together in the common conspiracy, should soon become very close. But Fucho told Delicate Blossom everything else about his relationship with Amy.

"Did you marry her in Japan?"

"No."

"Did she know of our pending marriage when you left her?"

"I told her. She made me promise not to go through with it, and I . . . I gave her my word."

Another long pause. Then she asked what his real relationship was with her. How they spent their time together.

This was becoming more difficult than Fucho had anticipated, but he felt he owed Delicate Blossom the whole truth.

"We talked most of the time. We held hands sometimes, and then we kissed a few times. That is all."

"Kiss? What is that?"

How innocent the girl was—how well brought-up she had been according to Chinese standards.

"A kiss is to press one's mouth upon that of another. It is a common practice between men and women in the West. When a couple kiss each other, they are supposed to be engaged to be married."

Delicate Blossom did not dwell on that for long. Her thoughts were pursuing a more important course.

"What are your plans for me?" she asked timidly.

"I hate myself," Fucho said, "but I cannot help it. We can only go on pretending to be husband and wife. We must do so before our families—especially before my parents and yours. We must not cause them any grief on our account. Perhaps, when they pass away into the Heavens, we may arrange a divorce."

"What is a divorce?"

"That is also a common practice in the West. It means that husband and wife can separate for good. Each is free to marry another person after a divorce."

For the first time a trace of vehemence appeared in Delicate Blossom's voice. "What a barbarian custom! You can divorce me, but I cannot divorce you. You may marry the girl any time you wish— I shall not hinder you—but I can never marry another man. You may have given your word to her, but I have given my pledge to my parents, who brought me up for you. You are my husband, for better or for worse. I'd rather die than associate with any other man!"

90

There was no reasoning with her. She had been raised too well according to the ideals of Fidelity. Fucho kept his silence.

"Can't you . . . can't you take her as a concubine?" she asked haltingly.

This touched Fucho most of all. He would have liked to yield to her self-abasing request, but something stronger made him speak.

"No, I cannot do that. For one thing, Amy would not agree. But it is more because of myself. I have learned that out in the West a man takes only one woman for wife, and no concubines. Then there is the example of my own parents. I believe it is right that a man should love only one woman. I may have given my word rashly and wrongly, but I must live up to my belief."

Fucho fully expected Delicate Blossom to give way to weeping, but not a whimper was heard.

After an unbearable hush, at last she murmured, more to herself than to Fucho, "Oh, how fortunate for her!"

"Why don't you blame me?" Fucho said savagely. "Why don't you rail at me? I deserve everything that you can possibly say."

Only his unreasoning anger provoked her to reply: "But what's the use? You are my husband. And you have already said that you cannot help yourself. You must be suffering as much as I am."

"Then why don't you cry? Why don't you weep?"

"I do want to cry, but the tears won't come. They seem to flow inward."

Fucho could no longer contain himself. His body shook and he moaned pitifully, "Oh, how I hate myself!"

Presently he heard a gentle whisper. "Do not torment yourself so. Trust me to do what you wish. I shall behave exactly as if we were man and wife. I shall never let our parents, or any others, suspect the truth. And when we have fulfilled our duties to our parents, I shall enter a Buddhist convent and become a nun. You may then marry that girl."

Fucho now understood what Delicate Blossom had meant. And he, in his turn, did not cry, but his tears rose within like an irresistible torrent.

Eight

AT DAYLIGHT FUCHO heard footsteps on the veranda, followed by a gentle rap at the door. The head matron of honor was calling them to rise, and Delicate Blossom had already answered. He jumped quickly out of the four-poster, making way for his bride and avoiding looking at her with deliberate effort. As soon as he had dressed himself he went to another room to wash, so that the maids could come in and help attire and adorn Delicate Blossom properly.

She joined him later in the outer chamber, but the three matrons of honor were with her, saving him the embarrassment of being alone with her. At the sight of him, her lips curled ever so slightly in a gallant attempt at a smile, and he lowered his head, abashed.

This was the day of the "Seeing-the-Face" ceremonials. The bride was to present gifts to the elders, and in return receive gifts from them. In all these visits the groom was required to escort her. Thus they proceeded on their mission, accompanied by the matrons of honor and by many maids bearing the various presents, all wrapped in red silk and enclosed within crimson lacquered boxes.

They went first to the court of Ho the Central Hall and Orchid, where they fell on the floor and kowtowed three times. But this time the parents did not accept the obeisances sitting. Wreathed in smiles, they stood while the newlyweds paid their respects. Then they helped them get up, the father the son, the mother the daughter-in-law, each murmuring at the same time, "All felicitations! All felicitations!"

Now Delicate Blossom presented her gift. It was a most expensive Ju-Yi—the word "Ju-Yi" means literally, "as you wish"—carved out of the choicest jade. It was shaped like a bow and was for use as an ornament—a symbol of happiness. In turn, Orchid gave her daughter-in-law the present they had long prepared for her. It consisted of four articles, four representing the four seasons and being considered a lucky number. They were a jade bracelet, a ruby ring, a pearl necklace, and an embroidered jacket of unusual excellence.

The parents bade the couple sit down. Fucho took his seat, but there was still something that convention required Delicate Blossom to do. Behind her stood two maids, one carrying two teacups on a tray, and the other all the essentials for making tea. Delicate Blossom poured fresh tea into the cups. Then she went to her father-in-law and mother-in-law respectively and placed a cup on each of the tea-stands nearest them. After that, she filled Ho the Central Hall's pipe with new tobacco. This done, she sat demurely by the side of her mother-in-law while all the matrons and maids withdrew to an outer chamber.

"How well brought-up you are, my own darling little daughter," said the delighted Orchid. "Now, children, you must have some refreshments."

On a near-by tea-stand stood a round silver container in the form of a lotus leaf. Orchid uncovered it, disclosing eight compartments, each filled with a different delicacy—olives, lotus-seeds, and other sweetmeats. She pressed an olive on Delicate Blossom.

"You must eat this, my daughter. This is the fruit of long life. This is to wish that you and Fucho may have a long life together, until your beautiful hair turns all white like your father's and mine."

Delicate Blossom took the olive dutifully. Then Orchid handed her some lotus-seeds.

"These you must take, my little girl. Plenty of them. These are from the plant of many seeds. May you and Fucho have many, many children!"

Blushingly Delicate Blossom ate a few. Orchid took her hand and fondled it.

It was hard to get away from Orchid, who kept telling Fucho how beautiful his bride was. The head matron returned to remind them they had to pay their respects to others, and then Orchid reluctantly let them go.

The other visits were much less elaborate. Their uncle and aunt would not have them kowtow more than once; the others would not stand for the ceremony at all. Everyone paid tribute to the exceeding beauty of the bride and to the good fortune of the groom. Though all were housed within the same compound, it took Fucho and Delicate Blossom a full forenoon to finish the round. When they returned to the bridal court, guests were arriving for the noon-time feast.

The women guests were entertained in the inner courts, separate from the men. Orchid was all joy and pride, delighting in showing off her exquisite new daughter-in-law. But she was considerate, too, and at the first chance she whispered, "You must be very tired, child.

Slip away to your court with a matron of honor, and take a good long rest."

Thus it was that when Fucho returned to the bedchamber, on an unimportant errand for his father, he was surprised to find Delicate Blossom there with her companion. Upon his unexpected entrance, she tried to hide the book she was reading, but Fucho saw that it was one of the Japanese volumes he had brought home. He knew that, unlike most Chinese girls of her time, Delicate Blossom had been well tutored in Chinese classics. But could she read Japanese too? The thought intrigued him throughout the rest of the day.

It was a long day for Fucho. The feast that started at noon did not end until late in the night. When the elderly guests finally took their departure, the younger ones, led by Ta-kong, trooped into the bridal court, dragging Fucho along. But they found Orchid sitting on a chair directly in front of the door to the bridal suite, barring their admittance.

"I know you want to play your pranks," she said. "I shall not deny you the pleasure. But not tonight. The bride and groom are too tired. Go now and come tomorrow evening."

"Oh, you are such a kill-joy, Grandma!" exclaimed Ta-kong.

"Enough, you spoiled brat!" scolded Orchid.

"But you stopped us yesterday, Grandma. Who knows what you will do tomorrow? My uncle marries only once, and I have no more unmarried uncles. I want to have my fun!"

"You'll have your fun tomorrow," insisted Orchid. "Tonight you cannot, unless you move me out of this chair by force. And that I dare you to do!"

Recognizing the determination of the old lady, the youngsters scattered reluctantly, much to the disappointment of Ta-kong.

After the last of them had left the bridal court, Orchid pushed Fucho and Delicate Blossom into the bedchamber, summoned out all the matrons and maids, and shut the door. Then from outside, she called, "Children, be my good son and good daughter. Retire at once. Good night."

Fucho and Delicate Blossom knew she was still loitering on the veranda, and they quickly put out the lights and went to bed. Presently they heard the old lady giggle as she moved away, supported by her maidservants. Alone again, they lay side by side in the same position as the night before. Both were extremely tired but could not sleep.

"You have done wonderfully well," Fucho said.

94

"It's not so difficult," replied Delicate Blossom, "when we have such trusting and considerate parents."

There seemed to be nothing more for Fucho to say. The silence lasted for minutes, while he fretted nervously. Finally, he asked if she were asleep.

"No," she said. "Just now sleep doesn't seem to come."

Then he asked if she would mind a question, and when she replied, of course not, he inquired about the book he had found her reading that afternoon.

"It was one of your books," she said. "A history of China written by a Japanese."

"And you can read Japanese?"

"A little," she said. "Not as well as I'd like to."

He was intrigued. How had she come to learn the language, he asked.

"It was when you were away in Japan. I was able to persuade my father and mother to get a tutor for me."

He made no comment. "But why did you have to read the book today of all days?" he asked gently. "Why didn't you get a little rest when you had the time? You must have been worn out."

"I want so much to learn what you have learned. I want to know you better, and I thought the only way might be through the books you have studied. Did I do wrong?"

"Oh no, no!" said Fucho hastily. She could have no idea how profoundly moved he was by her simple, straightforward answer.

"May I also ask a question?" she whispered presently.

"Of course."

"There was a paper between the pages of the book, written in Japanese. It is . . . it is a plan for an uprising in this province. It gives all the details of men and weapons needed for the purpose. How did it get there? What does it mean?"

Fucho's muscles tightened involuntarily. This was the plan he had drawn up with Sun Yat-sen and a few other trusted revolutionaries. Thinking that nobody in Yi could read Japanese, he had hidden it rather carelessly, and in the midst of the activities he had all but forgotten it.

"You need not tell me if you do not wish to," Delicate Blossom said softly. "But remember this—it is a wife's duty to die for her husband if need be, and I would willingly die for you."

Fucho drew a deep breath of relief. If he could ever trust anybody, he could trust this girl who considered herself to be his wife. And

95

suddenly he wanted her to understand his revolutionary activities. All at once he was telling her everything—how he had thought about the Manchus and their rotten Imperial Court, how he had argued with his father on the eve of his departure for Japan the second time, how he had joined Dr. Sun Yat-sen as soon as he reached there, and how they had conspired together to overthrow the Empire. He even told her that he had acquiesced to their marriage because of the revolution. The Manchus were on their guard, and the revolutionaries had found it increasingly difficult to smuggle in firearms from abroad. His wedding was considered a godsend. Her father being a present Minister of State and his a former Central Hall, not the least suspicion could be attached to him; so under the disguise of goods and gifts for the wedding, he had succeeded in smuggling a large quantity of weapons safely past Government customs.

Nor did he not neglect to impress on her the dangers he and the revolutionaries were taking. Again and again he emphasized the necessity of secrecy and caution. Now that he had told her, she must never disclose what she knew to any other soul, and most important of all, not to his parents and hers.

Delicate Blossom listened attentively and quietly, without interruption. When he came to the end, she thought for a moment before she said, "Your life is mine. Trust that I will keep all your secrets. But do be careful, yourself!"

There was no expression of terror, no question about his dire purpose. There was no attempt to dissuade him from continuing such a perilous course. There was no hesitation, no indifference. Indeed, there seemed to be only complete devotion to him, compounded with a womanly anxiety for his personal safety. And he, a husband who had refused to be a true husband to her! The more Fucho pondered, the more he marveled. Could there ever be such a woman? Yet she was lying there by his side. Any time he cared to, he could touch her.

"Do you fully realize the perils we are in?" he asked.

"Of course. If you are discovered, it would mean the extermination of our two families."

"And you think it right for me to do what I am doing?"

"That is not for me to say. From the standpoint of our families, perhaps you should have thought twice before you joined the revolutionary cause. But I also understand that you have aims higher than the well-being of our families. Had you consulted me before you

96

made up your mind, I might have spoken differently. But since you have already done so, what you want is now what I want."

Again a sense of wonder engulfed him. "Delicate Blossom . . . may I call you by your name?"

"Of course, Fucho."

"Why are you so good, so understanding, so patient with me? You accept everything I say without question. Tell me, Delicate Blossom —what a beautiful name that is!—is it because you consider husband superior to wife, because you think I am your lord and master, that you follow my inclinations blindly, whatever they may be?"

"Oh no," she answered in all seriousness. "A husband is not superior to his wife. Don't you know the old story in our classics? When a sage was once asked what the word 'wife' means, he said that it means 'equal.' You are not superior to me, nor my lord and master. You are my equal. More than that, husband and wife are counterpart each to the other, two yet one, separate and yet inseparable. Since we have already kowtowed to Heaven and Earth as husband and wife, I have no other life but yours. How, then, could I act independently of my own life? I will guard your secrets."

Fucho heaved a long, satisfied sigh. "I thank Heaven and Earth for giving me such a wife!"

But he made no move toward her.

2

WHEN DAWN CAME, Fucho's mind was made up in a secret resolve.

The head matron of honor tapped at the door, waking Delicate Blossom. Fucho smiled enigmatically at his bride and said, "There is something I must do, and show you, today. If I don't bring up the matter before the day is over, please remind me of it."

This was the last day of the three-day festivity, when the bride and groom were to receive the younger relatives and distribute gifts among them. But before they could do that, they must pay their respects to their parents. A single maid carried the implements for making tea, as well as some of Ho the Central Hall's favorite tobacco. This time Fucho and Delicate Blossom did not kowtow, but saluted with a deep incline of their bodies, their hands touching their knees. Dutifully Delicate Blossom poured the tea and filled Ho the Central Hall's pipe—the symbolic gestures of Filial Piety that a daughter of the house was obliged to observe toward her husband's parents, the first thing every morning for as long as she lived under the same roof.

Ho the Central Hall smiled. "Thank you, daughter. And now be seated, children. You rise too early, you cannot have had much rest. After today, you need not come at such an unearthly hour, my daughter. You may take as much time as you wish."

This was the most gracious concession parents could make to a daughter-in-law, and Delicate Blossom was grateful.

Orchid had already taken her daughter-in-law's hand and was fondling it. "Sit closer to me, my darling," she said. "Let me look more clearly at your face."

When Delicate Blossom did so, Orchid screwed up her old eyes in unblinking scrutiny. "There was an old woman who once taught me a trick," she went on. "She said that one can tell the difference between a maid and a woman by examining the eyebrow. A maid's eyebrow always stands out straight and even; when she is married, the eyebrow becomes ruffled. But bless my soul, your eyebrows are still the same as I first saw them—all straight and even! Are my eyes bleary with age, or was the old woman mistaken? Of course, she must have been mistaken!"

Seeing Delicate Blossom blush and hang her head, Orchid chuckled. "Your father and I are getting on with age. Nothing would gladden our old hearts more than to have grandchildren by you two. Most people prefer boys, but in your case we don't care which comes first—boy or girl."

And the old lady went on fondly until Ho Tao came to the rescue, and bade them return to their bridal court.

The young people were waiting there. According to the proprieties, they were expected to kowtow to the couple before they received their gifts. Fucho and Delicate Blossom waived these ceremonies, with one exception. When it came to Ta-kong's turn, Fucho frowned at the boy sternly.

"You have been so naughty, you imp, that you must kowtow."

The boy laughed outright. "You know how much I hate to kowtow. I'll do it, but understand this, uncle—I'll not kowtow to you. I'll kowtow to my new aunt only. She is so much smarter than you, and so much better-looking. When I grow up, I want to have a wife just like her. Only I'll not be henpecked! For this wish of mine, I'll kowtow to my aunt not only once, I'll kowtow to her three times."

And he fell on all fours, and knocked his little head resoundingly against the carpet thrice in quick succession. The whole bridal court roared with laughter.

Guests came and went as the day passed, and Fucho was never alone with Delicate Blossom. Late that evening the young people who had thronged the bridal suite were having the time of their lives at the expense of the newlyweds. This was the last night of the festivity, and even if she wished, Orchid could not have stopped them.

And now Ta-kong decided to have his revenge. He cried aloud so that all could hear: "Uncle, you made me kowtow three times to my aunt this morning. I dare you to do the same to her. We all demand that you kowtow three times to my aunt!"

He turned to the crowd for support, and clamorously they shouted their approval.

Delicate Blossom, sitting at one end of the bed, instantly recognized that this was a most atrocious prank to play on Fucho. No man in China would think of kowtowing in public to any woman, with the exception of his own mother, Her Majesty the Empress, or some very elderly relation. If he ever did so, even to his wife—especially to his wife—he would be a laughingstock. Delicate Blossom stole a glance at Fucho, expecting him to be infuriated at the proposition, but he looked quite calm. Emboldened by his passivity, some of the crowd, led by Ta-kong, began to drag him forward. They cleared a little space before Delicate Blossom and stood him there, trying to force him to his knees. At this, Delicate Blossom stood up, feeling it not right to accept such reverence from her husband, but Ta-kong rushed to his aunt with other children to help and drove her back to her seat.

"I want my uncle to kowtow to you properly," he shouted. "I want you to accept his kowtow sitting."

"Why don't you leave me alone? I'll gladly kowtow to her," Fucho said.

Delicate Blossom could scarcely believe her ears. And there was a shocked silence in the room.

"You will really kowtow to her of your own free will?" someone asked. "You are not going to trick us?"

Fucho nodded affirmatively and the children turned him loose. Delicate Blossom at once made another attempt to stand up, but the youngsters held her tightly.

Fucho knelt and kowtowed to her three times in the most proper and respectful manner. The crowd burst into loud laughter, but

Delicate Blossom understood. By paying her this homage, he was showing his penitence for what he had done to her. And her heart warmed toward him.

"My uncle has done what a man should never do to a woman," Ta-kong declared. "He has proved himself hopelessly henpecked, and he ought to be rewarded by my aunt. They must now hold hands!"

This was an even more indecorous jest. The boy well knew that no intimacy whatsoever between a husband and wife should be displayed in the presence of others.

Fucho was quickly pushed to sit down on the bed side by side with Delicate Blossom. With the help of the other children, Ta-kong began to pull at their hands to make them clasp together. If he had expected embarrassment and reluctance he was disappointed. Delicate Blossom let her hand fall quite naturally into Fucho's. Then she gave his hand a gentle squeeze to show her appreciation for his having kowtowed to her. This was their first physical contact, and Fucho's blood stirred violently. Though the others did not notice, he responded with a grip far firmer than hers.

The head matron of honor now stepped forward. "You all have had your fun. The hour is getting very late."

"I still have one request to make," yelled Ta-kong.

"If it is the last, I shall ask the groom and bride to accommodate you," the matron said. "If not, then I shall have to go and appeal to Grandma Ho."

"The request I'm going to make is no prank," the boy said. "I now ask my uncle and aunt to drink three cups of wine together, not separately, but both from the same cup by turns. I wish them great happiness."

The brat was truly clever, Fucho thought. He himself was inwardly delighted with the suggestion. It was carried out forthwith and the crowd dispersed.

3

FUCHO AND DELICATE BLOSSOM were again alone, lying side by side on the four-poster. The moon was full, much brighter than on the two preceding nights, and each could see each the other's face distinctly. After what they had gone through together, they no longer felt so awkward.

Delicate Blossom turned her head toward Fucho, who was watch-

100

ing her every movement, and whispered, "I must thank you, Fucho, for having kowtowed to me. You should never have done that. But now that you have, I am extremely thankful."

"It's I who ought to be everlastingly grateful to you, Delicate Blossom. I kowtowed to you entirely of my own free will."

He stretched forth his hand under the quilt and caught hers. When he gave it a tender squeeze, he felt a response even tenderer that loosed the passions that had been raging in his heart. Raising himself, he touched her lips gently with his own. Delicate Blossom remained silent, supine, immobile, her eyes almost closed, her lips slightly parted and tremulous, her breath coming faint and short. He kissed her again. It was nothing like the kisses he had experienced with Amy. This girl knew nothing about kissing. She kept her lips parted, and they were limp and moist. There was no responsiveness in them, only yielding—yielding without reservation, yielding with the willingness of the soul. It was far, far more delectable, far more sensuous.

Unsteadily his hand stole across her bosom. Fumblingly it unbuttoned her tunic. It touched skin so velvety, so magnetic, that the fingers tingled. Fucho thought of the divine alabaster of the Maiden of the Moon, and almost drew back for fear of committing a desecration, but the hand could not long remain away. It grew bolder. It felt its way about, made new exciting discoveries—and then, at last, it strayed downward.

Delicate Blossom seized the venturesome hand abruptly. "Are you drunk, Fucho?" she whispered.

"No," replied Fucho with difficulty but truthfulness. "I have never been as clear-headed in my life."

But Delicate Blossom would not release her hold. "Have you forgotten your resolution?"

"This is what I told you this morning I wanted to do today. Remember? Darling, please!" Fucho pleaded.

Slowly Delicate Blossom loosened her grip. . . .

When finally he lay limp and rapturous, his head close beside hers, he said tenderly, "Forgive me all the pain and anguish I must have caused you, my darling wife."

Delicate Blossom embraced him all the tighter and whispered, "All that was nothing, my dearest husband, compared to the joy you have brought to my heart."

They lay thus intertwined for a long time, both hating the thought of separation. Then Delicate Blossom said, "Just think,

101

tomorrow—or should I say today?—is the Homecoming Day for the bride, when we pay our respects to my parents."

Fucho understood her thought. "And now," he said, "I can face them with a clear conscience and call them my father and my mother."

"Perhaps I shall be able to bear you a child soon, as our dear parents wish so much."

"I hope it will be a daughter," said Fucho. "Father and mother won't mind, and I'd like our first-born to be a girl like you."

Delicate Blossom remained silent. Fucho was grateful, for he knew instinctively that Amy must be very much in her thoughts then as she was in his. Though Amy was nothing to him now, he felt he could not bear any mention of her name. When long minutes passed and Delicate Blossom still did not say a word, a sweet, balmy content descended upon him and he fell into a deep sleep.

Early in the morning, long before dawn broke, Fucho awoke of a sudden. It was a trick he had learned at the Japanese Military Academy; before going to sleep he would impress upon his subconscious the need to awaken at a certain hour, and would automatically wake at that time. Now he stealthily crept out of bed, stepped over to the writing desk, and began a letter. But when he came to the end, some unwary movement of his must have aroused Delicate Blossom, for she raised herself on the four-poster.

"What are you doing, Fucho? Come back to bed at once—you will catch cold!"

He walked over, a candle in one hand and the letter in the other, and sat down. "Come and read this, my darling."

Delicate Blossom crawled over to his side and hurriedly wrapped part of the quilt about him before starting to read what he had written. It was a letter to Amy. It reminded her gently but firmly that their past relations had never really gone beyond the stage of friendship, and told her that he was now married to his betrothed and that hereafter he and she, Amy, must continue as friends, but friends only.

When Delicate Blossom finished he said apologetically, "I meant to do this yesterday. I intended to write the letter and show it to you before . . . before last night. But in my confusion I got things in the wrong order. Will you forgive me, my dearest?"

Delicate Blossom put her arms around Fucho and hugged him tightly. Taking the initiative herself, she pressed her lips on his, and then took fright at her own boldness and in a flurry buried her

102

blushes in his lap. All at once, inexplicably she broke into convulsive sobbing. But muffled though her head was within the folds of his pajamas, her voice came out clear and singing.

"Oh, dearest . . . dearest . . . I liked . . . your wrong order!"

Nine

THE ENTIRE HOUSEHOLD of Ho was happy. Fucho and Delicate Blossom were lost in their love and their happiness with each other, and Ho the Central Hall and Orchid rejoiced. And if Ho the Central Hall and Orchid rejoiced, so did the rest of the house.

Ta-kong, for his part, had found a genuine hero and heroine to admire and worship in his boyish heart. Despite the naughty pranks he had played on them, the newlyweds took a great fancy to their spirited young nephew. Fucho regaled him with stories from his own experience—the lands where he had traveled, the people he had seen, and tales of the great heroes he had learned both in China and in Japan. And Delicate Blossom indulged him with sweetmeats and delicacies, and tended him with motherly care. Curling himself, feet and all, in a large chair, Ta-kong would watch and listen to them entranced, thinking that no couple on earth could be more wonderful.

It was some time after the wedding when Ho the Central Hall asked Fucho what he would like to do for a career. Would he take service with the Government? Or would he prefer joining the New Army that Yuan Shih-kai had organized? It was for Fucho to choose. The old man still had high connections in the Government. And even though there was no love lost between himself and Yuan Shih-kai, a word from Delicate Blossom's father, Minister Tan, to the head of the New Army would pull the strings. But Fucho would not do either. He said he was still young and his parents were growing old; his two older brothers were both in Government service and away from home. If his father and mother would bear with him, he would remain and wait on them in their old age.

Ho the Central Hall was deeply touched. He had always thought this son to be independent and ambitious, and had not expected him to sacrifice so much for the sake of Filial Piety. Orchid was pleased beyond measure. She so much wanted to have Fucho and Delicate Blossom live with them, and hoped to see her favorite daugher-in-law bear a grandchild before she herself joined the ancestors.

But what would Fucho do to pass the time? For this, the son had a ready answer. If his father would deign to approve, he would like to establish a high school in Yi. There was only one grammar school in the city, and after graduation the students had no place to go. Other children like Ta-kong who were tutored at home also needed additional modern knowledge. Partly to anticipate the old man's objections and partly out of his own convictions, Fucho proposed that besides the new courses he hoped to offer, he would also emphasize the study of ancient classics. If his father cared to do so, he himself could give the students the full benefit of his wisdom. At first, Ho the Central Hall viewed the proposition with some skepticism, but the last argument persuaded him. "Ah," he declared, "has not one of our sages said, 'To meet with the promising talents under Heaven and to be able to teach them—is that not a source of great personal pleasure?' I wonder how I have failed to think of this before. It is good of you to bring it up, my son."

Thus, with a substantial donation from the House of Ho, the high school was founded and became an immediate success. The Reverend Dr. Holt was consulted about the curriculum, and was drafted to teach English and physiology. Anna was invited to teach music and singing. Her presence in the school caused quite a stir, since it was the first time a woman had ever been employed to teach boys. Ta-kong clamored to join the school from the very outset. He was not of the high-school age, but Fucho set up a special preparatory class for younger students. Lan Yuwen, Widow Lan's son, enrolled, and he and Ta-kong became bosom friends.

In all the preparations for the school and in its subsequent activity, Delicate Blossom took a large part. She was not only wife of its founder and principal, but also his advisor and secretary. She graced everything with her feminine touch.

Nobody was as enthusiastic about the school as Ho the Central Hall. Each Wednesday afternoon a mass meeting of the students was held in the main hall, and Ho presided. Wearing his yellow jacket, a benign smile on his face, he talked to his heart's content about the merits of the ancient classics and about the eternal values of time-proven virtues.

Things would have been vastly different if Ho the Central Hall

104

had known the real purpose for which the school was established. The education of the young was truly one of Fucho's purposes, but not the main one. Only Delicate Blossom knew that the school was a revolutionary project which he had formulated with Dr. Sun Yat-sen in Japan. The latter had at first counseled Fucho to take advantage of his family connections and join the New Army of Yuan Shih-kai for subversive purposes. But Fucho was exceptionally sensitive about the virtue of Integrity. He might revolt against the Manchus with all his might, for he himself had never sworn allegiance to them; but to join the New Army or enter any Government service he would have to swear a false allegiance, and that he could not bring himself to do. Respecting his scruples, Dr. Sun had agreed on the plan Fucho proposed as a substitute. Thus, the school was to be a center for training and recruiting young revolutionaries in secret.

Fucho staffed the school with teachers who were fellow revolutionaries, and they all spread revolutionary propaganda skillfully and surreptitiously. Concentrating on the older students, they told them of the corruption and incompetence of the Manchu court. They inflamed the boys' feelings against the autocratic rule of an alien race, and successfully planted in their minds the idea that revolution was not only a necessity but also a sacred duty.

Still, Fucho felt frustrated. While making the plans in Japan, he had thought he could use the students to stage an uprising; now he knew that he could not. Most of the boys were too young, and Fucho became sentimental about them. They were the flower of the nation, the hope of China—they should not be sacrificed in a bloody upheaval, but must be preserved for the later reconstruction of the country. Only recently, one of Dr. Sun's chief lieutenants had staged an uprising far south in Canton. With barely a hundred men, the majority of them not much older than Fucho's boys, he had undertaken to storm the Viceroy's yamen and seize the city. The project failed miserably. Out of the hundred, seventy-two were killed in action or executed afterward. It was a gallant attempt, but a futile and wasteful one that should not be repeated.

"We cannot sacrifice the students, my darling," Fucho told Delicate Blossom one night, "but we must have men. Plenty of men. Men who are at once reckless and expendable. Reckless enough to take any risk, and expendable enough from the standpoint of the well-being of the nation. But where can I find such men?"

2

DURING THE NEXT twelvemonth, Fucho was distracted by other matters of more immediate and personal concern.

First, a daughter was born to Delicate Blossom. The event was celebrated in the House of Ho like a second New Year, and the grandfather proudly named the baby Li-hwa—Beautiful China.

Then tears followed laughter, as is too often the course of human life. Orchid, having seen her dearest wish fulfilled, joined her ancestors after a brief illness.

For a time after his mother's death Fucho was greatly concerned about his father's health. But gradually the old man became reconciled to the loss and settled down to a sort of routine. He seldom went out of the compound, and received few visitors. He loved Fucho's company most, and the son made it a point to be with him as much as he could. Ta-kong was put up in Ho Tao's bedchamber as his grandfather's roommate, and when Fucho and Ta-kong were away at school the old man would have Delicate Blossom bring the baby to him and he would watch them play. But he still looked forward to Wednesday and always found enough energy to go to the school and lecture on the ancient virtues.

Fucho became increasingly distraught with his secret problem, for two years had passed since the founding of the school and he was as far from accomplishing his dream as ever. Then, one day while he was with his father, the Commandant of the troops newly assigned to garrison the area, a part of Yuan Shih-kai's New Army, came to pay respects to Ho Tao. At the end of the interview the old man said, by way of apology, that since he was afflicted with old age and ill health he would not be able to return the call; he would send Fucho to do the duty instead.

Fucho welcomed the chance to observe the strength and morale of the New Army so that he would know how to deal with it when the time came. Aware of his education and eager to impress him, the Commandant granted his request to observe a company training on the field. At their approach, an officer ordered the men to present arms and then saluted smartly. The Commandant presented the officer to Fucho as Captain Tien Fong. He was a tall, powerful man with a large, ugly sword-scar on each cheek, which made his features extremely grotesque. The Commandant explained later that the Captain claimed to have acquired his wounds in a remote forgotten

106

battle. Fucho could not remember ever having seen the man before, and still there was something vaguely familiar about his bearing and carriage.

On the way home a sudden recollection came to Fucho, and his heart beat in wild excitement.

He had to be sure. For three days he had his fellow revolutionaries keep Captain Tien under close surveillance, and he himself collected as much information as he could about the man. Captain Tien was living in a rather poor section of Yi. He was married to a vulgar, frowzy woman of proportions almost as large as his own. They had no children. In spite of his limited income, the Captain was inordinately fond of wine, women, and gambling. Every time he received his monthly pay, he would squander it all in the first few nights in brothels and gambling dens. For the rest of the month he would be obliged to stay at home in the evenings, live on watery rice and preserved vegetables, and bicker with his wife as his sole pastime. It was understood that he was considerably in debt. Only a few days before, the owner of a gambling den had threatened that unless Tien paid up soon, he would go directly to the Commandant to seek restitution.

Nobody could tell where Tien had come from or what he had been, and the Captain himself was conspicuously silent on these subjects. He had strange friends who visited him only by night, and always in groups. They were so noisy, they frightened the whole neighborhood.

Fucho was sure, now. Late one evening, he went to the Captain's house accompanied by four of his comrades bearing two strongboxes. As they approached they heard the riotous hubbub that indicated the Captain's mysterious friends were there. All the neighbors' doors were closed, and no one was on the street. Considering this circumstance well suited to the purpose, Fucho knocked loudly on the gate.

It was opened by the Captain himself. He cast one look at Fucho and his companions, and his scarred face contorted in a dark frown.

"You!" he growled. "What do you want from me?"

"May I have a word with you?"

"I don't see why. Besides, I have company."

"I come with no ill will. I bring you gifts."

Scowling suspiciously, Captain Tien Fong shrugged his powerful shoulders. "You may come in for a minute then, but not your companions."

"How about the boxes? They contain the gifts, and they're quite heavy."

The Captain glanced contemptuously at the four men who held the boxes. "These?" He grabbed one strongbox as if it were weightless and tucked it under his arm, then did the same with the other. With a thrust of his jaw, he directed Fucho to enter the house, and quickly shoved the gate closed with an elbow.

It was a dirty, dreary courtyard, surrounded by a few ramshackle rooms. But by the lights within, by the shadows that flitted to and fro, and by the dreadful din, Fucho knew that scores of persons were making merry inside. Captain Tien led his guest to a corner room where there was no one except a woman sitting on a stool. Her size and slovenly appearance identified her as his wife, but Captain Tien did not introduce her.

"Get out!" he ordered. "I have some business with this man."

The woman left without a word. Captain Tien placed the strongboxes carelessly on a rickety table in the center, and Fucho surveyed the bare and miserable room. Tien saw his glance. "Quite different from what you and your like are used to, eh?"

"Everybody has to live," Fucho answered with a smile. "One place is as good as another. . . . Why don't you look at the gifts I brought?"

Captain Tien glared at Fucho, then lifted the cover of one strongbox. He leaped back at once with a savage oath. This box held the one-legged steel man—the unique weapon wielded by Fong Tienpa the Boxer.

"Son of a turtle!" Tien thundered. "So you did recognize me. Well—are you going to denounce me?"

"Why should I?"

The big man's yellow teeth showed. "You know there is a price on my head. You know there is a standing order for the arrest of all chief Boxers in general, and of me in particular. But you won't get out of this house because I'll tear your throat open with my bare hands!"

"I told you I came with no ill intentions," Fucho said calmly. "Why don't you look at the gift in the second box?"

Tien hesitated, but finally he lifted the other cover. The box was filled with silver taels. He grasped a few greedily and let them fall slowly one by one, making a clinking sound. His eyes narrowed on Fucho, and then turned on the silver taels again.

"There must be almost a fortune here. Why? What do you want

from me? A robbery? A murder? With such a gift as this, bygones are bygones. I am at your service."

Fucho shook his head. "There's more where this came from," he said. "Tell me first—how did you get those scars?"

"I did it myself," the Captain boasted, laughing. "No one is strong enough to do such a thing to me. It was when I changed my name from Fong Tienpa to Tien Fong to avoid arrest. Now Captain Tien Fong of the Imperial New Army, sir. Curse the Empress Dowager! Curse the Emperor! May they rot in the eighteenth grade of Hell! The same with the scars. I put a sword to my face and gave it a little twist. Twice. Nobody knows me any more—only my disciples. The scars work, but every time I go to a brothel the women are frightened."

"You speak of your disciples. Do you still have some of them around you?"

"All of them. Some have joined the New Army too, some are here in the other rooms now. Every one of them is at my beck and call."

"How many do you have in all?"

"At least five hundred."

Fucho was delighted. Seeing that the visitor had no more questions, Captain Tien turned to the silver taels. "Are all these mine? You haven't told me what you want me to do."

"I'll come again tomorrow at this hour. Make sure you are alone. I'll let you know then how you can make more silver taels."

3

DELICATE BLOSSOM'S INTUITION warned her against Fucho's relations with Fong Tienpa, alias Captain Tien Fong, and deep down in his own heart Fucho also had qualms. But he was young and full of confidence; he told himself that to build anew you first must destroy the old. And in the process of destruction, you must use destructive elements. When you start to build once more, there will be plenty of time to do away with those who are undesirable.

Moreover, the Captain proved to be more submissive than Fucho had expected. He introduced Fucho to his disciples, group by group. Fucho harangued them on revolutionary ideals and aims, and they seemed attentive and receptive. Perhaps there were other reasons for their malleability. Several had prices on their heads like Fong Tienpa, and nearly all were on the Government's black list. It would take only a word from Fucho to put them behind bars. But above all, Fucho held the pursestrings. These were penniless ruffians who had always lived from hand to mouth, and now for the first time they could count on a monthly subsidy. It was truly an example of the underworld saying: "She who has milk is my mother."

However, their expenses drained Fucho's financial resources. He spent all the generous allowance with which his father provided him, and dug deep into the school treasury. By the close of a year, he was almost at the end of his tether. Delicate Blossom was willing to sell her jewels, but that was not feasible because on ceremonial occasions she must wear some of them, and often relatives and friends would drop in and want to examine and admire them all. Sun Yat-sen had been traveling tirelessly abroad to raise funds from the patriotic overseas Chinese, but still he had not money enough to meet all his needs and could help Fucho but little. Desperate, Fucho wanted to stake everything on an immediate uprising, but Sun Yat-sen countermanded him, saying he must wait until all sides were ready.

Fucho knew that some of Captain Tien's "expenditures" had gone into gambling dens and brothels. One evening when he took the Captain the monthly pay for his men, he proposed some reductions.

"I didn't expect this from you." Tien frowned. "I looked on you as a big man who wanted to do big things. When you want to do big things, you cannot scrimp."

"Even a mint is limited by its capacity, and I am no mint."

"That I understand," returned Captain Tien shrewdly. "But it's not for myself that I grumble. It's my men I'm thinking of. Without ample money, how long do you think you can hold them together? If you have difficulties in raising money, perhaps I can help you there."

"Of course I have difficulties. Look at how much I've already spent!"

A broad grin, at once obsequious and scornful, spread over the Captain's grotesque face. "You—a son of Ho the Central Hall, with your inheritance—Give me your position, and I'd be able to raise tenfold what you have."

"But I haven't come into my inheritance," answered Fucho sternly. "And I hope I don't—for a long time yet."

Captain Tien suppressed his laughter. "No ill wishes to your ancient father. But can't you use your future inheritance as security to borrow money? Can't you get some 'Beat-Drum Money'?"

110

Fucho's sense of delicacy was outraged. "Beat-Drum Money" was the money a spendthrift son would have no scruple in borrowing, using his anticipated inheritance as collateral. While the father remained alive the creditors would not ask for its return, but as soon as the parent passed away and drums began to beat at the funeral service, they would press for redemption. Fucho recoiled at the thought, but he was driven to the wall.

"Even if I were willing, where could I borrow the money?" he asked hesitantly. "I need large sums, and the man who lends to me must be absolutely dependable. The whole transaction would have to be dead secret."

"Don't you know Ma Teh-lin?"

"My neighbor Ma? Of course. I have a nodding acquaintance with him, but he and my family are not on friendly terms. It's common knowledge that he bears grudges against my father."

"Isn't that all the better for our purpose?" replied Captain Tien cunningly. "He will be that much readier to loan you money. It will be an incentive for him to get at your inheritance."

"But he's the kind that might purposely make it known, just to shame my father and me."

"Have no fear," said Tien Fong. And he told Fucho about the conspiracy he had once plotted with Ma against the Reverend Dr. Holt. "You can see that Ma is as deeply implicated in the Boxers' Rebellion as I. You can denounce us to the authorities any time you wish, but we can't denounce you. Our crimes are deeds already done, all substantiated; yours are just intentions—we could not prove them. I'll go and tell Ma, first, that you have learned of our little felony. When you negotiate with him, just agree to any rate of interest he wants and I'm sure you will have no trouble at all getting your loan."

Their Imperial Majesties were both dead. They had died within three days of each other. Rumor had it that the spiteful Empress Dowager, knowing she had not long to live, poisoned the Emperor whom she never trusted in life and who was her nephew and not her son. But one thing was certain. His late Imperial Majesty had died without issue. A three-year-old boy named Pu-yi was chosen to ascend the Dragon Throne, with his father, widely known as a weakling, serving as Regent.

The prescribed period of official mourning was three years. For

111

the first six months, all officials, incumbent and retired, were required to don coarse white sackcloth and render ceremonial lamentations. Thus, every morning well before sunrise, Ho the Central Hall would repair to the Prefect's yamen, where he would join an august assemblage, kowtow countless times to the golden tablets, now shrouded in white, of the deceased sovereigns, and chant repeatedly, "Alas, my Empress Dowager! Alas, my Emperor!" Though the grief of many was no doubt feigned, that of Ho the Central Hall was real. Some had to rub their eyes hard to make a pretense of weeping, but tears trickled freely down the old man's cheeks.

The news produced a different reaction in Fucho. If he ever considered a moment opportune for revolution, it was now. He had money and he had men. The Government was in the throes of transition, and the Regent was no man to direct the affairs of the nation in such a crisis. Fucho urgently recommended an instant uprising to Sun Yat-sen.

The leader, however, feared that Yuan Shih-kai's New Army was still too loyal to the Manchu Dynasty, and too formidable for the revolutionary forces. But reports had been received that Yuan was secretly plotting for his own advancement and the Regent was becoming suspicious of him. It would be better for the revolutionaries to bide their time and let the two fall out between themselves.

Moreover, in Sun's opinion, the revolutionaries still did not have enough munitions to stage a major uprising—and that included Fucho. But Sun had discovered a foreigner who could supply any amount of firearms and guarantee their safe delivery at designated destinations; if Fucho wanted some of these, it could be easily arranged. The only difficulty would be the everlasting one—the means to pay.

Fucho indeed needed more munitions. As for the money, he no longer considered it a problem. By now his sense of delicacy had been thoroughly dulled. Ma had kept their transaction secret. And besides, Fucho thought, had not his own father taught him the ancient saying: "In order to save the nation, you must not flinch at destroying your own family?" So without further misgivings Fucho again went to Ma and asked for another loan.

Ma studied with meticulous care the properties Fucho offered as surety. Then, nodding approval, he said maliciously, "You understand, of course, that after this, were your father to die, you would have nothing left of your inheritance."

"Yes, I know," said Fucho, and signed the papers.

4

BECAUSE OF THIS transaction, three strangers made their appearance in the city of Yi. Two came together, claiming to be friends of Fucho's; they went straight to the high school and took up lodging there. One was a tall, grayish, lean man about the age of Fucho, called Chang Fa-foo. The other was a little younger, of a fair and rather pasty complexion, short and rotund, with promise of becoming quite corpulent in later years. His name was Tong Hsi.

The third was a foreigner, one John Hunt. He spoke Chinese fluently, was hail-fellow-well-met with everybody, and insisted that one and all call him "Johnny." He said that the sole purpose of his visit was to get "a glimpse of the interior," and that he did not know a single soul in Yi. He had written in advance, however, to the Reverend Dr. Holt as a fellow countryman, mentioning that he had found native inns as a rule very unsatisfactory and expressing a hope that Holt would put him up in the Mission compound during his short sojourn. Holt was happy to consent. Johnny Hunt's appearance in Yi did not attract much notice; by now the people were more or less accustomed to the sight of foreigners.

Hunt was fond of riding. On the day after his arrival, he hired a horse and went out for a ride in the countryside. When he returned, he told about the new acquaintances he had struck up. By "accident," he had run into the other two strangers, who were out sightseeing with Fucho. From that day on, he was often seen in their company.

Of course the three strangers were no strangers to one another at all, but bent on the same secret mission. The foreigner was the munitions dealer whom Sun Yat-sen had mentioned. The two Chinese were Sun's trusted comrades. Chang Fa-foo was the only one among the three who had been known personally to Fucho before; he had joined Dr. Sun in Japan about the same time as Fucho. Tong Hsi had been initiated into the revolutionary party later; he spoke English and knew Johnny Hunt well. According to Chang, Tong was handling most of the business between the revolutionaries and the munitions dealer.

Fucho liked to reminisce with Chang Fa-foo about the old times. It was only natural that one day Chang should ask if Fucho had heard anything from Amy.

Fucho started. He had forgotten her almost completely. Since writing her the letter, he had received neither a reply nor news of her. He knew he did not love her, had never loved her; it was only that circumstances had thrown them intimately together. Nevertheless, he had been sorry to be the cause of any bitterness for her.

"No," answered Fucho halfheartedly. "How has she been?"

Chang Fa-foo grinned. "Why don't you ask Tong Hsi—she is his wife! They were married shortly after you left Japan. They had barely met then; it surprised us all. We all thought she was head over heels in love with you, but apparently we were mistaken. Frailty, thy name is woman, eh?"

Fucho was glad to hear this news. Evidently Amy had not suffered much, or long—if she had suffered at all. Now that she was married he felt no more qualms about his own conjugal bliss. He sincerely wished only the best for Amy, and from that time on he became especially friendly to her husband, Tong Hsi.

In the meantime, Holt rather enjoyed the visit of his self-invited guest. Johnny Hunt was good company and from his own country; he was talkative and amiable. True, there were a few times when Holt thought he saw Johnny, in passing through the clinic court, leer at Anna, and especially at Widow Lan, in a manner that was not to his own taste. But he did not introduce him to them, and for the most part Hunt behaved quite well, never accosting or annoying the women. After all, he was a man of the world, and Holt felt he should overlook such trivial faults.

On what was to be Johnny Hunt's last night in Yi, the missionary thought it fitting that he wait for his guest's return. But the hour grew very late and Holt was tired. He went to Johnny's room to rest while he waited.

Finally he heard shambling steps in the courtyard, and rose from his chair just as Johnny appeared, barely able to stand. He was panting, his face was flushed, his jugular vein throbbed perceptibly, and his breath was strong with the smell of alcohol. Making no comment on his guest's condition, Holt gently helped him to a chair.

Johnny rested his head on the chair-back and looked up.

"Thanks, Logan. Thanks," he mumbled. Then, as Holt cushioned his head with a pillow, he stretched out his long legs and went on, "What a dingy hole I thought Yi was when I first came—but now it turns out to be a gold mine. Do you know where I've been?"

Johnny answered himself: "Why, Logan, at your next-door neighbor Ma's house. And what a lark! I bet you know—probably you've had a taste of it yourself, eh? During dinner, Ma paraded all his concubines for me. Nine of them, I counted. Oh, the way they walked with their bound feet—it was simply too much for me. What fiddlesticks about bound feet being a savage custom. It's the most civilized, the most luxurious, thing man ever invented to please himself with!"

Holt was disgusted. Hunt, his bloodshot eyes filled with a lustful gleam, wagged a finger playfully at him.

"I bet there's one thing you haven't done—you haven't got my guts. I asked Ma to let one of them sit on my lap, and that scoundrel agreed. I'd have preferred the sixth one, the prettiest of the lot, but she was unwilling. Probably has a temper. I had to be content with the next best, the eighth. She's a docile wench. What liberties I took—and that old rascal Ma just looked on and smiled. I had a pretty good idea he rather encouraged her."

Revolted, Holt said angrily, "Stop that! You're drunk!"

"I certainly am not!" Hunt made a manifest effort to appear wide awake. "Oh, Ma tried to get me pie-eyed—yes, he filled me with wine. And let me fool around with his women. He wanted me to give in on certain terms he'd been haggling about. Do you know what I did? I *gave* in, and still made plenty of profit."

Holt was lost for words. Hunt gave him a sharp, peevish glance and did not like what he saw.

"Don't look so damned self-righteous," he said loudly. "I know your kind, Logan. Your face is all innocence, but your heart's as black as mine. You and I are two peas of the same pod. If you're so pure-hearted, tell me this: Why do you have a woman doctor in your compound who's such a good-looker? Woman doctor, indeed! She just doctors your manly desires with her womanly ways!"

"Shut up, you . . . Just leave her out of this."

"So I touched your tender spot! My, you look stirred up. I am too, but in a different way. I have been, as a matter of fact, the whole evening—with those women of Ma's, with that piece of soft flesh on my lap, and that sweet rice wine, and all. Thanks to your damned self-righteousness, my feelings need an outlet. I'm going to that woman doctor of yours right now—I know where she lives. What's good for the host ought to be good for the guest too."

He rose and stumbled toward the door, but in a towering temper that matched his red hair, Holt barred the way. Blindly Johnny lunged forward, but he was no match for the missionary, who shoved him back roughly. Johnny fell over one of his own traveling bags. The lock gave, and the contents scattered over the floor—small

115

parcels wrapped in yellow oily paper, some with the wrappings torn. Holt knew at a glance they were samples of opium.

Hunt got to his feet and stuffed the parcels back into the bag. When he looked at Holt again, his eyes were fully clear.

He seated himself comfortably. "Well," he said cheerfully, "now you know my business, and other than holding your tongue, you have two alternatives: Either go and denounce me to the authorities, or else join me in partnership. I advise you not to take the first course. I enjoy the immunity granted all foreigners, so what can the rotten mandarins do to me? And your denunciation won't hurt, it'll only make you look like a traitor to your own people."

Holt listened with a growing amazement.

"No, the only course for you to take is the partnership, and I'm offering it to you purely from a business standpoint," Johnny went on. "You have a good reputation—nobody will suspect you—and you have a clinic and dispensary for a legitimate cover. Since the premises are owned by your Mission, the Chinese Government can't search them. And you have a good-sized compound which could be handy as a warehouse. I'm willing to take you into equal partnership. I had that in mind even before I came here—that's why I asked to lodge with you.

"Life is short, Logan, and to enjoy it you need money. Here is money—millions and millions. Three hundred million people, just think! If each one buys just a dollar's worth, that'll be three hundred million dollars."

Holt was shocked into silence, which Johnny Hunt mistook for hesitation. "You probably think the drug is harmful, but you haven't taken it and I have. It gives you a thrill you can't get any other way. It's the most humane drug on earth. You're a doctor—you ought to know. When you have pain, it soothes you and makes you forget. When you're weary and worn out, it revives you and gives you strength. I don't mind saying I've been genuinely moved by the wretched condition of the millions of coolies in this country—their hard life and pitiful pay. When they're fatigued, what comfort can we give them? Not your charities, your medical aid. Only this drug, and the more we can supply the less it will cost them. Then take the rich with all their concubines. There's so much demand on their energy they can't possibly cater to all of them. By selling them this drug we're doing everyone a good turn. The Chinese, rich and poor, know its merits; they call it 'the Balm of Blessings and Longevity.' In fact, I'm doing much better missionary work than you

116

missionaries are. Think how few converts you've made in your work, and how many I've made in mine."

Johnny nodded his head. "Oh, I know. You'll say that once you're addicted to this drug you can't stop. But that's not true; it's all a matter of will power. Take me, for instance. I can take opium or leave it alone. I've been with you over a week now, but have you ever seen me crave it? Of course not. There are thousands upon thousands like me, Chinese and foreigners alike. At any rate, the Chinese themselves know what's good for them. I don't mind telling you, many natives with high connections have a hand in this affair."

Holt was astounded. "You don't mean that my friend Ho Fucho takes a part in this traffic!"

Hunt regarded him sharply, pondered a moment. "I'll tell you everything, since we're going to be full partners. No, Ho Fucho has no part in the opium trade; his business with me is of a different kind. He's a revolutionary, a follower of Sun Yat-sen, and I sell him munitions. If you want to help your friend, you can have the firearms stored in your compound. Be my partner and I'll give you a share of the profits in that transaction too."

This was too much for the redheaded missionary. "You! It's you and men like you who turn nations and races against each other. Get out of this compound at once! And never come back!"

Ten

IT WAS OCTOBER, 1911. Ho the Central Hall was suffering from a severe attack of gout, and had grown half blind. He spent most of his time with his eyes closed, reciting the old classics by rote, book by book, chapter by chapter. The Reverend Dr. Holt was the only friend he would receive, and the missionary visited him intermittently and tried to alleviate his pain.

Fucho was away in the provincial capital, and Ho felt a terrible loneliness. His affection for his youngest son had increased with the years, but of late Fucho had many duties that took him away from home. Delicate Blossom and Li-hwa were the old man's only constant companions during those periods.

In the evenings, Ho looked forward eagerly to Ta-kong's return from school. This meant noise in the lonely house, activity, and arguments, for Ta-kong was always full of new learnings and new ideas. The old man could not agree with many of them, but it was stimulating to reason with his grandson.

Sometimes, Ta-kong brought his friend Lan Yuwen, and Ho marveled at the constrast between the boys—one impetuous, the other gentle-natured; one filled with brilliant fancies and dashing roguery, the other showing a steadiness and an understanding usually found only in an older person. Knowing Yuwen's sad background, Ho the Central Hall could not help feeling a secret compassion for the lad.

Because of his illness, Ho had not lectured at the school for two weeks, but this Wednesday was sunny and bright and he felt strong enough to talk. He was somewhat worried about Delicate Blossom, who seemed uneasy and anxious, and he volunteered to stay at home and keep her company. But she insisted that he go to the school and deliver his lecture; he suspected that she wanted to be alone.

The students were not gathered in the main hall waiting his arrival, as was usual, but were grouped about the campus, talking excitedly. Very few of the teachers were on hand, and everything seemed strange. Ho asked an old man who taught Chinese belles-lettres what had happened.

"Haven't you heard the big news, Your Excellency? Two days ago an uprising broke out in Wuchang, in the very center of the Empire. It was instigated by the rebel leader, Sun Wen. Most of the Imperial Army stationed there is reported to have gone over to the revolutionaries, and the Imperial Court is helpless. It has recalled from exile Yuan Shih-kai, whom—as Your Excellency knows—the Regent ordered into retirement only a little while ago. But it is rumored that the revolutionaries are too strong even for him. The New Army has been infiltrated by Sun Wen's men."

"Where did you hear this?" Ho demanded. "I cannot read the newspapers. My daughter-in-law reads them for me, and I have heard only that Yuan Shih-kai has been recalled from retirement."

"Of course. There is Government censorship, Your Excellency. But one of the servants of the school has a brother who is an operator in the telegraph office. He—"

"Send him here at once," ordered Ho the Central Hall. "I will teach him to spread such rumors! Doesn't he know that the penalty for that is death? Send him to me immediately."

118

The servant stuck brazenly to his story, despite Ho's censure, but the old man felt much better after castigating him.

"This is nothing of consequence," Ho said, turning to the few teachers who were with him. "As you may know, this accursed Sun Wen has tried before to give trouble to the Empire and has staged insurrections nine times. Nine times he has been quashed. Wuchang is far away, and official news lacks the wings of rumor. Don't be alarmed. Let us proceed with our lecture."

Many of the older students were missing, but Ho the Central Hall attributed this to the report he so firmly believed false. He forgot the pains of his gout, and shifted from the scholarly thesis he had prepared to what he considered a much more important message. He emphasized the two cardinal virtues which formed the foundation of Chinese culture—Loyalty and Filial Piety. He quoted the time-honored adage. "If you want to find a loyal subject in the Empire, go to the door which houses a filial son inside." Why did people go astray—why did they become traitors? Because they had not been properly brought up, because they had not been carefully educated. They were not filial sons to their parents, and so they thought it no sin to commit treason against their lawful sovereigns.

The students listened quietly, but Ho the Central Hall felt that they had absorbed his message well. He returned home with a sense of satisfaction.

When he alighted from his sedan chair, the gatekeeper reported that His Excellency the Prefect was waiting inside the guest chamber. Since the Prefect of the Prefecture was changed every three years, this was a much younger man, one Ho Tao did not know well. Wondering what the official's business could be, the old man dragged himself painfully forward to meet his guest.

The Prefect's face was white and grave. Before Ho the Central Hall could seat himself comfortably, he said: "Your Excellency, I have come under the instructions of the new Military Governor of the province—your noble son."

"What is this?" exclaimed the old man, startled. "Which son of mine? My two older sons are in Government service, but neither has written about being transferred to this province. And Military Governor—what is that? We have no such title!"

The Prefect hesitated for a moment respectfully. "Why, Your Excellency, it is your youngest son, Fucho. He is now Military Governor of this province of the Republic of China!"

"My son Fucho!" the old man repeated with utter dismay. "Republic of China! What are you talking about?"

"Perhaps Your Excellency has not been informed. Last night there was an uprising in the provincial capital, led by your noble son. It was successful. The former Viceroy was taken prisoner, and the commander of the garrison troops killed. The old Imperial flag with the yellow dragon was replaced by a flag with five horizontal bars— red, yellow, blue, white and black. The nation is declared to be a republic, with no more Emperors or Empresses—a President is to be elected by the people, to rule instead. Meanwhile, the leader of the revolutionaries, the most honorable Sun Wen, has been proclaimed Provisional President, and your noble son has been installed as Military Governor of the province. His columns are now marching in every direction in this province, taking over prefectures and cities. Only a few hours ago a contingent of his men reached my yamen. Most of the New Army stationed here joined them at once, and the few who resisted were quickly disarmed. I was given a choice. Either I be held prisoner, or I swear allegiance to the new flag and remain in my post as subordinate to your noble son."

"And you have chosen the latter?" the old man demanded angrily. "You degenerate!"

"But Your Excellency—I am doing no more than your noble son has commanded. His first orders were that I hasten to inform you he is safe, so that you may not feel unduly worried."

"But this cannot be!" Ho the Central Hall sounded dazed. "No, this cannot be. My Emperor! My Dynasty! My son! It must be someone else who bears the same name. Fucho would not do this."

"No," the Prefect said softly, "it is your own son, the noble and honorable Fucho. Otherwise, why should he send me to Your Excellency?"

"But Fucho has been such a filial son! In all our history no filial son was ever a disloyal subject. I am sure you are mistaken."

"The revolutionaries have a different idea of loyalty," explained the Prefect. "They say that loyalty should not mean loyalty to an Emperor or to a Dynasty, but to the nation."

The old man suddenly roused himself. "Begone!" he said loudly. "It is not fitting for a Central Hall of the Empire to speak to a traitor, a coward, and a knave. Take yourself from my sight!"

For a long time after the Prefect had left, Ho the Central Hall sat there in the guest chamber. His gout was extremely painful from his recent exertions, but he paid no heed. He tried to think, but his mind was blank. Finally some of the attendants helped him to his suite, where Delicate Blossom was waiting anxiously for him, holding Li-hwa by the hand. For an instant Ho's wrinkled old face shone with delight. Then abruptly it darkened.

"I am not well," he said harshly, averting his glance. "I want to be alone. Go back to your own court."

Delicate Blossom left, hurt, and Ho lay down on his bed, a lonely, broken, old man. He had barely closed his eyes when Ta-kong rushed in with Lan Yuwen, shouting boisterously. Even the ordinarily soft-spoken Yuwen seemed to have been infected with the excitement.

"Grandpa, awake!" Ta-kong cried, seizing his grandfather's hand. "Have you heard the great news? The Manchus are overthrown! We Chinese are rulers of our own country again. And Uncle Fucho is Military Governor of this province! Proclamations in his name are posted everywhere in the city, and people are talking about no one else. Listen—you can hear the firecrackers."

Ho the Central Hall tried to shut his ears against this treason, but the firecrackers sounded as if they were being set off even on the Lane of Eternal Stability.

Ta-kong's voice went on, making his grandfather's head and heart ache. "What a hero Uncle Fucho is! People say he took the provincial capital with only a few hundred men—some of them our older schoolmates. I wish he could have taken me along. Isn't this a glory for the House of Ho? Aren't you glad, Grandpa? And proud? Shouldn't we get a new flag to hang outside our gate, and lots of firecrackers? Why, if anybody—"

Ho the Central Hall jerked himself to a sitting position, both hands clapped to his ears. Out of the depths of his misery, he shouted furiously:

"Shut up, you worthless brat!"

2

Ho LAY MOTIONLESS and apathetic. A maid entered and announced that supper was ready, but he pretended not to hear. There were whispers outside on the veranda, and he could make out Delicate Blossom's soft voice, filled with anxiety. But he felt no pity for her. Presently she came in herself, carrying his most favored dishes on a tray, and called to him gently. He closed his eyes and did not answer, and she placed the tray on a stand near his bed and departed noiselessly. He left the food untouched. By the rustling movements outside, he knew she was still standing there on the veranda, watching and waiting.

He had no conception of time, but lay half-wakeful, half-unconscious. After a while he heard footsteps in the room. It was Ta-kong, for once walking on tiptoe, for once not blowing out the candles with mighty puffs but snuffing them silently. The boy went to bed without a sound, and was soon asleep. After a long time the old man heard Delicate Blossom go back to her own court, and he opened his eyes wide and gazed into the darkness.

Ho did not sleep. He was conscious only of an overpowering and agonizing emptiness. The pains of the gout no longer hurt him, but the anguish in his soul was terrifying. When the gray hours of the dawn were gone and the light of another bright day filtered into the room, he was not even aware that the brightness hurt his eyes. There were whispers again on the veranda, then Ta-kong's footsteps running into the courtyard from outside. When had the boy left his bed and gone out?

"New proclamations! New proclamations!" the grandson cried. There was a quick "Hush!" from Delicate Blossom, and Ta-kong lowered his voice. But Ho the Central Hall could still hear his excited words, and each one was like a death knell for the things he revered and loved.

"No more kowtows are to be used when people greet each other. What a wise ruling—I have always hated kowtows. Second, ah! there is an order for you to obey, aunt. Girls should no longer bind their feet, and all those who have already done so should have them loosened. Third, all queues are to be cut off—men are all around in the streets, ready with scissors to cut off any queue on sight. You should hear the people scream when their pigtails are snipped off. Pigtails! That's what the revolutionaries call the queues now. Do you know what I did, aunt? I went to one of those men with scissors, and thrust my head straight forward! See how much better my head looks, cleaner and freer?"

The old man had heard enough. Getting up, he dragged himself to a desk, picked up a comb, and began to comb his shaggy white queue with solemn care.

Delicate Blossom entered, followed by Li-hwa, bringing tea and his favorite tobacco and some sweetmeats. She curtsied, and inquired timidly after his health. He saw and pretended not to have

122

seen; he heard and pretended not to have heard. She stood hanging her head sorrowfully and awkwardly.

"Do you know—have you known of this thing all the time?" Ho said suddenly.

Delicate Blossom nodded. Li-hwa toddled forward and pulled at his hand, but the old man brushed the child aside. He spoke evenly. Even his anger had left him.

"Begone, woman. And take the child with you. You are his wife. You are not my daughter."

Li-hwa was crying, hurt by her grandfather's rude rebuff. Delicate Blossom opened her lips as if to speak.

The old man looked away. "Can't you see that your presence is pain to me?" he asked harshly. "Away with you—you and yours. Let me not see you again!"

Slowly, Delicate Blossom gathered Li-hwa in her arms and turned about. She hesitated, then broke into sobbing and ran out of the room.

For four days, Ho the Central Hall remained in his room. He spoke to no one, and ate only some rice gruel. His younger brother and sister-in-law visited him several times, but he glared at them silently. Delicate Blossom did not dare come again. Often he caught her watching silently from a corner of the courtyard, her eyes red and swollen. Every time she appeared, he picked up a book of ancient classics and gazed at it pointedly, although she knew perfectly well his eyes were so poor he could not read. All his nephews and grandchildren took care to stay away from him. In the night, Ta-kong would steal in furtively and creep to his own bed.

On the fifth day, not long after Ta-kong had left for school, Ho the Central Hall heard sharp reports, like firecrackers, coming from a distance. They drew nearer and nearer, and stopped just outside the house. Delicate Blossom, her child in her arms, hurried to the outer courts.

Understanding flashed upon the old man. In spite of the pains in his legs, he dragged himself forward and bolted the door of his suite. Then he fell exhausted into a chair.

Soon he heard the familiar footsteps—the footsteps that once had been so well-loved. They approached the door and hesitated, and he heard a brief fumbling at the latch.

Then the voice.

"Father! Father! I have returned, your son Fucho. Here we are on our knees—I and Delicate Blossom. We are kowtowing to you."

There was a succession of thumps on the hard brick tiles. The old man remained unmoved, silent.

"Father! Father!" Fucho cried in desperation. "I may have done great wrong in your eyes, unforgivable wrong. But I have meant well. I now beg your forgiveness. Will you not forgive your own son?"

"My son—*my* son?" Ho retorted. "I have only two sons. I know not another. *You* are not my son!"

Fucho's voice choked, but he went on, "We are doing obeisances to Heaven and Earth, and to the spirits of our ancestors. We are praying that they forgive me. Would you not forgive me for their sake, O my beloved father?"

"Heaven will not forgive you! Nor Earth! Nor my ancestors who begot me! You are nothing but a regicide!"

Delicate Blossom wept audibly. Fucho, too, sounded as if he were crying.

"Do not forgive me if you cannot, Father. But I implore you— take pity on Delicate Blossom. She has always been a filial daughter to you. She has never failed you."

"She is your wife. She is not my daughter. She is a stranger to me, just like you. Take yourselves away from me—you and yours! Take yourselves away to your Military Governor's yamen. You have no business here in the house of a Central Hall of the Great Ching Dynasty. So long as I live, let me not see you and yours again!"

The lamentations of Fucho and Delicate Blossom were becoming unbearable. Ho the Central Hall's younger brother, who had been watching silently at a corner of the court with his wife and other members of the household, now advanced to the door.

"Old brother," he said loudly, "it does not befit me to tell you that you are wrong. Yet you have gone too far. What wrong has Fucho done? He has overthrown the Manchus for us Chinese—in my opinion, he has added greatly to the glory of the House of Ho. If he has offended your sensibilities, he also has kowtowed to you and begged for your forgiveness. He is your own flesh and blood."

The old man was beside himself with fury. "So you have all been turned against me by his example? Even you, younger brother! Where is your sense of Loyalty? Where are the books you have learned? I don't want to live any longer in this cursed Republic! If this man who calls himself my son does not leave my house instantly with his wife and child, I will hang myself from a beam in this room! He is already a regicide. I am sure he will not mind if I hang myself. Let all this be on his conscience!"

He began looking for a sash to use as a noose, while the younger brother vainly tried to dissuade him. Now the whole household trooped to the courtyard and watched fearfully. At last Fucho spoke, tears running down his cheeks.

"Father, it shall be as you wish. Here . . . Delicate Blossom and I kowtow to you again. After this we shall leave. Farewell, Father!"

Three times he kowtowed toward the closed door, and Delicate Blossom did the same. Then they stood up and turned about. Delicate Blossom took Li-hwa from the arms of a maid. Looking neither to the right nor the left, Fucho walked out of the House of Ho, with Delicate Blossom following meekly behind.

3

THE NEXT MORNING, unannounced, the Reverend Dr. Holt came to see Ho. The old man had no time to bar the door, but he turned his head aside and did not bid his friend welcome. Taking no offense, the missionary sat patiently until innate politeness made Ho speak.

"I suppose you have come to exercise your powers of persuasion?"

"Why should I?" answered Holt. "You have your moral values, I have mine. Remember our old discussions on religion? I have never tried to force my beliefs on you, nor have I lacked respect for yours."

This surprised Ho the Central Hall. After a pause, he said, "I still presume you come at his bidding. Do you not?"

"Partly, yes. They stayed with me last night, and they are still in my compound. But in coming here, I also have a purpose of my own."

"Don't mention them again, please," Ho said. "Let us confine our conversation to the purpose you mention."

"I have been in China more than twelve years," Holt said slowly. "I love China well, as you know. There were times when I thought I understood your people, but now I find I do not. Frankly, I'm bewildered."

"About what?"

"About your action, for one thing. You feel that the virtue of Loyalty has been violated. That I can understand. What I do not understand is why a man like you, for whom I have the highest esteem, cannot differentiate between loyalties. There is loyalty to an individual, to a family, or to a dynasty. But there is another loyalty—and to me a greater one—to one's people, one's nation or race, or to humanity at large. Why can you not reconcile the two, when they come into conflict?"

"But we do make a distinction between loyalties," Ho declared. "We know what is greater and what is lesser. Unlike you, we do not see them as conflicting with one another. To us, Loyalty is a continuous, indivisible chain which starts with your self, with loyalty to your own person, to your ideals and beliefs. Then it extends to the family—loyalty to parents and ancestors, to your children and the generations to come. It goes further—to the nation, to the government, and the people. It ends finally with the universe —loyalty to the human race. In the Book of Great Learning, Confucius outlined the Four Loyalties in this order—rectify yourself, harmonize the family, serve the nation, and pacify the universe. No, Ho-Lo-Teh, Loyalty is a chain, and unbreakable—when you set one link of loyalty against the others, you lose the strength of the entire chain."

"Circumstances are often beyond man's control," Holt argued. "It may not be that you wish to break the chain; it may be that circumstance, or environment, compels you to choose one loyalty above the others."

"You should never let such a thing happen," Ho said. "And it is within your power to prevent its happening, since you deal with your own loyalties and not those of others. The whole Confucian doctrine is based on the idea that man must shape his environment, and not let environment mold him. He must do this not by violence but by convincing others—converting them, perhaps—to his own ways. He must do this through setting a personal example, practicing the ideals in which he believes, and living up to the standards of Loyalty, Filial Piety, Fidelity, and Integrity. If you have done all this and circumstances do not shape up as you intend, do not blame the circumstances. Blame yourself. Something is lacking within you that makes the circumstances unyielding. Therefore you must start again at the beginning, and rectify yourself."

The redheaded missionary sighed and smiled. He had never admired the old man more than he admired him now, as he stubbornly reiterated his Confucian philosophies.

"But life is short," Holt said. "If circumstances cannot be changed

126

easily by this long and arduous procedure, can't one try swifter and shorter methods?"

"No, not at all!" Ho the Central Hall answered firmly. "It is like the story your Jesus teaches. You cannot build a house on sand. You must build it on rock. To attempt to change an unrighteous environment by means you yourself cannot acknowledge as wholly righteous is to lead the people to even greater unrighteousness. Moral values will be confused and rationalized—there will be, no more, commonly recognized ethical standards, no cohesive, stabilizing force in society. The result will be utter chaos. No, there cannot be a shorter way. The Great Sage said, 'If you want to reach a goal in too much hurry, you may never arrive there at all.' He said again, figuratively, 'When a gentleman walks, he never takes a short cut.' "

"Then I am afraid many a Confucian gentleman must have died without ever achieving his aims."

"That may well be," Ho agreed placidly. "Like your crucified Jesus. But it is far better and nobler to have died in such an attempt than to lead the people into a dangerous and blind alley."

"The revolutionaries are not aiming at a blind alley," Holt pointed out. "They are setting up a republic. Isn't it better for the people to choose their own rulers than to have Emperors thrust upon them without their consent?"

"That I would not deny," Ho admitted. "In fact, it is one of the Confucian ideals. We are told that, some three thousand years ago, we too had Emperors chosen by the people—Emperors Yao and Shun—and their period is called the Golden Age of China. But perhaps this was all made up by the Great Master—as you know, he edited the Book of History as a way of guiding our thoughts. Yes— I am for such a system."

"Then why be so harsh on the revolutionaries and Fucho for overthrowing the Manchu Dynasty?" Holt saw the old man stiffen at his son's name, and he raised his hand. "Wait—let me finish. I know you are opposed to the use of violence, but without violence how could the revolutionaries succeed? The Manchus certainly wouldn't give up without a fight."

"Now I know that you came at his bidding," Ho the Central Hall said sternly. "Very well. I will tell you why I detest him and can never forgive him. Go back and repeat it to him word for word."

Holt waited while the old man drew a deep breath and tried to calm himself.

127

"The use of violence is one reason," Ho began. "But the deception and treachery he has practiced is far worse—not because I am a victim, but because he is doing infinite harm to our society by his example.

"We have a saying, 'Of the thousands of sins, adultery is foremost; of the hundreds of virtues, Filial Piety comes first.' The reason is this. Fornication is the most seductive and persistent of man's Seven Passions and his Six Desires. If one yields to the impulse without restraint, one will gradually give in to other wickednesses. Curb that passion, and you can learn to curb the others. On the other hand, Filial Piety is the principal link in the chain of loyalties. Once that loyalty is established, the others come more readily.

"Think what an evil that man who calls himself my son has committed!" Ho went on hoarsely. "He has for years practiced deception and treachery upon his own father. 'The heart of man is ever dangerous; the core of Truth is ever small.' He has suppressed the truth in his heart to its very core. If he can do this to me, what may he not do to others, now that he is hailed as a hero? He is doing infinite harm to society by his example.

"He is disloyal to me. Can he count on others to be loyal to him? He is without the small voice of Truth. Will the people keep theirs for long? I see nothing for China but endless deceptions and treacheries, endless evil-doing, and endless violence. It will be as your Holy Book says, 'They have sown the wind, and they shall reap the whirlwind.' It is not important that I do not forgive him. Others will do things to him far worse than not forgiving!"

The old man sank back on his bed with a feeble wave of his hand, exhausted by his long discourse, and Holt knew the interview was over. He shook his head sadly, and bowed his way out.

4

As BEST HE could, the missionary repeated the conversation to Fucho and Delicate Blossom. Fucho was plunged into despair, although Holt and Delicate Blossom tried to reassure him. If the affairs of the Republic made good progress—if he could prove to Ho the Central Hall that the revolutionaries could and would do much to benefit the country and the people—then his father's forgiveness would be forthcoming.

Meanwhile, his presence was urgently needed in the provincial

128

capital. Fucho went back that day to his post, with his wife and his child, and with a sorrow-burdened heart.

As if the long discussion of his beliefs had been a tonic, Ho the Central Hall began to feel in much better spirits. A sudden purpose had come to his mind. He ate his meals with relish, and when Ta-kong came in to go to bed, his grandfather smiled and spoke pleasantly to him. The boy answered cautiously, but that night he again extinguished the candles with mighty puffs, showing that he was returning to his normal self. Ho was pleased. It was Ta-kong's generation that he must think about now.

The next day was again a Wednesday. Ho the Central Hall showed impatience early that morning, and kept asking what time it was. He had decided upon a bold step—he would lecture once more at the school, and would denounce his own son before all the students.

As the plan grew in his mind, he determined to marshal his arguments more fully and forcefully than he had done with Holt. He would point out the enormity of the offense the revolutionaries had committed, not against the Empire, but against society. This lecture would warn the students of the danger and help them ward off the evil; it would cleanse their minds. Ho would not be acting out of spite, but for the protection of the younger generation.

In his eagerness to get to the school, he forgot to send word that he was coming. The teachers were surprised at his appearance, and the students were not assembled in the big hall. By the oblique glances, Ho saw that his break with his son had become generally known, but the teachers went out of their way to be courteous. The bell was rung to call the students together. Some arguments seemed to be going on during the process of assembling, but they subsided upon the entry of the teachers and Ho the Central Hall.

With his back to the audience, the old man began to drag his painful legs laboriously up the steps to the rostrum. What happened then was cruel and shocking. Behind him he heard a growing wave of impolite snickers. A voice called, "Pigtail! Pigtail!" and a wild, jeering chorus took up the word and flung it tauntingly.

"Pigtail! Pigtail!"

One stentorian voice bellowed through cupped hands: "We won't listen to a man with a pigtail! Let's get out!"

Ho the Central Hall, mustering all his courage and dignity, tried to turn to face his disrespectful audience, but he was still on the steps and his legs failed him. He heard the shuffling of hundreds of feet, and by the time he reached the platform and could look, he saw that only two little figures remained in the big hall—Ta-kong, and Widow Lan's son, Yuwen.

The old man's head whirled with dizziness. The younger generation had already been corrupted by Fucho's example! The proverbial respect of the Chinese for age—for an Honorable Elder—was no more. Ho the Central Hall, once a tower of strength and example, clutched the lectern for support, and a teacher hurried to his side.

"Take me home! Quickly!" Ho whispered.

He lay in his bed, exhausted and defeated. His younger brother and other members of the household came to see him, but he waved them all away impatiently.

After a while, Ta-kong and Yuwen entered the room. Ta-kong's nose was bleeding and he had a black and swollen eye, but his voice was loud with pride. "Why didn't you stay at school a while longer, Grandpa? You would have seen what I did to that big boy who started it all! Oh, he pummeled me some, but I kicked his shins so hard he fell down like a tree. If it hadn't been for Yuwen, I would have scratched his face into slices. They should never have behaved like that to you!"

The old man managed a slow, feeble smile. Encouraged, Ta-kong went on. "But of course you should have cut off your queue, Grandpa. The pigtails are out of fashion, you know. They are—they are against 'the current of the times.'"

Too weak to protest, Ho mumbled faintly, "Some time . . . some time . . ." He meant to say that some time he would speak to Ta-kong, but he could not finish. He fell into slumber that was almost a coma.

When Ho the Central Hall woke again, it was already dawn. As he turned his face away from the light, he sensed something strange and felt his head with his hand.

Then he raised himself from the bed with a scream of horror.

"My queue! *My queue!*"

Ta-kong was awakened by the pitiful cry. The old man stared across the room. In the extremity of his shock he once again saw quite clearly, as if the full powers of vision had returned. He saw a tangled braid of white hair, severed from its roots, thrown carelessly on the floor. He saw a large pair of scissors lying still open on a tea-stand. He saw the horrified, guilty look on the boy's face. Ta-kong had misunderstood him and cut off his queue the night before!

130

The old man gasped. His head jerked back as a sudden spasm ran through his body. His heart stopped.

5

Ho THE CENTRAL HALL was buried on a day of rain, at a scenic spot he had chosen long before in his journeys about the country-side. It was in the foothills of the high mountains southwest of the city of Yi, not far from the secluded wood where he had once chanced upon Widow Lan and saved her life—on the tip of an out-thrust hill, half-circled by lofty peaks that towered behind like a Chinese landscape screen. Here, Ho the Central Hall had buried Orchid. In deference to his often expressed wishes, only a simple stone was erected before the mound of earth. It bore this legend:

Here is the tomb of Ho Tao, a Minister of State of the Great Ching Dynasty, and also of Orchid, his beloved wife.

Only members of the House of Ho attended the simple ceremony. Fucho and Delicate Blossom came, with little Li-hwa, but they stood apart, watching the others make their obeisances, generation by generation, to their departed ancestor.

The downpour was ceaseless. When the mourners knelt to kowtow, servants held umbrellas over them. Li-hwa was sheltered by an umbrella in her nurse's hand, but as if doing penance, Fucho and Delicate Blossom stood bareheaded and were drenched.

Fucho's two brothers were there. They had voluntarily retired from Government service since the Revolution, and had returned home for the funeral.

When the ceremonies were finished, everybody quietly moved aside and waited to see what Fucho and Delicate Blossom would do. Ta-kong tried to join his uncle and aunt, but was restrained by his own father.

Their heads bowed, clothes soaked with rain, Fucho and Delicate Blossom advanced slowly and solemnly toward the grave, with the maid leading Li-hwa behind. They did not go to the front of the tomb, where mattresses had been placed for genuflections, but approached one side.

The ground here was virtually a pool of mud, but they did not seem to notice. They prostrated themselves and kowtowed three times. Then another three times. And still another.

Little Li-hwa, coached by her nurse, knelt behind them and touched everybody's heart by doing the same.

Delicate Blossom's body shook with her sobs. Fucho would not rise. He lifted his head a little, his face wet with both tears and rain.

"Oh, Father!" he murmured. "Forgive me! I dare not number myself among your sons, for you have forbidden it. Yet I will ever strive to be filial to you. I swear to you that I will maintain and cherish always the small Truth in my heart. I swear to you that I will do all I can to bring to pass such a rule in the country as you dreamed about. If I cannot fulfill this pledge, then let me perish in the attempt. Oh, Father, your unseen eyes must be able to see clearly through my entire being at this moment. Pray forgive me! And pray—oh, hallowed spirit of my beloved mother—intercede for me!"

Eleven

Fucho held that graveside vow close to his heart during the next twelve turbulent months of the infant Republic, and strove with all his power to uphold the ideals of Ho the Central Hall. But from the beginning, he faced tremendous odds.

The Manchus had not been overthrown by the revolutionaries, but by Yuan Shih-kai and his New Army. Except for certain units like the one commanded by Captain Tien Fong, the New Army had remained loyal, and with it Yuan could have stamped out all the uprisings. He chose to do otherwise. He made a secret proposal to the head of the revolutionaries, Dr. Sun Yat-sen: the New Army would support the revolution if Dr. Sun would yield Yuan himself the Presidency of the Republic.

Dr. Sun agreed.

Yuan then informed the Manchu rulers that the rebels were much too strong for the New Army. Unless they abdicated, he could not protect them. The Manchus abdicated.

Political affairs moved swiftly after that. Yuan and the revolutionaries had agreed to convene a National Congress in Peking to serve as the Legislature of the Republic, and to elect the President. Most of the revolutionary leaders, including Chang Fa-foo and Tong Hsi, succeeded in being named delegates to the Congress. Now the new political party came into the open under Dr. Sun's guidance, and became known as the Kuomintang—"the Party of the People of the Country." The Kuomintang went to Peking, attended the Congress, and elected Yuan Shih-kai the first President.

Then President Yuan sprang his trap. Under one pretext or another, he kept the National Congress in continuous session. No delegate could leave Peking without his consent, and so most of the revolutionary leaders were virtual prisoners in the capital.

Fortunately, Dr. Sun and a few other Kuomintang leaders like Fucho had not been delegates to the Congress and had stayed away from Peking. Now they saw the trap, and consulted one another through secret communications. The situation was grave. Their forces, with the exception of Fucho's, were mostly in the South, far from Peking. They were no match for Yuan; there was nothing they could do but hope and wait.

Fucho's position was the most dangerous of all. The province of which he was Military Governor was exposed and vulnerable; it also was so near Peking as to worry Yuan. It dominated the big port city at one of its corners—the very seaport upon which Peking depended. Yuan acted swiftly to take this port out of Fucho's province and establish it as a separate entity directly under the Central Government. Still, Fucho had enough troops to seize the seaport at any time and cut Peking's lifeline. This placed him in a precarious position. Nobody knew Yuan's mind. If he secretly viewed the Kuomintang as his enemies, then Fucho held a dagger at his heart and must be removed.

Fucho saw this, and worked tirelessly to consolidate his provincial strength. He drilled his troops mercilessly; he harangued them on democratic principles and the high ideals of Ho the Central Hall. But his troops were very young and inexperienced, except for the men of Tien Fong's command. Fucho had never trusted the former Boxer completely, but in this crisis he had to rely on him. So much so, in fact, that he made Tien Fong a general in command of a division of the provincial forces.

Delicate Blossom was worried about Tien Fong. She had seen him when she made public appearances with Fucho—she tried to set an example to the people by accompanying her husband and by loosening her bound feet—and, on several of these occasions had caught Tien looking at her with an unmistakable leer. She said

133

nothing to Fucho about this, but warned him that perhaps the general could not be trusted.

"You are quite right, my dear," Fucho agreed. "But he's not a bad soldier—he's illiterate, but he trains his troops well. So far he has not shown any disloyalty to me."

"But can you really depend on him? He deserted Yuan's New Army for you in the Revolution. I'm afraid he might desert you for Yuan in some future crisis."

Fucho smiled at her tenderly. "I've considered that. But Yuan is widely known as a man who never forgives an injury. Tien Fong can't go back to Yuan again—and Tien Fong knows it."

The Kuomintang leaders outside Peking, unsure of President Yuan's plans, chose Fucho as the instrument for a test. He was to urge Yuan to appoint as mayor of the port city a man who would give him, Fucho—as Military Governor of the adjacent province—the utmost co-operation. As candidates, Fucho named his two comrades, Chang Fa-foo and Tong Hsi—both then in Peking as delegates to the National Congress.

It was an impudent request, a presumptuous interference in the affairs of the Central Government, but it was a calculated risk. Yuan's reaction might reveal his true feelings toward the Kuomintang.

Yuan sent Fucho a handwritten special dispatch couched in gracious language, but still carrying a mild reproof. The President said he might have taken the matter amiss had he not been absolutely certain of Fucho's loyalty. As it was, the request—improper though it might seem—would be granted.

A few days later it was officially announced that Tong Hsi—the revolutionary who had married Amy in Japan—would be the new mayor of the big port city.

2

REASSURED BY YUAN'S attitude, Fucho redoubled his efforts to carry out the "Three People's Principles" advocated by Dr. Sun Yat-sen—a Chinese adaptation of Abraham Lincoln's deathless phrase at Gettysburg—government of the people, by the people, and for the people. He discussed his problems often with the Reverend Dr. Holt, whom he visited every time he was in Yi. He built schools, modernized roads, and established free clinics. He also tried, but

134

without much success, to reduce the excessive rents imposed on tenant farmers.

These reforms Fucho introduced on his own initiative, but meanwhile he enforced one of the country's new laws with the utmost vigor—the law that made opium traffic a crime punishable by death. Before many months Fucho's province was almost free of the pernicious trade; still, there undoubtedly was a trickle smuggled from the big port city, and Fucho suspected that his old neighbor, Ma Teh-lin, had a hand in the illicit traffic.

He owed Ma nothing now. The Central Government had declared that all loans negotiated for revolutionary purposes—after being approved by a commission—could be repaid from the national treasury. Fucho had felt great relief and pride when he summoned Ma, paid him in full, and warned him that neither he nor the Revolution now owed the old man anything.

Ma had been under surveillance, because Fucho well remembered that only the shining example of Ho the Central Hall had kept the miser of Yi from even more openly nefarious ways, and now Ho the Central Hall had been gathered to his ancestors. However, the surveillance turned up no concrete evidence against Ma Teh-lin.

In the port city, Mayor Tong Hsi co-operated with Fucho in the war against opium, and for a time the evil appeared wiped out. Then, quite inexplicably, the drug was in abundant supply on the black market. Fucho could even smell the fumes of opium pipes along the streets, and there was no law against smoking the narcotic at home. Calling in his police chiefs once more, he told them to ignore the small peddlers and find the higher-ups.

They made an arrest that shocked Fucho. They caught General Tien Fong red-handed.

Being a general, Tien Fong was under military jurisdiction. And as Military Governor, Fucho himself presided at the court-martial.

"I have given you position and honor," he told Tien Fong. "You have enjoyed larger allowances than generals receive in other provinces. So why did you do this?"

Tien Fong drew himself to his formidable height, and gave a sneering laugh that twisted his scarred face. "Position and honor? They mean nothing to me. I do what I like. I helped you overthrow the Manchus—not for you, but because they curbed my freedom. Your pitiful allowances are not enough for me—not even for one evening's gambling." He glared at Fucho. "I've had enough of your preaching. No need to preach to a man you're going to kill!"

"Who are your accomplices?" asked Fucho sternly.

"I would not have betrayed you if the Manchus had caught me before the Revolution. I'm a man of integrity among 'the rivers and lakes,'" he went on, using the Chinese phrase for the underworld. "Let me be torn apart by five wild horses—I will never whisper a name!"

"Is Ma Teh-lin one of them?"

Tien Fong grinned. "Don't be childish."

"The penalty for this crime is death," said Fucho, "but I remember your part in the Revolution. Name your accomplices, and I shall try to reduce your sentence."

Tien Fong laughed again in defiant mockery. "If I did that, I could never again wander among 'the rivers and lakes.' Go on and put me to death! The sooner death, the sooner my reincarnation. Eighteen years from now, I'll meet you again—"

Fucho sentenced Tien Fong to death.

The court-martial verdict had to be referred to the Ministry of War in Peking, and it came, eventually, to the desk of President Yuan Shih-kai. Yuan wrote to Fucho. He concurred with the Military Governor . . . he remembered that Tien Fong had once deserted his New Army . . . but Tien had also done much for the Revolution. . . . Therefore the President commuted the sentence to life imprisonment, and gave Fucho custody of Tien in the provincial penitentiary.

Not until the trial was over did Fucho learn of its residual effects. When Tien Fong was arrested, Ma Teh-lin had been frightened so severely that he suffered a stroke, and was half-paralyzed.

The province prospered. Throughout the country Fucho was known as "the Model Governor," and the province as "the Model Province." But now there were rumors that Yuan Shih-kai plotted a final showdown with the Kuomintang, and was seeking Japanese loans and Japanese munitions.

The crack troops of Yuan's New Army virtually surrounded Fucho's province. Fucho got in touch with Tong Hsi at the port city, and Tong promised to obtain arms and munitions from Johnny Hunt. But when these did not arrive in the following weeks, Fucho finally decided to make a hurried and secret trip to confer with Tong. Because Yuan's spies could be everywhere, he did not send word that he was coming but went to the Mayor's home late at night, when he could be sure there were no other visitors.

There was an awkward moment for Fucho when Tong Hsi received him with Amy, but his old sweetheart of Japanese student days greeted him simply as an old friend, and apparently Tong Hsi suspected nothing. Amy had reached a somewhat voluptuous maturity without losing any of the vivacity Fucho remembered; she was still very pretty, and obviously was able now to afford the most expensive cosmetics and perfume, as well as elegant clothes. The dress she was wearing fitted her tightly and showed every seductive line of her body.

Tong Hsi saw that his caller was hesitant to bring up the matter on which he had come. He smiled at Fucho, and said, "Amy has told me that you and she were very good friends in Japan. You know, then, that she's as good a revolutionary as you or I. You can say anything you like before her."

Fucho launched at once into a discussion of his military situation and his lack of munitions for any prolonged contest with Yuan.

"Ah, we know!" Amy said when he had finished. "Hsi and I have worried a great deal about it—haven't we, darling? But Johnny Hunt is a hard man to find—just now he's in Shanghai. Hsi can get in touch with Johnny's assistant tomorrow and perhaps settle everything. Then he can telephone you at your hotel."

Tong Hsi nodded.

"For that matter," Amy went on, "why don't you stay here tonight? We have so much to talk about."

Fucho expressed his thanks, but thought that would be most unwise. "If Yuan's spies saw us together, it would be the end."

He remained a little longer, however, and Amy discussed the military threat to his province with amazing astuteness for a woman. She asked questions about the disposition of his troops, so that Tong Hsi's municipal forces could be properly deployed to Fucho's assistance if Yuan attacked. Tong Hsi agreed; his forces were small, but they were Fucho's to command in any time of need. Warmed by such friendship, Fucho held back no secrets.

Next morning a special messenger came to his hotel with a sealed note. It was from Amy, and it urged him to go to a certain room in a hotel in a Concession—a hotel that was patronized exclusively by foreigners. The matter, she wrote, was urgent and gravely important.

Fucho frowned thoughtfully as he burned the note. He disliked the idea of discussing revolutionary plans in the foreigners' hotel.

137

But this was the port city, a town actually made up of several cities because of the foreign Concessions. Tong Hsi had no control over these richer and more populous areas, since under the so-called "Unequal Treaties," the foreign nations had their own troops and police and their own law courts. The Kuomintang had pledged to abolish the foreign Concessions and restore these areas to China. Then the schools and parks and other improvements which had been built by Chinese labor and paid for by Chinese taxpayers would be open to Chinese, as at present they were not—an atrocious practice of discrimination against the people on their own soil.

"Why must we meet at the foreigners' hotel?" Fucho asked himself again. But he realized that Tong Hsi probably knew best; perhaps it was safer there; perhaps Johnny Hunt's assistant was another American. Fucho put his worries aside.

There were only a few people in the hotel lobby, all foreigners who hardly noticed him. He found the room easily, and knocked. The door opened from behind, and then closed. A key turned, and he looked around to see Amy putting the key into a pocket of her pajamas.

She smiled. "Are you surprised?"

The pajamas were of soft, clinging black satin, the jacket open halfway to her waist, showing most of her plump white breasts.

"Where's Brother Hsi?" Fucho demanded, averting his eyes. "And Johnny Hunt's assistant?"

"Don't glower at me that way. There's no one here but you and me."

"Then I'm leaving!" Fucho said, turning to try the knob. Amy laughed mischievously, and patted the key in her pocket.

"You can't leave, Fucho. And there are important things to talk about—later. Right now, let's talk about ourselves. It's much more pleasant."

She moved close and tried to take his hands. Then she lifted her face to offer a kiss, and her sweetly seductive scent made his head whirl. He looked over her shoulder and saw the bedroom through an open door, with a huge bed, and Amy's clothing thrown carelessly over a chair.

"If you want to get out," she teased, "you'll have to take the key out of my breast pocket. Would you like to do that by force? There's an easier way. After a while—a long, wonderful while—I'll give you the key without any struggle at all."

138

"I'm going now," Fucho said firmly. But she laughed again, and caught his arm to pull him toward a sofa.

He realized the situation was not only delicate but dangerous, and now he cursed the looseness of his tongue the night before. Amy knew more than enough to ruin him or even to cause his death. He had to get out of this trap tactfully, diplomatically, if it were possible to do so.

He sat down on the sofa submissively, and she snuggled close beside him.

"Now, you're being a good boy," she giggled. "Take me in your arms, darling, and kiss me as you used to in Tokyo—when I wanted you to make love to me and you were afraid. There's nothing to be afraid of now. I'm a woman, no longer a—"

Fucho cut her short. "It would be very foolish, and very dangerous, Amy. Several foreigners saw me come in, and so did one Chinese servant."

"You know very well the foreigners can't tell one Chinese from another, and the Chinese boy is in my pay. Nobody is going to disturb us, darling."

Fucho tried to divert her attention. "Isn't this hotel reserved exclusively for foreigners—no Chinese allowed? How were you able to get this suite?"

"Ah," said Amy, beaming with pleasure, "that's my special privilege. Special privilege—what a satisfying phrase! What's the Revolution for but to get special privileges for us revolutionaries? Even foreigners give me special privileges now. I can get a suite here any time I like, and we can come as often as you wish, without any Chinese ever finding us out. I'm the Mayor's wife—remember?"

"Yes," said Fucho, disgusted. "You are Tong Hsi's wife. Remember that!"

"Hsi is a weakling, don't mind him. I lead him around by the nose. I loved you first, Fucho, and I always have loved you. Tell me that, too—kiss me—"

Fucho laughed bitterly. "And we used to talk about the need for preserving all the cardinal virtues, Loyalty and Filial Piety, Fidelity and Integrity. You said then that Fidelity was not for women alone, but for men and women alike. Now look at you! I know I hurt you, Amy, I've always been sorry about that. I'm honored you still have warm feelings toward me, just as I still have for you. But there's a difference now. We're both married, and you're wife of a friend and a comrade."

Amy took his face in her hands and looked at him. He breathed the scent on her wrists, and her nearness and her loveliness made his heart pound. But her laughter was a mockery of all he had just said; it angered him and put him on guard.

"Still the preacher!" she taunted him. "Still the child, even if you do look so much like a man. I love you for being both, but you need to grow up. Let me be your tutor, darling. We used to make plans to overthrow the Manchus. Well, the Manchus have been toppled. Let's have our own revolution. I'll overthrow Tong Hsi, and you'll overthrow Delicate Blossom."

Flinging her arms around his neck, she pressed her hot cheek against his face. "Love me, darling. Love me, and I'll go with you to the ends of the earth. Now, please—now!"

Fucho cast all caution to the winds and pushed Amy away rudely.

"Give me the key," he ordered, standing up.

For a moment she lay sprawled on the sofa, her jacket open, her breasts heaving, a burning look in her eyes. Then she drew a long breath and got to her feet, rearranging her clothing. Just as suddenly, she became quite composed.

"Did you think I was serious, Fucho?" she said without the slightest tremor in her voice. "This was a test, and nothing else. I wouldn't have let you touch me beyond a kiss. You see, without our knowing it, Yuan has bought over a good many of our former comrades; for all Hsi and I knew, you might have been one of them. So, for our own sake, I had to make sure you're still true to our revolutionary ideals, to the Cause. You have indeed proved yourself a trustworthy comrade."

"Give me the key," Fucho repeated, still wary.

She tossed it to him. "Go back to your hotel and wait for Hsi to telephone," she said, smiling. "You passed the test well, Fucho."

She extended her hand in a comradely fashion. Fucho clasped it, then shook his head in admiration. "Amy, you certainly had me fooled for a moment. You're not only a good revolutionary, but also a wonderful actress."

Unfortunately, Fucho too often was inclined to endow others with the qualities he wished to find. Moreover, his experience with women had been quite limited; he had known Amy, but not nearly well enough. She was far from being the embodiment of the spirit of the Revolution that he in his innocence imagined—dedicated to one sole purpose as she had been in his student days. There were things about her he could not even conceive:

140

For example, there was her recent illicit affair with one of the sons of President Yuan Shih-kai, which had enabled her and Tong Hsi to establish clandestine connections with Yuan without the knowledge of the Kuomintang.

Then Fucho's recommendation; it really had had little to do with getting Tong Hsi appointed mayor of the port city. Though Yuan had made the appointment in an outward concession to the Kuomintang, actually he wanted Amy and Tong Hsi to keep him informed of Fucho's moves and his military strength and weakness.

As for the sudden increase in the opium traffic that had led to the arrest and conviction of Tien Fong, this too had involved Tong Hsi and his pretty wife. It was they who were handling the smuggling in the big port city, and were getting rich from the trade.

Amy was a woman as ambitious as she was unscrupulous, as passionate as she was conceited about her own irresistible charms. If ever there was a man she could be said to have loved, it was Fucho. And she wanted him all the more ardently because she had lost him once before. There were extenuating circumstances in that particular instance, Amy had been telling herself, and she had not really blamed Fucho for going through with his marriage. But now! This was entirely different. Had Fucho been less virtuous and yielded to her advances in the foreigners' hotel, she would not have sent Yuan information on the disposition of Fucho's troops.

But Fucho had scorned her. . . .

3

THE TELEPHONE CALL from Tong Hsi reached Fucho later that afternoon, and he left for home greatly reassured. Arms and munitions would be forthcoming, and soon. The visit to the port city had proved quite successful.

There was now a railroad connecting Fucho's provincial capital with the port city, but the line took a circuitous route by way of Peking. Though it would have been a much faster way of travel, Fucho knew Yuan's spies watched the trains and he probably would be recognized. So he returned in the manner he had come, riding hard on fast horses along country roads. It was ordinarily a three-day journey, but Fucho was so eager to get home that he covered the distance in two and a half days and arrived at his yamen late at night.

Delicate Blossom was waiting for her husband. One look at her, one embrace in the privacy of their suite, and he forgot Amy. He might have admired her as a good revolutionary, but as a woman and a wife she could not stand comparison with Delicate Blossom.

Hand in hand they went to an adjacent court to see little Li-hwa sleeping, and then started back to their own quarters. Suddenly there was gunfire slamming against the walls of the yamen, and the shadowy, onrushing forms of men running everywhere.

Fucho seized Delicate Blossom and ran with her to their own room. Putting out the lights and grabbing a gun, he commanded her to hide under a bed. Outside, in the dimly lighted courtyard, he could see dark shadows trooping through the gates, their shapes grotesque and confusing. It all had the quality of a nightmare that would soon end. But the nightmare did not end, and then there was a huge shadow on the wall and he heard the raucous voice of Tien Fong.

"Don't shoot, Governor!" the big man shouted. Then he laughed —Tien Fong always laughed, and his mirth was somehow always obscene. "Don't shoot—you're surrounded! Think about your wife and child. Step forward, disciple! Take the child along, and let the Governor hear how she cries!"

Out of the darkness came a man carrying little Li-hwa in his arms. He took his hand from her mouth, and Fucho and Delicate Blossom heard her frightened wails.

"Don't cry, baby," Tien Fong laughed from the shadows. "Now, Governor, listen to me. Do what I say, and no harm will come to the child. Refuse, and I'll beat her brains out!"

Delicate Blossom clung to Fucho, sobbing, "My baby—oh, my precious baby!"

Fucho struggled up through numbness. The pistol in his hand was of no use now, with his child held hostage. "What do you want?" he shouted helplessly.

"Throw your gun into the courtyard and put your lights on. I want to talk to you as a friend."

"There may not have been many guards here, Tien Fong, but I have garrison troops not far away. They'll come and wipe you out."

Tien Fong exploded into another laugh. "You'll never hear of your garrison troops again, Governor. They've already been surprised and overwhelmed. Yuan's forces have taken over the troops you had on the borders too, and now I am the Military Governor of the Province, not you. Do what I say, or it's the child's brains!"

Fucho tossed the gun into the courtyard. Freeing himself from Delicate Blossom's embrace, he turned on the lights.

Tien Fong swaggered in, a pistol in his hand, his face the very personification of evil.

"Loyalty!" he roared. "You preached a lot about Loyalty, didn't you? Well, Loyalty is a flower on a dunghill. I'll take power and money instead."

Then he saw Delicate Blossom. She was pale, but held herself proudly erect. Tien Fong leered at her, but she faced him fearlessly and contemptuously.

"I suppose you're going to kill me," Fucho said quietly. "But at least spare my wife and child."

"I have orders to kill you—yes. Here—I can't read them, but you can. You can see what they say." And he thrust out some papers.

Fucho glanced at them and saw that Yuan had signed his death warrant.

"Very well—carry out your orders! But they say nothing about my wife and child."

Tien Fong looked at him intently, and he saw that Fucho was not afraid. The big man studied Delicate Blossom. Her face showed dreadful concern for her husband and her baby, but she did not cringe either.

Tien Fong had little regard for any of his fellow men, but here was courage and spirit—the one thing his raw and brutal nature respected.

"Babies. You're just babies. Governor, you sentenced me to death, you put me in jail, and all the time you didn't even know your jailers had been bought by Yuan. Now I've got you, and I've got Yuan's orders to kill you. Can you give me one reason why I shouldn't?"

Fucho said nothing.

The scarred giant paced the room, stopping finally to tap Fucho's chest with a huge index finger. "Do you remember," he boomed, "I told you once before that I'm a man of integrity among 'the rivers and lakes'? I take orders from no one. I owe loyalty to no one. But the rules of 'the rivers and lakes' must be obeyed. A good turn must always be returned. Now, can you think of a good turn you have done me?"

Still Fucho said nothing.

Tien Fong shook his large head. "What babies you are indeed! You will not even seize this chance to plead with me. I'll tell you then. You spared my life twice. Once in the Boxers' Rebellion, when I was about to kill your redheaded foreigner friend, Ho-Lo-Teh—though you are a crack shot and could have killed me, you shot me in the arm instead. And again when you caught me in that opium business. Yuan commuted my death sentence, true—but you could have executed me before that, or even afterward, Yuan or no Yuan. So—orders or no orders, if I kill you now what will 'the rivers and lakes' think of me? So I'll spare your life this time."

"What do you plan to do?" Fucho asked, tight-lipped.

"You and your wife and child will be taken to the port city. You can find safety there in the foreign Concessions. I'll report to Yuan Shih-kai—that son of a turtle—that you've escaped. Don't try to get away from your escort, or they'll shoot you down. And as long as I'm Military Governor here, don't ever come back to this province again. Do I make myself clear?"

For himself, Fucho would have preferred death at this disaster to his Cause, brought about by his own carelessness. But he could not choose for himself.

Tien Fong moved swiftly, and before dawn Fucho and his family were on their way to the port city. On the second night of their journey, they approached the hill where Orchid and Ho the Central Hall were buried. Their escort had the same respectful feeling for the old aristocracy, and they allowed Fucho and Delicate Blossom to go up to the tomb and make their last reverence. After they had kowtowed, Fucho said tearfully:

"Oh, Father and Mother, I now take leave of your graves. I do not know when I may return. I have not fulfilled my oath to you, Father. I have failed, but please forgive me. I shall try again. . . ."

BOOK II

One

AT THE TIME Ma Teh-lin suffered the stroke that paralyzed one side of his body, Jasmine had been his sixth concubine for nearly fifteen years. She was still just over thirty, and very pretty indeed for one who had come such a long and sorrowful way; looking back, she could remember only one brief moment of love and happiness.

Jasmine had come from a sandy, barren plateau known as Red Rock, where her father wore himself out trying to farm the impoverished soil. When she was eleven, her mother had died. The very clothes the poor woman wore on her deathbed were needed for the growing daughter, and so Jasmine's father had stripped the body and wrapped it in a rough cover of woven bamboo strips. He dug a grave behind their hut. There was no incense to burn and no wine to offer; he shed tears copiously and spilled, besides, a cup of water on the sandy earth.

Jasmine was the only surviving child of many born, and now she became the woman of the house and also worked in the fields. Cooking was the easiest of all her labors because the food was nothing but sweet potatoes and soya beans. When festival days came, her father sometimes bought a little vegetable oil, to be hoarded and used drop by drop.

She liked washing in the little creek flowing through the ravine that bordered the plateau. The water ran clear over a pebbled bottom, and small fishes swam there. Jasmine even gave names to the fishes and thought of them as her playmates. But there was one chore she hated. Each morning she had to descend three hundred stone steps to the creek and bring up a bucket of water for the day. Not until she was fifteen was she strong enough to carry a full bucket up the three hundred steps. And when she was fifteen, she showed other, and lovelier, evidence of maturity.

In dry years, her father labored prodigiously carrying barrels of water suspended at the ends of a bamboo yoke balanced across his sturdy shoulders, and Jasmine did all she could to help. She was well aware, by now, that her father was a tenant farmer. He did not own the land, and could not claim the whole crop that his labors produced. The land was owned by Ma Teh-lin, who not only owned all of Red Rock plateau but had other fields where water was plentiful and rice and wheat could be grown, and people could raise chickens and pigs and cattle.

As a child, Jasmine had never even seen chickens, pigs, or cattle. Her father could not raise them because on Red Rock there was simply no food for such animals. And there was a kind of mosquito that attacked the eyes of chickens; it bit them, blinded them, and killed them.

When Jasmine was growing up, she could never understand the man Ma. He had everything—rice, wheat, chickens, pigs, cattle—but he still demanded and took a share of her father's sweet potatoes and soya beans. When the crop was good, this share was about half. When the yield was poor, Ma insisted on seventy per cent—and then Jasmine and her father went hungry until the next harvest.

The only other hut on the plateau that was within shouting distance was the home of the Chis, who had come there a year after Jasmine's mother died. The Chis had leased the land after Ma's former tenants had been evicted, sadly in arrears on their rent. There was a woman past thirty and an overgrown lad of sixteen. Jasmine never knew the boy's real name. His mother always called him "Brother Ox," and he was, in fact, as strong as one. Mother Chi, on the other hand, was sickly; she coughed incessantly and sometimes vomited blood.

Of course, one had to think of the conventions. Jasmine's father was a widower; Mother Chi was a widow; Brother Ox was a boy, and Jasmine was a girl beginning to mature. Except for New Year's

146

Days when they exchanged courtesy calls, or on occasions when they borrowed utensils, they never even held conversation.

But one day Brother Ox saw Jasmine dragging a half-bucket of water up the three hundred steps, and he ran to her and tried to help. She waved him away.

When she had turned fifteen, strange things stirred within her body and mind. She saw Brother Ox watching her from a respectful distance and she found this pleasing. When she went down the three hundred steps to do her washing, Brother Ox followed her with a bundle of clothing. Blushing, he told her his mother was ill and he had to do the family washing. They washed the clothes a few paces apart, and kept stealing sidelong glances. Later, Jasmine did all the washing for the Chis—but Brother Ox came to carry her water up those formidable steps. So they were in love, but still innocent, and did not know about love.

One day Brother Ox came to the creek in the ravine with terrible news. He had found Jasmine's father bleeding terribly after having cut his leg with an ax; he had carried the man home, and now Jasmine was needed.

Although she summoned a herb doctor, her father's leg got worse. Soon their money was gone, and Mother Chi gave them what little she could. It became obvious, finally, that Jasmine's father had permanently lost the use of that leg, and he had to depend on a crutch that Brother Ox made for him. He could no longer do much work in the fields.

The next year was catastrophic. Brother Ox strove manfully to work both fields, but it was a dry season and the yield was poor. There was barely enough return to pay the rentals to Ma Teh-lin.

When the dreaded day of reckoning came, Ma's chief agent uttered an oath of surprise at sight of the miserable crop. Leaning on his crutch, Jasmine's father pointed dumbly at his disabled leg. But the chief agent shook his head.

"That may be a good excuse for you," he said, "but it is not a good excuse for us. We have our own jobs to consider. I might let you off, but sure as death Ma will not do the same with us. We will have to take the whole crop and leave nothing for you. If I were you, I'd look for other jobs at once. You may take it from me that Ma will not renew the lease with you again." And without another word the agents set about to move the crop.

Jasmine could contain herself no longer. Running out of the hut, she shouted, "Stop! Can't you see that we'll starve?"

All the agents laughed.

But the chief agent looked her up and down. "Well, I never thought a flower could grow out of a dunghill," he said, "but here you are. It's been only a year since I saw you, and you've grown into a woman." Then he turned to Jasmine's father and said with a sly smile, "May I have a word with you alone?"

The two went into the hut together to hold their private talk.

Jasmine had no idea what kind of bargain her father struck with the chief agent, but she was glad that the crop was left untouched. Now that the harvest was finished Brother Ox had more time to himself, and every morning he would be at the creek waiting to help her draw the water. Though she still would not speak to him, she smiled much more often, and they made a habit of lingering as long as possible as they climbed the steps. Then there was that morning when they became too bold, and arrived at the top together. Her father was leaning against a window of the hut, and she was sure he had seen them come up side by side. Hastily she whispered to Brother Ox to sneak down the steps to hide himself from view. She herself ran home all in a flutter, spilling a good deal of the bucketful of water, but her father did not scold her. He only looked at her tenderly and wistfully. He had behaved strangely of late.

That very evening when she was about to retire to her small room, her father asked her to remain for a moment. Though they had a lamp, they had not lighted it for many a day in order to save oil. The room was dark and she could not see her father's face, but his voice sounded tremulous.

"Jasmine, my little Jasmine, I have something to tell you. I have agreed to sell you as a concubine to our landlord Ma, to pay the rentals we owe him. It is the only way to save us both from starvation—me with my leg, and you with no future. But the bargain is not yet made. Ma has to have a look at you before he decides. He will come tomorrow. Put on the neatest dress you have, and do not do anything to displease him. Should the deal fail to go through, there will be nothing left for us but death. Be a good daughter, and help me."

Jasmine felt the choking in her throat, the paralysis at her heart.

"Do not think ill of me, my little Jasmine," her father went on. "Believe me, I do this more for your good than for my own. I know the lot of a concubine is bad, but it cannot be worse than ours. At times I had idle thoughts about pairing you with Brother Ox—he is a nice lad. But he has a consumptive mother who will be burden enough. And when you two grow up, what could you look forward to? It would be like me and your dead mother. I want Heaven to spare you the same fate. To be a concubine—I don't know—"

Jasmine realized she was not expected to answer, and so she said nothing. She heard him shift his legs and groan, and then she hastened to his side. But he pushed her gently away.

"From now on you must forget all about me," he said. "When my leg gets a little better, I shall make my way to the big port city. There perhaps I may find an odd job for a crippled man. Forget all about me, think of me as already dead. I thank Heaven you were born with good looks, so someone wants to buy you as a concubine. Go to bed and sleep. When you get up tomorrow, make yourself as pretty as you can."

It was the longest speech her father had ever made to her.

There was nothing Jasmine could say in reply. She went quietly to her own room, but she did not close her eyes that night. There was only one thing she was sure she must do. She must go down to the creek in the morning much earlier than her usual hour, to bring up her bucketful of water without Brother Ox seeing her. And this she did before dawn, before anybody in the two huts stirred.

All morning she went about her chores as usual, but she kept herself hidden inside the hut. Her father did not speak to her, nor she to him. Once, from a window, she caught a glimpse of Brother Ox standing like a scarecrow halfway between the two huts. She shrank back from the window and did not go near it again. When the sun was high, her father told her to change into her least-mended clothes.

Before noon Ma arrived. He came with an entourage, all riding on horses, but only he and his chief agent entered the hut.

After a humble salutation from Jasmine's father, which he did not deign to acknowledge, Ma said curtly, "My agent has told me what you have in mind. I already have five concubines, and I don't care about any more. Yet for your sake I might make a bargain if your wench is any good. Let me have a look."

When Jasmine's father called to her, she came out from her room, her head low.

Ma examined her closely. "Lift your eyes!" he ordered.

Jasmine obeyed automatically, though she felt her eyes had gone blind.

"Come nearer," she heard Ma say.

She inched forward a little, feeling as if she were about to faint.

"Ah, that's bad. Her feet are not bound."

Her father spoke up in haste. "But what can you expect from a poor farmer's daughter, honorable sir? Her mother died when she was not yet eleven. And we have so much work to do. But she is still young, not sixteen, and her bones are soft. Her feet can be bound any time you wish, honorable sir."

"But her skin is so coarse!"

"That's because she has worked so often in the sun, and we never have much oil in our food. Keep her in the shade and feed her with oil—in no time her skin will be as sleek as a newborn fawn's."

"Well, well," said Ma, not convinced. "That may be, yet that may not be. I'm afraid I am getting too soft-hearted. If I agree to this at all it will be out of sheer pity for you, but your price is too high. There are defects. You owe me a good deal, and the crop you have is less than half of what you ought to pay. I'll tell you what. I'll take both the crop and the girl, and we'll be quits."

Jasmine's father protested feebly, "But then I will have nothing to eat. And with my leg as it is, I cannot get a job anywhere. I will surely starve to death."

"The starving of one is not like the starving of two. These are my terms—take it or leave it."

Then Jasmine lost her temper. "Take your crop and begone!" she said between her teeth. "I'd rather starve to death with my father than be a concubine to you!"

Ma eyed her slowly, licking his lips. "They told me you were a spirited minx. I'd like the pleasure of taming you. Well, for that, I'm willing to take only half of the crop and you. This is my final word. If you don't like it, you may have your wish and starve together with your father."

Jasmine was about to defy him further, but her father spoke. "Let it be. Take her and take half of the crop."

"Of course, you know the rules of concubinage," Ma said. "Once the contract is signed and she is taken away from here, you must never try to see her again. You must never come to my house, and never communicate with her in any way. For all purposes, you two must each act as if the other were dead. Understand?"

Though her father's eyes were filled with tears, he answered stoutly, "Yes, sir, I understand."

"Then tomorrow I'll send my agent over with the legal papers. If you can't sign your name, you can affix your thumbprints. Once

150

that's done, he'll take away the wench and half of the crop. You may have the rest."

Ma departed, and Jasmine ran back into her own room. She threw herself on her cot, muffled her mouth with bedclothes, and wept.

After supper, when it was mercifully dark, her father said, "I must turn in now. It's best this way. Forget me, my little Jasmine. Forget me as if I had never existed. And live—live only for yourself!"

Jasmine could stand no more. She darted out of the hut and ran into the open field. When she was sure that her father had not followed her and she was safely out of his hearing, she fell on the earth and sobbed.

Then a voice as tormented as her own came to her: "Cry no more, Jasmine!" It was Brother Ox, crouching nearby.

"How did you get here?" she asked, raising herself.

"I missed you this morning down at the creek, and watched for you the whole day. I followed you when you ran out just now. I would not have disturbed you, only—"

"You know what has happened to my father and to me?"

Brother Ox hung his head. "I heard from one of Ma's men, when Ma was inside your house. Oh, how I despise myself! I wish I were as rich as Ma—then you wouldn't have to go away. Is it tomorrow?"

"Yes," Jasmine whispered. "But please don't watch when they come to take me away. I wouldn't be able to bear it."

Brother Ox pounded the earth with his fist, groaning. "I wish Heaven had never given me birth. Why should it make men like Ma so rich and me so poor? If I had the money Ma has, I would not buy you for a pack of sweet potatoes and soya beans. I would make all my gold and silver into nuggets, each as big as the biggest sweet potato, and give them all to you free."

"If it were not for my father, I'd rather kill myself than leave—leave this place. After I go away, please look after my father for my sake. His leg is not well yet and he needs care. The half of our crop will not last long, and he may not be able to find work."

"I promise, Jasmine. I swear to you that as long as I live I'll treat him like my own father. I swear that I'd sooner starve myself than let him know hunger."

Gratitude filled Jasmine's heart and she crept close to him. "There is not much I can give in return," she whispered, "but what I have, I'm willing to give to you, Brother Ox."

Clumsily and yet with a fierce tenderness, the boy took her in his arms.

151

The next day Jasmine was carted away by Ma's agent, along with a load of sweet potatoes and soya beans.

From that time on, Jasmine did not live. She only existed.

She considered her body no longer her own, regarding it as a mere chattel Ma had bought to use as he pleased. To begin with, since it was his wish to have her feet bound, she suffered the binding to be done in spite of the excruciating torture it produced. And thereafter she submitted to all Ma's cruel and perverted demands with an apathy and indifference that sustained her and enabled her to get along with him better than any of his other concubines.

To the delight of her sister concubines, there was no wife in the house. As far as Jasmine was concerned, she did not care whether there was or not. Ma's wife had died before he became rich enough to live in the compound on the Lane of Eternal Stability, and he had not remarried. Go-betweens had offered many a suitable match, and the second concubine herself had long entertained secret aspirations to become his wife, since it was she who had borne his two oldest sons, Pingnan and Pingshi. But to all such propositions, whether outspoken or insinuated, Ma turned a deaf ear.

The conventions conferred too many rights on a wife for his liking. She would be undisputed mistress of the house, with full control over both domestic spending and servants inside the compound. She would have the authority to care for and discipline all the children, whether or not she had borne them. Why, she could even interfere with her husband's love-making, for though she might not prevent him from taking a concubine, she could chase away any who displeased her.

The concubines liked the present arrangement very well. Under it, they were all equals and need not put up with anybody but their one and only lord and master. Among themselves, however, there was no love lost. Jealousy had a free and open field; with all except Jasmine, it ran rampant. But this amused Ma and gave him a sensual gratification.

The daily routine for Jasmine was simple, the same as that of all the other concubines. Ma had divided among his women the duties usually entrusted to the wife. Each of them in rotation had to supervise a different domestic function, such as food, clothing, the managing of servants, and the general taking care of the house, for half a month. Apart from participation in these occupations, each concubine took breakfast by herself, in her own court and with her own

152

children if she had any. The master breakfasted with the one with whom he had slept the night before. At noontime, all the concubines and all the children congregated in the big dining room for lunch. The master would join them or not, depending on the pressure of his business. Only at dinner would he be found together with all his concubines and with them alone. This meal was served in his private court, while the children took their supper in the dining room. It was the time when Ma decided with which one of his women he would spend the night. The last concubine he spoke to before he rose from the table would be the one chosen.

The luncheon, however, was the instrument through which Ma sought to instill in his children the sense of Filial Piety. No matter whether he was present or not, the seat of honor at the table—the one facing the entrance—was always reserved for him. Reserved, too, was the chair opposite him across the table. This was occupied by the concubine who happened to be in charge of food for that half-month. She had to serve as a sort of Mistress of Ceremonies on this occasion, the other concubines and the children being allowed to sit at random. But even the infants who could not feed themselves were required to be there, and would be waited on by their amahs.

Before food could be touched, a moment of quiet was expected. Then the concubine who served as Mistress of Ceremonies would raise her voice and ask:

"Children, who gives you this food to eat so that you may not suffer hunger?"

"Our father!" the children were obliged to shout loudly.

"Who has provided you with clothes so that you may not suffer cold?"

"Our father!"

"To whom do you owe your gratitude throughout your life?"

"Our father!"

Only after this little ceremony had been duly performed was the assemblage permitted to eat. If Ma happened to be present, he would lean back in his seat and smile with satisfaction. Even when he was not there, however, he was certain that the ritual was being observed, thus inculcating a wholesome sense of Filial Piety in his children.

But the food was miserable. When Ma was absent, the children—especially Pingnan—complained loudly immediately after the ceremony, and most of the concubines chimed in. All but Jasmine. Remembering her childhood fare at Red Rock, she thought the food wonderful by comparison.

153

When Widow Lan set up her shop across the street, the other concubines and their children devised all sorts of ways to smuggle in her dumplings. Jasmine followed their example, but mainly out of compassion for the Lans. Her heart went out to the young widow and her son; she wanted to give them as much business as she could.

Although Ma added several concubines after he bought Jasmine, she remained his favorite. If she had anything to complain of it was the restrictions imposed upon her movements, and those of all his concubines. Ma's inordinately jealous nature made him ever fearful that his women might have clandestine affairs with other men. As was the custom, the house was divided strictly into inner courts and outer courts, and Ma never allowed any man, servant or otherwise, to set foot inside the inner courts. He even went beyond the customary practice and forbade his concubines to take a step outside their restricted precincts. And what was more, he had arranged things so that his private court formed the very first inner court, and any outside access to the other inner courts could be gained only through his. Thus, in this strategic position, he could see to it that no violation was possible.

But unfortunately for Ma, though he could keep men out of the inner courts, he could not prevent them from growing up within. Only three years after Jasmine joined the household and not long after Ma acquired the eighth concubine, Pingnan reached the dangerous adolescent age of sixteen and Pingshi of fifteen. Pingshi was a surly lad who kept his thoughts to himself, but Pingnan was a born rogue. A few years previously, Ma had hired a tutor to teach them the classics, after a fashion. And when the Reverend Dr. Holt opened his English class, Ma had enrolled the two boys, not out of any esteem for the foreigner but to keep the Hos from getting the better of him. So, as far as the education of the boys was concerned, he felt satisfied that he was giving them all that was necessary.

But then he had an awakening. Though the two boys did their studies in an outer court with their tutor, they still slept in their mother's court and ate their meals with the other children. One day at luncheon Ma caught Pingnan ogling Jasmine brazenly; Jasmine was so ashamed that she lowered her head. Ma suddenly realized that his two oldest sons were now too grown up for the inner courts, and despite their mother's protestations, he ordered them to sleep thereafter in their tutor's court.

But he was much pleased with Jasmine's conduct at the luncheon, and not overly angry at Pingnan. He was counting on this oldest son to manage his vast properties when he grew old; he had always been fond of the boy, considering him a very chip off the old block—even to this early indication of prurience. Pingnan could do what he pleased with all the other women in the world—but not with his father's.

For months Ma secretly watched the movements of the two boys, and one night while he was with Jasmine, he got up suddenly and scurried to the eighth concubine's suite. There he found a giggling Pingnan rolling on the carpet with the young woman. At his father's unexpected entry, Pingnan bolted away, throwing back a brash explanation, "We had a game of hide-and-seek, and she lost!"

Ma wanted to give them both a whipping, but he returned to Jasmine silent and pensive. He could not afford to make a scene; if the matter became known outside, he would be a laughingstock.

The next day he decided to send his two sons abroad to study, Pingnan to France and Pingshi to Germany. And in order the better to hide his secret, miserly though he was he gave them a large send-off party to which all the notables of Yi were invited.

Jasmine remained Ma's favorite during all these fifteen years, merely suffering him with indifference, doing what she was told to do, disinterestedly and submissively, uttering no complaints, pressing no demands, and begging no favors. And therein, perhaps, lay her attraction for Ma. When he went to the other concubines—there were now eleven in all—he was plagued with supplications, grumbling, and reproaches. When he came to Jasmine, it was all docility and peace. Finally, as he had grown old and bought more concubines, he was distressed to find his virility waning. He smoked opium and took to other drugs also, but they were of little avail. It was then that Ma found solace only in Jasmine. When he was capable, she yielded to his desires; when he was not, she made no claims.

After Ma suffered the paralytic stroke, he bowed to the inevitable and sent word to Pingnan and Pingshi to return home and help him manage his affairs (the next boy in line, born of the third concubine, was but fourteen years old). Ma knew he should long since have asked the two older boys to return, their living abroad having been much too expensive for his liking, but neither had indicated any eagerness to come home and for his own reasons he had deemed it safest to keep them both at a great distance. No sooner had he sent them the letter, however, than he noticed a change in their mother. Every night when she came to supper—he still required all the concubines to take that meal in his private court—the woman acted haughty toward everyone else, and sometimes even toward Ma himself.

Again he turned to Jasmine. His crippling illness had made him still more dependent on her, and she ministered to his wants. Even in nighttime when, in pain, he had to rouse her from sleep for the meanest and foulest service, she never complained. He knew she had no affection for him, but her constant readiness to be at his beck and call amounted to devotion. And he who had never been moved by anything in his life was touched in his own characteristic way: he told himself he had really got his money's worth out of her. Before long, he allowed no one but her to take care of him, and bade her sleep in his room and wait upon him day and night without shift. The other concubines were outwardly jealous, but actually they preferred to leave her to do the thankless tasks alone.

Ma remained bedridden for two months, although his fears had by then subsided somewhat. Tien Fong had not betrayed him, and Governor Ho Fucho was unable to bring formal charges against him. At length, he received replies from his two sons. Pingshi could not return right away; he had to wait for his graduation from a school next summer. But Pingnan was rushing back and could be expected home any day. Ma received the news with mixed feelings.

Presently Pingnan arrived, fully grown up now, a young man of twenty-six. He wore foreign dress, of the latest Paris fashion, and also sported a mustache. Otherwise, he was the very image of his father, having the same build, the same sallow, pasty complexion, and the same narrow, piggish eyes.

His return caused quite a stir in the house. For appearance' sake, Ma summoned all the concubines to meet Pingnan in the room in which he himself was confined. Then, hurriedly, he bade one and all, including Jasmine, depart to their respective courts and leave him alone with his son. While the women were with them, he had watched Pingnan closely. The son had behaved most properly, talking little to any of the concubines except his mother. And he had paid no apparent attention to any of them—not to Jasmine whom he had once ogled, nor to the eighth concubine with whom he had previously frolicked, nor to the eleventh who was the youngest. After the concubines were gone, Ma spoke to Pingnan.

"I'm glad you are back, son. I am disabled and may not live long, and I want you to help me manage my businesses. Except for Ping-shi, all your brothers are young, so sooner or later all my properties will pass into your control and Pingshi's. But look after your other brothers and sisters well. I've already divided my estate into equal portions, but when I pass away, you and Pingshi may each take a double share. Give each of your other brothers a share too when they grow up. I have done well. You'll find out for yourself that even after such a division, your inheritance will be very large.

"As for your sisters, I haven't been able to match them off, especially the two grown ones by your first aunt. The good families of Yi are still jealous of me and reluctant to be allied with any of my daughters. But times are changing. You're young and you'll make new friends, and if you find any good matches for your sisters, marry them off. I've set aside a suitable dowry for each girl. These are not included in the main estate, they won't affect your inheritance.

"You owe me much, Pingnan. I've fed and clothed you all these years, and gone to great expense to send you abroad. And now I'm going to give you this huge inheritance. So do as I say—take good care of your brothers and sisters."

Pingnan nodded affirmatively. The old man, tired with the lengthy discourse, rested a while.

"Now, about my concubines, your aunts," he went on at last. "You're a grown man, so I can be frank with you. You know my idiosyncrasy—once a woman is mine I don't want anyone else to touch her. When I'm gone, keep them in this same compound. They needn't have separate courts as they do now; you and your brothers may like to use them—the courts, I mean. Put your aunts all together in two or three courts. Follow my rules, and don't let any man come near them. They have enough clothes to last their lives. They need only to be fed, and the food we serve here is not costly— women don't eat much anyway. So the burden on the estate will be next to nothing. But . . ."

Here the father stared distrustfully at his son and swallowed perceptibly.

"But don't you ever molest them yourself. You may have as many women as you like, but just leave mine alone."

Pingnan looked at his father and smiled wryly.

"You still think I'm a boy of sixteen, don't you? You can trust me, Father. I want to ease your burdens and help you get well quickly. As for women, since you're frank with me, I'll be frank with you. I have now seen more of the world than you have. I spent ten years

157

in Paris, where women are pleasing and most procurable, and I've seen night life in many other big cities both in China and abroad. I've had all sorts of women. Why should I care for your concubines, countrywomen as they are? Most of them are much too old for me anyway. But just to make you feel better, Father, from this very day I shall not sleep in any other court. I'll put up another cot right in this room and take care of you day and night, and you can keep an eye on me all the time."

Moved though he was, old Ma said hastily, "You needn't do that, son. Your sixth aunt is taking care of me, and she's a very good nurse."

"Then I'll put myself up in my old tutor's court, and come into this one only in the daytime to help you conduct your businesses. Without your permission, I won't take a step into the other inner courts."

Old Ma was thoroughly gratified. And Pingnan was as good as his word. He took his meals alone in an outer court, and absented himself conspicuously from the suppers at which the concubines were assembled. Whenever he found it necessary to speak to his mother, he asked her to come to his father's room and talked to her there in Ma's presence. Even when he had to discuss business with Old Ma while Jasmine was present, he hardly looked at her.

And what a business head Pingnan had! In no time at all, he had learned all the intricacies of Ma's multitudinous affairs, aboveboard and otherwise. He had all the figures concerning the properties, the investments and the loans, and the various usurious interests Old Ma charged, at his fingertips. The agents and servants of the house feared him even more than they had feared Ma. Where the father in his age was slow to catch an error, the son in his youth would spot it right away. The old miser who had never admired any person before came to admire his own son. And since his pains were growing worse, he soon told Pingnan to handle the estate entirely by himself. He merely wanted to be given an accounting at intervals.

Two weeks after this, however, something happened that caused the old man to view matters differently. One evening while his concubines were taking supper in the room next to his bedchamber, he smelled an unusual aroma. It seemed to come from food much richer than the poor fare he invariably ordered served in the house.

"What are you eating there?" he cried out.

There was a moment of silence. Then the second concubine made her voice heard. "Why, just the usual fare."

158

"Then bring some samples of the food to me!"

A pause, and then the second concubine answered again.

"We can't do that. It's all eaten up."

"You lie!" shouted Ma from his bed. "Ask Pingnan to come to me at once!"

The second concubine loudly passed this order to a maid, and presently Pingnan ambled in.

"Who has given orders to serve more costly food in this house?" Ma demanded.

"I have," Pingnan said nonchalantly. "Who else can give such orders? Food prices are falling, and I find I can provide better fare at the same cost. Is there anything wrong in that?"

The father was astounded. He had never before been so openly defied in his own house. Unconscious of the impropriety of his language, he cried out furiously, "Curse you, you son of a turtle!"

Pingnan's answer was derisive. "Now, now, be careful of the names you call me. Remember that I'm your own son, not that of a turtle. No doubt you know that turtle means cuckold. You don't mean that you yourself are a cuckold—or do you?"

Old Ma could barely speak. "Curse you, you liar! You cheat! You spendthrift!" he mumbled foolishly. "Food prices are always rising, not falling. If they're really falling, then you should have saved the expense. Serve the same food as before—and get out of my sight!"

For a minute Pingnan stood and watched his father with amusement; then he shrugged his shoulders and left. As he stepped out into the next room where the disputed supper had been laid, the old man caught him throwing a wink in the direction of the concubines, and heard a few titters in response.

Ma could not sleep after that. The pains of his half-paralyzed body worsened, and Jasmine was kept awake the whole night. Early next morning he sent for the second concubine, but she replied through a maid that she had suddenly been taken ill and could not come. Ma wanted to remove his business from the hands of Pingnan and so he sent for his chief agents. When none responded to his summons, he at last realized his son must have ordered them to disregard his commands. He had lost control of his whole household! He was no longer its lord and master—only a prisoner confined to his bed!

When supper came he was given his usual plain fare, but from the other room came the same savory smells. The second concubine was also there, making no mention of her illness but talking loudly and arrogantly and monopolizing the conversation, flaunting her presence. He knew it was useless to call to her. That would be only an added humiliation.

Since his illness, he had always kept lights on in his suite so that he could be waited upon at any time in the dark hours. This night, however, he bade Jasmine extinguish all the lamps. Notwithstanding his torment both in body and mind, he pretended to fall into a deep slumber. Jasmine was soon asleep.

Before long, Ma heard a man enter from the outer courts and walk boldly in the direction of the inner ones. Bitterness seized his soul, and he helplessly gnashed his teeth. The night seemed endless. At dawn he heard the same footsteps returning. They stopped outside his room, and a man's shadow appeared at the window. The man put his face close to the pane and peeked in.

It was Pingnan.

Old Ma fainted. When he regained consciousness that afternoon, his pain was terrible and he tried to call for Jasmine. But for a moment he lost his voice and could only blink around the room. Jasmine was nowhere to be seen. Could that ever-dependable concubine have deserted him too?

Then he heard excited whispers in the next room. It was Pingnan and Jasmine. Could the two be billing and cooing under his very nose? Ma agonizingly raised himself from the bed by one arm, lowered himself onto the rug, and crawled sidewise inch by inch. At last he reached the door. With one final desperate effort he hoisted himself up against the wall and leaned the good half of his body on it so that he could look.

Pingnan had driven Jasmine to a corner of the room and stretched out his two arms against the converging walls, holding her prisoner. He was playing with her like a cat with a mouse. But Jasmine was all defiance.

"Can't you see that he's dying? If I don't scream for help, it's for fear of awakening him. Touch me and I *will* scream!"

Pingnan gave a low chuckle. "Go ahead and scream. I've had all the others except the old ones, but it's you I want most. I've wanted you since my teens, and now you can't get away. I'm the lord and master of this house!"

"Haven't you got any decency? What you're doing is incest!"

"Mon Dieu!" retorted Pingnan. "You were a peasant girl. You should know the common saying among the farmers: 'Fertile waters must not be allowed to fall into other fields than your own.'"

160

"Have you no feeling for him at all—your own father?"

"That old turtle! The sooner he dies, the better."

Old Ma gasped and choked audibly, and at the sound Pingnan relaxed his hold and turned around. Jasmine fled to the old man's side.

Pingnan stood laughing, arms akimbo. "Well, well, see who's here," he jeered. "If it's not the old turtle himself, crawling out from his hole!"

Ma shook convulsively and moaned, "O Heaven! I should have heeded Ho the Central Hall!"

Then he stiffened, slipped sidewise, and fell heavily. His head crashed against the doorsill with such force that it broke his neck.

That very night, while his father's coffin was being nailed up, Pingnan came into Jasmine's suite. He attempted to violate her by force, but she fought him so desperately that he failed. Then, angrily, he ordered that she be locked in her room and denied food and fire until she chose to submit.

She was kept there, starving, for three days. Instead of her faithful amah, Mistress Chow, two amazons stood guard in the anteroom; she could hear them eating and smell the food. Had it not been for the stubborn stamina of her peasant stock, she would have yielded to Pingnan's wishes; as it was, she simply resigned herself to her fate.

On the third day, when Jasmine was growing weaker, she heard noises from the outer chamber. Presently the locked door was opened, and an anxious, familiar voice became audible.

"Mistress! Mistress! Are you alive?"

Mistress Chow rushed in. Clasping her chain of beads, she said excitedly, "The Goddess of Mercy be thanked! You're alive. You're safe. Safe, too, from the young master!"

Jasmine was too weak to answer.

"Mistress, you *are* safe," the amah repeated. "The young master will not annoy you again. The Goddess of Mercy has taken care of that. I'll tell you about it after I get you a fire and something to eat."

At her bidding, the two women guards brought in the brazier and took themselves away. The room began to glow with warmth and Jasmine felt a new interest in life. Mistress Chow brought a bowl of rice gruel, and while feeding it to Jasmine bit by bit, she told her story.

Pingnan had discharged her on the night Jasmine was put under lock and key. She had hastened at once to Widow Lan, who, though a woman doctor in the Mission compound, still lived in her shack. Together the two had immediately gone to see the Reverend Dr. Holt.

"I tell you, mistress, the foreigner is a good man. He remembers what you did for him in that Boxers' affair, and he is gratitude itself. He telegraphed at once to Governor Ho, but the Governor was away on an inspection tour and could not be reached, though he was expected here in Yi in a day or two. Today he arrived, and the first thing he did was summon our young master. I was there, hiding myself in the very next room, and I heard everything.

"And what a blackguard that man is, even if I now have to call him my master again! He told the Governor you had hidden some of the old master's jewelry which rightly belonged to him by inheritance, and that when he questioned you about this, you refused to answer and locked yourself up in your room to hide your guilt.

"But the Governor saw through that lie, and what a lecture he gave him! He reminded him that concubinage has been abolished by the law of the Republic, and then he got very angry. He said, 'However flippant your tongue may be, Ma Pingnan, remember there is a law against murder. If that sixth concubine of your late father's dies, I shall order an investigation at once—and if she has starved to death, I shall call it murder. And you will have to pay life for life, Ma Pingnan!'

"Mistress, I got so excited that I forgot everything and stepped out of my hiding place—and the young master saw me! He was really frightened of the Governor then, and he turned meek and contrite, and even hired me again, then and there, as your personal amah."

For ten days or so, Jasmine was left in undisturbed peace. She did not see Pingnan again. He had abolished the customary mass luncheons and suppers, and Jasmine, like the other concubines, could take her meals separately in her own court. Pingnan seemed willing to leave her alone, and she was happy that it was so.

Then, as if the Goddess of Mercy was indeed showering belated blessing upon her, Jasmine had word of her father. Mistress Chow had talked to one of Ma's agents, who had gone to the big port city and had seen her father there. "He is doing quite well," Mistress

Chow went on excitedly. "He owns a shop, and he has remarried but has no children. He inquired about you."

"Does the agent know my father's address?" asked Jasmine anxiously.

"Yes, he told me that too. But their streets have such strange names I just can't remember it."

Jasmine thanked Mistress Chow for bringing the good news. "It makes me very happy to know my father is alive and well. But you know the conditions the old master imposed when he bought us concubines. My father and I are forbidden ever to communicate with each other again."

"The Governor told the young master that concubinage has been abolished by the Republic," the amah said. "And it's true—I made inquiries. Now that the old master is dead, you are free to leave this house. You may go to your father if you wish. If the young master tries to stop you, we'll appeal to the Governor again, through our good friend Ho-lo-Teh."

Pingnan had already installed himself in Old Ma's private court, and Jasmine went there to see him without delay. She was agitated and awkward, but he was all suaveness. Bravely she expressed her wish.

"If that's what you want," he said not disrespectfully, "that's what you want. The law's on your side. But the law says also that all your belongings are mine. I'm sorry, but you must leave all your jewelry and furniture behind."

"That I'll do willingly."

"And you must leave all your clothes behind. You can take only a very simple suit, which you must wear on your person."

"That I'll do too."

"You must leave behind all the money you received from my father as an allowance."

"Little is left of the small sums your father gave me. You must allow me at least a trifle to cover the expenses of the trip. I would like to take Mistress Chow with me also."

"That is impossible. It's against the law."

"Then how can I get to the big port city? Perhaps you would be so good as to lend me the money? I will return it as soon as I meet Father. You can depend on it that I will."

At first Pingnan seemed to be immersed in thought. Then he smiled benignly.

"I'll be generous. I've always had a soft spot for you, so I'll do this

163

for you and for you alone. The agent who chanced upon your father is going to the city again tomorrow on my business. I'll have him take you and pay all the expenses of the trip. Of course, you can't take Mistress Chow along. And you may think it inconvenient to travel alone with a strange man—but you did that once before, when you came here, didn't you? Knowing you, I have no doubt you can fend for yourself where a man is concerned. If this arrangement suits you, you may leave early tomorrow morning with my agent."

Jasmine assented readily. She was about to take her leave when Pingnan clapped his hand to his forehead.

"I almost forgot that meddlesome Governor!" Pingnan said. "I'll have to have something to show you're leaving this house of your own free will—to go to seek your father. Wait, I have an idea. I'll write out a statement to that effect, and then you put your thumbprint on it. No, you better not put your thumbprint on my draft. The Governor might think I had made it myself. Take my draft to my brother, son of my third aunt; he's fourteen now and knows the characters. Let him copy out the statement for you, and you can fix your thumbprint on his copy in the presence of his mother and as many other concubines and amahs as you can find. Bring me the copy, and you may leave tomorrow with my agent."

Jasmine nodded her agreement. The young master might not be such a bad man after all. . . .

Jasmine made the journey with Ma's agent without mishap. They arrived in the port city one afternoon, and her escort took her to a house in a quite busy section of the town. It was a Western-type, three-story brick structure, very pretentious in appearance. Ma's agent explained that this was not her father's shop, but the place where he lived. Her father must be doing exceedingly well, Jasmine decided, to be able to live in such a magnificent building.

They entered, and a stout woman of about forty, muscular, hard-featured, and expressionless, met them. The man introduced her to Jasmine as her stepmother. Jasmine kowtowed respectfully and then asked for her father. The woman replied that he was still in his shop, but since her stepdaughter must be feeling tired after such a long trip, she would take her to a room on the second floor that had been made ready.

As Jasmine followed the woman up the stairs, she was amazed at the size of the building. On the second floor was a peculiar long

164

gallery with a formidable-looking rail along its open side. This was made of sharp-pointed iron balusters, densely spaced, taller than an average man; city people must be frightened to death of thieves, Jasmine thought. On the other side were ranged at least a dozen rooms in a row, and when Jasmine reached the gallery, as if waiting for her arrival, a number of women, varied in age and appearance, suddenly stepped out of these rooms and gazed at her with curious interest. Her stepmother did not introduce them, and Jasmine wondered if her father could have taken so many concubines.

As soon as she was ushered into her room she noticed the cold; for although it was winter, there was no fire inside. The room itself was divided in two by broad sheets of cheap cloth, strung from the walls like a curtain. In the part Jasmine entered, a bed stood against the far wall, and alongside the makeshift curtain there was a couch with opium-smoking utensils arrayed on it, ready for use. A square mah-jongg table was in the center, and sundry chairs and tea-stands on the sides. Jasmine went to the curtain, parted it, and looked in. The inner section, much narrower, contained a washstand, some dirty towels, and a covered wooden can which catered to human necessities and now gave off the foul smell of recent usage.

Jasmine drew back, beginning to feel afraid. Her stepmother was sitting on a chair by the door.

"Who are those women? What are they to my father?" Jasmine asked her.

The woman replied without expression, "They're your sisters. But they are no daughters of your father."

"What do you mean?"

"I don't know anything about your father, dead or alive," the woman said impassively. "And I'm not your stepmother, though you must call me mother now. The only thing I know is that I paid a man named Ma Pingnan a lot of money for you. I have the deed, and you are my property. You must do what I tell you."

"What is this place?" Jasmine demanded.

"This is paradise. This is where the Buddha of Happiness holds sway. This is what elegant people call a palace of pleasure, but the vulgar simply a whorehouse. Not a first-class whorehouse, mind you, nor second-class. Third-class! You have to be much younger to get into the other two."

Jasmine staggered back in horror. "Isn't there a law against prostitution?"

"Of course there is. But who obeys the law?"

165

"You cannot do this to me," Jasmine protested, her heart beating fearfully. "Wait until Governor Ho Fucho hears of it!"

"I have heard of that name. But what can he do here? We're inside a foreign Concession. We have no law but the laws of the foreigners—and they don't care a pin about us Chinese—least of all, about our fornications."

In desperation Jasmine bolted toward the door, but the woman sprang up and barred the way. Though Jasmine was strong, the bawd was heavier and stronger. And then she called out and several tough-looking men at once appeared out of nowhere. Jasmine stood terrified. The woman waved the men away and sat down again, as impassive as before except for a slight shortness of breath.

"You see, this sort of thing is useless," she said. "I could whip you for it—and I do whip my girls. But you're a newcomer, and newcomers must be taught."

"I'll kill myself before I will stay here!"

"I know how to handle that, too," the woman said. "I've been in this business over ten years. Newcomers all fall into three classes—babies, loonies, and ghosts.

"The babies cry and cry—and plead and plead. They think I have a heart. But I haven't. Nobody in this business can afford to have a heart, so you may as well save your tears.

"Then we have the loonies. What you did just now is one of their symptoms. They scream, they bite, they kick, they fight. Usually I can handle them myself. And if I can't, I have half a dozen men here, ready any time.

"As for the ghosts, they just want to do away with themselves. You needn't search this room for anything to help you do that. There's nothing. All the windows have steel bars, and the gallery railing outside is too high to jump over. And if you try to starve yourself to death, I've even found a way to deal with that. I simply call on Wang Da. He's a terror in this district, especially to people in my business. He's a disciple of that dreaded Old Head. You're a countrywoman and don't know these things, but in our business, whenever you meet with one of those gangsters you must go out of your way to please him. And with your looks I expect a good many of them will come to you soon, and often."

"G-gangsters!" In spite of herself, Jasmine showed her fear.

"Take this Old Head, their chief," the woman continued calmly. "The foreign mandarins ran Old Head out of the city once, but when they found he could control his men from outside just as

166

easily, they decided they'd better put up with him. Since then, they've made him Chief Police Advisor of all the Concessions—why, he has as much voice in running the city as the foreigners themselves.

"Old Head has the whole city divided into sections, with one of his men in charge of each section. In ours, it's Wang Da. He's the worst of the lot—afraid of nobody but Old Head. From the first he not only collected protection money for Old Head, but demanded a special privilege for himself. He calls it the 'right of the first night'—says he learned it from the foreign mandarins, whose ancestors used to work that way. In all the whorehouses except the first-class ones, where virginity brings a premium price and the protection money is exorbitant, he requires each newcomer to submit to his pleasure gratis, on the first night after her arrival.

"And, in a way, I'm glad he does. I've had many hold-outs among my newcomers, but Wang Da never fails to help me bring them to their senses. Never have I seen a stronger man. It takes him only a minute to force any woman to do his will. Afterward, the newcomers usually realize resistance is useless.

"Of course some of the ghosts—the third type I mentioned—will still try to starve themselves to death. Wang Da gave me the idea for dealing with them. I just get other men to repeat the same process. The more the ghosts refuse to eat and drink, the weaker they become, the less they can resist and the more men I thrust on them. And in no time at all they find it a great deal better to bounce up, take food, and receive customers as a good girl should.

"Well, I've told you all that's necessary. I'll leave you and let you think things out for yourself. Your door will be locked from outside for the time being, but after you've received three customers you'll be given the freedom of the house. Your food will be served here regularly. It won't be very good at present, but the more customers you receive the better it will get. Of course, the fewer the customers, the worse your fare."

Still without any expression whatsoever on her face, the madam went out of the room and locked the door. From outside, she said, "Prepare yourself. One of my men is grand-disciple to Wang Da, and he has already gone to inform him of your arrival. Wang Da will surely come tonight."

Jasmine's head was in a whirl; she could think now of nothing but her hatred for Ma Pingnan. Supper was served, and she ate for only one reason—to keep up her strength. When Wang Da came,

167

she would fight as she had never fought before, not for life but for death.

The night came, and along with it Wang Da. The bawd brought him in herself. She said merely, "This is Lord Wang," and then left.

Wang was a swarthy man of middle height, but Jasmine paid not the least attention to his appearance. As soon as he advanced near enough, she mustered all her strength and struck with her fist. Nimbly the man seized her arm, his fingers like claws of steel, and sharply twisted it around. Getting hold of her other arm, he gripped both her hands behind her back.

"Hey, little chicken, you want to battle a wolf?" he snickered.

He thrust his free hand into her collar at the back of her neck and yanked with brutal force. With a snap, her upper garments were rent apart and her breast lacerated with pain.

Not knowing what she said, Jasmine cried, "O Heaven! O Brother Ox!"

All at once the man loosed his hold and swung her around. "What did you say, woman?"

Jasmine glared at him fiercely and did not answer.

With surprising gentleness the man asked her again. "Just repeat what you said. It may be important."

Thinking that nothing worse could happen to her in any event, she hung her head and murmured, "I said 'O Heaven! O Brother Ox!' "

"What may your name be, woman?" Wang asked.

"Jasmine."

"Where do you come from?"

"The city of Yi."

"Where were you born?"

"A place called Red Rock in the Prefecture of Yi."

"What may this Brother Ox be?"

"A man I used to know in Red Rock."

"What is his full name?"

"I don't know. I know only that his surname is Chi."

Wang Da shouted loudly for the madam. When the bawd entered, he ordered curtly, "Have this woman's clothes changed. Give her the best you have, and take care of her yourself. I'll be off for a moment, but I'll be back soon."

After Wang Da's abrupt departure, his commands were faithfully carried out. The bawd remained in Jasmine's quarters. The noises of men and women making merry could be heard from the other

168

rooms, and several times attendants and painted girls came in to ask the woman for instructions on sundry matters. But she would not leave her post. She eyed Jasmine frequently, and Jasmine sensed in her still expressionless face a slight show of interest.

They did not wait long. Suddenly strange honks were heard outside on the street, but Jasmine did not recognize that these were the horns of automobiles. Such vehicles were still rare in China, even in the big port cities, and the unexpected descent of three motor cars therefore caused quite a turmoil. All at once the bawd's servants rushed in and reported excitedly, "Old Head is come! Old Head himself!"

The madam stood up, her face taking on the pallor of fright. Jasmine stood up too, mechanically following her example. All sound of merrymaking in the other rooms was at once stilled, and in the sudden hush, more than a dozen men could be heard trooping upstairs, then straight toward Jasmine's room. She stared fearfully at the doorway. Of the two men in front, she recognized one as Wang Da. But it was the other who caught her attention.

"Jasmine!" the man cried, after a second of incredulity.

"It's you, Brother Ox!"

And she fainted.

Two

JASMINE'S WEDDING was attended by all the foreign mandarins, and all the Chinese of any importance, including Mayor Tong Hsi and Amy. Old Head, or Brother Ox, or Chi Teh-shan (meaning a Mountain of Virtues of the House of Chi) as he preferred to call himself, had been faithful to his boyhood love and had refused even to take a concubine, let alone a wife.

The day after their meeting, Jasmine went for what she supposed would be a sightseeing ride. Brother Ox never moved about the city without at least three of his automobiles, one for himself and his chosen companions, the others filled with his bodyguards. The motorcade pulled up at a cemetery, which Jasmine first thought was a garden, and Brother Ox led her to two huge, ornate mausoleums, built side by side, with burning incense sticks and fresh flower wreaths abundantly displayed before them.

Brother Ox explained that she was now standing before his mother's tomb, and Jasmine dutifully prostrated herself and kowtowed. When she rose, he led her to the other mausoleum, and started to read the words engraved on the stone. This surprised her, for the Brother Ox she had known had been an unlettered country lout; in becoming the famed and feared Chi Teh-shan, however, he had learned to read. As he pronounced the beautifully carved characters slowly one by one, she realized that here was the grave of her own father and mother. And she fell to her knees and wept for a long time.

While they drove back to the Concession, Brother Ox related all that had happened since their farewell so many years before. Shortly after Ma Teh-lin had taken Jasmine away from Red Rock, Brother Ox's mother had died. He and Jasmine's father then sold what was left of their crops and set out for the big port city, Brother Ox carrying the lamed older man on his back most of the journey. Brother Ox soon found that by hawking fruits on the streets he could make a living for them both, and for his part Jasmine's father set up a fruit-stand not far from their lodgings.

They were doing well, when one evening Brother Ox returned to find Jasmine's father dead. He had refused to pay protection money, and a gang had beaten him to death. Brother Ox felt he had betrayed Jasmine's trust. He buried her father hastily in a deserted countryside cemetery, and next day he returned and set up the fruit-stand himself at the same street corner. As he expected, the gang returned to demand protection money. Brother Ox, stronger than any of them, maimed several of his assailants in the fight that followed, but there were just too many of them. He was down, with a knife at his throat, when an old man ordered the gangsters to stop. All those able to do so got up respectfully.

"Enough of this!" the old man said sternly. "He has injured a few of you men, but you killed his partner and beat him nearly to death. This lad has shown prowess, stubbornness, and loyalty. He strikes my fancy. Let me have him." And without a murmur the leader agreed.

After the old man had nursed Brother Ox back to health, he disclosed that he was chief of the secret Chin Society and asked Brother Ox to become his disciple. Brother Ox could not tell Jasmine much about the Society; he was bound to silence by a solemn oath. But he did reveal that he had become the so-called "Close-Door-Disciple" of his teacher. When a teacher in the Society took disciples, he ex-

170

plained, the first—called "Open-Door-Disciple"—and the last—"Close-Door-Disciple"—were usually the most important. Both were initiated by special ceremonies.

As principal teacher of the Society, the chief ruled it like an absolute monarch and could name the one to succeed him when he died. The choice usually lay between the Open-Door-Disciple and the Close-Door-Disciple. It was by this means that the leadership of the Chin Society had fallen on Brother Ox.

The organization of the Society was nationwide. There had been a rival society called Hung, but after Brother Ox came into power, through force and diplomacy he succeeded in unifying the two societies in the port city, making himself their joint chief and ending a long and bloody feud. Thus he had earned the nickname "Old Head" and become the undisputed master of the entire underworld in the foreign Concessions.

He explained to Jasmine that his influence of necessity was confined mostly within the big port city. The Chinese knew how to deal with the Chinese, and the government authorities, if determined, could always curb the activities of the secret societies; but the foreigners in the Concessions had little knowledge of Chinese ways. Nor were they concerned about the well-being of the Chinese. Wanting only to make money for themselves, they permitted traffic in opium as well as gambling and prostitution. And these constituted the secret societies' principal sources of income.

After his succession to the mantle, Brother Ox had sent many an agent to Yi to make inquiries about Jasmine, though of course he could not rescue her from concubinage. He had to content himself with removing the remains of her parents and honoring Jasmine's ancestors and his own mother by building the huge mausoleums. Only a few of his closest disciples knew he had once been called Brother Ox, and these he had told of his devotion to Jasmine. Thus had Wang Da been able to identify her.

"Others may call you Old Head," Jasmine said when he concluded. "You may like to be called Chi Teh-shan. But I will always call you Brother Ox."

"That is right and proper, my heart," he replied. "Brother Ox I was to you, and Brother Ox I shall always be."

"You yourself are good," Jasmine began in a troubled voice, "but some of the things your disciples do—such as Wang Da—"

Brother Ox put his arms around her tenderly. "Jasmine, if it had not been for Wang Da's badness, we would not now be together.

Besides, in this world of ours there is no good or bad. There is only strong or weak. Remember once by the creek at Red Rock you asked what the fishes eat? I quoted the saying 'The big fish eat the little ones, the little ones eat water-insects, and the water-insects eat mud.' Well, the world is just like that. We were water-insects then; we had nothing to eat but mud. Old Ma was a little fish, and he ate us. Now I'm a big fish here, and you must share the feast with me."

Jasmine sighed. "Must we always eat one another? What of the old proprieties—the things my old neighbor in Yi, Ho the Central Hall, used to talk about?"

Brother Ox laughed outright at Jasmine's naïveté until he saw the hurt in her face. "Don't be offended with me, my heart," he said quickly. "But you've been out of contact with the real world. Men like Ho the Central Hall are long dead, and nobody cares about the old proprieties any more. The foreigners don't know a thing about our proprieties, yet they are much stronger than the Chinese. The greatest man of our Republic is President Yuan Shih-kai. But he acts like the biggest fish in our midst—the whole country has become his private pond."

"Some people think and act differently, Brother Ox. What about my benefactor, Governor Ho Fucho? He's a son of Ho the Central Hall."

"True, he's an exception," conceded Brother Ox. "But I'm afraid his simple-mindedness may have caught up with him at last. I hear that Yuan Shih-kai has ordered his downfall."

"Oh, you must help him! For my sake!"

"For your sake, my heart," promised Brother Ox, "I will do what I can. But already it may be too late, and, after all, my influence is limited to this city."

But while Jasmine resolved never again to talk to her husband about the old proprieties, that very day Old Head sent for Mistress Chow, promising to install her in the house not as a servant but as an elderly relative. To please Jasmine further, he ordered Wang Da voluntarily to abolish his so-called "right of the first night" in the brothels, and though he could not do away with the many infamous activities of the secret Society, he promised himself he would go conspicuously into charities. Before long, he would discover that these new activities inspired by Jasmine not only gave her pleasure but also worked to his own advantage.

He would no longer be just feared, but also respected.

172

2

Brother Ox's information came from many sources. His entire organization was a secret intelligence service. His disciples, and his disciples' disciples, bound by a terrible oath and by the rigid traditions of the Society, had no right to keep any secret from him and were obliged to report any item of news that could possibly serve his interests. With every one of them, loyalty to the Society and its chief was above everything else. Although no high government officials belonged to the Society, many of their underlings did, and the intelligence they gathered was always sent to headquarters.

It was thus that Brother Ox learned President Yuan Shih-kai had conspired with Tien Fong and Tong Hsi and Amy against Governor Ho Fucho. But events moved too swiftly, the information came too late; before Brother Ox could warn the Governor, Fucho had already been ousted from his province.

It was a miserable Fucho who arrived at the sanctuary of the foreign Concession. In the last three days of his forced flight he had lost touch with the outside world, and so the first thing he did was to read the newspapers. The news astounded him. On the very night he had been ambushed by Tien Fong, President Yuan had ordered his troops to march into the southern provinces held by the forces of the Kuomintang. The revolutionaries had been taken by surprise, and Yuan's armies were meeting with little organized resistance.

Fucho hurriedly telephoned Tong Hsi at his office, identifying himself by the customary assumed name with which the latter was familiar.

The Mayor seemed momentarily stunned at hearing Fucho's voice, but then he exclaimed: "Thank God you're alive! I'll come to your hotel at once."

But Tong Hsi did not arrive at the hotel until late that night. He explained he was being cautious, lest he lead Yuan's spies to Fucho's whereabouts. When he asked how they had managed to escape, Fucho, not wishing to overinvolve Tien Fong, said only that he had discovered the ambuscade in time.

Tong Hsi relayed various messages that Dr. Sun had sent from the South, painting a far rosier picture of the Kuomintang position than the newspapers did. Fucho was encouraged. He did not know that the accounts quoted by the Mayor, though true, covered the Kuomintang leader's earlier communications, not his later ones.

173

"What are your plans now, Fucho?" asked Tong Hsi.

"There's little I can do here. I must go to the South and join Dr. Sun at once."

"I beg to differ," Tong said emphatically. "Our comrades are doing all right in the South. Your going there will not help much, but both Amy and I think you can still do a good deal here. You're known everywhere as a model governor, you're very popular with your own people, and many of your troops may still remain loyal to you in their hearts. Perhaps you'll be able to create a diversion in your province that will greatly help our comrades in the South. Why don't you wait here a few days and see how the situation develops?"

The argument was plausible and Fucho agreed.

"I want your advice," Tong Hsi continued. "You know that even while I was a delegate to the National Congress, Dr. Sun instructed Amy and me secretly to go along with Yuan on the surface. That's why, when you recommended me and our mutual friend Chang Fafoo for the mayorship here, Yuan preferred me to him. But naturally Yuan doesn't trust me. When I heard you'd been ousted, I wanted to resign my office and join Dr. Sun in the South, and Amy agreed. Since then, however, I've received a message from Dr. Sun urging me to do everything possible to retain this post, which, of course, entails some personal danger for Amy and me. As revolutionaries, we don't mind that, but we do have our scruples. Unfortunately— outwardly at least—we must do everything we can to curry favor with Yuan, and that will make us look like turncoats. It's against our principles and our new Christian religion. What do you think we should do, my friend?"

"Follow Dr. Sun's orders," answered Fucho unequivocally.

"If you say so, then my conscience feels much easier. . . . I must go now. You're perfectly safe in these Concessions, as you know. Why don't you go to the opera? Or have a good rest—you've earned it. In the meantime, I regret that I'll not be able to see you as much as I'd like, nor can Amy come here and pay respects to your wife. However, when I have important news I'll get in touch with you."

By the next day Fucho was already finding it irksome to be cooped up in his hotel. Delicate Blossom, seeing his restlessness, sent for Ta-kong, who was now enrolled in the Government University in the port city.

Since it was a Saturday, Fucho's spirited nephew had no classes. He came to the hotel in the afternoon, eager to learn of their sorry adventure, but Delicate Blossom warned him he'd better restrain his curiosity until his uncle felt better about the matter. The boy understood and diverted Fucho with hilarious anecdotes about his experiences in the University. That evening, Fucho put on a pair of dark glasses and the three of them went out, taking little Li-hwa along, to have supper in a good restaurant and talk about their plans for the next day. There was a Buddhist temple on the very edge of the Concessions, famous for its exquisite architecture as well as for the delicious vegetarian dinners the monks served. It was settled that Ta-kong would stay in the hotel that night and they would visit the temple the very first thing in the morning.

After dinner they saw a Chinese opera, returning to the hotel rather late. When they entered their suite, an attendant appeared and whispered to Fucho mysteriously, "You have a visitor, sir." And he handed him a card bearing the name Chi Teh-shan.

Fucho had heard of Old Head as a sinister power in the city. Though he had not met him, he was prejudiced against him because of his reputation; thus, Fucho's first impulse was to send his uninvited caller away. On second thought, he decided there was no harm in receiving the man. Telling Delicate Blossom to take Ta-kong and Li-hwa to an inner room, he asked the attendant to let the visitor in.

"To what business of yours do I owe this visit, Mr. Chi?" he asked coldly.

"No business of mine," answered Old Head. "Business of yours, Governor Ho."

Fucho was stunned. He had registered under an assumed name; he had been in the city less than forty hours and was certain he had not been recognized. He answered calmly, however, pretending to be baffled. "I am afraid you have made a mistake. I am not Governor Ho."

The visitor grinned broadly. "You must have heard of me, Governor Ho Fucho. I, Chi Teh-shan, never make a mistake. To prove my point, did not Mayor Tong Hsi call on you here last night?"

Fucho looked sharply at his guest. Further denials were useless; the man knew too much.

"Let it be then as the old saying goes," Fucho said, " 'Before a true man, not a false word should be spoken.' What is this business of mine to which I owe your visit?"

"Well spoken," answered Old Head. "And lest you are still suspicious of me, I'll tell you what I already know about you."

175

And he outlined in detail the movements of the family, including Fucho himself, for the whole day, as well as their plans for the morrow.

Fucho shook his head in amazement. "I can understand how you might learn about our movements by having us shadowed, but how could you learn our plans for tomorrow?"

"That nephew of yours," replied Old Head with a smile, "talked very loud at dinner, and the walls had ears. Well, now that I've produced my credentials, Governor, I want you to listen to me."

Old Head glanced at his wrist watch. "In about two hours this hotel will be surrounded by scores of men, all detailed to watch you. When you visit the temple tomorrow morning, similar arrangements will have been made there. If you so much as set your foot inside the temple, or if you choose to remain here much longer, it will be impossible for you to leave this city alive."

Fucho asked calmly, "Why do you give me this gratuitous information, Mr. Chi?"

"For your own good, Governor."

"And what do you think I should do?"

"I respectfully suggest that you and your family depart at once. There is a foreign steamship scheduled to sail for the South within three hours. You have barely enough time to make it."

"How do I know this isn't some trick to get me to leave the city?"

"What good would your leaving the North do me?" Old Head countered.

"But you've never known me. Why are you so concerned about my well-being?"

"I, Chi Teh-shan"—Old Head looked Fucho full in the face— "seldom explain my actions, but I will make an exception. It is as you have said, Governor, 'Before a true man, not a false word should be spoken.' A few months ago you saved the life of a woman in Yi. She was a concubine to Ma Teh-lin. But she happens to be a person very dear to me and she is now my wife. So I have come to save your life in return."

Fucho still hesitated.

"I know what is in your mind," Old Head went on. "You think you can still do something in your own province to help your cause, but I tell you you can do nothing. The commanders who are really loyal to you have been either killed or taken; the others have gone over completely to the other side. Tien Fong—or should we

176

call him Fong Tienpa?—is in absolute control. The secret hopes you cherish are wishful thinking. If nothing else can convince you of the truth, I think this will: It was Tien Fong himself who helped you escape from your provincial capital and sent you here under escort. That's a secret unknown even to President Yuan or Mayor Tong. Is it not so?"

There was no more doubt in Fucho's mind. "I am truly grateful to you, Mr. Chi. Since you know so much, can you tell me who is now plotting my assassination? Yuan Shih-kai, of course. But are there others?"

"I am afraid I cannot oblige you there. I have my own rules to go by. You have friends as well as enemies, you may suspect anyone you wish. But for your own safety, you must leave at once without letting anyone know of your departure."

"But I must at least inform my good friend, Mayor Tong Hsi."

"That is not necessary." Old head's voice was bland, although he knew it was Tong Hsi and Amy who had been ordered by Yuan to make the attempt on Fucho's life. "You can write to the Mayor later—you have no time to spare. Of course, I trust that you will never mention to anyone what passed between you and me here tonight."

"Of course not," Fucho promised.

"Well, then, I have already bought three first-class tickets for you, your lady, and your daughter, and your hotel bill is paid. If you will only pack your things, we can leave any minute—by the back door. In order not to attract notice, I have only one automobile waiting there instead of my usual three. If you and your family do not mind being crowded a bit, I shall serve as your escort. I will see to it, Governor, that you go safely on board, and that the ship gets under way on time."

Fucho called out his family to tender thanks to Chi Teh-shan. And with only Old Head and Ta-kong to see them off, they left for the South.

3

TA-KONG HAD OVERHEAD the whole conversation between his uncle and Old Head in the hotel. He had been permitted to go to the steamship, and while waiting for its departure, his aunt had told him about their flight from Yi. So it was a sad and disillusioned Ta-kong who returned to school. He had always considered his uncle an incomparable hero; now this idol was toppled from its pedestal. Fucho was by no means so wise and able as Ta-kong had though him to be, and he was no match for men of cunning and deceit like Yuan Shih-kai or Tien Fong. Why, he was not even as capable and as knowing as the notorious gangster, Old Head, to whom he owed his very life. Thus Ta-kong not only lost faith in his uncle but in his ideals.

Ta-kong's disillusionment had actually begun, however, when he entered the University two years before. While he had been tutored at home he had been allowed to read nothing but the classics, and the high school regulations regarding extracurricular reading had been no less strict. But here in the University the students could peruse anything they pleased. It was then that Ta-kong, like his fellow students, came across the vast hoard of Chinese fiction written in the colloquial rather than the classical language. A new world opened—he was thrilled at his every discovery, and his reading gave him a different view of life. It served, too, to strengthen the doubts about his grandfather's wisdom which had been growing in his mind ever since the Revolution. For Ho the Central Hall, while alive, had called this popular literature "Little Talks," warned him of its worthlessness, and forbidden him to have anything to do with it.

Ta-kong took special delight in two novels, which were read and reread by all the young men of the school, who vied with one another in reciting passages from memory. The two books were *The Three Kingdoms* and *The Tales of the Marshes*.

The Three Kingdoms, a historical novel based on real figures, is a long chronicle of the history of China in the third century, when, after a period of chaos, the country was divided into three kingdoms which warred ceaselessly among themselves. It gives a graphic account of the various strategies each of them pursued in war and describes man with candor and realism, from his utmost nobleness to his most abysmal depravity.

One godlike character in the book is so peerless, so loyal and true, that his name has become a legend. He and two other men were sworn brothers, the eldest of them later founding one of the three kingdoms. In an early defeat, the hero thought the other two had been killed. A king who admired his sterling qualities gave him refuge and bribed him with everything a man could want—women, gold, position, and honor. But then, at the rumor that his elder brother was still alive, the hero at once gave up all the king offered

178

and set out singlehanded on a long journey through hostile territories, braving all sorts of obstacles and perils, in search of the man to whom he had sworn brotherly love and loyalty. The account of this journey is so inspiring that its effect went far beyond what its author ever might have imagined. Later dynasties formally consecrated the hero as the War God of China, and temples were built throughout the land to worship him.

Not all the stories in the book are so uplifting. One tells of a king—the very one who had previously tried to bribe the War God—when he himself was facing a critical battle. His food supplies were running short; his men, on reduced rations, were panic-stricken. Fearing wholesale desertions, the king summoned his faithful quartermaster-general and asked for a frank report. The general said the provisions would last but three days more, whereupon the king replied that he knew a remedy for the situation, provided he be permitted to borrow something from the general. Unsuspecting, the general vowed himself willing, and the king had him decapitated on the spot. He had wanted to borrow the general's head! Parading the severed head on a tall pole, His Majesty's heralds proclaimed to the troops that there was no real shortage of food, that the supplies had been withheld by the guilty quartermaster-general to fatten himself, and that full rations would be restored at once. By this deceit the confidence of the men was regained and the battle won.

The second novel, *The Tales of the Marshes,* also had a vague historical background, but its characters are largely fictitious. They number a hundred and eight, yet each is endowed with distinctive characteristics.

Because of hard times, these people have joined together in banditry in a swampy land known as "The Marshes." The novel is actually a saga of revolt, bristling with complaint against social injustice; a sad tableau of man's eternal oppression of his fellow man—of the poor by the rich, of the weak by the strong, of the simple by the cunning. Whenever the author's naked account of such persecutions is unable to make the point, he resorts to insinuation, as in this song sung by his most insignificant character:

> The sun scorches the earth like fire burning,
> All the grains are half parched in the fields.
> The farmer's heart boils like water churning,
> The gentleman leisurely his fan wields!

179

When Ta-kong read this, he could not help but be affected by the picture it painted of inequality among men, and its prophecy of that terrible phrase yet to come—class struggle!

Although the leader of the band robs the rich to help the poor, and raises the banner of Loyalty and Justice, the author did not intend his hero to be a Robin Hood. His deeds are merely a façade, for he is a man of great cunning and deceit. In prowess and in bravery, the leader falls far short of many of his sworn brothers; in unscrupulousness and in craftiness he outdistances them all. He does not rule by seeking to forge his band together but by dividing them, unawares, into factions, each jealous of the others but all depending on him for support and guidance.

There was, of course, a moral here—that even among men who band together to fight injustice and oppression, injustice and oppression sooner or later are bound to result. But the author's pen was too adroit, his subtlety too well concealed, for the moral to be understood by youths as immature as Ta-kong and his fellow students. Though both *The Three Kingdoms* and *The Tales of the Marshes* must be considered among the masterpieces of the world's literature, the injury they did to the minds of the young Chinese of Ta-kong's generation is incalculable. Too many of them accepted the novels as gospel truth, and became so accustomed to deceit and treachery that they thought nothing of them. They took craft for wisdom, bluff for courage, and cruelty to one's fellow men as a means toward achieving what they supposed was humanity. The only way of life they admired was outsmarting others; the only motto they respected was the utterance of that infamous king who slew his quartermaster-general—"I'd sooner deceive the whole world than let anyone in the world deceive me!" Thus, without their realizing the consequences, a generation of cynics and opportunists was brought into being.

When Ta-kong had first enrolled in the Government University he had wanted to take Yuwen with him, but Widow Lan could not afford the expenses and so Yuwen went to the Missionary College, where the Reverend Dr. Holt had arranged a scholarship for him. Happily, the Missionary College was also located in the port city, and the two boys visited each other often. Ta-kong also found a schoolmate in the University who caught his fancy—a tall, strong, square-built lad named Li Chien, open-mannered but loud-mouthed.

Though he was in a class below Ta-kong's, they won each other's admiration because of their ability to recite the two novels almost passage by passage. Before long, Ta-kong introduced Li Chien to Yuwen. It was Ta-kong who proposed that they should follow the example of their heroes in *The Three Kingdoms* and *The Tales of the Marshes,* and become sworn brothers.

The term, to say nothing of the concept of, sworn brotherhood was one taken very seriously in China at that time. The Chinese had always ranked the relationship between brother and brother next in importance only to that between father and son, and higher even than that between husband and wife. As the common saying went, "Brothers are like hands and feet, wives are like clothes; one can change one's clothes, but one can never change one's hands and feet." And if born brothers were highly valued, sworn brothers were even more so, for the first relationship could be considered the result of Providence, but the second could be entered into only of one's own choice and will.

Li Chien knew that Ta-kong and Yuwen were already sworn brothers, although they had formed that relationship rather casually when they were children in Yi. Now the three reckoned their various ages. Ta-kong, being the oldest, was to be Big Brother; Li Chien was to follow as Second Brother, and Yuwen as Third Brother. This arrangement was very much to Ta-kong's personal satisfaction. As head of the three, he would be like the oldest brother of the War God's triad, who, with the support of his two sworn brothers, in the end had founded a kingdom of his own.

On Ta-kong's insistence, the boys observed the solemn ceremonies for taking the oath of brotherhood as these were laid down in the novels. One morning before the sun rose and before anyone stirred on the University campus, the three met at a secluded spot. They knelt down on the ground, and while Ta-kong and Li Chien kowtowed to Heaven and Earth, Yuwen bowed to his Christian God. Then they recited in unison:

"From this day on, we three do swear by all that is holy that we become brothers, closer even than brothers of blood. We shall share our lives in common—three lives in one and one life in three. If there is joy and happiness, we shall equally enjoy it. If there is pain and sorrow, we shall equally suffer it. It is our misfortune that we were not born together; it is our prayer that we die together. If any one among us violates this oath, may he be damned forever by all that is holy!"

181

Then Ta-kong and Li Chien kowtowed again, and Yuwen bowed once more. When they rose, they were sworn brothers.

4

THE DRAMATIC FORCED flight of his uncle caused Ta-kong to view the two novels from a new angle. Although in the past he had more or less accepted men like the War God as heroes, now they suddenly seemed to lose their luster. Was not his uncle in many ways like the War God? Yet what had loyalty and integrity availed him? His idealism might be admirable, but he lacked the capacity to make it work. He could not win an empire; he might even lose one. It was not men like Fucho who could achieve and consolidate power, but men like the king who beheaded his quartermaster-general in *The Three Kingdoms,* or the leader of the band in *The Tales of the Marshes.* Ta-kong began to study with closer attention the artifices and deceptions described in the two books.

He could not, however, avoid experiencing an inner struggle. At first he found it difficult to reconcile the ancient virtues he had been taught in early childhood with his present inclinations. Then, gradually, he rationalized that if power was what he wanted, he did not want it for himself; only to enable him to carry out what his grandfather, Ho the Central Hall, had always talked about— the establishment of an ideal state in the country, somewhat like the rule of the legendary Emperors Yao and Shun. Though he was vague about this Utopia, he was satisfied that such was his aim; and since the aim was good and noble, there could be nothing bad in the means he might choose to pursue it.

In this manner Ta-kong overcame his misgivings. No longer did he feel contempt for men like Old Head. On the contrary, he was greatly impressed by him and wanted to know more about the secret societies, especially about the details of their organization. Perhaps they would be of use to him in the future. However, in spite of his eager search for books which might give him such information, he found that little had been written. He did learn that of the two secret groups, the Hung Society had been founded first, as a revolutionary organization. This had been at the time when the Ming Dynasty was overthrown by the Manchus. Patriotic Chinese had banded together secretly to continue underground resistance, calling their organization the Hung Society. There was good reason for the choice of name, and its Chinese character. "Hung" sounds somewhat like "Han" (the Chinese usually call themselves the Han race). But the two characters also are written alike, except for one difference: the composite character that makes up "Han" includes one element not found in that of the secret-society "Hung"—the symbol for "mouth"!

Outwardly, the Society took on the appearance of a mutual assistance association somewhat like the Freemasons in the West; inwardly, its organization was different. Its secrets were strictly guarded, its discipline severe. The founders permitted its revolutionary aims to be known only to a select few of the top command, and after the founders died, the new leaders began to forget or neglect the primary purpose for which the Society had been established. But by then the organization had already grown into a tremendous force, and the benefits to its members were actually numerous and invaluable. Thus the Hung Society had thrived and spread.

The Manchus were aware of its existence. At first they tried unsuccessfully to suppress it, and then, early in the eighteenth century, a wily Manchu emperor applied a variation of the time-honored ruse—divide and conquer. Since he could not stamp out the Hungs, he would create a rival Society. Under his hidden sponsorship, this organization—named Chin because it sounded like the word Ching by which the Manchus called their Dynasty—grew by leaps and bounds. Before long the Chins were able to challenge the power and popularity of the Hungs, and thus began the feuds. The Hung Society never permitted its members to join the Chins, but the Chin Society had no such restrictions; the Chins had their men join the Hungs to spy on them.

But time is a great eraser of memory. By the close of the Manchu Dynasty, both the rulers and the societies themselves had all but forgotten the origins of the two groups. With the overthrow of the Manchus, the Hungs lost their primary reason for being and the Chins had no government to fall back on for support. Both soon degenerated into mere secret organizations which men joined for one purpose or another and which their leaders exploited for their own selfish aims. Finding that continual feuding harmed both and benefited neither, the two had made occasional overtures of peace or fusion, but it remained for Chi Teh-shan, alias Brother Ox, to seize the reins of both organizations in the big port city, and thus earn the nickname Old Head.

The more Ta-kong learned, the more he wanted to know, especially since he had met Chi Teh-shan in person. He planned to call on him and strike up a better acquaintance, but suddenly he came down with scarlet fever, then a much dreaded disease in China.

At that time, even in the port city, Western medicine was still not in use. The University authorities hastily advised Ta-kong's father of his illness, and also summoned the best native herb doctor. There was no hospital on the campus, so Ta-kong had to be put in a separate room far removed from the students' dormitory. Nor was there a nurse. The doctor insisted that someone attend the patient constantly, but all the servants feared the infectious disease and refused to do so. Here, clearly, was a job for the sworn brotherhood. Li Chien, the Second Brother, volunteered without hesitation to live with Ta-kong in the same room and wait on him day and night. For a full week he nursed his friend patiently and devotedly, relieved only occasionally by Yuwen, who had to have special permission to absent himself from the Missionary College.

Ta-kong was extremely grateful to Li Chien. "Second Brother," he remarked time and again, "I would not have lived through this illness without you and Third Brother. Especially you. You risked your life to save mine."

"Nonsense, Big Brother!" Li Chien would reply. "I'm doing no more than you'd be willing to do for me. Haven't we sworn that if we have pain, we shall suffer it equally? And that though we were not born together, we'd like to die together?"

Between the medications of the herb doctor and the nursing of Li Chien and Yuwen, Ta-kong recovered even before his father arrived from Yi. Neither Li Chien nor Yuwen caught the disease.

5

SHORTLY AFTER TA-KONG's recovery, and about a month before summer recess, a momentous event occurred in China. By then Yuan Shih-kai had, with Japanese assistance, established undisputed mastery over the whole country. Now common gossip had it that, with further Japanese assistance, Yuan would soon overturn the Republic and crown himself Emperor.

But Japan had her own plans. Seizing a time when the Western Powers were preoccupied with frantic preparations for the First World War, Japan secretly presented Yuan with "Twenty-one Demands" which, if accepted, would reduce China to a Japanese satrapy. Reluctant to yield to such exorbitant terms, Yuan haggled and procrastinated for months, until Japan lost her patience and delivered an ultimatum.

The news leaked out. The people as a whole had not awakened to full national consciousness, but the intellectuals, especially the students, were filled with indignation. Protest meetings sprang up spontaneously at the University, and Ta-kong threw himself into these agitations with such zeal that though he was only a sophomore, he was elected one of the leaders. At his suggestion, invitations were sent to other schools in the city, asking them to send delegates to a united conference at the University. All responded with enthusiasm except Yuwen's Missionary College, which forbade its students to participate in unauthorized outside activities.

Ta-kong boiled with excitment, for this was his first chance to practice all he had learned in *The Three Kingdoms* and *The Tales of the Marshes*. He was out to make himself the leader of leaders. And indeed, he soon became extremely popular and influential among the students.

Besides, he was attracted by one of the delegates—a girl.

There was only one girls' college in the city, and its students had never associated with the boys at the other schools. But this time the college made an exception and permitted one Yin Mei-yin to come to the conference. She had sharp features, triangular-shaped eyes, and no beauty to speak of except the bloom of youth. At his first sight of her, Ta-kong thought with amusement that if he ever wanted a wife this would be the last girl he would choose. She could not compare with his aunt, Delicate Blossom; however, when Yin Mei-yin started to speak, Ta-kong got a pleasant surprise. She was neither shy nor backward as Chinese girls generally were then, and she had a quick wit and a sharp mind. Realizing that she would make a valuable ally Ta-kong began to cultivate her friendship, and she seemed willing to reciprocate.

Ta-kong, Mei-yin, and the other students all had much to learn about organizing protests and demonstrations. The only move they could think of was to draft a petition to be presented to Mayor Tong Hsi as the highest Government representative in the city, and to send copies to schools in other cities. However, there was a heated debate when it came to drafting the petition. Most of the delegates wanted it to contain only a protest against the Japanese demands, but Ta-kong proposed that a passage be inserted to express their opposition to a change of regime from republic back to empire. His opponents argued that whereas the Japanese ultimatum was an established fact, the possible change of regime by Yuan was only a speculation. For a moment it looked as if Ta-kong had lost the day. But Mei-yin turned the tide: "We are not waiting to protest against the Japanese demands until we have accepted them, are we?" The matter was settled in favor of Ta-kong, and both he and Mei-yin were chosen to be members of the delegation that presented the petition.

Considering it beneath his dignity to give the students an audience, Mayor Tong Hsi asked his secretary-general, Chang Fa-foo, who was newly appointed to the post, to receive them instead. When Ta-kong's name was announced, Chang showed a sign of recognition. And Ta-kong realized at once that Chang was one of the two men who had visited his uncle in Yi before the Revolution. However, they did not exchange any personal remarks. Chang, all courtesy and attention, said the situation was by no means as serious as it might appear to the public, and assured them that the Government would not yield to the Japanese demands. He thanked the students for their demonstration, explaining that he felt it would, of itself, strengthen the Government's hand in negotiating with the Japanese.

Most of the students were satisfied. Ta-kong was not. Chang Fa-foo had completely ignored the subject of a possible change of regime, and Ta-kong brashly brought it into the open. At once he noticed a gleam of warning in Chang's eye, but this did not stop him. He insisted that that particular passage in the petition be singled out for President Yuan's attention. Shrugging his spare shoulders, Chang Fa-foo promised this would be done.

The delegation left the Mayor's office feeling highly gratified, but Ta-kong regarded the affair as his personal triumph. Because the hour was getting rather late, because he had a larger allowance than the others, and because he wanted to make himself more popular among them, he invited the whole group to supper and to a Chinese opera afterward.

The opera seemed made for the students' amusement. They were particularly delighted by one exchange between a bully and his victim:

"When I abuse you, you must not answer so much as a word," ordered the bully.

"Yes, sir," replied the helpless victim.

"When I beat you, you must not return so much as a blow."

"Yes, sir."

186

"When I slay you, you must not shed so much as a drop of blood."

"Yes, sir."

The students laughed merrily at this.

Then someone said, "Don't laugh! Don't you realize it's just the way the Japanese would like to have us? They want to kill us, but they won't permit us even to shed a drop of blood."

Struck, like the others, with the aptness of the comment, Ta-kong remarked, "Not only the Japanese. There are such people in our own midst. Take Yuan Shih-kai. Isn't his intention to treat the common people just that way?"

They all fell quiet at his words, and Ta-kong felt pleased with his own smartness. Then Mei-yin, who was sitting beside him, whispered: "Perhaps there's more truth than we think in what the bully says. That may be the only effective way to rule a nation. Who knows?"

At a loss for an answer, Ta-kong mused to himself: What a girl! What a mind!

When the opera was over, he saw Mei-yin back to her school and then started for his own University with her words still ringing in his ears. He had not asked her for an explanation because he did not want her to think his intellect was unequal to hers. But he knew he had not fully grasped her meaning.

Ta-kong had taken a short cut through a dark, deserted alley between the Concession area and the Chinese city, when suddenly, out of nowhere, dim shadows converged upon him. He had no time to put up a struggle, for the first blow stunned him. But before he lost consciousness he heard one of his assailants growl, "Trouble-maker! Let this be a lesson to you. What business is it of yours if the President wants to become Emperor?"

As his body hit the hard dirt of the alley, all at once he had a vague understanding of what Mei-yin had meant.

At dawn a peddler found him lying there. The peddler happened to be a great-great-grand-disciple to Old Head, and he immediately telephoned the headquarters of the Society. Thinking the matter a thing of no account, headquarters told him to inform the policeman on the beat, so in due course Ta-kong, still unconscious, was carried by ambulance to a police station in the Concession area. Luckily, a detective on duty there was one of the disciples Old Head had detailed to shadow Fucho at the restaurant, and the man recognized Ta-kong at once and got in touch with his chief. Before the foreign police officer at the station knew what was happening,

Ta-kong was taken to the house of Chi Teh-shan, where he was given the best medical attention and nursed personally by Jasmine.

Ta-kong was deeply grateful to the Chis, and during his convalescence began to call them Uncle Chi and Aunt Chi. While he was recovering, he gave a good deal of thought to a matter which had long been in his mind.

One day when Old Head came to see him, he said, "Uncle Chi, I want to beg a favor of you."

"Name it, boy," said Old Head, "and it's yours."

"Allow me to join your Society and become your disciple."

"You must be joking!" Old Head exclaimed in surprise. "You, a grandson of Ho the Central Hall—a nephew of Governor Ho Fucho!"

"No, I am serious, Uncle Chi, I want to become your disciple."

"But the rules of the Society are strict and severe. You have to obey your teacher's commands without question. Any violation means drastic punishment, and the initiation is harsh and rigid—you might not be able to stand it."

"If you could, Uncle Chi, so can I."

Old Head meditated for a second. Then his rough face relaxed in a broad grin.

"Who would think I'd live to see the day when a grandson of Ho the Central Hall wants to become my disciple! I haven't taken a disciple for years—I only let my disciples take disciples. Well, in your case I'll make an exception. Just as my late Venerable Master made me his Close-Door-Disciple, so I will make you mine."

Three

THE NEWS OF Fucho's downfall had rocked Yi from top to bottom. For days it formed the sole topic of conversation among the good people of this small provincial town. Even the more momentous national events that ensued—President Yuan's suppression of the so-called Second Revolution of the Kuomintang—did not arouse as much interest and excitement. In the opinion of many of the elders, men of Ho the Central Hall's generation, Fucho was being punished by Heaven for his unfilial behavior toward his father. The

188

landed gentry welcomed the news, for they had resented Fucho's attempt to reduce rentals. For the riffraff of society, such as the opium-smugglers, the change was heartening indeed, for was Fucho not their arch-enemy and Tien Fong a man of their own breed? Only the common masses who had tasted of Fucho's good government truly regretted his removal. But these people did not care to get into trouble with the authorities, and so they kept their views to themselves. There remained, therefore, only the Reverend Dr. Holt to deplore openly the sudden turn of events. Apart from the affection he had for his friend, he saw in Fucho's ouster a bad omen for the country he had come to love as a second homeland.

No one was more pleased with Fucho's downfall than Ma Pingnan. Had he been able to foresee events, he never would have sold Jasmine. His experience with Fucho, however, had taught him a lesson. In a country like China, it was not enough to be rich; to enjoy wealth fully and to keep trouble from the door, one had to be in the good graces of the authorities. It was lucky that Tien Fong—a sort of family friend—had become Governor. Ma Pingnan would have liked to resume the close and lucrative partnership in the opium traffic which his father had once enjoyed with Tien and which Ho Fucho had disrupted, but this, he understood, was no longer possible. Tien Fong, having all the provincial resources at his disposal, now needed no financial backing from the House of Ma. He had already made direct contact with Tong Hsi, Amy, and Johnny Hunt, and was not inclined to let anyone else cut in on his profits. Nevertheless, Pingnan went to the provincial capital to congratulate the new Governor in person. He called him generation-uncle and took him many gifts. Tien Fong was quite pleased with the tribute and Pingnan felt that cordial relations had been established.

However, this trip to the provincial capital had another purpose, for Pingnan was greatly troubled by a problem. He had discussed it with his mother, who agreed something must be done about it quickly: Pingnan had too many brothers and sisters. Besides Jasmine, only the eighth concubine was childless; even the eleventh one, the youngest of his father's seraglio, had borne a son while the old man was still alive and given birth to a daughter after his death. Though the father had left no will beyond the instructions he had personally given to Pingnan, it was the Chinese custom to give all the sons their rightful inheritance when they grew up, and the daughters their dowries when they married.

So far, only the two girls of the first concubine had come of age, but before long the boys would grow up and demand to participate in the management of the estate. The thought appalled Pingnan.

Shortly after his visit with the new Governor, he made it known to all the concubines that he thought his father had treated them abominably. It was against "the current of the times." It was inhuman. Why, in France where he had studied, men and women mixed freely. From now on there would be no more restrictions on the concubines' movements. They could have the freedom of the house and the city, and within the limits of their allowances, they could go shopping and sightseeing whenever and wherever they wanted. To show that he was sincere, he no longer stationed himself in his father's former private court where he could spy on them, but moved his office to an outer court.

Of course it was understandable that some conditions had to be attached to such liberality. To make sure that, on their unaccustomed forays, nothing happened to the valuables and jewelry his father had presented to them, he expected the concubines to hand these over to him for safekeeping. And there was another matter. He had no objection to their forming associations with other men, as they were free to do according to law. If any of them found a man after her fancy, she need only to tell him and he would gladly let her go free as he had Jasmine. But there must be no underhanded tricks.

The concubines were delighted. Their young lord and master was truly liberal and understanding. They had no knowledge of what he had done to Jasmine, for he had discharged Mistress Chow immediately thereafter; and when the amah was later sent for by Brother Ox, she was taken to the port city directly from her home in the country. Enthusiastically, they delivered all their valuables to Pingnan's custody, and like captured birds suddenly set free, they trooped out into the city. Pingnan secretly had them shadowed.

But if he had expected any results from this maneuver, he was disappointed; time passed, and not one woman came forward to confess she would like to leave with some man. Nor had putting them under surveillance done any good. The older women, especially the first concubine, remembered the rules of propriety and acted accordingly. And though many of the younger ones indulged in flirtations, they had their children to think of and they behaved with circumspection. The eighth concubine had no child,

190

but by now she had become Pingnan's own favorite and she desired no other liaison.

Pingnan was therefore forced to modify his plan. He began to put temptation purposely in the way of the concubines. The men-servants were allowed free access to the inner courts, and not a few of them were bold and attractive. Before long, several un-suspecting concubines had succumbed. Pingnan, listening to his men's reports, was vastly pleased.

Then, late one night in early summer, voices suddenly were heard in every inner court crying excitedly, "Fire! Fire! The house is burning! Run for your lives!"

Flames were indeed crackling furiously skyward from the outer courts, giving the appearance of a huge conflagration.

There was only one exit from the inner compound, and that was through Old Ma's former private court. Everybody—mistresses and amahs, grown-ups and children—darting headlong from their bedrooms, rushed instinctively in that direction. Several concu-bines, frightened out of their wits, bolted out with their lovers, just as they were—stark naked. But in the case of those who were innocent of any wrongdoing, Ma Pingnan had thoughtfully ar-ranged for a nude man to follow behind each one, and in their excitement the women did not notice. Two naked men even followed the two daughters of the first concubine. The only exceptions were the second concubine, Pingnan's mother, and the eighth con-cubine, his present mistress.

Abruptly, from all directions, fully dressed servants appeared, torches in hand. Loudly they expressed their astonishments at the amazing sight. "This is outrageous! We must take them to the master at once!"

Most of the women were genuinely surprised, and struggled desperately. The men struggled not at all. They were taken, couple by couple, into the big dining room, where Pingnan was waiting.

The fire, which had been set off by burning a large pile of hay in an empty space in the outer compound, now was under complete control.

"So this is what my late father's concubines have been doing behind my back!" exclaimed Pingnan, turning on his captives with manifest disgust. "Had there not been a fire, I never would have found you out."

Several of the concubines bowed their heads in shame. The two daughters sobbed incoherently, but their mother, the first concubine,

191

noted for her rash temper, was a woman who prided herself on observing the proprieties.

"This is a mistake," she declared indignantly. "I don't know about others, but I do know I've never seen this man who stands by my side. This is a trick!"

Pingnan snickered, "People caught red-handed invariably offer the same excuse. At least you might be original."

"What you imply is impossible," she protested. "I am forty-five, older even than your mother. Such passions as stir in younger hearts no longer stir in mine. I need not defend myself. My age is my defense."

"You talk of woman's passions. Well, let me remind you of the old saying: 'In her thirties, a woman is like a wolf; in her forties, she is like a tiger.' You're like a tiger now in your carnal desires. Why, even your two daughters appear to have followed your splendid example."

"I am innocent! And so are they!"

"Well, well!" Pingnan smiled slyly. "There's one thing about adultery—it can't be committed by one party alone. Let's see what your paramours have to say. Speak up, men! Deny it if you can!"

All three supposed paramours hung their heads and remained silent. Pingnan laughed aloud.

"See for yourself, woman!"

The first concubine turned ghostly pale. On this point, the standards of propriety were unequivocal; in the old days many a woman had committed suicide for charges far less serious.

"As Heaven is above," she cried wildly, "I have not committed this sin. Nor have my daughters. I'd sooner kill myself. I'll kill myself now to prove my innocence—and theirs!"

Pingnan chuckled. "I know you, woman. You might convince my father with those words, but not me. With you, it has always been, 'I'll kill myself for this,' or 'I'll kill myself for that.' But you have committed adultery and you have lived to this day."

Her face went white. "Give me a knife and I will cut my throat before your eyes!"

Pingnan shrugged nonchalantly. "Why do you need a knife? If you want to die, there's a well right outside in the courtyard."

Without a word the woman dashed out of the room. Her captors made a move to catch her, but it was too late. Everyone heard the sudden muffled splash.

A terrible silence followed. Then there was a violent commotion.

The two daughters struggled with all their might to follow their mother, but Pingnan bade their guards hold them fast.

"She is beyond rescue now. And she's not worth saving anyhow. She killed herself because she knew it was impossible to cover up her shame."

His glance swept over the other women. "You are all as guilty as she. Is there even one of you with something to say for herself?"

Except for the moanings of the two daughters, there was not a sound.

"Since you have no defense," he went on pitilessly, "you leave me no choice. You have committed adultery, you have sinned against my father, you have shamed my good name. I can either take you exactly as you are to the magistrate of the local court, and parade you in the streets of Yi so that everybody will know what crime you have committed, or else I shall take you in this manner all the way to the provincial capital and present you to Governor Tien Fong. He was a good friend to my father and he's a good generation-uncle to me. I'm sure he knows what to do with the likes of you."

Unspeakable horror seized the women. To be paraded in their present state was unthinkable. Unlettered and ignorant, they knew nothing about law and had an exaggerated fear of it. They knew of Pingnan's recent visit to the new Governor and suspected collusion, and terrified by Tien Fong's reputation for cruelty, they imagined that if delivered into his hands they would be given the lash, put to the rack, tortured, and then condemned to a slow and agonizing death.

"Oh, no!" one concubine whined in desperation. "Anything but that!"

Pingnan waited until the significance of these words had sunk deeply into the minds of the women.

"Well, that's what you deserve. It's what I ought to do. But considering that you were my father's concubines, I'm inclined to be a little lenient. Of course, from the very nature of your crime, I can only conclude that not all the children you bore in the name of my father are of his true blood. They must be bastards, like the two girls here—who apparently are girls no more! Well, if you agree to take yourselves and all your illegitimate offspring out of this house and never return, I might be persuaded to drop the charges against you."

The women were dumfounded. Only the third concubine summoned enough courage to protest.

"No, no! I swear by Heaven that my children are your father's, the same as you are. You cannot deprive them of their rightful inheritance and their dowries."

"Then swear by Heaven that you were not discovered side by side with your lover here."

"It was a trick! A trick you planned yourself. You want to rob my children of their due!"

"So we come back to that again," roared Pingnan. "I shall not bother to question your paramour now. I'll have him tell his story to Governor Tien, and I'll proceed exactly as I told you before. I'll let the Governor and the law-court declare your children illegitimate and order them out of this house by legal decree."

The third concubine fell back aghast. The women were confounded—they had no choice.

"You've had enough time to think," Pingnan said slowly. "If you're ready to do what I say, I have documents here on which you can affix your thumbprints. They are confessions that you have committed adultery and that your children are bastards. Once you sign your document, I'll let you go free."

The documents were passed around. Some of the women marveled that these could be produced at a moment's notice, but no one dared argue further with Pingnan; even in this minor detail he had planned to perfection. The concubines who had actually conducted illicit affairs were approached first; reluctant but resigned, they affixed their thumbprints. Once they had complied, the rest was easy—in the end, even the third concubine gave in. The two girls were ordered to sign similar papers admitting that both they and their mother had committed adultery and that they themselves were bastards, with no claim whatever on the House of Ma. They resisted so furiously, however, that Pingnan's men had to seize their hands and force them to press their thumbs on the documents.

That very night Pingnan drove all of them—women and children alike—out of his house. He permitted them to take nothing but the simple clothes on their backs.

2

THE DAYS THAT followed were an unmixed joy and triumph for Pingnan. At last he was the sole possessor of his father's vast riches.

Although the huge compound seemed quiet and lonesome after the concubines had gone, he reminded himself that sooner or later he could people it with his own women, whether concubinage was allowed by the Republic or not. But at the moment he was still too much enamored of the eighth concubine to mind. He slept with her openly and spoiled her terribly.

Even his mother had become jealous of the eighth concubine, and he liked that. Ever since his return she had reveled in being mistress of the house, and of late had become quite impossible, with her attempts to exercise control over him. It was high time to teach her a lesson.

The eighth concubine, though pettish and capricious, was docile and harmless by nature. Left to her own wits, she would not have been much of an adversary for the second concubine; but, incited by Pingnan, she assumed a different attitude. Before long, when the older woman put on haughty airs, the younger woman would show an even haughtier disdain; when the second concubine spoke one sharp word, the eighth concubine would reply with two. And to the chagrin of the mother, every time she appealed to her son he unfailingly took the side of his mistress.

Finally Pingnan's mother confronted him directly.

"Can't you see how scandalous your carrying-on with that woman has become?"

"What's so scandalous about sleeping with a woman?" asked Pingnan coolly.

"But she is your father's concubine!"

"There's no law against it. She's part of my inheritance, and I enjoy her just as I enjoy my other possessions."

"Aren't you afraid of what people will say? Have you no sense of the proprieties?"

"Only the servants know about what you call my carrying-on. I pay them and they're afraid of me, so they won't say a thing—unless you do. As for the proprieties, bah! You didn't have any compunction about urging me to chase out the other concubines and their children. Why should you care about my having a little fun with this one? I warn you—if you whisper a word about it, I'll tell everyone it was you who hatched the plot against the others."

The second concubine was forced to try another approach.

"I can't see why you should take such a fancy to her. She's no longer young. And she is certainly not beautiful—not even as good-looking as that Jasmine you sold off as a prostitute. Why don't you get married? Or at least get some mistresses younger and prettier than she is?"

"Enough of your tricks, old woman! I don't want to get married. I don't want a wife to restrict my freedom. I've had plenty of women in my young life, both foreign and Chinese, and this one happens to appeal to me. When I'm tired of her, I'll get rid of her without your telling me."

"You cannot talk like this to me!" the mother shouted. "You must remember you are still my son. Even if you like her as a mistress, in all decency you should make her behave more respectfully to me, your own mother."

"So now we get to the bottom of the matter! Well, understand this, old woman—I owe you nothing. The fact that you are my mother is pure accident. And for that, I've rewarded you enough. Never forget that I am the only master in this house; whoever is in my favor I'll raise in the household, you and anybody else notwithstanding. So long as you are quiet and obedient, you'll have your food, your clothes, and your allowance, but if you're not, don't think I won't take them away from you too."

No longer able to control herself, the mother stormed out of the room in a rage.

That very day, out of sheer malice, Pingnan announced that thereafter the eighth concubine would have sole supervision over all domestic spending as well as over the servants in the inner compound. The very first thing she did was transfer her rival's favorite personal amah to her own service. The mother's embittered heart smouldered like a volcano, but unlike a volcano, she could find no outlet.

A few months later Pingnan was given fresh cause for anxiety: Pingshi suddenly wrote that he was returning home. Pingnan believed his mother was behind this and had secretly communicated with his brother. He suspected a plot to take the management of the estate away from him. If any human being ever hated another, Pingnan hated his mother and brother then.

However, almost overnight, he outwardly changed his attitude toward the old woman, as a chameleon changes its color. He became filial and respectful, and at his bidding the eighth concubine, though with much pouting and frowning, also agreed to humble herself. Though she was still left in charge of the domestic spending and of the servants in the inner courts, she was made to consult her senior "sister" often. But the older woman was unforgiving and met all the advances of her son and his mistress with cold scorn. Now Pingnan was genuinely alarmed.

When the exact date of his younger brother's return was known, he hurried to the provincial capital and called on Governor Tien Fong, bringing many gifts, and also an invitation: He planned a welcome-home celebration for his brother; would his generation-uncle honor the occasion with his gubernatorial presence? The Governor did not wish to be bothered with such trifles, but Pingnan's tongue was as persuasive as his gifts were expensive. Tien agreed to come.

On the night before Pingshi's arrival, Pingnan unfolded a plot to his mistress. However, she felt quite squeamish about it, for the attachment she bore Pingnan was real. Pingnan reassured her, promising that she need not go through with the whole thing; he himself would make certain to appear in the nick of time. All she must do was simply scream at the top of her voice at the critical moment—scream so loud that Governor Tien and his entourage, who would be conveniently lodged in the nearby courts, could not fail to hear and rush to her rescue.

Pingshi arrived. While the two brothers had been in Europe, they had never sought each other's company, and this was their first meeting after a long separation. Pingnan eyed Pingshi closely. His brother had the same family build, but was shorter and stouter than himself. His eyes were narrow and piggish like Pingnan's own, but his complexion less sallow. After the initial scrutiny, Pingnan gave Pingshi a most heart-warming display of brotherly affections. He had Pingshi put up at once in the most luxurious of the inner courts—the one Jasmine had occupied, which also happened to be next to the eighth concubine's.

On the first night after Pingshi's return a banquet was given exclusively for the members of the family. On the second, a larger one was held for the business agents and associates of the house. At both banquets, Pingnan made it clear that he was glad his brother was back and that from now on they would be equal partners in the management of their father's estate.

The third night was to be the crowning event of the festivities. The Governor was to grace the occasion with his presence, and all the notables of Yi were invited—except the Hos and the Reverend Dr. Holt. Pingnan thought it better not to ask the American. There was no telling what might happen if he met Tien Fong, who had not only supplanted Ho Fucho as Governor but had also once made an attempt on the missionary's life.

Pingnan felt his plans were proceeding well. In the beginning, he had been afraid his brother might not fall into the snare. He remembered Pingshi as an ambitious lad, always dreaming about being the future Bismarck of China; but now, to his comfort, he discovered that the man fell far short of the promise of the boy. Though Pingshi still had his wild ambitions, he showed little intellect to support them. Pingnan had also been fearful his brother might yet retain some sense of the old proprieties, but there Pingshi turned out to be a man after his own heart—he ranted violently against Confucius. Moreover, Pingnan wormed one fact out of Pingshi, much to his own inward glee. It seemed that up to now the young man had never experienced any intimate relations with women. Sullen and surly, he had timorously approached girl's of his acquaintance several times, only to be rudely snubbed. Since then he had pent up his passions, and ungratified desire gleamed in his eye. Pingnan decided his brother would be easy prey.

At the outset, the eighth concubine took Pingshi's surliness for rebuff and was much discouraged. But enlightened by Pingnan that this was only a mask to conceal a lack of self-confidence, she persevered in her advances, and before the second day was over Pingshi was frequently found in her company, openly infatuated, blind to both his mother's mortification and his brother's apparent unconcern.

At last, on the afternoon before the Governor arrived, the eighth concubine told Pingnan that everything was ready. An assignation had been made between her and his brother for the exact hour he had planned. The very minute the Governor and his entourage retired to their assigned rooms, Pingshi would steal to her bed-chamber.

Tien Fong came, roaring and roistering, with his retinue. Unlike his predecessor, he did not travel with a mere handful of select companions; he descended with a hundred men, armed with pistols and rifles. They were a noisy and unruly crowd, and very hard to please. Huge as Ma's compound was, they crammed the outer courts to the full and many of the inner courts besides. They pocketed any small article they fancied and flirted shamelessly

198

with the maids and amahs. But Pingnan looked on and smiled. Only thus could he hope to establish himself in their favor.

At the banquet, he did his best to ingratiate himself with the Governor, starting off with a nice little speech calculated to flatter Tien's vanity. He lauded his physical prowess and his achievements in the Revolution. He called him a fighter against foreign imperialism and a savior of the landed gentry of the province. Tien Fong was vastly pleased, sometimes nodding his enormous head in approval and at other times contracting his ugly scars into bemused frowns in a feeble attempt at seeming modesty.

But Pingnan had miscalculated on one important matter: the Governor's capacity for wine. No mean drinker himself, Pingnan was no match for Tien. Every time he slowed down a bit, the Governor would clamor for more and insist that his host keep him company. Before the banquet ended, Pingnan felt quite tipsy, but Pingshi was completely sober. Notwithstanding the Governor's repeated pressings, the surly young man would not touch a drop of wine. The thought that his brother's mind was preoccupied with his coming tryst pleased Pingnan. It was obvious that the Governor had taken a dislike to Pingshi, and that pleased Pingnan even more.

Finally, the Governor and his entourage were escorted to their quarters for the night. As Pingnan had arranged, Tien Fong was put up in a court very close to the eighth concubine's; in fact, the two courts were separated only by Pingnan's own. The brothers said good night to the Governor, and then Pingnan saw Pingshi sneak away in haste. He returned to his own bedroom to wait. He needed only his mistress's scream now to dispose of his brother.

But he had drunk much too much, and a great drowsiness fell on him. What if he should miss the scream and not arrive at the critical juncture? Then the eighth concubine would be ravished by his brother. How strange that he should mind! He had always treated women as chattels, to be used for one's pleasure, as he had early learned from his father. But this woman was different; not that he loved her, for he knew nothing about love, but he couldn't bear the idea of another man's touching her. He began to understand his father's feelings. At length his head nodded with increasing drowsiness and he shook himself with a mighty effort, but it was in vain. Pingnan dozed off.

Awaking with a start, he looked at his watch. An hour had passed—what might not have happened in that time! Had the woman screamed at all? He listened: not a sound. With his heart

199

pounding fearfully, he took up the flashlight his brother had brought back from Germany as a gift, but he kept the light off as he made his way to the door of the eighth concubine's suite.

Inside, he could hear unmistakably suggestive sounds. So the woman had betrayed him! Well, he would have them both thrown out of the house. What stupid, impatient fools! They had neglected even to bolt the door. Turning the flashlight on, he rushed into the room and snatched the quilt from the bed.

And he uncovered a couple indeed! The woman was the eighth concubine, but the man was not his brother. It was Governor Tien! Pingnan stood frozen in consternation. Tien Fong, indifferent to his predicament, jumped out of the bed and grabbed a revolver.

Pingnan turned on the woman. "You strumpet! You deceived me!"

"No, no," she sobbed. "How could I know it was the Governor, not your brother? And the Governor is so strong—he had my mouth smothered before I could scream."

Tien took instant command. He shouted at the top of his voice and his men began to pour into the courtyard from all directions; torches were carried in until the whole court was light as day. In the forefront of the few people who entered the room were Pingnan's mother and brother. She averted her glance at the sight of the naked Governor, but neither of the pair looked at all surprised. At a word from Tien Fong, his men seized Pingnan.

Leisurely the Governor proceeded to clothe himself. "You've got a lot to explain, Ma Pingnan," he said. "You might as well tell it to everybody."

Pingnan collected his wits. "It's you who have to do the explaining—not me!" he protested indignantly. "I invited you as a guest to this house. How could you come here and violate my late father's eighth concubine?"

Tien Fong lit a cigarette. "Ask me a harder question than that! I came here at the specific request of your own mother and brother."

"That cannot be," retorted Pingnan. "They are no mother and brother of mine if they could dishonor my house so despicably!"

Tien Fong stepped forth and slapped Pingnan's face sharply.

"There's no more despicable wretch than you yourself," declared the Governor. "I know your kind. You can never tell the truth unless you're confronted with a direct witness. Well, we've got one."

He barked a command, and a woman was brought in—none other

than the former personal amah of Pingnan's mother, whom the eighth concubine had arrogated to her own service.

"Tell your story, woman," ordered the Governor.

By sheer accident, the amah said, she had overheard the conversation between Pingnan and the eighth concubine. Her former mistress, the second concubine, had been much kinder to her than her present one, and so she had confided to her old mistress what she had learned. She and the second concubine had managed to stop Pingshi in time, and together the three had gone to see the Governor.

Now Tien Fong said, "You've heard the story, Ma Pingnan. And I myself heard the remarks you exchanged with the eighth concubine when you came in here. Have you got anything more to say?"

Knowing he was cornered, Pingnan shrugged his shoulders helplessly. "The amah is lying, trying to discredit me. But Governor, you are my generation-uncle, and I've always treated you with respect and affection. Well, I admit I made a mistake in surprising you. If you like my late father's eighth concubine, you may have her."

"You want to bribe me with your mistress, eh? I admit I like her, and I'm going to take her away with or without your blessing. Who dares stop me? So you can see for yourself, Ma Pingnan, your offer is not much of a bribe."

Pingnan swallowed hard. "I'm sorry I inconvenienced you a moment ago, but I'll show you how sincerely repentant I am. I shall give the eighth concubine, for your sake, a dowry amounting to no less than one-fourth of my father's whole estate. I trust that will make ample amends to you, generation-uncle."

"That's much better," said Tien Fong with a cunning smile. "But unfortunately for you, the other side has come up with a higher bid."

Pingnan glanced quickly at his mother and brother. Both turned pale. He realized at once that not only had they made such a bargain with Tien Fong, but they were afraid he himself might turn up with a better offer.

Seeing hope, he plunged on recklessly, "Then I'll go higher. You may have one-half the property as dowry."

The Governor snorted. "That's no more than your mother and brother agreed upon. And remember, you have one disadvantage. You have given me—you acknowledge it yourself—a little unpleasantness and awkwardness. So I'm afraid the scales of justice are tipped in their favor."

Pingnan jumped at the insinuation. "I'll give you three-fourths of the property," he said eagerly. "See if they can do better!"

The pallor of his mother and brother deepened. The woman made a hasty move to speak, but Tien Fong gestured her to silence.

"I used to think there were no greater rascals in these parts than your father and me." He laughed uproariously. "But I've found one now. You out-rascal both of us, by far."

He paused for a moment, then went on, "No offense, Ma Pingnan—that's intended as a compliment. Of course, your offer is the best. How could your mother and brother top it unless they gave me the whole property? If you were in my place, you wouldn't hesitate to accept your own bid, would you?"

Hope throbbed wildly in Pingnan's heart; he would get out of this dilemma after all. Tien Fong threw his cigarette on the beautiful carpet and ground it out carelessly with his big foot.

"The trouble is, Pingnan, that I am not you. I'm not such a big scoundrel as you—I still go by the rules of 'the rivers and lakes.' I struck a bargain with your mother and brother: I am to take half of the property and the eighth concubine, and that's all I am going to take. I am also to run you out of the house for good. And that I'm obliged to do, whether you make me a better offer or not. A bargain is a bargain—that's the way it is with 'the rivers and lakes.'

"Get out of this house now, and never come back! You disinherited yourself with your own conduct. Just as you drove out the other concubines and their children, just as you intended to chase out your own brother, so do I now deliver the same judgment on you. I've had my secretary prepare papers for you to sign. I can't read them, but my secretary has read them to me. They state that you committed incest with your father's concubines, against our time-honored traditions, and that therefore you voluntarily surrender all your inheritance to your brother. Sign them! Then you will leave at once, with nothing whatever but the clothes on your back—the same terms you gave to the other concubines and their children. I never believed in Heaven, but by thunder and lightning, there indeed seems to be One who has made me hand out this justice to you."

Ma Pingnan knew when he was beaten. Without a word he signed the papers and left the house.

3

BUT ONCE OUTSIDE on the Lane of Eternal Stability, with the gates of the house where but a moment ago he had been undisputed lord and master closed behind him, Pingnan faced cold reality. It was early winter, and the north winds, frost-beaded, chilled him to the bone. He had no money at all, Tien Fong's men having even emptied his pockets of small change. He understood now how the concubines and their children must have felt when he drove them out of the house. However, unlike his former victims, he did not stumble around in aimless confusion. He leaned against a wall and tried to think things out.

Where could he go? Not to any of his agents; Tien Fong had already sent for them, meaning to have an instant and clear-cut division of the properties with Pingshi. His business associates? The hour was late; what lies could he fabricate to induce them to give him welcome? Their curiosity aroused, they would make prompt inquiries, and once the truth was out none would take pity on him. Friends? He had none. Since his return he had wasted no time on making friends; he had only business associates and agents. As for the notables of Yi who had attended the banquet this very night, he was quite certain many of them would not have come at all if he had not announced beforehand that the Governor would be present.

But as he was considering the notables, he suddenly had an inspiration. Of course he had a friend; at least he was sure he could depend on the man in this emergency. And at once, without hesitation, he headed toward the Mission compound.

He had to pound hard at the main gate for some time to rouse the gatekeeper, who was growing old. When the man finally appeared, Ma Pingnan said, "Please admit me to your master. I have urgent business with him."

The gatekeeper, lantern in hand, looked him up and down. "It's strange you should have business with my master—and at this hour! You have not even paid him a courtesy call since your return. You, his pupil in the English language! The only time you've been in this compound was when Governor Ho Fucho summoned you here because of the nasty trick you played on your father's sixth concubine. Since when have you remembered my master? And what business can you have with him? Anyway, he is asleep now, he had a hard day. He has performed several difficult operations and he needs a rest. Come back tomorrow with your business."

The gatekeeper was about to shut the gate again when Pingnan pushed inside.

He said contritely, "Is not this a house of God? Are not its doors always open to penitents? Well, I am a penitent now. Please go and announce me to your master."

The old man shrugged his shoulders and led Pingnan toward the Reverend Dr. Holt's suite. But he mumbled, "Ah, in truth we are not like some people. As the old saying goes, 'If you have a good conscience, what fears need you have even if evil spirits rap at your door in the dead of night?'"

Holt had been awakened by the loud knocks at the main gate. Thinking it was an emergency call, he made himself ready and then hurried out to the courtyard at once. No sooner did Pingnan see the missionary then he fell on his knees.

"Generation-uncle and teacher, I have come like a prodigal son!" he said, bowing his head low.

The Reverend Dr. Holt's breath was taken away for a minute. But he took Pingnan by the arm and said warmly, "Come into my suite, Pingnan, and tell me all about your troubles."

It was half truth and half lie that Pingnan told the missionary. He confessed frankly that he had committed many sins in the past, if not before men, at least before God. He did not blame himself unreservedly, but hinted he was more or less a victim of circumstances—first, because of his early environment, which was his father's responsibility, and later, because of his going to Paris, which he condemned as a city for offering too many temptations to a young man. Without Holt's asking, he admitted he had been cruel to the concubines and their children. At any rate, he was now repentant. Could he but be master of his house again, he would make amends to them.

Then he related—again half truth and half lie—the events of the evening.

Holt was touched, but not taken in. He knew of something which Pingnan could not have suspected. Shortly after Jasmine's rescue, Chi Teh-shan had written Holt a letter thanking him and Widow Lan for what they had done for his wife in Yi and giving an account of what had happened to her afterward. The letter expressed regret that since Widow Lan was a woman and a widow, Chi

204

Teh-shan could not write her directly; but it was accompanied by many gifts for both the missionary and the Lans. The two recipients were as delighted at the news of Jasmine's good fortune as they were shocked at the extent of Pingnan's depravity. But as they were bound by their faith to be charitable, they had kept the knowledge secret.

Then, not long after the compulsory exodus of the concubines and their children, gossip had reached the missionary's ears that Pingnan had had some unfilial responsibility for his father's death. The Reverend Dr. Holt was utterly shocked, and also filled with pity for the women and children who had been turned adrift homeless and penniless. He had asked Ah Wong and his two servants to search for them throughout the city. Some of them had already found their way into the Prefectural Home for the Destitute, which Fucho had established when he was Governor; the rest had vanished. For their sake the Reverend Dr. Holt made a small donation to the Home, but it was a source of regret to him that he had not been able to do more.

Knowing these things, the missionary had thought Pingnan unforgivable. But there Pingnan was, standing before him, full of seeming repentance.

Holt said slowly and not unkindly, "Is that all? Don't you think you have something more on your conscience to confess?"

Pingnan shook his head decisively. "I think that's about all, generation-uncle. Of course, my business practices may have been too sharp and not entirely aboveboard. I learned them from my late revered father and I didn't know any better. But I regret them too, now."

"How about your late father's sixth concubine?" asked Holt. "The one known as Jasmine?"

"Ah," answered Pingnan, looking down his nose shamefacedly, "what a sinful thing I did there! What a beast I was then! If I didn't confess that to you before, it was because I thought you knew about it already. Thanks to your friend Governor Ho Fucho, I learned my lesson. I made amends to the sixth concubine at once —I let her go back to her father free and even paid her travel expenses."

"Have you had any further news of her?"

Pingnan looked at Holt sharply, but saw only a gentle blandness on the clergyman's face.

"No. According to the agent who escorted her, he handed her

over safely to her father, who owns a small shop there. I trust everything's going well with her."

Holt's heart sank, and he bowed his head in silent prayer. When he lifted his eyes again, he said wearily, "What do you want me to do for you, Pingnan?"

"I don't ask much, generation-uncle. Since I no longer have a home to go to, I hope you'll give me lodging for the night."

"That, I'll do," said the missionary. And pointing to the room in which he had once accommodated Johnny Hunt, he added, "You may have that room as long as you wish."

"There's one more favor I must ask, generation-uncle. I can't stay in Yi, or anywhere in this province. Everybody will be so frightened of Tien Fong that no one will give me a job. I must go to the port city tomorrow to look for a living, but I have no money. May I borrow some from you? I shall return it as soon as I can, at whatever interest you may charge."

"It will not be a loan," the American said. "It will be a gift from me to you."

Pingnan was all thanks.

But Holt fixed his eyes on the young man, and went on with noticeable gravity. "There's one thing I want you to do in return. I want you to think about a quotation from Tennyson, a great English poet you may have heard of: 'The world will not believe a man repents; and this wise world of ours is mainly right.' Repentance, Pingnan, must be not only spoken but also felt. It must be supported by deeds. Go to bed now and sleep on that thought."

Pingnan promised faithfully to do so, but as soon as he laid his head on the pillow he fell instantly asleep. He had got all he wanted out of the missionary.

The next morning the Reverend Dr. Holt gave Pingnan a small sum of money. That young man again expressed profuse gratitude and then said his farewell.

"I hope you pondered well over the words I spoke to you last night. Have you nothing more to say to me now?" Holt asked.

Pingnan shook his head. "No. But if the money you have so generously given me does not prove sufficient, may I write to you for further assistance?"

The missionary sighed, and nodded.

After Pingnan's departure, Ah Wong came to Holt. Cocking his head to one side and assuming his most solemn mien, he said ponderously, "I have always known you for a good man. But up till now

I've never known what a gullible fool a good man can turn out to be!"

The Reverend Dr. Holt smiled. "Saith the Lord, 'I am not come to call the righteous, but sinners to repentance.' "

Four

SHORTLY AFTER PINGNAN left for the port city, momentous events took place. Spurred on by declining health and advancing years, President Yuan Shih-kai precipitately threw off all republican pretenses and donned the dragon-robes of Emperor. But in his haste to found a new Dynasty, he underestimated the wishes of the nation. The people might not know much about democracy, but they were dead set against reversion to a monarchy. Banners of revolt were raised in the Southwest, and hundreds of nationally known leaders, men like Ho Fucho, rushed to follow the standard. Universal indignation took hold of China. In the face of these violent eruptions, even Yuan's trusted henchmen quailed. One by one they swiftly shifted their allegiance and declared themselves for the continuation of the Republic.

Amy and Tong Hsi at once recognized which way the wind was blowing. Because of their acknowledged membership in the Kuomintang and their clandestine relationship with Tien Fong, they easily persuaded the Military Governor of that strategic province adjacent to Peking to take a similar step. That was the straw which broke Yuan's back. He died of apoplexy after a reign of eighty-three days.

At Yuan's death, the Vice-president assumed the reins of government in the name of the Republic. Honest but weak, he was not a man qualified to govern the nation in such a crisis. Union and peace seemingly were restored to the country, but actually the Military Governors of the provinces, emboldened by their triumph over Yuan, began to take the law into their own hands. They collected their own taxes and raised their own armies. They obeyed the orders of the Central Government when they wished to, and disregarded them when they did not.

They could not be removed by the Central Government, for they were stronger than it was. Nor would they allow free elections to be held in the territories under their control, as advocated by Dr. Sun Yat-sen, since that would obviously run against their interest. But among themselves, ambitions and rivalries collided; they engaged ceaselessly in feuds and intrigues and warred continuously on one another for more than a decade. President followed President in Peking, each more enfeebled than his predecessor, while the Military Governors became virtual independent tyrants in their respective provinces. It was an age of atavism for China, when the country reverted to chaotic medieval feudalism. It was the Era of the Warlords.

Tien Fong found the situation ideal. He was like a giant fish that glided happily and easily along with "the current of the times." Through his influence, Tong Hsi was able to retain his post as Mayor of the port city, and Amy was delighted that now they could make the most of it. But Sun Yat-sen and the other enlightened leaders of the Kuomintang viewed the whole situation with dismay. They had wanted a Republic. They had one now in name, but in the process of achieving it they had plunged the country into a worse plight than before.

Sun Yat-sen deliberated with his handful of faithfuls, among whom Fucho was always included. To realize their ideals, they would have to subjugate the warlords and unify the nation. But first they needed to gain a foothold to build up their own power. The Kuomintang, without a base, concentrated its efforts on the regions around Canton where Sun Yat-sen had the greatest influence among the masses. But their undertaking met with repeated reverses. The warlords whom they tried to convert were unreliable—even a trusted lieutenant of Dr. Sun's, a long-standing member of the Kuomintang, once he had attained a position of power succumbed to the temptation of becoming a warlord and turned against his own leader and Party. For men like Sun Yat-sen and Ho Fucho, these were the dark days of their revolutionary career.

They needed money badly. Dr. Sun could no longer raise funds from abroad because the overseas Chinese had lost faith in the Revolution. The Kuomintang was reduced to bitter straits. Then reports reached Fucho of Chinese who had moved to Southeast Asia, especially Malaya, where they were making enormous profits dealing in rubber—the price had skyrocketed because of the war in Europe. Fucho saw no reason why he could not succeed at the same game. He consulted with Dr. Sun, and before long he and Delicate

208

Blossom and Li-hwa set sail for Malaya. There, he sold his wife's jewelry and bought a rubber plantation. They worked hard to make it a success, for he wanted to make money, big money, and he needed to make it quickly enough to return and finance a revolution for the Kuomintang.

In the meantime, conditions inside China grew even worse. Except for a very limited number of Chinese, like the warlords and their parasites, only foreigners benefited from the chaos. Foreigners supplied the warlords with munitions and ran contraband goods with their collusion. They rendered all sorts of unscrupulous services, and seldom failed to amass fabulous fortunes. China soon came to be known as an "adventurers' paradise." And of all the adventurers, none was more venturesome and successful than Johnny Hunt.

Of course the foreign Concessions also benefited immeasurably. Protected by their home governments, immune from internal wars, they were the only oases of seeming order and safety in a vast desert of disorder and turbulence. Not only did millions of people pour into them for refuge, but also the wealth of the hinterland. The more improverished the interior became, the more enriched were the coastal trading ports. The more the Concessions prospered at the expense of the whole nation, the more the foreigners looked down on the Chinese as a race unfit to govern themselves. Although Chinese intellectuals were helplessly infuriated at the predicament of the nation, the secret societies which used the Concessions as bases of operation could not have been more pleased. Thus Chi Teh-shan, alias Old Head, notwithstanding his humble origins and questionable activities, became publicly acknowledged as the leading citizen of the big port city in the North.

During all this time, the common people were torn by wars, trampled by oppression, crushed by taxes and extortion. Those who could not afford to escape to the Concessions stayed on the land and bore their burden the best they could. The daring and the discontented took to brigandage. They prowled and plundered, preying upon the weak, and in turn were themselves prayed upon by those stronger than they. For the people at large, the world had indeed become like the one described by Brother Ox: "The big fish eat the little ones, the little ones eat water-insects, the water-insects eat mud."

2

BUT NONE OF these catastrophes had yet befallen China at the time Ta-kong was recovering from the wounds he received in the assault. His injuries were much more serious than the doctor had at first thought, and full convalescence was long delayed.

Ta-kong remained with the Chis. Jasmine cared for him as though he were her son, and Old Head treated him as his Close-Door-Disciple, though the initiation ceremonies had to be postponed because of Ta-kong's health. His parents made special trips from Yi, but he remained in the port city because it offered better medical facilities. Thus he missed hearing that Ma Pingnan had been driven out of Yi.

On Old Head's advice, Ta-kong had kept his mishap a secret from all except his sworn brothers, and the two of them visited him often. The Chis showed particular interest in Yuwen because he was Widow Lan's son; Mistress Chow was always especially glad to see him. But soon summer recess arrived and Yuwen had to leave for home. Li Chien, however, stayed on at the University to keep his Big Brother company. Ta-kong was grateful, but he never revealed to either of his sworn brothers that he was to join the secret Society and become Old Head's Close-Door-Disciple.

During his long convalescence, he had an unexpected visitor who came to see him quite frequently. This was Chang Fa-foo. When the man first called, Ta-kong did not wish to see him. He had suspected him, ever since Chang had received the students' delegation, of having a hand in the beating. But as he thought about it, he remembered the gleam of warning in Chang's eye and realized the man had tried to save him.

Ta-kong found Chang Fa-foo interesting company. Despite his age, Chang seemed to possess a youthful idealism that was appealing to an adolescent. He told Ta-kong he always preferred the companionship of the young; young minds were open and unformed, and could be kneaded with a view to the future, whereas old minds as a rule were rutted in dogma and prejudice. Chang regaled Ta-kong with exciting inside accounts of politics, and with stimulating analyses of the personalities involved—not unlike the stories of *The Three Kingdoms* and *The Tales of the Marshes*.

Once Ta-kong asked Chang Fa-foo about his uncle Fucho. After a moment's reflection, Chang answered, "He is no doubt a good man. He has retained his idealism, but he has too many scruples. He doesn't seem to understand that in order to achieve a big ideal you may have to sacrifice many small ideals. And his idealism is altogether too well-defined, all cut and dried. He never changes his ideals. Unlike him, I seldom stick to my ideals. I'm perpetually in search of better ones, and that's why I prefer young company to old."

Another time Ta-kong inquired: "Since you have such a low opinion of Tong Hsi, why do you work for him as his Secretary-General?"

Chang Fa-foo smiled. "You have much to learn in life. Even an idealist has to live, you know. As a delegate to the National Congress, a known member of the Kuomintang, I couldn't even get out of Peking without Yuan Shih-kai's permission. But here, as Tong Hsi's Secretary-General, I'm much freer to continue my search for higher ideals."

The answer satisfied Ta-kong. But the truth was somewhat less noble: Chang had secured the post in return to his promise to say nothing about the affair between Amy and Yuan's son.

"Tell me then, Uncle Chang," said Ta-kong, "who gave the orders to have me so badly beaten up?"

Chang Fa-foo averted his grayish face. "I don't know for certain. Yuan's spies are everywhere, and your activities in the University must have been observed. I suspected what might happen and tried to warn you in the interview, but you didn't heed me."

Chang had not told a tenth of what he knew. Amy and Tong Hsi, of course, had been responsible for the attack, not so much because Ta-kong was a fiery student opposed to President Yuan's dynastic ambitions as because he was the nephew of Ho Fucho. President Yuan had been much displeased at the ex-Governor's escape, and Amy and Tong Hsi had Ta-kong beaten in order to convince the President they had had no hand in aiding Fucho. Chang Fa-foo also knew about all the Tongs' other connections with Yuan Shih-kai, and for days had wrestled with the idea of reporting their betrayal of the Kuomintang to Dr. Sun. But the future of the Kuomintang did not look very bright just then. In Chang's own words, he was not pleased with the way his Party was going, and was searching for a more satisfying "ideal."

When Ta-kong was fully recovered, he was duly initiated by Chi Teh-shan as his Close-Door-Disciple. Then he returned to school, but because of his long illness he was demoted one year. This pleased Ta-kong because now he was in the same class as Li Chien.

Shortly after he began school, Ta-kong wrote a note to Yin Mei-yin inviting her to a Sunday luncheon with his two sworn brothers. He half-expected he would meet with a rebuff, for girls of marriageable age did not mix freely with young men. To his delight Mei-yin promptly accepted the invitation.

As was natural with a reunion of three sworn brothers, luncheon conversation turned to a discussion of *The Three Kingdoms* and *The Tales of the Marshes*. Li Chien was noisiest in showing off his knowledge, but Mei-yin surprisingly put in a word or two that indicated her studies of the novels had been even more penetrating. Only Yuwen remained silent.

"You've read the two books as closely as any of us," Ta-kong said to him. "What's happened to your enthusiasm about them?"

"Big Brother," answered Yuwen, "I must confess my excitement has waned. I read them again during vacation and found them different from what I used to think. The authors never intended to commend the deceit and craft of their characters, but to condemn it. This comes through distinctly if you read between the lines. And there's a moral lesson in the books which I'm afraid we've all missed."

"Bah!" exclaimed Li Chien. "That's just like you, Third Brother. You see a moral everywhere. You've been too influenced by the spirit of your religion and your man of God, the Reverend Dr. Ho-Lo-Teh."

Yuwen's face reddened. Acting as the Big Brother, Ta-kong sought to make peace between the two.

"As I see it," he said, "there's no real difference between your views. The practice of deceit and craft, when considered independently, must be unequivocally condemned. When they're directed toward a good purpose, then they may be condoned. One must have idealism, but one shouldn't have too many scruples. In real life, if one wants to achieve a big ideal he must be prepared to sacrifice some small ones. If there's any moral in those books, it's that."

But Yuwen stuck to his guns. "I beg to differ, Big Brother. What is idealism but a compound of ideals? How can there be a big ideal unless it's supported by lesser ones? Idealism is whole and indivisible. We talk about Righteousness. Can we fulfill our righteous purpose by committing unrighteous deeds ourselves? We talk about Justice. Can we be called just when we stoop to injustices? We talk about Humanity as the supreme goal. Can we reach it through a short cut paved with inhumanities? I'm afraid our minds have been poisoned by what that execrable king said: 'I'd sooner deceive the whole world than let anyone in the world deceive me.' The true idealist is precisely the opposite—he'd sooner let the world deceive him than permit himself to deceive anyone. That's the real moral the authors wanted to point out."

Both Ta-kong and Li Chien were surprised. Quick as his wits were, Ta-kong could not think of a rebuttal, but Yin Mei-yin spoke up.

"All authors are influenced by the prevailing thoughts of their times. The writers of these two novels were first influenced by the conventions and proprieties that had lasted for centuries. They wanted to picture society at its darkest and truest, but they couldn't completely shake off the effects of those conventions and proprieties. Second, they were influenced by a fear of the powers that be. The Dynasties always upheld those conventions and proprieties for their own good—to make the people more ductile and thus easier to govern. The authors were afraid that unless they put into their writing a traditional moral interpretation of events, their books might be banned and they themselves persecuted. That's how morals found their way unnecessarily into the books.

"As the world is now, I see nothing but wrong and evil as the two authors must have seen it, and I feel exactly as Omar Khayyam must have felt. You've all read his *Rubaiyat*. Most of it's rubbish, but I like one passage:

> " 'Ah Love, could you and I with Him conspire
> To grasp this sorry Scheme of Things entire
> Would we not shatter it to bits—and then
> Remold it nearer to the Heart's Desire!'

"But Omar too was influenced by the beliefs of his times. He was a Moslem and he believed in a Him. I don't. No offense, Yuwen, but if there had really been a Him, how could He have created such a mess as the world is, was, and has always been? If He is truly the Creater of all, then He is only a bungler and I have no use for Him whatever. Girl as I am, life for me has only one dream —I want to grasp this entire sorry Scheme of Things and shatter it to bits! To remold it can come later; I don't yet know my Heart's Desire. But if I could, I would certainly shatter the present world. If we could bring the authors of those books back to life, I'm sure they'd tell you this is the only moral they wanted to convey."

The girl's three listeners were astounded. Li Chien was particularly enthusiastic; he felt he could not have expressed his own sentiments better. Ta-kong looked on with envy. Why could he not have thought out these matters so trenchantly? Only Yuwen wondered what the girl's background must have been to make her think such dire and terrible thoughts?

But all agreed on the woes of China. Its sorry plight was born of two evils, they felt—the Feudalism of the warlords and the Imperialism of the foreigners. How could they overthrow these two yokes? How could they shatter them to bits?

Yuwen was of the opinion that for the time being they could only watch the situation and study their books. They were not yet mature or wise enough; they could afford to wait.

Li Chien said that was all right, but they should have their lines of action charted in advance. In order to defeat foreign Imperialism, they must first have a unified nation. And in order to unify the nation, they must resort to force. However, he thought the ways of the Kuomintang impractical: they wanted to stir up the people to revolt against the warlords, but the warlords were too deeply entrenched in power. The most feasible method, so far as he could see, was for the intellectuals of the nation—that is, themselves (Mei-yin excepted of course, since she was a girl)—to bore at the warlords from within. After their graduation, they should enlist under the warlords' banners; with their education, and with diligent application of the craft they had learned from the two novels, it would not be too difficult to outwit the present warlords, who were mostly unlettered, and soon gain a position of strength. The rest would be comparatively easy. They would sweep across the country like conquerors of old and drive the foreigners back to the sea.

Li Chien put forth the proposition proudly, but these thoughts were in fact Ta-kong's. Li Chien, under the Big Brother's influence, had accepted them *in toto* and taken them for his own. Ta-kong beamed on his Second Brother with approval.

"What do you think of it, Mei-yin?" he asked, turning to the girl for whose incisive intellect he had a deep respect.

The girl smiled with her triangle-shaped eyes. "I'm not qualified to be a warlord, as Li Chien has pointed out. But I don't think his way will work at all. You greatly underestimate the warlords. Some of them are gifted with an innate cunning, and all of them are more experienced in matters of craft and deceit than any of you.

214

Though many of them are illiterate, they know the stories of *The Three Kingdoms* and *The Tales of the Marshes* as well as we do. These books are, as Yuwen would say, their Bible. Besides, all of them distrust intellectuals."

"Then how, in your opinion, can we overthrow the warlords?" asked Ta-kong.

"By fighting foreign Imperialism first."

"How can we do that?" demanded Li Chien incredulously. "It's like the old saying: 'You aim to go to the north, but you turn the face of your horse toward the south.' "

Mei-yin replied, not looking at Li Chien but at Ta-kong: "Ask your Big Brother. He'll understand. The only way to overthrow the warlords is to rally the whole nation against them. But if you make your purpose known before you're ready, the warlords will be alarmed and will unite against you. You'd be stamped out by their combined force in no time. That's where the Kuomintang makes its mistake. It harps incessantly on their misrule and stirs up the people against them; that puts the warlords on their guard and the Kuomintang can't make any headway. But if you start by agitating against foreign Imperialism, it will be a different story. The interests of the foreign powers are so divided that they find it difficult to unite in concerted action. The foreigners are, after all, on alien soil; their governments may be strong, but they themselves are outnumbered. They wouldn't dare undertake ruthless suppression like the warlords. So, speaking relatively, it's much safer to stir people up against foreigners than against warlords.

"If you have the courage to continue to agitate against them openly, fearlessly, untiringly and systematically, the people will follow you. In their present mood, the masses long to find a scapegoat for all their miseries. It's good for their souls to pin the blame on the foreigners. If you take such a stand, you'll soon be hailed as national heroes, and the people will rally to support you. In the meantime, the warlords will be off their guard. Why, the general sentiment of the nation may even compel them to back you. But once you've reached a position of sufficient strength, what you want to do next is up to you.

"Oh, how I wish I were a man. Then I'd know how to plan my life!"

3

TWO YEARS PASSED uneventfully for Ta-kong. When he was a junior, he took a course in French. Though the professor was not much of a pedagogue, he had a good command of the language he taught, but he spoke Chinese with the accent of Yi. He called himself Nan Ping and had a sallow face and narrow piggish eyes. When Ta-kong first saw him he felt sure he had met him somewhere before. But when he asked, the professor denied he had ever been in Yi and said he came from a distant northeastern province whose dialect was much the same. Ta-kong accepted the explanation, not recognizing that the teacher was none other than his neighbor Ma Pingnan. Following the example of Tien Fong, alias Fong Tienpa, he had changed his name. Though Nan Ping was the reverse of Pingnan, he had been careful to choose entirely different Chinese characters.

During those two years Ta-kong saw Chang Fa-foo frequently. They no longer met at the Chis', but the older man often invited him out to dinner and sometimes took him to his apartment, a very comfortable one inside the Concession. Chang was apparently not married. Out of curiosity, Ta-kong once asked him the reason.

"Take it from me," replied Chang Fa-foo, "women are born hindrances to a man's search for higher ideals."

Ta-kong was perplexed at the remark. He thought of his aunt, Delicate Blossom, and of Yin Mei-yin. His sense of respect for his aunt forbade him to talk about her, but he told Chang of Mei-yin. He extolled her marvelous intellect, giving in detail her views on how the warlords could be overthrown by agitating against foreign Imperialism.

Chang Fa-foo listened with deep interest. When Ta-kong finished, he said meditatively, "Well, I may have to take it back in this instance. Says a great French novelist, 'All generalizations are false —including this one.' I'm not the only man who makes such mistakes. A seeker of truth and higher ideals always must be prepared to re-shape his views. But," he continued with a twinkle in his eye, "if you're thinking of marrying the girl, my boy, my advice still holds good. You know the old proverb, 'When a hen crows instead of a cock, it bodes ill for the house.'"

Ta-kong protested vigorously that his interest in Mei-yin was purely intellectual. But, as a matter of fact, he saw her more frequently than he did Chang Fa-foo. Almost every week end, except

216

his sworn brothers and take Mei-yin along. He treated her like a
when he had to attend on Old Head as a disciple, he would gather
boy rather than a girl.

One day Yuwen took him aside.

"Big Brother, do you think it wise to have Mei-yin with us all
the time?"

"Why not? She's stimulating company."

"She is that, all right," conceded Yuwen. "But I think her ideas
are extreme and ill-balanced. And there's something else."

"You must be thinking of the old proprieties, Third Brother.
They're all gone now, and a good riddance too. I admit Mei-yin was
unique at first, in associating with the opposite sex, but this last
year has seen quite a change. Many girls her age are taking to
mixing socially with boys. So what's wrong in having her with us?"

Yuwen responded seriously, "When a Chinese girl goes out with
a boy, she doesn't think of it as merely social. She's likely to consider herself almost engaged to be married to the boy."

Ta-kong laughed. "I'm sure Mei-yin is above that. Besides, there
are always three of us together. She can't possibly consider herself
engaged to all three of us at the same time."

"But there's the trouble," persisted Yuwen. "It's you who have
always invited her. Tell me, have you any serious intentions toward
her?"

"Of course not. I have a good deal of respect for her intellect,
but she doesn't attract me in any other way. She's the last girl on
earth I'd want for a wife. Besides, a wife is usually a hindrance to
a man who has ambitions to fulfill and ideals to attain. I shan't get
married for a long time."

"That makes it even worse," said Yuwen gravely. "Though you
may not have serious intentions toward her, she may have toward
you."

"Since when has my little Third Brother become an expert on
a young girl's heart?" said Ta-kong, laughing.

"Well"—Yuwen was sober—"many a time I've caught a glimpse
of her eying you, and not in pure and simple friendship. Please
stop seeing her. I don't want you to get hurt in any way, Big
Brother."

Ta-kong stopped laughing. "I think you're imagining things. But
I'll do this. Hereafter we three will take turns inviting Mei-yin.
Because I am Big Brother, and have more money than either you
or Second Brother, I'll stand all expenses, the same as before. But

that way she can't form any mistaken notion whatever, and you'll have nothing to fear."

This procedure was acted upon, but Mei-yin did not seem to notice the difference. She came to their parties as before and conducted herself as usual. Since the matter had been brought to Ta-kong's attention, he could not help surreptitiously observing Mei-yin. Whenever their glances met, he thought he caught a gleam of wistful tenderness in her odd-shaped eyes.

He felt no response, he did not care for her. Only his vanity was flattered.

Yuwen had another reason for not pressing his demand that they stop seeing Mei-yin. Unknown to the others, he had just learned that the Reverend Dr. Holt had been successful in obtaining a scholarship for him in a university in the United States. He knew that the moment of announcing his good fortune also would be most propitious for a forceful admonition to Ta-kong.

Sure enough, once the sworn brothers heard the news, Ta-kong gave a special party in celebration—limited, of course, to the four of them. After the party was over and they had seen Mei-yin back to her college, the three boys lingered in a nearby park. Yuwen was more than usually pensive, rehearsing what he intended to say. Li Chien attributed it to the sorrow of parting, and spoke up cheerily.

"Don't take it so much to heart, Third Brother. Our separation is temporary—only a matter of a few years. Remember our oath? Although we were not born together, we have vowed to die together."

"Yes," answered Yuwen with a sigh. "I'm wondering whether we can ever fulfill that sacred oath. The real world, I'm afraid, is different from what we think. When we finish our education, we may each have to pursue a separate life that takes us as far away from one another as this trip is taking me now."

"Nonsense!" declared Li Chien. "I shall stick to Big Brother like fish to water, and when you come back you'll do the same. We'll fight shoulder to shoulder to overthrow the warloads and the Imperialists. We will build our country again!"

"In the old days, when good friends parted," Yuwen said, "the custom was to make the occasion very solemn and to deliver farewell advice to each other. I'd like to follow that example now, and give you each a piece of my mind, if I may."

"Certainly," agreed his two friends.

Yuwen addressed Li Chien first, beginning formally, "Second

Brother, you cannot know how much esteem and affection I have for you. You have a nobility of soul that makes you, in many ways, not unlike the War God of *The Three Kingdoms*. But you also have his faults. You're too outspoken, too impetuous, too single-minded, too trustful of others. You talk of cunning, but you have no cunning. You tell everyone you want to use craft, but you're incapable of craftiness. This is your nature, and I love and respect you for it—but if you're not careful it may be your undoing."

"I'm grateful for your advice," Li Chien said. "I know those are my shortcomings and I'll always treasure your warning."

Yuwen turned to Ta-kong. "As for you, Big Brother, it's useless to say how devoted I am to you. What fault can I find with you? Your intentions are noble, you have many different talents. You're born to be a leader, and you're determined to be one. As sure as day follows night, you'll go far in this world; but there is one thing I must say to you—please don't associate with Mei-yin any more."

Ta-kong smiled. "If you still think I may want her for my wife, just put the idea out of your head."

"No, not that. So far as that's concerned, I'm convinced she means nothing to you. In the long run, she would get hurt, rather than you. It's just that I don't like her outlook on life. It's evil. You may be annoyed with me, but let me quote a word from Christ, 'I am come not to destroy, but to fulfill.' To destroy is nothing; to fulfill is everything. Yet to destroy is easy, and to fulfill is hard. There's so much in you, Big Brother—so much fulfillment you can offer this world. But Mei-yin thinks only of destroying; if you associate with her constantly you can't help being influenced by her. He who plays with fire will get burnt and he who touches pitch will be defiled. That could spoil all my hopes for you and even lead you to your own ruin in the end. For my sake, Big Brother, please keep away from her."

"Have no fear, Third Brother," Ta-kong said, deeply touched. "I will not disappoint you. I trust I have sense enough not to let anyone destroy me." Then he added, by way of amused after-thought, "Except perhaps myself."

After Yuwen's departure, however, Ta-kong did not heed his advice. He and Li Chien went out in Mei-yin's company as steadily as they had before.

It was toward the close of their senior year in school that Ta-kong at last found an opportunity to put into practice Mei-yin's idea of demonstrating against foreign Imperialism. The First World War had ended and the powers were meeting at Versailles to negotiate a peace treaty. The Japanese were demanding openly that all special rights and concessions which the now vanquished Germany had formerly wrested from China be transferred to them as a reward for their participation in the war. Most of the Allies—since it cost them nothing—were willing to agree to the proposal, but when this news broke, a feeling of dismay swept China. The country had been emasculated by the warloads, the Central Government was impotent beyond description. Thus, in the face of this new Imperialism, the nation was helpless.

But Ta-kong—whose views were heartily endorsed by Chang Fa-foo—and Mei-yin thought differently: the time was ripe. While Mei-yin stirred up the girls in her college, Ta-kong began inciting his own schoolmates. The youth of China were already partially aroused, their feeling of indignation spontaneous and universal. But Ta-kong and Mei-yin bent their energies toward a fixed purpose and whipped up the sentiments to fury. Under the joint sponsorship of their two schools, a students' association was formed consisting of all the student bodies in the big port city. A Central Committee was elected, and it was only a matter of course that Ta-kong be chosen Chairman, Yin Mei-yin Vice-Chairman, and Li Chien a member of the committee.

This time they knew better than to be content with a mere presentation of their protests. They were determined to flex their new muscles, to test their abilities in organization and agitation, and they put forth a daring proposition to the Central Committee: a mass meeting of all the students, to be followed by a giant parade starting from the very heart of the city and winding up in front of the Mayor's office. It would be a massive demonstration of the strength and unity of the students, a mighty display of the latent power of China.

Objections were boisterously shouted down, and the motion was carried. Amidst loud acclamations, Ta-kong was elected to direct the whole program, and Mei-yin and Li Chien to be his chief deputies.

It was a proud moment for Ta-kong as he addressed the huge assemblage of students. They were more than twenty thousand strong, overflowing the public square in the heart of the city and jamming the adjacent streets and beyond. As far as Ta-kong could see, faces were turned up to listen to him. He felt an exultation he had never known. This was life! This was where he must always be . . .

4

TA-KONG BEGAN WITH the speech which had been drafted by the whole committee, but after a few bursts of applause from the crowd he brushed aside the prepared discourse. His improvised words bristled with hints of fire and sword; he whipped his feelings so that they rose to a furious crescendo. He not only called for the withdrawal of the Japanese demands, but pledged himself and his whole generation to drive the Japanese back to the sea, leaving not a man on Chinese soil. Theirs was to dare and do! Theirs was to restore the glory of China or perish in the attempt!

The response was terrific. For a second after the dramatic end of his speech, there was a stillness in the vast square, heavy and frightening. Then the crowd broke into maddened applause. They brandished or threw their banners frantically in the air. They cheered themselves hoarse, rendering him homage.

He turned to the committee on the rostrum. Mei-yin was staring at him open-mouthed. Ta-kong felt a glow of triumph. Good; let her know there are things in this world only a man can do.

The parade began. Lashed to frenzy, the students shouted and sang wildly as they marched through streets lined with hundreds of thousands of bystanders. It was an unprecedented scene. As the students yelled their slogans and flourished their banners, many of the people wept openly.

At the head of the procession marched the Central Committee, and at the head of the Central Committee marched Ta-kong. He was flanked on one side by Mei-yin and on the other by Li Chien, who bore the largest standard of the parade.

As the three strode forward, Li Chien could not suppress his admiration. "Big Brother, you have outdone yourself today. What a speech! Did you discard the prepared one on purpose?"

"Oh, no," answered Ta-kong with self-satisfaction. "Today I discovered a great secret—the secret of how to handle a mob. Never be tame, always be bold. Never be conservative, always be radical. When I started out with the prepared speech, I noticed that where-ever it was bold and radical, I got applause. Wherever it was tame and conservative, I did not. So I decided to proceed on my own."

By now the procession had arrived in front of the municipal building, and the students assembled in ranks and demanded that Tong Hsi come out and receive their protest in person. The Mayor answered through an emissary that he would welcome a delegation at his office. This Ta-kong refused. Then Tong Hsi sent out his Secretary-General, Chang Fa-foo, but Ta-kong told his friend that the students wanted no one but the Mayor himself.

Half an hour passed, during which Ta-kong again harangued the crowd, pointing out the incompetence of the Government in general and the discourtesy of Tong Hsi in particular. The students raised such a din that Tong Hsi was at last forced to appear.

His pasty face was ashen, his porcine body trembling. When he spoke, he mumbled and stuttered, his voice so low that Ta-kong had to repeat his replies to the crowd. How could such a craven ever have been a revolutionary? Young and limited in his experience, Ta-kong had no idea how position, wealth, and soft living can weaken stamina and corrode the soul.

Ta-kong had no pity on him. He was not outrageously disrespectful, but by gestures and insinuations he made the man look a greater fool than he actually was. Before the eyes of all the students, Ta-kong wanted to expose the caliber of men who were at the helm of Government and to suggest what a contrast his own leadership would be when his time came. Tantalized and browbeaten by turns, Tong Hsi accepted everything Ta-kong said, without question and with servility. The students roared with delight.

At last, Ta-kong permitted the Mayor to escape back to his office. Then he turned to his audience again.

"Fellow students, you have seen for yourselves an example of the type of men who now hold high positions in our Government. Can we entrust the holy task of guarding our nation to such feeble and fumbling dunderheads? No, we cannot. We have only ourselves to rely on—we, the younger generation, the future masters of China! We cannot depend on others. None will fight the battle for us. None will defend our heritage for us. It is only in ourselves that we can find hope and strength—in our unity, in our solidarity, in our willingness to sacrifice everything, including our lives, for the land of our ancestors. This is not the end of our fight, it is the beginning. We must march on!"

He felt they had reached a fitting climax for the parade, and was waiting for a last ovation from the crowd before issuing orders to disband, when suddenly he heard a voice shouting shrilly through a megaphone at his side. It was Mei-yin.

"Fellow students! You heard what our chairman said. The fight is only begun. We must march on. We cannot disperse now and call it a day. We cannot be satisfied with merely registering our protest with our Government. We must face the enemy. We must go to the Japanese themselves and show our defiance. Onward, fellow students! To the Japanese Concession!"

Segments of the throng responded with turbulent fervor, but more of the students remained silent, perplexed. The suggestion was not within their original plans. Mei-yin spoke again, her voice ringing with passion:

"Are you afraid, fellow students? Are you men, or are you boys? Or should I say—worse than boys—are you girls? I am a girl, but I'm not afraid. Are you so chicken-hearted that you're not as brave as a girl? Onward, fellow students, if you are men! Onward, to the Japanese Concession!"

The mob, which consisted mostly of boys, could not suffer the taunt. They echoed back wildly and recklessly, "To the Japanese Concession! To the Japanese Concession!"

Ta-kong, vexed at first by Mei-yin's unauthorized intrusion, soon saw what a bold and imaginative stroke hers was. He did not intend to let her steal his thunder. With a wave of his hand, he motioned the assemblage to silence.

"Onward, men!" he roared. "We'll lead you!"

He joined arms with Mei-yin and Li Chien, and the three of them marched forward. Sheepishly the other members of the Central Committee followed, and the crowd stomped stormily along behind.

They came to the wide street that led to the Japanese Concession, and then arrived at the border of the Concession itself. The Japanese had piled sandbags and erected an impenetrable barbed-wire fence across the street. Inside the barricade a platoon of armed Japanese soldiers had been posted. Outside stood two stony Japanese sentries, firmly holding their rifles with bayonets fixed, ready for instant charge.

Ta-kong halted the march some three paces from the sentries and waited until the entire procession pressed behind him, jamming the street. The mob had now swollen beyond counting, for the students had been joined by thousands and thousands of onlookers. From every window of every building along the street, men and women and children watched tensely.

223

Ta-kong shouted through his megaphone and the mob fell momentarily silent. Then, at another order, they thundered in unison:

"Down with Japanese Imperalism! Down with Japanese Imperialism!"

Nothing can be more terrifying than a stupendous volume of human voices concentrated in an explosion of hate. The sound shook not only the near-by buildings but the hearts of all who heard.

When the last reverberations of the terrible roar died down, Ta-kong gave a signal for the students to sing. They sang songs of love for their country, songs of hate for the enemy, battle songs of the heroes of old, and new songs they had composed for the occasion. And intermittently and violently they shouted their slogan:

"Down with Japanese Imperialism! Down with Japanese Imperialism!"

But the frustrating barricade was before them; the Japanese soldiers stood guard and they could not advance. Suddenly, Mei-yin darted forward and tried to pass through the narrow passage at the center of the barricade. One of the Japanese sentries barred her way, and there was a brief unequal struggle.

The soldier threw the girl brutally to the ground. Enraged, Ta-kong bolted to her rescue, and the other sentry lunged from behind, his bayonet aimed directly at Ta-kong's back. Li Chien sped forward, his right hand still grasping the huge standard, and shoved his left arm between Ta-kong's body and the on-thrusting bayonet. The sharp weapon pierced his arm, and he fell with a groan. Then the platoon inside the barricade fired.

Pandemonium broke, and people fled in all directions. They milled and stampeded, uttering cries of fear and pain. But, unconscious of the uproar and of his own danger, Ta-kong dropped by the side of Li Chien and bent over him.

"Second Brother, you saved my life! Are you badly hurt?"

Li Chien made a gallant attempt at a smile. "My wound is not serious. Take care of yourself, Big Brother!"

Fury seized Ta-kong. He picked up Li Chien's fallen standard, and holding it aloft, rose before the two Japanese sentries.

"Down with Japanese Imperialism!" he shouted in their faces. "Down with Japanese Imperialism!"

The soldiers were no less frightened than the mob they had

tried to scatter. At an order from the officer in charge, the two sentries withdrew inside the barricade. The narrow gap in the middle was swiftly closed by additional sandbags, and the soldiers stood firmly behind with loaded guns. But they did not fire.

Ta-kong's brave example had a calming effect on the mob, and gradually quiet and some measure of order were restored. In the meantime Mei-yin had resumed her position at Ta-kong's side and many of the members of the Central Committee had also returned. The first-aid squads, which the students had previously organized now went into action. They picked up the wounded, gave the less injured what treatment they could, and carried away the more serious cases on stretchers. When Li Chien was borne off, he waved his good arm to Ta-kong and yelled, "My wound is nothing. Take care of yourself, Big Brother!"

There were no longer many onlookers. Those in the street had fled; the shops and houses on both sides had closed their windows and doors tight. But the students stayed on. Following Ta-kong's leadership, they continued to shout their slogans and sing their songs until the hour grew late and the Japanese brought up reinforcements. At last, after a consultation with the Central Committee, Ta-kong gave the order to disperse.

He and Mei-yin together went at once to see Li Chien at the hospital. Neither mentioned what had occurred, beyond a remark made by Mei-yin that Ta-kong was to remember: "You know, if we had really set our minds and planned the whole thing in detail, I believe we could have taken the Japanese Concession with our bare hands, by the sheer force of numbers!"

Two onlookers and one student had been killed by Japanese fire, and a child trampled to death in the stampede. Some three hundred persons, students and others, suffered either minor or major injuries. But overnight Ta-kong had become a national hero— a symbol of the fiery and indomitable spirit of China's youth.

The incident had widespread consequences. The example of the students in the port city was followed by student bodies in all the larger cities of China. Protests, parades, and demonstrations against the Japanese took place throughout the country. China's delegates to the Peace Conference at Versailles refused to sign the treaty which included the Japanese terms, and the Japanese were forced to drop their demands.

But Japan lodged a vehement protest with the Central Government in Peking about the incidents, especially the one in the port city. Using as a pretext the necessity of appeasing Japanese feelings to make greater gains in diplomatic negotiations, the Central Government dismissed Mayor Tong Hsi from his post, blaming him for having mishandled the whole business. All the wiles and intrigues of Amy and Tong Hsi were of no avail against this combination of circumstances. But the artful and astute Amy at least made their exit an honorable one. They held a press conference before their departure, and condemned the action of the Peking Government as cowardly and unpatriotic. And they further asserted that since a principal aim of their party, the Kuomintang, was to fight Imperialism, their sympathies had been with the students' movement all the time. Thus, when they went south and joined Dr. Sun again, they were immediately taken to the bosom of the Kuomintang and hailed as martyrs to the cause.

The incident also produced a curious side effect. Shortly after the bloody demonstration and some time before Tong Hsi's dismissal, Chang Fa-foo proposed to Amy that she use her influence to get him appointed Chancellor of the University. The students there evidently had got quite out of hand; it would be to the Mayor's advantage to have his own man watching over the young hotheads. The proposition sounded plausible to Amy; besides, she was in no position to refuse a favor to Chang, who knew too much about her affairs. She pulled the wires, and in due time Chang received the appointment.

However, Chang Fa-foo never would have been able to assume his post had it not been for Ta-kong. At first, the students were unwilling to accept him as Chancellor because they regarded him as Tong Hsi's stooge. But Ta-kong told them Chang was no ordinary official but an idealist, that he liked nothing better than progressive ideas and youthful companionship, and, moreover, he was his own personal friend. After that, Chang was inducted into the office without opposition.

By all logic of Chinese politics, Chang Fa-foo should have been displaced as soon as his principal backers, Amy and Tong Hsi, were gone. But now the University was considered such a hornet's nest that no one else wanted to be its chancellor. Thus was Chang Fa-foo allowed to retain his position for many years.

Immediately after taking office, he summoned Ta-kong and told him how valuable he had been. "You are to graduate this

226

summer, but when school opens again in autumn I want you to serve as my personal assistant. I need you to maintain contact with the students."

Ta-kong thanked him for the offer but said that he was thinking of going to the United States for graduate studies and to join his Third Brother, Lan Yuwen.

"That's a mere waste of time," said Chang Fa-foo. "You will learn a lot about America there, but nothing about China. I went to Japan when I was a young man, like your Uncle Fucho. But I've never been able to put what I learned to good use here. And mind you, Japan is much more like China than the United States is, or any other Western nation. You're a born idealist—you have great ambitions and capabilities. If you want to realize them fully, take my advice and stay in China. Study our own conditions and try to influence our own people."

Ta-kong was swayed by the argument, but not fully convinced. "I'll think it over. But if I accept your offer, will you try to secure a position in the University for my Second Brother, Li Chien? His family is not well-to-do, and he can't afford to go abroad. I was going to take him to the States with me if I could get my family to finance the trip for both of us. If I can't, then he'll need a job badly."

"Whenever a vacancy occurs at the University I'm pestered by hundreds of applicants, who all come with high recommendations. But if you agree to my proposal, I think there may be a position as assistant librarian available for Li Chien."

"Well then," said Ta-kong, "I'll give you my answer before the summer vacation is over."

The final examinations approached, and Ta-kong applied himself diligently to his studies. This was actually not necessary, because Chang Fa-foo had adopted the policy of making the examinations very easy in order to ingratiate himself with the students. Even Li Chien, who had spent much time in a hospital nursing his wounded arm, came off with flying colors.

At last the commencement exercises were over and they had received their diplomas. Yin Mei-yin had also graduated from her college, so the three of them were in the mood to celebrate with a special dinner party that evening. Then in the afternoon a telegram brought Ta-kong word that his father and mother were critically ill with cholera.

Though Ta-kong had been taken away from his parents in early childhood, and since his grandfather's death maintained close personal relations only with his uncle Fucho and his aunt Delicate Blossom, he still had a deep sense of Filial Piety. He wanted to hurry back to Yi, but there was no train available until the next morning.

Cheerlessly he went to the party with Li Chien, and, being worried and silent, failed to notice that Mei-yin was also acting very strangely. She was not only as quiet as he, but her air of gloom bordered almost on despair.

When they walked Mei-yin back to her college, however, she suddenly became very talkative. What was more, she did something she had never done before. Inserting herself between the two sworn brothers, she laid a hand on the arm of each. Ta-kong paid no attention but Li Chien, gallant as any Western cavalier, said that although the arm Mei-yin was holding was still bandaged, he was glad she could put it to such good use.

They came to a lamppost, and Mei-yin exclaimed that Li Chien's bandage had broken loose. He halted to straighten it, telling them not to wait, and Mei-yin half pushed, half led Ta-kong along a short cut toward her dormitory, which they had never taken before. It was a narrow path screened with clusters of shrubs and overshadowed with tall trees. Reaching a secluded spot, Mei-yin stopped. She took Ta-kong by both hands and lifted up her face toward his.

"Tell me, Ta-kong, what are your plans now?" she said softly.

Ta-kong was called back from his anxious thoughts with a start. But he did not withdraw his hands. "Perhaps I will go to America with my Second Brother to join my Third Brother."

"Haven't you ever thought of getting married?" she whispered.

Mechanically, Ta-kong shook his head.

"Don't you feel that you have met an ideal partner for life? One whose intellect is as keen as yours? Whose ambitions are the same? Who will be a helpmate to you always? And one with whom you can climb any heights, hand in hand?"

Ta-kong was taken aback. Yuwen's warnings returned with a rush. Why, the girl was actually proposing. What immodesty! And especially at this time, when she knew his parents were critically ill, what wanton lack of delicacy!

"I can't think of that now," he said shortly. "I can think only of my parents on their sickbed."

Abruptly Mei-yin dropped his hands. Without another word, she ran stumblingly toward her dormitory. Ta-kong had no wish either to call her back or to follow her.

228

5

TA-KONG'S PARENTS WERE dead by the time he got home. The sickness had struck violently and swiftly, and even the prompt attendance of the Reverend Dr. Holt had proved of little avail.

Ta-kong took the loss extremely hard. He had no loved ones any more. Unwittingly he had been the cause of his grandfather's death years before. The uncle and aunt he loved so dearly were now living in self-imposed exile, in faraway Malaya. His older brother and sister had been brought up separately from him since childhood, and he had no abiding affection for them. Now, with his father and mother gone, he felt as if all ties binding him to his family had been severed.

With Yuwen still in the United States, he did not have even a close friend in Yi. Dutifully, as a sworn brother, he called upon Yuwen's mother, Widow Lan. That lady had become the marvel of the city. She was not only widely famed for her medical skill, but had developed into quite a scholar in both Chinese and English. She was very kind to Ta-kong, but she was always busy and he did not see her often.

For the Reverend Dr. Holt Ta-kong entertained a deep respect, mostly derived from childhood impressions he had acquired from his grandfather and uncle. He had been too young to enroll when Holt first started his English class. Although he had once called the missionary "grand-generation-uncle" at the behest of his grandfather, he was unwilling to do so now—the term was out of vogue. Moreover, he did not think it fitting that he, who was known nationally for the bold stand he had taken against Imperialism, should abase himself in this manner before a foreigner. So he avoided meeting the Reverend Dr. Holt.

To his amazement, Ta-kong discovered that the family income once again had dwindled to an alarming degree. The taxes Governor Tien Fong had imposed on the province were excessive; the countryside was infested with bandits, and the rentals of farmlands could no longer be easily collected. This placed him in a very awkward position. When Ho the Central Hall died, Fucho had waived his own share of the inheritance and passed it on to his nephew. Legally, that share was Ta-kong's now. If disposed of, it would enable him to go to the United States and take Li Chien along too. But he also knew that if he were to take this drastic step, the livelihood of his many cousins—who had had only a classical education and lived off the estate, and whom he therefore considered parasites and held in contempt—would be put in grave jeopardy. Often he was on the verge of doing so, thinking his indolent kin deserved no better treatment; yet, speculating on what his grandfather or his uncle would have done under similar circumstances, he simply could not bring himself to take the step.

After the burial of his parents, Ta-kong returned to the port city. It was Old Head who made up his mind for him. He told Ta-kong that if he wanted "to succeed to his mantle" at all, he had better stay and work hard in the Society. Formerly, he had received special treatment as a student of the University, but now that he had graduated, there was no further reason he should not be regarded in the same manner as the other disciples. Henceforth, he must closely join in the activities of the Society and learn to administer the octopus-like organization. If he left for America now, he would miss his chance of ever becoming Old Head's successor. Ta-kong's ambitions were far above being the chief of a secret society, but still he saw enormous possibilities. Though Old Head was using the organization only to exploit his fellow Chinese under the protection of the foreigners, could he not wield it as a weapon to drive out the foreigners themselves?

Ta-kong decided to stay.

He went to Chang Fa-foo and told him he would accept his offer. Thus, when the University reopened in autumn, Ta-kong was installed as the Chancellor's personal assistant and Li Chien as an assistant librarian.

6

By DAY TA-KONG worked at the University; by night he helped Old Head direct the multitudinous affairs of the Society. His double life went undiscovered, though Li Chien complained that they did not have much time together after office hours. At first, Ta-kong was appalled by the criminality of many of the Society's activities, but Old Head pointed out that that was the only way to keep it in existence. As time went on, his heart hardened. One had to be prepared to sacrifice lesser ideals to attain a big ideal. The trouble with Old Head was that he had no big ideal. Wait until Ta-kong became the chief—he would provide the Society with a big ideal! And with a view to establishing himself firmly in the good graces of Old Head and his fellow disciples, he applied his more highly developed intelligence with even greater zeal to all their enterprises. As a result, the Society grew in profit and in influence beyond what Old Head had conceived possible. He was pleased, and his men came to respect and fear Ta-kong almost as much as they did their chief.

Ta-kong was a man of more realism than philosophy, and had no qualms about the Jekyll-and-Hyde life he was leading. As personal assistant to a chancellor of a university, he talked about ideals and idealism. As personal assistant to an arch-gangster, he dealt in crimes and atrocities. He felt no prick of conscience, and saw no incongruity in his two occupations. Both were means to achieve his great ambition—to make himself master of China and then to lead the nation on to glory and to the Utopia he had long envisioned.

But *what* Utopia? That was the only thing he was vague about.

One day Chang Fa-foo called Ta-kong into his office. Giving him some papers, the Chancellor said, "Read them here. I want to hear your opinion about them."

The papers were two pamphlets: a draft for an organization called "The Society for Study of Marxism," and a brochure on the theories of Karl Marx and experiments in Marxism such as then were being introduced by Lenin in Soviet Russia. Ta-kong was fascinated by the documents. He already possessed a casual knowledge about both Marx and the Soviet Revolution, but he had never studied either closely, considering the one an alien philosophy and the other a foreign uprising—and neither applicable to China. But this brochure was different. It was so terse, so precise, so inspiring. There should be not only political equality among men, it said; there should also be economic equality. The world should be a world of the workers, the toiling masses, the proletariat, and not a world of the *bourgeoisie,* the capitalists, the parasites. There should be no social classes among men. Society should be classless. From each according to his abilities, to each according to his needs. What an ideal! What a system! At last Ta-kong had the Utopia he had sought.

He was still immersed in the brochure when Chang, getting impatient, asked what he thought of it.

"Why, this is wonderful! Where did you get it?"

"Have you ever heard of a man by the name of Chen Tu-hsiu?"

"No."

"Well, he's the editor of a monthly in Shanghai, *La Jeunesse—*

we subscribe to the magazine, you can find it in the library. It's written in Chinese, but in the fashion of the times Chen has given it a French title. Nobody has any faith in our ancient rubbish; if you want to impress the public you have to show off your knowledge of foreign culture. Chen is a friend of mine, and because he knows and shares my progressive idealism he sent me the pamphlets. He has already founded a Society for Study of Marxism in Shanghai, and he wants me to form a branch here among the students. Do you think we can manage it?"

"Of course we can," answered Ta-kong enthusiastically.

So it came about that, under the Chancellor's sponsorship and with Li Chien's help, Ta-kong began to organize a branch society in the University. But he did not meet with the success he had anticipated. Most students were far more interested in reading the old novels than such dull and serious subjects; and besides, of all the Western nations, the Chinese had the lowest opinion of Russia. They thought the Russians the least cultured of the Occidental peoples, and remembered that under Genghis Khan and Kublai Khan China had once ruled as far as Moscow and Kiev, and that only recently Japan, an Oriental nation, had defeated Russia in war. They called the Russians "the Big Noses." Thus, they could see nothing exciting in anything Lenin might be doing in Russia. Moreover, the word Marx itself sounded in Chinese like the words that meant "horse feces." The students made much fun of that. They said that if they wanted an ancient philosphy, they could have their own Confucianism; if they wanted something new, they could have Dr. Sun Yat-sen's Three People's Principles. But what use did they have for "horse feces"?

Nevertheless, Ta-kong persevered. Then a year later something happened that gave his undertaking a boost. In a formal treaty with China, the Soviet Union renounced all the special rights Czarist Russia had wrested from her neighbor, and returned all her Concessions, including the one in the port city, to Chinese sovereignty. Lenin openly proclaimed that the Communist policy was to fight against international Imperialism, and that any nation suffering from exploitation and oppression could look to Russia for help. The Chinese people received the news with surprise, encouragement, and then a sudden upsurge of gratitude and admiration for Soviet Russia. And more students began to join the Society for Study of Marxism.

Shortly after, Chang Fa-foo asked Ta-kong to dine with him in his apartment. There was nothing unusual about this, but Ta-kong was mystified when Chang cautioned him not to tell anyone he was coming, not even Li Chien. He arrived at the appointed hour to find two other guests already present. One was Professor Nan Ping, who had taught him French but with whom he had not formed an intimate association. The other was a foreigner. He was a short, stooped little man of about fifty, affable in manners and scholarly in appearance. He wore thick glasses. Chang introduced him as Mr. Voitinsky.

During the dinner Voitinsky singled out Ta-kong. He spoke Chinese fluently, and questioned Ta-kong in minute detail both as to his understanding of Marx and Lenin and as to the progress and the difficulties of the Society for Study of Marxism. The little man seemed quite satisfied with Ta-kong's answers.

When dinner was finished, they retired to the study. Chang Fa-foo told the servants that they were not to be disturbed, and after making sure no one was eavesdropping he locked the door from the inside. At a nod from Voitinsky, Chang Fa-foo addressed Ta-kong.

"There is a very serious matter I want to talk to you about. I've already told you about Mr. Chen Tu-hsiu. He and some other like-minded men have seen fit to organize a Chinese Communist Party, and I have already joined. We see no way to fulfill our ideals and to save China from her woes except through Marxism. Before us is the glorious example of Soviet Russia. We think you are ripe to join our Party. Will you do so?"

Ta-kong understood now the reason for the secretiveness. He had no hesitation about joining the Party; in fact, since he had taken so much pains of late to study the Soviet Revolution in the Society for Study of Marxism, he had often thought of following Lenin's example and organizing a Communist Party for China. But now that the Party had been founded by better-known and more influential people than himself, he was quite prepared to join. Still he could not suppress his curiosity on another matter.

"Chancellor, aren't you already a member of the Kuomintang?"

"Oh, yes," replied Chang Fa-foo with a smile. "But that doesn't matter. The Communist Party does not forbid its members to participate in other political parties. On the contrary, it rather encourages them to do so, the one condition being that their loyalty must be only to the Communist Party. It's quite all right for me to continue my membership in the Kuomintang."

Ta-kong reflected that this was like the rule of the Chin Society, which allowed its disciples to join the Hung Society as spies.

"I understand you don't belong to the Kuomintang," Chang Fa-foo added. "Is that so?" Ta-kong nodded.

"Do you happen to belong to any political party, known or secret?"

Ta-kong considered the secret Society by no means a political party and accordingly answered, "No."

"Do you want to join the Communist Party?"

"Yes."

"Good," said Chang. "It is as I expected. Professor Nan Ping has also signified his willingness to join, and you are both to be initiated into the Party tonight. Comrade Voitinsky is here to conduct the initiation and help us organize our branch afterward. We have so much to learn from our Soviet Big Brothers."

Voitinsky asked Ta-kong and Nan Ping to stand up, raise their right hands, and swear a solemn prescribed oath. After that, he produced two papers and had them sign their names. Then he motioned for all to sit down.

"Hereafter," he said pleasantly, "Comrade Chang will give you two new comrades general guidance and direction in your daily work. Now, I will inform you of the basic rules of our Party."

Suddenly all affability was gone and his eyes sparkled behind his thick glasses like fiery stars.

"Our Party," he said, "is different from all other political parties. We do not want revolution only for China, we want revolution for the whole world. Consequently, we have more opponents than all other political parties rolled into one. Reactionary forces the world over—governments, capitalists, *bourgeoisie,* even down to small landowners and petty shopkeepers—by their social nature are bound to be our enemies. The only way to preserve ourselves from destruction, to keep our strength effective, to expand our forces against all odds, and to achieve our aims in the end is this—to build up our Party in such a manner as to give it the most rigid organization, the most ruthless discipline, and the most airtight security the world has ever seen. We learned that bitter lesson in Russia, now happily the Socialist Fatherland. The rules have been formulated for your protection. Do you understand?"

All nodded solemnly, including Chang Fa-foo. But Ta-kong reflected silently that howsoever rigorous the Communist Party

234

might be, it could not be as rigid and secretive as his secret Society.

"From this day on," Voitinsky resumed, "you three form a cell of the Party. Later on, the Party may create other cells in this city, independent of you and without your knowledge. But I tell you now that you are the first Communist cell here because I want you to know what an honor the Party has accorded you and what responsibilities you should feel toward the Party in return. Comrade Chang Fa-foo is designated as the leader of your cell. You two, Comrade Nan Ping and Comrade Ho Ta-kong, are to obey him absolutely and unquestioningly. This is the first rule of the Party. Every member must be attached to a cell, and every participant of a cell must carry out his leader's instructions implicitly, unthinkingly, and—yes, blindly.

"The leader's wish is your command. His word is your law. The leader—and nobody but the leader—represents the Party in his cell. All the Party directives are transmitted through him, and through him only. To get a promotion in the Party, you must depend mainly on his favorable reports. To disobey him in any way invariably results in dire punishment, sometimes in liquidation. Of course, the leader himself is a member of an upper cell, of which there is another leader to whom he must render total obedience, the same as you do to him. But that is none of your business. Even if you happen to know the members or the leader of the upper cell, you must not contact them unless they send for you. In time, you may be allowed to form lower cells yourselves and be designated as leaders, but you can do that only with your own leader's permission. In short, henceforth your lives are entirely at the disposal of your leader. He can make or break you. You must do nothing, either public or private, without his direction. Are there any questions?"

"You mean," asked Nan Ping, "even if I know Comrade Chen Tu-hsiu, the founder of the Chinese Communist Party, I cannot go to him directly?"

"No, you cannot," returned Voitinsky emphatically. "This is to protect you. Comrade Chen is now the recognized leader of the Chinese Communist Party, which circumstance he cannot avoid. But you are still an unknown Communist. To go to him might unnecessarily identify you with the Party, and that would imperil you, wouldn't it? There is also another rule which pertains to this matter."

"You mean, then," inquired Nan Ping again, "that hereafter

235

Comrade Chang will be our master in every aspect of our lives, including our private affairs?"

"Yes," said Voitinsky. "But not necessarily Comrade Chang Fa-foo. By the direction of the Party you may be transferred to another cell, or the Party may designate a new leader for this one. But in all aspects of your life, public and private, you are bound to obey your leader, whoever he happens to be at the moment. Take your occupation, for instance. You may have a very lucrative position, but if the Party, through your leader, asks you to give it up and go to a remote place to take a poorly paid job, you must not hesitate to obey. Or take marriage. I know that none of you here is married; that is good for our purpose in many ways. But if you ever want to marry, you must first secure permission from the Party through your leader. Or if, under certain circumstances, the Party directs you to marry some person, be she deaf or blind, it is not for you to object. Yes, from now on your life is not your own. The Party is your life. Remember: this is the only way we can forge our organization into an effective weapon; the only way the Party can act like one man with one mind, without being annoyed by divisive individualities; the only way possible by which we can ever hope to achieve our world revolution. Do you understand?"

Nan Ping took the explanation quite composedly. But Ta-kong inwardly was taken aback. The leader-member relationship of the Party and the teacher-disciple relationship of the secret Society were not too dissimilar, but the latter seldom interfered with the disciples' private lives. This rule of the Party went much further, becoming truly all-inclusive. Yet Ta-kong felt no grave uneasiness. Having broken his family ties, he did not mind taking a job anywhere at the Party's command. And as for his heart, it was still unattached. Perhaps by the time he wanted to marry, he would have risen so high from the Party ranks that he could choose any wife he wanted, without encountering objections.

"Now," Voitinsky went on, "we come to the second rule, which I just mentioned in replying to one of Comrade Nan Ping's questions. A Communist must not reveal his membership in the Party to a single soul without the permission of the Party. Not to his parents. Not to his wife or her husband. Not even to a fellow Communist. When comrades are directed to work together, naturally they know one another as such and there's no necessity for them to ask. When they are not, there's no reason they should know. You may suspect, or you may even know for certain, that some persons are Communists. But they may not know or suspect that you are a fellow Communist. To reveal yourself is to give yourself away unnecessarily, and might put you in unwarranted danger. To mix freely among ourselves would make us easy targets for the reactionary forces to discover and shoot at. And we would place our Party machinery in peril. No offense is considered more serious than to disclose your membership to anyone, including a fellow Communist, without the permission of the Party. The punishment without exception is liquidation."

The little man surveyed his audience darkly from behind his dense spectacles. This rule was something the secret Society had never conceived. Suddenly Voitinsky grew before Ta-kong into a person of gigantic stature.

"The third rule is that each of you must now take an assumed name. Comrade Chang Fa-foo already has one, and he, as leader of the cell, will think up assumed names for you two. Wherever possible, you must use your assumed names and not your real ones. In the archives of the Party a dossier will be kept for each of you under your assumed name. This is again for your protection. Take me as an example. Voitinsky is not my real name. If I am caught, the enemy will have a hard time learning my true identity and my background. And even if they chance upon the Party archives, they will find my activities entered under Voitinsky, but they will not be able to discover who I truly am.

"Now, both your identities and your assumed names are known to your leader, Chang Fa-foo. But in the upper cells your identities are known only to the leaders, not to the members. The same will be true with you when you form your lower cells. You must report the identities of your members to your leader, but to no one else. On all occasions, wherever a third person is present, when you speak of a member you must use his assumed name. Suppose Comrade Ho Ta-kong is permitted to lead a cell in which there is a member whose real name is Wang and whose assumed name is Koo. Comrade Ho must report both names to Comrade Chang, and in turn Comrade Chang must report them to his leader in the upper cell, and so on. But in your cell meetings, Comrade Chang and Comrade Ho must always refer to him as Koo, his assumed name, and not as Wang, his real name. In this manner Comrade Nan Ping, for instance, will be enabled to know all about the activities of this supposed Koo and join in discussions concerning him, yet Comrade Nan Ping will not know his true identity as Wang. This provides double security. It gives Comrade Wang security because his identity is known only to the direct line of leaders above him and to no one else. It also gives security to Comrade Nan Ping because even if he is caught by our enemies and tortured, he can honestly confess that he knows a certain Koo as a Communist, but not anyone named Wang. Do I make myself clear?"

All nodded. Ta-kong reflected that here was still another ingenious invention which the secret Society had not thought of. He said, "Would this not lead to great confusion? Who keeps track of all the real and assumed names?"

Voitinsky eyed him shrewdly. "A very intelligent question. Of course it creates a lot of confusion, even among the members in the higher echelons. But it's meant to. It confuses everyone but the top command. There, at the topmost of our layers of cells—at the very peak of the pyramid of our organization, so to speak—the air is clear and purified. For the top command, and only the top command, has a separate dossier in which all the real and assumed names of our comrades are entered. It is the holy of holies of our Party, the most vigilantly and closely guarded of our secrets. Can't you see the great advantage? It protects us members. It protects the organization. We are so intricately compartmented that the destruction or defection of one segment, even a very large one, will have no effect on the whole. Are you satisfied, Comrade Ho?"

In truth, Ta-kong was not only satisfied, he was impressed. He saw beyond the advantages to the Party machinery set forth by Voitinsky. He wanted to attain the unique position of leadership in the top command and exercise that transcendental authority himself.

"There is a final rule," Voitinsky said. "This is one in which you cannot falter for so much as a second, except at your dire peril. Fear none but the Party, and trust no one—not even a fellow Communist. Fear the Party as you have never feared anything. Whatever terror the enemy may hold out to you, know that the Party holds out a hundredfold. The most the enemy can inflict is death, but the things the Party can do to you are incalculable and immeasurable. Not liquidation, pure and simple. Torture, perhaps, crude and cruel. Or all these, and, in addition, the destruction before your very eyes of all those you hold dear. The enemy may relent. The Party is relentless. The enemy may have a short memory. The Party never forgets. The enemy may forgive. The party, never.

238

"Obey your leader absolutely, but don't trust him. Co-operate with your fellow Communists to the limit of your capacity, but place no confidence in them. This may sound paradoxical, but it's not. The path of class struggle and world revolution is paved with the skulls of renegades, those who indulge in deviationism and swing away from the Party line. They drain away our strength and weaken our solidarity. There's no enemy worse than an enemy from within—for them the Party has no mercy.

"It's your bounden duty as a comrade to ferret out these deviationists and denounce them to the Party. If you have any suspicions of a fellow Communist, report it instantly to your leader. If you have concrete evidence even against your leader himself, don't hesitate to approach the Party headquarters. Only under such circumstances, Comrade Nan Ping, is a contact over the head of your leader permitted. If you know something about your leader which should be reported to the Party and you fail to do so, when your leader is purged you will be too. But if you feel you must bring charges against your leader, take care that the charges are very well substantiated, for just as the reward for a truthful informer is beyond compare, so is the punishment for a false accuser.

"You may wonder why I do not exhort you to be loyal to the Party. I have no need to. I have no doubt that you are all loyal, Comrades. But let me ask you this: What is an expression of loyalty? Merely an utterance of empty words. To exact a pledge from you in this matter would be the easiest thing in the world. I might freely ask and you might freely give, and that would be good enough for other political parties. It's not good enough for us. Ours is a philosophy of materialism, through and through. We have no use for empty words, and so we don't demand any expression of loyalty from you. We see to it ourselves, by our own organization, that you are loyal, that you don't dare to be otherwise.

"The Party does not depend solely on your watching one another in this matter of deviationism; it has other means and other weapons. You may be the first Communist cell here now, but who knows whether another cell will not be formed in a day or two? It would certainly be done without your knowledge, perhaps without mine too. And its members would doubtless be directed to keep an eye on you, just as you will be asked sooner or later to watch the movements of others, surreptitiously. Then, there is a special, ultra-secret security organ within the Party whose sole function is to enforce loyalty and discipline. Its eyes are everywhere; it has never been known to give quarter to anyone who has gone astray. So, Comrades, beware!"

Abruptly Voitinsky's eyes softened and he again took on his scholarly appearance.

"Don't think ill of this method, Comrades. It has been devised both for the Party's safety and for your own good. None know better than we Communists that though the spirit may be willing, the flesh is weak. The Party watches over its comrades like a shepherd over his lambs. It does not want to see any of them stumble, and it takes care that they are not led into temptations. Comrades, abide by the Party line always, and you will be safe."

Voitinsky inquired whether there were further questions.

"Can you tell me, Comrade," Ta-kong asked, "what the relationship is between the Russian Communist Party and the Chinese Communist Party?"

"They are one and the same," replied Voitinsky. "Our revolution is a world revolution and our Party is a world party. The Communist Party is one. It merely has branches in different nations. Just as there are separate cells in our organization below, so there are separate branches above. The relationship between the Russian and the Chinese Communist Party is like the relationship of two cells in a branch."

"But in matters of general policy pertaining to our revolution in China, which branch of our Party has the authority to make the final decision—the Russian branch or the Chinese branch?"

"Neither," Voitinsky said. "In your studies in the Society for the Study of Marxism you've learned of the Communist International—the Comintern—the organization in which all the branches of the Party are represented. It's the top command of the Party, and there the major policies of our revolution in every corner of the earth are deliberated and decided upon. So far, the Communist International has functioned in the open in order to rally the toiling masses of all nations more easily to our standard. But when the Party has collected more strength, it may perhaps be wiser to let it go underground. But whether it is open or underground, you can be sure that it, and not any one particular branch, is the directing force of our world-wide revolution."

"But is not the Communist International dominated by our Russian comrades?" Ta-kong asked. Then, seeing Voitinsky glance sharply at him, he added quickly, "I beg your pardon, Comrade.

I am not making this inquiry to express any objection to such an arrangement. I only want to understand our Party better."

Voitinsky's lips flickered into a smile. "I'm glad you raised this question, Comrade Ho Ta-kong. I'm aware there is still a tint of old-fashioned nationalism in you, but I'm sure you will get rid of it soon. With world revolution as our aim, how can we have room for nationalism? Ours is a struggle by the working class as a whole against all the other classes the world over, not just a struggle against any particular ruling class in any particular nation. The proletariat everywhere are our brothers, and the reactionary forces in all countries are our enemies. It is true that the present Communist International is dominated by our comrades of Russian derivation. But is this not natural? So far, Russia is the only land where our revolution has succeeded and we have founded a Marxist state. In the process, our Russian comrades have acquired far more experience in revolutionary techniques than we have. And besides, Russia is pouring forth both money and men in all directions to help us obtain our goal. Is it not logical that we should entrust the control of the Communist International to our Russian comrades? Of course circumstances may change. Though our philosophy of materialism is most rigid in many aspects, it is very flexible in others. Who knows—by the time the Chinese revolution is completed, you yourself, Comrade Ho, may be a leading figure in the Communist International."

Voitinsky spoke well. His words were calculated at once to put the young man in his place and to excite his vanity.

Ta-kong felt a happy little flutter, envisaging a day when he would become not only master of China but also a central pivot around which the whole world milled in revolution. Eager to make up to this Soviet Big Brother, he said humbly, almost contritely, "Comrade, I agree with you entirely and heartily."

Then the conversation turned to the immediate objectives of the newly formed cell. The first thing was of course to recruit more members for the Party.

"Here is where the Party needs your services most," said Chang Fa-foo to Ta-kong. "Comrade Nan Ping and I can work among the professors, but among the students we have to depend on you. Your prestige is very high with them, and you have your Society for the Study of Marxism to start with. Comrade Voitinsky thinks it most important to recruit as many young students as we can. And here we count on only you to produce results."

Ta-kong was flattered. But he was also aware of his problem, and anxious not to have the Party later feel he had not come up to its expectations. Voitinsky saw his hesitation and bade him speak his mind.

"At dinner," said Ta-kong, "I told you about the various difficulties I've experienced in promoting the Society for the Study of Marxism. Now that we are going to go further, obviously we will run into more and far stronger obstacles. Not that I will not do my utmost to contend with them; but we must face facts. At present, I might be able to recruit two or three, but no more. I can see only one possible way to get better and quicker results. Though the Kuomintang has lost much of its popularity among our young people, Dr. Sun Yat-sen's name is still one to conjure with, and it would be a ready weapon for us. Can't we seek to co-operate with him nominally, but actually merely use his name to recruit more members for our Party?"

"Comrade Ho Ta-kong," declared Voitinsky, bringing his fist down on his knee, "you indeed have a sharp mind. I don't mind telling you that is exactly what the top command has decided to do. At this very moment, Comrade Lenin is sending a man to negotiate with Sun Yat-sen with that purpose in view. We're offering him both money and arms in exchange for his co-operation with the Chinese Communist Party. We know Sun has separately approached Great Britain and the United States for assistance, and been rebuffed by both of them. He cannot afford to ignore the helping hand we extend to him, and he will have to accept it on our terms. So everything, I believe, will soon come out in the way you suggest. You have a very good and practical mind, Comrade Ho Ta-kong. Use it for the Party, and I'm sure you will go far."

Voitinsky took a cup of wine and requested the others to do the same.

"To the inevitable victory of our revolution in China! To the unfailing loyalty of our new members!" he toasted.

All drank. Ta-kong was specially pleased. He did not notice that his fellow Communist, Nan Ping, alias Ma Pingnan, was watching him with a jaundiced eye.

Yet no sooner had Ta-kong left his comrades than he was troubled by a sense of divided loyalties. He was due at the headquarters of the secret Society; should he, or should he not, report his new adventure to Old Head? According to his pledge to his teacher, he should tell him at once. By the conditions imposed by the Party, he should remain silent.

He considered his dilemma from various angles and at last came to a decision. Because he had joined the Society first, it must be said to have prior claim on him. Besides, the rigidity of its discipline had long been proved, but that of the Party had yet to be. Moreover, loyalty to the Party, as Voitinsky pointed out, was not based on one's volition but was enforced by fear. Just now, there being only one Communist cell in the port city, he had no one to fear except Chang Fa-foo and Nan Ping. And so far neither of them had any suspicion of his connection with the Society. So if he wanted to make a clean breast of the matter to Old Head, it had better be now than later.

Old Head listened to the account and was not displeased.

"It may be a good thing that you have done," he said finally. "The way the wind is blowing, I can see the Society sooner or later getting involved in politics. I myself am flirting with the Kuomintang. It may be a godsend that you have become a founding member of the Communist Party in this city. We can ride on both horses. No matter which Party wins out, the Society will not lose. But there is one thing you must not do. You must never disclose your discipleship in the Society to your Party."

"That I promise," said Ta-kong. "But the program of the Communist Party is ambitious and its discipline is very severe. Sometimes circumstances may make it impossible for me to report plans and activities to you in full, Venerable Master."

Old Head cast a shrewd glance at Ta-kong. "That is all right. I have implicit confidence in your judgment and your loyalty. I shall not require you to tell me everything. But should you come across any doings of your Party that may seriously affect the Society or myself, I trust you will not fail to let me know at once."

This Ta-kong also promised. And his mind was at rest.

As Ta-kong had foreseen, he made little progress at first in recruiting new members for the Party. Besides his Second Brother, he was able to enlist only five students. Under the instructions of the Party, these were organized into three cells. He himself was appointed leader of a cell consisting of Li Chien and a senior student whom he had recruited immediately after his Second Brother. In turn, Li Chien and the senior were designated as leaders of the two lower cells, each with a pair of comrades.

Then electrifying news flashed across the country. In January, 1923, Dr. Sun Yat-sen announced publicly that he had concluded an agreement with one Adolf Joffe, a special representative of Lenin. In a statement issued to the public, that delegate of the Communist International openly proclaimed that Communism was not suitable to the conditions of China and that henceforth the Chinese Communists would not labor for the founding of a Marxist state in the country but would work under the leadership of the Kuomintang for the sole purpose of achieving national unification and full independence.

To the people on the outside, this was a great moral victory for Dr. Sun Yat-sen and the Kuomintang. But the Communist Party knew better. In exchange for material support from Soviet Russia, Dr. Sun had agreed to let the Chinese Communists retain membership in their own Party and at the same time join the Kuomintang, participate in all its activities, and create all sorts of disturbances in its name. Thus, ingenious Communist devices as yet unknown to an unenlightened world, such as United Front, Popular Front, Coalition Government, Infiltration, and Boring from Within, saw first light in China. Overnight, a couple of hundred comrades, all the Chinese Communist Party could then muster up throughout the length and breadth of the country, were transformed into full-fledged members of the Kuomintang. Because of the peculiar nature of their organization and the unmatched effectiveness of their techniques, they were soon to exercise a dominating influence on the Kuomintang far beyond what their small numbers warranted —an influence that most people at that time, including many genuine members of the Kuomintang, would not have thought possible.

This turn of events made Ta-kong's task much easier. He was now able to induce many more young and ambitious students to become nominally members of the Kuomintang, but actually Communists.

Presently a special directive came to Ta-kong from the Party headquarters. With the help of Russian advisers and Russian equipment, Dr. Sun was to establish the Whampoa Military Academy near Canton, and he had already named one Chiang Kai-shek as its superintendent. Ta-kong was ordered to proceed there immediately and enroll as a Kuomintang cadet. He was authorized also to select another young comrade to go along, and he chose Li Chien. The two sworn brothers left North China for Canton.

BOOK III

One

IT WAS THE fateful summer of 1926, and Ho Fucho was preparing to return to China with Delicate Blossom and their daughter Li-hwa.

It had taken longer than he expected to achieve the purpose for which he had come to Malaya. Behind them lay ten years of hard work and dedicated self-denial, during which they had built up the rubber plantation and other properties in Malaya. But now that he had enough money, Fucho was determined to go back to his homeland to help finance a revolution.

Dr. Sun Yat-sen, beloved founder of the Kuomintang, had died a year before. Fucho had resisted an impulse to rush to the side of the leader during his fatal illness. He was not quite ready to return then, since he wanted to dispose of his properties first, and he also knew Dr. Sun's death would precipitate a struggle for leadership within the Party. He did not want to be suspected of having returned to join in this contest. Fucho was not a politician but an idealist; he abhorred publicity, and wanted only to see the Kuomintang strengthened, the warlords overthrown, and his country unified.

He finally sold the rubber plantation and the other properties for cash, and found himself with a sum equal to two million dollars in American money. If they had so wished, he and Delicate Blossom and Li-hwa could have had ease and comfort for the rest of their lives. But they had come to Malaya to make money for the revolution. The sum was not enough for what Fucho had in mind, but it would help ...

Now he was filled with urgency. The events of the past two years —even during the time when Dr. Sun was still alive—had left him somewhat bewildered. Letters from his old comrades had all been burdened with a common and bitter complaint: the Communists had become a divisive influence within the Party; unless drastic steps were taken at once they would seize control of the Kuomintang. The old comrades had warned Dr. Sun; they wanted Fucho to write and add his voice to the admonitions.

All this had puzzled Fucho during these two years. He had thought nothing amiss when Dr. Sun first announced his agreement with the Communists. The revolutionaries needed any help they could find; it was good that Soviet Russia had offered military and financial aid. Besides, although Chinese Communists might have ideological ties with the Russian Communist Party, Fucho told himself that certainly they would always be Chinese first. And he thought there was nothing wrong with an ideology that laid emphasis on economic as well as political equality. This went with an ancient saying he believed true: "Within the four seas, all are brothers."

Nevertheless, the letters had alarmed him, and he wrote back asking for more particulars, more details. Nobody had any to give; there were many suspicions, but no specific facts. Fucho's old friends reminded him that since the agreement did not require the Communists to disclose their dual membership, no one could be sure just who the Communists were. They could be identified only vaguely as a group, and lumped under the contemptuous term of Leftists.

Studying these reports, Fucho feared that his old comrades might only have become jealous of the younger and more aggressive men who had risen in the Kuomintang's ranks. He wrote chiding them gently, quoting a Confucian saying: "The effort must be ours to make, but the glory of success need not be ours to own."

However, through the months of negotiating the sale of the rubber plantation, he looked out over the steaming Malayan jungles and fretted impatiently, eager to be on his way. From all accounts, miasmic mists were swirling over all of China too, so that no man at a distance could comprehend what was happening. The Kuomintang had been reorganized after Dr. Sun's death, and a new Central Committee chosen. Fucho was mildly vexed to find his own name had been dropped, but he was terribly shocked to see that a good many of his old comrades had not been elected. Only a very few of his once intimate associates, such as Tong Hsi and Amy, retained their membership in the Committee.

Chiang Kai-shek's name was prominent—he knew the man slightly. In Fucho's day, Chiang had been a junior member, not much noticed. Among the complete strangers on the list was a man named Mao Tse-tung. Fucho pondered this addition, wondering what Mao had done for the Party. It never occurred to him Mao might be a Communist. As he understood it, the Communists were so few in number they could not possibly have elected their own men to the Central Committee of the Kuomintang.

The fogs must have blinded people in China, too. Genuine Kuomintang delegates greatly outnumbered the Communist delegates at the conference to elect a Central Committee, but as Fucho had anticipated, the death of Dr. Sun had left them separated into factions. Their votes were divided; the Communists voted with a single voice, then traded and dickered with every faction. Fucho was to learn later that the Communists had captured nearly a third of the seats in the Kuomintang Central Committee.

He felt lost and out of touch; it was almost as if he were preparing to return to an alien land rather than to his own home. Delicate Blossom, in her wisdom and gentleness, pointed out that it was only natural he had not been retained on the Central Committee. He had been away from China for a decade, remaining aloof from political affairs in his single-minded zeal to make money for the Party. He had attended neither Dr. Sun's funeral nor the conference for the Central Committee election. Dr. Sun would have understood and applauded his motives in Malaya, but now Dr. Sun was dead. To others, Fucho might well appear a politically thwarted man who had gone abroad to recoup his personal fortune.

There was only one thing to do. Go back quietly, observe and study what was going on, and then offer the Party his financial support and whatever leadership he could. Fucho had the money remitted to a bank in Hong Kong; he could hardly wait now to begin the homeward journey. The Kuomintang had established a stronghold around Canton, and organized a brand-new army under Chiang Kai-shek, with the graduates of the Whampoa Military Academy as its nucleus. This army was feverishly preparing a "Northern Expedition" to overthrow the warlords and unify the nation.

But just as Fucho closed his affairs and left Malaya, the disturbing news reached him that the Kuomintang had become openly split. While Chiang Kai-shek's forces consolidated their position in Canton, the disgruntled old comrades had met in the North at a place called West Hill, and set themselves up in Shanghai as the opposition group. Each camp sent urgent messages to Fucho asking his support. The men at West Hill were his old friends, but his sympathies lay with the new Central Committee. The West Hill group appeared impotent; they did not have Chiang Kai-shek's army, nor any logistical alliance with a dependable foreign power, such as Soviet Russia, for military and financial assistance.

Although he grieved for his old comrades, Fucho sent identical replies to both sides, counseling patience, restraint, and forbearance. But he told neither side that he had two million dollars to donate to the success of the revolution, for in his heart was the dream that he could perhaps compose the differences between the two factions and once more bring unity to the Kuomintang. . . .

He hurried to Canton with Delicate Blossom and Li-hwa, arriving late at night, and registered under an assumed name.

2

AFTER BREAKFAST NEXT morning, when Delicate Blossom and Li-hwa had gone out for a sightseeing tour, Fucho sent for the morning newspapers. He was shocked to find them filled with vituperations against the West Hill group. The news dispatches were slanderously distorted; the editorials called Fucho's old comrades unbelievable names, and made it appear that they—not the warlords or foreign Imperialists—were the arch-enemies of China.

Fucho was more bewildered than before. He had intended going to Party headquarters this morning; now he thought it wise to study the situation first. He telephoned Tong Hsi, but finding both him and Amy out at a conference, he merely left a message for them. As he started to look up the number of another member of the Central Committee, there was a knock at his door. Thinking it was the hotel maid, he called, "Come in!"

Then, from the entrance, a man's voice exclaimed, "Uncle Fucho!"

Fucho immediately forgot all the worries of China. Here was his nephew, Ta-kong, grown up and in uniform. He rushed to greet the young man, to take both his hands and say over and over:

248

"Ta-kong! Oh, how glad I am to see you! Ta-kong—this is wonderful!"

Ta-kong beamed.

Fucho stepped back a little. "It's been ten years," he said. "Come over here by the mirror. Look! You've grown very much like me—only you wear a uniform and you're younger. Your face is more square, and your eyes brighter. I have your grandfather's eyes, softer and more hazy; yours shine like stars. But otherwise you could be taken for my son!"

"Don't you have a son, Uncle Fucho?" asked Ta-kong.

"No, only Li-hwa. But you have always been as dear to us as a son."

Ta-kong was visibly touched. "Where are my aunt and Li-hwa?"

"Out seeing the city. They'll be happily surprised when they get back. You've been a poor correspondent, Ta-kong—the last letter we had was when you graduated from the Whampoa Military Academy. . . . By the way, how did you ever find me?"

"I came to the hotel to look for a friend, and saw the register. I ran across the assumed name you used ten years ago in the port city, and took a chance."

"A Heaven-sent coincidence!" Fucho exclaimed.

It had been no coincidence, of course, but Ta-kong said nothing. He had risen high in the Communist ranks, and in addition to his army appointment he had the secret duty of organizing labor unions in Canton. He had an agent in every hotel to report arrivals and departures; his uncle's arrival had already been passed on to the High Command of the Communist Party.

If Fucho proved ready to support the new Central Committee and all its policies, the Communist Party would accord him a fitting welcome. If he were undecided, no stone would be left unturned to win him over. But if he were immovably opposed to it, he would be regarded as an enemy and dealt with as such.

"Uncle Fucho," Ta-kong said a little uneasily, "I suppose you've returned to join the Northern Expedition and the new Central Committee?"

"I am for the Northern Expedition," Fucho said. "I can't agree entirely with the policies of the new Central Committee. But never mind those things now. What about you? Are you married?"

Ta-kong smiled. "Remember the words of the Han Dynasty general you used to quote? 'While the Tartars remain undestroyed, what's the use of my getting married'?"

"Good for you!" Fucho laughed. "What's your rank in the army?"

"I'm a Division Political Commissar with the rank of colonel."

Fucho frowned. "I don't understand that. What's a Political Commissar—what are his functions in an army division?"

"Why, the authority of a Political Commissar is nearly equal to the commander of a division. It's his duty to see that the men are well fed, well clad, and well indoctrinated. He handles propaganda and public relations, and gains the good will of the people wherever the troops are quartered. On the march, he and his men go in advance to gather intelligence, spread propaganda, and stir up agitation."

Again, Ta-kong was not telling the whole truth. His most important job was to spy upon the commander. Chiang Kai-shek, the Commander-in-Chief, appointed commanders who were loyal only to him. The Communists infiltrated the army by concentrating on filling the posts of Political Commissars.

Fucho had been away a long time; he would not have understood.

"I suppose the Russian advisors introduced this system?" he asked.

"Yes," said Ta-kong. "It was invaluable in the Russian Army, and it's working well here. We have much to learn, uncle, from Soviet Russia and her great revolution."

He watched Fucho closely as he said this, but saw no sign of disapproval.

"True, I suppose," Fucho said. "At least the Russians succeeded in their revolution, and we haven't in ours." After a moment of silence he went on, "I can't tell you how glad I am to see you just now. I've been away too long, Ta-kong—I'm out of touch. You're probably the only man I can trust, here in Canton. I want you to advise me."

"I'll do all I can," Ta-kong answered guardedly. "Don't forget—as a junior member in the Kuomintang, I don't take part in high councils."

3

FUCHO BRUSHED ASIDE what appeared to be a modest disclaimer, and told his nephew all about the years in Malaya. Now, he said, it was his intention to go to the Central Committee, announce his two-million-dollar donation, and then—having proved his personal dedication to the cause—to call upon all the members of the Kuomintang, new and old, Rightist and Leftist, to make peace for the sake of the Party and its common goal.

Ta-kong listened with a growing amazement. Was it possible he and his uncle were only one generation apart? He had not been in politics long, but already he knew how unprincipled, how selfish and sordid and murderous, politics could be. Working as a dedicated Communist, he had quickly forgotten that there could be nobility in man. But secretly he would have admitted that Fucho's ideals were like a shaft of light in the darkness, and he was greatly touched.

However, cynicism soon got the upper hand over pride. There was only a slim chance that Fucho's example could unite the wavering members of the Central Committee and the West Hill group; there was a far greater chance that Communist machinations would doom the plan to failure, in which case Fucho's sacrifice would be in vain and he and his family would be paupers for nothing.

Callous though Ta-kong had become, he could not bear the latter possibility. He knew he would not report his uncle's plans, truthfully, to the Communist Party. But what else could he do?

How odd Ta-kong felt then! It was as if he had suddenly uncovered something from the past—something from the Age of Chivalry, say. Fucho had been away only ten years, but what he now proposed harked back to the time of the Crusades. Ta-kong realized his uncle was idealistic to the point of being incapable of fending for himself in the cutthroat, free-for-all struggle that politics had become. Fucho was too honorable a man for politics. And in that moment, humbled, Ta-kong felt a great sadness for what he knew was likely to come. . . .

"What do you think of my plan, my dear nephew?" Fucho was asking.

Ta-kong collected himself. "I'm afraid it won't work," he said hesitantly. "The rift between the Rightists and Leftists is too deep. Your personal example—however selfless and commendable—cannot bridge it."

"But we're all comrades!" argued Fucho. "Rightists or Leftists, we're working for the same goal. All we need is a little forbearance on both sides. Look at today's newspapers! You didn't know the old comrades of the West Hill Conference Group, but I did. They may differ in their opinions, but they are not the scoundrels the Party papers make them out to be. Why have their past records been distorted so foully? This sort of vicious, one-sided propaganda must be stopped at once! Who is responsible—who is now in charge of the Party's Publicity Department?"

"Comrade Mao Tse-tung is the head of the Publicity Department," Ta-kong said. "From all I've heard, he is a good and temperate man. In this policy line, he must be acting under orders of the whole Central Committee."

"He may well be a good man, but he must be a new member in the Kuomintang or I would know his name. And so he does not really know the old comrades, as I do. Why does Chiang Kai-shek tolerate such doings—why do not Tong Hsi and some of the others stop them? How have the differences grown so bitter and violent? Is it true that the Communists have incited the disputes?"

Ta-kong hesitated, then followed the Party line. "No . . . I'd say blame the Communists less than the Kuomintang, blame the Leftists less than the Rightists, and the Rightists less than Chiang Kai-shek and his group."

Fucho was startled. "Why?"

"Well, uncle, the Communists are few, to begin with, and they openly accepted—in their agreement with Dr. Sun Yat-sen—the Three People's Principles of the Kuomintang, and promised they would not seek to found a Marxist state in China. So I don't believe the Rightists when they say all Leftists are Communists."

"Maybe not," Fucho admitted.

"Some people are born more conservative, some more radical," Ta-kong went on smoothly. "There's the matter of age. You'll pardon me for saying it, but though the older people look on the young as reckless hotheads, the young know very well—in their own minds—that their elders are not progressive enough. And the trouble with our Party is the lack of leadership since Dr. Sun's death."

"I looked to the old comrades to supply that," Fucho said sadly.

Ta-kong shook his head. "The old comrades tried to monopolize things, but they've lost contact with the rank and file. They have no new ideas—their only justification is their seniority. And when they demanded that we break relations with Soviet Russia—how absurd! Russia is the only country that has given any assistance to our revolution!"

"You said you blame Chiang Kai-shek more than you do the Rightists. Why do you say that?"

"Because he has an insatiable ambition, uncle. His one aim in life is to make himself master of the Kuomintang, and then dictator of China. In the beginning, the difference between the Rightists and Leftists might have been mended—it was Chiang who fanned the sparks into a conflagration. He has risen to prominence simply because Dr. Sun appointed him as superintendent of the Whampoa Military Academy, and that led to his becoming Commander-in-Chief. He has to get rid of all the old comrades before he can realize his ambitions—that's why he has exploited the differences between the Rightists and the Leftists."

Fucho, still lost in his idealism, was aghast at hearing these charges. He did not question Ta-kong's veracity, but he did not know that here, again, his nephew was giving the Party line.

"But hasn't he done a good job as Commander-in-Chief?" Fucho asked haltingly. "Isn't the army better equipped and organized than ever before?"

Ta-kong shook his head scornfully. "It was the Russian advisors who really organized the army, and Russian money and arms that equipped it. All Chiang has done is to fill the military commands with his own men, loyal neither to the Kuomintang nor the country —just to Chiang. Don't I know, uncle? He's still also superintendent of the Academy, you know. When I was a cadet there, if I had groveled to him, I probably would have been appointed a Division Commander instead of a Political Commissar. What's more, if he hears you have come back, and learns about your donation, he'll be very frightened—he'll think you want to supplant him as Commander-in-Chief!"

"That's absurd!"

"Not as absurd as you think, uncle. Remember what Yuan Shih-kai tried to do to you—and did do to you? Well, you're as much a threat to Chiang now as you were to Yuan, then. There are many things Chiang could do to you. You must not think just of yourself —you must think of my aunt, and Li-hwa."

Fucho drew himself erect, and the younger man saw he had been taking the wrong tack. Fucho had never lacked courage. "If Chiang is what you say, then I shall proceed with my plan at once. I must do my best to bring back the old comrades and hold him in check."

Loving his uncle as he did, Ta-kong decided to break the Communist Party rule about revealing secret information. "Uncle," he said, "you've returned too late. I know that the Central Committee is going to expel all the members of the West Hill group from the Kuomintang. You won't even have a chance to express your opinion."

Fucho hardly believed this. "What's your advice?" he asked skeptically.

"You can't reunite the Rightists and the Leftists. You have only two alternatives. Forget all about donating your money for the present. Simply report your return to headquarters, and say nothing about your views. There may be things about the Leftists you don't like, but they are fast losing their confidence in Chiang Kai-shek. So ally yourself with the Leftists, secretly, and you may be able to replace him as Commander-in-Chief."

"I have no personal ambitions in this matter." Fucho spoke impatiently. "What is the other alternative?"

"Please forgive me for what I'm going to ask," Ta-kong begged. "But have you ever read *The Three Kingdoms?*"

Fucho chuckled. "Yes. Your grandfather used to forbid us to read those 'Little Talks.' But I read it in Japan."

"Do you remember a saying quoted often in the book? It goes, 'Of all the thirty-six stratagems, to get away is the best'?"

"No!" Fucho threw up both hands in a gesture of dismissal. "I won't run away from the purpose I've worked toward so long! I won't be a coward!"

"Uncle Fucho," Ta-kong said soberly and earnestly, "you must get away as soon as you can—the sooner the better—and take your money with you, if it's here. For the love I bear you, do not remain here! This is not cowardice, uncle. It is only that discretion is the better part of valor."

At that moment Delicate Blossom and Li-hwa returned, and there was no more serious conversation. Delicate Blossom greeted Ta-kong like a mother; Ta-kong marveled at the ripening beauty of Li-hwa, who showed every sign of being as breath-takingly lovely as Delicate Blossom had been as a bride in Yi.

Delicate Blossom ordered lunch served in the suite, and for a time they chatted happily. The sightseeing tour, Li-hwa reported, had been marred by the shocking slogans they had seen posted on every street: "Down with Confucius!"—"Down with Filial Piety!"—"Down with Fidelity!"—and many others.

Fucho turned on his nephew. "Are these the work of the Leftists?"

Ta-kong told himself miserably that his uncle, aunt, and beautiful cousin would never understand the reasoning in materialist dialectics behind those Communist slogans. Averting his eyes, he said lamely, "I told you, uncle, that there are some things about the Leftists you might not like . . ."

"Yet you want me to work with them?"

Ta-kong pretended not to hear. Looking at his wristwatch, he

254

exclaimed that he was late for another appointment, and made his farewells hastily.

In the hallway, alone with Fucho, he lowered his voice and said seriously: "Forgive me for not being able to tell you everything about the situation, uncle. But remember this: I love you and my aunt more dearly than I have ever loved anyone. For the sake of that love—for the spirit of my grandfather in Heaven whom you revere—take this advice from me. 'Of all the thirty-six stratagems—'"

Strangers suddenly appeared in the hallway, and Ta-kong dashed away without finishing his sentence.

4

AFTER TA-KONG'S DEPARTURE, Fucho made Delicate Blossom and Li-hwa take another tour of the streets with him so that he could see the slogans for himself. He returned to the hotel infuriated, and recalled the ominous words his father had spoken to the Reverend Dr. Holt. The Leftists were committing sacrilege—profaning Chinese culture and poisoning the minds of the people. Theirs was not a revolution but a betrayal. They were not uplifting the nation; they were demoralizing it. He vowed to do all he could to destroy their evil influence.

And he was angry with his nephew for daring to suggest that he work with the Leftists. Had Ta-kong forgotten the teachings of his grandfather? As for his charges against Chiang Kai-shek, Fucho told himself that Ta-kong probably had made them out of sheer spite because he had failed to secure an appointment as a Division Commander. Fucho felt ashamed that a member of the House of Ho, one whom he had loved as his own son, could have stooped so low. He was sure that if Chiang Kai-shek and his old comrades in the Central Committee had chosen to go along with the Leftists for the moment, it could be only because they needed Russian money and Russian arms for the Northern Expedition.

It was in that mood that Fucho heard a hotel boy announce that Tong Hsi and his wife had come to call. He would be glad to see Tong Hsi, but he remembered his last meeting with Amy in the foreign hotel years ago, and felt embarrassed. When they came in, however, he at once discovered his misgivings had been unnecessary.

Tong Hsi had grown very corpulent and was getting bald, but Amy had lost little of her vivacity and voluptuousness. Although

255

there were crow's-feet at the corners of her eyes, they were covered by heavy make-up. She looked remarkably chic in an expensive close-fitting gown.

Amy did most of the greeting, with Tong Hsi following like a well-trained dog. She saluted Fucho like a long-lost intimate friend, but nothing more; she shook Delicate Blossom's hand cordially, and looked at Li-hwa with genuine admiration.

Patting the girl on the cheek, Amy said, "How lucky for your parents to have such a pretty girl! I wish I could have a daughter like you. But unfortunately your Uncle Tong and I have no child of our own."

They settled into easy conversation. And apparently partly out of curiosity and partly out of a sincere interest in Fucho's welfare, Amy began to ply him with questions regarding his life in Malaya and his present intentions. Was it true that he had become fabulously rich? No doubt he had returned to join the Northern Expedition. That was indeed a wise move—the Expedition was sure to be a success. They had received enough aid from Soviet Russia for the purpose, and they had a capable leader in Comrade Chiang Kai-shek. Both she and her darling Hsi regretted that because Fucho had been absent from the country for so long, they had been unable to re-elect him to a seat in the present Central Committee. They themselves deplored the rift within the Party ranks and had done their utmost to heal the breach, but their mutual old comrades in the West Hill group simply would not listen to reason. They could not see that Russian help was indispensable to the revolution, and they took exception to the legacy of Dr. Sun, which stipulated close co-operation between the Kuomintang and the Chinese Communists. By the way, what did Fucho think of the new Central Committee and their policies?

Fucho was on guard. The most compelling question he wanted to resolve was why the Central Committee permitted such reprehensible slogans to be splashed all over the city, but recollecting Amy's views on the old proprieties, he did not raise the issue with her. He said he had worked hard in Malaya but had not made as much money as he wanted to. He held Chiang Kai-shek in high esteem; it was his understanding that Chiang had done an excellent job in organizing the new army. His opinions with respect to the split in the Party were like hers.

Amy was evidently pleased. She had been secretly charged by the Central Committee to sound Fucho out, and she felt she had sounded him out to her satisfaction. She threw a glance at Tong Hsi, and he picked up his cue.

"I have a formal mission on behalf of both the Central Committee and Comrade Chiang Kai-shek," he said. "I have reported your arrival to them and they are as pleased as can be. It's a godsend that you chose to return at this particular juncture. You should have let us know beforehand, so Comrade Chiang Kai-shek and all of us could have met you at the railway station as a reception committee. Now, in order to accord you a suitable welcome, I am directed by the Central Committee to invite you to attend its meeting tomorrow as a special guest."

Fucho accepted the invitation, and Tong Hsi and Amy arranged to pick him up next morning and take him to the meeting in their limousine. Then they left.

Fucho spent the whole evening composing the speech he wanted to deliver to the Central Committee. He would wait until later to talk about the unification of the Party; now he intended to speak on the importance of the ancient Chinese culture as a basis for the revolution. Had not Dr. Sun Yat-sen himself made it clear that he derived his Three People's Principles as much from the teachings of Confucius as from the Western civilizations? How, then, could the Party which professed to carry out his legacy to the letter, as in the case of co-operation with the Communists, fail to live up to his ideals? A nation without morals would be like a house built on sand. A revolution advocating the destruction of ethics would be like a man bargaining away his soul for power.

He discussed his speech with Delicate Blossom and Li-hwa, and they thought his arguments unanswerable. He concluded with a proposal that all such propaganda as the slogans he had seen be condemned at once by a formal resolution of the Central Committee. If this were agreed upon, he told his wife and daughter, then he would announce his donation forthwith.

Fucho's reception by the Central Committee next day was cordial enough. The chairman, a stranger to Fucho, welcomed him with befitting respect, and the few old comrades whom Fucho knew received him with manifest enthusiasm. Chiang Kai-shek sent his regrets; he had been unexpectedly detained at headquarters on urgent business in connection with the preparations for the Northern Expedition. Fucho was introduced to various other members.

257

Because he was so concerned about the propaganda of the Party, he paid special notice to Mao Tse-tung, who was in charge of the Publicity Department.

Mao was a man of medium height in his middle thirties, with a round face and slightly bulging eyes. He walked with a peculiar gait. Clenching his fists and keeping his arms close to his sides, he moved with his head turning this way and that, in a deliberate, lumbering manner. He was very sparing of words, but he looked harmless.

Fucho was taken to the rostrum by Tong Hsi and seated beside the chairman. He told that dignitary he would like, if permitted to do so, to address the Committee after he had been introduced. The chairman glanced at Tong Hsi in apparent surprise, but when he turned to reply to Fucho, he wore a disarming smile.

"Of course," he said. "We will be deeply honored if we can find time for it. May I ask on what subject you propose to talk, Comrade?"

"On the most important question now facing the Party—the moral basis of our revolution."

"Do you have a written draft of your speech?"

"No. I made some notes, but I did not bring them with me."

"Excuse me a minute," the chairman said hesitantly. Motioning Tong Hsi to follow, he then went down to the floor and beckoned several other members into a huddle in a corner of the room. Fucho noticed that Amy and Mao Tse-tung were among those he summoned. Presently, the chairman returned.

"I am exceedingly sorry, Comrade Ho," he said politely. "I have just discussed the matter with the chairmen of the various subcommittees. There are too many items of urgent business on the agenda today, but we shall arrange to have you address us at the next meeting. However, we would appreciate a written draft of your speech in advance."

Fucho was vexed.

The chairman now quickly called the meeting to order, beginning resonantly, "I consider myself especially privileged to preside at this meeting today, which is not only of the utmost importance to our Party, but in addition is graced by the presence of one of our oldest and most distinguished comrades. It is indeed gratifying that he has chosen to return from so far as Malaya, after ten years' absence, to give us guidance and render us support at this most critical

258

hour in the history of our Party. We would like to devote the whole meeting to listening to him, but because of pressing business we shall have to defer that pleasure until a later date. For the time being, we can only ask him to rise and acknowledge the sincere expression of homage that is due him. He is so famed for his past revolutionary achievements that he needs no introduction. Comrades, I give you Comrade Ho Fucho!"

Mechanically Fucho rose and made his bow. The members of the Committee, to a man, stood up and gave him a rousing minute-long ovation. Then, before Fucho could open his mouth, Tong Hsi and Amy were at the rostrum saying it was time to leave. The chairman extended him a hasty hand in farewell, and he was half-guided, half-hustled out of the room by Tong Hsi and Amy. They returned to the meeting after seeing him safely to their chauffeur-driven limousine.

Fucho arrived back at his hotel irritated and frustrated, but Delicate Blossom and Li-hwa tried to console him. It was understandable that the Central Committee might be burdened with urgent business. Why not write his speech now, as they had suggested—it might well become a historical document.

Fucho took cheer and began writing down his thoughts. He was still working at this task when, past noon, he heard newsboys on the street shouting loudly and excitedly, "Extra! Extra!"

Delicate Blossom sent Li-hwa out for a paper, and the girl soon returned with her pretty face the picture of anger and indignation.

"Father, look at this!" she cried.

Fucho took the paper and Delicate Blossom looked over his shoulder. The first thing that met their eyes was Fucho's picture—one he had had taken when he was Governor. Then they saw the headlines: "West Hill Conference Group Expelled from Party! Full Support from Old Comrade Ho Fucho."

In large bold black type was the resolution the Central Committee had adopted during the morning session, followed by the news of Fucho's arrival and his presence at the meeting, with the specific purpose—it was said—of expressing his personal endorsement of the resolution. After that, in smaller type, came an enumeration of "the enormous crimes" the reactionaries of the West Hill Conference Group had committed, and also a detailed account of Fucho's distinguished past record in the Party. There were also numerous telegrams and petitions purporting to be from various comrades and organizations demanding the expulsion of the West Hill group. But there was no mistaking that he himself was being used to the disadvantage of his old comrades.

Speechless with rage, Fucho suddenly recollected Ta-kong's words. The resolution had been decided upon in advance, and he had deliberately been made a cat's-paw. Well, the battle was on now between him and the whole new Central Committee. He would call a press conference and fling his denials at the Committee, denounce them for their trickery and depravity. He would fight them to the bitter end.

Just then there was a sharp rap at the door. Li-hwa opened it to disclose a tall, square-built young man, holding a tiny piece of paper in his hand. He wore a military uniform, but kept the visor of his cap drawn so low that the upper part of his face could hardly be seen.

"I think one of you must have dropped this in the hallway," he said loudly, extending the slip of paper.

Li-hwa shook her head.

Abruptly the stranger thrust the paper into her hand. "It is yours. It is important. It is for Governor Ho Fucho."

Then he turned on his heel, sped down the hall, and disappeared at the turn of the landing.

Fucho examined the paper. On one side was a number—36. He turned the paper over. On the other side were two Chinese characters —"This minute." The handwriting was familiar—it was Ta-kong's. Fucho understood: "Of all the thirty-six stratagems, to get away is the best!"

Fucho considered carefully. After all, his nephew might be right. The newspapers were all controlled by the Party. Even if he held a press conference they would not print anything that was not authorized by the Central Committee. If he were willing to stay here and go along blindly with the Committee, they would take advantage of his name wherever they could. Of a sudden, it dawned on him that since these men had openly announced to the world that he was a strong supporter of their policies, they could not afford to let him go elsewhere and publicize his real views. To silence him, they would not hesitate to resort to violence—even murder.

Quickly he made up his mind, and then explained his decision to Delicate Blossom and Li-hwa. They left Canton at once, as unnoticed as they had come. When, late that night, Ta-kong reported their unexpected departure to the High Command of his party, they had already crossed the border and arrived safely in Hong Kong.

Two

THE DAYS THAT followed were dull with misery. Fucho's mind
was in a state of ceaseless turmoil. He saw his name dishonored, his
self-respect outraged, and, above all, his hopes for his Party and
his country blasted. And as he suffered, so did Delicate Blossom and
Li-hwa.

The day after his arrival in the British Crown Colony, he had
intended to give a news conference to the free press of Hong Kong,
but as soon as he read the morning papers, he threw the idea over-
board in a fit of fury. The newspapers of that date (and for almost
a fortnight afterward) were filled with violent and vicious incrimina-
tions and recriminations from both Right and Left. Though the
Central Committee at Canton maintained a discreet silence about
Fucho, the West Hill Conference Group in Shanghai, his old intimate comrades, singled him out as the main target of their bitterest
venom. They called him a traitor, a renegade, a worthless and faith-
less opportunist. He had fled the country for the past ten years, they
charged, in order to shirk his duty as a Party member and to enrich
himself. And he had returned now only to cast his lot with the
Communists because birds of a feather would flock together and
because he saw in this adventure another profitable chance for
self-advancement.

Fucho's heart bled. His story would be no longer believed. Either
it would be interpreted as a cover-up to conceal the disappointment his self-seeking ambition had met at the hands of the Leftists,
or it might be construed simply as another ruse to further some of
his sinister and unscrupulous designs.

He was now cut off from both factions of the Kuomintang. He
was a Party member without a Party, a revolutionary without a
revolution. His entire being revolted against the Leftists in Canton.
Yet he could no longer go to Shanghai and ally himself with the
Rightists, for he would surely be ostracized by his old comrades and
suspected of spying for the Communists.

He talked of returning to Malaya and again starting a business.
He talked of going into permanent retirement and leading a life of

ease and leisure on the money he had already earned. Both Delicate Blossom and Li-hwa supported him in every momentary whim, but they knew his heart was not in what he was saying. And at the end of a fortnight, when the Rightist denunciations of him were at last beginning to simmer down, it was announced in Canton that the Northern Expedition had started its march to overthrow the warlords and unify the nation. This news that would otherwise have gladdened Fucho's heart now fell upon it like a stone. He felt no joy, only unfathomable grief.

Should the expedition fail, it would mean the ruin of the last hopes of the Kuomintang. If it succeeded, it would mean domination by a group of men who were devoid of moral principles and who wanted to destroy what was best in the Chinese people. And worst of all, Fucho could do nothing about it. He, the man who had toiled so hard, striven so long, and devoted his whole life so selflessly to the Cause, could not do anything to further the Cause. His oath to his father would never be fulfilled; his life was meaningless.

He could neither eat nor sleep, and in a few days he grew so thin and haggard that Delicate Blossom, patiently watching him in silence, became genuinely concerned about his health.

Then one gray dawn Delicate Blossom saw Fucho get up furtively and steal to a window. All these nights he had tossed fitfully about in bed, sleepless, while she had lain rigidly by his side pretending to sleep, aware of his every movement. But he had never done what he was doing now. Without a sound he opened the window and leaned out. It was five stories to the street.

A terrible thought seized Delicate Blossom. "Fucho!" she screamed.

He sprang back from the window, stricken by the fright in her voice, and quickly took her in his arms. Both of them burst into tears.

"Oh, Fucho, for a moment I thought . . . I thought . . ."

He held her close. "Dearest—it wasn't that. I could never do such a thing while we have each other. I was only looking to see if anyone was stirring at this hour."

"Your life is my life, Fucho," Delicate Blossom sobbed. "I want you to do whatever you feel you must—I'll help you. We can't go on like this! I cannot bear it, nor can Li-hwa."

"All I've been thinking of is Li-hwa and you, darling. I have a plan, but I can't bring myself to follow it."

"Tell me," she begged.

"There's no use in talking about it."

"Please tell me, Fucho."

"It's a dangerous and unlikely scheme, darling. I can't work with either side—you know that. The only possibility left is to start a revolution all by myself—a revolution that will not be tarnished by personal ambitions, that will aim at nothing short of realizing the ideals of our revered father and Dr. Sun."

"Can one man do that?" Delicate Blossom asked in astonishment.

Fucho felt suddenly alive and confident. "We faced difficulties in our province fifteen years ago. We had no money of our own then; now we do. But we need men, just as we did then. From all I can learn, the people in our province are worse than discontented with Tien Fong, and many of them remember the improvements I made there. Some of my former subordinates are still among Tien's troops, so I might be able to overthrow him and get control of the province. Once we had that as a base of operations, we'd be well on the way toward achieving our real revolution. It would be extremely difficult, but not impossible."

"Go ahead with your plan, Fucho!" Delicate Blossom urged.

"I don't dare," he said painfully. "When we decided to give the money to the Kuomintang, I felt that if the revolution succeeded we would never need to worry about a means of livelihood. Even if it failed, the Party probably would be able to hold Canton and its two adjacent provinces, and I'd still have some position to fall back on to support you and Li-hwa. But if this venture were to fail, Heaven knows where it might end. No, I will not gamble with your happiness and security, and Li-hwa's—possibly even with your lives!"

"I have no life but yours, Fucho. I have no security but in your security—no happiness but in your happiness."

"Think of Li-hwa, my darling."

Delicate Blossom smoothed Fucho's cheek gently with her hand. "Don't you know your own daughter? Her sense of Filial Piety is so strong that if she ever felt she was a hindrance in your life she'd wish she had never been born. We both know how intelligent she is. Sooner or later she'd be bound to find out she'd held you back. She would suffer then infinitely more than she is now."

Fucho bowed his head thoughtfully.

"Go ahead with your plan, dearest," Delicate Blossom said. "If you don't, you will eat your heart out—and mine and Li-hwa's too.

May Heaven bless you, my love, may the spirit of our dead father smile upon you and guide you from his grave."

Fucho took her hand and kissed it devoutly.

2

FROM THAT MORNING, Fucho became all cheerfulness and energy, with a purpose in life. And Delicate Blossom and Li-hwa, rejoicing at the change, put themselves completely behind his undertaking. They helped wherever they could, counseled him whenever necessary, and comforted him when he encountered temporary disappointments.

He began by writing countless letters to people in his province—friends, acquaintances, former subordinates, men for whom he had done some service at one time or another. They were casual letters informing them of his return to Hong Kong and inquiring in an offhand manner about conditions at home. To the Reverend Dr. Holt, with whom he had kept up an off-and-on correspondence throughout the years, he wrote a lengthy epistle and asked for answers to a list of specific questions.

Nearly all the letters were answered promptly. If the sentiments they expressed at hearing from Fucho were enthusiastic, the accounts they gave of the conditions in the province were even more encouraging to him. The people were thoroughly malcontent with Tien Fong's rule, far more so than Fucho had anticipated. Although none of the letters mentioned the Governor by name, many of them included the same quotation from the ancient classics, "Ah, if only the sun that scorches us from above could perish, I would willingly enter perdition with it!"

And Fucho's own popularity, it seemed, had soared in these years because of the sharp contrast. Several daring souls hinted pointedly that it would be great good fortune if they could have him back as Governor.

The reply of the Reverend Dr. Holt furnished the most objective analysis. Reading between the lines, Fucho could tell that his foreign friend was not unaware of the motive that had prompted his inquiry; though the missionary had tried hard to steer clear of the reefs of Chinese politics, there was no mistaking where his personal sympathies lay.

Fucho was particularly pleased with letters from three of his former subordinates who were now regimental commanders under

264

Tien Fong. All intimated that their troops were poorly and irregularly paid and often left to shift for themselves, and they also conveyed guarded complaints about Tien's misrule. They apparently thought Fucho was still working with Chiang Kai-shek, since they made mention of the initial successes of Chiang's Northern Expedition. It was clear, too, that they had no qualms about arranging a turnover at a price. Fucho felt that if they were prepared to do that for Chiang, they would do the same for him. All he had to do was act faster than Chiang.

He wanted to send confidential messengers to the three commanders, but there was nobody he could trust and so he hastily wired some of his former business agents in Malaya. Most were too busy with their own affairs, but after a lengthy exchange of telegrams two finally promised to come to Hong Kong.

Meanwhile, Chiang Kai-shek's forces were meeting with spectacular success. The Communists in charge of the Kuomintang Publicity Department had adopted a wily propaganda line, the possibilities of which that remarkable girl, Yin Mei-yin, had long ago foreseen. They proclaimed repeatedly that the Northern Expedition was out to unify the country, and intended to do so more by fighting against Imperialism than by overturning the warlords. This produced a double result: On the one hand, the people, aroused to an unprecedented pitch of patriotic fervor, welcomed the Expedition as a chance for national salvation; on the other, the warlords were not unduly frightened. As a matter of fact, they were provided with an easy escape from a tight corner—to save their skins they needed only to throw up their hands and join forces with the Kuomintang. Thus, before the year was over, Chiang's troops had taken control of most of the territory south of the Yangtze and were marching confidently toward the principal prize in the heart-land of China, the city of Hankow.

At last—after a number of demands for more money—Fucho's two agents from Malaya set out with sealed dispatches requesting the three commanders to name the specific conditions under which they would lend him their full support. Fucho himself, with Delicate Blossom and Li-hwa, went along as far as Shanghai, where he remained to await the commanders' replies. Shanghai was halfway between Hong Kong and his native province. Moreover, he knew the commanders would demand munitions, and nowhere in China could these be so readily procured in quantity as in Shanghai.

While Fucho anxiously marked time until his couriers returned, dramatic events were taking place in Central China. Hankow fell to the forces of the Northern Expedition. Then, a few days later, something happened that once would have been thought impossible. The British Concession in Hankow, symbol of Imperialism deep in the interior of China, was seized by a popular uprising—captured by a mob with their bare hands! And it was done in the face of armed British soldiers and in sight of British gunboats with decks cleared for action.

Neither Fucho nor the people knew that this incident had been well plotted in advance by the Communists; and Fucho did not dream that his nephew Ta-kong had taken a major part, utilizing his own experiences as well as the idea Yin Mei-yin had put into his head so many years before. With every move of the organized mob charted out beforehand, the British authorities had been taken completely by surprise. Overawed by the bedlam, unprepared for the audacity, they had lost both their wits and their nerve, and yielded the Concession without firing a gun.

The news stirred the whole nation as nothing had before. It struck fear and dismay into foreigners, and incited the people to wildest enthusiasm about the Northern Expedition. But Fucho did not share the common sentiments. Though he had avoided seeing any of his old friends in Shanghai, from casual talks with men in the street he gathered that the Leftists were now in absolute control of Hankow. Slogans like those he had seen in Canton were reported to be everywhere, and a campaign was being carried on from house to house, from school to school, denouncing the shackles of the old feudalistic proprieties. It was even said that women would soon parade stark naked in the streets to celebrate the good riddance of all sense of shame. Fucho prayed his own revolutionary move might succeed before the Leftists took another step northward.

The messengers returned at last. The three commanders were eager to cast their lot with him, but they needed both cash and munitions The minimum of cash required came to half a million dollars. Fucho hastily sent a messenger back with the necessary money, and his pledge that the munitions would be delivered at the designated places as soon as possible.

Fucho well knew that the only munitions dealer who could supply large quantities on short notice was Johnny Hunt. He called immediately at Hunt's office, only to learn that the American now worked in his home and that two days were required to make an appointment. So, again, he had to wait.

266

Johnny Hunt's home occupied a whole block of the most valuable land in the Concession area. The main building, constructed entirely of the finest marble, was the most ostentatious private residence Fucho had ever seen; no maharaja's palace in Malaya, no governor's mansion in Singapore or Hong Kong, could compare with it in splendor and extravagance. Fucho felt outraged—all this could have been made possible only at the expense of his own people. And now he himself was forced to do business with the man and enrich him all the more!

A secretary took Fucho to Hunt's private office, which was really not an office but a sumptuous sitting room. Hunt was not there. A voluptuous blonde lolled on a davenport, and the secretary exchanged a few words with her. She got up sluggishly, swinging her hips, and disappeared briefly behind the closed door into another room, then reopened it and gestured for Fucho to enter.

Inside, the first thing he saw was a huge teak couch, made by the Chinese especially for smoking opium in luxurious comfort. On it reclined Johnny Hunt, sucking on a pipe, with two exceedingly attractive girls, dressed as nurses, in attendance. One girl was lying on the couch opposite Johnny, engaged in the important business of kneading the soft black molasses of opium into a doughy substance ready for burning. The other was massaging Johnny's back.

Fucho had not seen Johnny Hunt since they had met in Yi; he never would have recognized him now. Though Hunt was about his own age, he looked twice as old. His ashen face was drained of all natural color. His eyes were lusterless and he could hardly keep them open. Pipe in hand, he made a feeble attempt to rise when Fucho appeared, but gave up and dropped his head back onto the pillow. Returning to his pipe, he smoked with furious puffs, and then handed it to the woman opposite, to be refilled.

At last he spoke to his visitor. "Please excuse me for receiving you like this—the cursed opium, you know. I seldom leave this apartment—I conduct all my business from here. What can I do for you?"

Fucho glanced at the two women and hesitated.

"They're all right," Hunt said. "They don't understand a word of Chinese."

Fucho stated his request.

Johnny Hunt answered with a sickly smile. "I'm glad you came to me; nobody else could possibly supply you in such a short time. You know, opium certainly stimulates the brain! I know my business as well as the palm of my hand. I can deliver the cargo to the recipients at the places you've specified in a week, provided you pay me cash in advance. Times are so unpredictable I can trade on no other terms."

"I am prepared to pay you cash right now," replied Fucho. "But can you make the delivery sooner?"

"No. I have to get some shipments from other places. A week is the best I can do."

"A week it is then. Now, what is your price?"

Hunt returned again to his pipe, and smoked even more furiously. Finally, he blew a last puff into the air and stared at Fucho, a strange gleam in his eye.

"For you, the price is a million and a half American dollars. Not a cent less."

"That's preposterous!" exclaimed Fucho. "You're asking twice the market price."

"These are my terms. Take it or leave it. Go to any other dealer and see if he has that much goods at hand and can deliver as promptly as I can. Yes, that's twice the market price, but I have a reason. When you were Governor you stamped out opium trade in your province and made me lose a great deal of money. If you become Governor again—which you well may, thanks to our little transaction—think what further losses I'll have to bear. It's plain common sense that I take these factors into consideration."

Fucho faltered. What Hunt said about the other munitions dealers tallied with his own findings. He had no time to spare, but if he yielded to Hunt's blackmail he would have only a few thousand dollars to his name.

With great effort, Johnny Hunt raised himself on the couch. "I have another proposition for you. If you promise that when you become Governor again, which I'm sure you will, you will co-operate with me and permit unchecked opium traffic in your province, I will not only give you, in the future, the commission I've been giving to Governor Tien Fong but I'll also come down now to the market price—that is, to three-quarters of a million. That's a very fair offer. I ask only your promise as collateral."

Fucho looked at him impassively. "Suppose I make the promise now and break it later?"

"I'll have to take my chances on that," retorted Hunt with a wry grin. "But I don't think it's much of a risk. Why are *you* sure I will deliver the goods after you have paid me cash in advance? Because I have the reputation of my firm to consider. Why do I trust your

268

mere word? Because I know your type of man; your word to me is as good as gold."

Fucho stiffened. "Thank you for the compliment. I will accept your price of a million and a half."

Hunt shrugged his shoulders and went back to his pipe. One of the girls handed him a telephone, and he alternated busily between it and the pipe. Presently a secretary brought contract forms, and Fucho signed and then handed over his check.

The now almost penniless Fucho was taking his leave when Johnny Hunt made a curious remark: "By the way, you haven't by chance heard from your old friend Tong Hsi?"

"I assume he is in Hankow."

"Ah," grunted Johnny Hunt, and they parted.

That afternoon Fucho dispatched his second messenger north. He was to advise the three commanders of the arrangements for delivery of the munitions and to ask them to meet Fucho the second day after the delivery, at any secret place they might designate. For reasons of security, Fucho cautioned that the place chosen must be either within the Concession area in the port city or in its immediate environs. Then he booked passage for himself and his family on a coastal steamship due to reach the port city a day ahead of his planned tryst.

Finally, he broke the news to his wife that he had already spent almost all their two millions. With a cheerful smile, Delicate Blossom told him not to be uneasy. What must be done must be done. . . .

Johnny Hunt had asked Fucho about Tong Hsi and Amy to make sure he knew nothing of their whereabouts. They were not in Hankow at all, but aboard a steamship on the Yangtze on their way to Shanghai. They arrived that evening and dined with Hunt in his apartment; their destination was the North. In the last days of Yuan Shih-kai, they had manipulated Tien Fong to declare himself for the Republic, as the Party well knew. Now they were entrusted with the mission of getting him to change—to shift his allegiance to the Kuomintang. If they succeeded, they were promised an even higher position in the new Government. They were not too concerned; Tien had already given them his assurance he would change colors whenever they wished.

During dinner, Johnny Hunt had one of his girls bring a portable set of opium utensils so that he could smoke between courses. As he relaxed, he looked up at Amy with open admiration.

"What an ingenious woman you are, my dear! But sure things

269

often have a way of going wrong. What if you get there and find Tien Fong gone—put out of the way, say, by somebody else?"

"What is this?" asked Amy, taking sudden alarm.

Johnny turned his head away and did not answer.

"You take everything too seriously, Amy," Tong Hsi murmured. "Johnny is only joking."

"You fool!" Amy snarled, then turned back to their host. "You have some information we don't have. I'm prepared to meet your terms. Tell me."

Johnny puffed at his pipe again. "It's not you, my old friends, that I don't trust," he said slowly. "It's your Party. It is getting so noisily antiforeign. I'm thinking of pulling all my resources out of this God-forsaken country. Why should I bother any more about your politics and your intrigues?"

"Bah!" replied Amy tartly. "I admit there are some radicals, even some Communists, within our Party. But mind you, to the people who really count, that antiforeign ballyhoo is only propaganda. We're just like the old Chinese saying: 'It is the same soup over and over—only the water is changed.' Isn't our position in the new Government a guarantee to you?"

"You mean I may continue to carry on my business as before?"

"Of course," asserted Amy. "In fact, it will work out better for you. Before, you had to dicker with many warlords; when we unify the country you will need to deal only with us."

"You mean I may continue my opium trade?"

"Why not? Hasn't it made money both for you and for us?"

That decided Hunt. After another pipeful, he told them of Fucho's visit and gave them full particulars concerning both the recipients and the destinations of Fucho's purchases.

Early next morning Amy and Tong Hsi left by train for a meeting with Tien Fong in his provincial capital—a full three days ahead of the time when Fucho's steamship was scheduled to sail from Shanghai for the North.

There is an old Chinese saying: "When a sparrow is intent on snatching a grasshopper, there may be a vulture stalking from behind." The Communists, having learned of Amy and Tong Hsi's mission, and having marked out Chiang Kai-shek and his group as their next target for destruction, forewarned Chang Fa-foo and other comrades in the North of the Tongs' coming and instructed them to keep a surreptitious eye on their every move.

270

3

FUCHO HAD NOT taken the train because of the danger in passing through Tien Fong's territory. Now, even as his steamship neared the northern port city, Amy and Tong Hsi and Tien Fong were meeting to decide on his fate. The munitions had been permitted to reach their various destinations, but the three commanders had been seized immediately. Under torture, which Tien Fong knew well how to inflict, all three had made full confessions, disclosing the details about their scheduled meeting with Fucho at a secluded hut.

There Tien was willing to let the matter rest. "So far as I'm concerned, Ho Fucho can go to the hut as often as he wishes. I feel I shouldn't do anything more. He was my superior officer once, and he treated me quite fairly. What harm can he do me now? He'll be sorely disappointed—and think of the pile of money he has lost! So long as he remains in the port city, I can always have him watched. No—if I were to do more, it wouldn't square with the standards of 'the rivers and lakes.' "

But Amy, once a woman scorned, was adamant. Her unforgiving nature had been aroused by their recent encounter in Canton, where she had observed the connubial felicity of Fucho and Delicate Blossom. And Fucho's unexpected departure from Canton had also caused her a good deal of discomfiture. She felt she had lost face in the Party because she failed to gauge Fucho's views correctly.

"You, with your standards of 'the rivers and lakes'!" she exclaimed. "I am the one who gave you the information about his plot, and I, not you, should have the final say!"

"Why are you so bitter against him?" asked Tien Fong curiously. "You may be the one who gave me the information but I'm the one he plotted against—and I'm not nearly so bitter. Besides, I thought he was your old friend and comrade."

"He's no comrade," Amy snapped. "He is a renegade from the Party—out to disrupt the plans of the Northern Expedition! Now, if you still want to join the Kuomintang and keep your position, do what I tell you!"

Tien Fong appealed to her husband. "What do you say?"

"Please, do what my wife asks," replied Tong Hsi.

Tien Fong's ugly scars settled into a grimace. For some reason he could never have explained—perhaps an instinctive respect for a man of learning and of courage—he had always liked Fucho. But now there was nothing he could do. . . .

271

At the hotel where his messengers had made reservations, Fucho and his family received reports that the munitions had been safely delivered and the meeting with the commanders arranged.

Delicate Blossom suggested that they call upon Chi Teh-shan and his wife that evening. It was their duty to pay respects to their benefactors, and this was the first opportunity they had had. Besides, useful information might perhaps be gathered from the powerful Old Head. Fucho objected. He was grateful to the Chis, but from all he had heard, Old Head had been flirting openly with the Kuomintang. Who knew on which side he really might be? Moreover, Fucho wanted nothing to do with the gangster until he had succeeded in his own revolutionary move.

Early the next morning Fucho breakfasted with Delicate Blossom in their suite. Li-hwa was still asleep.

"Is this not very early?" Delicate Blossom asked.

"Yes," Fucho said, looking at his wife tenderly. "But I must be extra careful. I want to take such a roundabout way to the meeting that nobody can follow me."

When he was ready to leave, he folded Delicate Blossom so tightly in his arms that he felt the fierce pounding of her heart.

"Don't be afraid, beloved," he whispered. "There is nothing to fear."

"I'm not afraid. There's no nobler man on this earth than you—and I cannot believe Heaven will let anything happen to you. Go, dearest, since you must."

Fucho lingered a moment at the door. "Will you say good-by to Li-hwa for me?"

Delicate Blossom smiled and nodded. And Fucho left.

Then, in spite of her firm resolutions, Delicate Blossom grew uneasy. A chill crept down her spine and her stomach felt bottomless. When Li-hwa arose, she tried to allay her mother's anxieties, but it was of little avail. By the time luncheon was served, food had lost its taste. The hours dragged.

Finally there was a knock on the door, and Delicate Blossom raced to open it.

It was Old Head. "May I come in?" he asked politely.

Delicate Blossom welcomed him with courtesy. "How kind of you to come here! By all rules of propriety we should first have called on you and Mrs. Chi."

Old Head remained standing. "Thanks, Madame Ho. But may I have a word with the Governor?"

272

"I am sorry to say he is not here. He will be back soon."

"Where has he gone?" asked Old Head anxiously.

Delicate Blossom hesitated.

"This is very important." Old Head's voice was grave. "I have just had most disturbing news from Tien Fong's capital."

Her heart standing still, Delicate Blossom at once told him Fucho's destination.

"I hope I am not too late," Old Head muttered between his teeth. He bolted out of the room.

The pursuit of an ideal demands time; time, to an idealist, is his most precious commodity. He needs time to study and contemplate and persevere, in reaching for his ideal—and Fucho had had ten years in Malaya to dream of what he could help his country become. He had also had anxious months of waiting while the Northern Expedition got under way, and he felt that time was running out.

He took three taxis in his circuitous journey to the rendezvous, and traveled the last leg on foot. When he came to the lonely hut in the woods, he was satisfied he had not been followed.

He knocked.

"Who is it?" asked a gruff voice.

"It is I, Ho Fucho."

And then there was no time at all. The door jerked open, and Fucho did not even see the guns before they blazed and roared and he felt a dozen bullets tear into his body.

"Delicate Blossom!" he gasped. "Oh, Father! I wanted to—"

Old Head found him later, and brought his body back to the private mortuary of the secret Society. He and Jasmine hurried to the hotel, worrying about how to break the news. But when they entered the suite, they saw Delicate Blossom knew and that made it easier. Li-hwa was lost in tears; Delicate Blossom seemed removed from grief, wanting only to be taken where Fucho's body lay.

At the mortuary she held Fucho's head for a moment in her hands, then turned to Jasmine and Chi Teh-shan.

"We have no friends left. Nor relatives, either, because Fucho always considered himself an outcast from his family. Please—Mr. Chi and Mrs. Chi—please take good care of Li-hwa. I shall be everlastingly grateful!"

Old Head nodded emphatically but could not speak.

Jasmine sobbed, "Don't worry, my dear! Everything we have is yours."

They saw Delicate Blossom put her hand to her mouth—but it was already too late. She had swallowed a deadly poison she had carried ever since she had urged Fucho to follow his plan in Hong Kong. She fell across her husband's body, dead.

Old Head and Jasmine sadly took Li-hwa to their home, and gave her parents the simple burial which Delicate Blossom, on their way to the mortuary, had told them Fucho always wanted. No obituary was released to the newspapers; thus the tragic end of Ho Fucho and his wife came to be known only to the very few whose interest it was not to let others know. After a time, Old Head and Jasmine wrote to the Reverend Dr. Holt. Even then, Old Head did not tell the whole truth, concealing the guilt of Amy and Tong Hsi.

The Chis treated Li-hwa as their own daughter and would have liked to adopt her, but they were too conscious of their own humble origins to speak of this for a while. And then one day they found the girl gone, leaving behind only a note saying that the port city was too full of sad memories for her. Jasmine wanted to search for her, but Old Head said no, that would be the thing Li-hwa least desired.

A few months later the forces of the Northern Expedition reached the borders of the province. Carrying out the bargain he had made with Amy and Tong Hsi, Tien Fong declared himself for the Kuomintang and was allowed to retain his post as Governor. As a reward for the Tongs, Tong Hsi was named chairman of the Political Commission for the Northern Provinces. He set up his headquarters in the port city, where fourteen years earlier he had been made Mayor on the recommendation of Ho Fucho.

Three

SIX MONTHS AFTER Tong Hsi's promotion, Lan Yuwen returned to China from the United States, a Doctor of Philosophy.

There was rejoicing in the Mission compound, but Yuwen's return did not cause much of a stir in Yi. Though Widow Lan had become famed in the Prefecture as a surgeon, and was especially esteemed by the poor, whom she served devotedly, she still retained her old aloofness in society and still lived in her old shack. It was more comfortably furnished now, and her former dumpling shop had been transformed into a sitting room. The walls were lined with shelves of books in both English and Chinese. Viewing them, Yuwen was very proud that his mother had been able to raise herself from total illiteracy to such heights of intellectual development.

A cot had been temporarily installed for Yuwen, and they sat on it now, talking alone.

"Now that you have attained the highest in education, my son, you must seek employment and then get married. In the old days we used to say that 'the greatest lapse in filial piety is the lack of an issue to carry on the family name.' I know things are changed. Still, I'd like to have grandchildren."

"Of course," agreed Yuwen, blushing. "But what I want most is to be with you, Mother. You've done so much for me that I want to show you some filial piety—even when I marry, I want you to live with me."

"I am glad you have preserved your sense of the old proprieties," Widow Lan said. "Too many young people hold them in contempt these days. Why, the Holy Scripture itself commands, 'Honor thy father and thy mother'! However, much as I should like to, I cannot live with you. I have my work in the Mission, but you will have to look elsewhere for work."

"Aren't there any jobs here in Yi?"

"You are just back, my son, and you don't know how bad conditions have become. The big cities may have a superficial appearance of prosperity, but the country at large has been impoverished by the constant civil wars and revolutions. Most of the people are without work, and many have turned to banditry for a living. Our old village, where you were born, is infested with bandits. Some of my patients come from there, and they don't have to tell me how they got their wounds. One of them, Kan Koo, is a well-known chieftain, though he appears to be a very good man. They all are very grateful to the Mission and to me, but I ask no questions, nor do I blame them. What else can they do, conditions being what they are?"

"But won't the Northern Expedition change all this? The country is unified, and the Kuomintang Government is more enlightened than the old warlords. When I was abroad I heard nothing but good about Chiang Kai-shek, and I believe he can bring peace and prosperity to our people."

"I hope so," said Widow Lan, "but I have my misgivings. Of course some other provinces may be better off. Tien Fong is still the Governor of this one—the man who used to call himself Fong Tienpa —and if there was ever a warlord, he is one. True, he has declared himself for the Kuomintang, though he has not mended his ways at all so far."

Yuwen's thoughts turned to a subject which had been in his mind all the way home.

"Mother, do you have any idea where my Big Brother, Ho Ta-kong, is now, or have you heard anything about him? You remember that he and I and another boy, Li Chien—you never met him—are sworn brothers. After I left for America we corresponded for two or three years, but then he stopped writing."

"No," said Widow Lan unhappily. "His parents died of cholera about a year after you left, and he came back to Yi then for a short while and visited me a few times. He was such a bright lad, so like his uncle, Ho Fucho, the former Governor. Did you know there is a rumor that Governor Ho has been murdered by Tien Fong? Anyway, Ta-kong has not written to any member of his family since he left here. And the Hos have done badly. What a pity! Ma Pingshi, who chased out his own brother with the help of Governor Tien, is flourishing, while the Hos have had to sell much of their property and even had to mortgage their house. When I heard about it, I went to them and offered to buy our shack at twice its value. They refused at first, saying that Ho the Central Hall had already given it to me, but when I insisted they finally took the money. It was the least I could do."

That night Yuwen did not sleep well. He was worried by the lack of news about his Big Brother, and disturbed by the cheerless picture his mother had drawn of the country at large. In the United States the papers had carried little news relating to China, and he knew only sketchily of the Northern Expedition led by Chiang Kai-shek, though he had gloried patriotically in its success. Unlike his Big Brother, Yuwen had no itch for power or position. He had returned to China with simple dreams: to lead a peaceful life, to be useful to society and to his country, to earn an honest living, to be with his mother, and to rear a happy family of his own. But if all his mother said was true, even these modest aspirations were beyond his reach.

Next day he had a serious talk with the Reverend Dr. Holt, who was able to give him more comfort. The situation in their province was in truth as bad as his mother had described, but the long-range prospects of the country as a whole were somewhat rosier. From his correspondence with other missionaries, Holt said, he had concluded that any collaboration of the Kuomintang with warlords like Tien Fong was merely a matter of expediency brought on by the struggle against the Communists. He blamed the plight of China on the Communists, not on the Kuomintang. The Communists were god-less men who wanted to overthrow everything good in the ancient Chinese culture; fortunately Chiang Kai-shek had seen this, and had now broken completely with them and had severed relations with Soviet Russia. He had allied himself again with the Rightists of the Kuomintang, the so-called West Hill Conference Group, and set up a new Government in Nanking with himself as Chairman. The Communists, outlawed, had risen in rebellion in the South, and Chiang Kai-shek was now engaged in suppressing them. The Kuo-mintang needed the support of the warlords to stamp out the Com-munists, but Holt had every reason to believe this was only a passing phase—it would destroy the warlords later.

Chiang Kai-shek, the missionary said, had recently married into a Christian family and had become a Christian himself. It was also gratifying to the Reverend Dr. Holt that Chiang had shown a pref-erence for Christians in the important posts. Tong Hsi and his wife, for example, were Christians.

But Holt did share the Widow Lan's opinion as to Yuwen's chances of finding a job in Yi. There was hardly any white-collar position available to a man of Yuwen's education; he could only enter Government service, but in this province all appointments were controlled by Tien Fong, who distributed them not on merit but on the basis of influence, bribery, or favoritism. It would be out of the question for Yuwen to serve under such a man.

In the end, the Reverend Dr. Holt found him an opening at the Missionary College in which Yuwen had studied before, and the young man returned to the big port city to serve as a professor in his alma mater.

2

YUWEN APPLIED HIMSELF with zeal, glad of the opportunity to study the conditions in his country. At first he was infected with Holt's optimism, but before long he had many doubts. By all reports, the Communists had been wiped out in the South, except for a band of one or two thousand men led by Mao Tse-tung, who had fled into the mountains. But now it seemed the Kuomintang was no longer paying any heed to exterminating the Communists nor even turning its forces against the warlords, as the Reverend Dr. Holt had hoped. Instead, it was like a house divided, and Chiang Kai-shek was hurling his whole might against the so-called Kwangsi generals, some rival Kuomintang officers in Central China, who contended Chiang had arrogated too much power to himself. Yuwen watched and was shocked; had China merely substituted new warlords for the old?

And even the old warlords were still entrenched in the North—apparently the only change achieved by the Northern Expedition was that they now acknowledged allegiance to Chiang's Government in Nanking. They had been shorn of no power and continued merrily in their evil ways, unmended and unchecked. What disillusioned Yuwen most was that Tong Hsi had fallen far short of the Reverend Dr. Holt's expectations. It was reported that he and his wife were in active collusion with the warlords and were enriching themselves.

Almost immediately after his arrival, Yuwen sought information concerning his two sworn brothers. He made inquiries at the University and even barged into the presence of Chancellor Chang Fa-foo. But Chang told him blandly that he had no knowledge of their whereabouts.

Yuwen then called on the Chis and learned the sad news that old Mistress Chow, whom he had known so well in his childhood, had passed away into the Ever-Happy Land of the Buddhas. The Chis treated him very kindly—Jasmine kept telling him how much she owed his mother, and inviting him to visit them often—yet when he asked Old Head whether he knew anything about Ta-kong and Li Chien, the chief of the secret Society merely answered vaguely that they were probably somewhere in the South. (The Close-Door-Disciple had advised his Venerable Master by way of their underground channel of communication that he and his Second Brother were now with Mao Tse-tung in his mountain retreat, but Old Head did not feel he could disclose this news to Yuwen.)

Yuwen had never been keenly interested in politics, but now he longed to discuss the country's troubles with Ta-kong and Li Chien. Somehow he did not feel as free to exchange opinions with his new associates as with his sworn brothers.

One night, especially lonesome, he went to the park where he had given them his parting admonitions years before. It was a beautiful autumn night, with a crescent moon; though the hour was rather late, there were still quite a few people on the grounds. He wandered back and forth, lost in idle reveries. The life of men, he told himself, is not different from that of birds, which flock together by chance and perch on the same tree; they share one another's company for a brief moment and then fly off and are separated for ever.

Suddenly, before Yuwen realized what was happening, a dozen or so uniformed men descended on the park from nowhere. They carried revolvers, brandishing them carelessly, and shouted to the people, "Get out! Make way for your betters!"

Most of the strollers scurried away, avoiding trouble, but a few hesitated, and they were at once roughly pushed out.

Yuwen, astonished at the sight, did not budge. One of the uniformed men advanced on him threateningly and shouted, "You there!"

"Is this not a public park?" asked Yuwen calmly.

"Right. But it's private from now until we leave."

"Then I have as much right to stay here as you."

"No. You haven't got the special privileges we have."

"This is outrageous!" Yuwen said indignantly. "In the old days only the Emperor had the special privilege you claim: wherever he made an appearance the people had to make themselves scarce. This was also the practice, I understand, with some warlords. But we have a republic and a Kuomintang Government now. Which are you? An emperor or a warlord?"

The altercation attracted more of the uniformed men, one of whom shouted, "This turtle-egg has no manners. Let's teach him how to behave to his betters!" And they leaped at Yuwen.

Struggling hard, he cried, "Take me to the police! Take me to a law court!"

The men roared, "We're the police. We're the court." And they started beating and kicking him.

Yuwen might have been badly injured had not a shadowy group of people just then appeared. A powerful flashlight was beamed on his face; then a voice cried, "Stop!"

Yuwen was released instantly, to his relief—and surprise also, for the voice was a woman's. Blinded by the strong flashlight, however, he could not see her.

She continued, quite pleasantly, "I must apologize for my bodyguards. Who are you, young man?"

"I am Lan Yuwen, a professor in the Missionary College. But who are you? And how dare your bodyguards treat me like this? What right do they have to chase the people away from a public park?"

"I said I was sorry. For what has happened, I am prepared to make amends to you personally."

"I do not want anything. I just want to know who you are."

The woman chuckled. "I will let you know by-and-by; now I have to take leave of you." And she began to walk off with her retinue.

Yuwen made a move to follow, but a bodyguard barred his way. Infuriated, bewildered, he heard a procession of motor cars roll off.

Several days later he received a letter bearing the name of a commercial corporation and signed by a secretary. It stated that the company was engaged in considerable import and export trading and that it needed the services of promising young men who had been educated abroad, especially in the United States. If Yuwen was interested, he could arrange for an appointment. Yuwen was well satisfied with his teaching position, but he had studied economics in the United States and he decided that if the offer proved suitable he might take it as part-time work.

Yuwen went to the address, and found a magnificent multi-storied building with modern offices and a large, busy staff. He was promptly shown into a private office, where a woman sat. He was quite surprised because businesswomen were still rare in China. The interview lasted only a few minutes, and then he was told that on the basis of his record, he had already been hired as a special assistant to the Board of Directors; and then and there he was paid two months' salary in advance—a thousand Chinese dollars in cash, almost triple what he was earning at the Missionary College.

Yuwen put the money carefully inside his wallet. "But what are my duties to be?"

"I will take you to see a Director at once," answered the woman, "and the Director will tell you." She rose and led him to an elevator marked "For the Exclusive Use of the Directors." When they reached the top floor she pointed to a door. "You go in there!" she said.

Yuwen knocked but there was no answer, and so he opened the door and entered. It was not an office, but a private apartment. He found himself in a parlor, expensively if somewhat garishly furnished. On one side, through an open door, he could see a commodious bedchamber with a beautifully carved bed, and on the other side a dining room.

A door closed behind him, and a sultry voice said, "Surprised?"

He turned, startled. He would have recognized the voice anywhere; it was that of the woman he had encountered in the park incident a few nights before. Though she must have been well in her forties, her make-up made her look much younger.

"You?" he exclaimed. "I—I am here to see a Director of the company."

"But I am the Director," answered the woman with a bewitching smile. "The entire Board of Directors, no less."

"Then you hired me as a special assistant. Why?"

"Please sit down," the woman said, immediately seating herself close beside him. "Why? To make personal amends for the wrong my men did you the other night."

"Then I do not want this job. I cannot take money under false pretenses."

"But there's no pretense on my part. I like you. I want you to be my special assistant, and I am sure you will provide exactly what I need."

"What do you mean?"

"You really don't know?"

Yuwen understood, and was shocked. The woman, emboldened by her own desire, stroked his cheek provocatively.

Her touch repelled Yuwen, but he was aware he was treading on delicate ground. There was no knowing what evil this woman was capable of. He managed a smile, trying to play his part as best he could.

"Since you obviously require special service, don't you think five hundred dollars a month is a little cheap?"

The woman giggled. "You're indeed a boy after my own heart—we shall get along well together. If you're not satisfied with my offer, what price do you suggest?"

Yuwen considered. To make the price prohibitive would not do; it would only arouse her suspicion. "Suppose we say two thousand a month?" he said tentatively. "And a guarantee of continuous payment for at least ten years? After all, who knows when you may become tired of my services?" He congratulated himself on the fact that these terms would be difficult enough to meet.

To his surprise the woman instantly said, "Agreed. However, I have my condition too. During these ten years I keep paying you, you must not dally with any other woman—not one. Tit for tat, my handsome one."

"That's fair enough. But what if I refuse?"

Her laugh sounded sinister. "I can have anything I want—anything! You can't escape me, my pet. From this moment, I shall have you shadowed day and night."

Yuwen saw a way out of his dilemma more clearly now. "I have no objection to your condition, but I will accept it only on my own terms."

"What are they?" she asked, admiring him for his assertion of maleness.

"First, you must have a legal contract drawn up—and sign it—stipulating that you are to employ me as personal assistant and to pay me two thousand dollars a month for at least ten years. Second—to use your own words—you, too, must promise not to dally with any other man during this period. Third, you must put your faith in me and have no one follow or shadow me at any time now or ever."

The woman looked at Yuwen calculatingly. "Your first two conditions sound all right, but I don't like the third one. How can I be sure you won't run away?"

Yuwen laughed. "Since when has a man been known to run off from so much easy, pleasant money? Anyway, these are my terms. Take them or leave them."

She flung her arms around him. "You win, my little fair face!"

Yuwen pushed her gently aside. "The contract first."

She withdrew reluctantly. "You cruel, tantalizing devil! Well, I'll have the contract ready tomorrow. Will you come at the same hour?"

"Of course, I will." He rose to leave. "By the way, you haven't told me your name."

"Why," the woman said in surprise, "I thought you already knew. I am Amy, wife of Tong Hsi, Chairman of the Political Commission for the Northern Provinces."

"I'll see you tomorrow," said Yuwen airily.

He escaped into an alley from the back exit of the building, goose pimples all over his body. The alley was deserted, but up on the top floor he caught a glimpse of the woman watching him from a window. He lifted his face, smiled, and waved his hand; Amy threw him a kiss. Then, making certain he was not followed, he took a bus to Old Head's house.

Yuwen told Old Head the whole story and asked for advice. At first, with a twinkle in his eye, that "Mountain of Virtues" saw no reason Yuwen should not accept the offer; opportunities like this for a poor young man to come by so much money so painlessly were few and far between. But Yuwen persisted in his refusal, and Old

Head, lost in admiration for him, offered to be of whatever help possible.

Would the secret Society, Yuwen asked, be willing to provide him with protection?

No. It was willing, but not able. Amy and her husband were powerful political figures and had a large private retinue. No matter how well-guarded Yuwen might be, there was no certainty of avoiding the fury of a woman scorned.

Could Yuwen go to the authorities of the foreign Concessions and ask for protection? No. The foreign police depended on Old Head himself to enforce law and order, and the foreigners were striving to establish good relations with the Kuomintang. They would not want to take issue with Amy and Tong Hsi on such a delicate and personal matter.

Could he appeal to the public through the newspapers, as was often done in the United States? No. The Chinese newspapers were mostly controlled. And anyway, it would be Yuwen's word against Amy's.

Could Yuwen approach Tong Hsi directly, tell him the whole thing, and ask for his protection against his wife? No. Amy could twist Tong Hsi around her little finger.

Could he return to Yi as a temporary refuge? No. Governor Tien Fong was working hand in glove with Amy and Tong Hsi. He would deliver Yuwen back to Amy immediately.

The only thing Yuwen could do, Old Head said finally, was to flee at least as far as Shanghai, which had the largest foreign Concessions, where Amy's influence would not prevail. Old Head added that there was not much time to lose—Yuwen was supposed to meet her again tomorrow afternoon.

Yuwen returned to his lodgings and wrote a note to the President of the Missionary College, regretfully submitting his resignation. He sent two other letters also, one to his mother and the other to the Reverend Dr. Holt, giving a rough outline of what had happened. Then he embarked on a ship for Shanghai.

3

Amy's thousand dollars now stood him in good stead. After he had spent two months in Shanghai looking for a job, he began to regret he had ever gone to the United States for additional education. He would have done better now if he had been apprenticed to a carpenter or a mason; with all his accomplishments, he could not earn a decent living. Of course, there were always the big foreign corporations where his knowledge of English and economics could be put to use, but he was unwilling to prostitute his talents to foreigners whose only aim was to make money out of his country. There were several missionary colleges in Shanghai, but he feared that since he had already disappointed one of them in the North, they might not be too eager to extend him welcome here. Then there were doubtless openings in Government services and Government universities—but he was disgusted with a Government that would raise people like Amy and Tong Hsi to power.

Finally, he ran into some fellow students returned from America, and found they were similarly frustrated. But they all put their heads together and an idea was born: they would establish a college of their own. An old rambling compound was rented as provisional campus; implements and furniture were purchased on the installment plan, and they pooled their books to form a library. Advertisements were placed in the newspapers announcing the opening and inviting students to enroll. The response surpassed their fondest hopes. At that time there were few schools of higher education in the country, and even well-to-do families had no place to send their children who wanted additional education. Moreover, Yuwen and his associates had purposely made their tuition fee so reasonable that it was not beyond the means of the lower middle class. The college became an instant success, and it gave Yuwen and his friends a useful purpose in life, as well as providing them with a modest livelihood.

Yuwen had time now to give thought to the woes of China. As he saw it, the people had to be restored to higher moral standards. His knowledge of the doings of Tien Fong, and especially his experience with Amy, had convinced him that the old structure of ethical conventions, so painstakingly built up by the sages of the past, had been too recklessly torn down; and nothing had been erected in its place.

In the United States, Yuwen had been profoundly impressed by the fact that even the smallest community had a church. But devout Christian though he was, he was broad-minded enough not to insist that everyone else be converted. There were Christians and Christians. Even Amy was a professed Christian. . . .

The important thing was, as Yuwen saw it, that everyone espouse a religious or ethical faith, raise spiritual values above material considerations, and unite with others to create a sense of right and wrong in the common community.

This idea, he knew, was Confucian and must have grown out of the tradition he had learned in childhood, but despite all the modern philosophies he had mastered, he could think of no better or more efficacious way of regenerating the nation.

The second thing the country needed, in Yuwen's opinion, was a government by law rather than by men. In spite of the nominal unification of the country by Chiang Kai-shek (for Chiang had, by this time, defeated his rival Kuomintang generals in Central China), no system of constitutional government had yet been established. On the contrary, Chiang and his men were loudly proclaiming that before the nation was ready for such a step, it must first go through two stages of political development—a "Period of Military Government" and then a "Period of Political Tutelage." During both these periods, whose duration was never defined, it behooved the people to submit to the domination of the Kuomintang.

If Yuwen had not been disillusioned by his personal encounter with Amy he might have thought this a plausible idea. He realized that there might be many good men in the Kuomintang far different from Amy and Tong Hsi, but still, people like Amy and Tong Hsi did occupy high and influential positions. The trouble with China, therefore, was not necessarily the presence of bad personnel within the Kuomintang Government; it was the lack of any system by which bad personnel could be effectively weeded out. As it was, the Kuomintang was responsible to none but Chiang Kai-shek, and Chiang Kai-shek to none but himself.

As Yuwen pondered the evils in the regime and the perils ahead for China, he first fully appreciated the true greatness of the founder of the country he had so recently left. Had George Washington been less noble and selfless—more susceptible to personal ambition, say, like Yuan Shih-kai, or Aaron Burr—he might have made himself a dictator of the United States and throttled the infant republic in its cradle. But only because, once having achieved supreme power, he relinquished it voluntarily, did he give the burgeoning democracy a chance to grow and develop a system of government by law for the benefit of all.

With the perspective of time and distance, Yuwen began to envy things he had not appreciated while in the United States. He wanted them for China—free elections so that he and his countrymen could choose their own government, a Bill of Rights so that all could be

285

protected from undue oppression. He wanted freedom of speech and freedom of the press so that the wrong-doing of the rulers might not go unchallenged and so that the public might be aroused to a greater awareness of their duties to the nation. He wanted Chiang Kai-shek to become another George Washington.

These convictions did not come to Yuwen suddenly, but were formulated slowly and gradually and after careful deliberation. To the public, however, his ideas were "against the current of the times." Although his emphasis on the restoration of moral standards was considered merely old-fashioned, his advocacy of a rule by law was regarded as near dangerous, it was so out of step with the announced policy of the Government. But undaunted by the initial unfavorable response and protected by the immunity of the Shanghai foreign Concessions, Yuwen preached his convictions, harped on them in his classes, discussed them in open forums, and wrote articles about them for several independent publications. Gradually he won recognition.

One day after a lecture in a girls' school, the faculty gave a reception for him. Gathered together there were a score or so of elderly old-maidish teachers who engaged him in polite but pointless conversation. While he sought refuge behind a cup of tea, he suddenly noticed a girl so lovely that she took his breath away. A trifle too old to be a student and too young to be a member of the faculty, she looked familiar to Yuwen and yet he was sure he had never met her before. She paused in the doorway as if undecided about entering, and her glance fell on him in a level, detached manner. Yuwen inexplicably felt his heart beat wildly. He turned to take up the lost threads of the dull conversation, and when he again looked at the door she was gone.

In the week that followed, he made discreet inquiries and learned that the girl taught English in the school. Her name was Leona Tan. She was highly esteemed by both the students and the faculty, and everyone was impressed by her exceeding beauty. However, Yuwen's informant added with a wry smile, if Yuwen had taken any fancy to her, he'd better forget it. She had odd but strong opinions and was, of all things, a misogamist. She maintained inflexibly that, for a woman, marriage could lead only to unhappiness: If she did not love her man sufficiently, it would end in disillusionment; if she did, the very intensity of her love might carry her to the depths of unsuspected tragedy. In the months Miss Tan had been at the school, she had shunned and disdained the opposite sex.

Yuwen, filled with dismay, told himself the young woman must have suffered some terrible experience that had left her with an indelible scar. And instead of being discouraged by the warning, his heart went out to her all the more.

He was invited to lecture at the Y.M.C.A., and the event was announced in the newspapers. As he rose to speak he saw the girl in a back row. He dared not look at her, and when he was finished she had disappeared. He wondered if she had come to the meeting purposely to hear him, or merely by chance. The uncertainty tormented him. He thought of asking his friend to arrange a party so that they could be introduced, but he knew that would be obvious and might offend Miss Tan.

Two weeks later Yuwen was asked to give a lay sermon at a community church, and once again an announcement appeared in the papers. Had she read it? Would she attend? He grew feverish with hope, and realized suddenly that he was desperately in love with a girl he had never really met.

He went to the church very early, and watched from behind the door of the vestry as people came in. Disappointment followed disappointment, and at last it was time for the procession. As he approached the altar, he turned for a last look and saw that she had just come in and was making her way toward the rear pew. Inspired by her presence, he surpassed his previous efforts.

After the service he excused himself to the pastor and hurried outside. The girl was a little ahead of him, and boldly he caught up with her.

"Good day, Miss Tan," he said politely.

She turned with a start, the trace of a frown clouding her beautiful face, and then nodded mechanically without speaking.

"I hope . . . I hope you liked my sermon."

After a second of hesitation, she answered matter-of-factly: "It was a good sermon—more ethical than religious, and more applicable to practical affairs than pure dogma. Now, if you please, I have to hurry back to school."

But Yuwen went on eagerly, "And how about my two other speeches—the one at your school and the other at the Y.M.C.A.?"

"They were good speeches too," she said curtly, and quickened her steps. Yuwen kept pace.

"I am glad to hear you say so. My views on the need to restore our moral standards are generally considered out of date. And my advocacy of a government by law is often condemned as too impractical and too radical. It certainly pleases me to have someone like you agree with me!"

The forbidding look returned. "If I have come to hear your speeches," she said pointedly, "and if I approve of them, it is only because they sound so much like the beliefs of my late father. There is nothing more. Nothing whatever. Now, will you please leave me?"

She went ahead, and Yuwen stood rooted to the ground. By all the rules of good manners he should leave her alone. But desperation seized him; if he let her go now, he would lose her forever.

He ran after her. "Miss Tan," he blurted out, "haven't we met somewhere before?"

The girl halted unwillingly. "Really? Where?"

"You remind me of someone I used to know," Yuwen stammered, ". . . my sworn brother's aunt."

Her smile was scornful. "And who may this sworn brother of yours be?"

"Of course, this may be all a mistake. His name is Ho Ta-kong, and he and I are both from the same place, the city of Yi."

Miss Tan caught her breath, then closed her eyes and swayed slightly.

"Are you ill, Miss Tan?" he asked, taking her arm.

"No, no," she answered, and stared at him searchingly. "Where is your sworn brother now?"

Briefly Yuwen told of his hunt for Ta-kong and his failure even to discover any information. When he concluded, her disappointment was plain.

"It is the same with me," she murmured, more to herself than to Yuwen. "I have tried to look for him everywhere. And I have also failed to find him."

Fighting down a twinge of jealousy, Yuwen withdrew his hand from her arm. "What is Ta-kong to you, Miss Tan?" he asked softly.

"He is a first cousin on my father's side. He's like a brother to me, the only dear one I now have left in this world."

Wild joy, mixed with incredulity, overwhelmed Yuwen.

"Then you can't be Miss Tan!" he exclaimed. "You must be Miss Ho! Why, you're the little Li-hwa I used to play with. Don't you remember me, son of Widow Lan and playmate of Ta-kong?"

"How could I? I went away from Yi to the provincial capital with my parents when I was scarcely three years old. But yes, now that I think of it, I do vaguely remember a little boy Ta-kong used to bring home—I called him Brother Lanny."

288

"How come you call yourself Miss Leona Tan?"

"Tan is my mother's maiden surname," she said sadly. "And Leona sounds like Li-hwa. After what happened to my parents, I wanted to forget all about my past."

"Let's forget the past then," Yuwen said. "Let's think only of the future!"

He offered his arm and she took it. They walked on together, and before the day was over both knew they were in love.

Three months later they were married. The Reverend Dr. Holt and the Widow Lan came to Shanghai for the wedding, and Holt married them at the Community Church. Widow Lan took care of their home while they took a week's honeymoon, and then spent another fortnight with them. These were the happiest days of her life.

Four

YUWEN WAS BLISSFULLY happy. Only a few days before, Li-hwa had presented him with his first-born—a boy—and both the mother and baby were doing well. He had just visited them in the hospital, and he felt thankful to his Maker and at peace with the whole world.

The college he had helped to found had proved a tremendous success. In little more than three years, it had expanded beyond recognition and now had thousands of students. The rambling old buildings had been remodeled and enlarged on premises presented to the school by several interested and wealthy merchants, and there was a sizable new library. Yuwen had become a well-known figure in the academic circles of Shanghai, and though his opinions were as yet not generally shared, he was widely respected as a sincere and learned scholar.

National affairs, however, had not progressed along the lines he had hoped. Chiang Kai-shek had embroiled himself again in a turbulent internecine war with another group of Kuomintang generals in the Northwest and had once more scored a smashing victory. He was now recognized by the public as the master of China, but many warlords who had supported him, including Tien Fong, still retained their old positions of power. Tong Hsi had become a member of the cabinet in the Central Government at Nanking, and his wife Amy was still pulling wires behind the scenes. The Kuomintang had continued their so-called "Period of Military Government," and there was no sign at all of the democratic constitution they had long promised.

Now, in the South, the nation faced a new menace. When Mao Tse-tung and his little band of Communists had fled into their mountain retreat several years before, they had barely escaped with their lives. But while Chiang was busy with one civil war after another, Mao's forces had built up their strength. Bandits and deserters joined their ranks; in three years they had grown into a horde of several hundred thousand men, and now roved and raided far and wide. Only a few months before, they had even captured a provincial capital and been strong enough to hold it against Government troops for a few days. Indeed, they were talking so openly of forming a "Chinese Soviet Republic" to challenge the authority of the Kuomintang that Chiang Kai-shek had gone to Hankow to launch a belated campaign against them.

The picture was scarcely one to cheer the heart of an objective patriot, but Yuwen was not very objective these days. Absorbed in his own happiness, he was disposed to be charitable and optimistic. Between Chiang Kai-shek and the Kuomintang on the one hand and the Communists on the other, however, his preference was plain. Chiang might be well on the way toward making himself dictator of China, but he had recently started a New Life Movement which rendered lip service, at least, to the old virtues. This, in Yuwen's opinion, was a step in the right direction. He was not anxious at all about the outcome of the conflict between the Kuomintang and the Communists. Despite their somewhat stronger resistance, he was sure the Communists would be defeated, just as anything intrinsically evil is bound to be subdued in the end. In Yuwen's lectures and in the articles he wrote, he still pleaded with the Government to take concrete measures toward establishing a rule of law, but he supported the Government strongly in its determined stand against the Communists.

This morning, in the trolley car riding back from the hospital to his college, his mind filled with his own happiness, he had the feeling that a fellow passenger was studying him intently behind a pair of dark sunglasses. Yuwen could see little of the stranger's face; there was a slouch hat pulled low over the glasses, and unlike most Chinese, the man wore a heavy beard, complete with side whiskers,

290

that concealed his mouth and chin. But somehow there was an air about him which Yuwen felt exuded friendliness.

At the next stop the passenger who had sat by the stranger got off, and Yuwen stepped over to the vacant seat.

"Mind if I sit here?" he asked.

The man inclined his head.

Yuwen sat down, and looking at him shyly, remarked, "Ah, I am so happy today, I could tell the whole world!"

Without turning his head, the stranger replied, "Tell me then."

He spoke with a marked Southern accent, and his voice had warmth and a familiar ring that caught Yuwen's fancy. Yuwen began talking about the birth of his son, dwelling with pride upon the infant's every feature. He spoke just as glowingly of Li-hwa and the wonderful and joyous life they were leading together. The man said nothing, though he appeared very interested; whenever Yuwen paused, he would encourage him to go on, with a gesture of his gloved hand or with a forward movement of his bearded chin.

When Yuwen at last felt that further discussion of his family might be ill-mannered, he turned to talking about some of his views on the future of China.

"I don't care about these things," the man said abruptly. "I am interested only in the drama of life. Please tell me more about your wife. Where did you meet her? And how?"

In his exuberant mood, Yuwen eagerly related everything.

When he finished, the stranger suddenly got up from his seat and, keeping his back to Yuwen, said, "Thank you for telling me of your happiness. I am happy for you too."

The car jolted to a stop. A man standing behind the stranger was thrown forward and collided with him, knocking off the slouch hat. In spite of the sunglasses, in spite of the beard, Yuwen would have recognized that forehead anywhere. It was Ta-kong!

Yuwen sprang up, elbowed aside the crowding passengers, and seized the man by the arm.

"You are my Big Brother! Why didn't you tell me?"

The man shook him off politely but firmly. "You must be mistaken," he replied in his Southern accent. "I have never met you before in my life."

He hurried out of the car, and Yuwen sank back on a seat and watched him go down the street. Even the walk was Ta-kong's.

That evening, back at the hospital, he recounted the strange incident to Li-hwa. She concluded that Yuwen must have been mistaken; that it must have been only a remarkable resemblance. For a week Yuwen took the same trolley back and forth, hoping to run into the stranger, but he did not see him again.

<h1 style="text-align:center">2</h1>

TA-KONG HAD SEEN Yuwen first in the car. A thousand thoughts immediately rushed into his mind, and his first impulse was to reveal himself to his Third Brother. However, having acquired the habit of subjecting every emotion to the demands of expediency, he was able to smother the impulse. It would be bad for himself; it might be even worse for Yuwen, because Ta-kong was a marked man with a price on his head.

But Ta-kong knew a great deal about his Third Brother. It was one of his duties to ferret out information about men like Yuwen. He was well acquainted with both Yuwen's reputation as a professor and his strong anti-Communist views; in fact, he had read all of his published articles. If Yuwen had not made his stand so clear, Ta-kong might well have sought him out shortly after his own arrival in Shanghai a few weeks before; he could not help feeling a deep attachment to the man with whom he had grown up and to whom he was bound by the ties of sworn brotherhood. But now he was sharply aware of an insurmountable barrier between them. He knew his Third Brother well. Once Yuwen had reached a decision, it would be as difficult to make him change his mind as to shake a mountain. They had parted company in the journey of life, and could no longer find a common ground. With a sigh, Ta-kong recollected the parting words Yuwen had spoken in the northern port city. Then he gave up his reverie as idle, unprofitable thought.

Still, Ta-kong had been sincerely happy to hear of Yuwen's happiness, and as he walked home after leaving the trolley, he could not help comparing his own home with that of Yuwen and Li-hwa. . . .

He could look back on many an affair with women comrades and feel neither regret nor squeamishness. His life, like that of all high-ranking Communists, was most irregular and hazardous. Often he led troops in guerrilla warfare, where the commander frequently ran greater risks than his soldiers. He had been sent on many secret missions where a false or unwary step might mean not instant death but unimaginable torture. These things were not calculated to calm a man's nerves; they tightened them until they clamored for release.

To take a woman—that was nothing; that was only a means of escaping from the realities of the moment; a momentary relief in a long continuity of anxiety and privation—it was a necessity. It was like killing an innocent man who happened to be in the way, or purging a turncoat who endangered the undertaking. It was good for the Cause. It was essential for his own well-being.

Standing so high in Party ranks was not without advantages, and he was also conscious of his own physical attractions. He could have had any woman in the Party he desired, except those who were married with Party approval and others who were monopolized by, if not married to, comrades ranking higher than himself. He laughed when his Second Brother, Li Chien, finally succumbed to the charms of a rather middling girl comrade. But, strange as it might seem, Ta-kong himself still held on to the vision of pure and innocent womanhood which he remembered in the persons of his aunt Delicate Blossom and his cousin Li-hwa. He dreamed of the day when he would find such an ideal. Of course it would be when he became the sole power in China; then he would put himself and the whole nation at her feet. Though he was already in his middle thirties, and had lived a life of gruesome realities and cold cynicism, in this one respect—dreaming of his ideal love—he was like a gangling youth.

Two months before his meeting with Yuwen, when Chiang Kai-shek's troops had encircled and tightly blockaded the guerrilla base at Juikin in Kiangsi Province, the Party decided to create an "Eastern Bureau" with headquarters in Shanghai. It was to have over-all direction of all the organizations and activities of the Party in East China. Its first task was to find some way to run supplies through the blockade. Mao Tse-tung's troops were not only short of munitions but had run out of simple necessities such as salt and edible oil. The second task, though not so urgent, was perhaps even more basic. The Communists had realized their strength was no match for Chiang Kai-shek's forces, so in order to survive they wanted a temporary peace with the Kuomintang Government. But they knew Chiang would never agree to this of his own will, and pressure would have to be brought on him. Since the eastern provinces were the most populous section, and Shanghai and Nanking the nerve centers of China, the Eastern Bureau was instructed to incite and organize public opinion there with the aim of forcing the Kuomintang to cease fighting the Communists and enter into negotiations with them.

Ta-kong was named head of the Bureau. Far from being daunted by the task, he took pleasure and pride in the unique distinction the Party had accorded him. If he could make this mission a success, the goal he had been striving for would not be so far out of reach.

With great care he selected a handful of assistants—all of them experienced comrades, and two of them disciples of his secret Society besides. These men had been inducted into the Party by him without disclosing their other allegiance. They were tough daredevils, not very intelligent, but they could be trusted. Of course he had also picked Li Chien, but Second Brother's wife was about to give birth, and Li Chien had to postpone his departure.

On the day he himself was to leave, Ta-kong was summoned to the presence of the High Command. Said the Comrade:

"We have complete confidence in you and we wish you every success in this matter of such extreme importance to us. You have sole charge of the East. You may even liquidate our topmost men if you deem it necessary, we shall not question your methods and decisions. We want only results. But you must know also that there are other comrades sent there to keep an eye on you."

"That is understood," replied Ta-kong.

"I have just received a message from our Top Command of the International Headquarters. It is a little out of the ordinary. As you know, the Party never tells a comrade who his watchers are, but in your case it seems to have made an exception—at least, with one of your watchers. Perhaps the reason is that the Top Command has attached the importance to your mission it well deserves. As soon as you reach Shanghai and get in touch with our branch there, you will be advised how to contact this agent. The message describes him as a graduate of Sun Yat-sen University in Moscow. You are directed to live with him while engaged in this work in Shanghai. You are ordered to do nothing without his knowledge. He is not to interfere with your plans, your decisions, and your methods of carrying them into execution in any way, but you have to keep him posted at all times. These are the instructions I am asked to transmit to you. I presume that he is only one of your watchers. There will be others unknown to you."

Ta-kong knew it was futile to ask for further enlightenment. Nor did he feel disconcerted by this arrangement, for he was thoroughly accustomed to the ways of the Party and entertained no fears for his own safety. So long as he kept to the Party line he would be always safe.

294

3

PROMPTLY AFTER REACHING Shanghai, he made his presence known to the local Communist branches and was received as their master. While he held conferences with their various leaders, he waited for the message that would lead him to the agent assigned to watch over him. At last it came.

"Comrade," a man said casually one day, "I am directed to tell you that you're expected at the east entrance of the public library at a quarter after its closing hour today. You will be holding a newspaper in one hand and a book in the other."

Ta-kong turned up at dusk and waited, alone, outside the closed library gate. A shadow emerged and whispered as it passed by, "Nine o'clock this evening. The corner of N. and W. streets."

On the dot of the hour a taxi pulled up in front of where he was waiting at the designated place. The rear door swung open and a hand motioned him to enter. The occupant was a woman, but her face, wrapped in a thick scarf, could not be seen, and she said nothing. Ta-kong too kept silent. The car brought them at last to a respectable middle-class residential section. When it let them out at a rather dim corner, the woman took Ta-kong by the arm and led him along a dark alley until they came to the back door of a house. She opened it and gestured him to go in.

It was a two-story structure of a kind very common in Shanghai, with a sitting room, a dinette, a servant's chamber, and a kitchen on the ground floor and bedrooms upstairs. It was well lighted and simply and inconspicuously furnished like any ordinary middle-class home.

Ta-kong made himself comfortable on a chair and waited for the next move. But his escort remained standing at a distance, with her back to him, the scarf still around her head. He thought that the agent he was to meet would appear soon or that he would be told to go elsewhere for the rendezvous.

Minutes passed. "Where is the comrade?" Ta-kong asked finally.

"What comrade?" came a low but distinct answer.

"The comrade appointed to watch over me—with whom I am directed to live."

"It is I, Comrade."

"You, a woman comrade?" Ta-kong exclaimed.

"That's right. The Top Command thinks you will be able to

carry out your mission more effectively if you and I live as man and wife. It will be more convenient for me to keep an eye on your activities, and also safer for you to assume the disguise of a married man—a much more natural disguise than your beard and your Southern accent. Any objections, Comrade Ta-kong?"

In spite of his long Communist training and experience, Ta-kong was taken aback. He knew a few of his comrades had entered into this sort of mock marriage, but he had not expected it would happen to him. And the woman had called him by his real name! Either she was very high in the Party ranks, or she enjoyed the complete confidence of the Top Command; otherwise she would not have had access to the private dossier and have learned his true identity.

"No objections, Comrade," he told her. "But why don't you face me?"

The woman drew aside her scarf and turned, smiling. It was Yin Mei-yin!

Ta-kong jumped from his seat in surprise. "Mei-yin! Since when have you become a Communist?"

Mei-yin beamed sweetly. "No questions, Comrade. Remember the rules?"

Ta-kong sank back on the chair. She came and sat closely by his side and took his hand fondly.

An elderly woman appeared from the kitchen bearing a tray, with vodka and a plate filled with the steamed dumplings which Ta-kong had always loved.

"Who is she?" he asked.

"She was my wet nurse when I was a baby, but she's our amah now—she's a comrade too."

The comrade-amah deposited the contents of the tray on a low table in front of them and went back to the kitchen.

"Go ahead and take the dumplings," Mei-yin said, as she poured the vodka. "If you're still the boy I used to know, you'll be able to finish the whole plate in no time."

Ta-kong chuckled.

Mei-yin handed him a glass. "Here is to our reunion! Or should I say, union?"

He drank, more at ease now, and looked at her objectively. Mei-yin had changed only slightly. She had added a little weight, and her features were no longer so sharp nor her breasts and hips so meager, which made her a bit more desirable as a woman. But her odd-shaped triangular eyes were still the same; they still shone with intelligence, and now and then with a hard gleam that was as cold as steel. Just now, however, she was gazing at him with unconcealed tenderness and longing. He recollected with a start what his Third Brother, Yuwen, had said long ago of her intentions toward him; and he felt confounded that they should become fulfilled now, and that they should be so far from his own expectations.

But all in all, Ta-kong concluded, this was the best arrangement under the circumstances. He had always had the highest respect for Mei-yin's intellect; she could be trusted to give him invaluable counsel. And since she seemed infatuated with him, he could be sure that she would send favorable reports to the Top Command. Even the necessity of living with her as man and wife suited his convenience; he wouldn't have to waste time seeking out girl comrades to satisfy his physical needs. Though the Party might regard the union as an authorized marriage, a divorce probably could be arranged as soon as this business was done.

So thinking, Ta-kong permitted himself to respond to her advances. They flirted and chatted about everything but Party affairs, carefully avoiding anything from the past which was unknown to the other, for that was tabooed. When the dumplings were devoured and the bottle of vodka was drunk, Mei-yin eagerly led Ta-kong upstairs.

The master bedroom was at the far end of the hallway, its door already open. A lamp covered with a pink shade provided the sole illumination, and under the rosy light was a large bed, with the quilt turned back invitingly. Ta-kong stood at the landing of the staircase a long while.

"What are you waiting for, my dear?" Mei-yin called impatiently from the bedroom. "Am I still nothing to you?"

Ta-kong sauntered in, and instantly she threw her arms around him.

At last her desires were fully gratified. Lying by his side and pressing every inch of her body against his, she whispered: "Darling, dearest darling, this is what I've wanted ever since I first set eyes on you! Now there will indeed be no heights in life we cannot mount together. Are you as happy as I am?"

Ta-kong replied with effort. The passions she had just displayed in the act of love were so intense, so possessive, so ferocious, they astounded and appalled him. And now that the deed was done, he remembered what Yuwen had said of her nature, and wondered

297

whether his Third Brother had been gifted after all with more clairvoyance than he had credited. What a mockery of his ideal love!

Involuntarily, he said: "If you loved me as much as you say, why didn't you keep yourself a virgin?"

Fury seized Mei-yin. She pushed him aside violently and sat up in a frenzy. The cold, hard gleam in her eye was not softened by the dim rosy light.

"You with your bourgeois ideas of virginity! A fine Communist you are! For harboring such fallacies, I could denounce you at once to the Top Command! What about you—how many women you must have gone to bed with!"

Then she flung herself on the pillow with her back to him and began to sob. "If I lost my virginity, it was because of you!"

Ta-kong laid his hand gently on her shoulder, but she shook it off. "How was I to blame?" he asked.

Through her sobs she managed to reply, "Because you refused me when I offered you marriage after our graduation. I could have gone with you to the ends of earth then—but you didn't care for me. I thought I had lost you forever, so I went back to marry the man to whom my uncle had betrothed me long before."

Ta-kong was contrite. By way of comfort he started to fondle her breast. She tried to put his hand away, but with only a mild display of persistence on his part, she let it stay.

"I'm sorry," he said, and asked her to tell him more about herself, since he had known nothing about her in their student days.

She told him, now, that her parents had been well-to-do people in a northern province. Both of them died during her infancy, and the whole estate was left in the charge of her only uncle, who feared that when she grew up she would claim a large portion of the inheritance as her dowry. So when she was fifteen, without her consent he betrothed her to a widower thrice her age who was willing to accept her youth in place of a dowry. She had rebelled, insisting she must have a college education before she would speak of marriage; actually, she hoped that with sufficient education, she would be able to make an independent living after graduation. Then she had met Ta-kong at the students' conference, and had fallen in love with him.

When Ta-kong then showed he did not love her, she had thought first of suicide. But she did not wish to die; she wanted to take vengeance on the world. There were no jobs, and finally she went back and married the man to whom her uncle had pledged her.

She despised and detested him; many a night, with that wretched senile snoring by her side, she could not close her eyes for thinking of Ta-kong.

Fortunately the man soon died, and Mei-yin managed to wrest a little money from his grown children so that she could return to the port city. She had searched in vain for Ta-kong, met some Communists, and joined the Party. Then Moscow established the so-called Sun Yat-sen University to provide an advanced course in revolutionary training for the Chinese Party cadre, and she enrolled and went to Russia. After graduation, she worked in the secretariat of the Communist International, which was where she had learned of Ta-kong's present mission. They were looking for an agent to watch over him; she had applied for the position and here she was.

Everything she had said was true except one thing. Her husband had not exactly died a natural death.

Ta-kong was touched by her story. He had wronged her, and he was sorry. Also, he realized that because of her intellect and her position in the Party, she would be an advantageous friend and a dangerous foe. He must quickly make up to her. But for such a woman, words could never be as convincing as actions. He braced himself and started to fondle her in earnest. Half spurning and half surrendering, this time she let him have his own way.

Soon she was in a state of ecstasy, and he in a state of exhaustion. He tried to draw away, but she held him fast.

"Oh, no, darling, don't stir! Stay close to me. I want you to belong to me always!"

And thus bound together, they went to sleep.

The next morning Mei-yin, beaming radiantly, produced a surprise. "Dearest Comrade," she said, showing him some papers, "here is something for you to sign."

Ta-kong at once recognized the marriage certificate of the Party. Evidently Mei-yin had already obtained permission of the Top Command for their marriage, and he knew that any idea of subsequent divorce was no longer feasible. So long as Mei-yin did not tire of him, it would be exceedingly difficult to get rid of her. He took the situation in apparent good grace, and signed the papers with a flourish. Forcing himself into what he thought was a suitable smile for a newly wedded husband, he said, "It's nice to have one's wife as one's keeper." A mischievous twinkle came into Mei-yin's eyes. "Even if I am for you, there are still others."

"Who are they?" Ta-kong teased.

"Now, now," she replied in the same vein, tweaking his beard playfully. "But just to reward my darling boy for his good behavior, Mama will let him into one little secret. When I left Moscow for Shanghai, there was another comrade taking a similar journey and I have an idea he knows you. His real name is Nan Ping."

Five

ABOUT A MONTH after Ta-kong ran into Yuwen, Li Chien arrived in Shanghai with his wife and his newborn daughter. The High Command had given Li Chien special permission to bring his family, for he was disguised as a refugee fleeing from war-ravaged land, and the addition of a wife and baby lent a convincing touch.

Li Chien and his family moved into a house which Ta-kong had prepared for them. It was at the other end of town, far from where Ta-kong and Mei-yin lived. The section was newly developed and the houses scattered, Li Chien's home being on the very edge of the Concession border. Its back door opened directly onto an expanse of farm fields, offering an avenue of escape. Ta-kong and Mei-yin were both satisfied with the location; in case of emergency, they too could use it as a temporary hide-out.

Li Chien was one of the very few entrusted with Ta-kong's address, and he took his family immediately to visit his sworn brother. The bond between them had been an enduring one. Never had Ta-kong undertaken a mission for the Party without Li Chien at his side. Whenever Li Chien discovered a secret, he had shared it with Ta-kong. Despite the general atmosphere of restraint and suspicion which the Party imposed, they could exchange opinions freely and in confidence.

Moreover, now that Ta-kong knew Yuwen and Li-hwa were lost to him forever, Li Chien was the only human being in the world he felt he could sincerely and safely love. He went out of his way to pour affection upon his Second Brother; he showed Li Chien's wife every attention, and played with the baby as if it were his

300

own. He said that as soon as it grew a little older and could say "papa," he would want it as his godchild.

At first Li Chien was surprised to see Mei-yin, but when Ta-kong told him of their marriage he was all felicitations.

"Ah," he exclaimed joyously, "this is really getting to be like old times. I'm very happy for you both—indeed, very happy for all three of us. If only we could have our Third Brother with us too! He was a strange one, all right. Remember how he predicted our lives would grow apart? I wonder where he is now. Perhaps still in the United States."

Ta-kong did not reply. He had told no one of his chance meeting with Yuwen, and Li Chien was too sentimental to be entrusted with the secret. He suspected Mei-yin knew Yuwen was in the city, but they had never discussed the subject. Mei-yin could hardly have forgotten Yuwen's dislike and his distrust of her—she would always resent him.

Ta-kong started to change the subject, but Li Chien looked at Mei-yin and chuckled, "Ah, but our Third Brother made one mistake. You know, Sister Mei-yin, he actually warned Big Brother against you? He said you had a very bad outlook on life—'Mei-yin thinks only of destroying.' He said you would be an evil influence over Big Brother."

Ta-kong smiled sweetly at Mei-yin and joined in the laugh. "Certainly she has a lifelong influence on me now. A dominating influence, I'd say, but all to the good."

"Good or evil, she is dominating enough," Li Chien said with a guffaw. "I have never seen my Big Brother dominated by anyone before. But if it is to be, I'm glad, Sister Mei-yin, that it's you."

Mei-yin smiled, but inwardly she was seething—she did not resent Yuwen so much as she did Li Chien. Yuwen was out of the picture; the gulf between him and Ta-kong could not be bridged. But Li Chien was here in their midst, and she felt his hold on Ta-kong was stronger than hers.

Next morning, at breakfast, Mei-yin and Ta-kong discussed the progress of his mission. Among other matters, he mentioned that he had not decided which of two positions he would give Li Chien: One was as second-in-command of the entire Eastern Bureau; the other was to take over the operation of the smuggling pipeline, which he himself had previously run.

Mei-yin silently discarded the first alternative at once because it would put Li Chien in daily contact with Ta-kong. Aloud, she said that although according to the Party directive this was a decision for Ta-kong alone, since she was his wife she had nothing but his interest at heart, and she thought the second position more suitable. The smuggling operation called for daring, courage, and an intimate knowledge of the terrain; and she knew of no other comrade, except Ta-kong himself, who was better qualified. The guerrilla base needed supplies desperately; the success of the smuggling operation was of much more immediate consequence than agitation or organizing public opinion. And notwithstanding Li Chien's proved capacities, propaganda did not seem to be his strong point; he was no theoretician and was not overly subtle.

Ta-kong thought her arguments sound and decided accordingly. Thus, for the first time since their schooldays, the two men were kept from daily association—with serious consequences, for the fact was that since schooldays Ta-kong had been doing all Li Chien's thinking for him.

Li Chien was essentially a man of action, not thought. Formerly he had been operating entirely within Communist territory or exclusively in the midst of his fellow comrades, but now he was thrust into an alien world. He did not talk to strangers, for that was forbidden; yet he could not help hearing conversations that aroused his curiosity about views which were sharply at variance with the Party line. He had been indoctrinated to regard all publications other than the Communists' as enemy propaganda and warned not even to look at them, but passing them day after day, he could not fail to notice some of their titles and headlines. His Big Brother easily could have quashed any such inquisitiveness. But Ta-kong was not there.

One night Li Chien found himself in the inn of a mountain village not far from Shanghai, where he had been exploring the possibilities of a new smuggling route. He was lonesome, and there was nothing to do. He saw an old and dog-eared picture magazine, and picked it up: It was probably capitalistic trash—he would not read the articles but simply look at the pictures. The photograph of the author of an article made him sit upright with a start. It was his Third Brother! Even to his name—Lan Yuwen!

Excitedly, Li Chien turned to the front page and found the magazine was published in Shanghai, and had been issued only a few months before. He flipped back again and dwelt fondly upon his Third Brother's photograph. Yuwen looked older, but more mature and more manly in his handsomeness. There was something else

302

in his face—a contentedness, a self-assurance not even possessed by Ta-kong. Consumed with curiosity and positive that Yuwen, with his background, had never been and could never be a capitalist, Li Chien threw his long indoctrinations to the winds. He read the article.

It gave him a rude shock, it was so boldly anti-Communist; but it also puzzled him. If Yuwen had come out foursquare for Chiang Kai-shek he would have known Third Brother was a Kuomintang stooge. But Yuwen was also pointedly critical of Chiang. Li Chien, too tired to think, told himself that if only they could argue the matter out as in the good old days, he and Big Brother would be able to persuade Yuwen without difficulty. Even if that failed, they would still have the solemn vow of sworn brotherhood to fall back on; by the simple rule of the majority, Yuwen would have to give up his ideas and follow their lead. They then would all be Communists, working for the same goal, and they would be able to fulfill their sacred oath together.

A perplexing thought occurred to Li Chien. In Ta-kong's new assignment, surely he must have gathered abundant information about magazines like this and about the writers who wrote for them—so he must have known of Yuwen's presence in Shanghai. Since it never occurred to Li Chien that Ta-kong could have intentionally concealed anything from him—that was against his whole conception of sworn brotherhood—Li Chien could only conclude reluctantly that Ta-kong's bureau had not been running efficiently. Important things had escaped Ta-kong's notice.

Being familiar with the severity of the Party discipline, Li Chien was now apprehensive about his Big Brother's safety. He decided to hurry back to Ta-kong, not only to tell him about Yuwen but also to warn him of his possible peril.

2

Li Chien returned to Shanghai posthaste. Though it was the practice, under Party security rules, never to meet at a regular place or at a regular hour, and not to meet at all except by prior agreement, he considered tonight an emergency and went straight to Ta-kong's house. Mei-Yin opened the door and frowned.

"Comrade," she said when he had entered the sitting room, "it is my duty to remind you that you have violated the rules of security. You have come here without permission. You are imperiling your leader, yourself, your fellow comrades, and possibly the whole mission."

"Don't worry, Sister Mei-yin," said Li Chien, laughing. "I was an expert in these tricks while you were studying them in Sun Yat-sen University. I made sure nobody followed me. But speaking of perils, there's a real one threatening Big Brother. Where is he?"

Ta-kong had already recognized the voice, and he came quickly down the stairs.

"What is it, Second Brother?" he asked.

"Do you know that Third Brother is here in this city?"

"Oh?" answered Ta-kong cautiously. "Have you seen him?"

Li Chien, who had expected an outburst of joy and surprise from Big Brother, tried to mask his disappointment.

"No, but I read one of his articles."

Before Ta-kong could answer, Mei-yin spoke. "There again, Brother Li Chien—as a comrade, you are not supposed to read anything except what the Party allows you to read. You are not in charge of the Publicity Department where such readings are in the line of duty. So how could you take it on yourself to read one of his articles?"

Li Chien turned on her angrily. "He is my Third Brother, isn't he?"

Mei-yin said nothing, and he calmed himself and went on to tell about the magazine in the village inn. "Did you know about it?" he asked Ta-kong. "If you did, why haven't you sought him out and made him join us? Why haven't you told me?"

"I'm sorry, Second Brother. Can't you see that it's best for us to forget him for the time being? It's impossible for us to get together on the old footing."

"Why?" demanded Li Chien.

"If you've read his article, you know his views. They're completely antagonistic to our Party."

"Then there is all the more reason for us to convert him to our Cause. I don't see as much difficulty there as you seem to. The solemn oath binds us together. And you being Big Brother, he will have to listen to you as I do. Moreover, anti-Communist though he may be, he is anti-Chiang Kai-shek too, and so we have some common ground."

Ta-kong looked affectionately at Li Chien. "How I wish everybody could be as single-hearted as you are! But, unfortunately, few are. We all know Yuwen well—you, Mei-yin and I. Yuwen forms

304

his convictions all by himself, and once he has made up his mind he will not change it. He's not like Chiang Kai-shek's followers—opportunists, bending like grass whichever way the wind blows. I'm sure many of them will rally to our standard once we get the upper hand of Chiang. But that won't be the case with Yuwen. He is basically opposed to our philosophy, he is against our way of life. Even though I grieve to say it, I'm afraid there's nothing we can do about him."

"Still," persisted Li Chien, "we must try. It's better to try and fail than not to fulfill our duties of sworn brotherhood at all."

"And thus," interrupted Mei-yin, "expose ourselves, our mission, and our Party to unnecessary and unknown hazards?"

"If you mean, Sister Mei-yin, that there's a possibility of Yuwen's betraying us when we approach him, I, for one, do not believe it! He may differ with us, but he would never harm us. He is our Third Brother!" Li Chien declared indignantly.

"True," rejoined Ta-kong, "but consider the matter from another angle. If we approach Yuwen, it may be more dangerous for him and his family than for us. You must remember we are marked men and the Kuomintang agents are lurking everywhere. While they may not be able to catch us, they surely will not be easy on anyone known to have associated with us. You yourself know how many innocent people have been tortured and put to death for that very reason. Since you love Yuwen as we all do, do you want to jeopardize him and his family?"

Li Chien admitted he hadn't thought of that.

"Then trust me, Second Brother," Ta-kong said earnestly. "The only thing to do is to forget Yuwen and to forget him completely."

"Forget?" Li Chien echoed. "I cannot forget one whom I have loved and sworn to love. Nor can you, Big Brother! I know you too well. Remember when you asked me to deliver the message to your uncle urging him to flee from Canton? You knew that by all the rules of the Party you shouldn't have done that, yet you did it because you loved your uncle and your aunt. And I delivered your message to him because of my love for you. And now you say to forget our own Third Brother!"

Ta-kong was aghast at this disclosure. Li Chien had taken for granted that Mei-yin was one of them and in every sense of the word his "sister." Now that the secret was out, Ta-kong covertly eyed Mei-yin, but saw only an amused smile.

He said, as lightheartedly as he could, "Ah, that was different,

Second Brother. It did no harm to the Party. Besides, we were young then and not in such responsible positions as we are today. Now we must think only of the Party. Our work here is a matter of life and death to the Party, and we must not let any private concern, however dear to our hearts, distract us from our duties. It is for the good of the Party, and also for Yuwen's own good, that we forget him."

Spiritlessly Li Chien rose and took his leave.

That night when Ta-kong was in bed with Mei-yin, he did what he could to please her, but she seemed detached while they were making love, more amused than aroused.

"A penny for your thoughts, darling," he said finally.

"Oh, nothing," she answered casually. "I was just thinking of the private dossier on you in the secret Party files."

He drew back so that she would not feel the pounding of his heart.

"You know, your record is all clear except for one place—the unexplained escape of your uncle from Canton. They suspected you had something to do with that, but they never got proof."

Bending above her, he said tightly, "I assume they will be given proof now?"

She brought him down and held him in a fierce embrace. "Oh, no," she whispered, "your secret dies right here within my bosom. Your life is mine. We must climb together, higher, always higher. I'd not hesitate to destroy anything that stood in our way—but I'll never hurt you. Only from now on, my own, you mustn't keep a single secret from Mama. And she'll always be at your side, taking care of you and seeing that you make no more false moves."

3

FROM THAT DAY Mei-yin redeployed the few operatives who had been assigned to her by the Party without Ta-kong's knowledge: She directed them to concentrate on Li Chien.

But Li Chien was attending to his business exceedingly well. Under his energetic management, the smuggling swelled from a trickle into a smooth and sizable flow. The messages that came from the High Command in the guerrilla base, though still demanding more, were not without praise for a job well done. Moreover, Li Chien was an old hand in the game of hide-and-seek. Though he did not suspect that Mei-yin was responsible for the special operatives on his trail, he knew he was no exception to the general Party rule and that his every movement was under close surveillance by unknown comrades, let alone Kuomintang agents. So he was particularly careful, and Mei-yin's men had a hard time shadowing him.

Li Chien was taking extraordinary precautions for a secret reason. If his Big Brother would not approach Yuwen and convert him to Communism, he would do so on his own. He could not afford to fail. Failure would result not only in punishment by the Party—it would expose Yuwen and his family to unknown dangers.

Whenever possible now—wherever he was certain he was unobserved—Li Chien looked for articles written by Yuwen and read them carefully. After he finished, he would close his eyes and attempt to refute them point by point as though he were arguing with Yuwen in person. Frequently he thought he had Yuwen cornered by Party dialectics, but then he would come across another article which made a new point that smashed all his arguments. And gradually Li Chien came to a frightful realization. He had exhausted the entire Party line and yet Yuwen stood unbent and unbeaten.

Then, suddenly, something happened to throw all the articles and Li Chien's replies into confusion—to say nothing of completely surprising both the Kuomintang Government and the Communists. The Japanese had struck in Manchuria! The news shocked and incensed the whole nation.

While Chiang Kai-shek was fighting the Communists in the South, while the young warlord in charge of the Northeast—a faithful ally of Chiang's—was beguiling himself with notorious courtesans in Peking, the Japanese put their long-planned designs on China into execution. Without excuse or provocation, they seized Mukden one autumn night, and then fanned out and occupied all of Manchuria without much opposition.

Li Chien, enraged against the Japanese, at the same time could not help but realize—as Yuwen must realize—that the Communists had been proved clearly right and the Kuomintang absolutely wrong. The Communists had advocated peace and unity, insisting that civil war must cease and the country be held ready to meet any foreign threat. But Chiang Kai-shek and the Kuomintang had embroiled China in so many civil wars—it was they who had supported that young, useless, profligate warlord in Manchuria—that they had failed to organize any effective resistance to the Japanese invasion. Eagerly Li Chien awaited Yuwen's next article, which surely could say nothing in defense of Chiang and the Kuomintang.

Meanwhile, he was proud to see the effectiveness with which Ta-kong swung his propaganda apparatus into action. In less than a fortnight, the sentiment of the people was turned overwhelmingly to the side of the Communists. Demonstration after demonstration was held, and demands grew that the Kuomintang Government cease fighting the Communists and immediately dispatch all its troops northward to resist the Japanese. The students of Shanghai were incited to proceed en masse to Nanking to present a petition, and the Government was so apprehensive that it suspended operation of the vital railway between Nanking and Shanghai for several days. The weakness of the Kuomintang position was fully bared, and the entire nation rose in protest.

Li Chien was as proud of his Big Brother's triumph as if it were his own, and told himself that the time was almost ripe for him to approach Third Brother and convert him to Communism.

Then another of Yuwen's articles appeared in a very influential and impartial magazine. It was entitled, "The Right Approach." Li Chien was stunned by Yuwen's arguments and conclusions.

The article made four points:

First, all past differences of all groups should be forgotten. It served no purpose either to blame Chiang Kai-shek and the Kuomintang, or the Communists. The most important thing was that civil war be stopped forthwith and that all military forces of the country be aligned to take a concerted stand against the common enemy.

Second, whatever Chiang's shortcomings, he remained the only man capable of leading the nation in the fight against Japanese Imperialism. His government was the government recognized by all foreign powers and acknowledged by most of the people in China. He had a force far mightier than the others. At this critical juncture when unity was needed, to try to thrust him aside was to throw the country into greater confusion and to leave it leaderless; to discredit his government would only weaken China's position and give aid and comfort to the enemy. Hence, all demonstrations against Chiang and the Kuomintang should cease at once.

Third, in order to prove himself truly capable of assuming leadership, Chiang should make clear that he was willing to introduce all necessary democratic reforms once the crisis was over.

Finally—and this was the most significant point for Li Chien—Yuwen said that despite the criticisms he had leveled against the

Communists in the past, he was prepared now to take their word that they were genuine patriots of China. That being so, there was only one thing for them to do. It would be futile to ask Chiang to fight the Japanese in the front while he had a huge hostile army in his rear; the Communists, therefore, should put their forces entirely at Chiang's disposal. If they did not trust him enough, they should at least go to Manchuria in a body to engage the invaders in action. Yuwen called upon the Communist Party to make such an announcement at once. Failing that, he called upon every Communist to surrender voluntarily and individually to the Government in order to prove that he was a genuine patriot and not a stooge of an alien power.

Hard as Li Chien tried, he could not refute these arguments. Although he knew of the connection between the Russian and the Chinese Communist parties, and of the Soviet domination in the Communist International, he had never considered himself a stooge of anybody, and to fight foreign Imperialism had been always one of his own as well as his Party's avowed revolutionary aims.

Here, now, was an actual case to put both him and his Party to a real test. Was not what Yuwen proposed essentially right? Should not his Party adopt it without hesitation? And if his Party failed to do so, what should he himself do?

4

UNBEKNOWN TO LI CHIEN, the article was to cause him more than anxiety. He had bought the magazine in a suburban bookstore, after making sure he was not followed; he had carefully determined that it was a conservative shop—not a single publication fostered by his Big Brother's Publicity Department was on display. Since all the books were Rightist—there was even a pile of the outmoded old classics for sale—Li Chien had no way of knowing that the bookstore was a front. It was operated by one of the principal agents of his Party in Shanghai, a former professor of French in the northern university where Li Chien had studied—Nan Ping, alias Ma Pingnan. The latter had recognized Li Chien, and had hidden in a back room. When he later learned what Li had bought, a malicious grin crinkled his narrow piggish eyes.

Nan Ping's assignment in Shanghai was, as Mei-yin had guessed, to watch over her and her husband. The Communist International, under the personal direction of Stalin, was then taking a direct hand in the Communist activities of China. As evidence of the importance he attached to Ta-kong's mission, he had arranged to have reports sent back by two of their ablest operatives. Each had been chosen for a different reason. Mei-yin, because the Top Command knew of her attachment to Ta-kong—she thus could be counted upon to report his activities in the most favorable light; Nan Ping, because of his jealousy of Ta-kong—he would deliver adverse and critical opinions. Sitting in the middle, the Top Command could thus form an unbiased, all-seeing, all-wise judgment.

Nan Ping was as anxious to find fault with Ta-kong as the Top Command had expected him to be, but so far he had not been notably successful. All things considered, Ta-kong had done extremely well. The smuggling of much-needed materials into the guerrilla base was a greater success than had been anticipated. Though the agitation and organization of public opinion against the Kuomintang had been developing at a rather slow pace, this operation had been acknowledged difficult by the Top Command at the outset. Then events had turned Ta-kong's way, and the remarkable speed with which he had swung the sentiments of the country to the Communist side was a tribute to his personal genius. Moreover, the Eastern Bureau, whose membership now numbered several thousand, was running efficiently under Ta-kong's direction.

Then, just when Comrade Nan Ping felt most embittered, Providence delivered Li Chien into his hands. Here was Ta-kong's most trusted lieutenant, known to be his sworn brother, committing the worst sin of all—he was thinking for himself. It was more than sufficient ground for Nan Ping to denounce him, but it was not Li Chien that he wanted to damage—it was Ta-kong. Nan Ping bided his time, hoping for evidence that would lead to Ta-kong himself.

Meanwhile, he followed Mei-yin's example and directed his men to watch Li Chien. Before long, Second Brother was being watched three ways—by Nan Ping, by Mei-yin, and by Ta-kong's own Discipline Squad. Mei-yin soon heard about the new group from her agents, but she kept her own counsel and ordered her men to double their vigilance.

Ta-kong was worried. His demonstrations against the Kuomintang, which at first had been wonderfully successful, now met a setback. What all the counter-propaganda of the Kuomintang had failed to achieve, Yuwen had accomplished with a stroke of his pen. "The Right Approach" was widely acclaimed; because Yuwen had always been critical of the Kuomintang, his new stand was all the

310

more influential. Writer after writer followed his line, and fickle public opinion once again swung to the other side. Anti-Government outbursts were reduced sharply; petitions were still drafted, but they were directed more against the Communists than the Kuomintang. Ta-kong and his Party were in trouble, and he knew it.

He discussed his worries with Mei-yin. He did not blame his Third Brother for their predicament; if Yuwen had not written that article, someone else would have come up with the idea. Still, a new line of propaganda to overcome Yuwen's arguments would have to be devised.

Mei-yin, to be sure, considered the simple and direct expedient of having Yuwen murdered. She kept silent on this, not because of any sworn brotherhood but because she realized Yuwen had become too prominent in the international metropolis. If anything happened to him, it might do the Party more harm than good. The days that followed the publication of Yuwen's article, therefore, were dark indeed for the Communists in Shanghai—all except Nan Ping.

Then, one evening Ta-kong returned home more anxious and troubled than ever. In the morning he had received an urgent report from his Discipline Squad that on the preceding night his Second Brother had gone to his Third Brother's house. Ta-kong had at once sent word that Li Chien should come to his home that evening. He would have liked to hold the meeting elsewhere, and without Mei-yin's knowledge, but he feared she also had been informed of Li Chien's movements and that hiding the meeting from her would only increase the dangers of the situation. Now, he debated how best to bring up the subject.

But she was looking at him with that amused twinkle in her eye. "A penny for your thoughts, darling," she said.

The intonation of her voice, a mimicking of his own words, told him that she knew everything.

"I've asked Second Brother to come here tonight."

"Comrade Li Chien is getting out of hand these days, isn't he?" she remarked. Before, it had always been "Brother Li Chien" or "Second Brother"; now it was "Comrade Li Chien."

Considering it best to pretend he was disclosing something she did not know, he told her everything.

When he finished, she patted him on the cheek. "That's good of you, my darling boy. You have not tried to keep this a secret. It's not good to keep secrets from Mama, you know."

But the next moment the amused twinkle returned to her eye. "This is a vile offense committed by Comrade Li Chien. You are going to report his conduct to the Party, I presume? It's your duty and mine as well, you know."

Ta-kong pleaded with her to wait. "You know what that would mean to Second Brother. No harm has been done yet, and he has served the Party well both in the past and in this present mission. Besides, he has risked his life many times to save mine. There are occasions you may not know about, but you must remember the time when we were students and demonstrated against the Japanese. And we three are not ordinary comrades—he and I are sworn brothers, you are my wife and his sister—"

"Even if I were disposed to overlook it," Mei-yin said, "there are others on his trail—Nan Ping, for instance. Suppose we don't report and he does?"

"But we *will* report the matter to the Party. I'll report that I specifically directed Second Brother to approach our former Third Brother because of our past relations and to sound out Yuwen on the possibility of writing another article and changing his stand. You'll report that I confided this to you some time previously. I am sure that both the Top Command of the International Headquarters and our own High Command will believe you and me, whatever different accounts they may get from others."

Mei-yin hugged Ta-kong to conceal her surprise at his ingenuity. She knew she could not very well refuse it, for that would make her openly against Ta-kong.

"You know what you are asking, my darling boy?" she murmured. "You are asking me to put you above the Party in my heart. If the Party knew of this, I'd be purged without question. If Mama does this for you, what will you do for her in return?"

Ta-kong knew too well what she wanted him to say. "I'll put you above the Party in my heart," he said.

"And above your sworn brothers?"

He nodded.

"Then I want you to show you really mean it. When Li Chien comes, be very harsh to him. Treat him as an ordinary comrade, not a sworn brother. He deserves it. He has endangered not only himself, but you and me."

So it was that when Second Brother arrived, he was confronted by a cold and stern Ta-kong. There was no friendship or familiarity. He was not even asked to sit down. In Mei-yin's presence, Ta-kong

312

demanded unceremoniously that he account for his unauthorized activity the night before.

Resentment filled Li Chien. He said perversely, "Since you know all about it, what's the need of my saying anything?"

"Why did you go there?" asked Mei-yin sternly.

Li Chien ignored her and addressed himself directly to Ta-kong. "I went there because I yearned to see my Third Brother. I am made of blood and flesh. I am not stone-hearted."

"Haven't you forgotten, Comrade," said Mei-yin, "that you're forbidden by the Party to see any unauthorized person? And in this case, an avowed enemy of the Party!"

"*Enemy?* He's no enemy! He is my Third Brother!"

"Did you talk to him?" continued Mei-yin, unperturbed.

"You know damn well I didn't."

"What did you do precisely?" asked Ta-kong, still keeping his voice austere.

"Why—I—just stood outside his house and peeped through a window."

Softly Ta-kong asked what he saw.

"A sight that filled my heart with happiness. Third Brother was writing at a desk, and his wife sat nearby knitting a sweater for him. They have a boy—he was toddling around playing with a toy. What a beautiful woman his wife is! And Third Brother hasn't changed much—he just looks more mature and more dignified. I'd have given anything to go in and embrace him!"

"Why didn't you, then?" pursued Ta-kong.

Li Chien looked at him in surprise.

"I don't know," he said wistfully. "Except that the place—the very air of the place—was so peaceful. So contented. I didn't want to disturb it. And I thought of your warning that I might endanger Third Brother and his family. I was like a plague that could contaminate them."

"Stop!" cried Mei-yin, the cold gleam flashing in her eyes now. "That's all nonsense, Comrade! You talk as if you admire a tawdry, worthless, bourgeois home life! You don't talk like a Communist!"

"What of it? You're going to report me anyway. I'm prepared to take the consequences."

"No," said Ta-kong. "But listen to Mei-yin. We're not going to report you in the way you think—and you deserve. We're going to say I directed you to seek out Yuwen to persuade him to change his views. When you got there, you decided it was useless and left

313

without seeing him. Understand? And for this, you have your Sister Mei-yin to thank! If I'd been left alone to deal with you, I might have been much harsher."

In his eagerness to ingratiate himself with Mei-yin and to smooth the feelings between her and his Second Brother, Ta-kong had tried to disguise his own sentiments. But Li Chien took him at his word. He resented any favors from Mei-yin, and was incensed against his Big Brother.

"What are you going to do with me now?" he demanded belligerently.

"We consider you overwrought," answered Ta-kong. "It's best that you leave Shanghai for a short time. I order you to take an inspection trip along the main smuggling route at once. You're to set out tomorrow morning without delay. When you return I trust you'll have come to your senses."

5

LI CHIEN RETURNED to Shanghai after an absence of more than a month. All those watching for his return were aware of it the moment he arrived, but contrary to the rules of the Party, he secluded himself in his house and failed to report his arrival immediately to Ta-kong's headquarters. Ta-kong was vexed, but excused him on the ground that he might have taken ill after such a long, strenuous, and nerve-racking journey. Mei-yin and Nan Ping, however, increased their vigilance.

A day and a half passed before Ta-kong had a message from Li Chien. It came not through any of their regular channels, but by one of the two comrades who were also disciples of Ta-kong's secret Society. Li Chien did not know the man as such, but he did know he was one of Ta-kong's most trusted followers. This comrade-disciple reported that Li Chien had stolen into his lodgings at night and given him the note after warning him of its extreme urgency and secrecy. It had to be handed to Ta-kong without anyone's knowledge.

The message confounded Ta-kong even more. It asked him to go alone to Li Chien's house in the evening, and not to tell anybody, not even Mei-yin. This was a flagrant violation of the rules of security that specifically forbade any inferior to make a direct request of his superior. But then Li Chien was his sworn brother.

Besides, the note said, it was a matter of life or death for both of them.

Ta-kong considered a long time. There was no telling what Mei-yin—and others—might know or do. . . .

Mei-yin knew enough. Her agents had reported that Li Chien was back, and when Ta-kong did not return home at the usual hour she was sure where he had gone. Long before, she had had duplicate keys made to Li Chien's house; in Sun Yat-sen University she had been trained to shoot, and for some time now she had been carrying a revolver.

One thing worried her: Nan Ping. She arranged for one of her men to station himself outside Li Chien's house with a supply of firecrackers, and to set them off if Nan Ping or any of his people appeared. This would arouse no undue curiosity, since the Chinese were in the habit of exploding firecrackers on any occasion.

Ta-kong reached Li Chien's home worried and exasperated, but determined to be firm. The moment he entered, however, he forgot his determination. Li Chien did not even rise to greet his Big Brother. He looked broken and ill, and slouched listlessly in his chair, his clothes disheveled, his broad shoulders sagging. His fleshy face appeared haggard and drawn, and his eyes were darkened with circles as if he had not slept.

Li Chien's wife had opened the door for Ta-kong, looking at him not with welcome but with wide-eyed fear. The baby was in her arms.

Ta-kong went to Li Chien, laid his hands on his shoulders, and said affectionately: "Are you ill, Second Brother?"

Without looking up, Li Chien shook his head slowly.

"Then what's the matter with you?"

"I was afraid you might not come. Mei-yin is such a stickler for Party rules."

"But I'm here—and I didn't tell Mei-yin."

"That's good," murmured Li Chien. "Sit down, and let's have a good long talk, like the old times."

Ta-kong sat down and waited. Impetuous and voluble as Li Chien had always been, his silence now was all the more unsettling. His wife kept glancing fearfully from one man to the other. The baby cried, but nobody heeded.

Ta-kong began gently, "You said in your note that this is a matter of life and death for you and me."

"Yes," answered Li Chien, a measure of animation returning.

"But I shall not talk about that now. I want to talk about the old times—you and I and our Third Brother."

"Proceed, then," Ta-kong said patiently.

"Remember our oath: Three lives in one and one life in three? Though we were not born together, we are to die together?"

"Yes. It is to our everlasting regret that Third Brother has parted with us."

"Ah, there!" said Li Chien, for the first time looking Ta-kong full in the face. "Can't you see also that it is we—you and I—who have parted with our Third Brother? Indeed, there is a way to bring us three back together again."

"How?" Ta-kong was on guard, now.

Li Chien caught the steely note in that one word. "Listen! Always in the past I've let you do the thinking for me. For this once, allow me to do the thinking for you. Please don't interrupt, Big Brother—I must speak."

"Go on."

"Well—I've come to the conclusion that Third Brother is right. Not you and I."

Ta-kong's face froze.

"Don't think I've come to this conclusion lightly or impulsively. I know I'm lightheaded and impulsive by nature—but this time it is not so."

And then, as if it were a confession—but in a way a challenge too—he told Ta-kong how he had resolved to convert his Third Brother to Communism, how he had read all Yuwen's writings, how he had debated with him mentally and had finally arrived at the shocking realization that Yuwen and not he had won the argument.

"That is when I went to his house and tried to see him. I had to. I had only a glimpse through the window, but it, more than anything else, was enough to convince me he is right and we're wrong.

"What is our way of life? Only circles and circles of fear! You may say this is necessary because we're still struggling with all reactionaries, because we're fighting against the Kuomintang and haven't yet gained full control of the country. But you know very well that is not so. Even after we achieve supreme power, there will always be the Party discipline, there will be always the High Command and the Top Command, there will be always the ceaseless surveillance of one comrade by another.

316

"High in the Party as you are, I know Mei-yin was deliberately sent here to live with you as your wife in order to watch you. You call that a marriage? Bah! Compare it with Third Brother's!

"And when I looked in Yuwen's window and saw him and his family, all at once I realized with horror the true nature of our way of life. He is happy and I am not. He is clean and decent. I told myself then that I couldn't face him unless I cleansed myself. That's why I fled."

As Li Chien paused Ta-kong's mind was in turmoil. This was nothing like what he had expected. If only this were not his sworn brother . . .

"Then you sent me on the inspection trip, and I went to our base in Kiangsi," Li Chien resumed. "It opened my eyes even wider. Third Brother is right: We have not been, we are not, and we never will be what we claim to be. We say we want to establish a new and better society, but we're destroying everything that is good, not only in our old culture but also in human nature. We have set up a Soviet Government in Kiangsi; but that Government, using the Kuomintang threat as a pretext, has introduced the most ruthless and cold-blooded measures to degrade, oppress, and trample the people. It has tried to destroy our old family system by forcing children to spy on parents and wives on husbands, and also by encouraging sexual promiscuity through a new marriage law. It has held endless public trials, executing people for no reason other than that they are opposed to its rule—and always in the most atrocious and savage manner. As if this isn't enough, Big Brother, you should know the real story behind the severe Government rationing of food. It says food is scarce, but with the foodstuffs grown inside its territories and the food I've smuggled in, there's more than enough to feed the entire population. No, it is using the food shortage as an excuse to deliberately and systematically starve to death thousands and thousands of people it regards as undesirable!

"And what makes me hate the whole thing the most is that we haven't the least intention of fighting the Japanese. What your Publicity Department puts out here is the falsest of false propaganda. We cry against foreign Imperialism, but we make no preparation whatever to quit the guerrilla base and go to Manchuria to fight the enemy. On the contrary, our plans are all drawn up to attack the Kuomintang forces in the rear as soon as they start north. And why do we do this? Because we are instructed to by the Communist International. Oh, how I hate to say it, Big Brother! Third

317

Brother is right again. We're nothing but stooges of an alien power!"

Old loyalties and ideals stirred briefly in Ta-kong's heart, but he controlled his voice.

"You know I could have you liquidated for this," he said.

"I know," answered Li Chien unflinchingly. "I've thought of that. You may not have brought a gun with you—mine is inside the drawer of the desk right beside you. If you wish, take it out and shoot me. Nobody will hear you."

Averting his head, Ta-kong asked in torment, "Why did you drag me here to tell me all this? Why didn't you go directly over to the Kuomintang? It would have been far better for you and me if you had simply deserted the Cause."

"It's because of you, Big Brother—because of our solemn oath. I can't go away without taking you along with me."

"Where to?" demanded Ta-kong involuntarily.

"As I see it, there isn't much choice. If you like, we can join the Kuomintang together. It might not be a bad idea, after all. With your position in the Communist Party, the Kuomintang will surely be glad to welcome you back to their fold. Then we'll be able to live our lives together with our Third Brother."

"That's impossible!"

"Well, if you wish, we might follow the example of your uncle— go to Malaya or some other foreign land and start our lives over. I've talked with my wife, and she is willing to follow me wherever you and I decide to go. You could take Mei-yin if you can persuade her. Once we make a success overseas, we'll ask Third Brother to join us. Or when peace is restored here, we can return and join him."

"That's also preposterous!" said Ta-kong. "Besides, the Party would pursue me to the ends of the earth."

"Then," said Li Chien, "there's only one other course left for you. Kill me, and be done with it. I've committed what the Party considers an unforgivable crime. You can only clear yourself by liquidating me."

Ta-kong bowed his head. His voice was only a hoarse whisper. "Not that I haven't thought of it—but Heaven help me, I couldn't!"

"What are you going to do then?"

"There *is* another way. I presume I can't change your mind. You've chosen your life, and I've chosen mine. I'll let you go free and make believe I never was here and talked with you. But flee!

Flee with your wife and baby right now. For tomorrow I'll have to order your liquidation and put my Discipline Squad on your trail."

Li Chien leaned back and smiled. "Big Brother, you're doing exactly what I thought you'd do. But I'm afraid it's too late. By tomorrow you will not have much of a Discipline Squad left, to say nothing of your whole Eastern Bureau. You see, I foresaw this possible loophole and closed it tight. I wanted to leave you no other choice. You must either kill me or go with me."

"What do you mean?"

"I knew your men and Mei-yin's would be waiting for me when I returned, so before I came back I mailed the Kuomintang secret police a full list of the assumed names and the whereabouts of all your personnel. Of course, I didn't give away your identity and your personal hide-out. I calculated it would take, at most, two days for the letter to get to the Kuomintang police. If they are a tenth as efficient as you, they'll have mobilized their forces by tonight."

Fury and terror seized Ta-kong, and he leaped up and took a menacing step toward Li Chien. "Damn you!" he shouted. "How could you do this to me!"

Li Chien fell to his knees and grasped Ta-kong's legs.

"Big Brother, can't you see I did it entirely out of my love for you? I want you to leave this life for good—to go away with me!"

Ta-kong tried violently to push his Second Brother aside, but Li Chien held fast.

"Run while you can!" Ta-kong cried. "I'll have to hurry myself if I'm to save anything from the results of your treachery!"

"It's useless, Big Brother. The Party will never forgive you for this, you'll be liquidated for sure. You can only save yourself by going with me or killing me."

Li Chien's wife, the baby in her arms, watched terrified as the two men scuffled, one striving to tear away, the other holding fast. Then a sharp clear voice was heard.

"Get up, Comrade Li Chien! You shall have your wish."

They turned. Mei-yin was coming through a back door, holding a revolver; there was a silencer on its muzzle. Li Chien stood up mechanically and separated himself from Ta-kong.

"I heard everything," Mei-yin said mercilessly. "I believe you are right. There is no escape for your Big Brother except to accommodate you according to your wish."

"No—no, Mei-yin!" moaned Ta-kong. "Please!"

Li Chien said calmly, "Big Brother and Sister Mei-yin, I have only one last request. My wife is innocent of this. Spare her, and look after my child."

Holding the baby close, the woman ran to her husband and clung to him, imploring Mei-yin dumbly with her eyes.

"Wait, Mei-yin!" shouted Ta-kong. "Wait!" And he leaped forward to shield his Second Brother with his own body. Just then, the firecrackers went off outside.

"Look out!" cried Mei-yin. "It's Nan Ping and his men!"

Ta-kong took a step toward the door. Mei-yin fired a single shot that struck Li Chien in the heart. He fell. His wife screamed and the baby cried, "Papa!" Mei-yin fired twice more.

Ta-kong ran toward her shouting, "Why? Why? Go ahead—shoot me, too!"

Then, above the sputter of firecrackers, footsteps pounded toward the house and someone hammered on the door. Mei-yin thrust the gun into Ta-kong's hand.

"Get hold of yourself," she whispered. "Nan Ping is outside!"

She went to the door and opened it. In rushed Nan Ping, leading several men, his piggish eyes flickering in excitement.

"We heard a woman's scream and what sounded like gunshots."

Then he saw the revolver in Ta-kong's hand and the sprawled bodies on the floor.

"What's this?" he demanded.

"I regret to inform you, Comrade," replied Mei-yin with composure, "that Li Chien has betrayed the Party to the Kuomintang, and Comrade Ho Ta-kong has found it necessary to purge him and his family."

She put her hand on Ta-kong's arm. "I am proud of you, Comrade. For the sake of the Party, you have not hesitated to kill your own sworn brother. But as you have just said, there's not a minute to lose. We have much to do to save the Party machinery from the calamity the traitor Li Chien has brought on us."

She pressed Ta-kong's arm, and he allowed himself to be led off. They went out into the darkness, leaving Nan Ping and his men standing open-mouthed.

Six

Li Chien's defection was a shattering blow to the Communists, and almost fatal to Ta-kong.

He had given away vital information, and despite all Ta-kong and Mei-yin could do, about a fourth of their comrades in the Eastern Bureau were caught up in a series of swift, devastating raids by Kuomintang police. Even worse for the Communists, the supply line to the guerrilla base was cut to pieces.

An angry High Command recalled Ta-kong and put Nan Ping in his place as head of the Eastern Bureau. Fearful and despairing, Ta-kong went back to the guerrilla base with Mei-yin—she had been ordered to accompany him and to watch his every move. He remembered Li Chien's advice about running away from Communist life; he remembered, too, Mei-yin's cold-blooded murders. He shuddered. There would be other comrades watching them both; he was now a marked man not only to the Kuomintang but within his own party. There was no place to hide, and no one to whom he could turn.

He saw that Mei-yin had found satisfaction in the disaster. She had saved Ta-kong from liquidation and she let him know, in every feminine way, that she was at last sure of her hold on him—she gloated because she held his life in her hand.

Ta-kong hated her bitterly. He might have grudgingly admitted that his Second Brother had to be killed; he might possibly have acknowledged that she had to kill Li Chien's wife, that harmless country girl no longer harmless once she had become an eyewitness. But so long as he lived, he could neither forget nor forgive the wanton murder of the baby, who could have done nobody harm.

Nor would he forget what Mei-yin was doing now. Ta-kong, a man who longed to dominate men, now found himself helplessly dominated by a woman.

There was only one way to fight this for the time being. Ta-kong swallowed his pride and pretended he was extremely grateful to Mei-yin; he went out of his way to submit to her every caprice. The Party laws on marriage and divorce were very lax, and not many couples lived together for long. Thus Ta-kong, a prisoner of circumstance and fear rather than love—love did not enter into it at all—found that his marriage to Mei-yin and their continual apparent devotion to each other were becoming a thing of wonder and admiration. They were being called the model couple of the Communist marriage system.

Then something happened that eventually would win back Ta-kong's self-respect. . . .

The guerrilla base was starving in that summer of 1934, and short rations and low morale go hand in hand. The Communist troops were reduced now from several hundred thousand to a mere thirty thousand. The High Command had been starving the people of the area under Communist control, and diverting food to the troops, but it was not enough. In studied and sober council, the Communists made a fateful decision: They could not hold the mountain base; they would have to move.

The forced march in search of a new base began. In the beginning it had no specified objective. The Northeast was out, since the Japanese had occupied Manchuria and its neighboring province Jehol, and the Communists had no intention of tangling with the Japanese. Besides, the central provinces that lay between were garrisoned by Chiang's most loyal troops. The West and the Northwest, on the other hand, were still controlled by old warlords who acknowledged only nominal allegiance to Chiang; their troops were more poorly equipped and they seemed less able to offer resistance. So the Communists sensed they should move first westward and then turn to the northwest—nearer the border of Russia, so that shorter and more direct channels of communication might be established with the supreme headquarters of Communism.

It was one of the great marches of history—one of the significant military movements of all time. But it did not look so historic or so significant at the time.

The thirty thousand troops were divided into several columns, loosely commanded by Comrade Mao. Ta-kong was given command of a column and took new heart—he was back in favor with the Party.

The initial outbreak from encirclement did not prove difficult; they had singled out the weakest Government position and overwhelmed it with one concerted attack. But from then on the going

322

was hard. Danger and enemy lurked everywhere; their route led them through territory under the control—more or less—of the Kuomintang. The people were openly hostile, which was extremely serious since they had to live entirely off the land once their rations were used up. The terrain was unfamiliar and confusing; worse still, to protect themselves from observation and pursuit, they could not use the highways and thoroughfares but had to depend on seldom-traveled paths and trails which were frequently all but impassable. By day they scattered and hid and rested; by night they moved and fled and fought whatever minor engagements had to be fought. They avoided Government strong points and serious clashes, and zigzagged, seeking always the soft spots, the places weakly defended. Sometimes, if they were in luck, they could make a dash of twenty or even thirty miles a day; but more often they covered only four or five. At times they could not move on at all. Short of rations, deprived of supplies, uncertain of the future, and plagued with hardships and hazards everywhere, the morale of the troops fell to its lowest ebb.

The Kuomintang could have crushed them then, and perhaps changed the course of history, but their sudden break-out from encirclement had taken Chiang completely by surprise. And since they themselves did not know where they were going, neither could Chiang. He ordered his crack troops after them, and rushed others to the Western provinces in the general direction they seemed headed. But he spread his forces too thin, and there was many a gap in his hastily established defense lines. In addition, Chiang had chosen as generals those who had been loyal to him, rather than those who were most able; not a few proved incapable of rising to the occasion—they let the Communists slip through their fingers. As for the old warlords, though each was anxious to prevent the Communists from settling in his own province, none was especially eager to put up a stiff fight to stop them from pushing on elsewhere.

So from one standpoint the Communist undertaking did not prove so impossible after all. But the human antagonists were only part of their problem; natural barriers, too, stood in their way—difficult passes to sneak through, rugged mountains to climb, turbulent streams to ford. And even above all these, stalking them every minute, pursuing them relentlessly, was an enemy far more dreaded than the Kuomintang—the daily specter of starvation. There was a time when they wandered for days near the borders of Tibet, hopelessly lost on the vast barren steppes known as the forbidding Grassland—where little besides grass ever grows and where few living things dwell—unable to sequestrate sufficient food even through systematic and merciless plunder.

This was no triumphant march. It had none of the wild, conquering flavor of the earlier expeditions of history. Genghis Khan and the savage Tartars would have scorned this mob of ragtag and bobtail. It was a hungry, pilfering, pillaging mob—but nonetheless a group of dedicated men, boldly led and cleverly directed. It suffered repeated and irreplaceable losses, either through natural hardships or through unavoidable encounters with Government troops; it had to fall back and regroup again and again; and yet it crawled forward. . . .

Ta-kong distinguished himself with the High Command, and endeared himself to his men. He fought in the thick of every engagement; he tended the sick and wounded. There were only two ponies in his column, meant for Mei-yin and himself, but whenever a comrade was disabled, Ta-kong walked and let the man ride.

It embarrassed and discomfited him—and yet evoked a grudging admiration—to see Mei-yin do the same thing. She was always at his side, in and out of battle; she gave her horse to another wounded man when Ta-kong walked. If he declined to eat until the last soldier had his meager rations, Mei-yin did too. And once, when Ta-kong was wounded and his column had been cut off from the others, Mei-yin took command in his name and held the troops together until the situation cleared.

He did not love her, he hated her. He knew that her love for him was strange and calculating, evil, unhealthy.

But they were useful to each other. Her body comforted him. The knowledge that she possessed him completely comforted her. The past was not forgiven, but it had been forgotten for the present. . . .

After more than a year, the Communists found themselves in the desolate waste of cave-dwelling Yenan, a small prefecture in Shensi, a province of the Northwest. It was not so near to Russia as they had hoped, but it had to do as a new base.

They had survived a march of approximately seven thousand miles—the "Twenty-Thousand-Li Trek." Of the thirty thousand men who had started, only a little more than five thousand remained.

Ta-kong gained great credit. His column had suffered the smallest loss of all.

324

2

THE COMMUNISTS, HOWEVER, were given but a brief respite in Yenan. Chiang Kai-shek was pouring hundreds of thousands of troops into the Northwest in hot pursuit, and by all reckonings the Communists were doomed.

But while Chiang harried the Communists, Japan did the same to Chiang. After the loss of Manchuria, Chiang had tried to slow down Japanese aggression by diplomatic negotiations, but in 1933 they occupied Jehol, and in 1934 they established the so-called "Manchukuo" and formally detached Northeast China from Chinese sovereignty. In 1935 they seized Chahar, a province adjacent to Jehol. And in this year, 1936, while Chiang was preparing to destroy the Communists once and for all, the Japanese were talking openly of annexing North China.

The Communists were quick to take advantage of the situation. They resorted again to their old idea of a pseudo peace with the Government; they raised aloft once more the standard of the "United Front." They proclaimed loudly that they were now willing to fight the Japanese under Chiang's command. And this time their propaganda met with greater success. Although at the time of the Mukden Incident many people still entertained vain hopes that the issue with Japan could be settled through diplomacy, now the entire nation realized it never could be. And besides, the Communist forces which formerly had numbered hundreds of thousands and had overrun several of the richest provinces of Central China now were reduced to a few thousands and driven to a desolate corner of the Northwest. Thus, as the Japanese threat grew into terrifying proportions, the Communist danger paled into insignificance. Even Lan Yuwen was brought around to this view. He wrote another widely read article pointing out the disparities between the two situations and supporting the idea of the "United Front."

Public opinion alone did not influence Chiang Kai-shek to abandon his determination to crush the Communists at any cost. The Communists themselves had prepared another ruse, in which both Ta-kong and Mei-yin took a large part: they bent all their efforts to subvert the armies Chiang had sent against them. They created such slogans as, "Aim your gun at the outsider, not at your countrymen!"—"Don't kill a Communist; he's a fellow Chinese!"—"Don't shoot a fellow Chinese, though he may be a Communist!" Their propaganda was so successful that it resulted in the "Sian Incident."

For this final campaign against the Communists, Chiang had depended mainly on the so-called Northeastern Armies commanded by one Chang Hsueh-liang, known as the Young Marshal—the very same warlord who had been responsible for the loss of Manchuria to the Japanese. His forces, evacuated from Manchuria after the Japanese occupation of the Northeast in 1931, now were sent to engage the Communists. But the men had no heart for the task; embittered by long exile, they longed to return to home and revenge themselves on the Japanese, and therefore were most susceptible to the Communist propaganda. The Young Marshal himself was a vain, capricious, immature, and unpredictable man. He had inherited the rule of Manchuria from his father, a notorious warlord of the old days, and now that he had lost it, he felt the well-deserved sting of public disgrace and secretly and eagerly sought to re-establish himself in the eyes of his countrymen. Besides, he was a man of pleasure, and before long it was rumored that he had fallen victim to the charms of a Communist woman-comrade disguised as a courtesan, and was being converted to the Communist cause.

Though these alarming reports had reached Chiang Kai-shek beforehand, characteristically he gave them no heed. If anything, he believed too much in himself. He had always befriended the Young Marshal in the past, and he felt sure he could be trusted. In December, 1936, he took a trip to Sian, capital of the Shensi province and headquarters of the Young Marshal, to look over the situation for himself. And there, in conspiracy with the Communists, the Young Marshal seized him.

For several days Chiang's life hung in the balance. Comrade Mao and others were for doing away with him forthwith, but Moscow sent different instructions. Germany and Italy were becoming a serious menace to Soviet Russia in Europe; Japan must be prevented from joining them and threatening the Communist Fatherland in Asia. For this purpose, it was best that Japan be dragged into a protracted war with China, and to make China's resistance effective Chiang Kai-shek was still needed. His armies were the strongest in the country, and his life must be therefore spared. Following Stalin's orders, the Chinese Communist High Command sent Comrade Chou En-lai to enter into negotiations with the captive Chiang.

Though Chiang had doggedly refused to compromise with the

Communists before, now he yielded. Not only was his life at stake, but he was more concerned that other of his troops, besides the Northeastern Armies, might succumb to the influence of Communist propaganda. If he was to be free to fight the Japanese unhindered by the threat of mutinies, it was imperative to come to terms with the Communists.

According to the provisions they agreed upon, the Communist-controlled territory around Yenan was to be recognized as an autonomous "Special Border Area," under only nominal supervision of the Nanking Government. The Red Army was designated as the Eighth Route Army of the national armed forces commanded by Chiang Kai-shek, but was allowed to maintain its independent status. Civil war in China was to cease once and for all, and a "United Front" was established to resist Japanese aggression. Barely a fortnight after his abduction, Chiang returned to Nanking and for a second time apparent co-operation between the Kuomintang and the Communists began.

A few months later, on July 7, 1937, the Japanese struck again, near the well-known Marco Polo Bridge just outside Peking, and now the fight was to the finish. China was not equipped to wage a modern war against modernized Japan, but she was not without her resources. Japan had her armies—China had her people, four hundred million of them. Japan had her cannons, her tanks, her airplanes, and her factories, which could turn out infinite quantities of armaments but China had her land, vast and unending—the farther the enemy penetrated into it, the more difficult the terrain became. Japan wanted a short war, China wanted a long one. Japan sought quick decisions on the field so that organized Chinese resistance could be wiped out in a few strokes; China was determined to preserve her strength, to entice the enemy farther and farther inland, and to weary and wear him out through sheer exhaustion. It was a race between time and space. Japan wanted to win both, but China was willing to trade space for time. When the war broke out, the Japanese militarists calculated it would take only three months. When the war ended, it had lasted two months beyond eight years. . . .

For China to fight such a war, there was only one source from which she could draw strength—the united and unconquerable spirit of the people. And at first the masses of China, young and old, rich and poor, literate and illiterate, stood up against the invader

327

to a man. China had never seen anything like it before in its history. The entire nation had suddenly achieved national consciousness, with every individual stirred up to ultimate sacrifice and heroism. Reverses followed reverses, but there was no faltering. Territories were lost, but there was no despair. Millions fled the Japanese, not merely to save their lives, but to reach the interior where they hoped they could help the Government. And countless other millions stayed behind Japanese lines, not simply to maintain their livelihood, but to sabotage and harass the enemy. Universities were moved in a body; professors and students alike set out from as far as Peking and walked thousands of miles to allocated new sites in the Southwest. What little industry China had was all removed inland. Machinery was carefully dismantled, and then borne on the backs and shoulders of men across endless rivers and mountains. Villages and cities were burned, often with the help of the inhabitants themselves, to leave the enemy nothing to live on— only scorched earth. It was a pathetic, dithyrambic, triumphant display of patriotism. It was a monumental self-expression of the inborn stamina of a people who refused to yield their birthright to another.

Chiang Kai-shek became the symbol of the inexorable will of the nation to remain free. He had been a stubborn man all his life, and now his stubbornness stood him in good stead. With resoluteness and dexterity, he managed to keep his main forces intact and to lure the enemy stage by stage into the bottomless quagmire that was the huge hinterland of China. The Japanese were bogged down and could not extricate themselves. And China, though battered and defaced, was neither broken nor beaten.

But the Communists had their own game to play. Under instructions of the Communist International, the Yenan High Command had carefully mapped out their plans. In a secret directive issued to the comrades, Mao Tse-tung made it clear that the policy of the Party was "70% self-expansion, 20% temporization, and 10% fight the Japanese." Pursuant to that policy, the Communists did most of their 10% fighting at the beginning of the war—actually, in a single brief action.

Responding to the universal patriotic fervor, they acknowledged a command from Chiang Kai-shek and sent out a column to engage the enemy on a Northern front. There they fought one molehill of a pitched battle, and through skillful propaganda made out of it a mountain of gallantry. They exaggerated the enemy's strength and fire power, and magnified their own difficulties and losses. In the face of the general retreat of Government armies which Chiang Kai-shek had ordered in line with his preconceived strategy of "trading space for time," the Communists found it easy to engrave on the minds of the uninformed public that the unique stand they had taken was nothing short of a heroic feat of arms. From then on the impression was widespread among the people that the Communists were fighting the Japanese in earnest and that their troops, man for man, general for general, were far better combatants than the Government troops. Once that impression was created, the Communists withdrew from any contact with the Japanese. They did not want to whittle down their strength by fighting the enemy; they wanted to expand their strength, and expand it fast—without conflict with the Government, if possible; with conflict, if necessary; but always at the expense of the Government.

But the Communists could not as yet proceed with their fixed plan of "70% self-expansion" because there was no place in which to expand. In front of them stood the Japanese, alongside were the Government armies. Even back at their Yenan base far in the interior, they could not expand, for, still suspicious of their intentions, Chiang had kept the "Special Border Area" surrounded with a superior loyal force. The Communist High Command was not sure what to do, and so appointed a special commission to study the problem. Ta-kong was designated as one of its members.

He and his colleagues pored over maps and gathered all sorts of intelligence, more about Government troops than about the Japanese. They infiltrated Chiang's armies and collected information about their movements. But the situation was too fluid. By the time the reports arrived, they were out of date. If they could only get hold of Chiang's military plans in advance! But that was all but impossible. Then Ta-kong hit on an idea, and promptly submitted it to the High Command....

3

MOST OF THE coastal provinces were already lost to the Japanese. Shanghai and Nanking had fallen; Canton and Hankow were about to fall. The seat of the Chinese Government had been moved to Chungking, far in the West, behind a barrier of impenetrable mountains.

Into this city, along with the Government, now came the so-called "Political Advisory Council." This was a new organ which Chiang Kai-shek had established at the outbreak of the hostilities as a concession to the popular clamor for democratizing the Government. But it was nothing like a parliament. Its members were appointed by the Government, not elected by the people. And it had no authority, except, as its name indicated, to give advice when called upon. But it had one power which the Government could not begrudge without defeating its own purpose—the power of criticizing the Government.

Under these circumstances, the Government was careful to see that the Council was composed mostly of loyal Kuomintang members. But it made one mistake—it named Chang Fa-foo a Councilor. That worthy had concealed his membership in the Communist Party and all these years had outwardly remained a faithful Kuomintang Chancellor of the Government University in the northern port city. However, now that the port city was lost, he came to Chungking and took his seat in the Council.

Naturally, under the agreement of the "United Front," the Government could not deny representation to the Chinese Communist Party, and a few prominent Communists were appointed. For appearance' sake, the Government also included a limited representation from the so-called "Minor Parties"—which, since any opposition in Kuomintang or Communist territories was forbidden, could operate only inside the foreign Concessions and, consequently, had little following.

In addition, to give the Council a more heterogeneous look, the Government selected a handful of "Independents"—among them, Chi Teh-shan, chief of the secret Society in the North. The Government realized his name was none too savory, but he had been flirting with the Kuomintang so long he could be trusted not to cause any trouble. For his part, Old Head was flattered not a little by the honor. He could have remained in the North, perfectly safe and unscathed, even under Japanese occupation. But inspired with patriotic fervor, that "Mountain of Virtues" chose to leave his Society in the hands of a disciple, depart from his comfortable home, and make his way to Chungking with Jasmine.

There was only one Councilor the Government had appointed with extreme reluctance—Lan Yuwen. His liberal views had been always regarded with disfavor by the Kuomintang, and his nomination was especially opposed by Amy and Tong Hsi. But because of his writings he had become too prominent and influential, and the Government had little choice.

If anyone took the Council seriously, it was Yuwen. Though he was not satisfied with the powers conferred on it or with the method by which its members were chosen, he considered the Council a step in the right direction. He took Li-hwa and their two children to Chungking (for now they had another son), and also persuaded his colleagues to move their college to a suburb near the wartime capital, so they could help educate the young in the interior.

There was a joyous reunion between the Lans and the Chis in Chungking. Just before Yuwen and Li-hwa got married in Shanghai, they had written the news to the Chis; and Jasmine and Old Head, pleased beyond measure at hearing from Li-hwa at last, and particularly happy with the man she had chosen, responded with a shower of gifts. Now that all four were in Chungking, they saw one another often and before long had developed an intimate relationship.

Besides the Chis, Yuwen and Li-hwa had another frequent visitor. Chang Fa-foo had taken an immediate fancy to them. As a fellow idealist, he expressed great admiration for Yuwen's idealism, and he told Li-hwa that he had been a great and dear friend to her late father. From time to time he gave them what he called inside information on Kuomintang politics. The accounts were invariably far darker than what appeared on the surface, and Yuwen and Li-hwa were often shocked. Yet they could not help but think there must be some elements of truth in what he said, for the top personnel of the Government had not changed in the last decade. Although Yuwen and Li-hwa might not know about other high personalities, they did know Amy and Tong Hsi.

Then, one evening Chang Fa-foo came to the Lans' in a state of great indignation. He had information! Of course, they both knew that Tong Hsi was in Chungking, occupying a key position in the cabinet, but did they know where his wife was and what she was doing? Now, when everyone was undergoing trials and privations for the country, Amy was in Hong Kong leading a life of debauchery. Not only that, she was using the British Colony as a base to smuggle into the interior huge quantities of luxury goods which the Government, to conserve foreign exchange, had publicly banned. Neither the Customs nor any other Government agency dared interfere with her operations, and she was reaping fabulous profits at the expense of the nation.

Yuwen was disgusted. Knowing Amy, he had no doubt this story was true, and he himself had seen various luxurious articles on display in some of the shop windows in Chungking. He asked Chang why he, as a longtime member of the Kuomintang, could do nothing about the matter inside the Government. The latter shrugged his spare shoulders. Just *because* he was a Kuomintang he could do nothing about it; however, someone else, he hinted pointedly, an independent and an idealist, could take up the issue in the Political Advisory Council. It might not stop the smuggling, but it would throw a scare into the hearts of corrupt people like Amy and Tong Hsi. It would be good for the nation, it would be good for the Government; it would be good even for the Kuomintang. But it would take a man with the highest degree of moral courage to speak up.

Yuwen hesitated. He did not wish to raise the question in the Council—for the sake of the Government itself, he deemed it better that he hold his tongue. Were he to speak up, the report might destroy the confidence of the people in the Government. And it would no doubt give aid and comfort to the enemy.

He had just about decided to say nothing when calamity struck Chungking. Out of the blue swooped Japanese bombers; it was the first time enemy planes bombarded the city. For months the Government had been talking of building a strong civil defense to cope with such an exigency, but when the enemy planes came the Government was caught completely off guard. The alert signals were not given till too late; hardly any shelters had been prepared for the inhabitants. In two raids on two consecutive days, half the city was laid in ruins and more than fifty thousand people were killed and wounded.

Yuwen and his family were safe in the suburb. By the end of the second day he had heard so many stories of horror that he felt, as a member of the Political Advisory Council, he ought to verify the reports for himself. Since the enemy was incapable—so far, at least—of launching a night raid, when evening came he set out on his inspection trip. What he saw was even more horrible than what he had heard. It was like a visit to Hell.

Many columns of fire were still burning, shedding a ghoulish light over the ruined city. The streets were full of craters and debris, impregnated with choking smoke and nauseating odors, and everywhere was the high sound of grief. The casualties were too heavy to handle. Here the well-to-do were collecting their dead and putting them into makeshift coffins; there the poor were carrying away corpses wrapped in rags or rough mattresses. Now and then Yuwen found mangled bodies, or parts of them, scattered along the wayside, cared for by none.

What incensed him most, however, was that the Government seemed to show little concern—nowhere were any responsible authorities rendering succor or giving directions to the people; they were left to fend for themselves. He found an old woman squatting like a hump of stone before the burnt ruins of a house, her body numb, her face tearless and vapid, her eyes frozen in a stupid stare. Except for her breathing, she might have been taken for dead. Onlookers, anxious and helpless, gathered about her, and from them Yuwen learned her pitiful tale. All her family—her husband, her children, her grandchildren—had been exterminated by a single bomb. She had been driven insane by grief and shock.

The sight of the old woman once again brought Yuwen's own mother, Widow Lan, to mind. The city of Yi had fallen to the enemy in the earliest days of the war, and for two years now he had not heard from her. He had written many times to the Reverend Dr. Holt through one foreign mission after another; there was never a reply. He had also besought Old Head to help, but he was candidly told that the Society, having withdrawn all its disciples into the port city, no longer maintained any connection with Yi. Right at this moment his mother could be sitting like this dazed woman, hoping against hope to see her dear ones again. . . .

Yuwen left the scene with a bitter rancor against the Japanese, and with an even bitterer feeling against the Government. Why had it failed to give the city an effective civil defense? And why was it even now neglecting its afflicted people?

The next day the Political Advisory Council called an emergency meeting to discuss the aftermath of the raid. When Yuwen rose to speak, he could no longer control himself. He did not confine his subject to the disaster that had befallen the city, but enlarged it to include the general conduct of the Government. He did not blame the local authorities alone, he censured the national government as a whole. He did not denounce Chiang Kai-shek personally, he condemned his associates, accusing them not only of incompetence but of corruption and flagrant disregard of the

333

interests of the people. Although he named no names, there was no question whom he meant. How could one occupy a responsible key office in the Government and yet engage in unlawful profiteering? How could one hold a high-ranking position in the Kuomintang and yet stay away from the wartime capital and luxuriate in Hong Kong? If the fate of the nation was to be continually entrusted to such people, how could the country expect to gain final victory over the enemy? It was a daring and scathing attack. Never before in any assembly under the rule of the Kuomintang had a man spoken so boldly as Yuwen did that day. When he sat down, he was greeted not with applause but with dead silence.

Naturally, no Government-controlled newspapers carried the story. But the Communist daily printed Yuwen's speech in full, and the news spread like wildfire. The next day the Kuomintang dismissed the incumbent Mayor of Chungking and replaced him. But inasmuch as the other charges leveled against the Government by Yuwen were deemed generalized and groundless, no action was taken.

4

THIS WAS THE moment for which Chang Fa-foo had waited, under specific instructions from Yenan. Now, his immediate problem was to get Amy to Chungking—for only she would have the necessary temerity and unscrupulousness for the Communists' proposition.

Chang went to see Tong, to tell him of Yuwen's speech. He was not alone; many other Kuomintang Councilors were gathered in the Minister's waiting room, and when Tong Hsi heard their story he flared up in anger. Chang Fa-foo took him aside and suggested that, all things considered, it might be best to halt the slander by urging Amy to come to Chungking at once. Tong agreed, an urgent telegram was sent, and a week later Amy arrived at the wartime capital by plane.

At once Chang sought her out for a private interview. Amy was just as eager to talk with him, to enlist his help in pacifying the Councilors.

"I understand from darling Hsi that you advised him to send for me," she said. "I would have come to Chungking long ago, but I was seriously ill and had to stop at Hong Kong for medical care."

One look at Amy told Chang what an unmitigated lie this was. The woman was well over fifty, but with her skillful make-up she looked not much older than thirty and was obviously in perfect health.

"You must have had a miraculous recovery," he told her. "You remind me of the good old days when you and Ho Fucho, your ex-beau and my late friend, were in Japan together. You don't look a day older."

"Flatterer!" Amy smiled. "You know that's not true—but I'm pleased nonetheless. Now, to be serious. I am in Chungking on your advice. I suppose my presence here should be sufficient to quash all malicious slanders against me?"

"Yes and no," answered Chang. "I have no fears about the other members of the Council, not even the Communists. But this Lan Yuwen seems to entertain a personal grudge against you and Brother Hsi."

Amy's face flushed visibly, and Chang Fa-foo wondered what could have passed between her and Yuwen. But she collected herself and said calmly, "I understand you have seen him often lately and have become a close friend of his. Can't you influence him on my behalf?"

"Lan Yuwen is a determined man. He has made up his mind about you two—he seems to know much more about you than I suspected, and he's collecting more information all the time."

"What can he possibly know?"

Chang Fa-foo shrugged. "My dear Amy, we've been through many things together. There's a good deal in your background that won't bear close scrutiny, as you know very well."

Amy laughed. "If you mean my little affair with Yuan Shih-kai's son, with which you used to blackmail me—it cannot be of any use to Lan Yuwen. If he breathes a single word, I shall sue him for libel. That little secret was of use to you only—you blackmailed me into appointing you Secretary-General to darling Hsi in the port city."

The conversation was proceeding better than Chang Fa-foo had anticipated. "Ah, Amy, you shouldn't speak of our little understanding as blackmail. Such an unfriendly word. Ours was a most cordial exchange of services that worked to our mutual advantage. But there are other matters, much more serious than your amours, that Lan Yuwen may get wind of."

"If you're thinking of my business enterprises—everything is legitimate. There is no law against an official's pursuing lawful

335

commerce. Besides, how else do you expect darling Hsi and me to support ourselves befitting our station, with Government salaries so low?"

Chang Fa-foo smiled mockingly. "And if you occasionally have to step a bit outside the law, I trust you have covered your tracks completely?"

Amy laughed again.

"Do you know who Lan Yuwen's wife is?" he asked suddenly.

"I don't care in the least who she is!" Amy said vehemently, frowning.

"Just Ho Fucho's only daughter—Ho Li-hwa!"

Amy started in momentary surprise, but her tone was non-chalant. "I wish her well for our dear old mutual friend's sake. But what has she to do with me?"

"Suppose Lan Yuwen should learn more about the conspirators who plotted the tragic death of his father-in-law and our dear old mutual friend?"

Amy's painted face was impassive. "That happened a long time ago. If I remember right, Tien Fong was responsible, and he had his reasons. What if Lan Yuwen did learn of it? Tien is fighting at the front—as a matter of fact, he and his men are guerrillas behind the Japanese lines. He wouldn't care a pin if Lan Yuwen preferred charges against him, and certainly it's no concern of mine."

"But it is not Tien Fong I am thinking of—it's the other two conspirators who plotted the assassination with him. From what I am told, Tien Fong was not at all anxious to kill Fucho. It was the others—particularly one who happened to be a woman!"

"What are you hinting at?"

"I am your friend, Amy," said Chang. "And as your friend, I feel I should tell you that an acquaintance of mine has some proof to that effect."

What proof, Amy wanted to know.

"Written testimony of two men who were employed by Governor Tien Fong. It seems that the conspirators were very careless when they plotted the murder, or else they placed more trust in Tien's servants than was warranted. Anyway, the two men overheard the whole conversation and have put it down in writing."

Amy was obviously alarmed now. "What does the testimony say? Have you read it?"

"No. But from what my acquaintance has told me, I thought

336

I should speak to you." He looked at her. "Especially since he's thinking of giving the testimony to Lan Yuwen—and you know what that means. Very likely he will raise the question in the Council and demand a thorough investigation."

"Let him! Ho Fucho was nothing but a traitor to the Party and to the country. He deserved what happened to him."

"You may have trouble explaining that view. You yourself called him dear old friend just a minute ago. And to many members of the Kuomintang, he is still remembered as an honored old comrade. He never was known to have harmed the Party, and his unexplained death has been always officially lamented by the Government. Then, there's the public—just think what the Communists can make of this in their propaganda! The people will swallow a good deal, but not murder. Especially a murder of a comrade by a comrade!"

Amy said nothing, but her face set abruptly in a flinty hardness.

Chang Fa-foo watched her carefully. "If you're thinking what I think," he said finally, "then I advise you not to try it. Lan Yuwen cannot be put out of the way as our dear old mutual friend, Ho Fucho, was. He is an idol to thousands of students, and a member of the Political Advisory Council. If there is anything that will stir this hitherto apathetic Council to unprecedented fury, it is to get one of its members murdered!"

Reading Amy's mind, he continued, "Nor do I think you can bribe him. I'm quite certain no amount of money will deter him from seeking vengeance for his father-in-law's death."

"No," said Amy, grinning. "I know Lan Yuwen cannot be bribed. I am not thinking of bribing him, but you—or should I say, your acquaintance?"

"You'd better say my acquaintance. I want nothing for myself. As your friend, I only want to persuade him not to pass on the testimony to Lan Yuwen."

Amy asked him to name the price.

"I think it very reasonable, considering the high stakes involved."

"A hundred thousand U. S. dollars? Two hundred thousand?"

"No. It's not money he wants."

"An office? The most I can promise is a Vice-Ministership, you know."

"He wants no office."

"Then what does he want?"

"Just some information from time to time, Amy. Information

337

which you and Brother Hsi can easily get, which will harm no one, but which my acquaintance needs."

"What information?"

"Information on our military plans and on the deployment of our troops."

Amy showed no signs of indignation. Finally, and rather hesitantly, she asked, "Is your acquaintance a Japanese agent?"

Chang Fa-foo debated what to answer. He would have liked to put Amy off the scent in that direction, but he was afraid it might be too risky. "Whatever my acquaintance is, I am sure he is not an enemy agent."

"Then he's a Communist?"

"That he could be."

"How can I trust a Communist?"

"Ah, Amy, you are in no position to distrust him. Besides, the Communists are our allies. Their troops are our own Eighth Route Army and they have a right to be informed of our military plans. And even if we keep the plans secret from them, they are bound to find out the deployment of our forces once the moves have been made. I'm not sure my acquaintance is a Communist, but if he is, all he wants is to acquire, a little earlier, information he has a right to know. What harm can come from that?"

"I'll take your acquaintance's terms," Amy said abruptly. "But the minute Lan Yuwen brings up any trumped-up charges, I'll consider the agreement broken."

"As long as you keep your part of the bargain, I am sure my acquaintance will keep his."

According to the agreement between Chiang Kai-shek and the Communists, the latter were allowed to maintain a delegation in Chungking and a newspaper, as well as a wireless station which could communicate directly with Yenan. This station was now put to use and the information that Amy furnished from time to time was rushed to the Communist High Command as soon as it was received. Ta-kong and his colleagues of the special commission studied the reports, and soon made a vital discovery. Although on the map the Japanese seemed to have conquered almost half of China, actually they maintained garrisons only in key cities and mounted guards over vital lines of communication. They did not have the manpower to stand watch over the vast countryside. Thus, behind the Japanese front there lay a boundless no-man's-land—

a genuine power vacuum. And what was more, both the Kuomintang Government and the Communist High Command had taken for granted that none of their troops could survive behind the enemy lines. Now, the facts belied this—quite a few Government forces, cut off during retreat, had been forced to stay behind. Tien Fong, for instance, led one such unit. Besides, new guerrilla companies were springing up, thriving, and maintaining contact with Chungking.

The Chungking Government had made no serious efforts to utilize and organize these scattered forces. Ta-kong and the other Communists saw their chance. The brightest prospect of their "self-expansion" beckoned to them like an enchanting vision, in the vast no-man's-land behind the Japanese lines.

From that day the Communists heeded no further Government instructions. When pressed by the enemy and ordered to retreat along with other Government troops, they did not do so. Nor did they engage the Japanese in battle. They merely slipped past the enemy lines and went into the wide-open spaces byond....

In most of the no-man's-land the Government had left no organized administration behind, and local leaders had risen overnight like mushrooms. Some were brigands or gangsters, pure and simple, who seized power by brutal force. Others were men of means and good standing who were thrust to the fore by their respective communities in an effort to preserve a semblance of order. Many, of course, were genuine patriots who, stirred by the noblest feelings, tried to forge their fellow countrymen into an effective fighting force and wage guerrilla war upon the Japanese. All, however, were jealous of their newly acquired power. It was not easy at first to induce them to submit to an outside authority.

But the Communists had several advantages. They came now in the name of the Government and in the capacity of the Eighth Route Army of the national armed forces. They spread the propaganda that in order to be patriotic, local units had to obey the Government and put themselves at the disposal of the Eighth Route Army. Since there was no other Government agency around to contradict them, their assertions were not, and could not, be challenged. As for the genuine patriots and the few troublesome intellectuals—force, of course, could be always depended upon as the final means of persuasion.

On the whole, the Communist success was immediate and enormous. Unbeknown to the Government and unhindered by the

Japanese, in a few months they were able to establish full control over the whole countryside of a northern province. Then they started to expand into a new area. Since this happened to be Ta-kong's native province, the High Command at first considered appointing him head of the expeditionary force. But Ta-kong was needed for more important work at headquarters, so comrade Nan Ping, who had been recalled to Yenan after the loss of Shanghai, volunteered, claiming that he had an extensive knowledge of the territory. He was given the command.

For the first few months everything went well. Nan Ping easily extended Communist domination over a wide portion of the mountainous area of the province, until he had come to the very threshold of the Prefecture of Yi. But here his expansion abruptly came to a halt.

Yi was of the greatest strategic importance and had to be taken at any cost. It was situated between the rugged mountains lying to the west and the fertile plains stretching along the east. So far, the Communists had confined their activities to the mountainous regions of the west, but to reach the rich plains of the east, there was only one practical passage—through Yi. If they could not gain control of that outlet, they would be bottled up in the mountains, unable to expand further.

But a formidable guerrilla force was entrenched in the country astraddle the coveted passage. Nan Ping first tried the methods of persuasion which had proved so efficacious with others; all in vain. Then he attacked it outright but that proved disastrous. What was even more humiliating to Nan Ping, the leader of the guerrilla force was one whom he had known personally, one whom he had always considered beneath his notice.

In desperation, Nan Ping reported the situation to the High Command and appealed for reinforcement.

Seven

THE WAR CAME to Yi with a disrupting, shattering force, long before the people of that inland town had heard a cannon shot. . . .

Their province was nearest Peking, and an immediate invasion was expected. Rumors came on the wind: the Japanese soldiers were following the ancient custom of barbarian conquerors—for three days after the capture of a town the troops were permitted unbounded license for rape and pillage. Governor Tien Fong had mustered his forces to defend the provincial capital, only a day's distance from Yi, but nobody believed he could hold it for long. Despair and desperation were rampant; young people talked of forming guerrilla bands in the mountains, but most of the population prepared to flee.

The pitiful and ceaseless exodus began by every road and every humble path. Parents, carrying children in their arms, stumbled along in blind terror. The young and strong bore the aged and disabled on their shoulders. Pushcarts and wheelbarrows, donkeys and horses, mules and oxen, poured out of Yi bearing the most precious of people's possessions. Many fled toward the big port city, hoping for asylum in the foreign Concessions. Some headed for the western mountains, knowing they were infested with bandits but hoping that a fellow Chinese, however rough, would be gentler than a foreign invader. Those who feared foreigners and bandits alike pushed aimlessly southward, guided only by the maxim: the farther away from the Japanese, the better.

Hysteria reigned along the Lane of Eternal Stability. The Mas were first to go. On the second day after the outbreak of hostilities, they secretly hired in advance nearly all the sedan chairs in town. Next day, Ma Pingshi, his mother, his wife, and their three children left for the port city in pomp and luxury, accompanied by many servants. Those sedan chairs that carried no human cargo were loaded with a superabundance of luggage; it was almost a pleasant, exciting holiday trip rather than a flight from terror.

The Hos were thrown into the greatest panic. Their fortunes had gone downhill, and they no longer had the means to escape as the Mas had done. Having been bred to gentility, they lacked the stamina of the poor, who could flee on foot. Still, they could not remain: the house was full of young wives and attractive grown daughters, and nothing horrified them more than the thought of tarnished family honor. Now, more than ever, they felt the lack of a Ho Tao, or a Fucho, or a Ta-kong—the family was without leadership, its strength gone.

Old Ho the Central Hall would have turned in his grave to see the males of the house, who were at sixes and sevens. Not one of the old proprieties was kept. Hair was torn and teeth were gnashed, and over and over they blamed one another. They needed

341

cash; they wanted to sell what remained of their lands, but the properties were out in the country and could not be disposed of quickly. In desperation, they turned to the people who held the mortgage on the house on the Lane of Eternal Stability and offered to sell. But these people needed money for their own flight, and refused. Panic-stricken, the scions of Ho put up a sign—the house was for sale to anyone at a desperately reduced price.

Widow Lan saw the sign one morning, and realized the tragedy that it foretold. She conferred at once with the Reverend Dr. Holt. They knew that the Hos could not accept anything gratis. The only solution was to buy the property for the Mission, which needed more space. Although authorization and money from Mission headquarters would take time, Holt and Widow Lan had their savings. And then Ah Wong and his wife Anna also expressed a wish to help. Word spread, and the gatekeeper, who was nearing seventy and had grown a white beard, came bent under a bag of silver. He had never trusted banks; this was his life's savings. He wanted to give it to the Mission. After that, the cook was not content until he had made a contribution. . . .

The transaction was settled at once. The Hos scattered, no longer a family, each one with his divided portion of money, and in his separate way. Holt watched them go, sadly. The house had been their ancestral home for centuries.

Meanwhile, Tien Fong neither faced the enemy at the provincial capital nor carried out orders to retreat southward along the railroad. He thought Yi a safer place instead, being near the mountains, and quartered his rabble of an army there for two days, putting on a great show of defense. He ordered people to stop fleeing, commanded them to dig trenches outside the ancient city wall and to erect barricades on the streets. What remained of the citizenry took heart, and turned to with a show of spirit. But on the third day, the town woke to a cruel shock. The Governor and all his aides, including the local magistrate and his staff, had fled the night before. Tien Fong had learned the Japanese had detached a special column from their main forces, with instructions to attack him or, if he escaped, pursue him until caught.

Blind, unreasoning panic gripped the town, and a new exodus began. But now hundreds of women and old people thought it was too late to flee into the mountains, so they ran to the Mission compound to seek protection under a foreign flag. The Reverend

Dr. Holt blessed his new purchase—he needed all the Ho compound to shelter the refugees.

Since there were more women than men, Holt crammed the women and children inside the House of Ho and put the men in the Mission compound. On all entrances to both properties he had United States flags flown, and had large signs painted in English and Chinese: "American Property."

Ah Wong and Anna were put in charge of Ho's house, and all the gates there were closed and reinforced with barricades of heavy furniture. Holt remained in the Mission compound, but here all the gates were kept open. The clinic was the only court free of refugees. Widow Lan stood inside, ready for any emergency.

2

AT FIRST THERE was the distant, desultory rumble of cannon, an ominous thunder that moved steadily and inexorably across the eastern plains. As the sound grew louder, the refugees huddled in the Mission in tragic silence; all Yi waited for the enemy like a cemetery.

Machine guns began stuttering outside the ancient city walls, where Tien Fong's partially dug trenches lay undefended. Smoke billowed high from the direction of the city's Northern Gate; flames thrust aloft, their forked tongues licking the sky. Soon the town heard the roar and rattle of motor vehicles moving along its streets.

From somewhere Holt heard a more sinister sound—a scream. He took up his post at the main gate of the Mission compound, his heart pounding. He was older, now, and not so redheaded; he told himself he had learned patience. He found the gatekeeper at his side, and that old worthy pulled at his white beard and glared up and down the Lane of Eternal Stability.

The Japanese came. Five jeeps and several trucks roared up and halted. A petty officer in the leading car shouted in perfect Chinese: "Is this the American Mission compound? Have you a doctor—a surgeon?"

The Reverend Dr. Holt stepped forward. "This is the American Mission," he said. "I am a surgeon, and we have another one inside."

"Then we have work for you. Do it well, if you want to stay in a whole skin!"

The petty officer ran to another car, saluted, and made his report. Several soldiers ran up to help two men out; both were officers—Holt saw from their insignia that one was a colonel and the other a major. He saw, also, that both had been wounded in the arm. The colonel had the look of a man who had some innate kindness; the major, a younger man, had bushy eyebrows and a sharply protruding mouth—he appeared surly and arrogant.

Holt introduced himself. The colonel shook his hand, and said in poor Chinese, "I am Colonel Shimitzu, commanding this expeditionary column. We ran into a land mine just outside the city—the whole medical squad got blasted." He indicated the major. "This is Major Miura, my chief of staff."

Miura ignored Holt's proffered hand.

The missionary took both men into the clinic. While Widow Lan looked at the younger man's wound, he examined the colonel himself.

"Colonel," he said, "this is a very serious injury. You will need expert care for some time."

"Ah," the Colonel said, "that's one thing I cannot possibly have."

Widow Lan had cut away the makeshift bandage on the Major's right arm, exposing a dreadful series of bone-deep lacerations. Holt gave this a quick look. "And the Major's wound is even worse! You'd both better stay here for treatment."

"Preposterous!" the Major retorted. "This is nothing in war. And we don't intend to let somebody else get the glory of capturing Tien Fong."

"Then you'd better send for the best surgeon you have," Holt warned. "Without proper care, you could each lose an arm or even your lives."

The Colonel shook his head cheerlessly. "Our best surgeons are with the main body of the army. We have none."

"Then stay here. Dr. Lan and I will take care of you."

"This is a trick, Colonel!" the Major exclaimed. "He's trying to delay us. Damn you Americans! Your sympathies are always with the Chinese."

"We have nothing but a professional interest in you," Holt replied evenly. "I've given you the best medical advice I know—take it or leave it."

The Major retreated into sullen silence. Beads of sweat glistened on his ugly face as Widow Lan probed and cleansed the wounds. All at once bedlam broke loose outside. Men shouted, and there was a sound as if rifle butts were being hammered against the walls of a compound. The white-bearded old gatekeeper burst into the clinic.

"Master! Master!" he gasped to Holt. "They have found where the women are hiding! They are already using a ram on the main gate!"

Holt paused in bandaging the Colonel's arm. "Colonel Shimitzu, you will stop them, of course. You *must* stop them!"

The Japanese shook his head. "This is war, unfortunately."

"But those women over there are not fighting you—they're noncombatants. Stop your troops, for God's sake! If you don't believe in God, I appeal to you in the name of humanitarianism!"

The noises outside grew louder. Widow Lan, finished with bandaging the Major's arm, stood in a corner of the room, anxiety on her face.

"Humanitarianism?" the Major scoffed. "That's only a theory based on human nature. You doctors should know more about human nature than I do, but I know this: in war, the physical urge in a man rises strongest. A soldier deserves to take a woman when he can find one. If I weren't wounded, I'd be out there with them."

Colonel Shimitzu strode toward the door, beckoning his chief of staff to follow. Holt barred the way.

"I warn you to respect the rights of a neutral!" he said sternly. "I am an American. Both this compound and that across the street are American property. I am not asking you to provide protection, Colonel—I am demanding it!"

"You've gone too far, American!" Shimitzu said, pushing his way past. "You must learn better than to threaten a Japanese. I thank you for your services and I require them no longer!"

He set off for the gate, followed by Major Miura and the sentry. Holt heard the loud thumping of a telephone pole being driven against the barricaded gate across the street, and ran hastily in that direction. Widow Lan followed, pale with fright.

Holt arrived in time to hear a splintering crash and see half the gate shattered and hanging crookedly from its hinges. The American flag was already in the dust. The pile of heavy furniture that had been stacked to buttress the gate swayed and toppled, and beyond it Holt saw the faces of helpless, terror-stricken women and children. He shouted at the group of soldiers who held the telephone pole; they sneered and spat at him, and drew back to make another assault. Then the white-bearded old gatekeeper ran across the sidewalk and put his back against the gate, his arms flung wide.

"Stop!" he cried pitifully. "For mercy's sake, stop!"

The soldiers lunged forward, and the battering ram struck. It made no crashing sound this time. Holt covered his eyes at the last agonizing instant; still, he heard the soft, soggy impact; he heard the soldiers grunting and shuffling back into the dusty street for yet another run. The gatekeeper's broken body remained impaled for a second on the shattered gate; then it sagged and fell forward, crumpling to the ground.

Holt ran to the old servant's side, his frenzy of grief giving him a blind, despairing courage. One look told him the gatekeeper was dead. He straightened to face the crew with the battering ram, barred their way, and waved his arms wildly.

"Kill *me*, if you dare!" he challenged. "Come on—kill me!"

The soldiers hesitated. A shout went up from their comrades, urging them on; then Colonel Shimitzu stepped forward and barked a single word of command.

The soldiers halted, and Shimitzu looked over his shoulder at the missionary.

"I'll stop this on one condition," he said. "If you'll go with me as surgeon for this expedition."

"That's impossible!" said Holt. "I'm an American, and a missionary. I cannot serve your army, nor can I leave my mission and these refugees."

Colonel Shimitzu shrugged. "Then I'm sorry. The soldiers consider this their rightful share of the spoils of war. What I ask of you is the only good excuse I have to make them stop—they will need your services the same as I. If you refuse, I can do nothing."

The impossible choice left Holt speechless. If he agreed, he still could not be sure that other Japanese troops might not come here; if he refused. . . .

Then he heard Widow Lan's voice calling from the main gate of the Mission compound: "Will you take me instead, Colonel? I'm as good a surgeon as Dr. Holt. I'll go with you if you will give full protection to the Mission premises and to the refugees, and if you will guarantee my personal safety."

The Colonel eyed her slowly, and with grudging admiration. "You'll do!" he said. "I grant the conditions you ask."

He turned to his troops and addressed them briefly. They looked disgruntled at first, but they dropped the battering ram. Officers and noncommissioned officers separated themselves from the mob, called out sharp orders, and the men immediately fell into well-disciplined formations.

The Colonel strode toward his jeep. "Get into the car with us," Major Miura told Widow Lan.

"But I must get some clothes, and my medical kit—"

"We can supply you with all that," he said gruffly. "You are now in the Japanese army, and you will obey my orders. Into the car!"

She obeyed silently. The Reverend Dr. Holt found his voice, and called pleadingly, "Dr. Lan! Dr. Lan—are you sure you want to do this?"

She looked at him, head high. "There is no other way," she answered simply.

"Then God bless you! Take good care of yourself!"

The jeeps rolled, and trucks filled with soldiers followed after. The dust of their passage swirled along the Lane of Eternal Stability and settled on the Reverend Dr. Holt, and on the wrinkled, bearded face of the lifeless old gatekeeper.

3

THE MOTORIZED JAPANESE column drove for the rest of the day in hot pursuit of Tien Fong. No stop was made to eat; the troops took their rations in their vehicles. Colonel Shimitzu handed Widow Lan a ration, which she found consisted of cold steamed rice and two small slices of salted fish. Although she detested the Japanese, she marveled as a doctor that they could wage war on such meager fare.

At last the column reached the edge of the mountains, and although they had encountered no resistance, the terrain had become increasingly difficult. At intervals a jeep scouting ahead would return to report that a bridge had been blown up, and the convoy would have to halt while it was repaired. The unpaved, muddy road slowed their progress. Major Miura turned to Widow Lan and loudly cursed all Chinese.

They passed through silent, abandoned villages, and frequently riddled them and the walls of deserted farmhouses with machine-gun fire; some places they set ablaze in wanton destruction. During the afternoon, four of Tien Fong's walking wounded were captured and brought to the Colonel's jeep. One by one Major Miura would question them about the retreating troops, learn what he could—and then cold-bloodedly shoot the man through the head with his revolver.

The first time this happened, Widow Lan uttered a little scream. "Oh, God! Why did you do that?"

Colonel Shimitzu looked down his nose, coldly. "This is war."

Major Miura, holstering his revolver, turned on her savagely. "Shut up, woman! Do you think I will leave them here to harass us from the rear?"

After that, she looked away and tried to shut her mind and her ears against the murderous crack of the gun. And she watched the mountains as night came on, a plan taking shape in her mind. They could not travel much farther. Though Widow Lan kept her face impassive, she began to hope.

This had been her country as a child. The very next village, a little larger than most they had already passed, was where she had played happily until she had been married and taken away by her husband. She prayed the convoy would stop there; she prayed that the troops would not shoot into the poor houses, or set them afire.

Then the scout jeep returned with reports that the village was deserted, and that it was large enough to serve as a bivouac. Instead of firing into the cluster of houses that loomed ahead in the fading light, the troops dismounted to spread out and encircle the place, closing in on the houses with fixed bayonets. They found nobody, but they did bring in several water buffaloes.

Sentries were posted as darkness fell. The officers moved into the most pretentious house in the village, and Widow Lan was given a medical kit and ordered to attend to the wounded. Outside, the soldiers had built fires; they were butchering the water buffaloes and roasting the meat, which they ate gluttonously. Widow Lan's heart sank—a water buffalo to pull the plow often represented the lifetime savings of a Chinese farm family. She refused the meat when it was offered to her, and ate only some steamed rice.

Colonel Shimitzu had been considerate enough to provide her with a separate room in one of the huts where the soldiers were billeted, but by the time all the troops were quartered, the space was no longer available. The men leered at her, although she was not touched or mistreated in any way. Still, the sense of womanly delicacy she had learned in childhood was strong in Widow Lan; though the times had changed, though she was now nearly sixty, and though as a doctor she had seen hundreds of human bodies, male

348

and female, she could not reconcile herself to the thought of sleeping in the house with all those men. It was July, and warm. She lingered outside the hut, leaned against a wall, and pretended to doze.

But she was not sleepy. She was trying to remember, very carefully, the location of a certain tumbled-down hovel somewhere in this cluster of huts—she was hoping that none of the Japanese had chosen it as a place to sleep.

If she could find the hovel, or even where it had stood, she had a chance of escape.

Widow Lan was remembering a legend and a ghost story—and yet the story was true in some respects. As a child in this village, she and her playmates had known about the plank trapdoor in the floor of the hovel, which was nothing more than an open shed. Under the trapdoor was a tunnel—that much was certain; then legend took over. The underground passage supposedly had been dug to connect with a larger natural cave, which opened on the far side of the mountain; wild goats had made a path up the steep cliff there, so that if one climbed he could come out overlooking the village and the surrounding countryside.

According to the legend, the shed stood on the ruined site of a mansion that had flourished centuries ago, and its owners had dug the passageway to hide their wealth from bandits. Another story said it was not a mansion at all, but a "black inn" where unwary travelers had been robbed and murdered. In Widow Lan's childhood the place had the name of being haunted, and none of the superstitious villagers would go near it. But some of Widow Lan's older playmates had been venturesome enough, before they fled shrieking in fright; to go into the shed, find the trapdoor, and report back on its location.

It was Widow Lan's only chance, now. The moon was bright, and sentries ringed the village; even if she were able to slip past them into the open plain, she would easily be found by morning. But if she could get into the mountains, it would be different.

She moved cautiously, keeping in the shadow of the huts to get her bearings. Most of the soldiers, tired and overfed on water buffalo, were already sleeping. The patrols moved listlessly, having nothing to fear.

Widow Lan rounded a corner and saw that memory had not failed her. The shed was still there, its ramshackle walls leaning crazily. She looked around cautiously, then darted across a moonlit strip and was inside. Now the Japanese medical kit came in handy, for it contained a small flashlight used in throat examinations. Widow Lan switched on the light and quickly surveyed the floor of the hovel, but was dismayed to find the trapdoor either gone or completely covered with the dust of years. She turned off the light and began to search another way—stamping her feet back and forth within the small enclosure until, finally, she heard a hollow sound and felt the ground giving beneath her weight.

With the knife from the kit she scraped at the earth. The layer of dirt was only inches deep: the knife struck wood—rotten—and Widow Lan worked feverishly to clear a small spot. She stamped upon the planks, they crumbled, and then she turned her flashlight into the darkness of a gaping hole.

Musty air came up at her, but she could see the floor of the passageway, and it was easy enough to lower herself into the hole. With the flashlight in one hand and the knife in the other, she went cautiously along the tunnel. It had been dug from solid rock; the walls were smooth and damp, and she could hear water dripping. The passage began to narrow, the roof lowered, and finally she found herself crawling on hands and knees. But the air smelled fresher, and soon she emerged from the tunnel and stood upright in a cavern fashioned by nature.

Now there was a real current of air. Spitting on her hand and holding it aloft to find which way the current moved, she went toward its source. The cavern turned several times, but she could feel the breeze on her face, and a few minutes later saw a patch of star-dotted sky.

She came out on what appeared to be a rocky shelf overhanging a deep, dark ravine—a stone dropped there took a long time to fall. Towering above her was a cliff; with the aid of the flashlight she determined it was the narrow, rocky trail, all right; it looked as if it had indeed been made by wild goats, for only they would be able to climb it.

But with the same dogged resolve that had taken her, when Yuwen was a baby, from her shack in Yi to the temple of the Goddess of Mercy, Widow Lan began the climb. She blessed the fact that now at least she did not have to do it with bound feet.

Yuwen! she thought sorrowfully. *Where is he now, and Li-hwa, and their children I have never seen?*

The climb was far more difficult and dangerous than the trip through the underground passage. She dared not look over the edge of the winding trail, lest she became dizzy, but she went valiantly on. The moon had become visible when she reached the top of the cliff at last, and saw a stretch of woodland before her.

Widow Lan sank exhausted, and piously gave thanks to God.

After a while she moved on, trying to orient herself. On the far side of the sparse wood at the edge of the cliff, she saw a cluster of lights far below, and knew she was looking at her own village.

The sight was thrilling. She stood for a moment, plainly silhouetted against the moonlight—and then, abruptly, she was seized from behind. A rough hand caught her throat; another pinned her arms behind her. She struggled, twisted around, and saw four men, their faces shadowed. They dragged her into the wood, and one of them struck a match.

"By Heaven!" he exclaimed. "It's the lady doctor of Yi! It's Dr. Lan! Release her at once!"

Widow Lan looked at him, and he laughed and struck another match. This man and one of the others had been patients of hers; she had suspected all along that they were bandits. The one who had recognized her said, "Please forgive us for laying hands on you, Dr. Lan. But how on earth did you get here?"

"That's a long story," she said. "I never asked you before but now I must—are you Kan Koo's men?"

"Yes. Kan Koo has been our leader for years. He has been your patient, too, I remember. He sent us here tonight to keep watch on the Japanese."

"Please take me to him at once!" Widow Lan said. She started, impatient to set out. The man looked at her and shook his head.

"Kan Koo is holding a conference five li from here. You could never walk that far. But you have been kind to us, and always refused payment—even gifts. Let us do something for you, now..."

The men produced two bamboo poles, laid them on the ground, and began strapping ropes around them—tighter at the ends, more loosely in the middle. Then they tipped the device on end, like a ladder.

"Dr. Lan, this will be your sedan chair. Use the middle rope for a seat, put your feet on the lower rope, and rest your head against the top one. Two of my men will take you to Kan Koo."

4

AN HOUR LATER, Widow Lan was carried through the door of a dilapidated temple of the War God, in the mountain wilds. It had been a large place, once, and the main hall was still big, but stars shone through holes in the roof, and although the War God and his two sworn brothers still sat on their lofty pedestals, their images were discolored and covered with cobwebs.

Burning straw torches illuminated the hall and showed a gathering of about fifty men. Kan Koo sat at the foot of the War God, on a chair covered with a tiger skin. No one had a uniform; all wore peasant garb and carried a weapon of some sort, rifles, pistols, shotguns.

Kan Koo, a man in his forties, was powerfully built, with a head like a leopard's, his face tawny and pockmarked, his eyes large and round. Bandit though he was, he had a good reputation—he dealt in plunder, but never turned to cruelties. He had never molested a woman. Even when he robbed a traveler, he left his victim enough money to continue his journey.

He rose, beaming, to greet Widow Lan and introduce her to the assemblage. Introductions were scarcely necessary; as she looked over the gathering, she saw that more of her patients had been bandits than she had ever suspected. A good-looking, athletic young man rose from the front bench and asked her to take his seat. He said he was Kan Koo's son, Kan Kan; his father had sent him to the Government University in the port city, Widow Lan knew, but he had returned to the mountains when war broke out.

Widow Lan told her story briefly, and Kan Koo asked a few questions about the strength and disposition of the Japanese column. Then he turned to the assembly.

"You have heard what Dr. Lan said. The Japanese have more than twelve hundred men. Any discussion?"

A man of about fifty rose. "You are our chieftain, and what you decide we will obey. But the Japanese not only have twice the number of our whole available force—they have cannon, machine guns, and a large stock of munitions. Even Tien Fong, with an army much bigger than ours and much better equipped, has fled. In my opinion, we should follow his example and go deeper into the mountains."

Young Kan Kan leaped up, his face flushed, his eyes flashing. "I watched Tien Fong and his army as they fled through the mountain passes, this morning. If my father had not stopped me, I would have waylaid and attacked them. We may not be soldiers paid by the Government, but we are Chinese! This is our land! This is the mountain that has given us sustenance and shelter. Let us never yield our land to the enemy—no, by Heaven! Let us fight!"

"But how?" asked a voice.

"Go down by the path Dr. Lan has just climbed. Surprise them under cover of darkness, and fight!"

There was a murmur of dissent. If the Japanese had discovered Dr. Lan's disappearance, the bandit force might well be ambushed.

"Then hold them at Tyrant Pass. Or farther back, at the narrower Ghost Gate Pass. They cannot bring their cannon that far into the mountains."

"But they have machine guns," the man who had counseled flight reminded Kan Kan. "Tien Fong apparently did not think he could hold them there."

"Tien Fong be damned!" the young man cried. "His courage is drained by soft living, his sinews emasculated by too many women. I speak for myself—I am a Chinese! I would rather die fighting at Ghost Gate Pass than retreat a step farther!"

Widow Lan saw that the sentiment of the majority was for flight. Kan Koo fidgeted on his tiger-skin chair.

"I truly do not know what to say," he began. "We know how to fight Tien Fong's men—they are not much better than we are. But the Japanese have better equipment, more men, and better organization. I am forced to conclude, although reluctantly—"

"Chief, may I suggest a plan?"

Everybody turned in surprise to look at Widow Lan. Kan Koo courteously said, "You certainly may, Dr. Lan."

"First," she said, "what is your stock of food? How long will it last you and your families, and the refugees who have come to you?"

"Our supplies would last us a month," Kan Koo said. "But the refugees number three or four times our own men and their families, and the refugees did not bring much food—some none at all."

"Then if you feed them," Widow Lan said, "the food will last only a week. Even if you flee deeper into the mountains and do not take the refugees, you can't replenish your supplies when they are used up. The mountains produce little food. Tien Fong is ahead of you, and he will leave little. Either you starve to death, or return to fight the Japanese—and when you return, remember you will be weakened by hunger."

The assemblage was silent. Kan Koo leaned forward intently. "Have you a plan, Dr. Lan?"

"Attack!" said Widow Lan.

"And send out six hundred men, poorly armed, against the cannon and machine guns of twelve hundred Japanese?" asked the man who had counseled flight.

"No," said Widow Lan. "Apply the strategy described in the ancient classic, *The Strategy of Sun-tse.* Attack when the enemy is divided and weak."

"Can we divide and weaken the Japanese?" Kan Koo asked dubiously.

"No. But they will divide and weaken themselves. Colonel Shimitzu and Major Miura are thirsty for glory. They'll push on at dawn in pursuit of Tien Fong. When they come to the village where I lived with my husband, the road forks—the main road turns past the tomb of Ho the Central Hall and runs eastward to the port city. The Japanese will not take this road, but will follow the other one into the mountains. But they will have to leave their heavy equipment and even their vehicles in this village, and pursue Tien Fong on foot. So they will divide their forces, leaving a guard of perhaps three or four hundred men to protect all that equipment and munitions. We will outnumber these, and we can attack and crush them."

"Bravo!" exclaimed young Kan Kan, his eyes shining.

"But we can't go by the mountain road," Kan Koo objected. "The main body of the Japanese will be on it."

"Use the goat path and the cave. By daylight, you can see their every movement from the cliff—you can estimate the number of men left behind. And by using the path and the cave, we can attack them from the rear, where we would be least expected. Pile up stones above Tyrant Pass and Ghost Gate Pass so they can be pushed down to block the road against any speedy return of the main body."

Kan Koo smiled proudly. "We had thought of that—against Tien Fong. The stones are piled and waiting."

"Splendid," said Widow Lan. "But don't block the road the minute the main body has crossed Tyrant Pass—Sun-tze said, 'Entice the enemy deep into the interior.' Lead them farther on—have ten

or twenty men show token resistance at Tyrant Pass, and then run—
have them decoy the Japanese for forty li, all the way to Ghost
Gate Pass. By then it will be nightfall. Just as the enemy approaches
Ghost Gate, block it. We'll have pushed the stones into Tyrant
Pass about noon—we will have the main body bottled up. The
village will have been taken. And when the main body turns back,
late at night, tired and confused, we'll be waiting for them at
Tyrant Pass. I quote from Sun-tze again: 'Attack not the enemy
when he starts out spirited in the morning. Attack him when he
returns wearied in the night.' "

Kan Koo sat in open-mouthed admiration, and forgot that he
was listening to a woman. So did all the others, and all suddenly
took heart. . . .

It worked. Shimitzu and Major Miura, eager to overtake Tien
Fong, left only two hundred men in the village to guard the vast
amount of vehicular equipment and supplies and munitions. They
had not concerned themselves at dawn when they discovered
Widow Lan missing; they did not find the underground passage or
the goat path.

Kan Koo led the assault on the village; his son, Kan Kan, took
a dozen brave men and lured the Japanese beyond Tyrant Pass. And
when Colonel Shimitzu led his men back that night, his own
machine guns opened a murderous fire from the heights at Tyrant
Pass, pinning the Japanese down in the narrow defile. At daylight,
Kan Koo's men swept down on those who were left, and only
Shimitzu and Miura lived to be taken prisoner.

Widow Lan was resting in a side chamber of the temple of the
War God when Kan Koo made his triumphant return and sent
for her. As she entered the main hall, everybody stood up. Kan Koo
stepped from his tiger-skin chair.

"Dr. Lan," he said, "you have given us a magnificent victory
and a wonderful surprise. Now I have a surprise for you." He
turned to face the assembly. "We have won a great victory and
captured supplies enough to last us through a long campaign. You
all know who made this possible. She is a woman, but by the War
God we all revere, she is a better general than all of us! So now"—
he bowed toward Widow Lan—"I have a proposition to make. I
am an unlettered man and know my limitations; that is why I sent
my son to the University to get a better education. But I have
plain, common sense. My brothers, I may have been fit to lead you

in ordinary times, but these times are not ordinary. We now need a more capable general, and we have one—Dr. Lan!"

He stepped forward and motioned Widow Lan toward the tiger-skin chair. She drew back in amazement.

"But that's impossible! I am only a woman!"

Kan Koo smiled. "Ah, yes—but in some ways a better man than any of us! What strategy you conceived! By the War God, I swear in all sincerity—by the War God I ask that you become our chief. The Japanese are bound to come again."

The discussion was long. It was unheard of, considering the status of women in Chinese society. But that status was changing under the pressures of war, and it was plain to Widow Lan that all of Kan Koo's men wanted her to become their leader. She argued until she had exhausted every objection, all the while growing more deeply touched. Finally, when Kan Koo told her that he had been considering dissolving the band so that each man could fend for himself in what was sure to be an unequal struggle, Widow Lan yielded.

"Then I have no choice." she said. "But there must be another chair placed beside mine, and you, Kan Koo, must sit upon it. You will never call me 'chief,' simply 'Dr. Lan.' "

"Agreed!" Kan Koo said happily, and the assemblage cheered. The second chair was immediately brought in. Kan Koo pulled it to one side, saying he could not sit on the same level, which again touched Widow Lan deeply.

"Among our trophies, Dr. Lan," Kan Koo said, "are the two prisoners. What is your wish? Shall we put them to death?"

Widow Lan parried cautionsly. "Was it agreed that you will abide by my decisions? Suppose I should want to set these men free?"

The entire hall was aghast. Widow Lan raised her voice. "This is an international war, and there are international laws governing the treatment of prisoners of war. I have learned this from the Reverend Dr. Holt. If we keep them prisoner, we must feed them. The alternative is to set them free. Will you abide by this decision?"

The silence was terrible, tangible. But Kan Koo sighed, and said, "Dr. Lan, you are our chief. We will obey your orders."

Colonel Shimitzu and Major Miura were brought in. Their uniforms were now torn and dirty, their wounded arms swollen and their hands manacled. No shock they had suffered compared with the discovery that Widow Lan was sitting in judgment upon them. and Widow Lan was shocked, in her turn, by a lesson in human

356

nature. Colonel Shimitzu walked head erect and shoulders squared. The formerly swaggering Major Miura had to be pushed forward, trembling and shivering in fright.

"Kneel, Japanese dogs!" their guards shouted.

Miura dropped and groveled; the Colonel stood stubbornly.

"Let him be!" commanded Widow Lan. She looked down at the Major and said, "Major Miura, you do not have a shred of humaneness in you, but I shall try to teach you a lesson in humaneness. Colonel Shimitzu—in ordinary times, I think you might pass for a good and honest man. Why then do you allow war to change your nature? I think you have an inner spark of kindliness, and I want you to keep it flourishing in your heart. Guards, unbind these men and set them free!"

Miura prostrated himself on the floor, kowtowed to Widow Lan, and was incoherent in his thanks. Colonel Shimitzu stood dazed, and then his face suddenly contorted with rage. Swiftly he snatched a long knife from the belt of one of the guards, leaped forward, and plunged it into Miura's body.

"Coward!" he shouted. "Disgrace to the Imperial Army!"

And before the guards could move, he plunged the knife into his own heart. *"Dai Nippon banzai!"* he choked, and fell dead.

5

IF ANY COUNTRY ever desperately needed the image and inspiration of leadership in the dark days that followed, it was China. Widow Lan supplied that image. Her fame spread widely, and she was undisputed ruler of a region that covered the mountain road and a wide fertile plain adjoining it. Twice the Japanese tried to destroy her band, twice they were defeated. They hesitated after that to send another expedition into the mountains; in their eyes she had become a nuisance but not a threat, and they had other uses for their manpower. By her interposition at the edge of the mountain, she was able to safeguard Tien Fong, who was farther up in the area, and at times she even helped him with supplies because (as she said) he was still the highest representative of the Government.

Her domain covered nearly half the Prefecture of Yi. She collected taxes legally and reasonably, not as the extortionist Tien Fong had done. The men under her command, who had been bandits before, were now uniformed militia, under pay. They liked this, and the people did, too. She was no longer called Widow Lan or Dr. Lan, but became known affectionately as "Mother Lan," or simply "Old Mother."

She could have been happy, but she worried about Yuwen, Li-hwa, and her grandchildren. She was disturbed, too, about the Reverend Dr. Holt and the American Mission. The Japanese had all but placed Holt under house arrest. His mail was censored—and Mother Lan knew her only chance of hearing from Yuwen was in that mail.

Three years after war had begun, the Japanese, realizing they lacked the manpower to police a land so vast as China, began to set up puppet regimes. Nor did they want for opportunist renegades. Installed as the Magistrate of Yi was Ma Pingshi, younger brother to Ma Pingnan (alias Nan Ping).

6

VENTURESOME MERCHANTS NOW began to smuggle goods past the Japanese lines, from the port city, and along the mountain roads. Mother Lan mounted guards at Tyrant Pass, Ghost Gate Pass, and Lion Head Rock, where the goods were examined. She threw out all that could be traced to the Japanese.

Then Communist propaganda began appearing in the luggage of supposedly innocent travelers. Taken before Mother Lan, these agents frankly admitted they represented the Eighth Route Army, and said all they wanted to do was to fight the Japanese.

Widow Lan was not at all taken in. She had read all Yuwen's articles, and was quite well versed in Communist tactics. She confiscated the literature, turned back the agents, and told them politely that if they wanted to fight the Japanese they could do it elsewhere.

Twice Communist emissaries came urging her to form an alliance with their commander, Nan Ping. She replied that since they both acknowledged allegiance to the Chungking Government, there was no need for private alliance. So far as fighting the Japanese was concerned, she did not see how the Eighth Route Army could help her, operating as it was far back in the mountains, even beyond the territory manned by Tien Fong.

But soon Widow Lan found herself facing a new problem. In the past refugees had come only from the east, fleeing the Japanese; now they straggled in from the west with alarming reports that the

358

Communists were trying to establish their dominion in the mountains. They were infiltrating local groups, either by persuasion or by ruthless force, and as soon as they established control, they spread the poison of individual spying—sons upon fathers, daughters upon mothers. To rid the people of the old conventional ideas, sexual morals were being relaxed. Anybody who disagreed with these teachings was summarily dealt with as a reactionary, and horrible tales of atrocities were told.

Widow Lan's men, although formerly bandits, had come from simple peasant stock and still cherished high regard for the proprieties in sexual and parental and filial relationships. What they heard now was an abhorrence, and the Communist killings far exceeded the bloodiest crimes any bandits had ever perpetrated.

Widow Lan, however, did not believe all the stories. She did not think the Communists capable of inflicting such inhuman atrocities upon fellow Chinese, especially in the face of foreign invasion. Nor did she feel any immediate concern for the safety of her own domain. Between her territory and that of the Eighth Route Army—serving as a sort of buffer state—still lay the zone under Tien Fong's occupation. Tien was still nominally Governor of the province; the Communists could not attack him without risking an open break with the Chungking Government.

But Widow Lan was in for a rude shock. One day Kan Koo, now stationed at Lion Head Rock to keep watch to the west, rushed back to headquarters—and with him were Tien Fong, his wife, and three bodyguards, all ragged and frightened. Widow Lan knew the woman well. She was not actually Tien Fong's wife, but the former eighth concubine of old Ma Teh-lin—Widow Lan had seen her many times on the Lane of Eternal Stability after the old man's death.

Tien Fong poured out his story. A column of the Eighth Route Army, commanded by Nan Ping, had advanced to the border of his territory. Since the governor supposed these troops were operating under orders from Chungking, he took no precautions against them, and his own men had fraternized with them at the border.

Just the night before, however, an old servant who had been in his household for years abruptly vanished—taking with him the full knowledge of the deployment and disposition of Tien's troops. When Tien discovered this, he immediately aroused his wife and three bodyguards—just in time to hear the first rattle of gunfire. He had scrambled up a wooded peak behind his headquarters, and from there he had seen the flaring torches of the Eighth Army column

359

advancing from all directions. And his men, instead of resisting them, were joining them in droves!

Their little party had fled through the mountains as swiftly as it could. He was here now not as Governor, he said, but as a refugee begging asylum.

Widow Lan knew this man's life had been filled with an extraordinary amount of evil, and that he deserved a thousand deaths. Left to her own inclinations she would have taken pleasure in throwing him to the dogs, yet as a Christian she had to forgive. And she could not but feel pity at the sight of him. No longer robust, lusty, and roisterious, he was now a debilitated, senile septuagenarian. He did not stand erect like the giant he had been in other days but drooped, shrunken and shaken. Even his ugly scarred face had lost its sardonic grimace. And there was one fact Widow Lan could not overlook—in name he was still Governor of the province, appointed by the Government to which she owned allegiance. She gave orders that the Governor and his small retinue be suitably accommodated.

Far graver matters demanded her instant attention. Now the buffer state was gone; the Communists had reached her threshold. She could no longer put off the issue; she had to choose, at once, whether to resist or submit. If she resisted, she would be fighting fellow Chinese and would be sandwiched between the Communists and the Japanese, with two fronts to defend.

In haste, she summoned all the leaders of her band to a conference. Her prestige had risen so high that ordinarily they listened to her opinions and accepted them in implicit faith. But this time, she told them, the decision must be theirs and she would abide by the rule of the majority. She stated the pros and cons of the issue as objectively as she could, and then insisted on a vote. The vote was unanimous. The Japanese had let them alone for a long time; her men foresaw no immediate danger from the east. Proud of their own fighting abilities, and even more fiercely proud of Widow Lan's generalship, to a man they voted to resist the Communists.

Widow Lan accepted their decision but did not share their optimism. She felt they might have underestimated the strength of the Eighth Route Army. True, the Japanese had adopted a more peaceful policy since the formation of puppet governments, but this could change overnight, and two fronts would divide and weaken her forces. She could not personally lead her men at both the east and

360

the west. Kan Koo, notwithstanding his great loyalty and courage, was what he himself had said—no general. Kan Kan, the best of all her lieutenants, was a bright and brave lad, but too impetuous and not to be trusted with independent command. For the present, she herself would have to do everything possible to meet the Communist threat. She drew up secret plans, and transferred as many men as she felt could be spared from the east to the west.

Next day, Nan Ping sent another envoy. She received him in state, with all her officers gathered to hear him. He was arrogance itself, and offered no alliance now but demanded immediate submission instead. The Eighth Route Army, he said, had taken control of the territory in the name of the Government. He denounced Tien Fong as a deserter and traitor, and on behalf of Nan Ping, commanded her to surrender Tien and his wife at once for rightful punishment.

Widow Lan could see her men were all roused to fury, but still she wanted to reach an amicable settlement if it was at all possible. She said that if the Eighth Route Army could produce written instructions from Chungking, she would accept their terms. Even failing such instructions, she was prepared to enter an alliance with Nan Ping. If the Communist commander would guarantee not to encroach upon her territory, she would furnish him in turn such material assistance as food supplies. But the envoy haughtily brushed aside these conciliatory proposals. He gave her a three-day ultimatum, and left angrily.

Widow Lan immediately repaired to Lion Head Rock. As she had calculated, Nan Ping did not wait for the expiration of the three-day limit but attacked at dawn of the following day. Because of Widow Lan's vigilance and foresight, however, his troops fell into ambush and suffered shattering defeat. A week later, he hurled another furious assault upon Widow Lan, and once again was outmaneuvered and beaten. Then he began mobilizing all the forces under his command, taking a whole month for preparations. He was certain, now, that by sheer force of numbers he could overwhelm Widow Lan's band. But she had laid another trap for him. Using the same strategy she had employed against Colonel Shimitzu's Japanese, she enticed nearly half of Nan Ping's men into Ghost Gate Pass and destroyed them there with murderous gunfire and boulders rolled from the mountainside.

It was then that Nan Ping, driven out of his wits, appealed for help to the Communist High Command at Yenan.

7

THE HIGH COMMAND found itself in a quandary. There were no troops to spare for reinforcement. The Communists had occupied extensive territories in the mountains, designated them as "Liberated Areas," and set up administrations for them without consent of the Chungking Government. But the people in these areas were still sullenly restive and sometimes openly intransigent. To transfer troops from such places to support Nan Ping would be to invite disaster.

On the other hand, something had to be done. The mountain road through Widow Lan's stronghold constituted the sole access to the vast fertile plains in the east; if the Communists could not control it they would be cooped up in the mountains where food was scarce and the population sparse, and the entire self-expansion program would fail. Because of this they had not hesitated to overthrow Tien Fong even though it meant risking open rupture with Chungking. And now they could not stop—they had to eliminate Widow Lan.

Moreover, there was an important psychological factor. If Widow Lan's successful resistance became generally known—as it would if it continued—the people of the "Liberated Areas" might be encouraged to revolt. She represented, therefore, not only the chief obstacle to Communist expansion, but also a threat to the acquisitions already made.

Yenan had respect for her generalship. But when Ta-kong read the news there, a sinister scheme immediately flashed through his mind. He kept it to himself, and did not broach it to the Party as a comrade was supposed to do.

Mei-yin, however, with her cold and cunning intelligence had thought of the same thing. Thus it was that Ta-kong received his new assignment: He and Mei-yin, disguised as refugees seeking shelter, were to proceed to Widow Lan's headquarters. Once admitted, they were to work for her downfall from within, while Nan Ping attacked from without.

Far-off memories of boyhood days in Yi ran through Ta-kong's mind as he listened, and he was filled with anger. No one but Mei-yin knew his old connection with Widow Lan . . . no one else could have submitted the plan to the High Command.

"Apparently you are not particularly enthusiastic about this assignment," the High Command observed shrewdly. "If you were not such a loyal comrade, I might be disposed to think you were putting personal sentiments above the interests of the Party. Or that you feel this task beneath the dignity of such a high-ranking comrade as yourself. You should not feel that way—you should remember that this mission is of the utmost importance. You have been chosen because of your family connections with this Lan woman. If you succeed, you alone will have been worth an army to us."

"I am not unenthusiastic," Ta-kong denied quickly. "I've been wondering how best to do the job. Wouldn't it be better to try persuading Widow Lan to join us, rather than try to destroy her? She is no ordinary woman. Remember that she raised herself from an ignorant and unlettered peasant to become a surgeon of wide reputation, able to read both Chinese and English. That proves her extraordinary mind. I've studied her operations against Comrade Nan Ping, and they were brilliant compaigns that rank with those of the best strategists. If I could win her over, she would serve our cause well."

"I wish you could," answered the High Command, "but I have my doubts. As mother to your sworn brother, Yuwen, she must share his views. You have my permission to try, but take care not to arouse her suspicions. This mission is so important that we're giving you only a month for it. You and Comrade Mei-yin will not be working alone. We had two agents in Tien Fong's camp—one of them is still with Tien as a bodyguard. He'll contact you as soon as you arrive."

But the boyhood memories still persisted. "Even after Widow Lan is defeated," Ta-kong said, "May I try to persuade her to join us?"

"I have said you have my permission to try. But the reasons you have advanced in favor of keeping her alive are outweighed by other considerations—which you know very well. Unless she chooses to yield, we must make such a terrible example of her that no one will dare follow in her footsteps. Comrade Nan Ping already has these instructions.

"Comrade Ta-kong, you have your orders."

BOOK IV

One

Unenthusiastic about his task, but unable to shirk it and therefore determined to perform it, Ta-kong left Yenan with Mei-yin.

Since they were part of the recognized Eighth Route Army, they had no difficulty traveling across territory held by Government troops. They slipped easily enough through a loosely held Japanese line, and reached one of the "Liberated Areas," where they conferred with Nan Ping; it was on the west side of the mountains, so that Widow Lan would not possibly find out. Then by a roundabout route—turning northward to Mei-yin's native province, which was under Japanese occupation, then boldly by train to Peking, and finally taking another train—they arrived in the capital of Ta-kong's province. Ta-kong had created quite an effective disguise by shaving off the beard he had worn ever since his Shanghai days. They were interrogated by the Japanese at several points, but since they carried little luggage and looked like an ordinary middle-class couple, they were permitted to continue their journey.

They stayed in the provincial capital overnight, and bought candles and incense-sticks, for three days from now was the anniversary of the burial of Ta-kong's grandfather, Ho the Central Hall. Ta-kong planned to reach his grandparents' grave, which was near the entrance to the mountain road and also near Widow

365

Lan's headquarters, that morning; since his grandfather had been Widow Lan's benefactor, there was every chance that she, too, would visit the tomb.

They avoided the main thoroughfare which went through Yi, and trudged country roads, the candles and incense-sticks strapped conspicuously outside their luggage. A detail of Japanese soldiers stopped them for questioning, and they encountered other inquisitive persons they suspected were guerrilla agents. They pointed to the candles and incense-sticks, and said they were on their way to render reverence at the tomb of their ancestors.

They were allowed to proceed. The countryside looked devastated and bleak; that night they were forced to sleep in the open. The next day they noticed a gradual change: More people could be seen in the fields and villages, and a degree of orderliness, security, even prosperity, was apparent. This was Widow Lan's domain.

There was also still another marked contrast with conditions in the Communist "Liberated Areas." There were no armed guards anywhere, yet everyone they met—every farmer, tradesman, peddler, and barrow-pusher—seemed a self-appointed sentry. Everybody was friendly, and gave them road directions cheerfully and politely, but both Ta-kong and Mei-yin were experienced enough in guerrilla tactics to be sure their every movement was being observed and reported.

That evening they stayed at an inn in the village where Widow Lan had lived with her husband, and which they knew was operated by Widow Lan's men. Ta-kong purposely engaged the innkeeper in conversation; he said they were refugees from the north, trying to get to Chungking. What about the mountain road? When the innkeeper answered that it had been closed for two months because of fighting between the Communists and the local guerrilla force, Ta-kong bitterly cursed the Communists for fighting against their own countrymen instead of the Japanese. This too, he was sure, would be reported to Widow Lan.

Next morning they rose early and walked the main thoroughfare, right past the entrance to the mountain road. Some two hundred paces on their right, the cliffs of Tyrant Pass rose sharply, with a row of barracks-like huts at the foot where uniformed men were standing guard. The tomb was only a short distance away now, on a hilltop at the turn of the thoroughfare.

Halfway up the hill, a sentry stepped from behind a tree and challenged them.

366

"I am a son of the House of Ho," Ta-kong shouted in a voice purposely loud. "I come with my wife to do reverence at my ancestors' tomb."

The sentry eyed the candles and incense sticks. "I would not stop anyone from that," he said, "but so far as I know, there are no more Hos in Yi—nobody has visited the tomb of Ho the Central Hall in several years. And anyway, I have my orders. You can't go up there just now."

"But why? I am truly a grandson of Ho the Central Hall. I have a right to revere my ancestors!"

"You'll have to wait. Old Mother is up there now."

Nothing could have gladdened Ta-kong and Mei-yin more. Ta-kong shouted, "Who is this Old Mother? How can she stop a son of the House of Ho?"

"If you're a Ho, you'd know Mother Lan. How do I know you're not a Communist?"

"Curse the Communists! If we were Communists, we wouldn't be here to venerate our ancestors!"

His shouting had the desired result. A soldier came hurrying down from the woods that concealed the tomb, and told the sentry that Old Mother had ordered the strangers to be brought to her at once.

They climbed the hill, and found Widow Lan looking down at them. Ta-kong halted, feigning astonishment.

"Why, it's you—Ta-kong!" Widow Lan exclaimed.

"Auntie Lan!" he cried in return, and then dropped to his knees. Mei-yin hesitated, but did the same.

Widow Lan ran to them and took Ta-kong's arm. "You don't need to do this for me, Ta-kong!" she smiled. "And this is your wife? I welcome you both with all my heart. Why, I haven't heard a word about you for sixteen or seventeen years."

Ta-kong breathed more easily. His one fear had been that, in spite of his use of an assumed name, Widow Lan somehow had learned he was a Communist. He rose. "They kept calling you Old Mother, and I had no idea it could be you—I thought you were still at the Mission. Is Yuwen, my Third Brother, here with you?"

"No," Widow Lan said sadly. "Since the war, I have lost track of him—I can only trust to God that he and his family are well." Then she brightened. "But did you know that Yuwen is married to Li-hwa, the daughter of your Uncle Fucho?"

"Why, that's wonderful news! Li-hwa was such a beautiful girl when I saw her last. But here—I've forgotten to present Mei-yin. If you will please excuse us, we want to do reverence to my grandparents."

Nodding approvingly, Widow Lan accompanied them to the tomb of Ho the Central Hall and Orchid. Ta-kong saw at once that the grave had a fresh wreath before it, and that it had been given excellent care. He and Mei-yin placed the candles and incensesticks in the stone receptacles, he lighted them, and then both prostrated themselves before the grave and kowtowed nine times, as properly and ceremoniously as any of his forefathers would have done.

Widow Lan was smiling when they arose. "Ta-kong, I remember how you hated to kowtow as a boy. It touches me, now, to see that you two remember Filial Piety—so many people seem to have forgotten it nowadays. If Ho the Central Hall were alive, he would be greatly moved, too."

Ta-kong felt a sudden involuntary pang in his heart, but then he saw Mei-yin was staring at him. Emotion had no place in her heart, and she was watching him for any trace of weakness. He heard himself thank Widow Lan for keeping the tomb in good repair, and then the older woman motioned to the two stone benches flanking the grave, and suggested they sit down and tell her about what had happened since last they met.

Ta-kong began their rehearsed story. He said he had lost touch with his Third Brother, Yuwen, after his graduation, when the Northern Expedition was launched. He would have written to Auntie Lan to ask where Yuwen was, but he had been in no mood to write a decent letter to anyone, having been disillusioned to see that all politicians, whether Rightist or Leftist, Kuomintang or Communist, were really working for their own selfish ends. He and his Second Brother, Li Chien, had fought in many a battle— always under Chiang Kai-shek. But they had not been promoted in rank because they refused to grovel even to Chiang. Then in a battle in the South against the Communists, Li Chien had been killed and he himself had been seriously wounded.

Mei-yin, in her turn, told how she had met Ta-kong at college, and how later, after she had come into a large inheritance in her native province, he had written her about his wound and his utter frustration. Their marriage had followed. Then the Japanese came, and Ta-kong had been eager to rejoin the Government and fight, but she would not let him, until now. Just last month the Japanese had confiscated their land to build an airfield, and now they were on their way to Chungking.

Widow Lan believed every word, because of her respect for the House of Ho. And she felt it was nothing short of providential that Ta-kong, a graduate of the famous Whampoa Military Academy and a veteran of many battles, should come along just when she needed experienced officers to help defend two fronts. With her own ears she heard Ta-kong curse the Communists because the mountain road was closed, thus confirming the report she had received from the innkeeper. She kept her elation to herself for the time being.

"But now you must stay here a while," she told them. "Seeing you two is almost like seeing Yuwen and Li-hwa. Come with me to my cottage, we still have many things to talk about."

Everything was working out as Ta-kong and Mei-yin had planned.

2

WIDOW LAN LIVED austerely, with only one servant, in the cottage halfway between the temple of the War God and a mountain village where most of her officers' families and now Tien Fong were quartered. She studied Ta-kong for several days, and was more anxious than ever for him to join her forces. She did not dislike Mei-yin, but found her somewhat dull; however, when she discovered that Mei-yin was adept at managing the household chores that had been a burden to her, she was thankful that both had come.

Meanwhile, she discussed battles and campaigns with Ta-kong, and was convinced that he was a born strategist and leader. She could also see that he was an expert in firearms, whereas Kan Koo's knowledge of that field was not at all scientific. She saw to it that Ta-kong accompanied her on several inspection trips to various outposts, and he volunteered suggestions for changes which Widow Lan saw immediately would lead to greater fire power, and increased combat readiness and efficiency.

Kan Koo, Kan Kan, and the other officers liked Ta-kong at once for his hearty, open manner, his rough soldierly talk, and—above all—the skill and dexterity with which he handled weapons of every description. But Kan Kan regarded him with special friendship, since he too had studied at the Government University in the port city, and now the two of them could laugh together at anecdotes about students and faculty members. Ta-kong told Widow Lan that Kan Kan reminded him of Li Chien. For his part, Kan Kan, being of a younger generation, revered Ta-kong almost with hero worship as the student leader who had defied the Japanese at the borders of their Concession.

Widow Lan, of course, probed Ta-kong on the subject of Communism, and got nothing but right answers—although Ta-kong could see little difference between the Communists and people like Tien Fong, with his misrule, his plundering and murders. She also talked about Christianity, and though Mei-yin kept her stolid silence, Ta-kong showed cautious interest, saying he saw no practical difference between Christian teachings and Confucian ideals.

Widow Lan disagreed. "Confucianism," she said, "is not a religion but a philosophy. Philosophy endeavors to enlighten man's intellect; religion strives to reach his soul. Religion is much more substantial in the trials of life—where philosophy instills only wisdom, religion infuses strength. A true Christian not only knows what he ought to do, but because of his faith, will persevere where a philosopher might falter."

Ta-kong seemed impressed. Sometimes Widow Lan—and a startled Mei-yin—would hear him say "Amen" to the grace she invariably spoke before meals.

Finally, the old lady made up her mind. After consulting Kan Koo, Kan Kan, and her other officers, she asked Ta-kong to join her band as one of her principal lieutenants. Ta-kong feigned some hesitation, while Mei-yin openly pressed him to accept.

This occurred barely a week after their arrival. All the while Widow Lan had been studying them, Ta-kong and Mei-yin had been studying her. They had come to the conclusion that she would never voluntarily join the Communists. Ta-kong's only hope now was that he might persude her to join the Party after she had been overthrown. Mei-yin, with feminine intuition, knew the hope was vain.

However, everything was working their way, beautifully and smoothly. And they still had more than twenty days left of the month the High Command had given them. . . .

Ta-kong joined up. Because the House of Ho was so well remembered, the news was received with enthusiasm throughout the whole area, except for one voice of dissent: Tien Fong's. The ex-Governor had purposely kept away, not wishing to meet Ho Fucho's nephew face-to-face. But when he heard that Ta-kong was being given a

370

responsible post, he came to see Widow Lan in the War God's temple, which served as a hospital where she looked after her patients.

"When I was Governor," he told her, "I received a great deal of intelligence from the national secret police. One dispatch in particular stuck in my mind. It directed me to put the House of Ho under surveillance because Ho Ta-kong had become a Communist and might use members of his family to spread subversion through the province."

Widow Lan was startled, but then considered the source of this information. Tien Fong most certainly had murdered Ho Fucho, and now understandably was apprehensive for his own safety.

"Do you have that dispatch, Governor?" she asked quietly.

"No. I burned all my papers when I left the capital."

"Was there any evidence that Ta-kong used members of his family to engage in subversive activities?"

"No," Tien Fong admitted reluctantly. "I could find nothing. Apparently he was then operating only in the South. But the secret police said he was one of the biggest Communists, under an assumed name."

Widow Lan asked what name that was.

"He used several but I remember only one. I could not believe it possible."

Widow Lan was stunned when he gave the name. It was, in fact, that of one of the very top Communists. She asked the former Governor why he had waited to inform her.

"Your connections with the House of Ho are well known. You would not have believed me."

Widow Lan reflected for a moment. "Thank you, Governor," she said at length. "I will consider what you have told me."

But there seemed to be one great flaw in Tien Fong's story. If Ta-kong were this big Communist, what was he doing here? Widow Lan did not consider herself or her activities important enough for such attention. Besides, Tien Fong was old and ill and embittered, as well as drunk most of the time. And Widow Lan still had her shining faith in the basic goodness of men in general, and in those of the House of Ho in particular.

She could believe no ill of Ta-kong.

Nevertheless, she proceeded cautiously. Before she named Ta-kong as deputy to Kan Koo at Lion Head Rock, she called both Kan Koo and Kan Kan to conference.

"You know the old saying: 'We know a man, we know his face,

but we do not know his heart.' Ta-kong is very dear to me. You know his connections; you have all expressed confidence in him and in his knowledge. But keep your eyes open, and observe him. Don't give him a separate command yet. I don't believe he is a Communist, but there are some who do. Watch him carefully."

Tien Fong had prolonged recourse to the bottle, and while drunk cursed Widow Lan's stubbornness. His bodyguards overheard, including the Communist plant, and Ta-kong was informed of Tien Fong's charges in short order.

Immediately he sent word to Nan Ping to arrange a trap and a sham attack in which he would have the opportunity to distinguish himself and convince Widow Lan of his loyalty. Kan Kan had been conducting ceaseless reconnaissance patrols beyond Lion Head Rock, and Ta-kong had already gone along with him on several occasions to familiarize himself with the terrain. He observed that Kan Kan was reckless to the point of foolhardiness, and invariably rode his pony far in advance of the patrols. Kan Kan merely laughed when Ta-kong cautioned him.

"We have the Communists scared out of their wits!" he boasted. "Why, we've whipped them so often that they flee at our shadows. Besides, I know these mountains like the palm of my hand."

"Does your father know about your tactics?"

"Heavens, no! Nor Mother Lan either. We should have taken the offensive here in the west, but she is too conservative. She is afraid the Japanese might strike from the east." He looked fondly at Ta-kong. "I like you. I liked you from the start. We're schoolmates, in a way."

Soon after Ta-kong had set the stage with Nan Ping's troops they went on a patrol again. Kan Kan had just been severely lectured by his father for taking unnecessary risks, and he blamed Ta-kong for this.

"I took you for my friend!" he said reproachfully. "And then you betrayed me to my father. Very well—most of you are cowards at heart, but not I, thank Heaven! I'll show you!"

He spurred his pony ahead. Ta-kong shouted for him to come back, but he paid no heed.

Then the trap was sprung. A single well-directed rifle shot, and Kan Kan's pony fell; another, equally well-aimed, and the boy's leg was shattered. Ta-kong reached his side at once, and everybody saw him beat off the attack and shield Kan Kan with his own body until the others arrived in force and the Communist snipers had fled.

372

Kan Kan, all apology and gratitude, was carried back on a stretcher. Kan Koo embraced Ta-kong, and Widow Lan hailed him as a hero; it was obvious that he had proved himself to her complete satisfaction.

What Tien Fong had told her could be only a pack of lies.

Widow Lan came to Lion Head Rock, attended to Kan Kan's wound, then sent him to the hospital in the War God's temple. She had probing patrols dispatched to the very outposts of the Eighth Route Army, but they found no concentrations of force.

At Ta-kong's request, Nan Ping had withdrawn his main body as far back as possible to give the deceptive appearance of weakness and lack of aggressive intentions.

3

TA-KONG NOW KNEW everything he needed to know: that Widow Lan's effectives numbered a thousand men, and that in her estimate —which was quite correct—Nan Ping's army was not much larger. Up to then, about nine hundred of her forces had manned Lion Head Rock.

"But what if the Japanese attack in the rear?" Ta-kong asked her. Widow Lan had delighted in telling him how Ma Pingshi had made her a number of conciliatory overtures, all of which she had turned down. Might not Ma lose patience? Ta-kong asked in concern.

"That puppet!" she said contemptuously.

Nevertheless, Ta-kong said Widow Lan should divide her forces into three parts, but keep them mobile. Put four hundred men at Lion Head Rock in the west, and two hundred at Tyrant Pass in the east. Station the other four hundred in the middle, at Ghost Gate Pass—these could be swiftly deployed in either direction.

Widow Lan agreed to the plan, and appointed Ta-kong and Kan Koo commanders of the two larger units. They would alternate between Lion Head Rock and Ghost Gate Pass every five days.

Ta-kong's third turn of duty at Lion Head Rock came just four days before the one-month limit set by the Communist High Command. Arriving at his post, he told his troops that they had rested more than enough in their five days at the quiet middle station of Ghost Gate Pass—they were getting soft. For three days he put them through exhausting and backbreaking maneuvers that left the men bone-weary. There would be more intensive training the following day, he warned, so they all should get a good night's sleep. Since there seemed no danger from the enemy, the night watch was reduced to one third.

Everything was in readiness. He had sent Nan Ping the password and complete plans as to where sentries were posted; Nan Ping also knew where the men were quartered and where the munitions were stored. And he had a special order from Ta-kong—his men were not to use guns, only knives and ropes.

An hour after dark, Ta-kong slipped out of the sleeping camp and took over command of Nan Ping's troops. Four men were assigned to each of Widow Lan's sentries, and two were detailed for every sleeping guerrilla soldier.

The attack came, swiftly, silently, and with overpowering force. In less than an hour, the Lion Head Rock garrison had been taken without a single shot. A hundred men were left to guard the prisoners, and then Ta-kong and Nan Ping, his men dressed in captured uniforms, moved swiftly upon Ghost Gate Pass. Ta-kong himself answered the challenges of the outpost sentries Kan Koo had stationed, and the attackers moved fast.

Kan Koo jumped out of bed in his pajamas at the first shots. He was wounded by a light machine gun that cut down most of the men around him. Nan Ping shouted a demand that he surrender; Kan Koo laughed contemptuously and put a bullet into his own head.

It was now midnight. Ta-kong left a hundred men to guard Ghost Gate Pass, and divided his remaining eight hundred into two columns: six hundred to attack Tyrant Pass, two hundred to climb to the mountain village and capture Widow Lan, unharmed. Nan Ping would command the former, he himself the latter.

Nan Ping objected strenuously, saying he did not know the terrain at Tyrant Pass, whereas Ta-kong did. He did not mention his real reason: Nan Ping had a private score to settle with Tien Fong and his wife, and intended that neither should escape.

"I will agree on one condition," Ta-kong told him. "Neither Widow Lan nor Kan Kan is to be harmed. I have the High Command's permission to try to persuade Widow Lan to join us."

Nan Ping gave his promise. Ta-kong led his troops on to Tyrant Pass, and struck while it was still dark. There was a sharp fight, but the garrison was overwhelmed. Ta-kong's only remaining worry was whether Widow Lan was safe . . .

It had been a night of horror in the defenseless mountain village.

374

Tien Fong's wife, the former eighth concubine of Ma Teh-lin, tried vainly to arouse her husband when the Communists descended, but he lay snoring inertly across the bed, dead drunk. Bedlam broke, and she looked up to see the piggish eyes of her former lover, Ma Pingnan.

Widow Lan had only two bodyguards with her. She dressed hurriedly, and quickly received reports that indicated all had been lost. She could have fled down the goat path and through the cave, which was but five li to the east of her cottage, if it had ever occurred to her to flee. But her place was here, doing the best she could for the people who had loved and trusted her.

"Where have you put my gun?" she called to Mei-yin.

"I have it here with me, Auntie Lan," Mei-yin answered.

"Then you keep it."

The rattle of gunfire rose, subsided, rose again. There were frantic cries that the Communists were coming.

Just then heavy, rapid footsteps stumbled toward the cottage from the direction of the temple of the War God. It was Kan Kan, still limping, with Widow Lan's other bodyguards, two convalescents and a soldier who had escaped from Ghost Gate Pass.

"Mother Lan, have you heard any news of my father?" young Kan cried wildly.

When Widow Lan sadly admitted she hadn't, he asked to go down with his men and find out what happened to him.

"No," she answered, "not with your wound. I have already sent one of my guards to investigate. You must be patient and wait."

But there was no need for further waiting. Loud reports crackled sharply from the direction of the village, and the sentry came running back, shouting, "The *Kung Fei* have come! The Communist bandits have come!"

"They have come for me," Widow Lan said calmly. "Kan Kan, take Mei-yin and all these men to the goat path. You still have a chance to escape."

The men protested loudly: "We can't leave you here, Old Mother! Come with us—we'll carry you on our shoulders!"

"No," said Widow Lan. "I am an old woman, and I am not afraid to die. If I go with you, I will be a burden to you. If I stay, I may delay their pursuit. Go quickly!"

But Kan Kan burst out in frenzy, "Go, you men! I'll stay here with Mother Lan and fight to the last!"

It was already too late. The pre-dawn dimness was suddenly alive with running shadows. Kan Kan limped to the roadside, hid himself behind a large rock and fired. The rest of the men scattered themselves around the cottage to protect Widow Lan. There was a sharp exchange of rifle fire.

The Communists fanned out to surround the cottage, and despite the resistance of Kan Kan and his men began closing in. Then Widow Lan, standing at the door, felt a jab at her back and turned to look over her shoulder. Mei-yin was pressing the revolver against her spine.

"Tell Kan Kan and the men to surrender at once!"

"You, Mei-yin! A Communist?"

"What else? Do what you're told, and no harm will come to you!"

Widow Lan ignored the command. "And Ta-kong? Is he a Communist too?"

"Of course. I don't have time for your silly questions. Order Kan Kan and the men to surrender this instant!"

Widow Lan turned grimly and called out, "Listen, my men! It will soon be dawn. Your only chance is to flee by the goat path. Run, all of you!"

"You stubborn old fool!" Mei-yin whispered. "Tell them to surrender!"

"Go ahead and shoot me!" Widow Lan answered, before she raised her voice to call again. "Run, I tell you! We have been betrayed—betrayed by Ho Ta-kong and his wife!"

Realizing what was happening, Kan Kan suddenly wheeled about and limped toward the women in the doorway. From behind Widow Lan, Mei-yin fired a single shot, and Kan Kan staggered, then toppled and fell dead.

The Communists now rushed in from all sides, and Widow Lan's men were quickly shot down.

Widow Lan returned sadly to her little sitting room. Ignoring Mei-yin, she sat down and bowed her head in a silent prayer. Presently she heard someone enter the cottage.

"Congratulations to you, Comrade!" a man called to Mei-yan. "What a night I've had with your comrade-husband!" He poked at Widow Lan's shoulder, "So this is the hag who has been such a problem!"

Widow Lan shrank from the touch, and opened her eyes.

"You are Ma Pingnan, son of Ma Teh-lin!" she exclaimed.

Nan Ping chuckled. "And what if I were, old woman? I also happen to be your undisputed conqueror just now!"

"You and your breed should never have been born," Widow Lan said scornfully. "I am sorry for anyone who has ever associated with you. I am even sorry for the Communist Party that has men like you for members."

"You miserable hag!" Nan Ping growled, and he slapped the helpless old woman sharply on both cheeks.

"You and you there!" he called to his men from the door. "Come and bind this she-devil hand and foot!"

Widow Lan suffered these indignities in silence. Mei-yin, unmindful of Ta-kong's instructions not to hurt Mother Lan in any manner, watched without concern. She had just learned something valuable: Nan Ping's real name was Ma Pingnan! She had once read his secret dossier in the Party holy of holies, and it said nothing about his name having been Ma Pingnan. The Party considered it a major offense for a comrade to conceal any part of his life from its top leaders. Clearly it was her duty to report this curious revelation to the High Command, but before she did that, she would talk with Ta-kong. The exchange between Nan Ping and Widow Lan suggested that this Ma Pingnan had had quite a notorious past in Yi. Ta-kong would have heard of him and could tell her more. Her odd-shaped eyes took on that cold gleam. Not only the vanquished was at her mercy now, but also the self-styled conqueror!

4

NAN PING LEFT the cottage in a fit of temper. He was not concerned at the disclosure of his true identity—in the excitement of the moment, he had all but forgotten the rules of the Party—but that inadvertently he had called himself "undisputed conqueror" in Mei-yin's presence, and he knew she would not forget. He was forced to admit that it was really Ta-kong who had overthrown Widow Lan—and now all Nan Ping's old jealousy blazed again. However well he had done for himself in the Party, Ta-kong had always done better. It rankled that he himself had been thrice defeated by Widow Lan, but Ta-kong had been able to bring about her downfall almost single-handed.

Leaving half of his men to occupy the village and guard the old woman, Nan Ping started down the steep path toward Tyrant Pass, and met Ta-kong climbing upward.

"How about Widow Lan, comrade?" Ta-kong called anxiously.

"She is taken alive and unhurt."

"And Kan Kan?"

"He was killed by your wife."

Ta-kong did not let his anger show in his face. However, now that both Kan Koo and Kan Kan had been killed, he feared it would become even more difficult to induce Widow Lan to join the Communists.

"How did things go at Tyrant Pass?" Nan Ping asked.

"It's in our hands. I advanced as far as the village at the mouth of the mountain road."

"And the other villages on the plains?"

"I didn't bother with them, their positions are too exposed to the Japanese. Widow Lan never armed them—she always told them that in case of Japanese raids they should simply flee into the mountains. You'll be able to occupy those villages without any trouble."

Nan Ping, pleased at this prospect of winning laurels for himself, hurried off to take charge of the whole operation. . . .

5

TA-KONG RUSHED BACK to Widow Lan's cottage and ran into the little sitting room.

"How could you do this to Aunt Lan, Mei-yin?" he shouted angrily. "Why is she tied? Didn't I tell you to treat her with affection and respect?"

Mei-yin's triangular eyes glared in resentment. Ta-kong had never talked to her so overbearingly before, and she was about to retort in kind when he winked at her. She understood, then, that this was a game she must play to try to win over Widow Lan.

Ta-kong hurriedly began to untie the old woman. When Mei-yin tried to help he elbowed her aside, pretending to be infuriated with her.

"Are you hurt, Auntie Lan?"

Widow Lan closed her eyes and refused to speak.

Ta-kong continued railing at Mei-yin. He was carrying the act much too far, she thought, and now he shouted, "You not only disobeyed my orders about Auntie Lan, but you killed Kan Kan!"

"I had to," replied Mei-yin. "It was either his life or mine."

Ta-kong saw the old woman's involuntary shudder at the mention of Kan Kan. He begged her to speak to him, but she bowed her head even lower and compressed her lips tighter than before.

378

Ta-kong turned furiously on Mei-yin. "Get out, woman! Can't you see Auntie Lan won't speak to me while you're here?"

A resentful rage seized Mei-yin. This was the old woman who had given the Party so much trouble. Her son had wrecked Ta-kong's mission in Shanghai—the same Lan Yuwen who long ago had said Mei-yin thought only of destroying. Well, she would prove him right —by destroying his own mother.

"Auntie Lan," Ta-kong begged when they were alone, "please forgive us. We were under orders—we had to do it!"

Widow Lan kept her eyes closed and would not even turn her head toward him.

"You must know I never intended to hurt you personally. I have permission from my High Command to save you from all harm, provided you listen to me."

Without opening her eyes, she murmured, "What have you done to Kan Koo?"

"I gave orders to take him alive, but he was surrounded by Nan Ping's men and I wasn't there. He was wounded, and he killed himself."

Tears trickled down her cheeks. "And my commander at Tyrant Pass?"

"He was killed in action, too. I would have given my life to avoid these tragedies. You must think of yourself now, Auntie Lan. You must forgive us and join us."

"Do with me what you will," replied Widow Lan, "but I'll never do that."

Then she opened her eyes sorrowfully. "On your way up here, did you see the hill where your grandfather is buried? Did you see the temple of the War God from whom you got your ideas of sworn brotherhood?"

Ta-kong bowed his head. Widow Lan rose and went into her bedroom.

Once Ta-kong and Mei-yin were by themselves, he could not help showing his distress. But Mei-yin acted the dutiful and loving wife, brought food and begged him to eat. Then she told him about the discovery that Nan Ping was Ma Pingnan.

Ta-kong was intrigued. He recollected that when he had begun to study French under Nan Ping at the Government University, he had felt there was something vaguely familiar about the man. Yes, he had heard gossip about Ma Pingnan when he was in Yi after his parents' death.

Mei-yin urged him to go to bed. She did not need rest; she would stay awake and keep watch. Ta-kong was tired indeed. He turned in, and Mei-yin sat in the sitting room, waiting for Nan Ping's return.

6

TA-KONG'S PREDICTIONS HAD proved true—Nan Ping occupied village after village without opposition, and at once put into effect stage one of the Party program.

This program, drawn up by the High Command especially for the "Liberated Areas," was planned in three stages. The first— which Nan Ping was instituting at this very moment—was all sweetness and light, to put the people at ease and off their guard. The second stage would come hard on its heels—the sudden injection of terror, made as dramatic and spectacular as possible by picking outstanding opposition leaders, liquidating them ruthlessly in public, and making them such terrible examples that the rest of the people would be shocked or stupefied into submission. The third stage was the intensification of regimentation—an endless and ever continuing campaign of indoctrination and organization, accompanied by systematic periodical purges to weed out the reactionary, bolster up the faithful, and bring the wavering into line.

So at each village Nan Ping called out the headmen, assembled the inhabitants, and harangued them. The only purpose of the Eighth Route Army, he said, was to fight the common enemy, the Japanese. The people could pursue their business as usual, for they had nothing to fear from his troops. Of course, in order to oppose the enemy more effectively, fuller mobilization was required, but it was no more than what every loyal and patriotic Chinese should do. And in order to assist the villagers, he would leave some advisors. He hoped the people would co-operate fully and voluntarily with them out of patriotism.

And sensing that the villagers cherished a profound devotion to their Mother Lan, Nan Ping assured them that the trouble between her and the Eighth Route Army was merely a slight misunderstanding, that he and his men had no wish to harm her at all, and that at this very moment his colleagues were doing their best to induce her to abandon her groundless prejudices and join them. Thus were the apprehensions of the people somewhat relieved, and Nan Ping marched on triumphantly and confidently to the next village.

At last, he arrived at the hamlet bordering the land controlled by the Japanese. While he was delivering his speech, his men seized a traveler coming along the main road from the city of Yi. Nan Ping broke off speaking and scowled at the prisoner. It was the American missionary—the Reverend Dr. Holt.

7

As Widow Lan had told Ta-kong, Ma Pingshi, the puppet magistrate of Yi, had made any number of overtures to her—all without success. Since she and her band had constituted as much of a threat to the successful Japanese occupation as they had to the Communists, Ma was at his wit's end.

Then he thought of a scheme. The old woman and the Reverend Dr. Holt were practically lifelong friends ... maybe he would be able to reach her through the missionary.

Ma visited Holt and laid his cards on the table. If Holt would see Widow Lan and persuade her to surrender, the Mission—which was curtailed severely—would have all its privileges and freedom restored, as well as receive a sizable grant.

Holt was not taken in, but he longed to see his old friend and so, with the blessings of the Japanese, he agreed to the journey.

Now Nan Ping found himself in a quandary. Besides his personal reluctance to meet with Holt, he was at a loss for a Party directive; so far, secluded in inland Yenan and in the "Liberated Areas" inside the mountains, the Communists had not come into direct contact with foreigners. Nan Ping's first thought was to denounce Holt as an Imperialist and put an end to him then and there. But most of the villagers had known the missionary for a long time and held him in great esteem. Of course, Nan Ping could detain Holt and then get rid of him in private, but if that were discovered by the villagers, it would jeopardize the first phase of the Party program. And if he took Holt to the mountain village to consult with Ta-kong, he would risk letting Ta-kong and Mei-yin learn too much of his own unsavory past from the missionary.

He finished his harangue and stepped down from the platform, hoping against hope that Holt's eyes were not as keen as Widow Lan's and that he would not be recognized.

But the missionary looked hard at him for a minute and then said quite animatedly, "Bless me, it's you, Pingnan! We haven't heard a word since you left Yi, and I've been worried about you all these years."

Nan Ping's heart sank, but the whole village was watching. He shook the missionary warmly by the hand. "My dear old friend! You were always so good and kind to me."

"Tell me, Pingnan, what are you doing here? Are you working with Dr. Lan?"

"Yes and no," answered Nan Ping. "I am commander of an expeditionary force of the Eighth Route Army, and we hope to work with Dr. Lan."

"The Eighth Route Army?" Holt frowned. "Why, that's the Communist army. I didn't know it had come this far."

"Yes," replied Nan Ping, loud and clear so that all the villagers could hear. "We are Communists, and we have our differences with the Kuomintang. We don't want a dictatorship; we want democracy for the country. But in face of the Japanese invasion, we have put these differences aside and have been incorporated into the National Government. We want nothing but to fight the Japanese. That's why we seek co-operation with Dr. Lan."

Then Nan Ping lowered his voice and asked, "Why are you here, Dr. Holt?"

The missionary hesitated, remembering that it had been Pingnan's own brother, with Tien Fong, who had chased him out of the house of Ma. So he countered, "Do you know who happens to be the present magistrate of Yi?"

"No, we have just arrived here."

"Then I must tell you, Pingnan, that it's your brother Pingshi."

Nan Ping chuckled. "So he's a Japanese puppet, eh? And I, a commander of the Eighth Route Army! We were always at odds, you know. But what has he got to do with your coming here?"

Holt explained that Pingshi had sent him to ask Widow Lan for her co-operation, and he begged to be taken to her.

Nan Ping at once saw a way out of his dilemma. He answered loudly:

"You know very well, Dr. Holt, there is nothing I wouldn't like to do for you. But to see Dr. Lan and ask her to surrender to the Japanese? No. Even if she agreed to see you, I, as a patriot of China and an officer of the Eighth Route Army, cannot allow it. Go back and tell that Japanese puppet magistrate, whom I no longer recognize as a brother, that his negotiations with Dr. Lan are off. When we finish with the Japanese, we'll know how to deal with puppets too."

Then, still protesting his friendship for the clergyman, Nan Ping ordered his soldiers to escort Holt back to the road. There was nothing the missionary could do.

Nan Ping was quite pleased with himself, but the incident bore unexpected consequences. Until Holt appeared, none of the villagers had known he was Ma Pingnan, a man from their own prefecture; now this news became the talk of the countryside. People not only remembered the good turn Ho-Lo-Teh had once done Ma Pingnan; they noted the exceptional friendliness the Communist commander seemed to show the foreigner.

Also, among Nan Ping's men was a lieutenant who was charged by the Party to report on him. Thus in due time two grave offenses found their way into the secret dossier on Nan Ping in the Party holy of holies—one his release of Holt without consultation with Ta-kong and Mei-yin, and the other, his having concealed his true identity from his leaders.

8

NAN PING DID not arrive until after dark. He and Mei-yin held a whispered conference, and agreed that all three prisoners—Tien Fong and his wife, and Widow Lan—would have to die in order to carry out phase two of the High Command's order.

Ta-kong was then awakened and brought to the sitting room, and Nan Ping, pretending he had just arrived, unfolded his scheme. The High Command, he said, had ordered that the reign of terror be introduced as early as possible. By the end of the next day Nan Ping thought his men would have had sufficient time to organize the villagers, so he proposed the executions be held the following morning.

This gave Ta-kong only a day and a night to convert Widow Lan, and he asked for more time. Nan Ping shook his head. As commanding officer of the expeditionary force designated by the Party to carry out these particular commands, he could in no way yield. In the end, Mei-yin suggested a sort of compromise: Tien Fong and his wife would be executed first. Widow Lan would see them die and might thus become more pliable.

That night Mei-yin slept well; Ta-kong could not sleep at all. Early in the morning he went outside the cottage and glanced into Widow Lan's bedroom. She was already up, sitting in a chair reading the Bible. He ordered breakfast for two, and carrying the food on a tray, knocked gently at the door. He entered at her calm

"Come in," but she gave him no greeting, merely glancing at him in a completely composed manner before she returned to her reading. He set places for two.

"Wouldn't you like to have a little breakfast, Auntie Lan? You must be very hungry."

Without reply, Widow Lan came to the table and took her seat, but before she raised her chopsticks, she spoke her usual grace. At its end, Ta-kong responded faintly, "Amen."

Widow Lan turned on him. "I wish you hadn't done that," she said sharply. "One can be false to men, but one can never be false to God!"

Ta-kong was abashed, and they ate silently. During the meal they heard noise outside, and saw villagers bringing up tools, lumber, and other building materials.

"What are these men doing?" asked Widow Lan finally.

"They're erecting something under Nan Ping's orders," answered Ta-kong hesitantly.

"What?"

"Scaffolds."

"There are three," said Widow Lan.

"Two of them are for Tien Fong and his wife."

"And the third is for me?"

Ta-kong hung his head.

Widow Lan said slowly to herself, "The Lord gives and the Lord takes. May the Lord's will be done!"

"Auntie Lan," Ta-kong protested, "have you no fear?"

"What fear need I have of men when I put my trust in God?"

"But these are not ordinary men, Auntie Lan, and their killings and cruelties aren't ordinary, either. You can't even imagine them. But you can escape—you can save yourself. I swear to you, Auntie Lan—I came here only with the purpose of getting you to join us! Just say the word, and no one can harm you. But if you persist in refusing, I'm helpless."

"Become a Communist?" she asked. "Be a member of a band that believes neither in God nor in morals—whose calculated policy is deception and terrorism? No! I can not, I will not, join you!"

"If you won't think of yourself," implored Ta-kong, "think of Yuwen! Think of Li-hwa! Think of your grandchildren! If you join us, you will see them again."

Widow Lan's eyes moistened, and for a moment she seemed

unable to control her feelings, but she held back her tears. When she finally spoke, her words sounded firm and not bitter.

"I was wondering if you still remembered Yuwen and Li-hwa. It's more for their sake than for my own that I cannot join you. I want them and their children to remember me as someone they can be proud of, not as someone they must despise. If I can't meet them again in this world, I am sure the Lord will let me meet them in the next."

Widow Lan went back to her chair and resumed reading the Bible. The hammering, the bustle of the workers, and the shouts of Nan Ping's men outside did not seem to trouble her in the least. Throughout the whole day she ignored Ta-kong.

When Ta-kong again told Mei-yin that he needed more time to convince Widow Lan, she replied coldly that Nan Ping had already issued the orders. Perhaps Widow Lan would change her mind when she saw what happened to Tien Fong and his wife. Ta-kong felt a revulsion toward Mei-yin he had never felt before; he remembered how cold-bloodedly she had shot down Li Chien, his wife and baby, and recalled painfully what Yuwen had said of her years ago. He hated her. He hated Nan Ping. But most of all he hated himself.

Next morning, the minute he heard Widow Lan stir in her room, he brought in her breakfast again. She was standing near the window, looking outside, and as he put the food on the table she spoke without turning around.

"There are many villagers assembled. Why?"

"They are here . . . to witness . . . and to take part in . . . the executions."

"I know many of them—they live in far-off villages. Some of them had to start early yesterday afternoon to make such a trip with their old folks and their young ones. Can't you even spare the old and the young?"

"Nan Ping's orders."

"They are all worn out—they look famished. Have you anything for them to eat?"

"They were supposed to bring their own food with them."

"Do they know why they were ordered to come?"

"No. They were told only to be present at a public meeting."

"How horrible!" Widow Lan declared. "What a terrible scene

385

for the children to witness! It will frighten them out of their wits—it will leave ugly scars in their souls when they grow up!"

Ta-kong sighed. "Auntie Lan, you can't understand or even conceive of the actions of men who use terrorism as a weapon. This is to indoctrinate the young, to inure them to strife and cruelty, to make them fear their masters all their lives. Don't you realize?"

Widow Lan saw Nan Ping ride up accompanied by mounted guards. "Is Ma Pingnan your superior?" she asked.

"No, but he's in command of this expeditionary force and in charge of the executions."

"What are your orders?"

"To persuade you, the best I can, to join us, Auntie Lan."

"And if you fail?"

"Then you will be turned over to Ma Pingnan—and I shall have nothing further to say."

Nan Ping and his guards got off their horses, and Nan Ping came toward the cottage.

Widow Lan said calmly, "Tell him I am ready."

"No. I've been given a little more time to persuade you. They won't come for you until they're finished with Tien Fong and his wife. Please, Auntie Lan, reconsider—please join us!"

"This is only a waste of time. You go and join your comrade Ma Pingnan. I never dreamed a grandson of Ho the Central Hall would associate and work with men like him."

She left the window and sat down to read her Bible. There was a shouted command outside, and the guard presented arms.

Ta-kong said, pleadingly, "Please, Auntie Lan! Listen to me! There's no time left—"

"*You* listen to me!" she said, with a curious smile he would always remember. "Your grandfather, Ho the Central Hall, was a great Confucian scholar, as you know. I've been wondering how he would conduct himself under my present circumstances—I am certain he would choose the same course, but I doubt he would be able to go through all this with the same composed state of mind. You see, as I told you before, here is the difference between philosophy and religion—philosophy gives men wisdom, but not necessarily strength. Religion gives both."

Ta-kong had no time for reply. Nan Ping, Mei-yin, and their retinue had already mounted the central scaffold, and a loud raucous voice was speaking through a megaphone—Nan Ping's voice.

"Bring forth the prisoners!"

9

A BRASS BAND of the Eighth Route Army started to play and sing the song which was popular with the Communists:

"Rise! Rise! Ye men who will not be slaves..."

Behind the brass band were two files of soldiers in full uniform, armed with rifles. Four of the men wore black pajamas and carried flogging whips. Then followed a muscular pair stripped to the waist, wearing only red pantaloons and red kerchiefs and each brandishing a sword. In their midst were two prisoners—a stooped old man and a woman. The man, hands tied behind his back, was led by a rope. The woman was half-shoved and half-carried forward by the soldiers.

They were Tien Fong, nominally still Governor of the province, and his wife, Nan Ping's former mistress.

The procession reached the space in front of the central scaffold. The uniformed soldiers withdrew to their stations on the flanks, and the two prisoners were left in the center, each with two whippers and a swordsman standing guard behind.

"Kneel down, prisoners!" an officer commanded.

The woman dropped to the ground, but the man valiantly tried to stand erect. Two whips cracked against his back and he fell in spite of himself.

Nan Ping looked down on his victims and addressed Tien Fong through a megaphone so that all the crowd could hear.

"Are you the reactionary and the enemy of the people, appointed Governor of this province by the corrupt Government of Chungking? Is your name Tien Fong and was it at one time Fong Tienpa?"

The Governor did not answer. The whips fell again. "Answer yes," ordered a guard, and Tien Fong mumbled a faint response.

Nan Ping turned to the other prisoner. "Are you Tien Fong's fellow reactionary and an enemy of the people, now his wife and formerly a concubine to Ma Teh-lin?"

The woman remained silent and the whips lashed out. But she had fainted.

Nan Ping directed his megaphone toward the entire assemblage. "You people! Has Tien Fong ever fought against the Japanese like the Eighth Route Army?"

He paused and waited for a reply from the mob. His planted agents among the villagers hastened to urge: "Cry out no! Cry out no!"

"No! No! No!" the crowd answered.

Nan Ping permitted an ominous frown to crease his sallow face as he surveyed the multitude. Again he put the megaphone to his mouth and roared, "You have to do better than that, you people! Only an enemy of the people will befriend an enemy of the people. No true people will ever fail to respond to a charge made against an enemy of the people. Has Tien Fong ever done anything good for you?"

This time there was a thunderous echo: "No!"

"Is not his wife his accomplice, his fellow reactionary, and an enemy of the people, the same as Tien Fong?"

"Yes!" returned the chorus.

"What shall we do with them?" demanded Nan Ping.

The people looked one to another. One of them, eager to establish himself in the good graces of his new masters, shouted, "Death!"

Then all the rest became fearful of being considered laggards, and instantly there was a terrific outburst—"Death!"

"So death is what you want," replied Nan Ping, his piggish eyes wrinkled by his smile. "You are the masters, you know. We, the Eighth Route Army, are merely your servants. You give the orders and we obey them. You want death for the enemies of the people— and death it shall be!"

He went on after a moment: "Now listen, you good people! You must have suffered a lot at the hands of these two, to feel the way you do. You must have hated them with all your hearts and souls. Here, indeed, is the chance for you to take sweet revenge. We, your servants, will not stand in your way. Soldiers, let the people wreak their justified vengeance upon the condemned. Let them walk past the prisoners, one by one, village by village, and do whatever they please with the enemies of the people—spit upon them, yell at them, beat, kick, and bite them. You guards are not to interfere!"

Immediately after this little speech, as if they had taken their cue from him, a group of villagers dashed from the edge of the crowd, yelling wildly. They did a kind of *danse macabre* around the prisoners, then filed past one by one—cursing, striking, and kicking the prostrate figures.

388

The majority of the spectators were puzzled and dismayed. The violent little group looked like ordinary villagers and dressed like them, but, not surprisingly, none of the inhabitants of Widow Lan's former domain could remember having seen them before. Now Nan Ping's agents told a group of genuine villagers to go forward and emulate the example of their neighbors. They hesitated at first, but prodded by the monitors and intimidated by threatening glances and gestures, they began inching forward, pushing the oldest man of their village ahead of them. This aged patriarch came to the side of Tien Fong and pronounced a mild denunciation against the ex-Governor. But when he approached the insensible woman he averted his eyes, unable to speak.

Nan Ping looked down from his commanding height, and called through the megaphone: "Behold, you people! Here is a friend to an enemy of the people! His look betrays his sentiments. He himself is an enemy of the people! Guards, take him away for punishment later!"

The old man was quickly seized and dragged away. The next man in line at once started to abuse the prisoners loudly and furiously—and so did all the rest of the mob that followed, one by one, village by village, young and old, men and women. When it was over, everyone was ashamed but none dared show his shame.

Nan Ping bellowed again: "The enemy of the people, Tien Fong, was appointed Governor by the corrupt Chungking Government. That Government has deserted you in the face of Japanese invasion. That Government has never done anything good for you. It has sent men like Tien Fong to tyrannize you. It has oppressed you—and neglected you—and forgotten you. It is not like us, the Eighth Route Army, who have come all the way from Yenan to help you and to save you from the Japanese. Yet I have no doubt that these enemies of the people, Tien Fong and his wife, are still clinging to the hope that there will be relief and succor for them from Chungking at this last minute. And I have no doubt there may even be some among you who still think you owe your allegiance to Chungking and not to Yenan. Then let the condemned be an example! Let Tien Fong and his wife look to Chungking for help! Let them cry to Chungking for help! Let us find out whether Chungking can see and hear them and save them from the death to which you people have sentenced them! Guards, strip the prisoners, and have each brought up to a side scaffold!"

Tien Fong desisted, but in vain. His wife, though now conscious, was too feeble to resist and could only moan. Both were stripped naked. The men in the crowd blinked vacantly; the women shut their eyes.

Nan Ping barked from above, "You people! Are you afraid of looking at the enemies of the people in the raw? Or do some of you still have a trace of pity for the enemies of the people?"

All the assemblage opened their eyes wide.

"Bind the condemned to the poles. Let them face in the direction of Chungking!"

Tien Fong and his wife were trussed up like fowls to the poles erected in the center of each scaffold. Their upper bodies were turned in a southwesterly direction so that they would appear to be kneeling to Chungking. Behind each of them still stood a swordsman and the men with whips.

Nan Ping raised his voice through the megaphone, "Condemned! Do you see Chungking?"

The swordsmen shouted from behind their respective captives, "Answer no!"

Tien Fong's wife murmured no, but the ex-Governor would not, until the whips lashed at his broad naked back and drew blood.

"No!" cried Tien Fong at last, at the top of his voice.

"Do you hear Chungking?" asked Nan Ping again.

"No!"

"Do you still hope that Chungking can save you?"

"No!"

Nan Ping repeated the three questions again and they were answered accordingly by the condemned. But when he commenced to ask the same questions a third time, Tien Fong blurted out defiantly, "Curse you, Ma Pingnan! Why don't you kill me at once?"

Nan Ping laughed. "So you think you can still talk back? You've already got two ugly scars on your face. I suppose you won't mind having one in your mouth. Swordsman, cut his tongue out!"

The two guards squeezed Tien Fong by the cheeks and forced his mouth open. Then the swordsman pulled his tongue out and cut it off by half. Blood spurted down over his naked body, and he groaned in agony.

Nan Ping directed his gaze on Tien Fong's trembling wife.

"That woman has been always a temptress," he said. "Even now she is trying to use her body to exercise seductive charms upon you people. Swordsman, cut off her breasts!"

390

The swordsman behind Tien Fong's wife made a grimace, then took a step forward. He drew out one of her breasts tenderly, held it out to give a better view to the crowd, and then sliced it off smartly with his sword. Before he did the same to the other, the woman had collapsed. The children in the crowd were too frightened to cry. Some men retched and many women fainted.

Nan Ping surveyed the throng with grim satisfaction and said sardonically, "I am disappointed in you people! You want revenge on your enemies, but you don't have the courage to go through with it. You have to learn better, and it's my duty to you to see that you do learn. Especially you women! You must follow the example of this intrepid comrade standing at my side. She's a woman like you, but she's afraid of nothing—she can endure anything—she will dare anything. Follow her example, both you men and you women! If you do not want to be enemies of the people, you must be ruthless to the enemies of the people!"

The mob was frightened into a show of stout-heartedness.

Nan Ping went on, "Now, you good people, shall we put the condemned to instant death?"

"Yes! Yes!" cried the mob, eager to see an end to this thing that had become as much a torture to themselves as to the condemned.

"Oh, no," returned Nan Ping grimly. "You are not being ruthless enough! These condemned don't deserve a quick death. In their hearts, they're still longing for a last-minute rescue from Chungking. Let us oblige them. Let them remain here as they are—as long as they can last. If they're hungry, let Chungking come and give them food. If they're thirsty, let Chungking come and give them a drink. Let them be exposed here day and night. Let them squirm and writhe in their hope. Let's see if Chungking can come and save them!"

Then Nan Ping rolled his piggish eyes around to scan the audience.

"And this will be a lesson to you, my good people. From now on, remember this: Don't ever rely on Chungking! Place your whole trust in Yenan!"

While all this was going on, Widow Lan remained inside her room with Ta-kong. Her eyes glued to the Bible, she never once left her seat or glanced out the window, but she could not help hearing. Her face was drained white.

Ta-kong said hoarsely, "Auntie Lan, you know now how cruel these men can be. Won't you please change your mind?"

Widow Lan held the Bible tight and answered sternly, her face flushed with indescribable contempt, "I'd rather be one of those who suffer than any of you who inflict the suffering!"

Then they heard Nan Ping's voice.

"Good people, this is not the end. You must not disperse. There will probably be a greater entertainment, a greater lesson for you. Officers, make ready the central scaffold!"

Ta-kong looked quickly out the window. Nan Ping, Mei-yin, and their retinue were descending from the scaffold.

"Auntie Lan, they are coming for you!" he said desperately. "For God's sake, say yes!"

Widow Lan stood up calmly. "For my God's sake, I say no."

Abruptly Ta-kong pulled the revolver from his belt and extended it to her. "Take this," he said frantically. "Kill me and kill yourself!"

Widow Lan shook her head. "No. I cannot kill you. You are grandson of Ho the Central Hall, my benefactor. Nor can I kill myself—my religion does not allow me to take my own life."

Ta-kong threw himself at her feet. His body shaking, his voice choking with emotion, he cried, "Auntie Lan, forgive me! What can I do? What can I do?"

Widow Lan put her hand gently on his head. "For what you have done to me, Ta-kong, I forgive you," she murmured compassionately. "But for what you have done to others, only the Lord can forgive." She paused. "There is, however, one thing you can do for me. If you could save me from the torture and humiliation . . ."

Ta-kong stood up in horror. But her eyes were clear, and her face calm and at peace. She nodded. "Yes, Ta-kong, I want it so."

He bowed his head and mumbled, "May your God forgive me!"

The bullet went through her heart.

Nan Ping and Mei-yin ran into the room, both demanding at once, "What's the matter?"

Ta-kong scowled at them darkly and said, "She went for my gun and I shot her."

Two

THE REVEREND DR. HOLT returned to the city of Yi tired and perplexed. He reported to Ma Pingshi the failure of his mission as well as his unexpected encounter with Ma Pingnan. Both the puppet magistrate and his Japanese masters were alarmed. Widow Lan alone had been a difficult problem; the addition of the Eighth Route Army constituted a real threat. They sent an urgent request for Japanese reinforcements.

Within a few days, however, many villagers who had lived on the borders of Widow Lan's domain were successful in fleeing into the city. Some of these had attended the monstrous "public trial," and had not only seen Tien Fong and his wife put to slow death but with agony and dismay had also watched afterward when the lifeless body of their beloved Old Mother was hauled out of the cottage and dumped on the central scaffold. Pointing at her corpse, Ma Pingnan had declared that she was a fine example for all those who dared to oppose the Eighth Route Army. And he added somewhat regretfully that though he had planned to put her to more refined tortures for the entertainment of the people, she unfortunately had been shot in an attempt to escape.

A few of Widow Lan's men who survived the slaughter at Tyrant Pass also reached Yi to tell how they had been betrayed by Ho Ta-kong. It was likely, they thought, that it was he who had killed Mother Lan.

When this news reached the Mission compound, Holt and his colleagues were shocked beyond description. Nothing that Ma Pingnan did would have surprised them, but Ta-kong was, after all, a grandson of Ho the Central Hall. . . . In their love for Widow Lan, they still hoped against hope that the report was not true, and many prayers were said for her safe deliverance. But as weeks passed and they heard nothing but confirmations of the tragic story, they fell into despair.

The Reverend Dr. Holt thought constantly of Yuwen and Li-hwa and longed to write to them, but he had no definite knowledge of their whereabouts. And besides, his personal freedom was being even more restricted by the Japanese. He was not allowed to communicate with any friends outside Yi. Word had got around that the commanding officer of the Communist expeditionary force had shown exceptionally friendly regard for the missionary, and the Japanese, who before had suspected Holt of possible secret collaboration with Widow Lan, now suspected him of collusion with Ma Pingnan.

The Japanese took other precautions, too. Notwithstanding Ma Pingshi's vociferous protests that there was no love lost between himself and his brother, they relieved him of his post as magistrate of Yi. However, he was permitted to retire to his ancestral home on the Lane of Eternal Stability.

By this time, many of the people of Yi had decided they might as well resign themselves to Japanese occupation. They did not like the Japanese, but Chungking was far away and the Communists were at their very threshold. Had it not been for what the Communists did to Widow Lan, they might have welcomed the Eighth Route Army with open arms. Now, fearful of their own fate, they wished the Japanese would send a larger force to garrison the area.

But Japanese reinforcements did not come. Instead, the foreign masters instituted a new policy which authorized the puppet governments to organize local militia units. These were to be lightly armed, but officered entirely with Chinese. The people welcomed the idea—they had no desire to set themselves up against their lawful Government, but they did want to protect themselves from the Communists.

The Japanese, however, had their own reasons for adopting this policy. On December 7, 1941, they attacked Pearl Harbor.

The Reverend Dr. Holt was arrested in Yi on that day. He was forced to leave the Mission in charge of the Reverend Wong Ming and Anna, and was hustled off to a concentration camp in the big port city. Because his sympathies were with the Chinese and he was reputed to have had close relations with both guerrilla and Communist leaders, he was considered too dangerous to keep in the North. The Japanese transferred him to a camp farther south, and then had to move him again a few months later. Taking advantage of the new situation created by Pearl Harbor, the Communists were making rapid inroads into the rural areas to the east and southeast; now they were descending in two columns, under the separate commands of Ho Ta-kong and Ma Pingnan.

The American missionary's second move put him in a concentration camp in Shanghai. The room to which he was taken was a large one filled with two-decked bunks, and when he first entered it all the inmates were out working except a sick man, old, bald, and wizened, lying on the bunk below the one assigned to Holt. As soon as the Japanese guard withdrew, Holt took a good look at the man.

This prisoner was a man of his own race, and evidently he was seriously ill. Holt had no medicine with him, but was anxious to do what he could. He felt the man's forehead; it was cold as ice. At the touch of the missionary's hand, the sick man opened his eyes slightly but for a moment could not focus them.

"You, Logan Holt?" he whispered.

"Yes," Holt answered. "But who are you? And what can I do for you?"

"You're a doctor," the man mumbled. "You must have drugs. Give me what you have. Opium, morphine, heroin—anything! Please!"

When Holt hesitated, the man shouted angrily: "Can't you see I'm dying without them? For God's sake, help me! I am Johnny Hunt."

Holt was shocked. Looking more closely, he saw in the shriveled and withered features some semblance of his former acquaintance.

"I'm sorry, Johnny. I haven't got any narcotics."

"But you're a doctor. You can manage to get some from the Japs."

"How can I? This is a concentration camp. The Japanese won't give us narcotics."

"Damn the Japs! Damn you for always being so damned righteous. I'm not asking for a favor, I'm willing to pay."

Holt shook his head.

Johnny writhed in agony. "I can't stand this any longer! At least you can do this for me, Logan—go to the kitchen behind this building and find a Chink they call the Rat. Tell him to come here at once. Tell him I want to go to the latrine."

"Just tell me where the latrine is, Johnny, and I'll help you get there."

"Damn you, Logan!" cried Johnny. "You can't. Only he can. Go and get the Rat!"

Holt hesitated, but when he saw Hunt's agony he decided to chance breaking camp regulations, and hurried out on the errand.

There were several men in the kitchen, but there was no mistaking the Rat—a short, spare individual who actually looked and moved like a rodent. Holt went to him and whispered, "Mr. Hunt wants you to go to him at once."

"He does, eh?" the Rat squeaked. And he began to pit-pat ahead of Holt toward the dormitory.

Johnny Hunt lay as if dead. The Rat laid a hand on him roughly. "So?"

Hunt nodded weakly without opening his eyes, and the Rat pulled him out of the bed and started to drag him toward a door. Holt made a move to help, but the Rat said, "No, you stay here. Camp regulations."

Holt had just finished unpacking his scanty luggage when Johnny returned, walking alone. His face was still colorless, but there was now a shiny glitter in his eye.

"Damn the Chinks! Damn the Japs!" he muttered as he sat on his bunk. "You know, Logan, if you could get the stuff for me, I'd pay you handsomely."

"You've just had a shot of morphine?"

"Right."

"And how much did you pay for it?"

Hunt looked at the missionary. "For this one shot, they made me pay a hundred thousand U.S. dollars!"

Holt was incredulous. "But you can't have that much money with you!"

"Of course not. These yellow devils have a list of all the cash deposits I used to have in the banks, and of the properties I hold in my name. They made me write checks at first. When my deposits gave out, they started making me sign away my properties. All legal and proper. The trouble is they keep raising the price! When I first came, a shot of morphine was only a thousand, and a good smoke of opium two thousand. God knows what they'll charge next time! So I really need your help, Logan."

"What can I do?"

"You're a doctor. I don't care where and how you get it—I'll pay you. What do you say to fifty thousand for a shot of morphine?"

"That's impossible!" Holt said. "I don't mean the price. I mean it's impossible to get narcotics from the Japanese in a concentration camp."

Johnny suddenly broke out into sobs like a child. "What will I do? If they keep raising the price, there's a limit even to my properties!"

"There's only one way," said Holt. "Quit of your own will. You *must!*"

Hunt turned on him. "I thought you were my friend. Any doctor knows it would kill me to stop taking drugs now."

"Yes, there's always that chance, but it's much less dangerous than the course you're taking. Anyway, one of these days they're bound to clean you out of everything you own and you'll be faced with the same problem—only worse. If you make up your mind to quit now, you'll have a better chance to pull through. Don't you remember what you said to me years ago in Yi? You said you could stop smoking opium any time you wished, that it was only a matter of will power. I think you have will power. So believe in yourself—quit right now! The first week will be the hardest, but in a fortnight I guarantee you'll be as hale and hearty as I am."

Johnny looked up half hopefully. "You really think I can?"

"I do."

"Then I will!" After a pause, he added shamefully, "When nighttime comes, I'll want to go to the latrine again. Don't let me!"

"Don't worry."

However, when they went to the mess-room for supper, Johnny was extremely wrought up. "It's the same damned rice again. My stomach won't take it. I'd rather go back to bed."

Holt had been watching him anxiously. "This is one of the symptoms," he whispered. "Pretty soon you'll have no appetite at all—only the craving. But I'm sure you can pull through."

Johnny nodded sullenly and went back to the dormitory. The missionary returned to find him lying limply on the bunk.

"If you think I've gone to the latrine again, you're wrong," Johnny said. "But the craving is back—I feel it in my very bones—and the Rat will come soon. Don't let him take me to the latrine!"

"I won't," Holt assured him. "When he comes, pretend you've gone to sleep. I'll know how to handle him."

2

NEIGHBORING PRISONERS INTRODUCED themselves to the Reverend Dr. Holt, and they were chatting together when the Rat made his appearance. He went past the rows of bunks with his scurrying, pit-pat gait, crying: "Anybody want anything? Fruits? Cigarettes? Candies? Any other tidbits? The usual prices—very reasonable."

At his voice, Hunt stirred convulsively. Holt quickly went to the bunk. "Cover your head with the blanket. Put your fingers in your ears."

Hunt gave him a blank stare, and Holt snatched up the blanket and pulled it over his head. Then he seated himself on the bunk.

The Rat approached, lowering his voice. "Does Mr. Hunt want anything?"

Holt shook his head.

"But he does," insisted the Rat. "He told me this afternoon to be here at this hour."

"Well," said Holt, "he has changed his mind. He won't want anything from you again, now or ever. Understand?"

The Rat fixed his round little black eyes on Holt. "You get out of my way and let me speak to him!"

"There's no rule against my sitting here," Holt said. "Mr. Hunt is asleep. And he has told me he doesn't wish to speak to you."

The Rat measured Holt's robust physique with his eyes and decided force would be of little avail. With a malicious squeak, "So!" he left.

When Holt uncovered Johnny's head he found him sweating all over, although his teeth chattered as though he had a chill.

"You've done wonders, Johnny," Holt said gently. "Just stick to it and you'll win!"

The missionary prayed for Johnny that night, but he slept very little. Johnny tossed and groaned; the other prisoners cursed him. Holt got down several times to feel Johnny's forehead—now clammy with sweat, now dry and cold as death.

At last the morning bell rang. Holt knew that after breakfast he would be assigned some sort of labor outside the dormitory, and might not see Johnny until the evening. The man was now in a state of coma, his pulse alarmingly low and weak. But Holt decided it would do no good to report his condition if the Japanese were indeed in collusion with the Rat, as Johnny had alleged.

Johnny's seat was vacant at lunchtime. As soon as the meal was over, Holt ran back to the dormitory and found Johnny sitting dejectedly on the bunk.

"You've gone to the latrine again!"

Johnny replied only with a slight shake of his head.

"Have you taken any narcotics?"

Johnny looked up defiantly. "I didn't break my promise! I didn't go to the latrine! I didn't send for the Rat! They came to me—the Rat and the doctor."

"And you let them give you another injection?"

Johnny looked down at his feet. Suddenly he burst out, "It's your

398

fault, Logan! You kept me from the latrine last night, and the injection they'd prepared for me spoiled. They put the needle to my nose and let me smell it. When I couldn't hold out any longer, they wouldn't let me have the shot until I paid double—four hundred thousand dollars!"

Holt shook Johnny by the shoulders. "Can't you see where you are going? Can't you see they'll raise their price—with or without excuse? At this rate, your properties will be gone in no time, and then no matter how you beg, they won't give you any more injections. What happened to your promise, Johnny? Where's your will power?"

"To hell with you, Logan! To hell with will power! My life is my own, and I'll do what I please with it!"

The bell rang again, signaling that it was time for the prisoners to go back to work.

That evening, Holt found Johnny in his place at supper, but Johnny refused to talk. Back in the dormitory, Holt said, "I take it the Rat will be here again tonight. I pray to God you'll be given strength to ignore him. You better pray too, Johnny!"

Johnny flung himself on the bunk without answering and pulled the blanket over his head.

In a short time the Rat's singsong voice was in the room: "Anybody want anything? Fruits? Cigarettes? Candies? Other tidbits? The usual prices—very reasonable."

Holt's anxious glance showed him Johnny still lying motionless, his head covered by the blanket. But before the missionary was aware of what was happening, the Rat had jerked the blanket away and was asking: "How about it, Mr. Hunt?"

Johnny sprang out of the bunk eagerly. Holt tried to bar his way, but with surprising strength Johnny pushed him aside. "Damn you, Logan! I've got a right to go to the latrine!"

"Sure, sure," squeaked the Rat. "The latrine." And he helped Johnny toward the door.

"Let them be," one of the other prisoners warned softly, "or you'll get yourself in trouble with the Japs for creating a disturbance. That dope fiend Hunt is hopeless. You're wasting your time. We tried to make him quit before you came."

Johnny Hunt was still asleep when Holt got up next morning. After breakfast, the missionary announced that he had to see the camp authorities on a matter of great urgency. He was taken to a Japanese officer, to whom he identified himself as not only a missionary but also a doctor. He explained to the officer that Hunt's addiction was so acute he might die at any time unless he could be weaned from the habit by slow medication. For humanitarian reasons, therefore, Holt proposed that Hunt be placed in his charge and that necessary medication be provided to effect a cure.

The Japanese officer was dubious. Why had the older inmates not reported the case? If Hunt was truly such an acute drug addict as Holt described, how had he survived so long in the camp without drugs? Perhaps Holt was using this as a pretext to gain access to narcotics for his own purpose. At all events, the camp had its own doctors and there was no need for the prisoner's services.

Holt was tempted to expose the whole business, but he held his tongue and demanded, instead, to see the Neutral Consul in charge of the interests of American citizens. The officer dismissed him bluntly. The Neutral Consul would make his monthly inspection in a fortnight, and if Holt harbored any grievances he could voice them then.

Holt returned to his work very much disconcerted. At lunch he was told that Johnny Hunt had made a complaint against him for having interfered in his private affairs. Holt was given a new seat in the mess-room; his belongings had been already removed to another dormitory.

The next day he was assigned to cleaning the latrines, a demoralizing job he was kept at for some ten days thereafter without shift. In one respect, he almost welcomed the work because he wanted to catch the Rat and his accomplices red-handed. But there were several latrines, and he never succeeded. As days went by, he worried more and more about Hunt. Though he knew how ill-gotten Hunt's money was, he now hoped there was plenty of it—enough to last until the Neutral Consul came.

On the twelfth day after he had talked to the officer, Holt was engaged in the distasteful chore of dipping up ordure and pouring it into a barrel to be sold as night soil. Though by this time he had become more or less inured to the work, he still could not help retching occasionally. Hearing a noise as if someone had stumbled and fallen outside the shed, he went out to see.

It was Johnny Hunt, crawling on all fours toward the door.

Holt helped him to his feet, asking, "Where's the Rat? Is he with you?"

"Take me into the latrine!" Johnny pleaded.

400

Holt led him in and stood him against the wall. Hunt inhaled a long deep breath.

"Logan, what a heavenly smell!"

Holt's stomach turned over, but he understood this particular depravity and mourned that Johnny was so far gone. He had been getting his shots here—now he associated the stench with the narcotics.

"Where's the Rat—where's the doctor?" Holt repeated.

"Damn the Rat and the doctor! Damn all the Japs and Chinks! I can do without them, Logan—I'm free! I don't have to have shots any more—I just need this smell!" And he drew another long breath.

Holt saw the ecstasy on Johnny's face, and stepped quickly aside and threw up. Finally he was able to return. "Have they cleaned you out of your properties?" he asked.

"Yep," answered Johnny. He breathed deeply and then broke into sudden laughter. "Not only me—they've cleaned out others too! Actually, I was cleaned out before you came, Logan. Other people have been paying for my shots—people you probably don't know, Tong Hsi and his wife Amy. They had too much unmovable property and were afraid the Japs would confiscate it—when the war broke out they transferred it to me, nominally, to hold in trust. But when they come back, they won't find anything left now."

Holt shook him roughly by the shoulders and said sternly, "What would you say to Tong Hsi and his wife if you met them again?"

"Why, what do you take me for, a liar? I'd tell the God-damned truth!"

"And if you should die before you meet them?"

"Then you tell them the truth for me, Logan. Tell it to Amy, not Tong Hsi. She's the one who wears the pants in that family!"

Holt was speechless.

Abruptly terror gripped Johnny Hunt. Choking and panting, he demanded, "What do you mean I might die before I meet them? I can live without the drugs, I tell you! I can live without a single shot! This smell—it will save me!"

He inhaled with effort, but his breaths grew shorter and his face turned blue. Beads of sweat started from his pores, drops of saliva trickled from his mouth. Holt ran out of the shed, calling loudly for help, and two guards came and carried Johnny Hunt away, unconscious. The next day he was dead.

3

BY THIS TIME the Communist successes behind the Japanese lines were of great concern to the Kuomintang. The Eighth Route Army had not only taken possession of the countryside in the northern coastal provinces, but was also expanding southward. Belatedly following the Communist example, Chiang Kai-shek dispatched loyal troops past the Japanese lines, to organize the southern countryside in support of the Government. As was inevitable, the Communist and Government forces clashed, and in a sharp engagement the Communists were overpowered. At once they raised their old hue and cry: The Kuomintang was not fighting the Japanese—it was fighting its comrades-in-arms! It stood not for unity, but for disunity! Not for resistance against the enemy, but for civil war in the face of foreign invasion!

The Government was not alone in being disturbed by the furious one-sided accusations resulting from this incident; Amy was greatly shocked—if for a different reason. For the past three years she had been passing the most confidential military information to Chang Fa-foo, knowing that it would probably wind up in the hands of the Communists. At first she had felt no qualms of conscience, since she thought it could not do much harm to the Government. But now she realized she was not working against the Government only; she was actually working against herself because her own interests were so closely tied up with those of the regime.

Of late, Chang had been particularly importunate in demanding information. He stood now in her private sitting room, his lean face all smiles. "I come here today with no special business, but only to bring you a present and some flowers."

"That's very sweet of you," said Amy, "but things have changed. When we first struck our bargain you admitted your acquaintance might be a Communist agent, but you said no harm could be done the Government since the Communists were our allies. Now the Communists are breaking with the Government—they've expanded their strength at our expense and have set up 'Liberated Areas' without our authorization. They've infiltrated many guerrilla units which acknowledged allegiance to the Government."

"What does all this have to do with our bargain?" asked Chang. "If the testimony of Tien Fong's servants—which, by the way, my acquaintance still possesses—had been given to Lan Yuwen, you and

Brother Hsi might have been no better off than Tien Fong. Anyhow, if Lan Yuwen knew, he'd certainly have reason to hate you even more than before."

"Ah!" exclaimed Amy. "Then you admit my information has helped the Communists gain an advantage over the Government. If this continues, it may eventually lead to the ruin of the Government and the Kuomintang."

"It's possible," conceded Chang Fa-foo. "But frankly, why should you worry? You're a shrewd businesswoman—haven't you feathered your own nest? Even in ordinary business, you must buy insurance policies—our bargain is your insurance policy."

"I want a stronger insurance policy. Say I were permitted to join the Communist Party. Then I might feel my interests were more adequately protected."

Chang Fa-foo knew the High Command had long ago ruled out this possibility. Amy was already completely in their power, and, besides, the name of the Tongs was altogether too disreputable.

"Can't you introduce me to your acquaintance?" Amy asked.

"I am not allowed to."

"Aren't you a Communist yourself?"

"What an imagination you have! No, at the risk of disappointing you, I am only like your good self, one over whom they have a hold."

"And what have they got on you, my friend?"

Chang shrugged. "You don't expect me to tell you that. One blackmailer is enough for me—I wouldn't like to add another."

Amy couldn't help chuckling. "So you still remember that little jest of mine." Then her painted face became serious. "You and I are in the same boat. What can we do?"

"Your stakes are higher," Chang reminded her. "But I have a suggestion: Let us of the Kuomintang openly break with the Communists and denounce them as traitors . . . and call on the people to resist them everywhere. Then we'll be able to answer their unfounded charges against us, and the people will know we're right and the Communists are wrong. And you, Amy, can privately persuade the Government to adopt this policy, even while you continue to furnish the required information. The Communists will be none the wiser."

Amy was convinced now that Chang was not a Communist. "You don't know the international situation as well as I do," she answered superciliously. "After Pearl Harbor, we, as a nation, received a tremendous boost. China is regarded today as one of the four big powers, with the same standing as the United States, Great Britain, and Soviet Russia. Chiang Kai-shek is a top leader of the free world, on the same level with Roosevelt, Churchill, and Stalin. We must not appear to be a house divided. No, as a matter of fact the Government's policy has been decided—we want to hush up the whole thing. We'll follow the old adage: 'Treat a big matter as a small matter, and treat a small matter as nothing.' We've already issued instructions to censor all news reports about the controversy between the Government and the Communists, so what you suggest is impossible."

Chang Fa-foo was delighted with the answer. This was what the Communist High Command had guessed. Hereafter the Communists would be free to make whatever accusations they wished against the Government; the Kuomintang would try to avoid any dispute, and hence would make no reply in return.

"In that case," Chang said, "it seems to me there's no course left for the Kuomintang but to negotiate with the Communists, as the Americans want us to. Perhaps we may reach an agreement. Then you and I, victims of the same blackmailer, will be safer."

"The Americans are such naïve people!" she said. "They want to send military aid to the Communist troops—they even suggest we form a coalition government! Of course we know better—we had a coalition government with them in the days of the Northern Expedition. But the Americans threaten to cut off our aid, so we must pretend to begin negotiating with the Communists, and then procrastinate—that's all."

Chang Fa-foo was pleased again, but did not show it. "Well," he said, "I suppose you'll have to go on furnishing information and I shall have to keep playing the messenger boy. You know, my dear Amy, if you were ever discovered to be a Communist spy, I'd no doubt be charged as an accessory and an accomplice."

"One thing you can be sure of," said she unsmilingly. "If I ever get caught I won't let you off easily. But I have a plan, which I didn't dare tell you until I was sure you were not a Communist. The big stick your acquaintance holds over me is Lan Yuwen. But what if I had Lan Yuwen arrested, and tried and sentenced to death by Military Court? We could charge him with the murder of Governor Tien Fong in conspiracy with the bandits—his mother was leader of the guerrillas, you know, and Tien Fong died a terrible death inside her territory. We could claim Lan Yuwen believed Tien Fong

404

responsible for Ho Fucho's death, and plotted with his mother to trap the late Governor. If you help me, I'll get you a Vice-Ministership and we'll rid ourselves of our mutual blackmailer."

Chang looked at her with grudging respect. The woman was even more unscrupulous and callous than he had thought. However, it did not suit the scheme of the High Command to put Yuwen out of the way at this moment; the Communists might yet use him to embarrass the Government.

"What a capital plan!" he said unenthusiastically. "I'd like that Vice-Ministership, and I wish you had thought of this earlier. But now it's too late."

"Why do you say that?"

"I told you I brought you a present. It's from my acquaintance. Why don't you unwrap it?"

Uneasily Amy opened the package. Then fear showed on her painted face. There was no gift inside, only a neat bundle of facsimiles of her own handwriting—photographic prints of the top-secret military plans she had copied and conveyed to Chang Fa-foo.

"What does this mean?"

"It means Lan Yuwen is no longer the big stick my acquaintance holds over you. This is. You see, he's angry with you and me, my dear Amy. With me because he thinks I haven't demanded enough from you. But above all, he's angry with you because he thinks you've shilly-shallied too much lately. He feels it was your failure to supply necessary information in time that caused him to suffer the reverses in the South. He doesn't want you to make the mistake again."

Amy sagged limply in her chair. Showing as much compassion for her as a cat would have shown a mouse, Chang Fa-foo continued, "I'm sorry for you, my dear Amy. You may be smarter and more ruthless than most people, but you're no match for my acquaintance. He knows exactly what's going on in our minds—he has eyes and ears everywhere. Be like me, Amy. The only safe thing is to obey his commands promptly and implicitly."

Three

FU-AN, THE OLDER SON of Yuwen and Li-hwa, was fourteen in the summer of 1945, and his brother Fu-sen was nine. The boys' names had been happily chosen. "Fu," which means "Return," was in memory of their maternal grandfather, Fucho; "An" means "Safety," and "Sen" means "Life." Return to Safety and Return to Life were symbolic expressions of the parents' hopes—as they wished that Ho Fucho could have returned, so now did they devoutly wish that their beloved China might soon come back both to safety and life. . . .

Yuwen's college had not yet opened for the autumn semester, but the two boys were in summer school and Yuwen and Li-hwa were at home alone. Ever since Yuwen's unprecedented outburst against the Government in the Political Advisory Council six years before, he had remained silent and inactive. He knew nothing of the tragic chain of events that had been set off, inadvertently, by that speech; he was not aware that his mother, Widow Lan, had been killed. Yuwen was silent from choice. He had seen both the Communists and the Japanese make full use of his criticisms in their propaganda, while the Government at which they had been aimed paid no heed. Thus Yuwen felt he had only given aid and comfort to the enemy.

Not long after the famous speech, Old Head had paid him a visit without Jasmine. It was a curious sort of call. After greeting Yuwen and Li-hwa, Old Head solemnly quoted an ancient saying: "Alas, it is from the mouth that comes Calamity!" He said this three times, then abruptly departed.

Yuwen and Li-hwa had looked at each other in perplexity. Then Li-hwa said, "I knew then, and I know now, that I made a mistake in going to the Community Church in Shanghai to hear your sermon, and in letting you talk to me afterward!"

"Why, darling, do you regret our marriage?"

"Not for a minute—not for a second. But you're constantly becoming more like my lamented father!"

She was afraid for him, and that was another reason Yuwen had held his silence. This summer, however, his mind had been active. Germany and Italy were crushed; the Allies were hurling their full might against Japan, and the victory for which China had been waiting eight long years was at last in sight. Now was the time, Yuwen felt, for him to speak out again; there would be serious problems of national reconstruction, and free elections and a rule of law would have to be established. Once more, Yuwen took George Washington for his model.

If Chiang Kai-shek initiated the proper reforms, he thought, the Communists would soon cease to be a problem. Yuwen sat down to write an article he hoped could be published in an independent magazine; though there were no such magazines now, they were sure to be resurrected after the Japanese had been beaten.

He had been collecting his material for several weeks, but when he finally began to write he found it difficult to overcome his expectant, anxious mood. Things were happening too fast. Ten days before, the United States had dropped an inconceivably destructive bomb on Hiroshima. Five days before, the Russians had declared war on Japan. The weeks—the hour—was filled with history. Yuwen switched on his radio.

"Rejoice!" it shouted. "Fellow countrymen, rejoice! The Japanese have unconditionally surrendered! Early this morning—"

Yuwen dashed upstairs. "Li-hwa! Li-hwa!" he cried. "The war is over!"

She threw her arms around him, murmuring tearfully, "Thank God! Thank God it's over at last! Now we'll see Mother soon, and we'll do our filial duty toward her. She must be more than sixty-five now, and no matter what she says she must come and live with us!"

Yuwen held her at arm's length. "I've always known I was the luckiest man in the world! My wife is the most beautiful—beautiful in body and beautiful in mind. She combines the graces of the West with the virtues of the East. You know, darling, our new-fangled, modern Chinese woman would not relish the idea of a mother-in-law in her home!"

Li-hwa kissed him.

"There's only one more thing I hope for," he said. "I want to find my two sworn brothers. Then my happiness and our happiness would be complete!"

Firecrackers began exploding outside, and an automobile suddenly pulled up before their door, its horn blowing loudly. The Chis —Old Head and Jasmine—rushed in without knocking.

"Congratulations!" Old Head shouted. "Congratulations to you, Yuwen! Congratulations to you, Li-hwa! Congratulations again to

407

you, my dear Jasmine! And to me, too—above all—congratulations, Old Head and Brother Ox!"

They shouted and laughed and hugged one another. Li-hwa apologized that she had not had time to tidy up the place. Jasmine laughed. "Just look at Brother Ox!"

Li-hwa and Yuwen turned to the "Mountain of Virtues." His long gown was not properly buttoned, and his silk jacket was not buttoned at all. His white hair had not been combed. One side of his face was washed, the other looked oily. He had toothpaste at one corner of his mouth, and when he smiled it was plain he had forgotten to insert his false tooth.

But Old Head laughed with them. "To hell with respectability on this occasion! I want to be Brother Ox again!"

He had hurried away, Jasmine said, because he knew the disciples of the secret Society would be coming in with their congratulations, and then there would be ministers and high officials—but Old Head wanted to celebrate only with Yuwen and Li-hwa.

"We're greatly honored, Uncle Chi and Aunt Jasmine," Li-hwa said. "You must stay for luncheon."

"Yes, and supper, too!" Old Head boomed. "But don't move, Li-hwa. I brought my cook along. He's at the market now, and he'll take care of everything." Then he turned to Yuwen. "What's on your mind, Yuwen? You look thoughtful."

"What I'd like to say," Yuwen began hesitantly, "concerns you, Uncle Chi. I don't want you to take offense."

"Speak up—speak up! For fifty years, Yuwen, I've been learning about the nature of men. I've known only two I judge to be really true—your late father-in-law, Governor Ho Fucho, and you. By your own nature, you two were incapable of evil. You, Yuwen, are a man far truer than my own Close-Door-Disciple."

Though curious, Yuwen let that pass. He knew it was a secret of the Society. Instead he said, "Well, now that the war is over, I suppose you'll return North and resume control of the Society. I know that you—and it—have done many good things. But I've also heard that . . . that . . ."

"Speak up!" Old Head thundered, his face reddening. "You mean you've also heard the Society thrives on crime, on evil? Right? You're critical of me for this. Isn't that so?"

Yuwen swallowed hard, and nodded.

"Then you insult me, young man!" shouted Old Head. "You shame me in your own house!"

408

"Please!" begged Li-hwa. "Please forgive Yuwen, Uncle Chi. He means well."

Old Head glowered. "So you side with your husband, young woman! You think he's in the right, and I'm in the wrong?"

"Yes," said Li-hwa, "I do. But we both love you dearly, and wish you nothing but good."

Old Head glared fiercely at them, then suddenly threw back his head and broke into a loud guffaw. Turning to Jasmine, he said, "Now—you see why I was in a hurry to come here? These are the only two friends I have in the world!"

He smiled at the younger people. "Forgive the little prank I played on you. Of course, I have led a very evil life in the past, by some standards. But the devastations of the war and the sufferings of our people have opened my eyes, I have already made up my mind. I will return and run my Society . . . but I'll direct my disciples to engage in nothing but legitimate and respectable business. I will go into charities and make myself respectable—not in the sight of others but in my own eyes. And don't call me Old Head any more—I want to be Brother Ox again."

Fu-an and Fu-sen burst excitedly into the room. "Papa! Mama! We've won the war! The school has given us a holiday!" Then they saw Old Head and Jasmine, and bowed ceremoniously.

"Good morning, Granduncle Chi. Good morning, Grandaunt Chi."

"Congratulations on the victory!" the Chis answered.

Old Head took out his wallet and withdrew a bundle of banknotes.

"Here, children. Go buy firecrackers. This is the day of victory—the day of new life for us all. Go buy all the firecrackers you can find!"

2

Now that it was all over, time seemed to crawl. The formal surrender was yet to take place, but as the fighting machinery ground to a halt the Japanese were directed to be ready to turn over the areas they had occupied. Partial lists of foreigners held in the concentration camps were published, and Yuwen learned from American friends that the Reverend Dr. Holt was in Shanghai.

Communications with North China from Chungking had not yet been restored, but those with Shanghai were. Yuwen was assigned the task of reclaiming his old college, which the puppet government in Shanghai had confiscated, and he managed to get aboard an American plane that was going to the coast city. He was extremely anxious to see his old mentor, the missionary, again, but there was an even more urgent reason to talk to the clergyman. Holt, if anyone, might be able to give him news of his mother.

As soon as permitted, Yuwen hurried to the concentration camp where Holt had known such trying days. The release of the prisoners was a dramatic and touching scene. People cried—people shouted. In the high emotion of the moment, utter strangers embraced each other. But nobody felt more joy of reunion than Yuwen and the Reverend Dr. Holt.

Yuwen took the missionary to his hotel, and each gave a brief account of his experiences since they had last met. Then Yuwen eagerly asked about his mother, whom he had not heard from for eight years. Perhaps while he was still in Yi, Holt had had some word?

The older man nodded. Watching Yuwen while he spoke, he gravely and eloquently related how Widow Lan had saved the women refugees on the Mission premises, and how—so Holt had heard—she had become one of the guerrilla leaders most feared by the Japanese in that part of the country. And then he resorted to a white lie. The Japanese had kept him under house arrest in Yi, he said; he knew nothing more about Widow Lan's movements.

But he planned to return to Yi at once and Yuwen decided to go with him. Holt told himself this was just as well. Even if he had disclosed the reports he had heard over and over, the son would have wanted to make certain of the sad truth for himself.

Railway connections with the North were still disrupted, so Yuwen booked passage for them both in a steamer sailing next day for the big port city. While he left to attend to some duties concerned with taking possession of the college, the Reverend Dr. Holt settled down to enjoyment of something that had been forbidden in the concentration camp—the perusal of the newspapers. Among the first items he saw was one saying that Amy, wife of Tong Hsi, had just arrived in Shanghai by special plane, and was at a Government house.

Thoughtfully Holt put the papers aside. With Johnny Hunt dead, it was his duty to tell Amy Tong what Johnny had done with her property. He tried to telephone her but the line was continuously busy, and so he went to call on her in person.

Amy received him cordially, ahead of a crowd of people waiting in her anteroom. This preferential treatment did not fool Holt. The popularity of Americans was at its height, and Amy was eager for the public to see she had American friends. Besides, he was a missionary, and she never lost a chance to show that she and her husband were devout Christians.

Holt stared at this woman he had never met, and saw a well-gowned, carefully painted woman, still voluptuous, and well preserved by every artifice against her years. In spite of his Faith, he could not like her.

"I have heard of you and your magnificent work in the city of Yi," Amy said. "My husband and I spent some time in the North before the war—I'm sorry I did not meet you then. You must have suffered all these years, as we all have. Did the Japanese treat you well? And what can I do for you?"

He thought, looking at her, that she had never suffered in her life. And her mind was not really on her charming little speech—she was worried about something.

"I want nothing for myself, but I bring a message from a friend of yours who was in the same camp—Johnny Hunt."

Amy's eyes gleamed. "Johnny Hunt! The best friend I ever had! Is he all right?"

"I regret to tell you that Johnny is dead." And then, as he related the details, he saw Amy's features set into a hardness no paint could conceal, and her eyes grew small and glinted with anger. She made him repeat the details about her property.

"Where is this man you called the Rat?" she demanded. "What's his real name?"

"We called him only the Rat. He disappeared a few days before the surrender—just as rats leave a sinking ship. I've no idea where he is now."

"Did Johnny Hunt . . . did he leave a list of the persons to whom he signed away my property?"

"Not with me. I don't think he was enough in possession of his senses to keep any records at all."

Amy's nostrils dilated; anger made her face a grotesque mask. In hysterical fury, she sprang up and beat her fists against the unfeeling walls, then collapsed in her chair again. "I am ruined—ruined," she moaned, and began to sob wildly.

Holt thought of calling for help, but just then there was a knock at the door and a footman entered.

"Madame, a Councilor Chang Fa-foo says he has urgent business with you."

The missionary was astounded at the change that took place in the woman. She controlled her sobs at once; in half a minute she looked cool and self-possessed.

"I am sorry, Dr. Holt," she smiled. "Show the Councilor in," she ordered the footman, "and see that we are not disturbed." She extended her hand perfunctorily to Holt but forgot to thank him.

As he went out, he exchanged nods with a lean, lanky, grayish man of more than sixty. He knew Chang by reputation, as former Chancellor of the Government University in the northern port city. Chang's business was none of his. . . .

But it was this business that had put Amy under such an emotional strain. The Russians, now in full control of Manchuria, had signed a treaty a few days before promising non-interference in China's affairs and support to the National Government, and pledging to evacuate Manchuria as swiftly as possible. But at the same time, they secretly urged the Chinese Communists to rush forces into Manchuria before Government troops could arrive.

Chang Fa-foo had been instructed to get from Amy all the latest Government plans concerning Manchuria.

She knew what he wanted. She had the information, but had hoped to fly secretly to Shanghai, recover the property she had entrusted to Johnny Hunt, and then leave China forever. Now, everything entrusted to Johnny was lost. She still had her sizable fortune from inland smuggling, but the loss represented the bulk of her wealth. She was sure she could recoup it all in time; the only thing was, she would have to put up with the Communists a little longer.

Chang Fa-foo gave her a sardonic smile. "Don't you know that my acquaintance is like the Buddha of a thousand eyes and a thousand hands? If you can charter a special plane to Shanghai, so can he charter one for me."

"Nobody's trying to run away. I had urgent business of my own here." She took a roll of papers from her handbag. "Here's what you want."

Chang Fa-foo examined the papers carefully. They were the Government's top-secret plans for Manchuria.

"Satisfied?"

"Yes, and no. I too have some private business here."

"What has that got to do with me?"

"Just this, Amy. I want you to have the Government appoint me

412

chancellor of a university in Shanghai, instead of my old post in the North."

"Are you asking me a personal favor?" she demanded coldly.

Chang Fa-foo smiled. "Not at all. This is a command from my acquaintance. He wants me to be near my dear old friend—so I can keep an eye on her—always!"

Amy shuddered. "You'll get what you wish."

Chang smiled again as he went out.

3

ON THE DECK of the steamship, surrounded by the dark infinity of sea and sky, the Reverend Dr. Holt first told Yuwen about the reports of his mother's death. Even then he did not break the news abruptly, but spent the whole first day of the voyage in a philosophical discussion of the meaning of life and death. Life, he said, is really only a brief earthly existence preordained by the Maker; death is a continuation of that existence in another form. The trials and tribulations of life are really immaterial; the soul itself, whether in this world or the next, is all that counts. . . .

And then, in the comforting darkness, he told Yuwen all he knew about Widow Lan's reported slaying. The final blow came when Holt revealed that supposedly it was Yuwen's own sworn brother— Ho Ta-kong—who had betrayed her.

For two days Yuwen could neither eat nor sleep. Holt left him completely alone, but when the ship docked he seemed resigned to his sorrow.

After Holt reported to his Mission headquarters, which had just resumed functioning, he and Yuwen boarded a train. The railroad was still running from the port city to the provincial capital, although the rest of the vast countryside seemed swamped with Communists and a terrible indecisive confusion. The road from the provincial capital to Yi had been kept in good order by the puppet regime, and the two men arrived in Yi the next afternoon.

Great was the joy of Ah Wong, Anna, and the cook, when they were reunited with the Reverend Dr. Holt—although each showed sadness at the sight of Yuwen. Wong Ming had discharged his duties well. In times of adversity, men always tend to turn more toward God, and now the Mission had a larger flock than ever before. But the people and the community had been impoverished by war; the church had been deprived of the support of Mission headquarters for several years. The two properties—the original Mission compound and the former House of Ho—were habitable, though badly in need of repairs.

Yuwen, believing but still daring through hope to disbelieve, ate his heart out in talks with Ah Wong, Anna, and Cook. The shack where his mother had lived so long had been sealed and locked by the Japanese, but the puppet magistrate gave him permission to open it. Memories of childhood flooded him as he looked around; the place had been looted of furniture and books, but in a corner, half-buried in dust, he found the little rolypoly mandarin doll of his childhood. He held this to his heart and went slowly back to the Mission compound, not even glancing at the House of Ho. He still did not know what to feel toward Ho Ta-kong. . . .

Nobody seemed to know where his mother was buried. The least of his filial duties was plain: He would have to go to the mountain village and search for her remains.

Holt objected strenuously. Yuwen was too well known an anti-Communist, and such an expedition would be foolhardy. Ah Wong, familiar with the local situation, was even more outspoken. The danger area, he said, was at the edge of the Communists' "Liberated Zone"; if Yuwen ever got inside this, he would never escape alive.

But when Yuwen persisted, both Holt and Ah Wong volunteered to go with him. He turned them down, and then the cook stepped forth.

"I know this countryside as well as any man," he said. "What is more, I can pass for a peasant better than most. And as for the Communists—bah! What have I to fear from them? If you will not take me with you, then I will go by myself!"

Yuwen was touched by such loyalty, and in the end had to agree. He and the cook disguised themselves as peasants, and set out for the mountain village, something more than a day's journey away.

"Now, remember," the cook said, out of the dignity of his advanced and honorable age, "I look much more like a peasant than you do, because I have not been educated abroad, or anywhere else. So—if we are questioned, pray let me do the talking."

This situation arose sooner than either expected. A detail of puppet soldiers stopped them at the Yi city wall. The sergeant in charge was a tall, personable man, with a kind face.

"We are farmers," the cook said. "We are on our way back to our farms, having sold our produce in the city—at a loss, of course. The times are hard."

414

The sergeant grinned. "You don't look like peasants to me. Why all this pretense?"

"Pretense?" the cook exclaimed indignantly. "As Heaven is above me, your eyes must be blind. I was born a peasant—I have lived a peasant—why, I'm every inch a peasant!"

The sergeant, still grinning, suddenly sized the cook's hand and turned it palm upward. "Not a blister, not a callus," he laughed. "Look, man—your hand is smooth and oily. It's a good thing you're trying to play your game with us. The Communists would cut off this hand for such a lie."

"Please forgive my companion's well-meaning falsehood," Yuwen said then. "We are not peasants. My mother was forced to live in a village a day's journey from here . . . and was killed by the Communists while I was in Chungking. I want to search for her remains, and this good man volunteered to accompany me."

"It's a better story than the other one," the sergeant admitted. He studied Yuwen, and with the intuitiveness of sergeants the world over, recognized enough character and bearing to make him come to attention. "I respect you for your sense of Filial Piety, sir, but the Communists won't. If you go on, I'm afraid I'll never see you again."

"My heart and mind won't rest until I've tried," Yuwen said simply.

"Go, then. It's your life, not mine."

They started, but the sergeant called, "Sir—did you say you have just come from Chungking?"

"I was there ten days ago."

"Then please tell me," the sergeant began eagerly, "what the attitude of the Chungking Government is toward men like myself? I've heard they call us puppets, collaborators, and traitors. But we are none of those things. The Government retreated far away and left us behind the Japanese lines . . . the Communists came near and frightened us; the Japanese asked us to organize for our own protection. And there was no work . . . nobody could get enough rice. We fought the Communists now and then, but never the Government—we've been patriots at heart. Now they say we'll be thrown into prison and tried as traitors!"

Yuwen hesitated. He had heard reports in Chungking, but the Government had not clarified its stand on the issue. As a matter of fact, Old Head had put it to him quite clearly: The Chungking Government was really on the horns of a dilemma concerning the people who had served the Japanese puppet rule. If they were drastically punished, many would be driven to Communism; if a softer policy were adopted, the Government would be denounced by the Communists for working with traitors to the nation. Meanwhile, large numbers of organized agitators only inflamed the situation.

"Unfortunately," Yuwen answered, "when I was in Chungking the policy had not been decided."

The sergeant blinked, then shrugged his wide shoulders. "Well, I guess it'll be every man for himself. If the Government doesn't want us, there are others."

"The Communists?" Yuwen asked sharply.

"Good luck, sir," the sergeant replied.

The road now became vastly different from the one Yuwen and Holt had followed from the provincial capital to Yi. A mile beyond the city gates, there was only stark impoverishment; two miles, and there was devastation and desolation, farmlands gone to waste. This was the no-man's land between the puppet regime and the Communists. In a little while, there was no sign of life anywhere. The cook began looking over his shoulder nervously; Yuwen was saddened at the waste of the area. They knew they must be approaching the "Liberated Zone"—the danger area mentioned by Ah Wong.

The road turned sharply, and they saw a lonely hovel a hundred yards ahead, and a woman stooped over a small cultivated plot of sweet potatoes. Yuwen moved forward at this first sign of a human, but the cook caught his sleeve.

"She must be a Communist!" he hissed.

"Very likely, but we're bound to meet them—more and more. I am very grateful to you for coming with me this far, but if you wish to turn back—"

"Turn back?" exclaimed the cook, with a fine display of indignation. "Why, I am neither afraid of the journey nor the Communists! I shall talk to the woman myself!"

Somewhat to Yuwen's amusement he ran forward. Yuwen saw them exchanging gesticulations, and then the cook came back in haste. "No use!" he shouted. "She's deaf and dumb!"

By now, Yuwen was near enough to see that the woman was well past seventy, and still working under the scorching sun to dig sweet potatoes and put them in a basket. In the vast desolation she seemed

416

a symbol of misery, and he felt a great pity for her. As he stepped closer, smiling, she looked at him vacuously and indicated her eyes and her ears and shook her head, but then he saw her glance at him a second time with a gleam of intelligence. As she bent again to her task, Yuwen took banknotes from his wallet and dropped them into her basket. The woman lifted her head and frowned at him intently when he indicated by a gesture that the money was hers. He turned to walk away.

"I wish to thank you for your kindness, sir!"

They whirled. Somehow, she did not appear so old, and the vacant look was gone from her eyes.

"So!" exclaimed the cook. "You're not deaf and dumb. You must be a Communist spy!"

The woman smiled slightly. "And if I were not, would I be here? And if I were not, you would go on to your death, wouldn't you? But since you've been kind to me, don't go on!" And then she looked oddly at Yuwen. "I shouldn't tell you this, but you resemble someone I knew and loved."

Yuwen gambled, his heart jumping. "My name is Lan Yuwen."

"Oh, praise to Heaven!" exclaimed the woman. She clutched his hand and began to weep. "Then there is truly a God, as she believed —her God has sent you! Of course you are her son—the same delicate mold, the same gentle smile. Oh, Heaven bear witness—here is my dear Old Mother's son!"

"And you?" Yuwen asked softly.

"I was your mother's amah! I served her for more than three years."

"And you can tell me about her, Nai-nai?"

"Don't 'honorable-grandma' me, sir! She talked a great deal about you. But why are you here?"

"To find her remains," Yuwen choked. "To take them back to Yi . . . if possible. You must know where she was buried."

There was a silence. "Sir, what a filial son you are! But—but she was not buried. She was burned to ashes."

Yuwen's grief overcame him. The woman said, "Do not feel badly. More than once she told me, 'From dust we come and to dust we shall return.' Perhaps she wanted this."

"How did she die?" Yuwen asked at last.

"I didn't see it, thank Heaven. Ho Ta-kong, the big Communist who betrayed her, shot her to death." Then she went on very gently, "I know, sir . . . I heard him tell your mother that you were his sworn brother! His wife said she knew you, too. Her name was Mei-yin. Oh, what a cruel, deceitful woman she was!"

Above the hammering of his heart, Yuwen heard his own words. "Was there a man with them named Li Chien?"

"No, sir," the woman said after deliberation. "But I heard his name. It seems to me that Ho Ta-kong said this Li Chien had been killed."

"Where are Ho Ta-kong and his wife now?"

"Who can tell where the big Communists are? They come and go, and never use their real names. But they're not here. I would guess they're in Manchuria—that's where most of the Communists have been going lately."

As Yuwen remained silent for a moment, the woman studied him. "About vengeance, sir," she said softly. "I remember how Old Mother used to read from her book. 'Vengeance is the Lord's,' she kept saying. 'It is not yours.' "

Then she looked at the shadows. "You must go—quickly. The sentry in the next post is a friend—I will not be questioned now. But when the watch changes in a few minutes, it'll be different."

"Will you go with us, Nai-nai?" asked Yuwen.

The woman made a gesture. "There you go again! No, I cannot leave. But I thank you from my heart."

"Your name—so that I can remember it in my prayers?"

She shook her head. "No. Because I am ashamed of helping the Communists. But go! Please, my old mistress's son—go!"

Yuwen and the cook retraced their steps. They did not see the sergeant again at the gate. Nobody bothered to question them there.

The next day, Government troops came by airlift and arrested the puppet incumbents, as well as the previous puppet magistrate, Ma Pingshi. They ordered the puppet garrison to assemble the following morning to receive instructions.

But that night, all the puppet forces in the area went over to the Communists.

Four

Yuwen returned to Shanghai with a secret resolve based on an old Chinese saying: "So long as I live, I vow never to share the same sky and sunshine with the Communists." He did not hate the Communists as individuals. He did not even hate Ta-kong or Mei-yin. He hated the system that had made them what they were, and he was determined to devote all his efforts toward destroying that system or perish in the attempt.

When Li-hwa rejoined him a little later with the children, for the first time in his life he hid something from her. He told her about his mother's tragic death, but made no mention of Ta-kong's part in the tragedy. And he said nothing about his secret resolve.

Fully aware of the strength of the Communists and their menace to the nation, Yuwen understood their designs on Manchuria and the reasons for their close collaboration with Russia. In his estimation, all North China was lost beyond recovery. The Government might send troops by airlift, retake key cities in token occupation, even keep vital communication lines in operation. But the vast countryside would be under Communist control. The situation indeed fit the Communist slogan: "Let them occupy the points! Let them occupy the lines! Ours will be the whole surface!"

Sooner or later the Communists would have their way. First the lines would be cut to pieces, then the points would be blotted out. And like a roaring sea the surface would rise and submerge all before it. . . .

Yuwen wanted to make the whole nation share his sense of imminent peril. But he found himself making very little progress.

At first, he pinned his hope on Chiang Kai-shek and the Kuomintang, and rewrote the article he had so carefully prepared in Chungking. He toned down his criticisms of the Government, laying much greater stress on the Communist threat. He advocated his proposed reforms strongly, but argued that they would enable the Government to gain broader popular support in its struggle against the Communists. The article was no longer a challenge to Chiang Kai-shek and the Kuomintang; it was an appeal.

But then Yuwen ran into unexpected difficulties. The Unequal

Treaties between China and the Western nations had been abrogated as a result of the war, the Concessions had been fully restored to Chinese sovereignty, and the city of Shanghai, with its five million people, was being administered as a single local administrative unit—with a mayor appointed by Chiang. This restoration was as it should be; but Yuwen now found disturbing consequences resulting from the change. Disgrace and humiliation to China as the Concessions had undoubtedly been, they had at least permitted some measure of freedom of the press. This was no longer the case. Yuwen could find no one who would publish his article. All important newspapers, periodicals, and even the major publishing houses—except the one paper allowed to the Communists—had become Kuomintang-controlled; and Yuwen's article, even in its modified form, was not acceptable.

Then he thought of putting his views before the Political Advisory Council, and took a trip to Nanking specifically for this purpose. No sooner had he arrived than he was called in by the Kuomintang and told to suppress his proposed speech. The American Government, through a special mission headed by General Marshall, was then trying its hardest to effect a compromise between the Government and the Communists. It would not do for Yuwen to express such views at this juncture. It might lead the Americans to think mistakenly that the Government was acting behind the scenes and had urged him to make the speech to disrupt the negotiations.

He returned to Shanghai frustrated, but he did what he could through the speeches he had occasion to make in public. The country at large, however, looked calm and peaceful on the surface. The Communists branded him a warmonger; and the general public, exhausted by a foreign war and fearful of a civil one, shied away from him as a prophet of gloom and doom.

In the meantime, heady with the triumph over the Japanese, the Government was going full tilt in a direction exactly opposite to what Yuwen would have wished. Chang Fa-foo, now Chancellor of the Government University in Shanghai, still visited him and Li-hwa occasionally, but they no longer needed his inside information to perceive the failings of the Kuomintang. Corruption in high places was the talk of the town, and the repressive actions of the secret police became daily more unjustifiable, more reprehensible, more widespread. The Government, by alienating the people more and more, was bringing the Communist danger nearer.

Yuwen felt like a man watching a gang of robbers approach his house; all the household was asleep, and he—the only man awake—was deprived of his voice and unable to arouse them.

One evening he returned home to Li-hwa, more gloomy and indignant than ever. It seemed a Professor Li, whom the college had left in charge during the Japanese occupation and who was reputed to be a millionaire in his own right, had bought some very valuable property during the occupation from one John Hunt, an American. The American, of course, was then in a concentration camp, but he had sold the property to Li through an agent, and the deed was signed by Hunt himself.

"Well, a few weeks ago," Yuwen continued, "a commercial company owned by Amy Tong—Tong Hsi's wife—told Li he had acquired the property through fraud, that it rightfully belonged to the company. After much argument, Li was persuaded to go see Amy Tong herself and take his title along. She received him alone, and when he produced the documents she flew into a rage and threw them into a fireplace, where they at once were burnt to ashes. Li threatened to go to court, but she just laughed. She said if he did, she would charge him with being an enemy collaborator."

"How terrible!" exclaimed Li-hwa. "Can't Li do something?"

"What can he do? Without those documents, it's his word against hers. And you know what would happen, with the courts in Kuomintang control. At any rate, Li doesn't dare go to court with the threat of collaboration hanging over him—and that backed by none other than Amy Tong! If he persisted, he'd surely run into far worse trouble than the mere loss of property."

"That's indeed awful—but no worse than what our neighbor Mrs. Wang told me today. The Wangs have only a small business, you know. They had some merchandise stored in a warehouse near the wharf—it represented about two-thirds of everything they possessed. Apparently, the Japanese Navy had commandeered part of the warehouse to store some of its supplies, and now our Navy has taken it over and sealed off the whole building, claiming that *all* the goods inside are enemy property. The Wangs also have documents to prove their ownership, as Professor Li did, and they've petitioned the Navy again and again. For three months now, the Navy has simply refused to listen. Mrs. Wang begged me to ask you to use your influence as a member of the Political Advisory Council. She left the papers with me."

Yuwen examined them and found them genuine. He flared up,

"This is a simple matter that should have taken only a week, at most, to check and settle. My God! It's things like these—this and what Amy Tong did—that make the people lose their confidence in the Government. Just look how popular sentiment in Shanghai has changed, scarcely three months after Victory Day! Remember, how in the flush of the triumph Chiang Kai-shek paid the city a flying visit—what a wild and joyful welcome the people gave him then! You and I both saw with our own eyes how they hailed him as a national hero; millions lined the streets for a sight of him, and thousands wept openly and struggled just to touch his clothes, as if his very person were sacred.

"And what do the people think of his Government now? They're calling all the officials Chungking Men—after the Peking Man! A fine thing, to be compared to a man supposed to have lived about a million years ago—who was certainly more brute than man. And the people say these Chungking Men are interested in nothing but appropriating for themselves the five Chih—Fan Chih, swanky houses to live in; T'iao Chih, gold bars to accumulate; Ch'eh Chih, automobiles to ride in; Lu Chih, women to enjoy; and Hsi Chih, actresses to amuse themselves with. O God! What is our country coming to? And this, with the Communist evil threatening to engulf us all at any moment!"

Li-hwa attempted to cheer him up. "The Americans are trying to help us. They may force our Government to adopt some reforms."

"Who can help those who don't help themselves? Who can force anyone to reform who does not want to reform himself?"

"But the people haven't lost faith in Chiang Kai-shek."

"What's the good of being a leader if he can't control his own men? People like Tong Hsi and his wife are still in the Government; there's little change of high personnel for years. Take Uncle Chi—there is a man worthy of our admiration! We know what he was, but the war opened his eyes and he has completely mended his ways. Why can't Chiang be as good as the mere head of a secret Society, a gangster? I don't mind saying I'm beginning to lose my faith in Chiang. . . ."

Nevertheless, the next day he started working for the release of Wang's merchandise. He plodded from authority to authority, to no avail. Then one evening about a fortnight later, Mrs. Wang rushed to the Lans' house in tears. Her husband had kept a constant watch over the warehouse, she said. The night before, the Navy had sent over some lorries, broken the seals off the warehouse and carted away the merchandise, then sealing the building anew. Her husband had followed the lorries to a shop not far away, apparently owned by some men connected with the Navy, and the merchandise was now being sold there as its own goods!

Bitterness filled Yuwen, and at once he wrote a strong letter to the Standing Committee of the Political Advisory Council.

The letter went unanswered. The Committee had received too many such letters, and simply passed them over to the Government. But popular resentment, though suppressed in newspapers and publications, had so grown by this time that the Government was at last compelled to do something. As before in Chungking, it minimized the matter, making no drastic change in its personnel and no attempt to seek out the wrongdoers and punish them. It merely made a scapegoat of the incumbent mayor of the city and replaced him with another.

Yuwen was thoroughly disgruntled. But the new mayor actually turned out to be someone up to his own standards of what a public servant should be. Though his powers were limited to local administration, he introduced some sincere reforms of which Yuwen approved. In his eagerness to grasp at anything that would bolster his faith in Chiang Kai-shek, Yuwen welcomed this improvement and felt a glow of new hope.

Besides, his time was now occupied with other matters. He was elected president of his college, and the unfamiliar duties of his office kept him busy for days. Then, with the local administration of Shanghai at last somewhat bettered, a new circumstance developed that made him feel the Communist threat more keenly than ever. This time the danger did not appear from far off; it turned up right on the campus of his college.

The tempo of unrest in Shanghai had been rising in an alarming and seemingly uncheckable crescendo. Not a week passed without a demonstration, a strike, or a riot of some kind. Yuwen felt instinctively that the disturbances were Communist-inspired, but what troubled him most was that the students of his own college participated in them.

Could Shanghai, so far from the Communist-controlled areas, be so heavily infiltrated by Communists? Yuwen suspected it was. Ever since the days when Ta-kong headed the Eastern Bureau, the Communists had concentrated on Shanghai; it was the economic and industrial center of China, and produced more than half the total revenue of the Government. If they could create constant turmoil, they could disrupt industrial output, bring about economic and social chaos, and thus weaken the Government's strength and shake the people's confidence in it.

For this purpose, they had been relying mainly on two groups which they had helped to organize and extensively infiltrated—the labor unions, and especially the student associations, which they considered the more effective. The students were better educated and therefore more able to stir up the public; and the people, usually inclined to be more sympathetic toward the young, were likely to overlook the students' excesses more than the workmen's.

But Yuwen was alert to the danger at his own door. Typically, he did not try at the outset to prevent his students from joining in the disturbances. Trained in philosophy, as he was, he began studying Communism in earnest. He re-read many of the Communist books and also read some he had not read before, from the writings of Marx and Lenin down to those of Stalin and Mao Tse-tung—anything he could get hold of. But this time he read from a different angle. He did not study them for their philosophy, which he knew was spurious; he studied them with the specific view of probing deep into the Communist system or organization and their tactics of subversion. Finally, after almost a year had elapsed, he felt he had learned enough to enable him to put his ideas to a test in his own college.

First, he minutely screened the personnel of his faculty, making sure none of them had Communist leanings, and also took pains to know as many students, individually, as possible, and made them feel he was one of them. Then he introduced the practice of Wednesday mass-meetings, which he had learned from Ho the Central Hall in the high school in Yi. Unlike Ho the Central Hall, however, he did not lecture to the students; he let them elect their own presiding officers and run the discussions themselves. But he attended every meeting as one of them, with the same rights or privileges. Every possible issue of the day concerning either school or country was brought up for open discussion, if not by the students then by Yuwen himself. And where the students failed to analyze thoroughly, Yuwen would explain his own analysis of the issue, never mentioning the Communists but anticipating every turn and twist they could take. He never requested the students to accept any specific interpretation; he let them make their own decisions by the simple rule of majority. Before long, the student body of the college was able to withstand all the pressure the Communists applied to them.

Of course the Communists could not permit this to go on. They centered their attention on Yuwen's college, sending many of their ablest young agents to enroll in the guise of students. But Yuwen was able to spot them quickly, expose them to their fellow students, and have them expelled.

Then Yuwen turned the tables on the Communists. He had now learned their technique so well that he could put it down systematically in writing. He made copies of this exposé and started distributing them among the authorities of other colleges and institutions, exhorting them to follow his example and rid their establishments of Communists.

In due course, a copy reached the desk of Chang Fa-foo. He was now head of the Communist Eastern Bureau, and he knew that if Yuwen's advice were followed it could spell an end to all Communist infiltration—not only in schools but also in labor unions, not only in Shanghai but everywhere else. Yuwen had become a threat to the very existence of the Communist Party. Urgently Chang reported the matter to the High Command and proposed that Yuwen be put out of the way at once.

2

THE REPLY FROM the High Command came swiftly. Yuwen had learned too much; the sooner he was destroyed, the better. But he was too prominent an anti-Communist—if anything happened to him, suspicion inevitably would fall on the Communists. Moreover, the Party was on the point of breaking off negotiations with the Government, and at this particular moment it was especially important to avoid making a bad impression on the people. There was no question that Yuwen had to be done away with, but in some way so that the blame would be placed squarely on the shoulders of the Kuomintang.

Chang Fa-foo cudgeled his brains until all at once he remembered what Amy had once proposed. He made due preparations, and then went to call on her.

Amy now spent most of her time not in Nanking with her husband but in her luxurious home at Shanghai. She had recovered all her lost properties, and actually had gained even more. All these assets had been converted into solid, dependable foreign exchange and been safely deposited in foreign banks. Fully prepared for a quick getaway, she found she could not take the final step. The older she grew, the sharper was her greed. Therefore she was particularly unhappy to see Chang Fa-foo.

After the usual exchange of insincere banter, she asked him curtly what he wanted this time.

In reply Chang produced a paper which looked somewhat like a news magazine. It was one of the "Mosquito Papers," so-called because they could bite at anyone and anything. With the rigid Government control of publications, many irresponsible and disreputable literary hacks were driven to use these vulgar and sometimes obscene journals to make a living; they were printed furtively in obscure printing shops and distributed through perambulatory hawkers.

"I never read such trash!" Amy said. But as a matter of fact, she was addicted to Mosquito Papers because she enjoyed gossip and because her dissolute nature took pleasure in things lewd and sordid.

"But this concerns you," said Chang Fa-foo. "Read it."

Amy began a casual perusal, and was startled into attention. She read it again with great care. It was not put out in the usual cheap print of most Mosquito Papers; it was well printed and excellently written in a style that was vaguely familiar to her. She had no idea that the paper was fresh out of a Communist press and that the authors had done their best to imitate Yuwen's style. The whole paper consisted of only one article—an account of the postwar doings of Amy and Tong Hsi.

It was not slander, but completely factual data substantiated with names, places, and figures. Among other things, it detailed how many "Enemy Properties" the Tongs had taken over on behalf of the Government and then sold for personal gain. It listed how much foreign exchange they had procured under one guise or another, in flagrant violation of the control laws proclaimed by the Government. The author concluded with the promise of another installment to follow soon, which would lay bare the whole past of the Tongs.

"O God!" Amy exclaimed. "Who wrote this?"

"Why, the writer's name is on the back cover. Can't you read the characters?"

"Of course I can read the characters, but I don't recognize them."

"Pronounce the name," directed Chang Fa-foo.

Amy did so. Though the characters were different, the syllables rang in her ears: Lan Yuwen!

426

"That contemptible dog! Why didn't he use his own name?"

"And be sued for libel?"

"I'll have the paper banned at once!"

"I know of no better way of making it popular. The whole country will be agog for the appearance of the next article."

"Yes," Amy admitted ruefully. "The second article must be prevented at any cost. I must go to Nanking at once and consult with Hsi!"

Chang Fa-foo left, deeming it no longer necessary to press the point.

Three nights later, Amy and Tong Hsi had a single dinner guest in their official mansion in Nanking. This was the little-publicized Chief of Secret Police of the Government, an inconspicuous, swarthy man in his forties. His only notable characteristic was his skin—a ghastly blue in color—like the blue of death.

After dinner they returned to the drawing room, and because of their intimate relationship Amy did not mince words. Bluntly she came out with her proposition to put an end to Lan Yuwen. The man had always been critical of the Government, he had proved an inveterate troublemaker, he should have been disposed of long ago. To make away with him would be to render an invaluable service to the country.

To her surprise, the Chief of Secret Police was hesitant. "Madame," he said, "there is nothing I wouldn't do for you and the Minister. But right now we should perhaps let the matter wait." He eyed Tong Hsi significantly. "As the Minister probably knows, in spite of the Americans' mediation, negotiations between the Government and the Communists have utterly collapsed. The Communists in Manchuria have completed their training under the Russians, and the Russians have given them enormous military stockpiles which they seized from the Japanese. The Communists are now ready for the first time to engage our forces in positional warfare, and fighting should flare up at any moment. If we win, well and good; if we lose, Heaven knows what may happen. That's why Generalissimo Chiang Kai-shek has sent all our crack troops to Manchuria and left the South nearly defenseless. That's why he himself has gone to Peking to direct the operations. Under these circumstances, Madame, we have to be extremely careful in the rear— we must not precipitate any trouble, such as the arrest of a prominent man like Lan Yuwen would stir up."

"Who asks you to arrest him?" asked Amy.

"My mistake," answered the man, his blue face turning bluer. "Let's say—his disappearance. The result will be the same. It will create an uproar."

"That's precisely why I've chosen this particular time. The outbreak of war will cause so much excitement that the people will pay no attention to minor eruptions. The disappearance of Lan Yuwen, if you handle it right, as I know you can, will be hardly noticed."

"But what if Generalissimo Chiang hears of it?"

"He is not here, is he? Besides, he will be so busy at the front he'll have no time for trifles in the rear. We have covered up for you in the past, haven't we? What are you afraid of?"

The face of the Chief of Secret Police remained expressionless. He could hardly say that from other intelligence he suspected Tong Hsi and Amy's backing could not be depended upon much longer.

"What is your wish, Minister?"

"Do as my wife asks, please," replied Tong Hsi. "Her judgment in such matters is infallible."

The Chief sighed. Though he might feel the day of Tong Hsi and Amy's influence in the Government were numbered, there was no telling about Chinese politics. This pair had squeezed out of many a tight corner in their long career; they might yet manage to again. To play safe, he decided to put all the cards on the table.

"Though you have not said so, Madame, would it be indiscreet if I asked whether the most recent cause of your anger against Lan Yuwen is an article, allegedly written by him?"

Tong Hsi paled, but Amy's face was inscrutable. "Who told you so?" she asked calmly.

"No offense, Madame. My job is to know. I am informed that while you bought most of the copies off the market, a few have unfortunately fallen into the hands of your enemies inside the Kuomintang. They are reprinting the article and distributing it in the highest circles. They are talking about formal impeachment."

In his eagerness to exploit Amy for his own purpose, the Chief of Secret Police had overshot the mark. Tong Hsi's face went dead white.

"What of it?" Amy retorted. "This is not the first time we've been under attack—nor, I am sure, will it be the last."

"I am ever a great admirer of your courage and sagacity, Madame —but you may need it all now. Your enemies have sent special agents down to Shanghai to investigate, and it is said that they've found all the facts in the article confirmed by the records in the Government archives."

Just then there came a tap at the door, and Amy's confidential servant appeared.

"I would not have disturbed Your Excellencies, but Chancellor Chang Fa-foo has just arrived from Shanghai and wants to see Madame at once."

Behind the servant's back, Amy saw Chang's lanky shadow in the hallway. The Chief of Secret Police rose.

"I thank you for a very enjoyable evening—our conversation has been most enlightening. I'm sorry I have another appointment; perhaps we can resume our discussion at a more convenient date."

Amy extended him a limp hand, but Tong Hsi could scarcely stand up to bid him good-by.

Chang had already brushed past him into the room. At the sight of Tong Hsi, he drew up short. Absorbed in the urgency of his own mission, he had not bothered to find out whether Amy was alone.

"It's good to see you, dear old comrade," Tong Hsi mumbled. "What brings you here?"

"To see you two friends, of course," answered Chang with a seeming heartiness. "You look well." He cast a sidelong glance at Amy and she shrugged, indicating that she could not help her husband's presence.

"Oh, no," Tong Hsi said spiritlessly. "I am not well. I am very tired."

"Then why don't you retire?" said Chang. "I don't mind. I can talk with Amy. My taxi is waiting outside, and I have to catch the next train back to Shanghai."

Tong Hsi looked at the clock on the mantel. "Then you have only a quarter of an hour to be with us. I have too few chances to talk with you."

Amy stared at her husband. "You do look terribly ill, darling Hsi. Why don't you go to bed and let me entertain our old friend alone?"

"I need company to get away from my own thoughts," said Tong stubbornly, shaking his head. "I want to be with Brother Chang for this short while."

The clock ticked on, and Chang Fa-foo looked desperate.

Amy took Tong Hsi firmly by the arm. "Be a good boy, darling. Go to your bed!"

With a sudden outburst of childish rebelliousness, Tong Hsi

shook her off. "You have treated me all my life like a small boy.
I am not a boy—I'm a man!"

Tong Hsi had never behaved like this before. Amy tried to pull
him up roughly from his seat. "Can't you see that whatever I do is
all for your good? Can't you see Brother Chang will not feel at ease
while you remain here?"

A light of cunning stole into Tong Hsi's eyes, and he sank back
on the sofa. His corpulent body was too much for Amy. "What
is there between you two?" he demanded. "I have heard that you've
been meeting each other very often in Shanghai. And why this
hurried trip here tonight, Chang? Either you tell me your business,
or I'll stay here all night if need be!"

A cruel grin spread over Chang's gray cheeks. He had no fear of
this man; his hold over Amy was enough. "Well, my good friend,
I do have private business with your wife. If you won't leave us,
you'll have to hear it, too."

Then he turned to Amy. "I want all the Government's military
plans for the forthcoming campaign in Manchuria. I want them
delivered to me within three days."

"What do you want those plans for?" Tong Hsi demanded,
shooting up from the sofa in fright.

Chang Fa-foo glared at him impatiently. "Amy knows why I want
them. Don't try standing in my way now. I want the plans delivered the same way the other information has been delivered
these past years."

Tong Hsi looked at Amy in disbelief. She averted her face.

"All along, the Government has suspected a leakage of its military
secrets," Tong Hsi said slowly. "So it's you—you, my wife! Why did
you do it?"

Chang Fa-foo said coldly, "Because I have a hold over her, my old
friend, and it's a hold over you, too. I have no time to explain, but
unless you deliver the plans within three days, you'll find a pretty
tight noose around your fat neck, just as she'll find one around hers!"

"But you are a Kuomintang yourself," Tong Hsi said. "Oh, my
God, you're not a Kuomintang! You're a Communist spy!"

Chang Fa-foo laughed as Tong Hsi drew back in horror and
fell on the sofa, gasping for breath. Tong's features contorted and
he started up, then fell back in the convulsion of a paralytic stroke.
He could neither move nor speak; only his eyes were alive.

Amy hurried toward the door, but Chang Fa-foo stopped her.
"Do I get those plans?"

430

"Please, I must send for a doctor!"

"You can do that afterward. Finish this business first."

"How can I get them now, with him so ill?"

"I'll show you what a good friend I am, Amy. I know you've been planning to make a getaway for a long time, but you've never had a ghost of a chance with all our men watching you. Before you could set your pretty feet on a plane or a ship, we'd have you stopped and denounced. But if you deliver the goods within the prescribed time, I'll let you go. Tell the Government you have to take your husband abroad for medical treatment, and we will let you go scot-free."

"How can I trust you not to go back on your word?"

Chang Fa-foo smiled. "You're a clever woman, Amy. You should be able to reason it out for yourself. After you've done this, we'll have no further need of your services. And if you and your husband go and live abroad with your ill-gotten wealth, we can always point to you in our propaganda as concrete examples of Kuomintang corruption. That way, you'll be more useful to us alive than dead. May you live long and well!"

Amy hung her head in silent agreement, and Tong Hsi stared wildly with his glittering eyes, unable to speak.

Five

AMY AND HER paralyzed husband went abroad safely. Manchuria was lost to the Communists, and the cream of Chiang Kai-shek's troops were wiped out in a single pitched battle near Shanhaikwan, which separates Manchuria from North China.

At first the Government tried hard to conceal this disastrous defeat from the public. But there was another grave matter it could not possibly hush up. The Government had relied too heavily and too long on the printing press, and the country was now suffering under the accumulated woes of its worst inflation. But what was more, the Government could no longer afford to print the old currency, known as the Fapi. It required special papers and ink which had to be imported from abroad, so that the Fapi actually was costing the Government more in foreign exchange than its nominal worth. In desperation, and without seeking some basic remedy, in August of 1948 the Government suddenly announced the issuance of a new currency, the Gold Yuan. The Fapi was to be converted to the Gold Yuan at twenty thousand to one. In addition, anyone who owned foreign exchange, or gold in any form weighing more than two ounces, must surrender it to the Government in exchange for Gold Yuan at a fixed ratio. And all commodity prices, regardless of consideration of supply and demand, were to be frozen from the date of proclamation. Violations of these orders were to be summarily punished by death.

Yuwen realized that this so-called Gold Yuan Reform was no reform at all, but he was in the minority. The people had suffered too much from the old Fapi; they still retained a lingering faith in the Government, and blindly hoped the Gold Yuan would turn out to be a salvation. For days and days, within the period designated by the Government, hundreds of thousands lined up before the Government banks, waiting patiently for their turn to convert their Fapi, or gold, or foreign exchange, into Gold Yuan. Yuwen had little to exchange. His savings were insignificant, the scanty jewelry Li-hwa possessed was not of gold, and the gold wedding ring he had given her weighed less than the proscribed two ounces.

Barely two months passed before catastrophe struck. The Government had gone a-printing again, and the Gold Yuan was flooding the market—just as the old Fapi had before. Though prices were still frozen, all commodities had vanished. The public had emptied the shops of all goods in a desperate attempt to preserve the value of their money, and shops were unable to replenish their stocks at the old prices. Foodstuffs disappeared in the same fashion, and the populace was struck with stark terror. Thousands were imprisoned by the Government for violations of the Reform, and quite a few publicly executed. But all in vain. At last the Government was forced to rescind its order and give up the pathetic self-styled Reform, but not before countless millions had been bankrupted and ruined, and the last shred of confidence in the leadership of Chiang Kai-shek and the Kuomintang was lost.

After the resumption of hostilities, the Communists had stopped all open agitation in Shanghai for fear of reprisal, and for a brief time Yuwen was no longer troubled with their subversive activities in his college. But he was confronted by a far more frightening picture—of all China being lost to the Communists. What was he to do?

If the Communists were to conquer the whole of China, he would not even have a foothold to fight from. It did not occur to him to flee—he lacked the money, and if he fled he could not fight. But if he stayed, he knew what awaited him—he would be denied every freedom and sooner or later liquidated.

There *was* one thing he could do. He could track down Ho Ta-kong—the man he used to call Big Brother—and Yin Mei-yin. Not merely to revenge his mother, but to perform the final service he could render his country. . . .

Li-hwa's worries, on the other hand, were more concrete. The inflation which had reduced the national currency to one-millionth of its former value had swallowed up their meager savings overnight. The salary from the college was paid in paper money, worth hardly anything. For more than two months they had been living on jewelry she had sold without Yuwen's knowledge. There was nothing left except her wedding ring, and it wrung her heart to think that in a short time she would have to part with it too. She refused to think what might happen afterward.

Yuwen returned for supper and Li-hwa did her best to look cheerful, but all through the frugal meal he appeared pensive.

"What makes the philosopher so glum today?" she asked after the boys had gone to the kitchen to clean up the dishes.

Yuwen attempted a smile. "I was thinking of our friends in the North—Dr. Holt, Uncle Chi, and Aunt Jasmine. We haven't heard from them for some time—I hope everything is all right."

"Of course it is. Dr. Holt is an American, and the Communists will think twice before they do an American harm. As for the Chis, who else can take better care of himself and his own?"

"You may be right. But I had two most surprising visitors today who gave me some very disturbing information. The first was Chang Fa-foo, who came in like his old self with what he called 'the inside dope.' According to him, the Government commander in Peking is negotiating for a surrender to the Communists, and only feeble resistance by some of Chiang's remaining troops is expected at the big port city. This will enable the Communists to join their main force in Manchuria with their guerrillas in North China. Then they'll make a dash for Nanking and Shanghai, and in Chang's estimation it should take them no more than a month or two to capture both cities."

"He may be exaggerating as usual."

"No, my dear, not this time, I am afraid. Then he asked what my plans are, and I said I intended to remain here as long as possible,

433

and then, if Shanghai falls, to try to remove the college farther south beyond the reach of the Communists, as we moved to Chungking once before. He ridiculed this, predicting the Communists would occupy the whole country before the year is out. No, the only thing for me, he said, is to stay in Shanghai and work with the Communists. I was shocked and told him so—I had never expected to hear such advice from him, a Kuomintang. And how he laughed! Then he gave me the surprise of my life. He said he is a Communist!"

"Chang Fa-foo a Communist!" exclaimed Li-hwa.

"Yes, and a very old one. He confessed quite proudly that he's been a Communist almost since the founding of the Chinese Communist Party. He said bluntly he didn't mind admitting this to my face because I couldn't do him any harm; the Kuomintang has always considered him a loyal member and me an undesirable element."

"Oh!"

"He also said he'd been directed to approach me on behalf of the Communist High Command. In spite of my anti-Communist stand, apparently the Party has decided to forgive me. They feel I'm a well-known figure, and would like nothing better than to have me work with them after their conquest of China. I thought it wise not to answer too quickly, so I said I'd give the proposition serious consideration."

"I begin to understand Chang now," mused Li-hwa. "His being a Communist explains many of his past actions—"

"That's not all, though. Half an hour later, who should turn up in my office but the Chief of the Government Secret Police! He came to warn me that the situation in Nanking and Shanghai soon might become very grave, and that I and my family are forbidden to leave the city without express Government permission. He said if men of my standing were known to have fled, it might further shake the confidence of the people. So, you and I and our children are now under close surveillance by the Secret Police."

Li-hwa could hardly conceal her concern. "What are we going to do?"

"Well," Yuwen said dismally, "the Government has forbidden us to leave. The Communists have invited us to remain. And we have no money to go anywhere anyway. If the worst comes to worst, we may have to accept Chang Fa-foo's offer."

"You can't mean that!"

When Yuwen did not answer, Li-hwa went on, "This is not like you, Yuwen. If I know your thoughts at all, you think the Communists will use men like you for the moment to delude the people —and once they've consolidated their control they'll liquidate all independent-thinking men without mercy."

Yuwen still said nothing. "And your concern for the Reverend Dr. Holt and Uncle Chi and Aunt Jasmine has betrayed your thinking," Li-hwa persisted.

Yuwen summoned cheerfulness to his face. "I can never keep anything from you, dearest."

"No, ever since you returned to Yi and learned of Mother Lan's tragic death you've acted strangely," she said. "I know your bitterness against the Communists, but there's something more than that. Can't you tell me?"

For a second he thought of confiding the whole truth about Ta-kong, but then he reasoned that there was no need for her to suffer too.

"It's really nothing," he answered briskly. "Still there's one thing we can do. On the slim chance that Chang Fa-foo may be right—may it please God that he turns out wrong—we must move our college to Canton despite the warning of the Secret Police; that hasn't frightened me but only made me aware of the gravity of the situation. I'll go to the trustees and ask if they can raise the necessary funds, and then I'll secure official permission for the move from the Ministry of Education."

But although Yuwen applied himself feverishly to this task, his labors were of little avail. Most of the Trustees had been bankrupted by the inflation. Then the dreaded news came that the big port city in the North had fallen. The Peking commander had surrendered to the Communists without a fight. And still Yuwen and Li-hwa had heard not a word from either the Reverend Dr. Holt or the Chis.

But they were deep in their own troubles too. The family finances had been reduced to such straits that Li-hwa could no longer delay parting with her wedding ring. She planned to go to the black market that very day.

2

THE DOORBELL BUZZED, and when Li-hwa answered there were Old Head and Jasmine. Jasmine looked older and a little fatigued, but Old Head—now well over seventy—was as jaunty as ever.

Li-hwa seized each by the hand, and forgot her troubles. She also forgot that there was no food in the house. Old Head chuckled, and said he had to talk to her alone. A while later the two boys returned from school, and finally Yuwen. He brightened up as soon as he saw the unexpected guests.

"No questions now, philosopher," Old Head told him. "I'll tell you everything by-and-by. First of all, we're going to have dinner in the best restaurant in Shanghai. I know how poor you college presidents are, and I have a private room already reserved. I'm hungry as a starved ox."

They had the most expensive dinner Shanghai could provide. It gave Old Head and Jasmine pleasure, as it gave Yuwen pain, to watch the two boys eat so voraciously. He silently wondered where and when they would have a meal like this again, and marveled too how Li-hwa could look so at ease. But Old Head was plying him with wine. Finally Yuwen could stand the suspense no longer.

"How did you escape, Uncle Chi?" he whispered.

Old Head roared in reply, "Why do you speak like a thief plotting a crime? The Secret Police won't hear you—all the adjoining rooms are occupied by my disciples."

Yuwen expressed surprise the Government authorities had not warned them against leaving the port city.

Old Head laughed. "The Mayor gave me a private dinner and hinted gently that I'd leave at my own peril. But what could he and the Secret Police do to *me?* We stayed as long as I thought it safe, and when it was safe no longer we made our way here."

"And what are your plans now?"

"We're going to Hong Kong."

"Is that safe? Once the Communists conquer all China, the British Crown Colony may be next."

"No. I have reason to believe that the Communists will not try to take Hong Kong for a long time."

Then, at last, Yuwen asked if they had heard anything about the Reverend Dr. Holt.

Jasmine answered this sadly. "We wrote and pleaded with him to come with us. Brother Ox even sent a special messenger to Yi to warn him that the Communist Hate-America campaign is genuine— that under Communist rule no freedom of worship is possible and it would be far wiser for him to get away while he could. But he simply refused to listen. Now, may his God preserve him well!"

436

Old Head sighed. "You know, you Christians are crazy—I can't understand it but I admire it; some day I may decide to become a Christian myself. But now, Yuwen, what are your plans?"

Yuwen told of his unsuccessful attempt to raise funds to move his college to Canton.

Old Head nodded. "Of course. Your plans will never work out, though. Who is going to squander his money on a lost cause? I have inside information—not only from the Communists but also from Government circles—Chiang Kai-shek is going to flee to Taiwan, and Heaven knows how long he'll be able to hold that tiny island. The entire mainland will be lost before the year is over."

"What should I do then, Uncle Chi?" asked Yuwen spiritlessly.

"I have everything arranged for you. You'll come with us tonight —on the steamship we have booked for Hong Kong. I've already bought four extra tickets."

"Hong Kong? Tonight? That's impossible, Uncle Chi! Not to speak of other matters, don't you know that my family and I are being watched by the Secret Police?"

Old Head smiled. "It's not for nothing I've been in Shanghai two days before coming to you. Three of those police are now being entertained by some of my disciples in the restaurant across the street. Before the meal is over, they'll be dead drunk. As for embarking on the ship, I have seen to that too."

"But what about my college? My colleagues? No, Uncle Chi, I can't do it."

"That's one thing I didn't think of beforehand," said Old Head. He frowned for a moment, then grinned. "I can't give you money to move your college to Canton or elsewhere in China—that would just be so much down the drain. But when we get to Hong Kong, I'll donate all the funds you need to establish another college there, and you can write your colleagues to join you."

Yuwen was speechless.

"What more have you to say, philosopher?" asked Old Head.

"Please don't think I'm ungrateful, Uncle Chi—you're about the most wonderful person I've ever had the honor to know—but I can't accept your proposal. Take Li-hwa and the boys with you. Look after them well, as I know you and Aunt Jasmine will. But I cannot go."

"Why?"

"Because I feel that as a Chinese, my place is in China and nowhere else. I must fight my battles here. I must live and die here. I must continue to speak out against the Communists as I have spoken against the Kuomintang. I can do that best if I stay here."

"Perhaps you are saying this with your eyes open," said Old Head reflectively. "Perhaps not. But you are even more of a marked man with the Communists than I. Not to speak of your strong anti-Communist stand, you wrote a little dissertation about their tactics which they don't like at all. Just for that, if for nothing else, they will liquidate you for sure."

Yuwen expected Li-hwa to make a vehement objection, but she remained curiously silent.

Old Head said, "And you have the example of your late father-in-law. Why can't you go abroad and try to stage a comeback like him?"

"Things are different now. In my revered father-in-law's days, China was ruled by warlords. Bad as they were, he could return to China from Malaya at any time he wished. But if we leave China now I'm afraid we can never return until Communism is overthrown. To fight Communism effectively, one must do it on one's own soil and among one's own people. No, Uncle Chi, let me stay here."

Yuwen's own voice was choking, but he was proud that Li-hwa spoke no word of protest.

Old Head looked at him carefully. "As I said before, there is some craziness in men like you that I admire. If that's what you want, Yuwen, that's what you want. I ordered a special wine to celebrate the occasion. Now I use it to bid you farewell. Waiter, the wine!"

Old Head served the wine himself, giving even the two boys a cup. He served Yuwen last. With everybody standing, he bumped his own cup against Yuwen's merrily.

"Let's all drink together. May we have a reunion sooner than you think!"

They all drank.

A minute later Yuwen murmured, "Li-hwa . . . darling . . ." and slumped unconscious on his seat.

When Yuwen woke next morning, he was at sea with his family on their way to Hong Kong. . . .

Six

THE REVEREND DR. HOLT had ample warning, in that year of 1948, that the Communists were coming to the city of Yi. Chi Teh-shan and Jasmine wrote him repeatedly, urging him to leave; his Mission headquarters notified him that the United States Government had ordered the evacuation of all American nationals from China. This meant that financial support of the Mission would be indefinitely suspended, and if Holt stayed he would be on his own.

But the once-redheaded missionary from Newton, Iowa, had been in China so long he felt he was more Chinese than American. This was his home, and these his people. He gave no thought to personal danger; he would not court martyrdom, but neither did he fear it. At most, he could not have many more years to live. Ever since that distant time of the Boxer Rebellion when he had been so miraculously saved from death at the last moment, the Reverend Dr. Holt had considered his continuing earthly existence only a renewed lease on life by the grace of God; therefore it should be wholly dedicated to God's service, without reserve. . . .

So he stayed. Financially, he was not worried. After the Japanese war, Mission headquarters had approved his purchase of the House of Ho and repaid him in full. In turn, he had refunded the contributions to Ah Wong, Anna, and the cook, and given the gatekeeper's share to his heirs. When he sent Widow Lan's portion to Yuwen and Li-hwa, it was promptly returned as a donation to the Mission, as Widow Lan would have wanted it to be. Holt kept this as an emergency fund, added to it his own savings, and since there was no modern bank in Yi, stored the money in a box in his bedroom.

The people of Yi knew the Communists were coming, and many of them called on him and begged him to stay. He could tell quickly which of his visitors were genuine and which were not. The genuine spoke of their own need of the Mission and his services; the false discussed politics. Some of them were Communist agents, others sympathizers. He listened to all, courteously. He would stay in Yi.

There was no resistance. The town of Yi fell quietly, without dramatics, without a shot, as soon as Peking surrendered; it lay inert and helpless, a victim of the creeping, insidious poison. In a short time everybody was calling everybody else "comrade." Streets and market places were given new names—the Lane of Eternal Stability was now called Lenin Lane. The little Communist army which took over Yi was exemplary in discipline and courtesy, in striking contrast to the rough Kuomintang troops. Trained Party cadres moved into the town's civil offices, acting honestly and working hard; Holt noted that all conspicuously lacked any sense of humor, but he conceded that the decadence of the old and rotten officialdom had been cleaned up.

He watched with interest and also misgivings the organization of the people. There were organizations for men, for women, for the old, the middle-aged, and the young—everybody was organized. Everybody was assigned work for the Cause: guarding a city gate, patrolling a street, watching for reactionaries, spying on his neighbor. Everybody had to attend discussion meetings. Communist dogma was dinned ceaselessly into the ears of the townspeople, who had to repeat it by rote and be prepared to be examined and interrogated. This was called "Study and Practice."

Everyone was required to make a clean breast of all past wrongdoings in deed and thought, in contrast to his now enlightened state —this was called "Open and White."

Those reckless souls who denied they had ever done anything wrong were not mistreated—they were merely subjected to questioning so endless that they had time neither for home nor business, and found themselves confronted by countless witnesses, friends, relatives, and acquaintances with better memories. In the end, everybody confessed and was then supposed to be happy again. They called this, "Speak and Accord."

It seemed to the Reverend Dr. Holt that the Communists were going out of their way to be kind and considerate toward him. True, his congregation was dwindling steadily. The people who had once attended his Sunday services were now out guarding a gate, or spying on a neighbor; they had no time for religious worship. But Holt hoped, charitably, that this would level off in time.

One thing he openly disliked. The city had been divided into "blocks," and each block had a leader. If a friend or a relative called at any house in a block, the visit had to be reported to the block leader within twenty-four hours. No doors were to be closed, even at night; the leader could walk in at any moment for a check on any house. American-born Logan J. Holt considered this an unwarranted intrusion upon personal privacy. Moreover, the more honorable citizens had not wished to become block leaders, and he saw that most of these posts had been given to people who formerly would have been considered the scum of society.

There were only three houses and Widow Lan's old shack on what had once been the Lane of Eternal Stability, but they were divided into two blocks—the shack and the House of Ho in one block, the Mission compound and the House of Ma in the other. The leader of Holt's block had been selected from the many residents now living in the House of Ma. Nobody remembered his real name, but everyone called him "Laughing Face" because he wore a constant expression of mirth. He was past thirty, a mason by trade, and had been a genuine workman, good-natured and honest. He took his duties seriously, but was never officious or fault-finding; Holt was sure he had been especially selected to impress the American.

The missionary also resented the fact that no one could go out of the city without a travel permit from the Public Safety Bureau. One had to apply to his block leader, giving full particulars about the proposed journey. The application was then submitted to the Public Safety Bureau.

Holt wanted to go to a nearby village to visit members of his church, and Laughing Face obligingly forwarded his request. Next day a uniformed official came from the Public Safety Bureau, with questions.

Why did the foreign comrade desire to make this trip? If his village friends were already Christians, why should he converse with them? They had work and discussion meetings, and their time was precious. There were reactionaries lurking in the countryside, eager to blame their atrocities upon the People's Government. Would not the foreign comrade consider his own safety, and withdraw the request?

Holt explained himself blue in the face. The Public Safety comrade was overwhelmingly solicitous, and spoke not one impolite word; he simply went on for hours, considering and arguing . . . if he issued the permit and something happened to the foreign comrade, he would die of remorse . . . he would be punished by his superiors . . .

In the end, Holt saw that it was hopeless and withdrew his request.

"Ah, I am so happy, foreign comrade!" exclaimed the Public Safety man. "You have spoken and accorded!"

Holt never applied again.

A dozen outspoken anti-Communists and a few suspected Kuo-mintang secret agents had been rounded up and taken away immediately after the fall of the city—nobody ever heard what happened to them—but the situation, for the most part, remained quiet. Then after a while, a campaign called "The Turnover of the Poor" was launched, and a score of the wealthier people—generally unpopular with the community—were singled out for severe punishment.

Ma Pingshi, the former puppet magistrate, was one of these. He was nearly sixty now; after the Japanese war he had been sentenced to three years' imprisonment by the Kuomintang Government as an enemy collaborator, but he had bribed his way out of prison half-way through the term and had been living in his ancestral house.

The Communists descended upon Pingshi. His wife and three children were sent to a Reform Camp, the location of which was secret. He and his mother—she was a fat, doddering woman in her late seventies—were each given a broom and ordered first to clean up the whole compound and then to leave it forever. This was called "Sweep the Floor and Leave the Door."

After that, workingmen and their families moved into the House of Ma. Ma Pingshi and his aged mother were allowed to move into Widow Lan's old shack, with its broken windows and leaking roof, and were given permission to beg for food on certain restricted streets. No beggar could beg outside his assigned area, and no one could give alms to a beggar not authorized to beg in that area.

However, Ma Pingshi and his mother were luckier than most. Impecuniousness had become politically fashionable in Yi; nobody was eager to give food to the "enemies of the proletariat" lest he be considered a reactionary. Beggars in other parts of town—many of them people who once had been rich—suffered terribly, but the two Mas could depend on the Reverend Dr. Holt. The missionary could not bear to see them starve, though it was difficult to feed them, especially after the Communists introduced a rigid system of ration-ing. Under this, the people were divided into several categories. For the Party cadre, there was abundant food; for the Dependables, the ration was adequate; for the Doubtfuls, it was not quite sufficient; for the Suspicious, it was a starvation diet.

Holt and his staff were classified as Doubtfuls. They had to tighten their own belts to feed Ma Pingshi and his mother, but feed them they did.

The missionary had grown accustomed to having no one at his

442

religious services except Ah Wong, Anna, and the cook. Patients had kept coming to his medical clinic in considerable numbers, but then one morning it was empty. Holt sent the cook out to ask his family what had happened; the cook's wife was dead, but he had many children.

He returned after dusk, infuriated. All his children had treated him more coldly than a stranger—there was total lack of Filial Piety. Finally a grandson—a boy of eight—had called him a foreign spy to his face.

The Mission compound expected danger, then. But nothing happened. Laughing Face made his regular inspections, and said nothing. The cook could still buy the regular food rations from the market; the other three stayed in the compound. The Reverend Dr. Holt, grown old and gray in the service of the Lord, looked far back down the years and remembered another time of ostracism, a half-century ago. . . .

But in those days he had been able to blame his troubles on one man—a man who, fortunately, had turned out to be rational, wise, and kind. He could not pinpoint his present troubles. No single man was responsible for what had happened to the Mission; there was only an organization. It was faceless, a stupendous and shapeless thing. And it had no heart.

2

EXCEPT FOR FORMOSA and a few small offshore islands, the Communists had completely mastered all of China by the spring of 1950. This was the fiftieth year of the Reverend Dr. Holt's missionary work in Yi, and events had run full circle: Just as in the beginning, there were now only four people in the Mission compound. Holt was nearly eighty, Ah Wong was slightly younger, the cook was almost seventy, and Anna was in her middle sixties.

But all four had lived good and simple lives, and were quite hale and hearty as the golden anniversary of Holt's tenure approached. Holt did not know it, but his colleagues were planning a celebration. They passed up the anniversary of his actual arrival in the town of Yi—they knew very well that he dated the beginning of his missionary career from the day he had been received by Ho the Central Hall—and that was to be the date honored.

For a long time, these four had been taking their meals together in the central room of Holt's suite in the inner court. Usually, as the fare was very meager, the table was simply laid. But this evening Anna spread their best linen, put out their elegant silver, and lit five candles.

Holt knew why they were there the moment he saw them, but he pretended ignorance and asked, smiling, "Why this pomp and circumstance, Anna?"

"It's for the celebration of your anniversary. Don't you remember?"

"Of course," he answered with a laugh. "Too bad we can have no banquet. We will just have to eat the candles."

"This is to be a real celebration. Wait and see!"

Presently Ah Wong dashed in from the kitchen carrying a fat roasted chicken.

"Where did that come from?" Holt demanded. "Have you used all the ration coupons for the whole month?"

Ah Wong cocked his head on one side in the old way and answered solemnly, "Have no fear that you will go hungry the next thirty days. But I cannot tell you where it comes from—that is Cook's secret."

He sped away to the kitchen, and scuttled back and forth several times with more dishes. There were all sorts of meat, cooked with vegetables and condiments. There was also a large fish, very rare in inland Yi, fried with ginger and soya bean sauce. The court was filled with piquant odors the missionary had not smelled for many a day. And then the cook emerged finally with a tray loaded with bowls of steaming rice, his face wreathed in a triumphant smile.

"Master, haven't I done well for your celebration?" he chuckled.

"Well! You have done wonders. I only hope you haven't done anything foolish."

"I didn't get the food for this celebration," replied the cook. "You did, Master."

"Let's not talk riddles. I have not set foot out of this compound for weeks!"

"Nevertheless, it was you, Master. Oh, Master Wong and Mistress Anna and I wanted to save our ration coupons for this occasion, but since you eat with us, if we had done that you would have suffered. So I went to the market this morning at my wit's end. I walked past the food stalls many times and wondered what to do. It happened that the Comrade Market Supervisor was away for a moment and one of the meat dealers noticed me. I told him that today is your

444

fiftieth anniversary in Yi and we wanted to celebrate. Before I knew it, the man thrust meat into my basket. Then before he knew it, other dealers put in their wares too. So I got all these for nothing. They are presents from those good men to you, Master."

Holt was deeply moved. He bowed his head, as did the others, and gave his thanks to the Lord, and then they began to serve while Cook went on with his story.

"Though the credit of getting the food must go to you, Master, I must claim the credit of bringing it back. You have no idea how the experience strained my nerves. There I was with my basket loaded— and the Comrade Market Supervisor returned. I was frightened to death! But the meat dealer, a nimble man, covered the basket with a piece of cloth, and I walked right past the Comrade Market Supervisor without a tremble—though my heart was bouncing inside like a wild deer!"

Holt gave the cook all the credit that was his due. Then he noticed a small boy stealing into the courtyard in the twilight, an urchin about ten years old. He looked hungry, and pitying the lad, Holt opened the door and asked if he would come in and eat with them.

The urchin cast him a disdainful look and glanced at the dinner table.

"So! I have smelled right. You are having a feast, you foreign spies!"

Then the boy spat, and ran out of the court.

Holt returned to his chair, more pained than offended, until he noted that the cook was trembling.

"Are you ill?" he asked anxiously.

"No, no," the cook stuttered. "But we are ruined! I understand now—remember my grandchild who called me a foreign spy? He told me he belonged to a special children's squad. 'Odor-Smelling Squad,' he called it. The boy who was just here was from that squad. Oh, we are ruined!"

Ah Wong cocked his head to one side. "What's eaten will not be seen, though it may have been smelled. Let's finish this food quick, and nobody will be the wiser."

The Reverend Dr. Holt laughed, the cook felt somewhat reassured, and they fell to with gusto. But in a short time they heard somebody in the courtyard, and Ah Wong opened the door to find the block leader, Laughing Face.

"So the little comrade of the Odor-Smelling Squad is right," he said, looking at the table. "You are indeed having a feast. I am no troublemaker—but may I ask where you got the coupons to buy all this food?"

Holt rose and decided on a lie: "Comrade Block Leader, this is the fiftieth anniversary of my humble work in Yi. We have saved our coupons for weeks."

"I don't see anything wrong in that. And I remember now, you have been here fifty years, Foreign Comrade. My best wishes to you!"

"Won't you join us?" urged Holt. "We don't have food like this often, and you have always been so considerate of us, Comrade Block Leader. We shall deem it a great honor."

Laughing Face wavered. According to the rules he should not, but the food was tempting, and as a native of Yi he had always esteemed Holt. Furthermore, he had just received some information which seemed to bode quite well for the future of the missionary. All smiles, he sat down, and as the dinner went on he became more expansive than ordinarily he dared to be.

Even with their guest, there was still some food left after the meal and Holt, after thanking them all, said he must give the leftover to the Mas.

Laughing Face stopped laughing. "Foreign Comrade, I wish you hadn't said that. I have known for some time that you gave food to those reactionaries, and I did not report you. But if others had reported it, I would have been blamed for not doing so. Please be careful in your speech and actions hereafter, Foreign Comrade. At any rate, the Mas are here no more."

"What do you mean?" Holt asked.

"If you walk past the shack, you will find out. The Mas were taken away today. It is said that a big public trial is going to be held."

"When will this trial be?"

"I don't know, but I expect after the 'Return of the Heroes.' You see, Foreign Comrade, now that we have conquered all of China, the Big Comrades of the Party are being allowed to return to their native places as Heroes, which they rightly are. When they fought against the Kuomintang they had to use assumed names, but now they have revealed their true identities. Yi is especially distinguished as the birthplace of two most important comrades—Comrade Ho Ta-kong and Comrade Ma Pingnan, both born on Lenin Lane. I am living in the very compound in which Comrade Ma Pingnan drew the first breath of life! It is expected that Comrade Ho and Comrade

446

Ma will return to Yi as Heroes soon, along with Comrade Ho Ta-kong's wife, Comrade Yin Mei-yin."

Holt was disturbed by the news and remained silent. But Laughing Face, an unobserving person, did not notice this and went on speaking.

"According to the rules, I shouldn't have given you this information in advance, but I have done so because you are such a good man and because I felt you would be pleased with the news. So far, you have not fared very well under the new Regime, but now everybody in the Party is talking about your relations with the two Heroes. You have been a great friend of the Hos for generations. And we all know of Comrade Ma Pingnan's friendship for you."

3

THE COMMUNIST HIGH COMMAND had decreed the "Return of the Heroes" partly to gratify the vanities of those few thousand faithful comrades who had joined the Party before the now-famed "Long Trek" and who had toiled so hard and so hazardously for the Cause —to give them a dramatic psychological reward, to let them revel in pomp and glory in their respective birthplaces, to permit them to vent their feelings where previously they had been contemned as outcasts or even condemned as criminals.

But this was only a side issue; there was another far more important purpose. The Communist ideology meant to create a new world, a different society, a brand-new kind of man. All the people, male or female, young or old, were to labor for the commonweal, and none would be allowed to deviate. However, the people were still steeped in false traditions, conditioned by memories of the past —too individualistic in thinking to work whole-heartedly for the collective aim. The past was wrong; all past interpretations of the past were wrong. So the histories had to be rewritten, and the future built, entirely according to the Communist ideology.

The High Command realized that although the Communists had conquered the mainland of China, their position was far from secure. Formosa was a threat; Chiang Kai-shek was not much of an adversary now, but he was supported anew by the United States—the arch-enemy of Communism. Inside China, there were even greater perils. Counting all the Party cadre and the Communist armed forces, the High Command numbered a following of barely more than one-hundredth of the population. The remaining ninety-nine hundredths were, of course, reactionaries—latent and potential "enemies of the people." Though they were being subdued, organized, and brainwashed with methodical care, the High Command knew that if an opportunity were afforded they might rise in opposition to the New Regime.

The High Command saw two possibilities. One was to intensify the Hate-America Campaign, to furnish the country with dramatic proof of American enmity, and to whip up the sentiments of the nation to unprecedented fury against Capitalist Imperialist nations in general and against the United States in particular. The other was to liquidate, by means of one mass purge, all possible reactionary leaders, great or small, so that the people would be not only shattered and stupefied, but deprived of any potential leadership, and organized opposition would be rendered impotent.

To heighten the effect of the gigantic purge, an element of surprise would have to be introduced and a spectacular occasion devised for its launching. What better scheme than to plan the mass liquidation on the very heels of the "Return of the Heroes"? Quite naturally, when the people had celebrated the homecoming of their famous native sons, they would expect the New Regime to display magnanimity and relax controls. Then was the very moment when the most horrifying shock would be dealt them.

The plans were carefully drawn up. The country had been divided into areas, each with an Executive Council which controlled all military, civil, and judicial authorities. The Councils were peopled with trustworthy comrades, natives of their respective areas, and it was these men who were entrusted with carrying out the mass liquidation.

For the northern provinces immediately adjacent to Peking, however, a different arrangement was made. With Peking now capital of Communist China, the seat of the High Command, the provinces near the capital had to be made doubly secure. So a special commission was created, with temporary headquarters at the big port city, to direct the mass purge in this region. Three commissioners were chosen with particular care from among the most trusted comrades who hailed from this part of the country.

The chairman of the Commission was selected by the High Command because his dossier in the secret Party files was singularly free from black entries. His loyalty had been tried on many occasions and never found wanting; he was a superb organizer and an outstanding military commander. Since the conquest of China, in just

448

reward he had been made head of the Department of Organization, one of the highest and most powerful offices of the Party. His name: Ho Ta-kong.

The second member of the Commission was the Chief of Secret Police of the New Regime, and understandably not many could equal this comrade in cunning, callousness, and cruelty. True, there were two black entries in his secret dossier, but the High Command had appointed him Chief of Secret Police not despite his blemished record but rather because of it. With such a record, the High Command could have him liquidated at any time.

There was a popular misconception—still current today—that the Secret Police was all-powerful in a Communist state. Actually, it was but a weapon in the hands of the High Command. With Communist cells so heavily compartmented, the Secret Police itself could not help but be infiltrated by Party members. Though the Party knew the identity of every member of the Secret Police, the Secret Police had no similar knowledge about the Communist membership at large. As a result, the High Command could follow everything that went on within the Secret Police, but the Chief knew nothing about the designs of the Party except for what the High Command chose to let him know. So the High Command felt no uneasiness in putting the Secret Police in charge of a man like Comrade Ma Pingnan.

The third member of the Commission was Ho Ta-kong's wife, Comrade Yin Mei-yin. She was chosen for two reasons: In her own right, she had risen very high in the Party ranks. The Communist International had designated her as a liaison comrade between its headquarters and the Chinese Communist Party; thus, her appointment to the Commission would help assure further cordial relationship between the High Command and the Socialist fatherland. Moreover, Comrades Ho Ta-kong and Mei-yin were celebrated for their mutual devotion. If the appointment of Ma Pingnan might have miffed Comrade Ho somewhat, her selection would no doubt appease him.

Ta-kong, however, was not at all pleased with the arrangement. If he resented Ma Pingnan's appointment, he resented Mei-yin's even more. But above all, he hated the very idea of being named head of the Commission.

Ta-kong had by now nearly attained the height of his ambition. He was in his early fifties, the youngest comrade in the top structure of the Party pyramid, and was only a few steps removed from the ultimate goal—the High Command itself; he needed only to bide his time. He was thoroughly indoctrinated with Communist ideology. He believed in Socialism, and was keenly aware of the necessity of consolidating the power of the New Regime. Nevertheless, he was more than a little shocked by the stupendous blood-bath the High Command planned for the nation. He did not mind killing people in war, but the purge would be slaughter, pure and simple.

Ta-kong had extended Communist "Liberated Areas" into the fertile provinces of the eastern coast more swiftly and more successfully than any other comrade. He had been the first to steal into Manchuria after the Japanese surrender, and had laid all the groundwork for Communist expansion there. And it was he who had returned with a vengeance, trapped Chiang Kai-shek's crack troops in one furious campaign, chased him to the limits of the South, and driven him off the mainland of China. The Party had recognized his outstanding achievements and rewarded him commensurately, never suspecting that there was an additional reason for his feverish activity: He was trying to forget the most abominable incident of his life—the betrayal and killing of his Auntie Lan.

He had hated Mei-yin for having killed Second Brother and his family; now he despised her for having caused him to kill Third Brother's mother. Yet, to prevent his career from being wrecked, he had to be particularly nice to Mei-yin. The more he detested her, the more he strove to appear devoted. And he had to satisfy her inordinate sexual demands, her appetite having grown rather than declined with age; every time he thought of that, he felt shame and revulsion. But he had hidden his sentiments well, and Mei-yin did not suspect.

He knew he could neither resign from the Commission nor show any leniency in the conduct of its affairs. Mei-yin and Ma Pingnan were sadistic—they were sure to become suspicious if he tried to temper the purge with justice and mercy; for his own safety he must pretend to be as callous and as cold-blooded as they. As the sole balm for his conscience, he decided to let them do the shameful work.

Thus, obediently he moved his headquarters temporarily to the big port city and called the first meeting of the Commission.

"Comrades, we all know the wishes of the High Command," he said. "I am exceedingly glad that you two have been named members, especially since the High Command must know how busy I am with the affairs of my Department. Comrade Pingnan, as Chief of Secret Police, it is on you and on your office that the burden of this mass liquidation must inevitably fall. So I would like you to make up the preliminary lists of names, arrange for the public trials, and carry out the subsequent executions. Comrade Mei-yin is my wife, and I trust her implicitly. Whatever you two decide, I will approve."

Ma Pingnan's piggish little eyes glittered—he had feared working under Ta-kong would be much more difficult.

"Comrade Chairman, I shall not fail you," he said rather obsequiously. "I have already drawn up the lists of names. Would you like to look them over?"

From his fat briefcase he took out a thick volume and presented it to Ta-kong. It was filled with tens of thousands of names, province by province, prefecture by prefecture, village by village. Ta-kong hardened himself, glanced over it carelessly, and then pushed it to Mei-yin.

"You look it over, dear. A few more or less don't matter."

Mei-yin began to peruse the volume with visible delight, like a child who has been given a new toy.

Ma Pingnan watched her with pleasure. "You can see for yourself, Comrade Mei-yin, with what great care I and my men have prepared these lists. Look under Yi, where both Comrade Chairman and I were born. The list is headed by my own mother and brother. I put their names in myself. As the old adage says, 'In the cause of great justice, you must not hesitate to destroy your own kith and kin'!"

"That's splendid of you, Comrade," said Mei-yin affably but with a note of amusement. "Yet if my information is not incorrect, wasn't it your mother and brother who chased you out of your own house with the help of Tien Fong? We've already disposed of him. And now we're going to dispose of your mother and brother. You will have your vengeance, and all in the cause of great justice."

A little abashed, Ma Pingnan added in haste, "But they deserve liquidation. They were capitalists, they must be eliminated in our class struggle."

"Of course," agreed Mei-yin. "But here, this is the list of my own native district. I don't find my uncle's name."

"Yes," Ma said, "my men made quite a search for him. Unfortunately, there is indisputable proof that he died in the Japanese War."

"The lucky turtle!" she cursed. "But I see only the names of my uncle's offspring, not any of my ex-husband's."

"You have the wrong page, Comrade," chuckled Ma Pingnan. He

451

leaned across and found the right spot. "See, they are all here. Since they all have become very poor, my men did not list them at first. But I put them in because of you."

Mei-yin examined the names carefully. "Yes, they're all here. What do I care about their being rich or poor, good or bad? Their minds are all filled with bourgeois poison. I am like you, Comrade. In the cause of great justice, I too do not hesitate to destroy my kith and kin. Every one of them!"

"Have you some of my Hos on your list, Comrade Pingnan?" Ta-kong asked casually. Actually, he was suddenly sickened by the realization that had his grandfather, Ho the Central Hall, been alive this day, the old man would have headed the whole list.

Ma Pingnan was extremely apologetic. "I assure you, Comrade Chairman, that under my personal orders my men have done their utmost to look for them. Your illustrious House has been our main target in Yi. But as you know, they sold their property and left the city during the Japanese war, and all seem to have vanished into thin air."

"Not even one, Comrade? Indeed, this does not speak well for the efficiency of your police! But perhaps they may have simply died. Lucky for them, in truth!"

For a fortnight thereafter, Ta-kong remained aloof while Ma Pingnan and Mei-yin continued with their detailed preparations. But two days before they were to leave for Yi in the much-heralded "Return of the Heroes," the Commission received a new order from the High Command. It was instructed to seize all Americans still remaining in the area, to charge them with espionage, and to hold a special spectacular public trial in the port city so that a spy scare could be stirred up in the country against the United States.

According to the statistics of the Secret Police, only one American was left in the area—the Reverend Dr. Holt. Ta-kong was greatly disturbed by this development. What a stupid and stubborn fool the missionary was to have stayed behind! But as Chairman of the Commission, he had no choice: He issued orders for the arrest of Holt and all the staff in his little Mission.

452

Seven

ON THE NIGHT before the "Return of the Heroes," the Reverend Dr. Holt, Ah Wong, Anna, and the cook were arrested. Separated at once from the others, Holt expected to be sent to a prison, but instead he was taken to a three-story Western-style building which had belonged to an affluent family before the change of the regime, and now was used as headquarters for the local Secret Police.

The missionary found himself in a room on the second floor, with iron bars newly installed at the windows, which looked out on a large square, and a little loophole in the thick door. The room was furnished not only with a bed but also a chair and a writing desk.

"Comrade," he asked the officer who was with him, "am I a prisoner? If so, with what crime am I charged?"

"You are a guest of the house for the moment," the man answered. "If you co-operate fully, you may be free to return to your compound soon. Up to now, you have not taken part in our 'Open and White' campaign, like the rest of the people. We only want a confession from you."

"Confession of what?"

"Of all the sins and crimes which you have committed, which you have intended, and which, though you may not know about them consciously, may have lain in your subconscious. You must probe deep and bare all these sins and crimes to us. If you cannot do it yourself, we shall be ready to help you."

"I have committed no crime that I know of," Holt said, "though I have committed many sins. I do not acknowledge you have the right to demand a confession from me, but I see no harm in making one."

"Splendid! We know you can handle a Chinese brush—go ahead and make a clean breast of everything."

"Why can't I do it in my own compound?"

"That's not practical. One always tends to cling to old ideas in an old environment. We have picked this new environment to enable you to become more reflective, more clear-headed, and more penitent."

"Where are my friends?"

"They are engaged in similar 'Open and White' work."

"Can I see them?"

"No, they cannot be disturbed."

"Well, it is late now, but I shall write out my full confession the first thing tomorrow."

"That's impossible. Confessions are best when written on first remorse. The sooner you finish, the better."

Holt put on his reading glasses and took up the brush. The officer left, but a guard remained outside the door. Holt collected his thoughts and began to write. He had sinned because he had not done as much for the Chinese people as he ought to have done. He avoided evaluating his contributions in religion, for he felt the subject might not be to the liking of the comrades, and said nothing about his acts of charity, for he remembered well the Lord's command: "When thou dost alms, let not thy left hand know what thy right hand doeth." Mostly he emphasized the shortcomings of his medical work; sequestered in the interior of China and lacking the latest medical publications, he had not kept up with the progress of modern medical science as he should. There were cases, he had realized later, he could have treated better, and some he had failed to cure because of his ignorance.

He finished the confession and gave it to the guard outside. He was just about to retire when the officer who had spoken to him before stormed rudely into the room.

"You call that a confession? I have read every word. If you say these are all your sins, then you are the most arrant liar I have ever known!"

"But I put down everything. I have never lied in my life."

"Then write out an account of your whole life. Start from the very day you were born, up to the very minute we took you. You have lived almost eighty years; in all that time you must have committed many sins and crimes. Why, for instance, did you leave your country? What made you come to China? Did you commit some crime in the United States? Or did you come here for some ulterior motive? Who supported your Mission? How was the money raised? Don't give us the usual hackneyed answers missionaries always give; they are nothing but lies. Give us the truth!"

"But my fellow missionaries *have* told the truth!"

"So you're going to be stubborn! Well, I'll be patient with you—

454

for a while. Write out the full story of your life and let us judge it for ourselves!"

"That will take time, and I'm very tired. Can't I write it out tomorrow?"

"No, do it right now. You'll get no sleep until you've finished."

For the whole night Holt was kept wearily at the desk. As soon as he finished a page, it would be snatched away for examination. If he stopped writing for a minute—and there were many times he felt himself doze involuntarily—a guard would come in and shake him roughly.

By the early morning he had written a complete, if somewhat hasty, account of all the important events of his long life. Gratefully he looked at the bed. But now a different officer entered, walked up to Holt with a smile, and then suddenly slapped him sharply on both cheeks.

Sleep forgotten, Holt rose to his full height in dignity.

"Lies! Lies! You have been writing nothing but lies!"

"I resent the remark," retorted Holt, "even more than the slaps!"

"The slaps are nothing," said the officer. "Your confession is useless—there are too many gaps in your story. You have omitted too many things."

"I have omitted nothing important."

"Ah, but you have! For instance, you say you are not married. But did you ever have a girlfriend back in the United States? If so, then who is she? You came to our great country so young. You cannot deny you are made of flesh and blood. Have you had affairs with our women? If so, how many, and with whom? I don't mind telling you, that woman in your Mission, Anna Wong, has already confessed you have often made love to her."

"That's a despicable lie!" cried Holt. "Anna would never say that of her own will!"

"Then there used to be a Widow Lan in your Mission. She was supposed to be very beautiful in her young days. Did you have sexual relations with her?"

Holt seethed in helpless fury. "Dr. Lan was a woman I held in great esteem—I honor and respect her name. Must you slander even the dead?"

"So!" taunted the man. "Your present behavior only testifies to your own willful omissions. You have denied making love to Anna Wong. You have denied having had sexual relations with Widow

455

Lan. But you have not denied that you had a girlfriend back in the United States. So there *was* a girlfriend in America! Yet you made no mention of the fact in your confession. By the same token, we can see you must have omitted many other important things. Now, be 'open and white'! Bare all your secrets. It is useless to hide anything. Write again, and write in full."

"I refuse to write any more," said Holt firmly. "You will not believe anything I write anyway."

"By the refusal, I take it you admit openly and freely that you have many things to hide in your past. And you, a missionary, a self-styled holy man!"

"I have nothing to hide!"

"Then why do you refuse to fill in the gaps?"

Holt was at a loss how to answer. "All right," he said finally, "I'll do what you want."

Thus he was kept writing again for the whole day. But no matter how much he wrote, there were always more gaps to fill and more details to explain. He was given food, but he had no appetite. Sometime in the afternoon he heard continuous outbursts of firecrackers outside on the streets, and he knew the so-called Heroes had returned.

He was forced to continue writing through the second night. His vision blurred, his head ached maddeningly. For a brief instant he fainted, but he woke with a start and knew by the sting and the tiny red spot on his arm that he had been given an injection of a stimulant. He refused to write further.

The officer who had slapped him before entered. "Go ahead and write," he commanded. "Confess you are an American spy."

"But I am not an American spy!" protested Holt. "And I have written everything you want to know."

"Oh no, you haven't! For instance, in your room we found a box which contains several thousand U.S. dollars. Where would you get so much money if you are not a spy? And what do you plan to use it for? Did you squeeze the money from your Mission funds, like the old rotten Kuomintang officials?"

"This is a simple matter to explain."

"Then explain it in writing."

Holt was anxious to clear his good name, and he resumed writing. One question led to another, and he was kept at the desk throughout the next day.

On that day—the third—he was interrupted by the huge mass meeting outside in the square to celebrate the Return of the Heroes. Though forbidden to go to the window, he could hear the endless eulogies paid them, and then each Hero speaking briefly, followed by tumultuous applause and cheers. At the end of the meeting came a stentorian announcement; the people were told to be at the square early the next morning to see a spectacle of great magnitude.

Holt was too preoccupied to feel any curiosity about this. He was now persistently pestered with charges that he had been spying for the United States, and had to answer one absurd question after another.

He was still writing when night came, and then he was suddenly seized from behind. Gagged, blindfolded, and bound hand and foot, he was carried to a car, driven somewhere, and finally dumped on a hard floor. They released his bonds and gags and left him alone.

This, he knew, was a prison, but the cell was pitch-dark. Out of the blackness came a fearful cry of pain that chilled his blood—it was like the wild scream of some dumb animal. The Reverend Dr. Holt realized he was somewhere near a torture chamber. From that moment, time became a nightmare and the room an inferno. Holt put his fingers to his ears, but he could not completely shut out the groans of men, the wails of women, the weeping of the old, the whimpering of terrified children. Again and again his spine would freeze as he heard the sudden piercing cries of agony.

After an eternity of horror, gray daylight lit up the dark cell and armed guards came. Holt was almost glad to see them—even physical torture itself must be better than the nightmare of listening. Once more he was blindfolded and bound, and carried off.

This time, when the blindfold was removed, he found himself back in the room of the Secret Police headquarters. Although he was untied, several guards crowded around him and forced him to stand before the window, facing the square.

The officer who had slapped him said, "How lucky you are to have a box seat. Look!"

The whole town of Yi had gathered, thirty or forty thousand men, women, and children, but the square was as silent as if the throng were not even breathing.

At the far end, three persons sat on a canopied platform—two men and a woman. These, he knew, would be the Heroes. Flanking the platform and lining the streets that enclosed the square were files of armed guards, both in and out of uniform.

But what struck Holt most was a dozen rows of men and women

immediately in front of the platform. All were kneeling, their backs toward him, and he saw they all were made fast with ropes.

Now, a master of ceremonies announced a name, and at once a comrade stepped forth with a megaphone and read a confession. The crowd listened with awful silence. When he was done, one of the Heroes rose and spoke through a loudspeaker: "My good people, you have heard the crimes voluntarily confessed by this enemy of the people. What is your will toward him?"

Holt recognized the voice as Ma Pingnan's. Then he heard the silent throng erupt into a frantic uproar: "Death! Death!"

He made an attempt to withdraw from the window but was pushed back by the guards. Though he closed his eyes against the scene, he could not stop his ears from hearing. The process was repeated over and over again.

Fearfully Holt waited for the names of Reverend Wong Ming, Anna, and Cook. Hundreds of men and women were condemned that day, and the missionary knew most of them—some were his own Christians. And all of them were charged with the crime of being enemies of the people.

On and on the monstrous thing dragged; it was becoming monotonous. But so far the names of Ah Wong, Anna and Cook had not been announced. Then, when it was already past noon, Holt heard Ma Pingnan bellow:

"My good people and my fellow comrades, we have come to the last of the enemies of the people we have discovered this time. Doubtless, there are still others hidden in your midst, but you people can have complete confidence in the People's Government—we will ferret them out. In the meantime, you must keep a sharp eye on everybody—yes, even on those whom you hold most dear lest they should be enemies of the people, working for your ruin from within. If you ever find such creatures, be it your father or mother, wife or husband, son or daughter, you must denounce them without hesitation. I myself will set you a good example. As a fitting climax to this public trial today, I give you my own brother and mother—Ma Pingshi and a woman nee Yang!"

Pre-arranged wild and frenzied cheers came from the crowd.

"And I have another surprise for you. In the cause of great justice, no one must hesitate to destroy his own kith and kin. I am proud to present, therefore, several former reactionaries who have seen the light and who wish to redeem themselves today. I consider it a privilege to call on the regenerated Mas—Ma Pingshi's wife and three

458

children. His wife will denounce her husband and her mother-in-law! His children will denounce their father and their grand-mother!"

Holt's head whirled. Was this the China he had known—the China he had loved so well? He opened his eyes and stared. In a haze he saw Ma Pingshi's wife and three children each take the stand and speak his piece in succession. But Holt's mind was so numbed with shock he did not understand a word.

"Countrymen and comrades," proclaimed the master of ceremonies, "the public trial is adjourned. But the executions are to take place outside the East Gate. Let us march these enemies of the people there on their own feet. Let us make them dig their graves with their own hands. Let us witness their last whines, and rejoice. Rejoice, countrymen and comrades—rejoice in the triumph of the people over the enemies of the people!"

Then the well-coached crowd, starting to move, broke out into a mighty song:

"Rise! Rise! Ye men who will not be slaves . . ."

2

The Reverend Dr. Holt was turned around by his guards.

"Confess!" the officer snarled. "Confess you are an American spy!"

"I am not a spy. And I have confessed in full."

"So you are still stubborn, eh? There is nobody we cannot break. Last night you heard the tortures we can inflict. You saw how every enemy of the people has confessed to his crime. So far we have given you only 'the softening process,' but if you persist in being contrary we know what to do."

"I am ready to submit to your tortures, but I cannot confess that I am a spy."

"All right," returned the officer grimly. "If that's what you want, we'll oblige you."

At that moment, however, another officer entered, smiling.

"Comrade," he said, "let me have a word with this old foreigner." Then to Holt, he said: "You are a missionary. You are a man of God. You have your beliefs, and stick to them. Is that not so?"

Holt said gratefully, "I am glad some of you understand."

"You are," continued the newcomer, "a Christian, a follower of Jesus?"

"Yes."

"You say your Jesus suffered crucifixion to save mankind?"

"Yes."

"Then, as a true Christian, should you not follow the example of your Jesus? To save the lives of others, would you sacrifice your own?"

"Yes."

"You also say you love your enemies?"

"Yes."

"Then according to your belief, you ought to be ready to sacrifice your life for the sake of others—your friends as well as your enemies. Am I wrong about your belief?"

"You are not wrong," answered the Reverend Dr. Holt. "But there's no point of talking about this here."

"Indeed, there is," returned the officer with a smile. "You must understand that your life is already doomed; whatever you do cannot change your fate. But we have been ordered to make you confess that you are an American spy, and unless you do so, it will mean the death of us. So you can see why my comrade here is so eager to use torture to extort a confession from you. Of course, in spite of your belief, you may not care to sacrifice your life for our sake, since we are your enemies, but think of your friends—Wong Ming, his wife, your cook. Needless to say, if you persist in your refusal, it will mean endless torture for every one of them, and also the cruelest deaths possible. So this is a simple question of asking you to live up to your beliefs. If you are the good missionary you claim to be, you will confess you are an American spy and save both your friends and your enemies. If you are a bad missionary, then you will refuse to save all of us. Now, Ho-Lo-Teh, are you a good missionary or a bad missionary?"

Holt was too confounded to argue, too deeply troubled by the thought of what these men could do to his friends.

The man continued, "I know you are a good missionary—you will save all our lives. So I have your confession already written up. You need only to sign it."

He seated Holt at the writing desk and put the brush in his hand. Then he produced a folder of papers, turned to its last page, and pointed to the place where he wanted the missionary's signature.

"Can I have my reading glasses?" asked Holt. "Some of your men took them last night."

"Can't you write your name without them?"

460

"I don't know. The words are all blurred. If I sign without my glasses, it may look very clumsy."

"That's all right so long as it is in your own handwriting. Go ahead."

The brush still in his right hand, Holt held the folder away from his eyes and turned to the first page. The officer let him, thinking that the old man could not read anyway without his glasses. Holt gazed hard, and suddenly recognized a few characters. It was the name of the girl he had known in Baltimore so long ago. Then, to his utter amazement, he made out vaguely that she was described as a United States secret agent—and had induced him to come to China for purposes of espionage. He threw down the paper in horror.

"This is infamous! I can never put my name to this!"

"Why?" asked the officer, still smiling.

"I can wrong *myself* to save you, but I will not wrong others!"

The man flared up in anger. "You foreign devil, you are going to sign this!"

Ordering his men to hold Holt fast, he grasped the missionary's right hand, which still held the brush, and forced it to scribble the three large characters—Ho-Lo-Teh.

"Now you have signed the document with your own hand! If I were you, I would not deny it—not ever. It wouldn't change the results, and will only give you more pain and misery. You will be put on preliminary trial tonight—and I'll see you in Hell!"

For the first time in days Holt was left alone. He prayed until he felt at peace, and finally fell into a welcome sleep. When they woke him, he rose silently and followed the guards. He expected to be taken on another long trip, but was led only to a room downstairs.

The chamber he entered was arranged like a courtroom, with many officers and clerks and a raised tribunal. Seated on this were the three Heroes. At the right was Ma Pingnan, his sallow face wearing a wry smile; Pingnan actually nodded as Holt walked into the room. At the left sat a plain-looking woman with odd, triangular eyes—this, Holt knew, would be Ho Ta-kong's wife. But it was upon Ho Ta-kong himself, at the center, that the missionary fastened his stare.

He had not seen Ta-kong for more than a quarter of a century. He could still discern a vague physical resemblance between him and his grandfather and his uncle. But whereas both the grandfather and the uncle had always looked gentle-mannered, this man was ferocity itself. He glared at Holt without the least hint of recognition, his face glum, fierce, and inscrutable as a mask of stone.

Without ceremony, Ho Ta-kong announced matter-of-factly: "This hearing is called to make a preliminary examination of the charges of espionage brought against the prisoner, one American named Logan J. Holt. Comrade Pingnan, what evidence have you collected against the prisoner?"

"We have collected much, Comrade Chairman," Ma Pingnan replied obsequiously. Then, motioning to an officer, he ordered, "Produce the first item of evidence."

The box in which the missionary had kept his American dollars was placed on a table. "This," explained the officer, "is the American money the prisoner hid in his bedroom and used for espionage purposes."

Ta-kong addressed Holt sternly. "Do you acknowledge that this money is yours, prisoner?"

"Yes," answered Holt. "But—"

"There can be no 'but,' prisoner," reproved Ta-kong. "In this court the accused is permitted only to answer yes or no. Any other evidence, Comrade?"

"Yes," said the Chief of Secret Police. "We have his testimony that he willfully killed many of our countrymen under the guise of being a doctor. Here is his own account in his own handwriting."

He passed to Ta-kong the first confession Holt had written, and pointed out the specific passages in which the missionary admitted his failure to cure some of his patients. Ta-kong read the account carefully. Then he lifted unsmiling eyes to Holt.

"Prisoner, do you acknowledge that this is your own writing?"

"Yes, but—"

"I said no 'but.' Comrade Pingnan, continue."

Ma Pingnan whispered to an officer behind him, who cried, "Bring in the witness!"

The cook was dragged forward in chains, barely able to walk. His eyes were glassy and wild, and he did not even recognize Holt.

"Comrade Chairman," reported Ma Pingnan, "this man has been employed by the prisoner for years, nominally as his cook but actually as one of his agents. This man has fully confessed he is an accomplice of the prisoner in the crime. He is not well educated— he cannot write much, nor does he speak well. However, he can make himself very clear on the main points of the issue."

Ta-kong glanced at the cook carelessly. "Are you a spy?"

462

"Yes, sir," answered the cook, "I have been called a spy. I am a spy."

"Is your American master a spy?"

"Yes, sir, my master has been called a spy. He is a spy."

"What espionage have you done for your American master?"

The cook acted as if he did not understand the question. He went on repeating like an automaton: "Yes, sir, I have been called a spy. I am a spy. Yes, sir, my master has been called a spy. He is a spy. Yes, sir, I have been called a spy. I am a spy. Yes, sir, my master . . ."

"Take this witness away!" ordered Ta-kong. As the cook was dragged out, he asked Ma Pingnan if he had any other evidence or witnesses.

Pingnan looked somewhat ill at ease. "But Comrade Chairman, don't you think we already have sufficient evidence to convict the prisoner?"

"The High Command wants a special public trial for the prisoner in the port city, with everything legal and watertight. We have to introduce credible confessions as well as creditable witnesses. The witness you have just produced can hardly be said to be presentable, let alone creditable. If I were you, I'd ask your men hereafter to be more careful in their treatment of such important witnesses."

The secret policemen in the room paled, as did their Chief. Ta-kong said, "I understand the prisoner has two other accomplices—one man and one woman. Can you produce them as witnesses?"

"Those two are very stubborn, Comrade Chairman. So far my men have been unable to persuade them to confess their crime. Give us a little more time—I am sure we can do so."

"That does not speak too well for the efficiency of your department, Conrade Pingnan. Have you secured a confession from the prisoner himself?"

Ma Pingnan had been reluctant to produce the document Holt had been forced to sign. "Yes, Comrade Chairman," he said hesitantly. "But he is an aged man. His eyesight is impaired, and his eyeglasses happened to be broken. So his signature is not as good as it should be."

"Let me see it."

Ma Pingnan handed over the document, and Ta-kong examined the signature with great care. Then he remarked, apparently more to himself than to others, "I think this will do."

A smile of relief flickered about Ma Pingnan's piggish eyes.

Ta-kong addressed Holt, "Prisoner, do you acknowledge that this document is your confession and that this signature is your own?"

"No!" answered the Reverend Dr. Holt.

"But I have seen you write your Chinese name before. This certainly looks like your signature."

His pent-up fury bursting out of control, the Reverend Dr. Holt uttered the first blasphemy of his life: "Damn you, Ho Ta-kong! If you're your grandfather's grandson, you should know very well that this confession cannot be my confession nor this signature my signature!"

The comrades in the room were shocked at the outburst; no one could speak like this to the dreaded head of the Department of Organization. Instinctively the guards moved toward the prisoner, but Ta-kong stopped them.

"No, Comrades! This man is a special prisoner, to be brought to public trial in the port city, in a whole skin. Chief of Secret Police Ma, here, will find ways and means to convince the prisoner that he is wrong without making him unpresentable either physically or mentally. Guards, take the prisoner away! The hearing is ended."

After Holt was hustled off, Ta-kong turned to Ma Pingnan with a smile. "I have just received word from the High Command to hold the public trial in the port city at the beginning of next month. So you have about a fortnight to finish your investigation."

Ta-kong leaned back comfortably in his chair. He had kept himself fully informed about the case. As head of the Department of Organization, he controlled the many Communist cells which had been carefully planted in the Secret Police with the approval of the High Command. In addition, unsuspected even by the High Command, Ma Pingnan's personal orderly was a disciple of Old Head's secret Society.

Ta-kong had called this preliminary hearing for a definite purpose; and he had achieved it. Though he knew that in the long run it would be impossible to save Holt, at least he wanted to spare the missionary as much physical pain as possible. Besides, he liked nothing better than to see Ma Pingnan discomfited. Thus, while acting the atrocious inquisitor as his part required, he had also been able to publicly warn the Chief of Secret Police and his men against the excessive use of torture in this case.

Then he heard Mei-yin speak: "Comrade Pingnan, I know how

464

difficult your task is. Should you fail to secure a genuine confession from the American spy in time, don't hesitate to ask for my help. I am sure I know a way to make him confess voluntarily. . . ."

3

THE COMMISSION RETURNED to the port city. While outwardly Ta-kong applied himself with his usual zeal, inwardly he was in great stress. There was a war going on within him for the mastery of his soul. He tried desperately to conceal it from Mei-yin, but he could not help becoming more and more withdrawn. He lived in constant fear that by an unwary remark or an unwitting look, he might give himself away to her. But Mei-yin, in her sadistic preoccupation with the mass purges, did not notice—she complained only of his physical flabbiness. Perhaps his nerves were strained from overwork and he needed a vacation. As soon as the public trial of the American spy was over, she said, they would spend a fortnight in the Summer Palace near Peking, built by the old Empress Dowager. It would be a sort of second honeymoon.

Ta-kong drew cheer from the secret information he obtained about the progress—or, rather, lack of progress—in the missionary's case. Ma Pingnan and his men had failed miserably to extort a confession from their prisoner. They had given him the electric treatment. They had filled his chest with water until his lungs almost burst. They had subjected him to systematic starvation. But beyond these they had dared not go, for fear of doing him more injury, and Holt had stubbornly refused to write even one more word. Reverend Wong Ming and Anna also benefited from Ta-kong's warning to the Secret Police. They, too, had to be preserved as presentable witnesses.

Then one day Mei-yin had a long, large, heavy boxlike structure, fully covered with black cloth, brought into the building, which was a branch office of the Department of Organization but which now served also as the headquarters of the Commission. She had it stored in a room in the basement, installed a special lock on the door, and kept the key herself.

The month ended. Ta-kong summoned another meeting of the Commission.

"The mass purges in our area have been carried out according to plan," he said. "The only thing left is the public trial of the

465

American spy. Comrade Pingnan, have you all the necessary confessions and witnesses?"

Ma Pingnan was deeply worried now. "Can you grant me some little more time, Comrade Chairman?"

"I wish I could—but I fear that the High Command will not. We have our orders."

In desperation Ma Pingnan privately sought out Mei-yin and asked her help. Smiling mysteriously she told him she was confident she could secure the confessions, provided the prisoners were brought to the headquarters for interrogation by herself. But permission to use these premises for such a purpose could be given only by Ta-kong, and since relations between him and Ta-kong had been none too favorable in the past, she suggested Ma had better do something about getting back into Ta-kong's good graces—and quickly.

So that night, to Ta-kong's surprise, the Chief of Secret Police asked for a special interview.

"Look, Comrade Chairman," said Ma Pingnan most ingratiatingly. "See what I have brought you—a gold-plated revolver made in Czechoslovakia. I could get only two, and have already presented one to the High Command. I saved this one for you, Comrade Chairman."

Ta-kong liked the weapon well. He examined it and saw that it was loaded. However, he thought the High Command would not be pleased to hear he had accepted a similar present from the Chief of Secret Police. He said, "But I cannot accept such an expensive gift, Comrade."

"Nobody will know," answered Ma Pingnan. "You know, Comrade Chairman, quite a few people would like to see bad blood between us. But I have only the highest admiration and respect for you, and I beg you to accept this as a token of my esteem."

Mei-yin fondled the revolver lovingly. "It is indeed a beauty, darling, and if you don't accept it you make those rumors appear true." She dropped the gun into Ta-kong's coat pocket.

"Well then, my thanks for the present, Comrade Pingnan," Ta-kong said. "What may I do for you in return?"

"I ask nothing for myself, Comrade Chairman. But pursuant to the duties of our Commission, Comrade Mei-yin and I would like to use the basement of your headquarters for the interrogation of the American spy and his two accomplices, Wong Ming and his wife. We need your permission for this."

466

Ta-kong remembered the boxlike thing under the black cover, but he could not very well refuse the request. Since Mei-yin had evidently had a prior understanding with Ma Pingnan, the Chief of Secret Police could report the Chairman for refusing to cooperate with the members of his Commission.

Ta-kong grudgingly consented—especially when he saw Ma was taking along only his personal orderly, who was a disciple of the secret Society.

Ma Pingnan acted swiftly. He had the prisoners already waiting just outside headquarters, and they were brought to the basement. The three commissioners, accompanied by many guards, descended, and Mei-yin unlocked the door and ushered them in.

In the middle of the room was the box.

The Reverend Dr. Holt, Ah Wong, and Anna looked tolerably well, and Holt had even been given a new pair of eyeglasses. Though this was the first time they had seen each other since their arrest, they dared not speak. At Mei-yin's bidding, they were lined up on the other side of the box, facing the three commissioners.

Mei-yin dramatically pointed to the box. "Guards, take the cover off."

Everyone in the room, prisoners and inquisitors alike, craned his neck to see.

It was not a box, but rather like a glass coffin—though it was not a coffin either. Through the glass, the viewers could distinctly see that the top, bottom, and four walls were lined with row upon row of sharp steel nails.

Mei-yin took special delight in the horror she saw on the prisoners' faces.

"Take the lid off."

Then Mei-yin unwrapped a package containing a large piece of raw meat and told a guard to put it on the bottom of the box. "Place it down gently—let's see how the nails work."

The nails were so sharp they pierced the meat instantly. Everyone in the room shuddered but Mei-yin.

"I ordered this from abroad when we first planned our mass purge," she explained. "I wanted to save it for special occasions like this."

Then she turned to the prisoners and spoke quite softly, "Prisoner Anna Wong, I want you to confess that your American colleague is a spy and that both you and your husband are his paid agents. If you refuse, I shall have you stripped and placed inside this glass

467

box, and let your husband and your American friend watch you bleed and writhe till you die. Understand?"

Anna fainted in the arms of her guards. Reverend Wong Ming turned ghastly pale; his head, cocked on one side, shook violently back and forth as though it were bumping against an unseen wall. Holt closed his eyes in mute prayer.

"Guards, strip the woman of her clothes!" Mei-yin went on relentlessly.

Holt opened his eyes. "May the Lord forgive you! But if you will spare my colleagues, I will confess to whatever you want."

Mei-yin smiled triumphantly. "Will you write out by your own hand whatever we choose to dictate and sign it with your own name?"

"Yes," affirmed the Reverend Dr. Holt. "But there must be nothing in your dictation that will incriminate my colleagues. If you do that, then put me in the glass box and I will not confess to a thing."

Mei-yin turned to Ta-kong and Ma Pingnan. "Will that do?"

"Yes, yes," answered Ma Pingnan quickly. "Unless Comrade Chairman thinks otherwise. The public trial is only for Ho-Lo-Teh—if we have his confession we have no need of anything else. Don't you agree, Comrade Chairman?"

Ta-kong hung his head in the manner of a nod.

"All right, American spy," Mei-yin exultantly cried to Holt. "Come to the desk and write out what I dictate. Guards! Take the other two prisoners away."

4

TA-KONG LEFT THE room. He wanted to be alone, and went to a sort of sitting room in the basement, his mind awhirl. The last few weeks of the mass purge had been a trial for his soul. For the first time in his life he had lost not only his convictions but also his ambition; life no longer held meaning for him. He wanted to think and yet he could not. He was like a prisoner, shut up forever in a tomb.

He had no idea how long he had sat there before the door opened and Mei-yin came in.

"Darling, I've been looking for you everywhere. Why didn't you remain? Ma Pingnan and I made up the fanciest cock-and-bull story of espionage ever. It's all finished now, and Comrade Pingnan is doing the proofreading. The American spy writes beautiful Chinese calligraphy, you should see it for yourself. But why do you look so dejected, darling? When you become the High Command, you must put me in charge of the Secret Police."

"Oh, stop it!" snapped Ta-kong involuntarily.

"Why do you look so frightened? These walls are soundproof, no one can hear. You have always wanted to be Number One in China. You can hide your thoughts from others, but not from Mama!"

Ta-kong turned his head away.

Mei-yin moved until she could look him in the face. "You know, you've been acting quite strange this last fortnight. Is it because of this American? Be careful, Comrade! If you don't watch your step, if you let your personal feelings get the better of you—as you almost did in the case of that traitor Li Chien—you may yet come to grief. But Mama will look after you—and see to it that her silly boy's career goes higher and higher."

Ta-kong strove to suppress his mounting irritation. "You're talking nonsense, Mei-yin. You know perfectly well that whether we go higher depends not upon us but upon the Party and the High Command."

Mei-yin studied him closely for another moment. "We've been married nearly twenty years now, but always you have worn a mask with me—the mask of a perfect and exemplary Comrade. Outside of what was permitted by the Party, you never exchanged any intimate thoughts, never talked about your career and your ambitions—and you've never discussed the High Command. I grant the mask might have been necessary when we were struggling to reach to the top, but now that the top is near at hand, it has become quite tiresome. After all, I haven't slept with you for twenty years without knowing your ambitions—you want to be nothing short of the High Command. Just as the High Command himself wants something even higher."

"What can be higher for him? He's already Number One in China."

"Number One in China is not enough for him. He is dreaming of becoming Number One in the entire Socialist camp, perhaps even in the whole world."

"He hasn't got much chance with Comrade Stalin still alive."

"Ah, but Comrade Stalin is aging fast. Every time the High Command heard Comrade Stalin was ill, I saw how he smirked to himself. And when Stalin dies, he believes he will become the acknowledged leader of the Socialist camp."

"But surely some Russian comrade—Malenkov, Molotov, or someone else—will succeed Stalin. The Russian comrades will be always our Big Brothers, the High Command notwithstanding."

"But he thinks differently, and not without good reason. He feels we Chinese Communists—and especially he himself—have made a great contribution to the cause of world revolution, as indeed we have! Lenin and the Russian comrades may be credited with the development of the Communist Party machinery, but it is we who devised and perfected the technique of military subversion from within a country. Look at the East European Communist countries! None of them became Communist through the efforts of their own Parties—they were converted to Communism only by Russian military occupation. But China is wholly different. We had little help from Russia except for what they taught us about Party organization; and all the time we were fighting Chiang Kai-shek and his clique; save in the very end, we fought against tremendous odds. But because we succeeded in developing this technique of ours we won, and now the High Command, as you well know, has set up schools to train Communists from all corners of the world—Southeast Asia, Africa, and Latin America. When these trainees return to their own countries, our influence is bound to spread. They will not look to Moscow but to Peking for instruction and guidance."

"But Soviet Russia still remains the greatest industrial power in the Socialist camp, and as such will continue to dominate the other Communist countries and Parties."

"Yes, that's what's troubling our High Command. Basically, he believes, as we all do, that China should be the leader of the future —not any other nation, even Soviet Russia. And indeed, that's the rightful place due us. Hasn't China been the greatest nation in her known world throughout her history, except for the last hundred years? Haven't we Chinese always called our country 'the Middle Empire' and our race 'the Celestial Race'? Nothing, I gather, will ever satisfy us Chinese, and especially the High Command, until this glorious position is restored to us. That's why the High Command keeps hammering on the idea, 'The East Wind must prevail over the West Wind.' But, as you've said, he is worried about our industrial backwardness. To catch up with Russia, he is now beginning to talk about taking some Great Leap Forward to industrialize China. But there, I think, he will run into a blind alley.

470

No, there is only one short cut that can make China the greatest nation on earth."

"Why don't you report it to the High Command?"

Mei-yin's triangular eyes narrowed. "You're being very obtuse today, or are you trying to put on that mask again? Report it to him? You know how his mind works; it's none too quick, but exceedingly devious and thorough. My only fear is that he may think of it before you succeed to the High Command. We can use this to make ourselves masters of the whole world."

In spite of himself Ta-kong could not help showing interest.

Mei-yin grinned an ugly grin. "Remember back to our young days, when you and I and your two good-for-nothing sworn brothers discussed ways to overthrow the warlords and fight Imperialism? That stupid Li Chien was for fighting the warlords first and Imperialism afterward, but I told him the only way to overthrow the warlords was by pretending to fight Imperialism first. Events proved I was absolutely right. So, today, the way to make China the greatest nation on earth does not lie through industrialization. We may take some Great Leaps Forward, but don't forget others are leaping too; we have lagged so far behind, we cannot hope to catch up with them soon. There is only a short cut possible, and that is another, and bigger, world war."

"But that's impossible!" exclaimed Ta-kong. "We haven't got the industrial power to wage a modern war. And the United States has the atomic bomb; it would destroy us in no time."

"But the Russians have told us they're producing their own atomic bombs. All we have to do is let Russia and the United States destroy each other."

"How?"

"By doing just what our High Command is doing now. Preach our technique of military subversion and incite Communists in the backward nations the world over to follow our example. The Russian Comrades are bound to object, for that would inevitably result in the expansion of our influence. Yet they can't very well call us to a halt, for with Communism avowedly dedicated to world revolution, they would lay themselves open to a charge of deviationism. But whether or not the Russian comrades object, whether they assist us or not, we will vigorously pursue our military subversion of those backward countries—in Asia, in Africa, in South America—until the time comes, as it surely will, when the Capitalist nations will get fed up and a third world war will result. And once

471

it starts, where will the nuclear weapons fall? On the highly industrialized targets, of course! Since we have so little industry, not many bombs will be wasted on us, but most will be concentrated on North America, West Europe, and Soviet Russia. Sooner than we think, the countries in those areas will be reduced to ruins, and the industrial power they are so proud of now will be wiped out. So here is the short cut for China. It is not to try to leap forward in industrialization to catch up with those countries, but to drag them backward through a war so that they'll all fall behind. Out of this war there can be, and will be, only one victor: China."

Ta-kong listened, horrified. "You don't know what you're saying. You're not a military man. You have no idea how dreadful those weapons can be. Even if we don't get hit by so many as others, half of our population may be wiped out."

"But that's precisely my point. Ours is the largest population on earth—over six hundred millions. Even if the bombs destroy two-thirds of the people of every country, we still will have two hundred million people left. And with the industrial differences wiped out at one stroke, we will become then the greatest nation on earth. And if you happen to be the High Command then, we two will become the masters of the whole world."

Ta-kong felt an utter revulsion. Suddenly, he seemed to hear his grandfather Ho the Central Hall reciting a familiar passage from Confucius: "What is a gentleman? He is a man who has an overpowering love for his kind." If that were true, then what could this woman be who was now standing before him? Was she human? How could she talk so unfeelingly and calculatingly about destroying countless hundreds of millions of her people just to gratify her own greed for power?

Yet at the same time he could not help but marvel at Mei-yin's intellect, as he had done so often before. From an inhuman point of view, her scheme was all too feasible. The more he pondered on it, the more he feared for the future of mankind. And knowing the High Command as well as he did, he had no doubt that sooner or later he would hit upon the idea and then there would be no checking him. How could Evil be endowed with so much genius!

Then he heard his grandfather's voice again: "When a gentleman walks, he never takes a short cut." Yes, the Evil always seeks after short cuts, so it is easy for him to find them. But the Good is not prone to look for short cuts, so he seldom understands what the

472

Evil is capable of. It is not that Evil is gifted with more genius than Good; it is just a basic difference in mental attitude. And he realized there was nothing in Mei-yin for him to admire, but everything to despise and detest.

He felt beaten, cheated, and infuriated. But what made him most bitter was the knowledge that so long as this woman lived, he would continue to be dominated by her. An irresistible urge to rid himself of this domination seized him, cost him what it might. He said suddenly and grimly, "I have no use for your short cut. I am going to retire—to quit."

"What do you mean?"

"Exactly what I say. I am going to tender my resignation as chairman of the Commission, as head of the Department of Organization, and from all my other offices."

"You know very well you can't. The Party will not let you."

"What can the Party do if I am determined to retire? I have worked enough for the Party, haven't I? If I want to quit working now, who's going to stop me?"

A cold gleam flashed in Mei-yin's odd-shaped eyes. "If nobody will, I will. I'll never let you quit until we have reached the very top together. If you desert me now, you will not quit, you will be liquidated!"

Ta-kong broke into a laugh. "Go ahead and denounce me. I know what cards you hold against me. As long as I wanted my career you had a hold over me, but now that I want my career no longer, I have nothing to fear from you. Yes, I did once send a warning to my uncle and help him escape from Canton. Yes, I did not kill my Second Brother, his wife and baby—you did. Yes again, though you may never have known this for sure, I shot my Auntie Lan to save her from the cruel tortures you and Ma Pingnan intended for her. Those are the cards you hold against me, aren't they? But I intend to tell these things to the High Command myself. I am sure that in consideration of my other services, he and the Party will forgive these trifles."

Mei-yin's eyes now held a malicious twinkle. "But, dear," she said, "these are not the only cards I hold."

Mei-yin stepped near to him, and stroked his chin playfully, "Tell me, have you ever heard of the term 'Venerable Master'?"

Ta-kong's heart missed a beat. When Old Head fled the mainland, he had left his "mantle"—all his authority—to his Close-Door-Disciple. Ever since then, the members of the Society had recognized Ta-kong as their Chief and called him by that appellation whenever they were alone.

"I suppose that when people hold someone in very high respect, they may call him by such a cumbersome title," he said stiffly. "But what has that got to do with me?"

"Don't take your Mama for a newborn baby!" sneered Mei-yin. "We hold the High Command in the highest respect, but we don't call him Venerable Master. No, several times I have overheard your men calling you not Comrade, but Venerable Master. I've also caught some of them referring to you in private as 'Young Old Head.' I can put two and two together. You are successor to the old Old Head, Chi Teh-shan. You are the new Chief of the secret Society. You have inducted hordes of your disciples into the Party, and put some of them in key positions. The High Command will forgive you many things, but he will never forgive this threat to his own power. If the High Command knew of this, you would be liquidated instantly, retirement or no retirement!"

Ta-kong reached to steady himself and his fingers brushed Ma Pingnan's revolver, which Mei-yin had dropped into his pocket.

"I've had my suspicions for years," Mei-yin went on, "but only after Chi Teh-shan fled to Hong Kong did I know for certain. However, you need not fear me, Venerable Master, so long as you are with me. You want to rule the Party through your secret Society, and to rule the country through the Party—but I want to rule all through you. If you listen to me, all will be well. If you don't, then before you can ever think of destroying me, I shall destroy you!"

Ta-kong's face became an unreadable mask, which Mei-yin took for tacit submissiveness.

"Now, Venerable Master, or Comrade Husband, we understand each other perfectly. You do what I say, and there are no heights we cannot climb together." She smiled at Ta-kong. "Comrade Ma Pingnan must have finished his proofreading now. I shall ask him to come here, and we'll discuss the arrangements to try the American spy."

Going to the door, she summoned a guard to fetch Ma Pingnan. Then she returned to Ta-kong, still smiling.

"After the trial, we shall have our second honeymoon. Ma Pingnan is coming now—don't look so glum, you fool! Look affectionate and devoted!"

It was the last straw. Choking out a cry, Ta-kong drew the

474

revolver and fired point-blank. Without a moan Mei-yin fell to the floor.

The Chief of Secret Police rushed into the room, but Ta-kong was waiting at the side of the door. Thrusting Ma Pingnan's own gun into his hand, Ta-kong began to grapple with him as though struggling for the possession of the weapon. He shouted at the top of his voice:

"Help! Help! Come quick, men! Ma Pingnan has shot my wife!"

5

PINGNAN WAS MADE fast with rope and put under lock and key in the basement. At Ta-kong's orders, his men—all disciples of the Society—sallied out of the building and quietly captured the handful of police Ma Pingnan had brought with him.

Ta-kong's plans had now taken shape. He had long known that loyalty inspired by voluntary devotion, such as in the Society, was much more dependable than loyalty enforced by sheer fear, as in the Party. None of his disciples would betray him; they would do what he bade and say what he told them to say. He felt perfectly safe.

He collected his thoughts and went into the room of the glass box. The Reverend Dr. Holt was still there sitting by the desk, waiting his fate. Ta-kong came to the missionary's side, and bowed humbly.

"Reverend, forgive me my inability to help you until this last moment. But I am glad I can do so now. I will help you escape right away."

"You?" Holt stammered in disbelief. "*You* help me, Ho Ta-kong? Escape? How and where?"

"A Scandinavian freighter will sail for Hong Kong in an hour. One of my men will take you on board and escort you to your destination."

Holt still could not believe his ears. "Pardon me for being suspicious, but is this another trick of yours?"

"Reverend," Ta-kong murmured in shame, "I must have been a very bad man indeed, if you cannot believe me even now. What I tell you is from my heart."

"But your comrades—Ma Pingnan and your wife. Surely they haven't agreed to let me escape, too?"

475

"I have killed my wife and seized Ma Pingnan," said Ta-kong, his voice scarcely a whisper.

"All because of me, Ta-kong?"

"No, not because of you. Because of my own conscience."

"But doesn't that put you in great danger? What are you going to do?"

"This is a chance I must take, but I think I can manage it. Reverend, there's not much time left; are you ready?"

Holt nodded. "I don't know what to say. I don't know even how to thank you."

Ta-kong turned and beckoned Ma Pingnan's orderly forward. "Disciple, I understand you have no family and no blood relations. Is that so?"

"That is so, Venerable Master. Only through the benevolence of the old Venerable Master was I brought up to manhood."

"How would you like to see the old Venerable Master again? Would you like to go to Hong Kong and serve him there?"

"Yes. I'll do whatever you command me, Venerable Master."

"Take as much money as you need for the trip. Bring a Department car to the back door and wait for my American friend. When he comes out, drive to the wharf—no Secret Police or Public Safety men will dare stop a Department car. But guard my American friend well—as if his life were your own. Do you understand, disciple?"

"I do, Venerable Master."

"Good. When you arrive in Hong Kong, take my American friend at once to the old Venerable Master and report to him. But you must not let anyone else know what has happened. Discreetly let out that it was Ma Pingnan who ordered you to help my American friend escape. Is that clear?"

"Yes. I understand perfectly, Venerable Master."

"Then go. And fare you well, my own disciple!"

"Farewell, Venerable Master. May my humble eyes be given a chance to see your august and illustrious countenance soon."

Ta-kong turned to the Reverend Dr. Holt.

"You will have to board as a stowaway to escape the authorities, but once the ship is at sea you can reveal yourself to the Scandinavian captain. There will be more than sufficient funds for your fare, and when you reach Hong Kong my old Venerable Master will take good care of you."

"Who is your old Venerable Master?"

"An old friend of yours. Suffice it to say that it was through him that I repeatedly urged you to leave the country before the change of the regime."

Holt began to understand the matter more fully.

"When you see my old Venerable Master," continued Ta-kong, "please give him this message. Always I have begged him not to tell a thing to my Third Brother, Yuwen, and his wife, my cousin Li-hwa; but tell my old Venerable Master that he can tell them all now. I have no time to explain these things to you, Reverend— but tell Yuwen and Li-hwa, two of the dearest people I have ever loved and still love, that I have suffered and am suffering from terrible memories. Ask—ask them to forgive me, if they can!"

The Reverend Dr. Holt was deeply moved. "The Lord will have mercy on you, Ta-kong. I feel sure Yuwen and Li-hwa will somehow find it in their hearts to forgive you."

Ta-kong's eyes were filled with mute gratitude. "Tell Yuwen I am glad my old Venerable Master got him out of Shanghai. Tell him he is right about the necessity for a rule of law for China.

"Tell him that I remember well, though much too late, the parting advice he gave me years ago—especially the quotation from Christ, 'I am come not to destroy, but to fullfil.' Tell him also that I now remember the Confucian teachings my grandfather used to try to instill in me: 'The heart of man is ever dangerous. The core of truth is ever small. One must be forever refined and single-minded. One must always hold on to the Truth at its very core.' "

"I understand, Ta-kong."

"I have always wanted power—power only," Ta-kong whispered. "This bloody purge has opened my eyes at last. You have suffered much these days, Reverend, but you can't imagine how much more I have suffered—watching so many innocent people tortured to death before my own eyes, and knowing countless others were butchered by my order. Being active in the Communist Party is like riding a tiger—you cannot dismount. And even if we succeed in fully mobilizing manpower and resources, and thus build China into one of the strongest and greatest nations on earth—even if we succeed in this aim, who is going to benefit by it? Not the people; only the few. The few will have their glory, but the people only their chains. At the very best, the nation will merely be turned into one vast monstrous anthill, with numberless soul-less and spineless ants toiling day and night—without laughter and without joy, without meaning and without hope. And if the worst comes, who knows whether an even more dreadful fate may not be devised for them...?"

Abruptly he stopped and looked at his watch. "It's almost time, Reverend, but you must not go on board until the very minute the ship is about to sail."

"Can Reverend Wong Ming and his wife Anna come with me?"

"No, Reverend. While you were writing your confession, Ma Pingnan had them remanded to jail. Escape is impossible. But to put your mind at ease, now that they are no longer needed to testify against you, no immediate harm will come to them."

"How about the cook?"

"There's not much that can be done for him, but I'll see what I can manage."

Holt asked about the trumped-up confession, but Ta-kong said he'd have to keep it as evidence. "After your departure, Reverend, I'll immediately report to the High Command that Ma Pingnan was indebted to you for the good turn you once did him, and went out of his way to protect you. He did not extort any confession from you; Mei-yin did. When he saw he could no longer save you he helped you escape, and when Mei-yin discovered him he shot her."

"What a tortuous life you must still live, Ta-kong! Only the Lord can judge whether you be right or wrong."

Ta-kong, however, was not listening. He was looking at his watch again. "It's time to leave, Reverend."

He led Holt to the back door, then grasped the missionary's hand warmly. "The car is waiting for you, Reverend. You will be in good hands."

Then—in that brief moment—the Reverend Dr. Holt was struck by the remarkable resemblance Ta-kong bore to his grandfather and to his uncle. Unlike the two other Hos, this one had always looked so fierce and grim of purpose; but now, in this instant of parting, all the grimness and fierceness seemed to be gone and only the heritage of generations of gentility remained.

Holt bowed his head and marveled at the miraculous workings of the Lord. Once before, his life had been saved by the two older Hos; and now, for a second time—and under these incredible circumstances—it was to be saved by this third Ho. He said fervently, "God be with you, Ta-kong!"

"The same to you, Grand-generation-uncle!" Ta-kong replied, a twinkle in the eye.

The missionary felt a twitch of nostalgia. He had not been ad-

478

dressed by this title for decades. It took him back half a century. Once again he was new on the Lane of Eternal Stability, and he was paying his first visit to Ho the Central Hall. And a little urchin with dark rolling eyes had, at the behest of his grandfather, just suppressed a naughty giggle and called a red-haired young foreigner—"Grand-generation-uncle."

The ship was on the open sea. The Reverend Dr. Logan J. Holt knew that if he had any sense he should have gone to bed, yet he had stolen up on deck. Out of the black night the words of a hymn rang in his ears:

Sing with all the sons of glory, sing the resurrection song!
Death and sorrow, earth's dark story, to the former days belong!
All around the clouds are breaking, soon the storms of time shall cease,
In God's likeness, man awaking, knows the everlasting peace.

He turned his head in the direction from which the sun must soon rise. He thought he caught a streak of dawn breaking. But when he cast his glance coastward, the mainland was still enveloped in darkness.